French Tales of
Mad Scientists
(Vol. 3)

FROM THE SAME PUBLISHER

French Tales of Mad Scientists (Vol. 3)

by
**Georges Eekhoud, Edmond Haraucourt,
Jules Lermina, Jean-Marc Lofficier,
Eugène Thibault** and **Gaston de Wailly.**

Translated by
**Brian Stableford
Fletcher Pratt**

A Black Coat Press Book

ISBN 978-1-64932-311-8. First Printing. June 2024. Published by Black Coat Press, an imprint of Hollywood Comics.com, LLC, P.O. Box 17270, Encino, CA 91416. All rights reserved. Except for review purposes, no part of this book may be reproduced or transmitted in any form or by any means, electronic or mechanical, including photocopying, recording, or by any information storage and retrieval system, without permission in writing from the publisher. The stories and characters depicted in this novel are entirely fictional. Printed in the United States of America.

TABLE OF CONTENTS

EDMOND HARAUCOURT

Introduction

Here are more French science fiction stories featuring the character of the mad scientist in all of its wicked, dangerous aspects.

We outlined an history of this most fruitful theme that runs through French science fiction like a live wire in our first volume; and therefore, refer our readers to it.

Here, we shall mention some of the most common features of the character:

Usually bearing the title of doctor or professor, the mad scientist is competent in many sciences and techniques at the same time; he is both an Albert Einstein with revolutionary ideas, and a handy Gyro Gearloose, capable of putting his crazy theories into practice.

The mad scientist usually displays obsessive behavior and use dangerous or at least unconventional methods to achieve his goals without the least regard for destructive or ethical consequences. He may be motivated by revenge, trying to punish a real or imagined slight, often related to his work. This narcissism and excessive pride generate a megalomania which leads him to want to overcome the laws of Nature, to despise human beings, to "play at being God" and to ne unable to maintain normal human relationships, which can lead him to live as a hermit.

Visually, his laboratory is generally cluttered with Tesla coils, Van der Graaf electrostatic machines, Jacob's ladders, perpetual motion machines and other spectacular scientific instruments, not forgetting test tubes and distillation equipment where brightly colored liquids bubble, from which disturbing vapors emanate.

I'll conclude with a real-life anecdote. Already in the 18th century, when alchemists and sorcerers were not yet forgotten, Professor Guillaume-François Rouelle, a French chemist and apothecary, demonstrator at the *Jardin du roi* (current National Museum of Natural History) warned his students:

"Do you see this cauldron on this brazier, gentlemen? Well, if I stopped stirring the mixture it contains for a single moment, an explosion would ensue that would make us all jump into the air!"

A moment of distraction, and his prediction came true: a terrible explosion was heard, all the windows in the laboratory were shattered, the chimney collapsed, and the incorrigible professor's wig was removed to the ceiling!

Jean-Marc & Randy Lofficier

KERMESSES

PAR

GEORGES EEKHOUD

DESSINS DE FRANS VAN KUYK

H. KISTEMAECKERS
ÉDITEUR

Georges Eekhoud: *Tony Wandel's Heart*

By the end of the 19th century, the expanding genre of French scientific romance began to attract the attention of established writers, many of whom dabbled therein. These included the Belgian writer George Eekhoud (1854-1927), whose collection Kermesses *(1884) included the remarkable moral fantasy "Le coeur de Tony Wandel," here translated as "Tony Wandel's Heart," in which the progress of medical science is viewed with a scathingly skeptical eye. The socialistically-inclined Eekhoud took leave to wonder whether such potential technologies as heart transplantation might enable the rich to become vampirically parasitic upon the poor in ways that Karl Marx had not imagined. This story, too, is a comedy, but the tenor of its humor is far darker than that of Robida or Mouton, reverting to the scathing abrasiveness of Voltairean satire.*

Eekhoud was a Belgian novelist of Flemish descent, but writing in French. He was a regionalist, best known for his ability to represent scenes from rural and urban daily life. He tended to portray the dark side of human desire and write about social outcasts and the working classes.

Born in Antwerp in a fairly well-off family, Eekhoud lost his parents as a young boy. When he came into his own, he started working for a journal. First as a corrector, later he contributed a serial. In 1877, the generosity of his grandmother permitted the young man to publish his first two books, Myrtes et Cyprès *and* Zigzags poétiques, *both volumes of poetry. In the beginning of the 1880s, Eekhoud took part in several of the modern French-Belgian artist movements, like Les XX (The Twenty) and La Jeune Belgique (Young Belgium). Kees Doorik, his first novel, about the life of a tough young farmhand who committed a murder, was published in 1883. Eekhoud received some guarded praise by famous authors like Edmond de Goncourt and Joris-Karl Huysmans who both sent him personal letters. For his second prose book,* Kermesses, *not only Goncourt and Huysmans praised him, but also Émile Zola, about whom Eekhoud had written an essay in 1879.*

B.S

I.

If I can believe the Saturnian Chronicles published after the disappearance of our planet, it was about the year 2250 that human science attained its apogee. Cures for the rabies virus and cholera microbes were known, the result of stubborn research by physiologists. The new anthropology was vertiginously ad-

9

vanced from earlier discoveries. Within institutions like phalansteries,[1] placed under the protection of their originator Charles Darwin, specialists controlled the selection of the human race, while a little-known scholar triumphantly solved one of the most redoubtable unknowns of the universal equation.

It was a surgeon from Flanders, Doctor Van Kipekap, as bold and steadfast as all his countrymen. Incessantly investigating the causes of the phenomena of life, he believed for a long time, with Christopher Wren and Denis,[2] that it was possible to substitute for the vitiated blood of a decrepit man that of a child or an adolescent. He took up and extended the experiments begun by Brown-Séquard [3] in past centuries; especially traveling to nations where capital punishment still existed, in order to operate on the condemned. The trials of his predecessors had

---

[1] A phalanstery–*phalanstère* in French–was a kind of commune envisaged as the key social unit in the socialist Utopian schemes of Charles Fourier (1772-1837). The word was derived by running together *phalange* (finger-bone) and *monastère*, the former word being used in the sense carried forward by subsequent proponents of the notion of the corporate state. It was actually Charles Darwin's cousin, Francis Galton, rather than the evolutionist himself. who repopularized the idea of "eugenic" selection, which had previously been advocated by Fourier.

[2] In 1657, Christopher Wren (1632-1723), the great English architect, borrow some equipment from William Harvey–who had demonstrated the circulation of the blood some 30 years earlier–in order to carry out a pioneering series of experiments in animal blood transfusion. A series of injections of lamb's blood into human patients was carried out in Paris a few years later by the natural philosopher Jean-Baptiste Denis (1625-1704); although the first three patients reported that the treatment had been beneficial, the fourth died. Denis was subsequently sued by the widow, and although the court decided that he was not guilty of negligence, he was ordered to desist from further experiments. Blood transfusions were then outlawed in France until the 1800s, although experimentation was revived in England in the 1790s by Erasmus Darwin (Charles's grandfather).

When Eekhoud wrote "Tony Wandel's Heart" in 1884, there was no similar history of attempted organ transplantation to which he might have referred, although a Dutchman named Job van Meeneren had claimed to have used a bone graft from a dog to repair an injury to a human skull in 1668; a temporary skin graft using skin from a cadaver was allegedly carried out on a burn victim in 1881. The issue of tissue compatibility came into sharper focus in 1901-03, when Karl Landsteiner began the research that led to his categorization of the A/B/O blood groups in 1909.

[3] Charles-Edouard Brown-Séquard (1817-1894) was a French physician and physiologist, one of the creators of opotherapy–better known in English as organotherapy–whose treatments used bodily fluids extracted from various organs.

been carried out on dogs, rabbits, a freshly-amputated arm at most; he was the first to give life to a decapitated head.

One of these resurrections crowned his career as an anatomist. Finding himself in Japan, and learning of the imminent decollation of a rebel soldier, he contrived to subject the mortal remains, following the work of the executioner, to his favorite manipulations. As usual, he waited until the severed head had lost its sensibility, little by little; when the eyelids were closed, the eyes dull and the nostrils immobile, he used a pump to force fresh red blood, free of any clots, into the arteries of the brain. Then, all the invited dignitaries saw the head, formerly inanimate, gradually come back to life, reopen its eyelids and flare its nostrils. The bloodless complexion was reinvigorated, the eyes shone.

As the injection continued, the mouth grimaced, the teeth grated, the eyeballs rolled grievously, teardrops formed. Then, someone having called the murderer by his name, the pupils moved slowly to the side from which the call had come, and the frightfully weak voice of the condemned man asked: "What do you want?"

At that moment, a panic took hold of the breathless and petrified audience. Everyone ran for the door. Even the experimenter's assistant abandoned his side. They knocked over the apparatus, the pump, the receptacles and the head itself–which rolled on the floor, bouncing and howling, trying to nip the legs of the fleeing dignitaries, hampered by their formal attire.

After this scene, three months passed without the doctor pursuing his explorations further.

He took them up again and extended them, armoring his nervous system to proof himself against any surprise, but they no longer succeeded in satisfying him. The phenomenon of resurrection only lasted as long as the continual introduction of blood by means of an artificial and mechanical process.

He tried to recall to life individuals killed by disease and encountered obstacles even more considerable. Often, the new fluid conducted into the cadaver was insufficient to galvanize it. The doctor attributed this failure to the exhaustion or contamination of the organs. It was important that the flowing flesh, the regenerative juice, could reach the channels and reservoirs that required it. The problem came back to the renewal of the essential parts of the body. But which? To replace them all would be wildly fanciful.

Van Kipekap did not hesitate for long. Impulsion being given to the blood as it left the heart, it was this organ that attracted the attention of the doctor. Another consideration, even more serious, dictated his choice. Like Aristotle and Ficinus, he placed the soul in the heart–in contrast to Plato and Descartes, who lodged it in the brain. In his eyes, the heart represented not only the origin and motor of circulation, but the key principle and very source of life. By the substitution of a healthy heart for an exhausted one, he would rejuvenate old men, cure the sick, and realize the fabulous Fountain of Youth that he and his predecessors had expected to obtain by mere blood transfusion.

With this belief, he returned to his experiments in vivisection, in order that his hands might cultivate an indispensable skill and quickness. The extraction of the heart involved an initial large incision made in the breast near to the sixth true rib, then a first section to separate the superior and inferior *vena cava* from the right auricle, a second stroke of the scalpel to detach the heart from the pulmonary artery, a third to disconnect the pulmonary veins and the left auricle, and, finally, a last flick of the wrist to sever the aorta.

When one bears in mind that it was necessary to carry out this extraction in two individuals–to place the healthy heart in place of the contaminated organ, to reattach by means of ligatures the stumps of the veins and arteries to the corresponding junctures in the breast of the individual to be caulked, and to sew up the percardium and the flesh of the thorax–one will understand the innumerable slicings that Van Kipekap carried out on all the beasts in creation, secretly and in seclusion, before experimenting on his own kind.

In the end, he considered his "training" sufficient, and had only to await an opportunity to confront the final test. It came along.

At the hospital in N***, on the Scheldt,[4] where Doctor Van Kipekap had his clinic, he observed one day two neighboring beds occupied by an old invalid and a young injury-victim. Both were dying, with the difference that the former was succumbing to sickness and senility while the other, built to last for a long time, was perishing accidentally.

The innovator had his demonstration.

Having solemnly summoned the most illustrious doctors, his interns and the great men of Flanders, he chloroformed the two patients, carried out point for point the little program so often repeated on innocent stray dogs and congenial rabbits, effectively attaining the substitution of the healthy and intact heart of the man in his prime for the worn-out and degenerate organ of the septuagenarian. The wounded man died, while the invalid awoke following a recuperative slumber, completely transfigured, as vigorous and hearty as a 14-year-old.

Among Van Kipekap's colleagues, some hailed it as an unqualified miracle, others as a fraud or a conspiracy. All of them challenged him to repeat the marvelous experiment. Van Kipekap asked for no more, and succeeded a second time. He operated repeatedly with the same facility. Then the envious bowed down.

Meanwhile, the news of the prodigy spread, dazzling and resounding, to all four corners of the world. Humankind in its entirety glorified this Fleming, who had equipped it with near-immortality.

---

[4] There is no Flemish town on the river Scheldt–Eekhoud uses its French name, l'Escaut–whose name begins with the letter N. The formulation is a joke, the reference being to Eekhoud's birthplace, Anvers, or Antwerp, whose name begins with a syllable not dissimilar to that letter's pronunciation.

In truth, the finding only benefited those people rich enough to afford to regain their youth. Such as they would be able to change their hearts as they changed their clothes and their mistresses. With the introduction of a new heart into the economy, the other machinery of the human clock was repaired.

It became very difficult to obtain exchangeable organs, because a well-constituted rogue that fate had delivered to a tragic death—and who, having been declared lost, consented to be separated from his irreproachable heart for the benefit of a millionaire mortgaged by old age and excess—did not turn up every day, at the appropriate moment. In normal times, one could only shop around for that desirable article in certain heroic categories: masons fallen from scaffolding, miners surprised by an explosion of fire-damp, railway-passengers crushed by an impact with the buffers, victims of cut-throats, and the same cut-throats in the hour of their expiation.

The heart became the luxury item par excellence, the monopoly of Croesus. Prices soared in proportion to the youth and vigor of the subject. Speculation became involved; the human heart was quoted on the Bourse like any other commodity. Despite the extraordinary prices commanded by that engine, supply invariably fell short of demand. Only war caused a lowering.

The only opportunities for repair extended to the middle classes arose by bombardment. Then, one might witness the most extraordinary of spectacles. Valetudinarians and incurables would drag themselves along in the wake of armies, in breathless anticipation of the following day's butchery, their longevity awaiting the violent suppression of thousands of the able-bodied and spirited. On bloody chessboards where black men were throttled by white, these gentlemen's surgeons and lawyers, lugged around on litters, leaned out over mortally wounded young recruits and conscripts, extending their instruments and pens. From those blond youths who were already dying, the vampires asked nothing more than to sign on the dotted line before witnesses. The surgeon took the place of the minister and the man of law to perforate and butcher each expiring soldier with all expedition. They went in this manner from one body to another, providing a prelude to the mutilations of the rooks and vultures.

Inevitably, abuses occurred and justice armed itself with new laws. In times of peace, many a conscienceless industrialist did not shrink from procuring by crime that which politics was tardy in delivering to him. Assassins supplanted conquerors. The courts investigated abominable affairs of the abduction and murder of children.

Thus, the discovery of Doctor Van Kipekap only profited the tiniest minority of humankind, while worsening the lot of the majority of men in exposing their robustness and their very blood to the ferocious covetousness of the powerful. Serfdom was kept alive under guises as various as ever: prison-seed, hospital-haunts, gallows-birds, cannon-fodder, pleasure-fodder and scalpel-fodder.

II.

At that time, one of the compatriots of Doctor Van Kipekap of N*** on the Scheldt was a poor devil of a paver named Tony Wandel. He was a simple Christian soul in a body worthy of the Homeric era. Married to a blonde pauper, who was his equal in resignation and as beautiful as the legendary burgesses of Anvers and Bruges, the father of three little ones as chubby as Rubens cherubs, he toiled steadfastly six days a week, his piledriver or mallet falling rhythmically and incessantly on the flagstones. He was never idle, except when he had to be; he would have considered it stealing from the four innocent creatures who comprised his paradise on Earth had he wasted a quarter of an hour of the working day or a *sou* of his wages in the pursuit of drunkenness.

Tony Wandel experienced neither envy nor rancor in comparing his lot with that of the aristocrats of N***. He endured the weather as God sent it to him, considering himself unrivalled in that he was able to feed, house and clothe his own.

On Sundays in summer and other holy days, after vespers, the humble family walked lovingly along the river bank. They inhaled the briny breeze, the fragrance of new-mown hay beneath the dikes, the invigorating perfume of tar. Their eyes would follow the flight of white sails over the greenish carpet of the waves or the corkscrewing smoke of a ferry-boat. Less contemplative, the children would rush up and down the slopes gathering armfuls of selected flowers, while wallowing farm animals and shy horses greeted them with a neigh or a whinny.

As evening approached, after the beneficial walk, they would snuggle together under the vaulted ceiling of an inn at the town gate, pounded by the vibrations of the organ and the dance, and share a *waterzoei*–the Flemish *bouillabaisse*–and slices of bread with white cheese spiced with garlic, all accompanied by a delectable *uitzet*, the beer of beers. They would go home as night fell, contentedly taciturn, the parents carrying their two youngest in their arms.

Thus they labored all their life, while the grey and monotonous weeks went by like a rain-filled sky that Sundays crossed with rainbows. But this humble outcast's felicity suffered an eclipse. One day, the housewife waited much longer than usual for the paver to return for his supper. Anxiously, she ran to his workplace. There she learned from her husband's gang-mates that he had been knocked down while lending a hand–helpful as ever–to decouple a carriage, when the horse, whipped by the impatient driver, took the bit in its teeth and succeeded in starting up the heavy vehicle, one of whose wheels had passed over the paver's legs. She would find the wounded man in the hospital, but–his companions added, shaking their heads–perhaps with two limbs fewer.

Having heard this sad anthem, Nellie hastened to fly off in search of her man. They had exaggerated. The amputation of the paver's limbs would not be necessary, but the poor devil would be crippled for life and would be unable to walk without crutches.

He recovered, but what good was that? No more working for six days, no more walking on the seventh. Little by little they ate through their savings, selling the most elegant of their clothes. Soon, they were heavily in debt, the baker's tally-stick covered in countless notches. Then privation attacked the rosy cheeks of the wife and children.

After that, there was no other recourse left to the paralytic than begging. Every day, leaving the sick woman to look after the little ones, the cripple undertook his painful and humiliating pilgrimage. Tony Wandel, whose muscular arms would still have been able to lift a pick or a mallet with ease, was reduced to extending his hand, at the risk of being taken for an impostor, confused with vagrants and paupers.

Once, when he was backed up against the door of a church, wringing his heart and thinking of his poor angels, telling himself that for love of them he would open his veins and nourish them with his blood, Tony was accosted by a little man in the prime of life. The man had a fresh complexion, thin lips, eyes of different colors, a face framed by salt-and-pepper mutton-chop whiskers, a sly manner and a paunch; he was dressed in black, ornamented and wearing spectacles. In a jerky and metallic voice, this personage subjected the young invalid to a kind of interrogation.

The trusting Tony willingly told the stranger his troubles; although the lad was rather prolix in narrating his adventures, and a chronic lisp stretched the lamentable tale even further, the unknown lent a complacent ear to the hymn of complaint–and, by an approving nod of the head, encouraged the paver to continue.

This mysterious interlocutor was none other than the illustrious Doctor Van Kipekap. While listening to the young chap, the surgeon was staring intently at his new acquaintance. His inquisitive eyes seemed to want to penetrate the outer tegument to analyze the blood and the humors. When the beggar fell silent, the doctor continued his questions.

"And, except for this little misfortune... I beg your pardon, this catastrophe... which has deprived you of the use of your legs, tell me, my dear friend– permit me this familiarity, for your appearance is infinitely agreeable to me– have you ever had any serious illness?"

"I never took to my bed except to make love or to sleep, before this calamity taught me its other functions..." After a pause, the good-hearted fellow added: "At present, I'm in remarkably good health for a useless creature. My stomach aches with an imperious clamor for a nourishment that my arms can no longer earn..."

"Truly, you experience hunger! Adorable young man! A providential encounter! Will you show me your tongue? I'd like to eat it... Will you permit me to take your pulse?... Excellent. And may I put my ear to your chest? There! Perfect! A heart that might beat for a hundred years without missing a pulsation.

Sixty-five beats per minute: the normal figure..." He had counted them on his chronometer.

The innocent Tony submitted to this auscultation with all his original deference. The doctor seemed more and more enthusiastic and expansive. He rubbed his hands together. His face became cheerful. He pronounced words that had no significance for the paver in a voluble manner.

"Marvelous constitution!... Solidly build!... Irreproachable well-being! Twenty-three years, and thus beyond the climacteric age! [5] No bile... Blood-supply generous, neither too thick nor too fluid!... Here's one who fits the bill! There are none but the world-weary, malnourished and badly housed, who bring together a similar combination of physiological virtues." Abruptly, he demanded of the cripple: "So, my lad, if I've grasped the moral of your fascinating story, we no longer hold hard to that she-devil life, and we'd quit it without regret, on condition that our entry into the realm of moles would benefit our widow and orphans?"

"Alas, Monsieur, that's exactly what I think. A tragic death is better than a tragic life!"

"Well, comrade, what if I took you at your word and asked you to abandon the remainder of your days in exchange for a fortune guaranteed to those you leave behind?"

"I would accept!" the market-trader replied resolutely. "On condition that you show me a Christian door whereby to make my exit from life. Suicide leads to damnation..."

"But a sacrifice like the one you shall consummate to save your family is no longer called a suicide!" said the artful doctor, recalling his casuistry.

"Do you think so, Monsieur? In such a matter, a person of your importance is better able to discern rightness than we mere sheep. Tell me what must be done; I'm your man."

"Marvelous! I was right to come your way, and your character does not give the lie to your physiognomy. Shake my hand! Your widow will gain 500,000 florins before the Sun sets or I'll give away my name."

"My widow! Five hundred thousand florins!" the beggar repeated, as his heart was squeezed by anguish–although hope soon reinflated it.

"Ah, we manage our affairs briskly, my young friend. The bargain set up, the bargain concluded. It will be necessary to do away with you this very day... But before I summarize the details of the transaction for you, and the manner in which we shall fulfill our mutual obligations, would you like to accompany me to a place more suitable for confabulation? Not least because idlers are spying

---

[5] A climacteric is a period in human life when a considerable change in one's state of health is supposedly likely to occur. In the 19th century, such key phases were popularly considered to be multiples of seven and three–i.e. the ages of 21, 42 and 63.

on us, intrigued to see a ragamuffin like you in conversation with the famous Doctor Van Kipekap. We must keep it to ourselves, you understand..."

Luckily, they found themselves in the proximity of a local tavern. Van Kipekap led his placid captive into a room sheltered from eavesdroppers and both of them sat down at a table before a revivifying collation and a delicious flask of dessert wine, which sat in their glasses like liquefied rubies. Then the doctor began to tell his story.

III.

The great man, loyal to his fatherland and a confirmed burgher of N*** on the Scheldt, also counted his among his fellow citizens his principal client, the extremely rich banker Trekkenpluk, a moribund sexagenarian who wanted to recover his health and a new youth at any price, in order to enjoy the fabulous wealth from which death threatened to separate him. For several years, he had been in search of a willing bumpkin who would sell him a sturdy heart, guaranteed faultless by physicians.

Unfortunately, fate had delayed the moment of its acquisition. The number of suicides was diminishing, and suicides skillfully procured at the banker's behest had killed themselves too abruptly, shooting themselves in the heart, not wishing their precious viscera to profit their survivors. As soon as the news reached him that a pauper was on the brink, Van Kipekap, always on the lookout, would dispatch his best bloodhounds to the hovel, but they always arrived too late; the hanged man, who was taken down completely cold, had already danced the last *bourrée*.[6] Assassins were too conscientious in finishing off their victims and maliciously put the scaffold's caterers off the scent. Then, there were the wounded transported to hospital, who presumed to die without forewarning the financier who was animated by the most generous sentiments in respect of them.

As he scoured newspaper obituaries posted by those ingenuous physicians of slaters and plasterers, who verified at their own expense the laws of gravity and falling bodies, the sick man felt the rancor of those capitalists who, consulting a list of successful lottery numbers, perceive that one of theirs is only one figure removed from the winner of the grand prize. Disgruntled, he proceeded to read the *Accidents, crimes and disasters* notices:

Rue Morgue, this morning, a young (here he pricked up his ears) *manual laborer, a native of the region* (the region! robust and vigorous, then! the reader enticed himself) *18 years of age* (the best age to become useful to an aged millionaire in a heart operation) *being exceedingly drunk* (worthy alcohol! helpful drunkenness!) *fell two stories from the rafters.* (The banker got excited.) *Griev-*

---

[6] A *bourrée* is an Auvergnian dance, whose tune was sometimes played at executions. The word also means a bundle of firewood.

ously wounded in the left temple (ah! ah!) *the unfortunate was carried into a neighboring house* (I shall take your awkward health, rustic adolescent!) *at No. 7, to which our eminent practitioner, Doctor Van Kipekap, happening to be in the vicinity of the accident scene* (what flair the dear doctor has!) *charitably ran in order to extend the assistance of his art to the young proletarian, free of charge.* (Tee hee–that joker Van Kipekap! One knows what your help is worth in cash!) *Unhappily* (what! What does that mean?) *the illustrious physiologist was only able to certify the death* (Help! I'm choking) *of the imprudent yokel.*

The page slipped from the banker's hands as he frothed at the mouth epileptically, howling like a maddened cat. "The imprudent yokel!" he repeated. "Truly, these journalists abuse the art of euphemism. It's thief, blackguard, kidnapper he should be labeled. Eighteen years old! Misfortune! And that Van Kipekap came running to certify the death! Still an eagle, that one! What awaits a society that produces such monstrosities? That's the third scoundrel's heart lost to me!"

To heap misfortune upon misfortune, not the slightest threat of war or revolution was visible on the political horizon. Kings were no longer jealous of one another; the people seemed to have been permanently tamed; anarchists, Fenians and nihilists had been idle since time immemorial. Diplomats wore forced smiles and Prussian captains were going to rust, along with the strategists' compasses. France had given up trying to civilize its neighbors and make them happy in spite of themselves; she did not even attempt the least massacre of the Indo-Chinese or the inhabitants of the Algerian-Tunisian borders.

And old Trekkenpluk was flickering like the flame of a lamp running out of oil; he was at risk of taking his place in the parade filing past Pierrot-la-Mort, just like the lowliest breadwinner. Horrified by the idea of a dénouement whose prognostications were multiplying hour by hour, he clung desperately to existence.

His heirs, distant cousins, imposed themselves upon him in his home in order to fall upon the spoils as soon as he passed on. His flunkeys were not waiting for him to die before robbing him; phenomenal pilfering was the rule in the rich unfortunate's dwelling, and the staff exacted frightful damages in wine and meat. His companions in debauchery, epicureans as egotistical and as hard as he, took great care not to trouble the quietness and animal carelessness of their last days with the pathetic spectacle of this sybarite on his way out.

IV.

While the doctor related these facts to his interlocutor, the dazzled Tony repeated aside the fantastic figure of "500,000 florins!" whose syllables sounded like the clink of gold coins.

18

The vastness of the offered sum vanquished his hesitation. He imagined an opulent future for his family: his wife lodged in a palace as great as the Beffroi,[7] she and the kids dressed in silk and lace, lying in a feather-bed, the table laid with a eternal Cokaygne,[8] a festival of black puddings that would not run out until Judgment Day. He saw them drinking from jugs full of delectable uitzet and sadly raising a toast to the salvation, if not the health, of their poor father.

The doctor roused the evangelical lad from his reverie mingling regret and consolation and, as if he had read his mind, proposed a toast to the future orphans and the widow-to-be.

"And now, young man, if you so desire, we shall go to the home of my client, the notable banker Van Trekkenpluk, who is at this moment in time the richest man in Flanders, but also the most pitiful."

"Let's go," said the paver, simply.

An advancement brought them close to the courtyard of the church where the two men had met. Poor cab-horses, heads burrowing deep into their nose-bags, were chewing their miserly oats while their coachmen were taking turns to buy rounds of drinks from the counters. Van Kipekap hired a fiacre, helped the cripple up, sat beside him and gave the coachman the name of the Flemish Croesus.

The carriage stopped outside a door with pretentious *mascarons*,[9] that of the Trekkenpluk townhouse. A Hungarian servant opened it to them and led them through hallways and corridors as vast as cathedral naves, stairways of serpentine marble, and suites of rooms hung with Gobelins tapestries, furnished with lacquered cabinets, dressers wrought by silversmiths charged with fine Chinese porcelain. Persian carpets stifled the noise of the doctor's footsteps and the cripple's crutches.

Passing from landing to landing they encountered clean-shaven and sullen valets with feather-dusters under their arms, with whom the Hungarian exchanged frightful winks. It was the unwonted presence of the pauper that unset-

---

[7] The reference is presumably to the Tour de Beffroi, a famous landmark in Bruges, although the word *beffroi* had previously been used as a generic term for fortified towers.

[8] The land of Cokaygne (whose many other spellings include Cockayne, Cockaigne and, in French, Cocagne and Coquaigne) is featured in an anti-clerical satire about a land of ease where no one has to work or fulfill any religious duties because food is abundant–the ducks are ready-roasted–and the weather always fine. Its origins are presumably Norman, although its best-known representation in England is a 14th-century poem that begins by comparing Cokaygne very favorably with Paradise (which, being controlled by God, still exercises constraints on human desire and behavior).

[9] A *mascaron* is a large design in the form of a mask; they are usually found in pairs.

tled them, but Doctor Van Kipekap was a powerful man; everyone trembled before his skill, and although the banker's relatives knew about his schemes for the moribund, none would have dared incur the wrath of so prodigious a man by shutting the door on someone in his company.

After a long walk, Tony and his introducer entered the old man's bedroom. They found him stretched out on a chaise longue, enveloped in furs, breathing in a labored fashion. With his yellow skin pasted on his bones, the vitreous expression of his eyes, the inertia of his limbs and the bitter rictus contracting his violet lips, he presented the appearance of a living mummy.

With careful discretion, the doctor brought Trekkenpluk up to date with the morning's events and presented him with his news and precious intelligence.

"An opportunity that will not arise again!" he whispered, leaning over the moribund. "Five hundred thousand florins for him, and the same for me. It's a good bargain!"

The sick man appeared to be reanimated by this last chance of salvation. A flame lit up his hollow eyes, and he inspected Tony from head to toe, with an expression of covetousness so ferocious and so sulphurous [10] that the paver almost ran away.

"I say, doctor," he whispered very softly in his friend's ear, "your client seems devilishly keen to have my life! A nasty-looking villain, with all due respect..."

"But a magnificent payer, on the other hand..."

"You're right, doctor." And with that, Tony resigned himself to his fate.

No time was lost. Two ready-stamped formal contracts, drawn up long before, were filled in by the two parties. Tony signed with a cross, like the knights of the Middle Ages. Then Van Kipekap supplied the patient with a check for half a million, made out to the impending widow Wandel, payable the same day at the Trekkenpluk Bank.

"May I deliver this *billet doux* to my darling myself?" asked the honest chap, with a trusting smile.

"Did you not understand the terms, my friend? You shall not see your wife again..."

"My God! To die without embracing my irresistible little chickens! But I give in–the sight of them would surely wipe out my resolve. Say, doctor, that you'll put the inheritance into my wife's hand."

"Willingly. Before nightfall, the treasure will be in your home..."

"Thank you, greatest of doctors; I'm sorry for the trouble I've put you to..."

---

[10] *Safre*, here translated as "sulphurous", can refer various yellow substances, including cobalt oxide and saffron, but the implication here is presumably infernal.

"Not at all, my boy," protested the surgeon, who was insensitive by nature and profession but slightly taken aback by such forbearance and candor. "Now let's get on, for the honorable Mr. Trekkenpluk seems very low today and we can't spend too long chatting..."

On Van Kipekap's orders, and with infinite care, the domestics lifted the old banker–who squealed and moaned all the while–on to a stretcher. They deposited him, more tightly wrapped up than ever, on the floor of a ready-harnessed carriage in the courtyard. The operator and his "subject" got in, with their backs to the coachman.

"Where are we going, doctor?" the young man asked, as two vigorous horses set the carriage in motion.

"Straight ahead! To find a suitable spot, my excellent friend–somewhat isolated, sheltered from any troublesome surprises, where we can properly expedite our little business..." Smiling with encouraging good humor, he clapped Tony on the shoulder in a familiar fashion.

Huddled in front of them, old Trekkenpluk coughed, his face convulsed. Looking at him, the doctor became alarmed and consulted his watch; then he stuck his nose to the window-glass to see how far they had traveled.

An elegant instrument-case and a portable pharmacy had been transported from the surgeon's fiacre to the banker's carriage. Van Kipekap made the moribund take a powerful sleeping-draught, whose effect was immediate.

"He'll not wake up again unless he awakes rejuvenated!" the scholar said, with a certain solemnity.

"In my trade, we call it repairing when we replace the worn-out stones in the road with new ones. The road becomes bad for the old–it's a repair job that we're going to carry out, isn't that so, doctor?" And Tony sang an old workmen's song:

"*On, on, honest paver,*
"*Dig and level the road.*
"*While the Angelus sounds*
"*In the distant tower,*
"*The resonant plink* [11]
"*Of your falling pick*
"*Adds amen to the prayer.*"

Meanwhile, the horses burned up the road.

After an hour of the frenzied journey, they reached the edge of a beech forest. They came to a halt, and the doctor invited Tony Wandel to get down and follow him. They left the road immediately and went into the thickets. Tony car-

---

[11] Eekhoud has *plainte argentine* where I have been content to use "plink;" I hope the latter can carry the double implication of a metallic sound suggestive of complaint, while wreaking less havoc upon the scansion of what is presumably the author's own composition rather than an authentic laborers' song.

ried the heavy instrument-case, in a manner somewhat reminiscent of Jesus carrying his cross.

After a hundred paces, Van Kipekap took his companion by the arm again. "How does this seem to you, Tony, my friend? Does the place suit you? An unknown poet would choose no other to exhale a final objurgatory sonnet... ah!"

The place was a sort of clearing. A single magnificent beech towered over the middle of a meadow surrounded by densely packed trees. At its foot the ground was raised. The noble tree [12] cast a great shadow on the grass for several meters around, for the ardent August Sun was unable to transmit its rays through the centuries-old branches.

Tony made no reply to the doctor's question. He understood that the moment had arrived to say his *in manus*.[13] Here or elsewhere, it mattered little to him. With his nose in the air, Van Kipekap noticed a branch extending from the trunk two meters above the ground and almost parallel to it.

"Ha!" the amiable scholar exclaimed. "Here's one that will make an adorable gibbet!"

"As you wish, Mijnheer!" sighed the lad, resigned but slightly melancholy even so. He had not yet attained the age of consistency. The hot bright Sun, the birds fluttering in the foliage above them and the edge of the immutably blue sky reminded him of the happy excursions of yesteryear, along the Scheldt. He sighed deeply, and within his breast the great heart that he would soon give up contracted and expanded convulsively.

Meanwhile, the doctor, confident of the stoical boy's acquiescence, drove half a dozen nails into the trunk of the tree, which would enable the suicide to climb up to the sturdy branch. Then he took from his pocket an elegant cord made of hemp and silk, as slender as a shoelace but of proven tensile strength, and extended it to his companion with his most engaging smile.

"When you're ready, dear friend, I am at your disposal..."

"Doctor," the lad declared, pale but resolute, "may I ask you one more favor?"

"Speak, my brave boy, but let's be quick–you know that someone's waiting for me..."

"Tell Nellie how much I adore them, that it's for love of them that I'm going and that I didn't want to see them. You'll give them good advice too, won't you, doctor? Because this unexpected fortune might go to their heads..."

"Put your trust in me. I'll take your family in hand. Is that all?"

---

[12] The word Eekhoud uses here is *marmenteau*, which has no simple English equivalent; it emphasizes that the tree in question is preserved as an ornament, forbidden to the woodcutter's axe.

[13] This reference is to a Latin prayer offered up by those about to die; coincidentally, it is given in full in the text of "The Red Triangle" (see Note 123 for a translation).

"God will repay you, doctor! Permit me to embrace you..."

"Gladly, for you're the most determined chap I ever met! No recriminations or sniveling–I like that! We're here, eh? For your convenience and mine, you'd do well to take off your smock."

Tony, always deferential, put himself in his shirtsleeves. The placid fellow threw away his crutches, not without gazing at them with a certain emotion. Then, supported by the doctor, he succeeded in hauling himself up onto the branch, on which he sat himself astride.

Van Kipekap had prepared the noose, whose knot slid smoothly enough to make an English executioner jealous. Tony fixed the cord to the branch and slipped it around his neck.

"Doctor...?" he stammered, at that moment.

"What is it now?" said the other–with a certain impatience, for the moribund in the carriage preoccupied him even more than this excellent proletarian dough.

"Doctor, may God bless you, and my heart serve the old man well..."

"Amen!"

"Wait! One... two... three..." He did not count as far as four; his fingers opened, he lost his balance and pivoted around his seat. His legs lost their grip and he fell, retained four feet above the ground by the cord abruptly tightened by his weight. The cord snapped his neck.

The poor wretch thrashed about atrociously; even his cataleptic legs found their vitality again for that last solo dance.

"The excellent market-trader!" murmured the hard-baked man, confronted by this painful scene. "Let's cut his suffering short and get busy with the other."

With his scalpel between his teeth, taking the same route as the paver with the agility of a squirrel, the doctor rejoined his patient and operated on him in no time at all. Carrying the precious organ, he ran back to the banker, unconscious in his carriage. There, he successfully completed the prodigious work that he had already carried out so often.

The carriage returned at full speed along the road to the house. Hunched over the body of his patient–who was prostrate on the cushions, as limp as a defrocked priest–Van Kipekap continually lifted a silver spatula to his withered lips.

After a few minutes of terrible anxiety, the doctor let loose a loud hurrah. The polished blade became dull. Trekkenpluk was breathing.

V.

When the banker woke up at dawn the following morning, after 17 hours of sound sleep, the old man was no more. Black hair, thick and solidly-anchored, garnished the scalp that had resembled a reef constantly washed by the waves the previous evening. The grooves in his forehead had been filled in and firm flesh had filled out his flaccid cheeks, colored in a most attractive fashion by vivid blood. The hollow and dull eyes were reilluminated in their orbits and the crow's-feet marking their outlines had also disappeared. Instead of a livid and bloodless pout, his lips had recovered the incarnadine of former days, and even his teeth–loose exposed stumps, which he had been on the point on replacing with ivory dentures–were solidly planted in their sockets and impeccably enameled.

This rejuvenation was not confined to the head, but extended to the entire body. It had recovered its stature. The adipose muscles, bundled around the cartilage, stood out as sharply as they had at 20. The thorax bulged. He had recovered the sturdy solidity of adolescence. When he threw himself from the foot of his bed, he scarcely recognized the hearty well-built fellow smiling at him with an insouciant air from the full-length mirror in front of him.

With that, a divine humor possessed him. In a daze, juggling with his shoes, washing himself with childish glee, putting his arms into his trousers and his legs into his sleeves, he nevertheless contrived to get dressed while yodeling, warbling and dancing, without even taking the trouble to summon his manservant. The latter, however, who was snoring in the next room, woke up with a start, extremely intrigued by this *aubade*. As he saw him come running, his mouth in an O, Trekkenpluk struck a new *entrechat* and let out a loud burst of laughter.

"Ha ha! Hee hee! Pom pom! Tra la la! The ineffable head! Why are you looking at me like that, you utter fool? Well?"

The old servant could not believe his bulging eyes. There before him was his master at 30 years of age–the age when Trekkenpluk had first engaged the rascal. But no, the laughing and bizarre Trekkenpluk who had surged forth from who knew where, in the place of the pitiful parishioner of yesterday, was even healthier than any of the Trekkenpluks previously known to Klaes. Never, at any moment in his life, had the rich man's visage been invested with that welcoming and benign expression.

"Well, Klaes, my old servant, I've caught you out, haven't I?" trumpeted the banker. "You've got a peculiar way of waking up a dying men. I'd have been able to cough up my wretched life and let out a death-rattle like a locomotive, while Klaes thought only of coming to wish me bon voyage. Anyway, I've no desire to go, joker that you are! I'm staying with you, and as I hate sullen faces, I'm increasing your wages tenfold. Do you hear, thief? Now run along, you rascal, and butter me ten slices of bread... Yes, ten, not one less. And smarten up my coffee, all right!" [14]

Laughing at the old domestic's stupor, he pranced past him nimbly and excitedly, quit his room and went down the stairs four at a time. His titanic merry laughter and his burbling song, intercut with apocalyptic animal cries, reverber-

---

[14] The final phrase is rendered into English in the original.

ated from landing to landing, filling the dreary corridors and awakening echoes of a pyramidal gaiety that the sumptuous palace had not known for a very long time, if ever.

All the flunkeys were scandalized, but they played their parts in the resurrection philosophically, for they were all well satisfied with the new arrangements that Trekkenpluk made with them. It would have been proclaimed a miracle had not Doctor Van Kipekap long since accustomed Flanders and the world to similarly improbable phenomena.

Trekkenpluk's heirs ground their teeth on finding him as fit as a fiddle and easily capable of sending them all fleeing back to the miserly means on which they had subsisted before their copious pillage. The resuscitated banker, after amusing himself with their discomfiture, took pity on them and endowed them henceforth with pensions with which a king in exile would have been content.

His generosity extended from his family to the vast army of employees slaving away in his offices. Previously he had worked them like slaves, and no commander had ever treated his natives so odiously, but now he rained money down upon these poor helots and awarded splendid pensions to bureaucrats worn out in his service. In place of the peevish, fumbling and implacable overlord whose mere appearance in the office corridors had scared the hungry legion half to death, the reheartened paper-pushers, well-ballasted in the gut and the wallet, came to know the ideal boss, a King of Cokaygne, as blooming and enlivening as a Sun.

The petrified soul of yesteryear no longer existed. Along with the heart of humble Tony Wandel, the evil plutocrat incarnated all the virtues of the evangelical paver. The result of this particular transposition of organs had even surpassed the boldest speculations of Van Kipekap himself.

Trekkenpluk's new qualities seemed far more considerable by virtue of being manifest in the midst of a bourgeois oligarchy that was avaricious and materialist, still worshipping the golden calf and a hundred times harder on the poor world than the worst of feudal aristocracies and absolute monarchies. His colleagues in big business, the stockbrokers and financiers, believing that he had gone mad, tried to exploit him and transfer his millions to their own pockets. They soon came to see their error. Generosity had not injured the banker's intelligence; they could not fool him any more easily now than in the past, and their underhand speculations were even turned to the profit of the "pigeon" that they intended to pluck together. He remained doubly superior to them, by his commercial genius and his absolute probity.

But of all the consequences of the two-part operation carried out by Doctor Van Kipekap, the most unexpected and amazing was undoubtedly the banker's marriage to Tony Wandel's widow. This seemingly-extraordinary union was determined by psychic phenomena, which Doctor Van Kipekap did not allow to escape his observation, and which he recorded in *The Mysteries of the Afterlife*, a work collected in *The Saturnian Chronicles* after the demise of the Earth.

VI.

It often happened that the refitted banker thought about Tony Wandel, his gentle and benign savior, but–contrary to what one might suppose–he never experienced any remorse at having sought the generous lad's final drop.[15] He did not consider himself in the least to be the instrument of the paver's horrible end; no, he reported his thoughts of that humble martyr with melancholy sincerity and wept for him as a tenderly-cherished brother, another self torn away from earthly preoccupations by an ineluctable law. He never conceived of Tony's shade as a pitiful and wrathful phantom coming to reproach him for his atrocious bargain, but rather as the sympathetic face of a twin or a double given a spiritual quality, intervening to inspire him in every act of his new life.

The banker submitted with such docility to that influence from beyond the grave that, on the night when Tony Wandel exhorted the solitary dreamer to espouse Nellie, he welcomed this strange injunction as the most rational solution in the world. On the following day, the conformed bachelor instructed Doctor Van Kipekap to go propose this marriage to the paver's widow.

The inconsolable creature rejected the impious proposition with horror, and did not wait for the doctor to finish before showing him the door. The somewhat crestfallen Van Kipekap reported this negative result to his capricious client.

"Nevertheless, it is necessary," sighed the banker. "The other wishes it; he issued the instruction again last night. I must present myself to the eyes of that wounded lioness..."

So Trekkenpluk went to see Nellie. He came unannounced into the room where she was. When he told her his name, she was already staring at him, and the syllables of the execrated name were unable to destroy the indescribable sympathy that she had felt for the intruder from the moment of his appearance.

In vain, she summoned to her aid the memory of the horrible bargain that had deprived her of the best of men; the revulsion no longer came. An imperious instinct, more powerful than her reason, stifled her rancor and showed her, in the very executioner of her first husband, the person fated to replace that beloved spouse in her unhinged heart.

What infernal illusion was misleading her? To what aberration had she been delivered? In the caressing inflexions of the voice of the visitor she had long abhorred, though, and in the gaze of those moist and emollient eyes, she found a striking reminder of the dead man for whom she had shed so many tears.

---

[15] I have rendered Eekhoud's improvised portmanteau word *chapechute* as "final drop" rather than translating it literally (as "escapefall"); it is impossible to preserve the alliterative effect.

The two men were quite different in their stature, features and coloring. Tony was as fair as the banker was dark, and yet they resembled one another in an incontestable fashion. Their features showed no correspondence, but in spite of that, the outline, the expression and the demeanor were identical. The supernatural light brightening their two masks had to be the same. It was as if the soul of the dead man inhabited the body of the present visitor–and that impression on the helpless woman become so pressing and so obsessive that all her hatred for Trekkenpluk melted like a mere prejudice.

At the same moment when he extended his hand to her, she advanced her own. He did not even have to ask her anything; in falling into his arms she accepted. They loved one another as Tony Wandel and Nellie had loved one another. When Nellie had made him a father, he lavished as much affection on his children as those of the paver–but no more.

Now, when Tony's smiling and radiant shade appeared to the banker, he saw it approach the young Wandels as little Trekkenpluks, and embrace them all with an equal and virile tenderness. And before dissipating into vapor with the retinue of ghosts that escorted the grey dusk, the well-wishing phantom finished up by touching his lips languorously to the irreproachable forehead of their mother. And the ecstatic banker found that last caress as natural as the others, feeling no jealousy at all. That became their way of life thereafter. No remorse or bad feeling ever divided the dead man and the living. Had they not, at present, the same heart?

VII.

Trekkenpluk eventually reached 40 years of age for a second time. On the morning of that anniversary, with his conscience at ease and full of the joys of living, he devoted himself cheerfully to his business affairs and silently prayed to Providence that he might be permitted to bring as much happiness to those around him as he enjoyed himself.

An unusual commotion in the street drew him out of this edifying reverie. The passers-by were drawing together, exchanging a few words, then parting at a run–and from one end of the town to the other the sinister rumor was carried: "To the fire!"

The banker did not wait for other news to follow on the heels of the idlers. The fire had started in one of the sinuous back-streets of the plebeian quarter, whose tall buildings sheltered large families of menial workers. One of these hovels was burning like a giant brazier and the foremen had no thought but to stop it spreading to the neighboring buildings. The chain of policemen and the cordon of soldiers respectfully gave passage to the rich burger, who was also invested with the most important civic honors.

Trekkenpluk learned that all the tenants had been able to escape in time except for one woman and two children lodged under the eaves. They were condemned to death, according to the official rescuers; it was impossible to get up to that height.

The flames were roaring in the stairwell and, from one moment to the next, the cracked walls were crumbling. Before long, the first-floor windows had shattered and were darting tongues of flame as red as the doors of a blast-furnace.

The fire, leaving the ground floor, climbed like a conqueror assaulting a hill. Three more staircases and landings and it would reach its victims; three more floors and, an implacable Moloch, it would daze, asphyxiate, lick its lips over and then devour those innocent sacrificial victims.

Trekkenpluk's great heart was squeezed by that thought. Every time a gust of wind drew drifting clouds from the roof, the banker anxiously interrogated the dormer window of the attic in which the unfortunates lived. He urged the firemen, the soldiers and the people on. Around him, strong young men folded their arms nervously, dazed or whining like old women.

Why were they hesitating to conduct themselves like heroes? In their place, Trekkenpluk would not have hesitated for a second. But had he the right to risk his own life? He had a duty not only to his own children but to the paver's widow and orphans. Despairing of awakening a sentiment of valor and duty in these tremblers, he tried at least to ignite their cupidity by promising a fortune to whoever saved one of the wretches–but in vain. No one budged.

The firemen continued phlegmatically to do what was strictly required of them. One of them could be seen, axe in hand and coils of rope on his arms, undermining the walls neighboring the furnace. Jets of water, projected from a distance, evaporated in the Gehenna with a rabid hiss, but the flames, exasperated by this hostile element, immediately reared up as if to defy it. The rhythmic rattle of the pumps was audible, the cracking of the beams, the blare of the signal-horns; the acrid odors seized one by the throat.

"Move back!" an officer commanded.

Trekkenpluk did not hear. He had perceived the silhouette of a blond child at the threatened dormer, waving its chubby arms.

"Please get back, Alderman; it might crumble at any moment!" the officer said to Trekkenpluk.

But the latter was no longer there, having thrown himself on to the soaring ladder.

There is no means of overtaking him. By way of salving consciences, the jets of the pumps are directed in his direction. He has vanished into the opaque swirl. He is lost!

A few seconds of anguish. A miracle! The smoke dissipates. He reappears, carrying a woman on his back and a child under each arm. He is coming back down the middle of the ladder.

At that moment, the sinister cracking sounds are redoubled. The walls are shaking; in the interior, the beams are crumbling; the scourge that sees its prey escaping increases its vehemence tenfold.

Trekkenpluk has only time to throw the children and their mother one by one into the blankets that hundreds of hands are now holding taut at the foot of the ladder. His noble example has enlivened the timorous. The three condemned having been saved, it is his turn to jump to safety.

Too late! The section of wall against which the fire-ladder is leaning collapses with a great noise, sending a fountain of flame and smoke up into the sky like a cluster of fireworks.

Down below, that black inanimate mass emerging from the cinders and the rubble... is Trekkenpluk.

Two firemen have seen him. They manage to reach him, because the collapse of the wall has stifled the flames on that side. To pick him up, to carry him away, takes no more than a second.

A triumphant acclamation salutes him–but, deprived of consciousness, his eyelids closed, the sublime alderman of N*** cannot hear the *vox populi* as he is transported back to his house. He cannot see the tearful mother, who is on her knees as the stretcher passes her by, and who, full of fervent gratitude, kisses the hafts of his litter as if it were bearing the relic of a miracle-working saint.

VIII.

"What do you think, doctor?" It is the exceedingly soft voice of Trekkenpluk, laid out on his bed. His body presents the appearance of a single horrible wound, from the soles of his feet to the top of his skull. Van Kipekap, recently arrived, contemplates with a professional eye this rarely encountered case, this superb living burn. From the viewpoint of his doctor, an indefinable smile has illuminated the charred visage of the sick man.

Van Kipekap wrinkles his nose, clears his throat and mumbles: "A new heart transplant might perhaps save you."

"No, no more of that. This time, I expire voluntarily. How much time have I left?"

"Oh, four hours... but, I repeat, before then I might be able to lay my hands on another mortally wounded man, younger and in better condition than you..."

"You know my resolution... don't insist. Besides, what good would the introduction of a new heart do? To supply me with a rascally heart, to resuscitate the original Trekkenpluk or to convert me into a specimen even more unpleasant...? No, I propose something else, impassioned operator that you are. Tell me at once whether my heart–the heart of Tony Wandel–still remains sound."

"As sound, albeit less vigorous, as it was ten years ago."

"Oh well, this 40-year-old heart, guaranteed fault free, will perhaps be the good fortune of one of your clients... especially as I shall abandon it to him gratuitously. Speak, Van Kipekap; don't you know anyone?"

"You don't mean it, my old friend."

29

"Absolutely. On one condition, however; if I desire that Tony Wandel's heart profit the recipient of your choice, I also demand that my disinterestedness contribute to the well-being of humanity, as was the case in the first instance. Therefore, doctor, you must endow the client who is not only in the most abysmal physical state, but whose gangrenous soul is also in the greatest need of redemption. Do you understand me?"

"So well that I already believe I know the individual in question. What do you think of the academician Foudrapiot?"

At the invocation of the grotesque and venomous metromaniac,[16] the patient forgot his excruciating [17] pain and his abominable martyrdom and could not help bursting into laughter.

"Oh, that will be an excellent joke!" He even attempted to bring his scorched hands together to applaud. "I wonder who the regenerated Foudrapiot will scandalize the most in the Academy–his official concubine, who entertains him like a *Sigisbé*,[18] or the *Jeunesse* [19] who scoff at him and riddle him with epigrams. Doctor, make haste to inform the bewigged pedant... and come back with him presto..."

Two hours later, the transshipment accomplished, Trekkenpluk expired and the septuagenarian rhymer was carried away from his house, plunged in anaesthetic slumber, in possession of the heart of the late and much honored Mijnheer Trekkenpluk, dignitary of N*** on the Scheldt.

---

[16] A metromaniac (Eekhoud's *métromane*), is an obsessive composer of verses. Although recognized by Webster, the word has fallen into disuse in English. The name *Foudrapiot* appears to be compounded out of *fou* (mad) and a derisory diminutive of *drapier* (draper).

[17] *Cuisante*–the word I have translated as "excruciating" carries a double meaning in French that is particularly acute in this instance; it also means "easily cooked."

[18] *Sigisbé* is a French form of the Italian *cicisbeo*, a term popularized in Venetian high society; it refers to a young man who serves as an escort to a noblewoman but is not her lover–although they often served as screen for actual lovers, functioning as alibis rather than chaperones.

[19] *Jeunesse* means "youth" but I have retained the original here because it obviously refers to the contributors to the francophone periodical *La Jeune Belgique*, which was taken over by Max Waller in 1882, soon becoming the central forum of an assertive movement that took aboard the ideas and ideals of the Parisian Decadent movement. It was a key showcase for writers like Maurice Maeterlinck, Georges Rodenbach and–of course–Eekhoud. The sentence in which the reference occurs is a symbolic comment on the ostentatiously respected and impatiently envied status of venerable members of the Académie Française, who had to die before their precious seats became available to younger aspirants.

IX

Two days after the death of the banker five young men, artists all, who generally led a Lenten life, were assembled in a tavern in the Rue des Chats at N***, the local eating-place where they dined least frugally. This time, the meal had taken on the proportions of a blow-out, to judge by the number of unsealed and "decorked" bottles strewn confusedly about the table. Each of them, miner-va on fire,[20] had been taxing his wits since the soup to sustain a never-ending flow of wit, paradoxes, epigrams, caricatures, etc.

None was chattering as much as the purveyor of this feast, Frank, a painter whose spirited and artistic intransigence made a delightful contrast with his dan-dy's physique, his languid, vaguely Lamartinian style,[21] his long fine hair, his exceptionally vivid blue eyes and his spiritual mouth, a trifle contracted by the pleat of thought–which is generally the pleat of suffering.

Today, he was exultant; he had obviously sold a painting and was eating and drinking, with his hot-headed coterie, the greater part of the price.

He was bragging without pausing for breath, and his harsh, strident voice was as shrill as a horn.

"My faithful friends, my Lords, as we Gauls are... I offer you an enigma: a bare-foot, red-haired, hypocritical, cunning, mellifluous poet, artificial but a very definite third-rater; a Conventioner [22] brandishing a sword of gilded card-board at the committee-meetings of beer-drinkers, scornful of the decorations obtained by his friends but flaunting in his buttonhole the following day the rib-bon awarded him the evening before; an abominable *caloyer*,[23] a critic of Punic

---

[20] A minerva was a kind of printing machine named after the Roman goddess of wisdom; Eekhoud, speaking figuratively, obviously has both meanings in mind.

[21] Alphonse Marie Lamartine (1790-1869) was a celebrated French poet–elected to the Academy in 1830–whose work bridged the transition from Classicism to Romanticism. He was also a noted orator and became Minister of Foreign Af-fairs in the provisional government set up after the Revolution of 1848, when many other French literary men, including Victor Hugo and Eugène Sue, also obtained political offices–with the result that they were all sent into exile after Louis Napoléon's *coup d'état*.

[22] *Conventionnel* was the term used to refer to members of the National Conven-tion established in 1792, which lasted until 1795, although it is here being used in a figurative sense.

[23] Eekhoud has *colir*; although Webster recognises "colire" as an English ver-sion of the term he gives it as an alternative form of the allegedly more familiar *caloyer*, which I have therefore used. Webster defines a *caloyer* as an Eastern Orthodox monk; Larousse adds the detail–which is preseumbly what Eekhoud had in mind here–that Chinese *colirs* were entitled to go into people's homes for the purpose of administering public censure.

faith,[24] anathematizing the endeavors of the young and patrial,[25] having recourse to malign interpolations to injure true poets; an emitter of froth,[26] faggoter [27] of cantatas, compiler of farragos, philosopher gaga,[28] dealer in second-hand writings, paper-spoiler and wholesale butcher. May Apollyon [29] deliver us from the vile beast!" [30]

Someone scratched at the door of the *cénacle*.[31]

"Come in!" said Frank.

"Pardon this intrusion, gentlemen," the newcomer stammered, bowing. He was a fat man with a round, jovial face and eyes of different colors, like Eulenspiegel.[32] "I am at your service. Twenty-four hours ago I regained my literary virginity. I have sent my resignation to the Academy and *La Jeune Belgique*. I

---

[24] Punic faith (*foi punique*) is an ironic synonym for treachery.

[25] *Patrial* survives in English–it means "pertaining to the fatherland," so Frank is referring to the fellow countrymen of the object of his spite–but the French word I have translated thus, *patriale*, was already obsolete when Eekhoud used it, thus fitting the general tenor of this florid speech.

[26] I have translated Eekhoud's *écumeur* literally, as he appears to intend it, although the French word is very rarely used in that way; its most familiar usage is in the phrase *écumeur de mer*, meaning "scourer of the sea"–i.e., a pirate.

[27] Eekhoud's fagoteur has an untranslatable double meaning, its straightforward translation (equivalent to "bundler") being supplemented by an implication of making a mess or putting on fancy dress.

[28] Eeekhoud's *gaga* is translatable as "doddering," but leaving it in place probably conserves more of the intended implication, even though it makes the phrase slightly awkward.

[29] Apollyon is the angel of the bottomless pit (Revelation 9:11), best known in England by virtue of his deployment in John Bunyan's *The Pilgrim's Progress*.

[30] Vile beast is a slightly deflatory literal translation of another of Eekhoud's improvised portmanteau words, *malebête*.

[31] *Cénacle* was the term–borrowed from the conventional label for the room where the Last Supper took place–that Charles Nodier adopted for the early meetings of writers central to the Romantic movement; it was subsequently adopted by similar literary groups.

[32] Thyl Ulenspiegel (1867) by Charles de Coster was an ostentatiously patriotic Belgian transfiguration of the legend of Tyll Eulenspiegel [Owl-glass], whose life as a prankster–very loosely based on the 14th-century exploits of a real German individual–was popularized in a famous collection of tall stories. Its first printed version dates from 1559, although it was probably written in 1483. The text in Kermesses renders the name as Uilenspiegel.

have burned my cantatas and pulped my quinquennial elucubrations. I am thus depalmate.[33] I make honorable amends and swear:

"*That my leonine verses to bring down venal Art*

"*Will discover the masculine vigor of Juvenal.*" [34]

"Well roared, lion! [35] For an academician, that's not too bad. But who are you, personage a hundred times more enigmatic and abnormal than the enigma I was posing to these gentlemen?"

"I am—or rather was—the answer to the enigma."

"Foudrapiot, then?" the flabbergasted five proclaimed.

"Himself, milords!"

"That's a good one!" cried Frank, who was the first to recover from that entirely natural astonishment. Seized by a fit of nervous gaiety, he flung his champagne in the face of the new member, saying: "*Jaune Belgique* hereby baptizes you *Jeune Belgique*! [36] Now tell us, I pray you, about the stages of your stupefying conversion." [37]

X.

At this point, the *Saturnian Chronicles* suffer a break of continuity. In all probability, the following documents in the sequence dealing with the avatars of Tony Wandel's heart would have been destroyed in the supreme cataclysm during which the Earth disappeared, along with other important traces of Man's exit from the Cosmos.

We do not know what literary services the rejuvenated and converted Doctor Foudrapiot rendered to his country, but everything leads us to suppose that the old fellow showed as much generosity as an artist as he had formerly shown as a contemptible pedant. Nor is it known how he perished, or who was the fourth possessor of the marvelous organ. What we can guarantee, however, is that it did not disappear with the poet Foudrapiot.

---

[33] Eekhoud's *dépalmé*, which I have translated literally, refers to *les palmes* [*académiques*]—decorations for services to education.

[34] These lines—*Que mes vers léonins pour tomber l'Art vé[nal]* / *Trouveront la vigeur mâle de Juvenal*—are presumably a quotation, but I have not been able to identify their source.

[35] Eekhoud renders this sentence in English.

[36] Eeekhoud's play on words is probably intended to recall the phrase *rire jaune*, which means constrained laughter, signifying a certain embarrassment on Frank's behalf. In France, unlike England *jaune* (yellow) is not the color associated with cowardice, although it is sometimes associated with treason.

[37] The reference to *les étapes...de conversion*, here translated as "the stages of...conversion" recalls the title of a significant autobiographical work by the French feuilletonist Paul Féval, *Les étapes d'une conversion* (1877).

Thus, it emerges from a few pages that escaped destruction that in the 2640s, the heart of the proletarian from N*** on the Scheldt entered into the economy of Tsar Esbrouffripoff.[38]

Abruptly vulgarized,[39] the day after this imprudent acquisition the autocrat made use of his absolute power to proclaim a democratic republic throughout the Russias, and abdicated immediately after issuing this marvelous ukase.

Esbrouffripoff went off to plant cabbages in Siberia ground cleared by several generations of nihilists and manured by their excrement. A fanatical boyar, more Tsarist than the Tsar, ruined by the new regime, sought out the hermitage of the tyrant who had thrown away his throne and stabbed him with a dagger.

The organ, cause of so many perturbations, was not yet tamed, for we find it again, in 2700, back in its country of origin, Flanders, beating beneath the uniform of a General given to gout and grumbling. The ailing veteran, restored to his feet by the influence of this purchase, did not long survive the operation. Commanded by a philanthropic monarch to go forth and civilize a population of so-called savages, he took his role as a legislator seriously and did not massacre the barbarians in question in order to civilize them more rapidly.

One day, the dark-skinned folk, badly advised by traitors, rose in revolt against their benign conqueror. The General refused the pitched battle that the rebels offered him and even forbade his troops to snipe at them. With his arms folded over his breast, he went on his own to confront the mutineers personally. After a few words of appeasement and paternal reproach, he declared himself ready to die beneath their assegais if they judged his death profitable to their country and their race. The savages, disconcerted by this stoicism, surrendered immediately.

This result, which might have been expected to delight the civilizer King, was, on the contrary, very badly received. One of the magnanimous General's officers, sent to the land of his birth to give an account of these events, did his commander some disservice at the Court and represented him not only as a milksop unworthy to command an army but as an ambitious schemer intent on the absolute sovereignty of the colony.

Recalled to Europe, this new Columbus, the excessively peaceful warrior, was court-martialed, convicted of desertion in the face of the enemy and stripped of his arms. His denouncer inherited his rank and his power, to the great

---

[38] The first part of the Tsar's surname is obviously derived from *esbrouffer*, meaning to bluff, while the second adds a Russian suffix to a noun derivative of *riper*, meaning to scrape, skid or scalp. Eekhoud would not have had the modern Anglo-American "rip off" in mind, but the intended effect is much the same.

[39] Eekhoud's *encanaillé*, here rendered as "vulgarized," usually referred to aristocrats mixing with the lower orders–"going slumming" would be the best translation of the modern employment of the word, although it would be inappropriate to use it here.

delight of the metropolitan militarists. After all, the fat epaulettes and the braid-trimmed kepis said to one another, what good was a commander who did not exterminate several thousand individuals for the greater glory of strategy, tactics and prrr...ogress?

Whether the condemned man make a deal with the recruits, or whether the members of the firing-squad–who were all his friends, his children–trembled as their eyes were obscured by tears, not a single bullet touched his heart... and that obstinate heart survived to protest against triumphant iniquity.

XI.

Doctor Van Kipekap, by applying his discoveries to his own frame, had similarly prolonged his own existence, but without attaining the moral perfection obtained at a single stroke by the banker Trekkenpluk. In possession of his third heart, he was still the same skeptical and materialist scientist, assisting with a sort of wicked joy in the perversion of humanity.

He loved, by means of study and a reasoned choice of organs, to graft a vice to a defect, to magnify a tendency to evil into explosions of crime. A new Wandering Jew, he traveled from continent to continent, comparing subjects with one another, contriving combinations of rogues and unpublished pedants.

However, this diabolical experimenter soon discovered that the differences between the organs became less and less noticeable. They all resembled one another in their baseness. Van Kipekap could transform a miser into a sensualist, a hypocrite into a homicide, a gossip into a slanderer, but he was no longer able to convert one of these "cases" into a fundamentally good person.

Eventually, the doctor acquired the conviction that no greater honesty and human virtue existed than there was in the heart of Tony Wandel, by virtue of its cosmopolitanism and its relationship with all the classes of society in consequence of its peregrinations. He discovered that, in this case at least, the immutable Christian goodness of the element always drew the same triumphant reaction from everybody to which it was introduced.

One day, when Van Kipekap found himself in Borneo, he learned that two colonists occupying neighboring plantations had quarreled over the barbaric treatment inflicted by one of them upon his slaves. The other had taken their part. Their master not having listened to reason, their defender had challenged him to a duel.

This quixoticism, to which he was no longer accustomed, made the doctor think. Might I be mistaken?, he asked himself. Might I find, in this new country, a match for Wandel's heart?

Van Kipekap was asked to accompany the adversaries to the battleground. He agreed, but requested to make the acquaintance of the challenger beforehand, thinking: An individual who consents to risk his life on behalf of pariahs is evidently a madman, unless he is the present possessor of Tony's heart! And he ran in double-quick time to the house of the chivalrous colonist.

Van Kipekap was not mistaken. This neo-Batavian [40] was indeed the moral heir of the Flemish proletarian. His name was Kemps de Salardinge.[41] He related how, as a fallen and ruined nobleman who had become a soldier, he had been a member of the firing squad that had executed the General. Knowing that he was ill, given up for dead by his doctors, he had had the sacrilegious idea of appropriating the heart of the condemned man. With the aid of one of his friends, a Jewish surgeon, the operation had been successfully carried out.

While the doctor listened to the story of the enriched and redeemed jonkeer Kemps' adventures, a singular and demanding desire was born in him for the first time. Until now, he thought, this absorbent pocket she-devil has completely metamorphosed the individuals in which she had lodged. But it would be interesting to see whether, set in contact with the blood of Doctor Van Kipekap, she can overcome the strong spirit, impassiveness, cold mathematical reason and will-power that have marked his passage on our planet. If only I might try. It would be a conclusive experiment, at least, and I would be able to observe every phase... Van Kipekap has a stronger constitution than his decrepit brothers. I defy this crazy heart to reduce me to the wishy-washy state of this entire Wandelized series and to make me act in a fashion that reproves my experience and my love of logic!

The more he thought about it, the more he was tempted by this supreme test, and the more obsessive and attractive the idea became.

"Providence!" he cried. "Supreme Being that I deny, do you accept the wager? My soul is the stake. I will believe in you if you can reduce me to the sheep-like role of your Christians. If not, I shall die as I have lived, blaspheming against you!"

At that moment, the doctor wished that his new friend might be the loser of the duel.

Chance granted his wish. During the first engagement, Kemps de Salardinge's breast was punctured by a thrust of the foil. He fell to the floor, blood flooding abundantly from his mouth.

Van Kipekap, having thrown himself forward, anxiously, to examine the wound, realized–but without saying anything, and hiding his satisfaction–that the blade, skirting the lung, had not perforated any essential organ. The wound-

---

[40] Batavia is an antique name for the Netherlands (also applied to a port in Java, the capital of the Dutch East Indies). Eekhoud's neo-Batave reflects the fact that the Low Countries had been briefly renamed *la République de Batave* [The Republic of Batavia] following their conquest by French Revolutionary forces in 1795.

[41] This surname has the customary uncomplimentary associations, sale meaning dirty and ardent implying fervent enthusiasm.

ed man had escaped with his life–but the doctor, to the contrary, exaggerated the gravity of the situation.

"Carry him to my house. Leave me alone with him. None of his family or his friends may come to see him; if that condition is met, I might perhaps save him."

Everyone, having faith in the genius of the illustrious man, submitted to his will and even gave him their effusive blessing.

"You shall have news in eight hours," he told them as he left.

Shut up in his residence again–having no one with him, save for poor Kemps de Salardinge, but a servant who was terrified of him and a pupil whose soul was damned–the doctor carried out his abominable project with all the care, caution, method and calmness that he put into the least of his experiments.

When the time had passed, the wounded man's nearest and dearest presented themselves at the practitioner's house. The latter was atrociously pale, his features drawn, his eyes red, his appearance revealing–perhaps for the first time–some trace of emotion.

Without speaking, he led them to the bed on which the cold body of the noble Kemps de Salardinge lay. The doctor received the family's thanks with embarrassment, and refused any payment. The wound, they said, must have been incurable, since this magician had been unable to save their overgenerous relative. They inherited a fortune and were perfectly ready to forget good old Kemps and Van Kipekap's unusual appearance.

XII.

The swaggering surgeon and positivist atheist lost the bet he had laid with Providence. As soon as he had taken possession of Tony Wandel's heart, he began to cast off his old self. He awoke completely dismantled. He could recall the past but, instead of taking pleasure in his memories, deriving strength from them and discovering a logical connection between past and present, he recoiled in dismay, seized by horror and disgust. His scientific knowledge, his carefully elaborated works and his irrefutable documents all fell apart, broken like waves upon a new and imperious force that had absorbed his being.

He, the eternal laugher, the calculator as certain as an algebraic proof, with sarcasm and negation forever in his mouth, first experienced scruples and then remorse. He even shed tears over the assassination of the wounded man confided to his care, for it was certainly an assassination–a word at which he had previously jeered–that he had committed, and he could no longer silence his conscience with the aid of sophism and casuistry.

That disowned conscience spoke now of implacable justice. No, science did not purify the evil; science did not justify the crime! That was what Tony Wandel's heart contained: the despotic tormentor conscience.

In addition, going against everything antecedent, scornful of himself and his former ideals, there was now a profound pity for humankind in him, while loathing degraded, defiled and diminished machinery, figures and automata. This belated pity was exasperated by the idea that he might not be able, in spite of all his good will, at the cost of heroic effort, to render to his brothers their primordial nobility.

Ah, if he could only dedicate a thousand hearts of this extinct species to that task, perhaps he might avert the end of the world and its inhabitants!

Tony Wandel's widow, the paver's children and the banker's, were dead. The other beautifully-ensouled inheritors of the chosen organ had not had the time to found families in their turn. So the doctor–the last receiver of the treasure–admitted despairingly that which a banker, an artist, a general, a missionary, a colonist and so many other powerful people had only been able to realize under the impulsion of Tony Wandel's heart. He, a simple physician, a man of scholarship and theory, experienced it even more painfully.

He dreamed then of sacrificing himself for the salvation of humankind; he knew the sublime thirst for death–for a redemptive death like that of a second Nazarene...

XIII.

At that time, the Episcopal seat of N*** on the Scheldt was occupied by Cardinal Willebrord Gelof, a fanatical, authoritarian, intolerant prelate clinging obstinately to life. Old and crippled as he was, he still made his lax diocesan flock tremble beneath his crozier.

The time arrived when Gelof demanded from the surgeons a renewal of health and vigor. However, the members of Monsignor's orthodox entourage were aware of the upsets caused in the world for several centuries by Tony Wandel's heart. The chapter of Canons having no desire for the operation to change this prince of the Church Militant into an apostle worthy of the first era of Christianity, the strictest precautions were taken to guarantee the provenance of the organ to be embodied in their master's debilitated frame.

It was of this Cardinal that Doctor Van Kipekap thought.

A priest worthy of Christ might perhaps be able to deliver the last children of Adam from their abject state. It was a matter of deceiving the vigilance of the archbishop's familiars and spies and of providing the moribund prelate with exactly that evangelical heart abhorred by Pharisees and the Rich.

One evening, while wandering meditatively through the streets, he was interrupted by a barricade of heavy paving-stones. A team of artisans was in the process of repairing the road. They had dug a trench and were bent over in a row, hindquarters in the air, bare-armed and open-necked in their shirt-sleeves, tamping and heaving by turns with their rammers and mallets. Laborers moved back and forth, carrying sand and stones in wheelbarrows, running obediently in response to the impatient calls of older men. The ruddy light of several resinous torches, planted at the level of the earthworks, illuminated the bronzed and hairy workmen. Velvet waistcoats, caps, bottles and haversacks were heaped up on either side of the pavement. There were old uncles there, skinny and wrinkled, dry as firewood, beside sinewy adolescents whose shining eyes and vermilion mouths stood out feverishly within dirty faces already grooved by coarse precocious labor. The hour sounded in a church, the bell striking in harmony with the heavy *demoiselles*. [42] The doctor was suddenly reminded of Tony Wandel and his harrowing refrain:

"*On, on, honest paver,*
"*Dig and level the road.*
"*While the Angelus sounds*
"*In the distant tower,*
"*The resonant plink*
"*Of your falling pick*
"*Adds amen to the prayer.*"

While he contemplated these nocturnal workers, rocked as in a cradle by the suggestive rhythm of their movements, he observed a poor devil in the company whose appearance was more downcast, hungrier and more extreme than the rest. In a sudden flash of inspiration, he saw the realization of his project. He approached the stout workhorses and took the world-weary one aside.

"Would you like to earn a fortune, sleep in a feather-bed, eat and drink as you desire?" he said to him, straightforwardly.

He had to repeat the question, for the other seemed lost.

"Yes? Well, get your coat and follow me."

The paver obeyed, moving like a sleepwalker, and fell into step with the doctor. The others, fully occupied, did not notice his disappearance.

First, Van Kipekap went home and wrote a few letters, which he sealed and left on his desk. They were addressed to his assistants and contained his last will and testament. He opened a drawer and took therefrom a handful of gold, which he slipped into the vendor's callused hand.

"This is a deposit. In three days you will return here and say that you have come on my behalf. The person who will receive you has orders to pay you 100,000 francs in cash. It's up to you to earn that fortune. I've welcomed you into my home; one good turn deserves another, and I want to return your visit. Off to your hearth..."

The other, still phlegmatic, believing himself to be dreaming standing up, decamped with his extraordinary benefactor. Having passed along the Rue des

---

[42] It is not obvious why the pavers' implements should be nicknamed *demoiselles*, but the reference is probably to the stick-like bodies of damsel-flies rather than to actual maidens.

Va-Nu-Pieds into the Impasse des Roses,[43] they came to a halt before No. 48, a sordid, moldy and unplastered edifice eaten away by parasitic plants.

"This is your nesting-place–a few steps from the archbishop's palace? Everything's working out marvelously. Oh, one more question: you're a bachelor or a widower, I hope, without children or a partner?"

"Alone as a plague-victim."

"Let's go up, then."

They went into a somber passage, at the end of which they found a tortuous stairway, a veritable goat-track, to which a greasy cord served as a handrail. The doctor was not put off by the darkness or the nauseating odor. Beneath the roof, the paver pushed open a door; they went into the wretched hovel and the master of the house lit a tallow candle.

The doctor looked around with a satisfied expression; these miserable lodgings seemed infinitely agreeable to him. He consulted his watch.

"Ten o'clock! Good. Now, my brave Tiest Tinkeltang,[44] take off your muddy britches, your patched waistcoat, your greasy cap, your stockings–pardon me, but they're indescribable–and your threadbare slippers. I'll get undressed in my turn; I'll put on your clothes and let you have mine, including the accessories: jewelry, fastenings, watch and chain... That done, you'll leave, and as you are obviously rich, you'll have no trouble finding somewhere to stay. Don't think of coming back here or of telling any living soul about your adventure, and in three days the promised treasure will be yours. Is that understood?"

"Yes, Mijnheer!"

To disguise themselves required only a few seconds.

"And now goodnight, Tiest Tinkeltang; I won't show you out."

Left alone, Van Kipekap prepared with superb firmness of purpose the setting of the drama on which the curtain of his centuries-long life was about to fall. While he went back and forth in his final apartment, however, dressed like a starveling, incoherent maudlin phrases, ejaculations of a fantastic verve and wild prayers fell from his lips.

"The forest was more beautiful, my gentle Tony, and the beech-tree from which you swung was a lot better than that filthy joist... the cord is similarly inelegant... but today's hanged man is not worth as much as you, my sublime ancestor..."

---

[43] The Rue des Va-Nu-Pieds might be translated as "Vagabond Street;" an *impasse* is a dead end, the roses for which this one is named having the same metaphorical significance that they bear in such English phrases as "a bed of roses" or "coming up roses."

[44] Tiest Tinkeltang is presumably a stereotypical pauper in Belgian or Dutch literature or legend, but I have not been able to identify the source of the name.

Having climbed up on the stool, his head lodged in the hangman's rope, he took a long look through the skylight. Day was breaking, grey and dull, over the billowing rooftops.

"It must be six o'clock in the morning. There's the tenants tumbling down the stairs to go to work. My assistant has orders to wake the Archbishop at this very moment. The operators can be here in a trice... let's get on with it!" He added, with passionate fervor: "May God and Tony Wandel pardon me! And may my heart be useful to Cardinal Willebrord!"

No one said amen, as once had been said beneath the majestic beech-foliage. He sent the stool rolling away with one kick, then struggled and thrashed about, prey to the supreme visions of imminent death.

At the climax of the spasmodic dance, a band of liveried lackeys came into the room, cut the cord and bore the hanged man away to a carriage where the surgeons–colleagues and heirs of the doctor–were waiting.

No one recognized the ragged and grimy hanged man as the opulent, eternal and cheerful Van Kipekap. The Senior Curate, the most suspicious, objected even so that the suicidal paver might be a second Tony Wandel. They laughed at him, and the organ extracted from the still-living hanged man's chest was encased, without further investigation, within the breast of the valetudinary prelate.

When, eight hours later, the fraud was made known, it was too late; the prelate, having the full use of his legs, did not stick around to hear the frightful proof a second time, and found himself much improved by his purchase. He had not waited as long as his predecessors to continue the worthy tradition of Wandelism.

XIV.

Willebrord Gelof began by renouncing purple robes, well-furnished apartments, delicate food and the pleasures of his palace. He sold his horses, his carriages and his gold plate, and gave the proceeds of this liquidation to the hospices. He was seen walking in the streets of the town, wandering in the surrounding countryside, dressed as a simple pastor, giving alms to the poor, exhorting the recalcitrant, proclaiming the religion of Christ.

At first, the Canons and the Senior Curate through that it might be a transient phase, but the generous folly and Christian humility of their superior increased day by day. The incandescence of his clergy became overwhelming when Gelof had the house pulled down, dismissing his parasites and regurgitating the holders of fat stipends and pious sinecures. They still dared not make any overt accusation against him, but while they bided their time, they secretly and slanderously spread abominable rumors about his private life.

Gelof had the clear vision of ancient theologians; the Eddas, the Vedas and the Koran revealed to him the symbolic meaning of the mysteries mocked by new religions, and he found the eternal and unique thread connecting all these incomplete cults to the sole verity. Gelof, disciple of Christ, preached these doctrines publicly. He dared to proclaim that Jesus was the founder of the socialist school and the first republican.

Then, the Pharisees howled and openly challenged his authority. They went to the Pope, denouncing his teaching as a pulpit of pestilence and the treason of Protestantism. They made a show of stepping aside as he passed by, spitting in front of him and drawing away. Gelof heard them murmuring with viperish hisses: "It's blasphemy: we must be rid of it, because it's poisonous!"

He was soon removed from office. The enthronement of his successor at N*** on the Scheldt was attended by much pomp and from that day on he was no longer spared.

In his sermons to the pastoral laborers and to the bandits of the region, the gentle apostle exalted charity above all else. The sophists ordained a punishment of death against anyone who would be so bold as to preach theological virtues.

His heresy was named Wandelism.

Governments and potentates, worked on by ministers of religion, turned an equally evil eye upon this dispossessed Bishop who took the side of the humble and the weak. Nevertheless, Gelof always condemned rebellions and prevented civil war. The Jacquerie [45] summoned him in vain to put himself at its head. After that, the little people, the hungry poor, turned against him. He spoke to them of a future life, of the compensation of their ordeals, of eternal reward. They mocked him, and distrusted him as an accomplice of rich oligarchs, all the more so as preachers of every sort sprang up like vermin from a sewer to exploit the evil passions of these desperate men.

No human authority or philosophy would have been able to hold back that tide. Discord was coming into its own. Populations became profligate in the pursuit of their oppressors, and the liberators of the day before became the persecutors of the day after.

The whole world was soon swimming in blood, and everyone was a victim.

Meanwhile, one man alone remained upright, bringing words of hope and peace, invoking the Gospel and Infinite Love. Barefoot, without pause, he traveled the world, interposing himself between brothers armed against one another. His soul was anguished by the sight of these universal excesses and he shed tears of blood over all these afflictions, but everywhere he went he was shouted down and execrated. The false priests saw him as a dangerous competitor, the despots as an accomplice of the protests of the crowd, and the populace as a spy, their tyrants' turncoat.

And everyone cried *Noël!* on the day this man, whose Christian virtue none could suspect, and whose generosity none could count up, was arrested in Flan-

---

[45] The original Jacquerie was a peasant revolt of 1357-58, although the term eventually became applicable to any popular uprising. The name Jacques is often applied generically to peasants.

ders. They would soon be rid of this nuisance, of this cynical mocker who still dared to acknowledge God and Heaven while the Earth returned to Chaos. He was delivered by common agreement to prosecution by his former Episcopal chapter, who consigned to the stake the placid apostle whom the claws of leopards and tigers had spared in the remotest deserts.

On the day of his execution, advertised well in advance to the four corners of the world, there was a pause in the massacre, so that the torture of the common enemy, to whom the whole human race had put a stop, might be smugly enjoyed in peace.

Myriads of curiosity-seekers flooded from every direction, their swarm spreading out into the fields and the slopes of the hills surrounding the place of execution–and those who would not be able to see his death-throes were hoping that the wind might at least bring them the delicious fragrance of the odor of charred flesh and the sweet music of his heart-rending cries!

At about five o'clock on a winter afternoon, the *cortège*, organized with theatrical precision, took him to one of the hills overlooking the town. To reach the summit where the stake was set, higher than the throne of Emperors, the old man had to climb 60 steps. When he appeared, in a white robe, and was attached to the stake, a mighty *hosanna* was raised by the innumerable crowd.

This shout, released by those who could see the sacrificial victim, was propagated for months, echoed from mouth to mouth, into the heartlands of the most obscure countries, beyond the oceans, by the entire human race, immobilized in the same ferocious angst, the same expectant sacrilege.

The flame was put to the pyre. It grew slowly, coquettishly, then rapidly, frenetically.

The martyr looked straight ahead, drowned in dolorous serenity. In the furthest reaches of the landscape, he saw, overwhelming the facing hill, a Babel of extravagant domes, which the setting Sun striped with cinnabar and ochre, and which stood out sharply from the lava-blackened horizon. The priest made out the twin columns of porticoes as high as cathedral spires–and above the principal pylon, in front of a vast succession of terraces extending in stages into the sky, was a white bust of Justice.

And this glorification of the Justice of men, facing the plateau one which the flesh of the last Just Man was being consumed, was a kind of supreme irony, an irreparable defiance hurled at the Creator by that rabble of fallen creatures.

At intervals, livid fulgurations scored the sepulchral firmament. The fire of joy, lit by delirious humanity, projected the shadow of its enormous tongues of flame as far as the distant walls of the Temple, with the magnified silhouette of the patient at its center.

Vaguely at first, that immense and fantastic black silhouette appeared to detach itself from the walls; then, as nebulous as a whirlwind descending into a valley, it passed over the town, overhanging the roofs of the Bourses, the Warehouses, the masts of ships, the chimneys of factories and the dungeons of arsenals like a funeral canopy.

The myriad fascinated eyes, distracted by the execution, were now looking to the side from which that terrifying storm cloud was advancing. The attendants turned their backs on the pyre.

The atmospheric phenomenon, borne by an angry wind, accompanied by the noise of thunder, headed for the plateau of the auto-da-fé. The closer it came, the higher the flames became, revivified as if by the breath of a powerful bellows.

But the storm was taking form. The clouds draped a mantle of darkness about a person of tall stature, with a phosphorescent visage, a vulture's beak, bloodshot eyes and a lipless mouth.

The apparition gained the stake's summit in a single stride. In its hand, it carried a long dagger, which it plunged into the martyr's breast–who was burned to waist-height. When the dagger was withdrawn therefrom, a red bleeding heart was impaled like a fly on its point.

The executioner lowered his arm; the palpitating organ fell off and rolled on the ground. Then the dreadful personage stamped its boot upon the heart of Tony Wandel: the last immaculate heart.

The clamor of the World died down, for the instrument of its hatred was named the Antichrist.

And afterwards, deprived of its last vestige of Goodness, that world had nothing to do but die...

Jules Lermina: *The Elixir of Life*

Jules Hippolyte Lermina (1839-1915) tried his hand at various clerical jobs, before turning his hand to freelance journalism. In 1867, he founded a political periodical, Le Corsaire, *which led to his being imprisoned. He was soon released in response to protest—from Victor Hugo, among others—but promptly repeated his crime, founding a new journal called* Satan, *and was imprisoned again.*

After the disastrous French defeat by the Prussian army at the Battle of Sedan (1870), Lermina was released and launched into a new career: writing popular fiction. Although his left-wing views did not change, he seems to have contented himself for the next decade with simply making a living. The great bulk of his work consisted of crowd-pleasing entertainment in the great tradition of the French roman feuilleton. *He consciously set out to be a loyal disciple of Eugène Sue and Alexandre Dumas; he wrote a Suesque* Mystères de New York *under the pseudonym "William Cobb" and produced two sequels to* Le Comte de Monte Cristo.

Shortly after 1880, when she was in her early twenties, Lermina's daughter Marie-Pauline married one of the bouquinistes *who kept stalls on the banks of the Seine, Henri Chacornac (1855-1907). Lermina presumably provided the financial backing for his son-in-law to move up-market; he opened a shop at 11 Quai Saint-Michel in 1884 under the title* Librairie Générale des Science Occultes, *that being his specialty as a second-hand book-dealer. The shop and its associated publishing enterprises were just in time to cash in on a remarkable explosion of interest in the occult, and they became very successful.*

Two of Chacornac's most avid customers were medical students at the University of Paris who had been entranced by the works of the pioneering lifestyle fantasist Eliphas Lévi (Alphonse-Louis Constant) and had been initiated into the esoteric discipline of "Martinism," founded by the 18th century mystic Martinez de Pasqually (1727-1774): Gérard-Anaclet-Vincent Encausse (1864-1916) and Augustin Chaboseau (1868-1946). Encausse, the Spanish-born son of a chemist, who used the signature Papus (allegedly meaning "Physician" and borrowed from a document called the "Nuctemeron of Apollonius of Tyana," faked by Eliphas Lévi) went on to become one of the central figures of the Parisian occult revival.

Encausse joined the French branch of the Theosophical Society shortly after its formation in 1884 but left within a year, dissatisfied with Madame Blavatsky's particular brand of mysticism. He then got together with two of Chacornac's other clients, Joséphin Péladan and Stanislaus de Guaita, who were to become his chief rivals as flamboyant lifestyle fantasists, to form the Kabbalistique Ordre de la Rose-Croix. Their triple alliance did not last long, because Péladan split to form his own neo-Rosicrucian Order, while Encausse, Guaita and Chaboseau decided to concentrate a revamped version of Martinism. Although he eventually completed his medical training in 1894, Encausse was frequently distracted from his studies; in particular, he took a leading role in a meeting held on 20 April 1889 by 80 delegates of some 34 occult groups and societies to organize a massive "Spiritist Congress" that was held in Paris on September 9-15 of that year. He persuaded Lermina to accept the honorary presence of the first session and give the opening address.

Encausse went on to join the Parisian branch of the Order of the Golden Dawn and numerous other organizations, gaining sufficient reputation as a modern magician to be entertained by Tsar Nicholas II on several visits to Russia (during which, he insisted, he had warned Nicholas in vain about the evil influence of Rasputin), but was always outshone by Joséphin Péladan, partly because the latter integrated a prolific and moderately successful career as a novelist into his career as a lifestyle fantasist. Eliphas Lévi had only turned to lifestyle fantasy when his own career as a littérateur had failed to take off, so it is hardly surprising that Encausse had literary ambitions too. He and Lucien Chamuel founded a publishing enterprise called the Librairie du Merveilleux in 1888, spearheaded by a Revue called L'Initiation, thus going into open competition with Chacornac, but Chacornac eventually bought Chamuel out in 1901. In the meantime, however, L'Initiation paid considerable attention to the literary aspects of the occult revival, publishing work by such Decadent heroes as Villiers de l'Isle-Adam and Catulle Mendès, as well as work by Lermina.

Exactly how much Encausse (as "Papus") contributed to the two Lermina stories whose separate publication he arranged, and for which he wrote prefaces, is unclear, but it seems probable that A brûler, conte astral [For Burning; an Astral Tale] (1889) and L'Elixir de vie [here translated as The Elixir of Life] (1890) ought to be regarded as collaborations.

Although he had sold stories to the first series of the Vernian Journal des Voyages, launched in 1877, Lermina became a much more frequent presence in its second series, launched in 1896. Most of his contributions were straightforward adventures stories, similar to those he had written earlier, but he also provided such lively and interesting serial scientific romances as To-Ho le tueur d'or, [46] Mystère-Ville [Mysteryville] (1904)[47] and L'Effrayante Aventure (1910)[48]. Lermina would probably have done more in the same vein had he been able to do so, but was then reaching the end of his career and his life; he died in 1915.

---

[46] *To-Ho and the Gold Destroyers*, Black Coat Press, ISBN 978-1-935558-34-7.
[47] *Mysteryville*, Black Coat Press, ISBN 978-1-935558-27-9.
[48] *Panic in Paris*, Black Coat Press, ISBN 978-1-934543-83-2.

Although L'Elixir de vie *would nowadays be considered an occult romance by virtue of its employment of animal magnetism, the whole point of the narrative is to challenge the justice of the decision that had been taken by the French* Académie de Médecine *to rule that Mesmerism was pure charlatanry and had no place in the canon of scientific medicine.*

The story's hero, presumably modeled on Encausse—although it is the villain of the piece, Monsieur Vincent, who shares one of Encausse's own forenames—takes a strictly scientific approach to the enigma that confronts him, which is why he takes so long to accept what is blindingly obvious to the reader. That is not, however, the most interesting aspect of the tale as an example of proto-science fiction; by contrast with many other 19th century tales of "psychic vampirism"—here, too, Lermina anticipates Arthur Conan Doyle, who published The Parasite *in 1895—*L'Elixir de vie *is by no means a straightforward horror story, and it comes remarkably close to endorsing the monster's excuses by virtue of an explicitly Darwinian argument that was to be reiterated incessantly in the revisionist vampire stories that became fashionable in the last quarter of the 20th century.*

B.S.

Foreword

Can human life be prolonged? This is a question that, sooner or later, secretly or otherwise, presents itself to the investigative mind of the scientist, whether he is an alchemist or a professor of the Collège of France.

The spiritualist school, which considers life as something immaterial, complete and existing independently, furnishes audacious and solid research evidence, but the cold positivist argumentation of the Ecole de Médecine de Paris came along to destroy these beautiful dreams in the name of pure experimentation, making life no more than the more or less perfect result of chemical actions accomplished according to laws operating within the intimacy of tissues.

The struggle between these two opposed tendencies is curious to observe. Bichat,[49] sensitive to the effective power of life, defined it as "that which resists death"—a poor definition in philosophical terms, but excellent for the physician who, sooner or later, will establish the curative force of that mysterious power. Claude Bernard[50] claims to know what it is and, inverting Bichat's spiritualist definition, had made the study of life the constant preoccupation of his research.

---

[49] Marie-François-Xavier Bichat (1771-1802) was a significant pioneer of scientific physiology, but found the burden of past assumptions about the essentially "spiritual" nature of life difficult to shake off.

[50] Claude Bernard (1813-1878) was one of the most accomplished French physiologists of the 19th century, renowned for his work on the nervous system.

Superlative results regarding the particular functions of various organs have been acquired by this approach, but the goal to be attained seems to draw increasingly further away, and Bichat's celebrated adversary declared himself defeated in one of his last works.[51] I quote from memory: "life is what makes the egg of a chicken and the egg of a nightingale, which are similarly constituted chemically, produce a chicken on the one hand, and a nightingale on the other."

Without wishing to dwell too long on this question, which is overly entangled with "first causes," let us posit the existence in human beings of a force that incessantly renews elements that are used up and conserved the form of the body. The experiments of Flourens,[52] feeding madder to animals, have proved, in fact, that the most durable and most resistant cells of the human body, bone cells, take a maximum of *one month* to renew themselves. The result of this, as Maldan[53] has remarked, is that a person that we see after an interval of three or four months is no longer the same, materially speaking, as the one we saw before. The physiognomy has not changed, though, nor has the general form of the body; there must, therefore, be some kind of force within the person that conserves acquired forms independently of the incessant renewal of the cells.

Where, then, is this force to be found?

In human beings it is carried everywhere by a little cellular element, the blood corpuscle, which restores the force to organs that have need of it and which then goes in quest of a new provision of the force for itself before returning. This is called circulation. If corpuscles are prevented from reaching an organ, the organ soon dies, which indicates to us that the blood corpuscle is the seat of the force, which is nothing other than life.

One primary, rather coarse, means of restoring life to someone who lacks it is, therefore, to infuse him directly with a certain quantity of living blood corpuscles. This is called transfusion, and it is the method of rejuvenation used by certain rich Orientals.[54] But the force in human beings is not only fixed in this

---

[51] Papus gives a reference here to "Claude Bernard, *Science expérimentale.*" The book, which was a definitive attempt to revolutionize medicine by the introduction of the scientific method to its research and practice, is actually entitled *Introduction à l'étude de la médecine expérimentale*; it was published in 1865.

[52] The physiologist Pierre-Jean-Marie Flourens (1794-1867). Lermina must have known his son, Gustave, who was one of the leaders of the Paris Commune and died during the insurrection in 1871.

[53] Papus gives a reference to "Maldan, *Matière et force*, Dentu, 1882." I have not been able to obtain any more detailed identification about the author.

[54] The suggestion that rich Orientals used blood transfusion as a method of rejuvenation is, of course, a myth. Christopher Wren, the English architect, had carried out a pioneering series of experiments in animal blood transfusion in 1657 and a series of injections of lamb's blood into human patients was carried out in Paris a few years later by the natural philosopher Jean-Baptiste Denis (1625-

perpetually-circulating element; nature has lodged a little of it throughout a series of reservoirs in which the force is condensed, subject to tension, accumulated in order to be released later in response to need. These reservoirs are nervous ganglions, often gathered into a plexus, and their ensemble constitutes the mysterious system of organic life represented by the sympathetic nervous system. All around the heart, all along the vertebral column and inside the abdomen are found *reserve centers of vital force*; all the organs that operate without being subject to the action of our will do so under the influence of these centers.

Now, a fact long known to the Hindus and Orientals is that life thus stored in reserve can *emerge from the human body* and act at a distance. A man who possesses the secret of that action can, therefore, cease to draw upon on the blood that ought to revivify him—a procedure worthy, at most, of the ignorant—and have recourse to the vital reserves, invisibly attracting to himself the force that he requires. To those who doubt the action of life outside the human body, I shall cite the delicate and rigorous experiments of William Crookes [55] of the Royal Society of London on Psychic Force and its action at a distance—action verified by mechanical measuring devices.

Have we, then, you might ask, fallen back into the domain of Animal Magnetism and Spiritism? Call it what you will; it is unimportant. It is a matter of actual, indisputable facts, which the Académies will admit in a few decades.

Since I have strayed into the terrain of occult science, why should I not extrapolate the hypotheses to their conclusion in telling you the origin of human life, according to the occultists.

You will accept, I suppose, that life is held in reserve in the ganglions of the sympathetic nervous system. Where does it come from before being condensed there? From blood corpuscles, either directly or via the intermediary of the cerebellum, if one believes the admirable but unfortunately little-known

---

1704). Although three of Denis' patients reported that it the treatment had been beneficial, the fourth died and Denis was subsequently sued by his widow. Blood transfusions were then outlawed in France until the 1800s, although experimentation was revived in England in the 1790s by Erasmus Darwin. In 1890 such experiments were still highly likely to do more harm than good; no headway was made on the issue of compatibility until Karl Landsteiner categorized the A/B/O blood groups in 1909.

[55] Papus gives a reference to "William Crookes, *Force Psychique.*" William Crookes (1832-1919) was the most famous physicist caught up by the vogue for spiritualist trickery. In 1870 and 1871 he published two papers on "Experiments on the Psychic Force," which were rapidly translated into French. The wide reportage given to a demonstration of the supposed abilities of mediums that he staged for the Royal Society caused something of a sensation in France.

work of Dr. Luys.[56] Where does a blood corpuscle obtain the force that it carries everywhere, under the influence of the oxidation of hemoglobin? From the air that bathes and vivifies all the living beings on Earth, either directly or in solution.

Setting its chemical composition aside, where does the air come from? An occultist of high repute, Chardel,[57] shows that the terrestrial atmosphere results from the action of the Sun on our Earth; the Air is a modality of the solar Force. The primary origin of Life is, therefore, the Sun; by a series of successive transformations, it is eventually lodged in a nervous ganglion in the form of human life. When I burn wood, do you think I am doing anything other than extracting the sunlight that the wood had condensed when the plant was alive? The same is true for life in all its modalities.

A third means, even more mysterious than the preceding ones, therefore consists of secretly going in search of the vivificatory elements in the Sun itself—but then we are dealing with Magic, a word that rings false in the ears of contemporary scientists and literary men take the responsibility for trying to make them understand it better than we do ourselves.

In fact, authentic centers of research exist in our own day in which Magic is studied in all its branches: The *Groupe independent d'études ésotériques*, which publishes the journal *L'Initiation*,[58] treats these questions, and numerous researchers—Stanislaus de Guaita, F.-Ch. Barlet, Julien Lajay, Polti et Gary, Augustin Chaboseau—apply the Occult Science to our various contemporary sciences. The list of Mage-Littérateurs grows every day, representing every school, from the ultramontanist Catholic Joséphin Péladan, the initiator of the movement, to the charming poet Gilbert-Augustin Thierry, passing through the

---

[56] Papus inserts a reference to "Dr. Luys, *Le Système nerveux*. Paris, 1865." The reference is to Jules-Bernard Luys (1829-1897), a significant pioneer of physiological psychology; the actual title of the book cited is *Recherches sur le système cérébro-spinal, sa structure, ses functions et ses maladies*.

[57] Papus inserts a reference to "Chardel, *Esquisse de la Nature humaine*, 1840." The reference is to Casimir Chardel (1777-1847); the full title of the work cited is *Esquisse de la Nature humaine expliquée par le magnétisme animal*, and its original publication was in 1826.

[58] Papus gives the address of this organization as "58, rue St.-André-des-Arts, Paris," but modestly refrains from mentioning that it is his own. In the same spirit, he does not mention that all the researchers he cites were either his friends and collaborators or contributors to his journal. "F.-Ch. Barlet" was the pseudonym of Albert Faucheux, a disciple of Guaita who subsequently became very interested in astrology. Little is known about Lejay or "Polti et Gary" save their signatures; the latter collaborators had published a book on "the theory of temperaments" in 1889.

Catholic socialist Paul Adam and the poets Alber Jhouney, Victor-Emile Michelet, Paul Marrot and L. Mauchel.[59]

Here, therefore, is a new school rising over the horizon, a school simultaneously scientific, artistic and social, and in the name of all its partisans I thank Jules Lermina for having lent his talent as a writer to the exposition of the thesis that life can be mysteriously infused from one being to another: the redoubtable secret of the Elixir of Life of the ancient alchemists and Oriental initiates.

But can one become immortal?

Ask Doctors Brown-Séquard and Variot,[60] or await Jules Lermina's next novella.

Papus

I

It was scarcely three months after I had presented my thesis and finally obtained the title of doctor that had been the ambition of my youth. With what joy I had written to my worthy father, with what emotion I had opened the letter

---

[59] As with the previous list, all of these were writers who were personally know to Papus or, at least, contributed to his journal. Thierry was perhaps the most notable, attracting warm praise from Anatole France, although Paul Adam—whose relevant work only forms a tiny minority of his huge output—was the most successful. "Alber Jhouney"—the signature used by Albert Jouney—had made a considerable impact in 1887 with *Le royaume de Dieu* but his career proved meteoric. Mauchel was presumably only known to Papus by his signature, which appeared on an article on "Balzac occultiste" that Papus reprinted in the special issue of *La Plume* he was invited to edit in 1892.

[60] Charles-Edouard Brown-Séquard (Papus has "Brown Sequart") succeeded Claude Bernard as professor of experimental medicine at the Collège de France in 1878. In the 1880s, when he was in his seventies, he began to promote the hypothesis that human rejuvenation might be achieved by the transplantation of animal testicles—a practice enthusiastically taken up by his colleague Serge Voronoff, who made the practice notorious (many of the transplanted "monkey glands" were rejected, and some infected their hosts with syphilis). A physician who signed his academic papers G. Variot was the first person to carry out an experimental trial of Brown-Séquard's thesis at the Hôtel-Dieu in 1889; that news must have been hot off the presses when Papus penned this preface. Brown-Séquard had worked extensively in America (with Alexis Carrel, the tissue-culture pioneer) and in London; while resident in London he was a near neighbor of Robert Louis Stevenson, who used him as a model for Dr. Jekyll (and thus, tacitly, Mr. Hyde).

bring me, along with his warm congratulations, the 500-franc bill that would permit my installation in Paris.

A physician in Paris! At the age of 27! It is necessary to have experienced these illusions to understand their full force, to reveal all their savor. I was esteemed by my professors. I had passed my examinations with exceptional success; I had, during those years of study, made a few fast friends; was it not inevitable that the future should seem radiant?

It is true that my resources were slender; I knew that my father, a small farmer in the Sarthe valley, was making a considerable sacrifice in sending me a small sum of money, and that I could no longer count ion anyone but myself— but I had faith in myself, in my passion for work and in *science*, which is indulgent to those who love it sincerely.

I therefore set resolutely to work, taking the *agrégation* as my next objective,[61] which I had decided to pursue while starting in practice. I was strong, I was sober; in sum, I fund myself in excellent condition, and I had best admit that I have now arrived at, and gone beyond, the goal that I had set myself.

It would be disingenuous on my part to insist on the hardship of my early days, which I sometimes rather miss: those days of youth when bread dipped in a glass of water seemed so good. In sum, I was, at the outset, comfortably lodged, thanks to easy-going suppliers—which some angrily call creditors, but were in truth my financial backers, since it is necessary, on pain of death, for a man who has no capital to obtain a few advances. I was properly furnished, comfortably dressed and, if I economized somewhat on nourishment without anyone being aware of it, I maintained a smart appearance and a healthy physiognomy.

I cannot say that clients flocked to my door; however, I religiously followed the prescriptions I had written at the time, in my conscience and on the copper plaque nailed above the building's coaching-entrance: *Medical Practitioner, consultations between two and five p.m.*—a healthy dose, as is evident.

I was only occasionally disturbed in my work, and I would have been able, if I had wished, sometimes to neglect the confinement to quarters that I had fixed, but I respected the word I had given, and in any case, imagine if a client had come while I was absent! I hardly ever went out before 6 p.m. and, after a rapid and frugal meal, hurried home, always fearful of missing the opportunity that would inevitably present itself eventually.

Needless to say, I also looked after everyone in the building for free.

One evening in September, I had lit my lamp early and I was studying assiduously, dreaming of the day when I would be able to proclaim my ideas and theories from the height of a professorial chair, when I was snatched from my

---

[61] *Agrégation* is the French qualification entitling someone to teach in a *lycée* [secondary school] or *collège*.

reverie by a loud ring of the doorbell. Leaping out of my chair, I hastened to the door and opened it, holding a lantern aloft in order to examine the visitor's face.

It was a lady dressed in black, but whose external appearance did not present any of the romantic characteristics that one might suppose. She was about forty, and plump, with rather coarse features. She was weeping. I hurriedly introduced her into my "consulting room" and, a trifle loquaciously, I put myself at her disposal.

I soon perceived, however, that he poor creature was in such a state of agitation, and had, moreover, climbed up to my fourth-floor apartment in such haste that it was impossible for her to utter a word. I had not been in practice long enough to be unsympathetic to human weakness, and I was just about to get her a glass of water—with sugar, if you please!—when she murmured: "Monsieur, I beg you… come, come quickly… my child…"

A sob cut the speech short—but had she any need to say any more? She had need of my services—and for a child!

I have always adored those little creatures, and it had been one of the most heart-rending things I had experienced to stand at the foot of a crib, powerless and ignorant, saying: "Oh! Meningitis! What an enemy!"

"I am under your orders!" I exclaimed, grabbing my hat. "Do you live far away?"

"No, no—the next house. Pardon me for coming here, but it's precisely because it was so close…"

It would have been unbecoming and futile to be wounded by that excuse. I affirmed once again that I was ready to follow her, and we went out.

Walking beside the woman in the street, I questioned her. What illness was her child suffering from? For how long?

"It's my daughter! She's dying, Monsieur! Six months ago, she was so healthy, so strong, so beautiful…"

"How old is she?"

"Ten. You see, Monsieur, I'm a widow. I live alone with my daughter. We don't see anyone except Monsieur Vincent…"

"Monsieur Vincent?"

Had the poor woman thought that she detected—mistakenly, to be sure—a certain suspicion in my tone? She immediately added: "Oh, he's an old man, Monsieur. Sixty, perhaps 70 years old… but so good, and he loves my Pauline so much!"

We had reached the house. We went up to the second floor and went in to an apartment that was neat and respectable. It was perfectly in order. From the dining-room, which served as a point of entry, we went into the bedroom. There, at the first glance, I saw the girl she had called Pauline lying on a little bed next to her mother's.

It is strange that sickness and death, contemplated in hospital during a period of internment, do not produce one hundredth of the effect that we feel at the bedside of our first patients. My heart had suddenly become constricted, and I felt myself grow pale.

The poor child was white, so white that she seemed no longer to have a single drop of blood in her veins. Beneath her blue-rimmed eyelids, her eyeballs seemed dull and grey, and her long, thin hands were extended on the bedclothes, where their pallor stood out even more.

"A candle!" I demanded, sharply. And I leaned over the bed, examining with profound attention the poor creature on whom Death had already set his finger, as evidence of an inevitable summons. It was anemia in its final phase. But what lesion could have caused that state?

Under interrogation, the mother repeated to me, in greater detail, that her daughter had always been sturdy, that she had been in perfect health six months before, and that everyone had admired the lively bloom of youth that was already evident in her little girl.

"And it can't be said," the poor woman continued, while weeping, "that there has been the slightest change in our life. We've been living here for three years. The apartment is airy, overlooking the gardens. I don't send Pauline to school; it's our neighbor, Monsieur Vincent, who gives her lessons, and he's too reasonable to have pushed her too hard."

In truth, I was almost afraid to touch the poor creature, whose sudden exhaustion alarmed me in its seeming inexplicability. I could not convince myself, however, that there was no means of saving her. Aided by her mother, I sounded her chest with minute care, and I established—with veritable amazement—that she there was no sign of any defect. The heart was sound, and I could not perceive the murmur characteristic of anemia there or in the neck. The lungs were equally sound and well-developed. Beneath that consumptive thinness, the vital framework was exceptional, with no symptoms of lymphatism.

The mother was not poor; with a little pension she had inherited from her husband, former member of the Paris guard, she had an annual income of two thousand francs. In addition, the old man she had mentioned, Monsieur Vincent, took his meals with her, and paid well.

Unfortunately, the young girl had not received any regular treatment. With a stubbornness based in an irrational mistrust, the mother had never called a doctor, contenting herself with anodyne remedies—water in which iron nails had been boiled, or some such. And now I was constrained to admit to myself that all my efforts to reanimate that organism, so strangle depleted, would not result in a prolongation of life, even for a few days.

I sat there, crushed and defeated, despairingly awaiting an inspiration that could not possibly arrive.

The mother watched me silently, doubtless reading the poignant thoughts that my face betrayed. I did not yet know how to hide my impotence beneath banal and consoling phraseology. There was no merit in that; a physician ought to act upon the brain as on any other organ.

At that moment, we heard the sound of footsteps in the next room.

"That's Monsieur Vincent," said the mother.

The door quietly came ajar—but at the same moment, I saw the little girl sit up and turn her head, her hands reaching out in the direction from which the almost imperceptible noise had come.

I supported the child and, to my great surprise, felt a supreme effort in that poor body, as if she wanted to escape from my arms. The door closed again, and the girl fell back, dead.

I let out an exclamation, simultaneously surprised and desperate. That excessively swift and painless death, that sudden extinction of the vital flame, amazed me, and I experience a sort of rage against my intelligence. For, in truth, I did not understand what had just happened before my eyes at all; it seemed to me that I was prey to a nightmare.

The mother, with a heart-rending scream, had hurled herself upon the poor motionless corpse. I moved away from the bed and mechanically, as if embarrassed by the futility of my presence, opened the door and went into the first room.

That was when I saw Monsieur Vincent for the first time.

Clear of complexion, he was wearing a grey, almost white, coat. He was of medium height, rather plump, but what struck me immediately was that it was impossible to estimate exactly how old he was. His hair was white and cut short, forming three distinct peaks on his forehead and his temples, but his face was so fresh and so rosy, and his eyes were shining so brightly, that I honestly asked myself whether I was looking at an old man or a young one whose hair—by virtue of a predisposition less rare is generally believed, with respect to the pigmentary tissue—had become discolored in his adolescence. And yet I remember full well that the dead girl's mother had spoken of Monsieur Vincent as a septuagenarian.

He was standing next to the window, looking sad—but not as much, it seemed to me, as I might have expected. He bowed politely and interrogated me with his gaze.

"She's dead," I told him.

A sudden contraction disturbed his face, and in that reflex movement I saw all his features become creased, displaying the thousand wrinkles that are a sure indication of old age. The appearance of freshness was entirely superficial. Moreover, doubtless by virtue of an afflux of blood to the heart, provoked by emotion, his complexion had suddenly taken on a yellowish, parchment-like tint; the skin had crumpled beneath his prominent cheekbones. Within the space a second, a death's-head had imprinted itself on his face—and without saying a word, seizing his hat with feverish haste, Monsieur Vincent ran to the exterior door as if possessed by a terror he could not master, opened it, and literally fled, with a vertiginous rapidity.

I thought that the abandonment of a friend at the supreme moment would be a new cause of despair for the poor mother, and I was all set to go back to her, in spite of the falseness of my situation, when I heard a knock on the door.

Thinking that Monsieur Vincent, gripped by remorse, had decided to come back, I opened it immediately. It was two neighbors in search of news of the little girl. When they were informed of the catastrophe, they shook their heads.

"It was bound to end this way," said one.

"What do you mean?" I asked, sharply.

The woman was about to reply when the mother, having heard the sound of familiar voices, came out of the bedroom and threw herself into her neighbor's arms, sobbing.

My role was finished; I bowed and went out, experiencing a sentiment of inexpressible relief at leaving that house in which my sensibility had been put to such a stern proof. Even so, I went down the stairs slowly, oppressed by an anguish whose nature I could not precisely define. It seemed to me that I was leaving an inexplicable mystery behind.

Just as I was passing in front of the concierge's lodge, he stopped me.

"Well, Monsieur Physician?" he said, inviting a response.

"I was called too late," I hastened to reply.

The man looked at me with astonishment, as if he could not comprehend. I gave him a few rapid explanations. He swore violently; them brandishing his fist at an invisible enemy, he groaned: "Oh, the bandit! When I think, Monsieur, that she was a colossus of heath, so pink and fresh!"

"How long has she been ill?"

"Six months, Monsieur—six months exactly."

"Who were you calling a bandit just now?"

"Him! That old tocasson[62] who had nothing but skin on his bones, and who came to nourish himself via the mother at the daughter's expense! Oh, he's certainly profited!"

"What?" I cried. "Do you think she's died of starvation?"

"Well, of what else, then?"

"Come here, husband, and don't get mixed up in other people's business!" shouted a female voice from the depths of the lodge. "It's the doctor's business to find out the truth!"

"At the end of the day, that's true!" said the concierge, breaking off the conversation unceremoniously.

---

[62] There is no English equivalent of this *argot* term that can convey the full complexity of its meaning. It was sometimes used to refer to a worthless horse, but Lermina—who co-authored a dictionary of *argot* and was sensitive to its subtler inflections—is using it here because it was primarily applied, with similar contempt, to old women who are trying to look younger than they are. "Mutton dressed as lamb" is the most similar expression that English can offer.

II

I went back home, feverish and almost angry. The first time that someone had made an appeal to what it pleased me to call my science, I had bumped into a desperate case; brutally, death had barred my way, and I seemed to hear the words of supreme despair murmuring in my ear: "You won't go very far!"

I was not only suffering from that egotistic sentiment of humiliation, though; the anguish I had felt a little while before had increased. To drag myself out of it, I tried to organize my thoughts, to gather together the facts I had observed and to obtain therefrom a response to the doubts that were irritating me.

The child's condition did not correspond with any known observations. I opened my books one by one, but could find nothing that satisfied me anywhere. The sick girl had not presented any of the classical symptoms, and that as exactly what troubled me most: the absence of symptoms seemed more certain with every passing moment. Was it necessary to believe, in accordance with the concierge's insinuation, in ill-treatment, in starvation? In addition to the mother's appearance, though, the profound and unfeigned affection that she had for her daughter giving the absolute lie to any such supposition, the physical state of the patient provided formal contra-indications to that hypothesis.

During the short time in which I had been able to examine her with my stethoscope, I had been particularly surprised by the healthy state of the vital organs. There had evidently been a loss of vitality, slow or rapid, but it had not been brought about by any of the accidents that ordinarily leave easily-detectable lesions in an organism. But why had the two neighbors seemed to find something that was inexplicable to me so easily understandable? Why had the concierge seemed, in his rapid interjections to be accusing the strange person I knew as Monsieur Vincent—who, it is true, had made a poor impression on me at first, but whom no indication permitted me to suspect. And where would such suspicions have led me? So horrible can certain hypotheses be that I stopped myself, and once again, combining my observations, acquired the conviction that there could be no possible basis for them.

Then again, I repeat, there are faces that do not lie, and that of the mother radiated the most perfect honesty. She loved her daughter, had never left her. No, no, it was futile to follow a trail that everything demonstrated to be false and slanderous.

In the end, that examination of reason and conscience exasperated me to the point that it was impossible for me to remain alone any longer. I needed to hear human voices, to exchange ideas, to refresh my brain in the flow of current banalities.

I went out.

When I went into the circle of light projected by the gas-lamps in the brasserie, from which emerged the moving silhouettes of young people, there was a clamor of greetings. Since I completed my thesis, they had not seen me three times—and amicable gibes rained down upon me as hands that drew me forwards, forcing me to sit down in front of a pile of saucers, the obituary obelisk of vanished tankards. I could not resist; the noise and exuberance restored my serenity.

It was necessary for me to explain my perpetual reclusiveness, to justify my ingratitude to my old friends, to confess my ambitions and my hopes, but above all to clink glasses, again and again, while absorbing the horrible alcoholic dilution that people decorate in our great country with the name of beer, and whose principle virtue—particularly appreciated by its vendors—is to condemn the unwary to a raging thirst, the mother of repetition.

Under that brain-inflaming influence, until the moment my stomach began to ache, my ideas became clearer. I resumed the active perception of facts and, at the same time, felt an invisible desire to recount the strange adventure in which I had been involved that night. Naturally, I was not long in succumbing to it, and I narrated the incident in a single breath.

As it concerned a child—the eternal problem that excites the most skeptical—they listened to me attentively, and no one jeered when I confessed the dolorous emotion that my ignorance had caused me to experience.

"Listen," said Gaston Dussault, a young doctor whose great merit we all recognized. "I don't claim to be able to give you the key to the puzzle that you've put in front of us. My observation will be of a more general character, and—alas!—scarcely encouraging in nature. There are two phases in a physician's life. The first—his youth—comprises ardent curiosity, a desire to conquer evil, a devotion that no one can discourage. That's also the time of unrelenting hard work, 25 hours of reading or writing a day, burning one's eyes on the wicks of smoky and malodorous candles. Now, while we're swotting away like that, life goes on, actively, rushing around and outside of us. We stuff our ears so as not to hear the noise that humankind is making, the vast illness suffered by the lungs, the heart, the brain. We demand of others that science should do everything, that the past be heaped up in weighty and pricy volumes, and we don't have time to learn the secret of life and death in the only book that's always open, with schematic illustrations that are always new, sincere and conclusive—and that book is here…"

With a circular gesture, he indicated the boulevard. The gas projected its white bands, though which the tide of strollers rolled ever on.

"There's the great manual of internal and external pathology," he continued. "There's physiology in action. What do we see of all that—we, the young, riveted to the hospital or the dissecting-room? And this is a volume, a chapter, a paragraph in the vast medical encyclopedia that is society entire." He paused, then cried out in a tone whose sincerity struck us forcibly: "Ah, to have the time—which is to say, the money of everyday life—and to consecrate it entirely to reading the human library, that universal dictionary in which every man is a page, to spell it out, to transcribe it, to annotate it… and after that, to practice medicine! What am I saying? After that, medicine would be practiced—for then one will have autopsied, not cadavers but living beings, brains, breasts and hearts. Ten years of observations accomplished with the supreme courage that we put into shuffling the cinders of erudition, and the true flame would spring forth!"

"But after the forced labor to which we are all condemned," I cried, "less than half our lives remain…"

"To become the second man who is in every doctor," he went on, "the discouraged, the skeptical, the ignorant, the banal and routine practitioner who aims for the *Croix d'honneur* and the Académie. When we escape from our books, we're blind, and no longer see human beings…"

At that moment, I let out an exclamation and put my hand on his arm. "Look," I said.

He followed the direction of my pointing finger.

"Who's that?" he asked

"That's the old man I was talking about just now—Monsieur Vincent."

Indeed, lit by the harsh light of frosted glass, the old man was moving forward slowly and painfully, and I shivered in contemplating the incredible change that had come over him, in scarcely an hour, since I had last seen him.

He seemed to me to be pale, thin, stooped and worn out. At each step he dragged along the asphalt he looked around, turning his shaky neck, whose vertebrae I imagined I could hear cracking.

"Hey!" cried one of our neighbors. "That's old Thévenin. He's not dead, then?"

"So it is," Gaston went on, having looked at him more attentively. "I didn't recognize him at first."

"Who's Monsieur Thévenin?" I asked, impatiently.

Without answering me directly, Gaston continued, as if talking to himself: "I met him a few months ago. He was alert and rejuvenated…"

"Since I believed myself, on seeing him an hour ago, that I was facing a man still young… it's possible, after all, that grief has produced this metamorphosis…"

"Come on," said Gaston, touching me lightly on the shoulder. "I'll tell you what I know about him…"

Monsieur Vincent—I shall continue to give him that name, which really belonged to him; his name was Vincent Thévenin—had passed through the zone of illumination whose center we occupied. I got up hurriedly and followed my comrade.

Within a moment we had picked up the old man's trail again. He was going along the boulevard, lost in the cheerful and laughing crowd enjoying the luxuriant and vivifying summer evening. His narrow back seemed to belong to some macabre character.

"Talk," I said to me comrade. "Quickly, tell me what you know about that person, who interests me, frightens me and irritates me all at the same time."

"Let's follow him first," said Gaston. "I know his past; I'd like to know something of his present."

I was obliged to restrain my impatience. Adjusting our pace to that of Monsieur Thévenin, we disposed ourselves so as not to lose sight of him.

I noticed then that he stopped in front of every café, remaining on the threshold and seeping it with his gaze, doubtless searching for someone…perhaps a woman, Gaston suggested, laughing. Indeed, he paused preferentially in front of the establishments frequented by the young women of the quarter.

"I was only joking," Gaston added. "Besides the fact that Thévenin has always been chaste, he must be more than 100 years old…."

"A hundred!"

"I'm 35," my interlocutor went on, "and when I was 15, the person who told me Thévenin's story affirmed that he was already alive in 1789."

The old man had, however, resumed his course—or, rather, his silent glide, which gave him a fantastic character. The further he went, the more he seemed to be bowed down by an increasingly heavy weight. His apparent feebleness was accentuated. In truth, we were beginning to dread that he might get to the point of evaporating into the air and disappearing entirely.

Having reached the extremity of the boulevard, he stopped, as if hesitating over which direction to take. It was getting late, though, and the strollers were becoming scarce. Because we were very close to him, almost close enough to touch him, we saw him sketch out a gesture that had both anger and discouragement in it, and he set off into a side-street.

We did not lose track of him, and soon saw him cross the street and march straight to a coaching entrance, in front of which a fat woman—evidently a concierge—was imbibing the fresh evening air, dandling a plump and sturdy boy of six or seven on her knees.

Scarcely had the lad caught sight of Thévenin when he leapt down from his mother's lap and ran towards him. He hurtled into the old man so hard that we feared for a moment that the latter would be knocked over. Quite the contrary, though; with a strength that astonished us, Thévenin seized the boy in his arms, lifted him off the ground and embraced him for a long time.

"Poor man," I murmured, sympathetically. "He's thinking about the dead girl."

The fat woman called her boy back, however, remonstrating with him and shouting: "Let the gentlemen go! Little imp! I beg your pardon, Monsieur Vincent…"

He replied by softly stroking the cheeks of the little boy, who had come back to hug him.

"Oh, I know you're the Papa Gâteau of all the little children," the woman went on, "and as soon as they see you in the distance, they run to you…"

The concierge stood aside to let Monsieur Vincent pass, but he did not go in. He seemed to hesitate. Then he said, timidly: "Wouldn't you like to entrust him to me? I'd teach him so many beautiful things!"

"Oh, with pleasure Monsieur Vincent. But you know that he stays in the country, with his grandmother. To borrow him for a week, I need to kick up an almighty fuss… and the air's so good out there!"

Monsieur Vincent did not insist. He embraced the child once again and disappeared into the long corridor. He seemed veritably rejuvenated.

Gaston drew closer. "Is that really the scientist Monsieur Vincent Thévenin who just went in?"

"Yes, Monsieur. Oh yes, a scientist, and such a brave man! A father to all the children, you know—and they know it well, the little rogues. They're under his feet all day long."

"He lives here?"

"For 10 years…"

"I knew him slightly at one time He seemed to be very old…"

"You'd never believe it! Why, six months ago, he was so worn out he could hardly draw breath. Suddenly, bang! It was like the wave of a magic wand. I don't know what he came up with to cure himself, but in less than a month he was as back on his feet, as right as rain—to the point where, if I'd been a widow…"

She laughed frankly, like a woman who could admit a certain licentiousness into her character without anyone holding it against her.

"How old do you think he is?" I put in.

"Oh, a dried-up husk. Ninety-five, at least!"

"That's the man," Gaston continued, when we were some distance away, having resumed our walk. "Highly-esteemed, highly-respected, loves children. What do you think?"

"Nothing—I'm waiting to hear his story."

"It's quite simple, in sum—I mean, for us, who don't admit the impossible as scientific fact. Monsieur Vincent de Bossaye de Thévenin is the last descendant of a great family, which emigrated during the French Revolution. His father was one of the hundred shareholders, at 2400 livres in the famous Mesmer, whom he followed to Switzerland—where, as you know, the celebrated thaumaturge was resident until his death in 1815. Monsieur de Bossaye senior came back to France with the Bourbons and died soon afterwards, leaving a son—the man in whom we're interested. Vincent followed the lessons of Carra and Saussure, qualified in medicine, and became an associate of the famous Deleuze, who was nicknamed the Hippocrates of animal magnetism under the Restoration.

"After that, he broke entirely with academic routine. For some years he was secretary of the Société Magnétique founded by the Marquis de Puységur, and he eventually became the secretary, the alter ego, of the Marquis de Mirville, the director of the Société d'Avignon and author of a very strange work on *Spirits and their Fluidic Manifestations*.[63]

I interrupted Gaston excitedly, exclaiming: "In sum, this great scientist is a spirit... a madman!"

"Why get carried away like that?" Gaston went on, smiling. "The man who, 100 years ago, could have foreseen the electric lighting of railway stations would have seemed worthy of being shut up in a lunatic asylum. Science begins with a minimal fact and grows by hypotheses." He became more animated. "A madman! Do you think that Crookes, who discovered a new metal, thallium, and posed the irritating enigma of the radiometer, whose visible functioning still remains inexplicable, is a madman?[64] Well, study his latest research and tell me is you don't feel *something* becoming shaky within you that you thought quite solid.

"To get back to Monsieur Vincent, though. About 1825, that man—who combines the astonishing patience of a fakir with the active perseverance of a seeker—was the universally-acknowledged and respected leader of hat bizarre population of magnetizers and their patients, who were much more numerous than is believed, whose good faith was not under the least suspicion, and who had the passions and courage of the apostolate. Alexandre Bertrand and Georget

---

[63] This list of celebrated Mesmerists runs through several of the principal names associated with the tradition; Jean-Louis Carra (1742-1793) was one of its earliest scientific investigators, whose *Examen physique de magnétisme animal* was published in 1785, but the date of his demise makes it unlikely that Vincent can actually have been his pupil. It is unclear whether the reference to "Saussure" is to the Swiss physicist Horace-Benedict de Saussure (1740-1799) or his son, the phytochemist Nicolas Théodore (1767-1845), but if the former is intended the same criticism applies. Chronology makes it far more likely that Vincent could have been an associate of Jean-Philippe-François Deleuze (1753-1853), who wrote an extensive *Histoire critique du magnétisme* (1813-19). Armand-Marie-Joseph de Chastenet, Marquis de Puységur (1751-1825) founded the Société Harmonique des Amis Réunis before the Revolution of 1789; the descendant society of which Vincent was secretary is fictitious. Charles-Jules-Eudos de Catteville de Mirville (1802-1873) is a more likely employer; the work cited, *Pneumatologie, des esprits et leurs manifestations fluidiques*, was published in 1854.

[64] Crookes' radiometer, or "light mill," which he demonstrated in 1873, did indeed pose an intriguing puzzle, whose solution is still subject to some controversy. It consists of a set of vanes mounted on a spindle inside a partially-evacuated glass bulb; when exposed to light, the vanes rotate.

were his pupils—and yet Thévenin never allowed his name to be spoken. He did not get directly involved in the famous quarrel with the Académie, which, despite Husson's report, ended in an absolute refusal of the erudite company to take magnetism seriously. You know that that decision dates from 1837, on the initiative of Dr. Dubois d'Amiens? [65]

"Dr. Thévenin did not protest. On the contrary, he seemed to lose interest in the matter and broke with his adepts—but I know from a reliable source that he did not abandon his studies. The man from whom I obtained all these details, who was one of Thévenin's last pupils, told me, a few months before his death, that his master's science terrified him—that's the very word he used. And he added: 'Don't think that any sleight-of-hand is involved, or any charlatanism, let alone those cerebral *disequilibrations* that can explain everything in the interests of money or pride, if not folly. Monsieur Vincent is the coldest, the most strictly positivist man I've encountered in my entire life. He has never worked by trial and error, leaving it to chance to decide whether his observations are well- or ill-founded. He proceeds slowly from one point to the next, step by step, submitting each progress obtained to the most minute verification. Perhaps it's because of that very slowness that I have so much trouble following him; my imagination continually carries me away, drawing me on to false trails. He goes straight ahead, without deviating from the determined track by an iota.'

"You will understand how curious I was to obtain details. Science, indeed! But what science? To all the questions I asked him, my friend replied with a discretion equivalent to a refusal to divulge his master's secrets. However, this is what I was able to find out. Monsieur Vincent was not preoccupied with second sight or the prediction of the future. His studies were uniquely devoted to the physiological, or even physical, fact of a radiant force—the exact term more recently employed by Crookes—emanating from the human body, and whose action, attractive or penetrant, can be exercised at a distance without the aid of a material conductor. From there to hypnotism, and especially to suggestion, is only a single step.

---

[65] The names cited in this paragraph refer to the clash of ideas that occurred when the controversy regarding animal magnetism came to a head in the late 1820s and 1830s. Fréderic Dubois d'Amiens (1799-1873) was the secretary of the Académie de Médecine de Paris who published the report that convinced the society to dismiss all such practices as quackery—a document whose partiality was stridently criticized by Dr. Husson of the Hôtel-Dieu, who had encouraged the practice of magnetic medicine within the hospital by Pierre Froissart, Jules Depotet de Sennevoy and a physician surnamed Georget. Alexandre-Jacques-François Bertrand (not to be confused with Alexandre Bertrand the archaeologist) was one of the most important academic analysts of the practice; he published *Du magnétisme en France et des jugements qu'en ont porté les sociétés savantes* in 1826.

"With the audacity of youth, I went to Monsieur Vincent's house and attempted to obtain his confession. A very singular man, in truth, who made an impression on me like no other I have ever experienced. While I spoke to him, under the authority of my friend's name—who was no longer alive by then—to offer myself as a sort of successor as his pupil, Monsieur Vincent stared at me. And, strangely enough, I felt an effect that was neither somnambulistic numbness not hypnotic fascination—but it seemed to me that an irresistible attracted was being exercised upon me. Don't misunderstand me: my body itself wasn't drawn towards him, but something that emanated from the entire periphery of my body, as if some impalpable, ethereal substance were being projected towards him through my pores. The effect didn't last more than a few seconds, however, and then suddenly ceased.

" 'How old are you?' he asked, abruptly.

" 'Twenty-six,' I replied.

" 'You work too hard,' he said. 'You're expending yourself too quickly and too soon. Take care—be more economical with yourself.'

"I didn't quite understand, feeling young and vigorous—with the reservation that, after the singular effect I've just mentioned, I felt a sort of lassitude, as if I had overstretched myself.

"I tried to get back to the subject that had brought me, but he interrupted me. 'Don't expect anything from me,' he said, rather rudely. 'In the present state of knowledge—or rather, in the face of universal ignorance—it's forbidden for me to communicate what I know to anyone.'

" 'But why?' I asked. 'Why not help us, we young folk, to fight against the stupid routines?'

" 'Why?' he concluded, raising his head and fixing me with his gleaming eyes. 'Because... because my science is criminal!'

"And then, without my having asked, he launched into an amazingly eloquent speech, sketching a complete, encyclopedic picture of present-day science for me. There was not a system, not a theory, nit a discovery that he had not studied and verified. With a sarcastic verve that sometimes became ferocious, he flagellated the prejudices, timidities and laxities that arrested all researches on the threshold of real science. An unparalleled prophet, he predicted for me ten years ago, the modest progress that we have accomplished since then; he saw, positively, beyond our horizon, and without any charlatanism, by the force of deductions whose authority I appreciated myself. And when he had finished, he added, dismissing me with a gesture: 'I refuse you my science, which is criminal... yes, criminal—for it augments, increases a hundredfold, the terrible inequality that creates victors and vanquished in the struggle for existence!'

"Following that enigmatic speech, I had to leave—taking with me, I confess, an impression of terrified admiration. Yes, in a few minutes of conversation, that man had appeared to me as a sort of superhuman being, superb and sinister at the same time. Was it a nervous predisposition? It's possible. However, if I wanted to describe in a single phrase the strange concept that had leapt into my mind, suddenly and irrationally, like those phrases that sometimes obsess the memory without any appreciable cause, I would tell you—please don't laugh at me—that that man put me in mind of a savant vampire. What does that mean? Even today, I'd have difficulty explaining it clearly. Try if you want to—another time! It's late. Let's go home."

"One more thing," I said. "Did you see Monsieur Vincent again?"

"Yes, I've run into him several times—sometimes old, worn out, as he appeared to us this evening; sometimes, on the other hand, rejuvenated, lively, rosy-cheeked and robust."

"And you believe he's a centenarian?"

"Recall the dates I cited, and draw your own conclusions."

A moment later, we went our separate ways. Alone in my apartment, by the light of my lamp, I soon resumed my interrupted studies.

People often laugh at the rapidity with which children pass from one idea to another. One moment, all their attention is focused on something, when a fly takes off and their train of thought is suddenly modified, and they forget whatever held their interest so forcefully a second before. Is the difference between children and adults really so vast, after all? The importance of the facts that attract their attention is, in reality equivalent, and can similarly be measured by the varying intensity of their sensations. The movement of a cat leaves us indifferent, but a passing skirt tears us away from our present reflections and sometimes carries us far away from the road we were following.

Can I tell what circumstances prevented me from following the definite plan that I had formed of seeing Monsieur Vincent again and subjecting him to closer scrutiny? I would find it very difficult. New impressions, some trivial, some more serious, were superimposed on that one; from time to time, the memory of that strange individual crossed my mind, but in the fashion of a vague vision without precise contours.

Weeks, months and years went by, and brought about important changes in my situation. My father died, leaving me a tiny fortune amassed *sou* by *sou*, with the superb tenacity of the peasant who deprives himself of everything in order to ensure his child's future. The clientèle had arrived, and I had given up my professorial ambitions. Finally, I got married and, after a legal but brief interval, became the father of an adorable daughter.

Obviously, Monsieur Vincent and his criminal science were far from my thoughts. More and more years went by. Prosperity arrived; my studies of nervous diseases and my experiments with hysterics had caused something of a stir. My daughter grew more and more adorable and adored. I was happy, and yet I had a history, for the Académies welcomed my communications and the journals printed them. An epidemic of cholera brought me decisively into the light and won me a benevolent decoration from the government.

It was exactly 10 years since I had spent a few hours chatting on the sidewalk with my friend and mentor Gaston about the person in question—I had even forgotten his name—when chance, which rules all our lives, reminded me of him in circumstances even more bizarre than the first time.

One of my colleagues, Dr. F***, the director of a sanitarium, wrote me a note asking me to call on him when I had the time, with a view to examining one of his patients.

Finding myself overloaded with work at the time, I put off responding to his invitation for a few days. When a new, more urgent letter arrived, however, I hastened to see him. The case that he wanted to talk to me about was most interesting, and fell precisely within the purview of the specialist studies to which I had devoted myself. It was a matter of the very curious phenomenon of multiple personality and, for several hours, we dedicated ourselves to experiments over ever-increasing interest. Fearing that we might exhaust the patient completely, however, we fixed a further appointment for the following day.

We went into the garden in front of the magnificent establishment, known and admired throughout Europe, and my colleague slowly led me through it, telling me the results of his personal observations of the subject we had just been examining. Just as we reached the main gate and were exchanging a farewell handshake, a little boy ran out of a pathway fringed by laurels and privets, raced towards the doctor and threw himself into his arms.

The latter lifted him up and said: "My son, Monsieur—eight years old... and a fine fellow."

He was a handsome child with delicate features, but he seemed a little pale to me. I caressed him, thinking about my little daughter, so pink and lively, and I said: "Why were you running so fast? One would think that you were running for your life." It was a banal question, to which I attached no importance.

"Oh, just for fun," the scamp said. "To tease Monsieur Vincent."

"Monsieur Vincent!" I exclaimed. "What Monsieur Vincent?" The name had struck a chord in my memory like a clarion call.

With a certain irritation, the child replied: "Pardon! There's only one Monsieur Vincent... that's Papa Gâteau!"

Papa Gâteau! There had been a Monsieur Vincent with that nickname 10 years before!

"He's a very singular individual," my colleague put in.

"Would that be Vincent Thévenin?"

"The very same. Do you know him?"

"He's not dead, then?"

"Ah, you too!" said the doctor, laughing. "You thought he'd disappeared. Not at all. 110 to 115 years old, my dear chap. And they say that madness isn't a certificate of longevity!"

"And how long has he been in your establishment?"

"About four months—and he was admitted in very curious circumstances. I'll tell you about it tomorrow, for I have to get back to my daily duties now. It's 6 p.m…"

"6 p.m.! I'm late too. We'll discuss Monsieur Vincent tomorrow."

"As you wish, my dear colleague."

I threw myself into my carriage, closing the door behind me. I was in a singular state of agitation, bitten by an indescribable curiosity. Within a second, I had remembered everything: the little apartment in which I had been patiently waiting for clients who were to arrive; the poor mother running to me for help; the funereal bed on which the little girl was lying. I asked myself whether, faced with the same mortal problem, I would have been any more adept today than I had been then—and, in truth, I shivered, telling myself that I was no more able now than then to comprehend that catastrophe. I tried to salvage my pride by supposing that certain symptoms had escaped my diagnosis that I might now perceive at first glance, but I knew that I was lying to myself. No, I had found nothing, and were I summoned in identical circumstances today, I would still find nothing!

That blow to self-respect, and the sincere regret of the researcher, was then juxtaposed with the memory of Monsieur Vincent, that strange, almost fantastic creature who was alive, still alive, everlasting in spite of the abominable senility that had had disturbed Gaston and me so much as we followed him through the streets. By what miracle had he resisted the crushing weight of a century, to which a further 10 years had now been added?

I recalled the inexplicable words that Gaston had reported to me: "*My criminal science multiplies a hundredfold the terrible inequality that creates victors and vanquished in the struggle for existence.*" And also the words that my friend had let slip, like the expression of a reflex: "savant vampire." Those coupled words did not, in reality, present any meaning to my intelligence. But I repeated them mentally, like the terms of an insoluble problem, the expression of an algebraic unknown.

Until I returned to my study it was impossible for me to extract myself from this obsession. Fortunately, my work, the occupations of the evening and sleep, eventually rescued me from that abnormal state of mind. In the morning, the haunting had vanished and all that remained of the emotion was a curiosity that no longer seemed to be at all unhealthy.

At the appointed hour, I met up with Dr. F*** again. He seemed to me to be anxious. Interrogating him with an interest dictated by the sincere sympathy that he inspired in me, I learned that his son's health had been giving him cause for concern for some time. He cut short these confidences, however, gripped one again by the passion for research, and we went to the infirmary to see the patient we had examined the previous day. For several hours, we were absorbed in the study of amazing manifestations of catalepsy and hypnotism. Then we came back to the doctor's study in order to compare notes.

"Now," I said, permit me to remind you that you promised me yesterday to talk at greater length about your inmate, Monsieur Vincent."

"I haven't forgotten, and I'll do better than tell you from memory. I have the custom, on the admission of my patients, of writing down the interesting circumstances of our initial interview." The doctor got up, opened a box and took out a few sheets of paper, which he handed to me, saying: "Read that while I take care of a few things I need to do—I'll be back soon."

Left alone, this is what I read:

Today, April 15, 1888, at 6 p.m., I was handed the card of a visitor who was asking for an immediate interview. It bore the name of Vincent de Bossaye de Thévenin, of the Faculty of Medicine of Paris. I started in surprise. As an alienist, I have made a special study of the history of animal magnetism, and I recalled having encountered that name in an era that was already distant. It seemed to me that it must have been borne by a contemporary of my grandfather, or at least of my father. I gave instructions for the person who had proffered the card to be introduced immediately, and a moment later I saw an old man come in, showing unequivocal signs of decrepitude throughout his body, while singular vestiges of youth subsisted in his parchment-like face. His gait also testified to a certain vigor.

Monsieur Thévenin bowed; I returned the gesture and invited him to sit down, then asked him the reason for his visit. "I have come," he said, in a voice that had no senile tremor, "to ask you to admit me as a resident—paying, of course." He made the last remark hastily, as if relying in advance to a possible objection.

"Pardon me," I said, "but are you really Dr. Thévenin?"

"The former pupil of Mesmer, the friend of Puységur. That's me."

"You must be very old?"

"109 years."

"Don't take the objection I must make to you amiss, but don't you know that my establishment is specifically designed for mental patients?"

"I know that," he said. "My request is all the more justified. I'm mad."

Well-accustomed as I am to all kinds of eccentricity, this seemed to me to be a trifle excessive.

"You'll permit me to doubt that," I said. "You appear to me to be in full possession of your reason."

"You're mistaken," he said, with the same calmness. "I'm mad—and, I emphasize this point—one of the most dangerous madmen in existence."

"Very well. But since you're a physician, and one of the most knowledgeable, you've doubtless analyzed your condition, and can easily give me the reasons for your peremptory affirmation."

He fixed his eyes upon me with a strange penetration. I understood how, in his prime, the man had contrived to be one of the most fervent and convinced adepts of magnetism. He remained silent for a few minutes, surrendering himself quite placidly to my observation. Then I continued: "Accepting your hypothesis, you are doubtless experiencing, at this moment, what I would call a lucid interval?"

"That's an error."

"I believe that I have considerable experience, however, and I cannot discover in your features or your expression any characteristic symptom of mental alienation."

"The most dangerous kinds of madness," he said, "are those that the human eye cannot detect." And he added, in a scarcely-perceptible voice: "I have been mad for 50 years, and no one, even among the most knowledgeable, has suspected my condition."

"But in the final analysis," I cried, "of what does this madness consist? Do you have visions? Do you evoke the dead? Do you believe yourself to be Mohammed or Jesus Christ? Are you made of glass? Are you not yourself?"

"I am," he replied, curtly, "a man who cannot die—and, until today, has not wanted to."

"So, according to you, it's solely thanks to your will that you have lived 110 years?"

"That's correct."

"You possess an infallible means of prolonging human life?"

"Not the life of another, but my own."

"The Great Work!" I cried. "The philosopher's stone."

"Not alchemy, in the sense that you mean."

"And do you intend to tell me what this means is?"

I had observed by now that I was dealing with a particular kind of reasoned monomania, and I was attempting to press the subject forward on his own terrain.

"I can't tell you," he said, emotionlessly, "for two reasons..."

"Which are?"

"The first is that, by revealing my secret to you, I would be running a great risk, in the present condition of society, of being treated as one of the worst criminals..."

"Do you admit your own culpability?"

"No, in the context of the superior law of the struggle for existence. Yes, in the view of reigning prejudices..."

"Have you killed anyone?"

"Yes," he replied, without hesitation.

"Have your crimes been discovered?"

"No."

"Have they given rise to pursuits directed against the innocent?"

"No."

"Your victims, however... what became of them? Have you got rid of them?"

69

"No."

"But no one has perceived that they died a violent death?"

"No one."

The madness was becoming increasingly distinct. "You mentioned two reasons that impose silence on you. What's the second?"

"I keep silent," he went on, in an earnest tone, "because one of two things would happen. Either, knowing my secret, you would be powerless to make use of it, or, having succeeded in using it, you would commit the same crimes that I have committed."

"Some poisonous preparation, presumably," I said, smiling, "which leaves no trace."

"Don't try to find out—you won't succeed. Let's cut this short. I'm coming to you, as an alienist, and I'm saying: 'I'm mad, dangerously mad. Will you intern me?'"

"A voluntary admission would give you the right to a voluntary exit. I can only admit you on condition of having total authority over you. For that, it would be necessary for you to submit to an examination by two physicians, whose certification would be my guarantee. Do you accept that condition?"

"Yes—but in my turn, I have conditions to make."

"I'm listening."

"My objective, in entering your establishment, is to die. So long as I'm free, I'm certain of staying alive, not having the courage to make no further use of my secret. Here, I cannot do that, and nature will take its course. I demand to be treated like your other inmates, with the sole difference that no one from outside should be admitted to see me."

"Don't you have relatives, friends?"

"I'm alone, quite alone. No one has any claim on me."

"I can assure you that your desire will be respected, unless you are summoned to appear before a superior authority."

"Oh, that's of no consequence to me. So, no one, except for you and the members of your staff, will be able to see me. On the other hand, I can assure you that no one will perceive my madness, and that I shall not be subject to any fit or fury, or any eccentric fantasy. Besides, if you observe the treaty that we are signing here faithfully, I shall be dead in three months."

"You realize that the surveillance exercised by the warders precludes any possibility of suicide?"

"Oh, they won't be able to do anything against me."

"You know, too, that before being interned in the place of your choice you will be searched, so minutely that it will be impossible for you to conserve any substance that might permit you to kill yourself?"

"They can't take my 110 years away," he said, smiling for the first time since the beginning of our conversation. "I know how much life remains within me... about 12 weeks."

All discussion being futile, I had only to accept my strange client, who fixed a very high price of admission himself, in exchange for which he demanded a very comfortable...

Here the doctor's manuscript ended. A note was written in the margin: *Building 2, no. 17.*

I had read these lines with profound interest, and when I had finished, I experienced a sensation of disappointment. Monsieur Vincent remained no less enigmatic to me than before.

My colleague came back in. "Well?" he asked. "What do you think of the former mesmerist?"

"I don't really know what to say. It's hardly an ordinary madness. But I'm thinking that Monsieur Thévenin entered this establishment on April 15 and it's now September 10, and he's still alive—his infallible diagnosis was mistaken."

"Absolutely."

"How has he behaved since he's been your guest?"

"I've never encountered a more docile inmate, or a more agreeable business arrangement. He submitted with the best possible grace to the examination of two of my colleagues, who did not hesitate to confirm my diagnosis of monomania. He was, in fact, a rather banal example of rational rectitude on all points but one. Thus, his situation being regularized, I had no other objective than to make his final years—or his final months—as pleasant as possible. I installed him in a detached building with a rather spacious garden. Two nurses were specially attached to his service. He has assembled a scientific library of the most curious sort, and seems to be working. Only one detail confirms his mental derangement. For an entire fortnight, he spent several hours a day lying naked on the ground. He warned me in advance, adding that he was attempting an experiment. As it was June, in a relatively warm spell, I did not think I ought to oppose him. He soon desisted of his own accord.

"During the first month, I didn't notice any change in him. From mid-May on, however, symptoms of decrepitude began to manifest themselves, and when he made his first singular experiment in June, I thought that he had predicted the date of his death accurately in fixing it at three months. When the fit of nudity—excuse the expression—had passed, we resumed our ordinary relations. I confess that I had rarely encountered as much erudition and boldness in the observations of any of my colleagues. If that man did not have the double monomania of magnetism and what I call his pretended vital will, I would proclaim him one of the greatest savants of the day.

"At the beginning of July, I perceived that his strength was declining further and further, but without any diminution of the lucidity of his mind. I must admit that I felt sorry for that centenarian, alone, abandoned by everyone, spending his final days sitting in an armchair in search of revivifying sunlight. I discovered one day that he adored children, and I brought my little boy to see him. I can't describe the expression of joy that lit up his face. If I hadn't known him so well, I would almost have been afraid of the gleam that suddenly came into his eyes.

"As for my little Georges, his sympathy was unhesitating. He ran to the old man as if he had known him for years. There was a sudden friendship, as children often conceive. Since then, not a day has gone by when Georges hasn't spent several hours with him. The effect of that distraction on the centenarian has been such that, since then, he seems to have found a veritable new youth. Yes, it's as if a restorative blood were running through his veins. His thinness has disappeared, and I wouldn't be surprised if he has a new lease of life. He has an astonishing constitution."

"But didn't you tell me, when I arrived, that your son is giving you some cause for anxiety?"

"Oh, a little weakness—summer fatigue... and he's growing. I'm not worried. Two months ago, he was full of beans. That will come back."

For a few moments, I was gripped by a singular desire to see the singular individual that I had only seen before in rather bizarre circumstances. I said as much to my colleague, but he observed that the agreement he had made prevented its satisfaction. Was he not formally prohibited from introducing into Monsieur Vincent's presence anyone not part of the establishment's personnel?

I had to give in. I did not insist, and I took my leave of my colleague, resolving to put the incoherent, almost crazy, ideas that were haunting me painfully completely out of my mind.

And yet, I had a sort of inexplicable fear within me, which was making my head spin. Like Pascal, I saw a gulf open in front of me—and in its utmost depths, I could see a sneering face, which had the features of Mesmer's pupil!

III

I had resumed my work and had once again put the aggravating memory of that individual out of my mind when, one morning early in November, I received a telegram that caused me an inexpressible emotion.

It was signed by Doctor F***, and read as follows:

My child is dying. I appeal to all my friends. Come.

I bounded out of my armchair. A few minutes later, I leapt into a carriage whose driver, enlivened by the promise of a large tip, whipped his horse vigorously.

I cannot say that the telegram surprised me. Hidden beneath the everyday preoccupations that I had made into a rampart against the visions of remembrance, there was a latent thought of which it seemed to me that the news was the explosion. Monsieur Vincent's silhouette, graven in the lobes of my brain, was inseparably linked with that of a child, the poor girl that I had seen long ago, dead before having died, and who had left me that impression—absolutely inadmissible from the viewpoint of true science—of having had the life, the animating force, drawn out of her. And here, once again, the appearance of that centenarian, stubbornly alive, was confused with that of a child, so vigorous, it seemed, six months earlier, but dying today!

I was not conscious of the length of the journey, so absorbed was I in my meditations, and when the carriage stopped, when the driver got down opened the door, and called, "We're here, sir!" I staggered out like a drunk, not knowing where I was or where I was going. It was by instinct, and instinct alone, that I set off along the long ash-lined driveway that led to the main building, after being admitted by the concierge.

When I arrived at the front steps, a male nurse who seemed to be on sentry duty greeted me. Without even asking my name he preceded me into the house and opened a door, introducing me into a drawing-room in which, at first glance, I recognized four of my colleagues, undoubtedly summoned as I had been by the telegram, who shook my hand silently.

After a brief silence that I did not venture to disturb, incapable as I was of stringing two words together, one of them spoke. They had examined the child. They had all established that the organs were sound and that they presented no natural characteristic that might give rise to fear of a fatal outcome. However, in spite of their common diagnosis, they could not pretend that the situation was not grave. The child was suffering from a kind of exhaustion—that word struck me—of the vital faculties, without there being any appreciable lesion to explain the degeneration.

At that moment the father came to join us. He was in a state of despair that was painful to see. Having lost a wife he adored two years before, he had trans-ferred all his affection to the little creature that an unknown malady was about to take away from him. He saw me and came to me, wanting to talk to me—impeded by the sobs that filled his throat, however, he took my by the hand and drew me away.

A moment later, I was beside the bed; mute and chilled, I recognized with horror with same appearances that had left an ineffaceable distress in my mind ten years earlier. The child, seemingly drained of blood, was no longer moving. It was a total exhaustion, as if all his blood had run out of an invisible wound, and the illusion was so complete that I asked the poor father, in a stammer, whether there had not been any hemorrhage.

He replied in a low voice. The child had not suffered any accident; the de-pressive effect had developed slowly; then, all of a sudden, in the last few days, the acceleration of the malady had taken on a lightning rapidity. Even so, he had still been running around the garden the day before.

"Is Monsieur Vincent still alive?" I asked, suddenly, obedient to an im-pulse beyond my control. I could have sworn that another personality than mine had spoken through my mouth, so involuntary were the words.

The father did not seem surprised by my question.

"Yes, he's quite grief-stricken. He was so fond of my little Georges, who returned his affection in full, for he never wanted to leave him. It was necessary to carry him away to bring him here—and he still resisted in spite of his weakness. It was like an attraction from which he didn't want to remove himself. But what does Monsieur Vincent matter? Examine the child and tell me—oh, I beg you—how he might be saved…"

I did not have the courage to proffer the generous lie. Even if my colleague still preserved some hope, how could I doubt? And yet… an obscure idea sprang up within my mind.

We stayed together in this fashion, the father not daring to question me any further, dreading to hear words from my lips that would be a sentence of despair, me not daring to be drawn into the mysterious path along which I felt myself slipping irresistibly.

Suddenly, a voice like a feeble breath escaped the child's lips. "Monsieur Vincent!" he sighed.

"He still wants to see his friend, you see," said the father.

But I had already launched myself towards the widow—and paring the curtains, I saw the man pass by on a pathway, attended by two nurses, heading for the house. I released an exclamation. "On your life," I said, addressing the father, "don't leave your child for a second—and whatever I do, whatever anyone might tell you about me, say that I'm acting on your orders."

"But what do you mean?"

"Don't forget—on your orders."

And without explaining any further, for I saw that the child was trying to get up, I threw myself outside.

At the foot of the front steps, I saw Monsieur Vincent, about to climb up.

"I forbid you to take another step!" I said to him, seizing him violently by the arm.

"Who are you?" he said. "What do you want with me?" And, turning to the attendants, who had paused, he said: "I want to speak to your master."

"And I repeat that you shall not pass. I'm acting on the instructions of Dr. F*** himself, who orders that you be returned to your lodgings immediately." I gave the nurses my name; they did not think it appropriate to disobey me. Besides, I had passed my arm insistently beneath that of the old man, and I was dragging him away rapidly. He did not have the strength to resist me.

"You," I said to one of the attendants. "Go to your master and tell him that I'll come back in half an hour, and that I'm making a supreme effort to save his child."

We had arrived at the lodge. I made Monsieur Vincent go in, and the two of us found ourselves alone in a little garden, over which the trees extended a vault of autumnal foliage.

I was finally face to face with the man! I stared at him.

He was very pale, and in his white and puffy face his eyes were like two shiny black holes.

We remained thus for a few seconds, looking at one another like two enemies studying one another before a duel. I was prey to a certain anger, which was making me tremble, but which must have communicated an excessive glare to my gaze—for his eyes seemed to flee mine.

Suddenly, I reached out towards him, touched his shoulder, and said: "Monsieur Vincent de Bossaye de Thévenin, you are a murderer!"

He did not reply, but this time, in his turn, he looked me full in the face.

"Oh, don't try to fascinate me," I said, sneeringly. "I'm not a child, and you shan't kill me…"

He raised his head, in a challenging manner. "What do you want from me?" he asked. "I don't know you…"

"But I know you, Monsieur Vincent. Do you remember a poor mother who came in search of a physician ten years ago"—I cited the street and the date—"for her young daughter, who was dying? Do you remember the physician you met in the outer room? And that…"—I emphasized every word, slowly and distinctly—"…one minute earlier, on hearing your footstep, the poor little girl had made one last effort to go to you, and had fallen back dead in my arms…"

"Ah! That was you!" said Monsieur Vincent.

"Yes, it was me, who also saw a strange phenomenon: the almost instantaneous metamorphosis of a vigorous man with a fresh complexion and relatively robust appearance, into a pallid, worn out, exhausted old man."

"Go on."

"Do you remember, again, that on that same evening you attempted to persuade a good woman, the concierge of the house in which you lived, to entrust her child to you?"

"That's right. She refused."

"That was ten years ago… and I find you again here, still living—you, for whom death is lying in wait. Living… while over there a child is dying, without any internal injury, without any scientifically detectable illness. Do you understand now, Monsieur Vincent, why I prevented you from going into that house, into which you were introducing yourself in order to steal from those dying lips the last breath of a life, to which your own is attached?"

"Come in," said Monsieur Vincent, pointing to the door of the lodge. He spoke with perfect simplicity, without irritation. I obeyed him, and we went into a study whose walls were completely hidden by bookshelves. He invited me to suit down, and did so in his turn. "What are you suggesting?" he asked,

I had recovered my calmness; I knew that I would obtain nothing from the man by intimidation. I resumed with more composure: "I'm not suggesting—I know…"

"What?"

"You've devoted yourself since youth, for almost a century, to the practice of magnetism. What your means of action are, I don't know. Present-day science is in the process of discovering the laws of hypnotism and suggestion, but it has not yet obtained the results that you have researched and attained. I'll use your own words; your science, according to you, is criminal: it multiplies a hundredfold the terrible inequality that the struggle for existence creates between the victors and the vanquished. I'm basing my assertions on your own confession, which I have, and I tell you that you are a murderer! Dare you tell me that I am not on the track of the truth?"

Monsieur Vincent let his head fall into his hand, appeared to reflect for a few seconds, then sat up straight and said: "Why didn't I meet you sooner?"

"Are you regretting not having the opportunity to teach me your abominable science?"

"No science is abominable," he replied, gravely. "The scalpel in the surgeon's hands might be a murder weapon; the hypnotism and suggestion that you mentioned might be instruments of crime..."

"Your science, according to you, is nothing but criminal..."

"Don't say that. Between it and the use that I have made of it there is all the distance that separates good from evil, the remedy from the poison..."

"You admit that!"

"I admit it. I horrify myself, not so much because of the crimes I have committed than the cowardice that led me to commit them..."

"The cowardice that leads to you attack children!"

"No, that's not it. The cowardice of not wanting to die."

"Explain yourself—for it seems to me that I've been carried away by a nightmare."

"Yes, I want to talk. But I must demand that you swear on oath..."

"To do what?"

"You're a man of science. I'll reveal the supreme secret to you, but you must make a solemn promise never to use it yourself..."

"Do I need to swear to not being a criminal?"

"And never to reveal it to anyone..."

"I swear it."

"Listen to me, then. There are three distinct phases in a human being's life: one of radiance, from infancy to the final limits of adolescence; the second of consummation, which lasts until the end of middle age; then the third, which is old age terminating in death.

"Every living organism—especially the human, which is the most complete expression of life—exhales during the first period of excessive vitality. A child absorbs more vital fluid than it consumes, and radiates the excess from its entire being. In the second phase, a creature consumes as much as it absorbs; there's an equilibrium of force. In old age, that equilibrium is broken; the absorption is inferior to the consumption; the vital expense is superior to the acquisition—which results in enfeeblement, which results in death.

"Now, in the present state of science, it seems to you impossible—does it not?—that a man, an old man, might beak the laws of nature and, by the exercise of a particular skill, steal from a child, for example, the vital effluvia that are in excess; to attract to himself, by means of a sort of endosmosis, all the fluid of which only one part, the exterior, is at his immediate disposition. That is, however, the truth. Yes, I am a criminal; yes, I am an assassin, because for forty years I have contrived to rejuvenate myself perpetually, a new Aeson.[66]

"Yes, I've killed children, but not, as the ignorant might be able to believe, or Johann-Heinrich Cohausen foolishly invented in his *Hermippus redivivus*,[67] by absorbing the air escaping from a child's lungs, or in the fashion of the legendary Vudoklacks,[68] by sucking their blood... no, by drawing into myself the excess of vital fluid that escapes from their entire organism...

"Ah, if only I had had the courage to stop at that! But I swear to you that there is no intoxication more profound, more addictive, more insanely pleasurable than that! When the warm and revivifying fluid penetrates the chilled limbs; when the assimilation takes place, penetrating the pores, insinuating itself into all the organs, it's unparalleled, entire absolute pleasure...it's the sensation of resurrection, if a cadaver were able to feel its own rebirth!

"And still I cried out to myself: 'Stop! But you must stop!' And still my entire being continued to drink these effluvia... and I killed! And I murdered! And the only remorse I could feel was for a thirst unslaked!

---

[66] In Ovid's *Metamorphoses*, Aeson, the aged and estranged father of the hero Jason, is restored to youth by means of Medea's magic.

[67] Johann-Henirich Cohausen (1665-1750)—Lermina gives the forenames as Jean-Henri—was a German physician well-known in his own country for his satirical sense of humor. *Hermippus redivivus* (1742) is a joke, which offers a tongue-in-cheek account of a method of human rejuvenation supposedly based on the work of the alchemist Jan van Helmont, which involves old men breathing in the exhalations of young girls, allegedly impregnated with vivifying "salts." Humor does not always translate well, however, and the hoax was not so obvious to all of the readers of the French and English versions of the text. The English translator did his best in the edition of 1744 but the demand that generated a second, expanded edition in 1749 was probably somewhat credulous. That text inspired both William Godwin's *St. Leon* (1799) and Percy Bysshe Shelley's *St. Irvyne* (1811), two of the most significant Gothic novels dealing with the theme of longevity.

[68] I have left this word in the idiosyncratic form that Lermina uses; he is presumably misquoting from memory a word that is spelled in various different ways in French references to Slavic vampire lore and is usually rendered into English as *vorkalaka* or *vyrkalaka*.

"Through my fingers and my gaze—oh, the gaze especially!—that attraction exerted itself which gives the victim a sensation of self-abandonment, not painful but delightfully intoxicating…"

He talked. He went on an on, the old wretch, with an orgasmic voluptuousness in his voice and his eyes… and I did not interrupt him, perhaps because of fear. How can I know?

Sensing that I was spellbound by his horrible and sublime infamy, he told me everything: what passes had to be made by the hands, what direction it was necessary to give to the gaze—and I listened, burying that hideous information, which intoxicated me like some poisonous liquor, in the utmost depths of my soul.

"And now that I've told you everything," he finally cried, "It's necessary that I die. Take me to the child!"

"Horrid old man!" I cried. "Do you want me to serve as your accomplice?"

He leaned closer to my ear—and, in truth, it seemed to me that his voice was like some subtle liquor, which flowed into me…

"You, whom I have initiated," he said, "do you not understand that *our* science also gives us the power of restitution? I am only alive by virtue of what I have stolen from that child, and I have told you that I want to die."

And I obeyed. I could not do other than obey him.

We went up the front steps together; together we went into the house; together we went into the drawing room, where the four physicians were still talking in low voices, and from there into the bedroom where the child was dying…

The child, who had recognized the footfalls of Monsieur Vincent, sat up, his eyes turning to him, his arms reaching out to him…

That was the supreme moment, the atrocious instant that I remembered, and which had preceded—as a blow precedes pain—the death of the little girl.

The physicians were behind us. The father was standing up, uncomprehending but hoping—as the desperate do—for a miracle.

I saw the child's body quiver, hesitate between two movements: to surge forward or to recoil.

Monsieur Vincent looked at him with dilated pupils, and he advanced slowly, his hands seemingly inert but active… as I, who knew everything, could see.

The child lay back gently. Monsieur Vincent was still approaching. Finally, he placed his hand on the little invalid's forehead. And suddenly I saw—oh, I cannot doubt it!—a rosy tint extend across the boy's face, clarify his lips, at the same time as gleam lit up in the depths of his dull eyes. And I understood full well, myself… and myself alone. The man was *reinjecting* into the child the life he had stolen.

"Your child is saved," said the old man, in a voice that was no more than a whisper. Then, turning to the physicians and standing up straight, he said: "Messieurs, you will bear witness to the fact that Doctor Bossaye de Thévenin, the last surviving pupil of Mesmer, has resurrected a corpse..."

So saying, he shuddered, and would have fallen down if I had not caught him.

"Carry me back to the lodge," he whispered to me.

I lifted him in my arms. The body was no longer heavy.

I deposited him on his bed. There, obedient to his ultimate wish, I remained beside him, and he talked to me at length—at great length—in a voice that grew ever weaker. He confided to me things that no mortal ear had ever heard, and which made me shiver. Those things I know, and can never forget— and I am afraid of old age, which will come, and which can render one criminal.

The child lived.

Monsieur Vincent died the following day.

One of my colleagues ran into me a few days later and said: "Did you see that old charlatan? How he tried to claim the honor for a natural reaction?"

As for me, I know—and I am afraid of my science.

Edmond Haraucourt: *Dr. Auguérand's Discovery*

"La Découverte du docteur Anguérande" *[translated here as Dr. Auguérand's Discover] by Edmond Haraucourt (1856-1941) appeared in seven parts in 1910 in* Le Journal, *but not quite as a serial. The first part appeared three weeks before the second and there was a fortnight's gap before the third appeared; that must have made for slightly difficult reading, and no one ever got a chance to read the story* en bloc *during the author's lifetime. Small wonder, therefore, that it has remained unknown and unhailed, even among dedicated fans of antiquarian proto-science fiction. It is, however, a very remarkable story, whose scope and sarcasm are slightly undermined by the inevitably awkwardness of their presentation.*

At a much later date, Isaac Asimov was to complain bitterly about the dire effect on speculative fiction of what he dubbed the "Frankenstein complex"—the tendency of writers about technology to use the same story-arc as Mary Shelley's novel, introducing a new technology only to cause it to run amok, thus requiring destruction. Whatever its convenience as a plot-formula, and the reassurance provided by the apparent restoration of the status quo *in the conclusion, the endless repetition of this ritual, in Asimov's view, was bound to breed an extremely unhealthy technophobia in its readers. The problem facing writers wanting to do things differently, of course, is that if new technologies are* not *introduced into stories merely in order to be canceled out again, the project of literary extrapolation becomes much more difficult and the results much less likely to provide readers with a comforting sense of closure.*

"La Découverte du docteur Anguérande" is one of very few scientific romances not only to recognize this problem but to react against it, decisively and fiercely. It deliberately inverts the formula, so that when the new technology makes its definitive appearance, it is not the invention that runs amok but the society into which it is introduced. Whereas Victor Frankenstein was represented as "the new Prometheus"—J. B. S. Haldane was later to complain that biological inventors following in the footsteps of Daedalus actually got an even worse literary deal than Promethean chemists or physicists—Haraucourt's biological inventor is explicitly likened to Christ, recapitulating God's role by bringing humans the gift of new life. Whereas Frankenstein became the archetype of a whole species of "mad scientists" threatening to upset worlds whose sanity is taken for granted, Anguérande is represented as a quintessentially sane individual caught up in a whirlwind of violence that exposes the inherent madness lurking just beneath the surface of civilization. The story thus became the first, if not the ultimate, parody of the Frankenstein complex, and warrants classic status of a sort on that account.

Classic or not, though, it is easy to see that "La Découverte du docteur Anguérande" *was not calculated to win its author any widespread popularity. If what he had done to Paris in* "Cinq mille ans," *in a relatively good-humored fashion, had seemed to some readers to be a mortal insult, then what he did to it in* "La Découverte du docteur Anguérande," *in a spirit of fervent wrath, was ten times worse; not only did Paris become an insane city stupidly rejecting the gift of life, but it did so partly because the good doctor had won entirely sane and reasonable support from Germany: the arch-enemy of all French scientific romance. If that support automatically made Anguérande a traitor in the eyes of the Parisians of the story, it presumably did exactly the same for Haraucourt in the eyes of his Parisian readers—as he had obviously known that it would.*

B.S.

I. Doctor Auguérand's Discovery

The affair was old. People hardly talked about it anymore except to laugh at it; even in scientific environments they only persisted in making it the subject of some joke. As for the newspapers, they never mentioned it anymore, considering the subject exhausted and monotonous. Society people, having once been passionately for or against, imitated the indifference of the press. Professor Patrice Auguérand's bluff was gradually relegated to the category of old legends.

In fact, nineteen years had already passed since the loud publicity provoked by his discovery; the elixir of long life that he claimed to have found in 1922 had not yet immortalized anyone by 1941, and even Dr. Auguérand had got nothing out of it but numerous annoyances and notorious ridicule. It was generally regretted that a man of such ability had compromised the glory of his career by a fantasy unworthy of him, his character and his previous endeavors. No one understood why he had yielded to the temptation of facile advertisement and thrown his name into the streets; his high reputation in science, his considerable fortune and his declared taste for quiet pleasures ought, logically, to have kept him safe from any such adventure, which could not be explained either by a need for money or an appetite for popularity.

But so what? The most serious men have their weaknesses. Besides, Monsieur Auguérand had paid for his, and had paid dearly; his moment of celebrity had been rapidly followed by universal derision. Under the pressure of jeers, and even catcalls, he had been obliged to abandon his positions of responsibility one by one—first his dean's chair, and then his chair in histology; in the meantime, he had renounced his clientele, or it had renounced him, and not one in eighteen years had been seen at sessions of the Académie de Médecine or those of the Institute.

"He's sulking," said some.

"He's ashamed," said others.

And everyone said: "He was wrong."

Whether it was out of vanity or resentment, sadness or rancor, the fact was that the old master lived alone. A bachelor with no family, having only distant relatives in the provinces, and cultivating no other friendships than that of the silent Thismonard, his inseparable companion, he lived a rather mysterious existence in his vast property at Neuilly. No one went in to the house except for tradesmen and the domestic staff, which was numerous but bizarre: all his servants were Chinese. He had doubtless been led to that organization by the increasing difficulty of finding tolerable domestics in France. He could at least, like so many others, have found French-speaking Chinese in the employment bureaux; on the contrary, he only admitted to his service Celestials ignorant of any European language, and it was even said that he had them come directly from Manchuria or Korea. A former professor from Canton served as both his interpreter and butler.

The staff in question never went out and talked even less.

It was known, however, that the professor had built three outhouses in the grounds of his house. One was minuscule, but constructed like a fortress or a prison, whose doors were reinforced with iron and windows furnished with bars; it was known as the laboratory. The second housed a veritable menagerie, in which the doctor kept animals of various species, mostly mammals. The third, large, well-lit and hygienic, fitted out like a sanitarium and provided with a garden, constituted a hospice. Poor old men were received there gratuitously, cared for with all expenses paid; their number was estimated at round thirty, and equity obliged one to believe that these hospitalized individuals did indeed receive good care, since the ministerial officers had never had occasion in eighteen years to go into the building to certify a death. In addition, the reports of sanitary inspectors unanimously attested to the perfect state of the premises and the people.

"What can be going on in there?" insinuated colleagues whose retrospective jealousy had not consented to disarm them.

Cattle, sheep and deer grazed the grass of the grounds. Neighbors who were too close or intolerant complained of hearing, during summer nights, the roaring of wild beasts and the croaking of frogs.

"He's gone mad, since that business!"

"Or at least obsessive."

"It's a scandal that, in this day and age, a madman is permitted to squander such sums lodging and nourishing dotards and animals, when millions of citizens have so much difficulty getting by."

"Only half a century ago, the poor died of hunger or cold; now, at least they have the right to a pittance and shelter."

"Which doesn't mean that aren't still rich people to be brought into line."

Things had reached this point of ironic or anodyne hostility when, on the fourteenth of July 1941—the anniversary of a date once famous but largely neglected now[69]—a twenty-line article appeared in an evening newspaper and re-awakened attention.

Hazard, wrote the journalist, *is a great master. It procured us the surprise, this morning, of being in attendance at an unusual marriage, celebrated in the Maison Syndicale*[70] *of the twenty-seventh arrondissement in the Boulevard de Neuilly. Two inmates of the famous Dr. Auguérand were joined in legal matrimony. The husband had counted no less than seventy-one autumns and the wife admitted an almost equal number of springs. Bawdy, however, and replete, the ruddy-faced lady was more reminiscent of a Jordaens than a Velasquez;*[71] *she had the manner of an excessively young actress playing an excessively old role. After the sacramental words, the septuagenarian, clad in a suit with a mauve cravat, offered the sexagenarian an arm free of ankylosis, and the couple made their exit as one exits at twenty. Were they going to pick strawberries? One might believe so, and they gave one to think as much, so advantageous, even triumphant, were the expressions that they were both exhibiting. Smiles, which were not mocking, greeted them as they crossed the thresholds, and there was even a certain amount of applause, when Dr. Auguérand, a witness to the marriage, appeared behind them. Is that couple, perhaps, the result of his work, emerged from his test-tubes? A serious advertisement, then, for the elixir of life?*

One final sentence, which we ask permission not to reproduce, indulged in wordplay and risked a joke that the press and public of 1940 will not find inadmissible.

No more was required. On the morning of the fifteenth of July on, reporters hastened to the Villa Auguérand and solicited interviews with the professor or his associates. The Chinese porter greeted them with speech reminiscent of birdsong, but whose syllables were so musical and unintelligible were that they were sufficient to bar any passage. The journalists persisted in vain; they were forced to restrict themselves to vague depictions of the outbuildings, and the very vagueness of their descriptions leant the abode a renewal of mystery. All afternoon, airplanes circled over the grounds, trying to discover some scientific or intimate detail.

---

[69] The storming of the Bastille—the beginning of the Revolution of 1789.

[70] The Maison Syndicale in Central Paris became the central focus of trade union activity in Paris following the Courrières Mining Disaster of 1906, which caused and enormous scandal, having been not merely he worst such disaster in history but the first to be widely reported in the Press. It is not surprising that Haraucourt, writing so soon after the disaster, was inclined to suggest that similar institutions might take over the functions of the local mairies in future.

[71] The Flemish master Jacob Jordaens (1593-1678) and the Spanish court painter Diego Velasquez (1599-166) represented rival schools of portrait painting, the former being less formal and arguably more robust.

The doctor had become enigmatic again, and his affairs interesting, at least for two or three days. He was in demand again, but he remained inaccessible. The reporters who came in the evening, like those of the morning, heard nothing but chirping from Chinese lips. For want of anything better, they invented. One of them overstepped the mark; the claimed to have observed the married couple by night, passing before their open window in an aircraft, and furnished an exaggerated account of them; one of his colleagues riposted with diametrically opposed, and even more sensational, affirmations. Polemic ensued. Then, people wanted to know, at any price; the public ear demanded the truth.

It got it.

It got it via the voice of the faithful Thismonard, to whom one journalist had the idea of paying a visit. The confidant replied, in substance:

"There's no reason why I shouldn't talk to you. If my glorious friend has kept himself in seclusion for such a long time it's not, as some have said, because of a sentiment of rancor or ruffled pride. He doesn't deign either to complain or to reproach anyone. People have laughed at his discovery, but far from taking offense, he deems that people have a right—almost a duty—to doubt; the benefit that it brings to humankind is too considerable for it to be welcomed without a measure of the skepticism that is elementary prudence. Besides, I have nothing to say that you don't already know; there is no essential modification to be made to the declarations of 1922.

"At that time, Auguérand's discovery was conclusive and total, and had been for ten years. But ten years added to a life is not sufficient to demonstrate that one can prolong the normal duration of life; a Macrobian fact can only be proven by the lapse of time. That is why Auguérand wanted time to go by. The Macrobians[72] that he is able to present today will bring you thirty years of experience, not the ten that they were able to do when you talked about them for the first time. We would have liked to wait for another ten years, but if the academies estimate that the present figure suffices and permits them to repent, my friend Patrice asks no more than to reserve a god welcome for them. As soon as they have formulated the desire, he will assign them a date and receive them. You can print that."

Interrogated as to the nature of the results obtained, Monsieur Thismonard replied:

"In order to be conclusive, our experiments had to be carried out, and have been carried out, not only on human beings but on various animal species, especially mammals, which furnish us with specimens exhibiting varying degrees of

---

[72] The Macrobians were a people described by Herodotus, perhaps somewhat fancifully, who allegedly lived in the Somalian peninsula during the first millennium B.C. According to the historian they were not merely the tallest and most handsome of humans but had mastered the secret of longevity, enjoying an average lifespan of 120 years.

vital resistance, and have served in consequence for us to draw up comparative tables from which the conclusion emerges that we can triple the duration of life. For example, rodents, such as hares, rats or rabbits, live for an average of four years; we maintain them for twelve. Bulls rarely surpass their fifteenth year; we can take them to thirty-two, and even to fifty by maintaining them in a state of virginity.

"As regards the human species, one cannot be ambitious for such a large augmentation for them. Indeed, if we compare humans with other species, the proportional calculation of the three phases of growth, maturity and senility lead us to conclude that people, reaching puberty at sixteen, ought normally live for a hundred and ten or a hundred and twenty years; you know that they don't last as long, in spite of the promise that they have at the moment of puberty; thus, they wear themselves out more rapidly. Proportionally, thy exhaust their vital resistance more rapidly than other animals do.

"Why and in what way? Evidently, by virtue of the one thing that distinguishes them from other species: the soul, the idealists will tell you; the nervous system, the materialists will say: their passionate and intellectual expenditure. In consequence, we do not hope, save in exceptional cases and curiosities, to produce Macrobians three hundred years old, but we are certain of being easily able to prolong the useful period of a human existence—which is to say, their physical and intellectual virility—until the hundred and tenth year. It will be even easier to take subjects who expend less—imbeciles and the chaste—to a hundred and fifty. I confess to you that that is not our aim; we attain it by virtue of the logic of the situation, without having wanted it.

"We are not philanthropists, in the outdated meaning that past generations attached to the word; we think in the same way as our time, which is utilitarian, practical and socially economical; the 20th century no longer has to entertain unproductive consumers, useless mouths and impotent limbs; we do not render youth to decrepit individuals, because, on the one hand, we do not have the ability, and, on the other hand, we do not care to. To conserve for society, for social cooperation, robust strength, by doubling it and perhaps tripling it—that is what is important to us, and that is what we are realizing. You can print that."

The journalist did not hesitate to do so; he would have said more if he had been given the means. He concluded by declaring that Academy and the Faculty, thus given the means to verify, and, if necessary, to rectify their premature judgment of 1922, had a duty to inform themselves fully on a question of universal interest, to enlighten the country and the world, and, if there was a need, to make honorable amends for their initial errors.

The learned bodies were reluctant to suffer the humiliation of soliciting an audience with an independent scholar who had severed all connections with them, but public opinion, which had scarcely deigned to mock the inventor a few days before, had abruptly turned around. Millions of people, renewing the hope of prolonging their lives, even for half a century, demanded the truth. Imposing processions passed through the streets of Paris; a few disturbances occurred.

The minister sent the official scientists an invitation that was as good as a command. A committee of inquiry was appointed. On the twenty-second of July, it expressed to Dr. Auguérand, by letter, the desire to hear his communications regarding the cases of longevity he had observed. An appointment was made, for nine o'clock in the morning on the twenty-fourth of July, for the designated committee-members to present themselves at the villa in Neuilly.

II. A Memorable Meeting

On the twenty-fourth of July, the committee members delegated by the Académie des Sciences, the Académie de Médecine and the Faculté presented themselves at the door of the establishment that popular parlance was already designating by a famous abbreviation, the AC: the Auguérand Clinic.

In spite of the care that the scientists had taken not to divulge the time of this visit, no one in Paris was unaware of it. An enormous crowd gathered at the edge of the city. In the first row, the reporters were waiting, recognizable by their automatic telegraph apparatus. The members of the crowd, visibly nervous and impatient, argued among themselves—but it was worse when the delegates got out of their cars. Immediately, an almost hostile agitation was manifest in the first rows, and the people at the back, braver because they were less visible, sounded anonymous whistle-blasts.

To tell the truth, for nine days, opinion had scarcely been favorable to the representatives of official science, who were caught in a dilemma.

"If Dr. Auguérand really did discover a means of tripling human life thirty years before, you're guilty of having rejected it out of paltry jealousy, thus depriving us of such a benefit. If, on the contrary, he's merely a charlatan and visionary, you made the mistake of not cutting short the deceptive hopes that he put into people's minds. In either case, your duty is to be sure, and you're sinning by negligence, you whom we pay to know what we don't know, on our behalf!"

The door closed on the dear masters. Three representatives of the press accompanied them in order to telegraph the news in the course of the session. The great dailies, speculating on public curiosity, and counting on the worldwide publicity that the event promised, had installed their Hertzian transmission apparatus on the threshold of the city and the paper's headquarters, in such a way that here and there, in Paris, London and Berlin as soon as at Neuilly itself, the crowd would be able to read, in white letter projected on black screens, the details of the communications made by the inventor and a summary of the technical discussions. New York would receive the cable only a few minutes later.

A quarter of an hour went by, seeming very long. Suddenly, the sound of an electric bell provoked a movement of heads and shoulders in the front rows, with a murmur that gradually propagated to more distant ranks. A reporter raised his hand toward the screen and switched on the receiver; binoculars were aimed. The dispatch appeared.

9.45. Reception at door of house. Exchange of civilities. Cold courtesy. Reserve on both sides. Dr. Auguérand seems confident, but devoid of arrogance. To his left, his faithful friend Thismonard, is smiling with a triumphant air that authorizes every hope. Committee members introduced into a vast, severe and glacial room where seats are arranged in a semicircle. Chinese domestics standing at all exits, barring the passage of anyone wanting to wander around the building. The doctor, with his back to the old 19th century fireplace, prepares to make a preliminary speech. Session open.

This initial telegram only furnished few elements to the commentators; they concentrated, however, on the phrase relating to Monsieur Thismonard, whose triumphant attitude "authorized ever hope." That was sufficient to create a current of opinion, still indecisive but already favorable, so strong was the desire to see the conquest confirmed. That was why the disillusionment was sharp, even violent, when, ten minutes later, the second dispatch was inscribed:

Auguérand speaks, explains his system. I do not prolong human life, he says. The expression is inexact, unscientific to the highest degree. I have never said any such thing. It is madness to pretend that one can reform the laws of nature; by the very fact that they are laws, they must be recognized as fixed, logical and immutable. Science can only aspire to understand them, to penetrate the secret of their functioning, so long mysterious, and to discover the conditions of their best return.

The street greeted this preamble with a sequence of whistles, which immediately announced total defeat; from the start, Auguérand's failure was proclaimed definitive; the egotistical hopes of the world, resuscitated for a week, were about to be dashed for the second time. In Berlin and New York the consternation was profound; instantaneously, share prices fell on the Bourse. But in Paris and London, outbursts of laughter covered the disappointment.

Professor Auguérand continued:

"Life is a perpetual resistance to death. In a great many animal species, however, individuals, yielding to the solicitations of instincts that corrupt them, have progressively rendered the race in a less resistant condition. Thus, one can say that they have voluntarily restricted the duration of life, since that diminution of the duration is the mediate consequence of a dissipation to which they consent.

"Death is the total of millions and millions of partial, successive deaths that beings accept or impose on themselves without being aware of it; very few animals live out their normal lifespan; the human species is, with a very marked prominence, the one that deteriorates the most rapidly of all. Why? Because humans abuse their strength more than the others. The comfort and relative security of their material existence have been able to provide relative compensation for the prejudice caused by an excessive expense, but that purely negative attenuation of harm is incapable of compensating for the effects of positive vice.

"The logical remedy, the only one that could bring the human animal back to maximum longevity, would consist of returning the abuser to the simplest conditions of nature, from which, on the contrary, humans are increasingly removing themselves. But that remedy is illusory, because humankind would refuse its application, and will refuse it even more forcefully the more social organization augments the possibilities of existence.

"Thus, common sense obliges us to anticipate that the maximum duration of human life, already briefer today than it was twenty thousand years ago, will be further reduced in generations to come—and since the logical remedy is logically impracticable, we shall be forced, Messieurs, to have recourse to accommodations. In other words, if we cannot prevent humans from ruining themselves incessantly and without respite, let us try to ameliorate the effects of those repeated ruinations whose total is premature death."

Further booing welcomed this theoretical verbiage, incomprehensible to some, devoid of surprise for others, which was displayed on the screens like a categorical confession of impotence or a bluff ill-concealed by the words. The impression on the street was, moreover, only a reflection of that of the scientists.

Indeed, at that moment Dr. W. Letigre made the observation, not without irony, that the task in question was merely that of the most elementary medicine. The silent Touposcoff, in his customary fashion, went to the window, looked out over the garden and took out his watch to signify that he was wasting precious time. Professor Axilo was studying the ceiling through his platinum-rimmed spectacles and tugging his filamentous beard.

Monsieur Sigismund Ricardos of the Académie des Sciences Morales et Politiques, a statistician, took advantage of the interruption to recall that one of the 19th century precursors of the then-embryonic science of statistics had already noted the influence that mode of life exercises on the relative duration of existence; in that epoch, he said, the two categories of subjects attaining the most advanced ages were ecclesiastics and agriculturalists; by contrast, artists, writers, advocates and physicians were at the bottom of the scale of vital resistance.[73]

---

[73] Haraucourt's "precursor" of statistical science is evidently fictitious, given that the actual 19th century French pioneer of this kind of analysis, Jacques Bertillon, continuing the work of his father Alphonse, found a diametrically opposite result with respect to the clergy, proving that, along with bachelors in general, they died younger, on average, than married men—from which he concluded that celibacy reduces life-expectancy. The English social scientist Herbert Spencer (a confirmed bachelor) interpreted the figures in a different way, suggesting that the cause and effect were the other way around: that sickly individ-

"From these statistics and others," Letigre added, "our predecessors felt able to conclude that excessive nervous strain, duplicated in sensual and intellectual forms, provokes the maximum exhaustion, and that alimentary intoxication, the effective cause of atherosclerosis, is secondarily manifest as a generator of precocious senility. Thus, love less, think less, eat less, and you will live longer."

General hilarity underlined this sally. The faithful Thismonard smiled with his imperturbable confidence.

Auguérand replied: "Thank you, Messieurs, for recalling observations that rejuvenate me in my turn, since they evoke the memory of my beginnings, the point of departure of the labors that were to lead me to the double discovery of which I have the honor of informing you today."

On reading this, an immense clamor went up from the exasperated crowd.

"Enough!"

"Down with Auguérand!"

"Enough!"[74]

"Basta!"

"Bravo Letigre!"

"Genuch!"

"Hurrah for Touposcoff!"

"Down with Thismonard!"

"Enough!"

The noise of the howling city-dwellers reached the hall. The Academicians, feeling that they had the support of public opinions, became restless in their seats. Several members, following Touposcoff's example, got up to go. Thismonard, motionless beside the fireplace, listened to the racket and seemed delighted. A pantogram[75] announced this confident attitude to the street. The indignant cries redoubled in volume. This time, however, the manifestation fell

---

uals unlikely to live long were more liable to be rejected as potential marriage partners, often having no recourse but to go into the priesthood.

[74] This exclamation is rendered in English, the previous one—and the next—having been a translation of "Assez!"

[75] The word *pantogramme* [pantogram] is probably improvised from *pantographe* [pantograph], a mechanical copying device. Haraucourt might have known that a device for copying images telegraphically had been patented in 1843 by the Scottish inventor Alexander Bain, and that a giant version of it built by Giovanni Caselli had sent a message from Paris to Amiens in 1856, displayed on a big screen like the one featured here. Bain's telegraph system, potentially the best and most versatile of all the candidates for 19th century development, would probably have integrated such a system eventually but it was ruthlessly annihilated by Samuel Morse, who would brook no competition.

flat, for Auguérand had just extended his right arm in a gesture of appeasement, and he resumed speaking in a tranquil manner.

Then, on the black screen, they read:

Auguérand says: "Messieurs, I have simply found a means of recovering the quotidian losses, and, in consequence, of attenuating the resulting degradation. By the diminution of these partial deaths, I delay by as much the term of their total—which is to say, definitive death. I confessed to you just now that I cannot prolong life, but I can restore it very nearly to its normal duration, which had progressively diminished. In that way, not only can I extend the term of individual existence, but I can maintain subjects in their useful maturity for a number of years that varies between double and triple the present figures."

Sensation in the learned assembly. Thismond inspects the audience, beaming. Everyone is on their feet. Precipitate dialogues in low voices.

Touposcoff, surrounded, says slowly: "He's making fun of people!"

Legrand-Gauthier, very somber, but known for not exhibiting any hostility to anyone, poses a question: "If I understand correctly, my dear colleague, it's a matter of a double therapeutic treatment of the nervous and circulatory systems?"

Auguérand replies: "Exactly, my dear colleague. With your permission, we'll go together to examine the evidence that I feel duty-bound to submit to your competence."

General movement. Thismonard heads for the exit and leads the way.

This dispatch, so abruptly affirmative after the disappointment of the preceding communications, disconcerted the public. Was it a joke? The inventor, by his own confession, could not prolong life, but could nevertheless double or triple it? Many did not understand. A few sensed that the master had wanted, by playing with words, to unmask his adversaries and increase their discomfort. Others saw in his language, not a contradiction but a legitimate distinction and the mark of a scientific mind.

For the immense majority, however, which is simplistic, one fact stood out above all others: Auguérand can triple human life!" On the boulevards of Paris, in London, Berlin and New York, the news spread like lightning.

"Is it proven?"

"Not yet."

"He's introducing the committee to the subjects on which he's been experimenting for thirty years."

"By noon, we'll know."

Bets were made in London and New York. Already, Auguérand, discredited a few moments before, was being laid at evens.

Stock exchanges rose everywhere.

III. The Macrobians

Third pantogram, posted at 10.30 a.m.:

*Thismonard leads the committee members to the menagerie, as if Augué-
rand does not deign to present these preparatory examples himself. On the way,
the cicerone explains that short-lived animals have been very precious for the
study of the cure, its procedure and effects, since they alone permitted the
demonstration, within a lapse of thirty years, of tripled existences. The cages are
maintained with a curious concern for hygiene and quietude. It has been observed, in fact, that the proximity of carnivores is sufficient to abridge the lives
of prey species, by reason of the nervous expense occasioned in the latter by the
presence of potential peril; same observation in respect of males lodged in proximity with females. All the cages are equipped with a card recording the animal's pedigree, its date of birth, its diet, and the average duration of life of an
individual of the species.*

Let us cite in passing:

*Cats, mean duration, 16 years; typical obtained, 32 years; maximum, 46
years.*

Cows, mean duration, 20 years; typical obtained, 52 years.

*Bulls, mean duration, 15 years; typical obtained, 32 and 34 years, with
trimestrial heifer; bullock, 45 years.*

Hares, 4 years, attaining 12.

*Rabbits, duration 4 years; impossible to extend beyond 8 (irreducible las-
civiousness).*

*Dogs, ordinary duration 20 to 24 years; impossible to extend beyond 45
(cynicism).*

*Deer, maximum duration, 40 years; impossible to extend beyond 90 (annu-
al excess of genetic instinct).*

Rats, 4 years, attainment 12.

*Pigs, 20 years; typical obtained 50, reaching 60 (undeserved reputation;
much more chaste than namesakes of the human species).*

Horses, duration 35, present specimens 60; still increasing.

Etc.

The complete official list will be published in due course.

This paragraph of the pantogram provoked mediocre applause; it only excited the Animal Protection Society, which had become very influential in 1941,
and aged spinsters. As for the mass of the public, it was somewhat hesitant to
conclude a perfect similarity between citizens and animals.

It is also necessary to remark that advantages so clearly marked in favor of
chastity and even continence, were of a nature to cool the enthusiasm of French
people; several men cheerfully declared their hostility to a cure that required so
great a sacrifice as an initial premium; many women did not hesitate to give

them loud support. To this criticism, moderate spirits objected that it would be permissible for anyone not to triple a lifespan by privation, but simply to double it while not depriving oneself of anything. Shopkeepers seemed full of confidence. Nevertheless, by a rather typical particularity, a sharp discontentment was manifest in Marseilles; the Cannebière declared that the very principal of such medication was an attack on the liberty of love, and the Bourse fell, while Stock Exchanges continued to rise elsewhere—notably in London and New York, where the premium attributed to good morals could not fail to obtain official approval.

Fourth pantogram, posted at 11.20:

Victory! Triumph! Doubt seems to be no longer permissible. Auguérand leads the committee into the human sanitarium. Thirty-three surprising subjects, men and women, all armed with their duly certified documents. The comparison of birth certificates with the present appearance of the individuals presents unimaginable contrasts.

M. Léonard Latude (the groom of 14 July), 71 years old, looks about 45.

The widowed Mme. Mathillat (the bride), 69, scarcely looks 38.

Marguerite Bouldeboul, 83, looks 60.

M. Alexis Perlot, 76, certainly doesn't look 50.

Mlle. Andréa Froussotte, 56, looks 30.

Her daughter Jeanne, similarly unmarried, 30, seems 22.

Etc.

The complete official list will be published in due course.

The subjects were interrogated by the committee members; the Demoiselles Froussotte were ausculated. They male subjects registered their strength with the dynamometer. In the hydrotherapy room, Alexis Perlot, completely naked, lifted weights.

The committee, visibly impressed, maintained reservations nevertheless that might have been deemed excessive. Legrand-Gauthier finally broke the silence and, in a slow but categorical voice, affirmed his amazement. Touposcoff objected that the concordance of cases, while establishing a presumption in favor of the theory, could not be considered as scientifically conclusive. Letigre declared himself satisfied.

Thimonard made the observation at this point that the results obtained were far from representing the maximum possible, since the treatment had only produced its effects from the date that the subjects had begun to follow it. (Scientific hilarity.) All that it had been possible to accomplish was to maintain them at that age, without rejuvenating them. The quinquagenarians had remained quinquagenarians.

"A subject who is submitted to the cure in his thirtieth year conserves the vigor of his maturity, in all its forms, for a half a century."

Touposcoff asked whether continence was indispensable to the efficacy of the treatment.

Thismonard reassured him in these terms: "Absolute chastity being unnatural, it is inadmissible, nor even supposable, that it will be necessary, much less indispensable. Only moderation is required; in this as in all things, *in media stat virtues*—virtue resides in the median.

"The exact median?"

"No, the just median."[76]

An evident relaxation had been established for several minutes. The famous Professor Graunerr, who had not said a word thus far, nor given any sign of approval or disapproval, took the floor authoritatively and addressed the assembly.

"Out of devotion for science," he said, "I am ready to run the risks of the treatment personally."

"That heroism, my dear master," Thismonard replied, "will reward you, albeit belatedly."

This riposte provoked malicious remarks. It was, in fact, well known that Professor Graunerr would reach the age of retirement in 1942; several candidates were already canvassing support for the eventual acquisition of his chair. His maintenance of his responsibilities would produce numerous disappointments among his colleagues.

The beginning of the pantogram reporting all this had given the masses as profound emotional shock, but the end was given a poor welcome. The public was unanimous in criticizing the journalist who was mingling details of excessively particular interest with the great questions of general interest. The intrusion of such petty matters was judged inappropriate and utterly unwarranted.

"What do individual egotistical concerns matter in a debate in which the future of humankind is at stake?"

People scarcely suspected then the importance of the two remarks made by Messieurs Graunerr and Thismonard, nor the formidable conflict that had just been inaugurated, unknown even to the interlocutors. People were only to comprehend subsequently the social gravity of the problem unexpectedly posed upon the world. For the moment, the joyful emotion of the conquest took precedence over all other considerations. The eleven-twenty pantogram left no room for doubt; the cause was won for Dr. Auguérand, and also for humankind.

Half an hour later, all the peoples of the Earth were publishing the enormous news:

Human life can be extended!

---

[76] This old joke refers to the longstanding French political principle of the *juste milieu*, which refers to a fair compromise rather than an exact partition, as the phrase could also be construed. I have employed "median" rather than "middle" or "mean" because the text has already established a principle of statistical pedantry that mathematically-minded readers will doubtless appreciate.

At midday, the Bourse registered the highest rise of the century. The antipodes, where it was the middle of the night, and where dispatches were anxiously awaited, celebrated the event with sudden and general illuminations.

The following pantogram, dated ten past noon, related that the session was concluding with a visit to the laboratories.

The inventor presented his two elixirs. Their employment was very simple: once a week, three drops in a glass of water, taken on an empty stomach. The price of manufacture was virtually negligible—one franc fifty a liter. M. Sigismond Ricardos of the Académie des Sciences Morales, immediately calculated that at five centigrams a drop and 156 drops per person per year, one liter would be sufficient for the annual treatment of 128 individuals—which would require, for each one, a total expenditure on ten centimes a year.

Interrogated as to his intentions relative to the sale price of the product, the doctor declared that he had no intention of indulging in commerce. He would deliver his formula to the International Codex, but only on the expiration of the thirtieth year that he had assigned to the interval of its study—which is to say, in five months' time. Until the first of January 1942, in order to avoid chemical analyses and counterfeiting, he would keep the secret of his formulae, and no quantity of elixir, however small, would leave his house. In the meantime all the people who so desired could present themselves at the clinic in Neuilly; a dispensary would be installed for their use in the villa's garden, and glasses of water would be provided free of charge for immediate consumption. It was recommended in the strictest possible fashion that no more than one glass per week be taken; the abuse of the treatment might present serious dangers.

The committee declared itself sufficiently enlightened. Professor Graunerr, having not eaten, asked to begin the treatment immediately. Dr. Auguérand poured him three drops of the yellow elixir. Graunerr raised his glass solemnly and, saluting the learned company with his gaze, he said: "I drink to the future of science"

"And to yours," replied one voice.

Smiles. Applause. The session ended. The committee was to reconvene at the Institut at three o'clock, to render its definitive verdict, which was henceforth not in doubt. Auguérand received warm congratulations; he showed the delegates out. There was an exchange of civilities—which, this time, were cordial and frank.

When the gate of the grounds opened to let the committee members out, a thunderous ovation acclaimed Auguérand, who immediately retreated.

In Paris and various other capitals, the disinterest of the inventor gave rise to the enthusiasm of some, the anxiety of others and the surprise of all; it was too abnormal a circumstance not to cause astonishment in an essentially practical epoch in which every invention represented a capital and every enterprise a business affair. That excess of generosity doubtless concealed some secret plan? It remained incontestable, nevertheless, that the benefit of the discovery would be accessible to all, rich and poor, without distinction. Henceforth, everyone, save for accident or disease, would have the means, or at least the hope, of remaining on Earth for a hundred and fifty or two hundred years. Human genius had finally conquered Duration, as it had previously conquered Space.

"Hurrah for Auguérand!"

The day was not to go by without alarm, however. At four o'clock, while the committee was in session at the Institut, a cablegram arrived from Chicago addressed to the doctor, which announced the formation of a company to exploit his discovery, and offered him twenty million dollars for the purchase of the patent. The different services of the daily press were then so meticulously organized that five newspapers received copies of the dispatch before the original had reached its destination. The boulevards were informed at the same time as the doctor.

What would he decide, in the face of such a strong temptation?

At five o'clock, it was learned that he had refused.

At five forty, the committee rendered its formal judgment, attesting to the reality of the results obtained by the treatment and only maintaining reservations with the regard to the chemical composition of the elixirs, unknown from then until the following first of January.

At five fifty, the representative of a London-based company, outbidding the American one, offered Auguérand eight million pounds sterling, equivalent to two hundred million francs.

The doctor's second refusal caused delirious enthusiasm in the world's population. In every language, people were glad to recognize in that noble gesture the proverbial disinterest of the French character, which had not degenerated at all.

Everywhere, successive editions of newspapers were printed. Every city saw agitation in its streets; the houses were empty, factories abandoned, work suspended. Old men, who were greeted with acclamations as they passed by, displayed faces radiant with joy, as if the discovery were only relevant to their decrepitude, although they would obtain less profit from it than anyone else.

Then, suddenly, upon that universal exuberance, that triumphant certainty, the great evening newspapers fell like an icy shroud. Reason had just spoken—too late, as always. An impression like that of a sleeper awaking from a crazy dream abruptly disconcerted the still-hallucinated minds. An immense malaise enveloped the terrestrial globe. In the depths of all human pupils, an anxiety emerged. The name of Graunerr was bandied about, leaving behind it a wake of anguish. Young faces became somber, and the old men were seen hastily returning home...

IV. Make Way for the Young!

It is necessary to confess that the movement began in France, in a light-hearted manner; is that country, where it is said that everything ends up in songs, one might say that everything begins in caricatures, which are pictorial songs.

The first to appear was the one by *Pal*, at six-thirty. It represented Professor Graunerr, in a toga and bonnet, standing on his doctoral chair, with one hand raising a cup from which he was about to drink, and the other blessing, with three drops, the crowd of candidates laying siege to his position. A few were reaching out with clawed fingers toward the desired placement, while others, probably touched by the benediction, were fleeting with dolorous expression. The caption read: "I'm drinking to my future!"

The second caricature, by *Témoin*, appeared in the cinema at six fifty; it depicted a thin old man, decrepit and doddery, in the countryside, who threw his spade away in despair and lay down in a furrow, as if to die of exhaustion there; he got up immediately, with great difficulty, and went up a hill to a thatched cottage, and the scene shifted to the interior of the house. Like a dying man opening his own tomb, the old man opened the door and came in; from a chest he took a bag of copper coins, emptied it on to the table and counted his treasure weeping. His three sons arrived, followed by their three wives and kids. The old man divided his money into three piles; he was put to bed and the bed surrounded, while they waited for him to die. But then the door opened again, and Mephistopheles appeared, wearing Auguérand's face; three drops of the elixir, and he moribund was standing up, cured and valiant. Then the drama:

"Give me back my money!"

The sons hesitated, the daughters-in-law protested, lecturing their men and preaching resistance. The rejuvenated old man took hold of his staff furiously and, alone against all of them, forced his heirs to give in one by one; all sent away, they went out cursing, while the little children, between the legs of the grown-ups, shook their fists at their grandfather. And the old man picked up his spade to go back to the field.

"You shan't have my land!"

In the next act, the children had grown up and become men, fathers to their own children, whom they watched grow up and multiply, to the extent that the cottage filled up with successive generations, too numerous for its restricted size, where they were crushed, choking, against the walls. They had all drunk the elixir, and no one was dying any longer—not even the lusty ancestor, who was driven by vital exuberance to be excessively familiar in corners with his own descendants, in conformity with the ancient laws of incest.

Finally, a saucepan was placed on the table, and the ancestor got ready to distribute the meal to his hungry family. He plunged a ladle into the enormous vessel and brought out the only potato, which everyone was expecting, and everyone could see; having taken it between his thumb and forefinger, he raised it up in front of his face, as a priest does with the host in order to present it to the faithful, and gobbled it up.

The piece was entitled: *The Last Communion.*

There was no laughter; everyone understood its economic message. In any case, if they had not understood, the editorial in the *Judgment Public* arrived just in time to make it precise; it appeared at exactly seven o'clock. It said

It's decided, then. The date is memorable in the auspices of stupidity. To-day, the twenty-fifth of July 1941, a benefactor of humanity, who naively imagines himself such, has endowed the world with a previously-unknown scourge, the worst of all those that science and history have recorded thus far: social plethora! How can it be that public common sense was not able, from the first moment, to see through this terrifying utopia? With a disconcerting candor, people have welcomed Dr. Auguérand's success and the demonstration of his discovery; it is done; the triumph is complete; we shall all live for a hundred and fifty to two hundred years! Which is to say that five, six, seven or even eight simultaneous generations will be competing for the jobs and food that are hardly sufficient for two or three.

No one has understood that, by virtue of this fact alone, we shall be abruptly reduced to the necessities of primitive barbarism, to the bloody struggle that once hurled our ancestors against one another, all the more determined to destroy those who are nearest to them, on the same continent, in the same province, in the same village and in the same family, competitors for the same wealth. We had succeeded, after two hundred centuries of murder and two centuries of philosophy, in putting an end to war, at least for a while. You are reestablishing it with a joyful heart, more ferocious than it was before, more necessary than it was before, armed with the formidable means that progress has given it, and without mercy, because victory or defeat will be a matter of life or death for every people.

By multiplying us to excess, you are condemning us to kill one another! Abortion and infanticide, which were crimes, will become duties. If you do not succeed, by means of international laws, in restricting the fecundity of women, there will no longer be any security on the planet, which will run red with indispensable murder. And how can you arrive at diplomatic agreement, what police will monitor you and suppress the increase in population among neighboring people, desirous as they will be to develop their numerical superiority—a desire and effort that will tend logically to mutual annihilation?

The *Drapeau Rouge*, the organ of the moderates, struck the same note:

In what animal species do you observe the coexistence of eight generations? You are returning to us, you say, the initial number of our years? All right, we'll take your word for it. But do not take the inference that you are restoring the natural order, for you are, on the contrary exiting from it, since that order is no longer what it was in the earliest days of the race. Then, the small number of humans permitted them to live much longer, which was possible but has ceased to be. Where do you see the available space? Are you going to popu-late Saturn, or would you prefer to conquer the planet Mars?

To triple the duration of the individual is to triple the number of individu-als; two thirds will be in excess; as soon as you add them it will be necessary to get rid of them. How? Many by violence and the rest by disease. For that natu-ral law, which you claim to be in error, will bring order to the fantasies of sci-ence and reestablish the equilibrium disrupted by your actions. Your benefit is only theoretical; the harm you do will be real. The dead will perhaps not be the same individuals, and they will die differently, but just as many will die, for our proportional disappearance is demanded by the economy of nature as well as political economy. Increases in poverty, disease and hatred, international wars, domestic crimes—that is what you are bringing us; that is your birthday gift! There is every reason to be proud of it. Thank you, Dr. Auguérand!

The *Balai* published an even more violent article, whose title alone is enough to convey its tenor: *Let's kill the old!* That deliberately excessive cynical piece obtained less credit but further disturbed the anxious minds of old people. A few thought it wise to declare, at the family dinner, that they had no intention of taking the treatment. Very rarely was any credence given to these asser-tions—which were, in any case, never sincere, for all those who made them had simultaneously made secret plans to visit the dispensary at Neuilly the following morning.

Let us hasten to add that families could be found, in fairly considerable numbers, in which worthy individuals rejoined in the idea of conserving the au-thors of their days and nights for longer, along with the delights or annoyances that those days and nights involved.

The evening was marked by a certain effervescence in the brasseries of the Latin Quarter. Professor Graunerr was roundly abused there, especially among medical students, who were more directly interested. There was much comment on *Pal*'s caricature; according to all the evidence, the movements in high places delayed by maintenance of a pontiff and others who would soon follow his ex-ample would produce stasis in all the echelons of the medical hierarchy, and the slowness of promotion could only be further accentuated henceforth. The younger generations foresaw themselves treading water interminably, con-demned to vegetate indefinitely...

By eleven o'clock that night, the opinion had become unanimous; the name of Graunerr was no longer spoken without the accompaniment of insulting epi-thets and substantives borrowed from zoology. At that very moment, a summons to a meeting launched by the president of IASUE (the International Association of Students and University Employees) was circulated through the cafés, invit-ing the comrades to gather in the great hall of the Maison Syndicale at midnight to discuss what action to take.

An immense procession immediately formed, under the rallying cry: "Down with Graunerr!" When the file attempted to cross the bridges, it was driven back by the police; a rather hectic skirmish ensued, but without any serious incidents. At midnight, the streets suddenly emptied, the students having gone to the Maison. The meeting lasted more than three hours; numerous speeches were made there, all hostile to the reform. The president's oration was cheered:

"To hell with living longer! To succeed—that's what matters!"

A motion was passed demanding that a delegation be sent immediately to the Ministry of Information, in order to present the grievances of the young and to demand the pure and simple maintenance of the rules presently in place for the retirement of teaching staff.

"What about the private clientele? Will you have a law to constrain them from continuing to going to the old men for as long as they survive? You'll be competing with their glory, won't you?"

Consternation followed this interjection, then a clamor: "Down with the old men!"—soon followed by "Death to the old men!"

For ten minutes the agitation was extreme; in the overheated room, faces and brains were congested with anger; without discussion, a motion was adopted setting up an action committee to organize a demonstration that same morning at the Auguérand Institute. The agenda was suspended without the session closing; the students went *en masse* to gather at the villa in Neuilly, preceded by a red and gold corporative banner bearing the motto: *Make way for the young!*

The reassembly was fixed for nine o'clock, in front of the Fontaine Michel.

For the rest of the night there was calm in the streets, if not in minds—for the world of the schools was not the only one to become agitated, and there were soon multiple proofs of the fact. Shortly before daybreak, the violet placards of the anarchist faction were displayed on the walls: *The bourgeois are perpetuating themselves!* Paraphrasing the article in the *Balai*, the leader of the proletariat urged the faubourgs to open revolt against the intrusion of this new abuse, of which the poor would bear the brunt, as always.

"It is with your lives that they will increase theirs! In prolonging your existence, they are prolonging your misery, in order to exploit it for longer! They're insulting you with illusory benefits and underhanded promises! Don't let them get away with it! Break the fratricidal dream of the exploiters in the egg!"

The *Cloche d'ébène*, a free newspaper was distributed by the thousand at factory gates; it announced for the afternoon a challenge to Clément Boeuf: "We summon the government to declare, yes or no, whether it intends to introduce disturbance into the social order and introduce to the peace of the world a ferment of individual and national hatreds."

Thus France, which had once preceded other nations in the path of adventurous reform, and which had now become pragmatic, the old France of epics, was reduced to preaching prudence and dogmatizing about egotism! At least it must be recognized that in that, as in everything else, it went from one extreme to the other and remained faithful to its character, if not its program, since it was ready to put the brake on innovators with the same passion with which, previously, it had given them free rein.

Immediately, Germany took the opposite stance to the thesis sustained here; the official press declared that all progress must be welcomed, under pain of obscurantism, and that, if it brought difficulties in application or secondary inconveniences resulting from side-effects of the principal benefit, that was no reason to reject it, but rather toward the problems off by remedies that remained to be found and would be found.

"France is wrong; it ought to be proud of its brainchild and of the progress that, once again, is emerging therefrom!"

Was Germany sincere and truly disinterested? Was it not trying, by flattering our proverbial vanity, to bring about a reversal of French opinion? Did its affectation of liberalism not conceal the already-nascent hope of further increasing, in favor of the Germanic lands, their numerical superiority, and of finally crushing us?

The *Cloche d'ébène* affirmed it: "We will not be duped by the Alboche!"

The idea caught on; after two hours, the supporters of Auguérand and his method were deemed to be affiliated to the interests of Germany; they were the *Alboche*. By contrast, the adversaries of longevity inevitably became the promoters of national defense; they were the *Frangins*.

Once again, two parties were born and constituted, furiously irreducible, as is fitting as soon as it is a matter of life and death. And the sun rose, radiantly, in the clear sky on the day of the twenty-sixth of July, which would decide the fate of future humankinds...

V. Alboches and Frangins

Thus, the question had unexpectedly become political and national, and two irreducible parties had formed on the night of the twenty-fifth and twenty-sixth of July: those who thought in the German fashion and wanted to prolong life, the Alboches; and those who thought along the French lines and claimed, in rejecting Auguérand's invention, to be maintaining the fraternity between individuals and peoples, the Frangins. The struggle commence with the day. Within the first hour, in fact, it became known that the Syndicate of State Functionaries, Employees and Workers had called a general strike for the day of the twenty-sixth; that it was demanding the strict application of the rules to all the title-holders of administrative offices who reached the age-limit; that it was demanding from the minister an immediate formal undertaking not to effect in future any prolongation of employment capable of hindering due advancement—under threat, in case of resistance, of continuing the strike until the petitioners received satisfaction.

All public services came to a stop: the mail, refuse collection, transport and the innumerable monopolies. Paris was about to be deprived on bread by the administration, of vegetables and fish by the railways, of meat by the abattoirs, of the greater part of its vehicles, of light—and, in consequence, of theaters. Food prices shot up instantaneously. Departing trains remained in the stations; the others stopped mid-route; no French steamship lifted anchor, but several made ports of call wherever they happened to be, awaiting telegraphic instructions from the Syndicate.

At seven o'clock it became known that the UOLS (Union of Officers on Land and Sea) had joined the protest.

The government panicked. A hastily-convened Council of Ministers affirmed that the demands were legitimate and the acquired rights were to be respected; they saved face by saying that Dr. Auguérand's discovery was too recent and too uncertain in its range to permit the introduction of any modification whatsoever to the laws and decrees relating to various age limits.

"Very well—but what then?"

"Then people will live, thanks to the elixir, but will no longer have a means of living? At sixty years, a third of life, people would have interminable days before them—twice as many as behind—but no bread for those years, and no right to earn their bread? Is that logical? Is it just? Is it even possible?"

The Minister had thought, by reaching an agreement, that he was begetting himself out of a major embarrassment, but he had merely ended up creating a new one. The adversaries of reform were certainly not soothed, for they mistrusted official promises, and they had a strong suspicion that the Minister had not found a solution to a difficult problem, but had merely displaced it, and even aggravated it further.

As for those who wanted to take advantage of the discovery and get their hands on the treatment while it was free, their number had probably only diminished in a minuscule proportion, but their serenity, and most of all they joy, was significantly corroded. One was obliged to suppose that they uncertainty of material existence would deter a good third of those future appetites; their number scarcely counted any tenacious partisans save for the sick, who would not consent to give in, valetudinarians who were rubbing along, the rich who had their bread guaranteed and petty pensioners who were content with very little.

"Them again! Will it be necessary, for another century, to pay the pensions of those useless creatures? What a burden for the Treasury—what an ever-increasing burden! It will end in bankruptcy, and in the meantime, an increase in taxes will be unavoidable to nourish these still-healthy idlers to whom the right to work will be refused!"

Thus, the drinkers of the elixir became social parasites, and the responsible government found itself driven, by the very urgency of matters, to dread the reform, to fear its budgetary consequences, and, in consequence, to oppose it in principle.

"To Hell with Auguérand! The animal has backed us into a fine corner!"

The Treasury Minister, a fellow possessed of a subtle intelligence, proposed that the affair be gently put to sleep.

"Difficulties of this sort," he said, "seem new, but aren't. Our situation is analogous to that of any government confronted with an innovator whose discovery threatens to disrupt the established equilibrium and the adopted harmony. There aren't two ways of governing, but only one that's good; a little more difficult today than before, but it's still the only one: roll the client over to safeguard the moment. History can therefore point us in the direction of the remedy for our situation. It's identical to that of the Church in confrontation with Galileo, another genius who proposed an inconvenient truth. It's important to obtain a retraction of that truth. Do we lack the coercive means that our predecessors possessed? You possess others. If Auguérand is disinterested, it will be more expensive, that's all, and it will certainly be less expensive than adopting his system.

"If we can't buy the doctor, let's buy his judges; let's address ourselves to the technical committee and extract a second report from them, full of restrictions. The mistake was not thinking of this plan yesterday, when it would have been less costly; a graver mistake, I regret to say, was the official dinner offered to the inventor by the President of the Republic. We're pressed for time, but we can still repair the situation. The note issued by the council this morning constitutes excellent preparation for this retreat.

"The declaration we need to obtain from the committee members is this: 'The public has drawn exaggerated conclusions from our report; Dr. Auguérand's discovery is real, but it does not have the enormous scope that has been credited to it; it seems to be able, in truth, to increase life by a few years, but it is important to be wary of the excess of philanthropy that will draw opinion to admit too rapidly that which is insufficiently demonstrated.'

"One point, that's all. As to what this declaration will cost us, don't worry about it; I'll find the necessary funds. The question, returned for further study, will become akin to that of Galileo in a quarter of a century: our successors will untangle it."

The Minister of Police accepted the mission of handling the negotiations; he did, in fact, hold various information of a highly confidential character relating to some of the honorable committee members, excellent strings that permitted him the hope of acquiring a prompt acquiescence to the administration's desires.

The president was the first to be summoned. Professor Graunerr promised to renounce the treatment, ostensibly, and only to continue it under the title of a scientific experiment, *in anima nobili*.[77] On Axilo, there was leverage via Rus-

---

[77] Moved by nobility.

sia, and on Touposcoff via the princes, and on Letigre via the ladies. But Legrand-Gauthier as seized, as soon as the subject was broached, by an indignation of Corneillian proportions.

"Auguérand is a man of genius! His discovery is an immense benefit! You won't stifle it like this!"

He threatened to reveal the plot to Thismonard. He could only be reduced to silence by a charge of indecent behavior motivated by the complaint of a neighbor; he would have to be released the following day, in recognition of the fact that he had merely put his nose to her window, but a respite of twenty-four hours was sufficient to liquidate an affair of State.

While these maneuvers kept the corridors of officialdom busy, the streets went crazy.

At eight thirty-seven Thimonard arrived, breathless, at the Neuilly clinic; he exploded into the doctor's study and threw a stack of newspapers on to the desk.

"Oof! What a crowd! It took me three hours to get here, and I wouldn't have managed it if I hadn't had the idea of going round via Suresnes."

"Are there that many people?"

"Fantastic! You've taken precautions?"

"I think so, we've made arrangements as best we could,"

"I'm pleased to see you so calm. You're ready for anything, then?"

"Damn it! You're asking too much of me; I've made the best dispositions I can, and it wasn't easy. When I got back from the Élysée last night after the banquet, I got down to business. I worked all night. We have six dispensaries, and enough elixir for two thousand people, or thereabouts. For the first day, you'll admit that that isn't bad. Tomorrow, we'll do better."

"What's that you say? Tomorrow! Who's talking about tomorrow? It's a matter of today; there might not be a tomorrow. Have you read the papers?"

"I haven't had time."

"So you don't know anything about what's happening in Paris?"

"No. What?"

"Rioting, perhaps a revolution."

"Bah—in honor of what saint?"

"You, you fool."

"Me?"

"Listen to the street, you Archimedes. Can't you hear that, in the street?"

"Last night, I saw the unemployed forming a queue outside the gate, doubtless in the hope of selling their place to some well-off bourgeois; they exchanged a few revolver shots to punctuate the darkness.

"Don't laugh! It's not the time. Hurry up and understand. All Paris is up in arms. A general strike has been declared. They don't want the elixir, they don't want longevity, and they don't want you!"

"What?"

"You're a public enemy, a disturber of the universe—and as if that weren't enough, you're a national peril, an agent of Germany, an Alboche! The tricolor rosette is a rallying call against you. It's patriotic to detest you. That's where we are! It's a tight spot!"

The inventor slowly extended a hand toward the newspapers.

"Yes," said the other, "look at them, for your edification—but time's pressing."

Auguérand unfolded a paper and scanned it, skeptical at first, then stupefied, reading headlines or odd sentences at hazard, his eyes wide.

Suddenly, he blushed with shame. "Oh, Thismonard! The youth of the schools?"

"That's where the movement began."

"The workers too?"

"You're working to exploit them."

"And the civil servants! The army!"

"You're hindering promotion."

"They're losing their heads. Someone's leading this campaign. Who? My colleagues?"

"No one. It's happening all by itself."

"Come on, come on...I don't understand. It's pure madness."

"Madness? Wisdom? Even I've started to wonder who's right—you or them."

Auguérand let himself fall into an armchair. "Fifty years I've worked, and worked for them...for you know, my friend, to what aim I've worked doggedly, and that I didn't want either their money or their applause. You've seen me at work, you've followed my thinking every day and my lifelong efforts. To become in the end...what? An evildoer!"

"That's what you are! Your discovery is inconvenient for the immense majority of individual interests; thus, it is being suppressed—and you'll suffer the same fate, if you resist."

"Ah! Their justice..."

"That's not the question, or not yet. They will talk about justice over your coffin and in books. In the meantime, hold your nerve, be worthy of yourself! For the moment, it's a matter of warding off the blow. They're marching on Neuilly. At this moment, the students are setting out, banner at the head."

Auguérand screwed up the newspaper, threw it on the floor.

"Be bold, Patrice! I like you better that way—you're more like yourself."

"You said that they're marching on Neuilly."

"To demonstrate, nothing more—but don't trust that; there are too many of them. Many men united have need of brutal gestures. Expect trouble!"

"A handful of loudmouths, in sum..."

"Hundreds of thousands!"

"But the police..."

"General strike: no police. Besides, the government won't compromise itself for you."

"The President and his Ministers seemed delighted yesterday evening—even to excess, for their eulogies almost overwhelmed me."

"Yesterday! The wind has changed. They've let you go. You're the Alboche. Anyway, what could the brigands of the Sûreté do against such an avalanche? It would need the army—which has joined the strike. You can no longer expect anyone. You're on your own."

"That will scarcely change me..."

"What is going to change is the situation. Here it is—listen carefully. The queue of the unemployed extends as far as the Porte Maillot. There, it's a crush—a barrage of humans and wheels. All the carriages in Paris are cluttering the Étoile and the twelve avenues. The provinces are arriving by car and airplane. The whole field at the airport is white with wings. Fortunately, the Metro, the Tube[78] and the Telegraph have stopped. Fortunately, too, the students have set off too late; they won't be able to catch up with you. All that's in our favor."

"And everyone's against me—everyone?"

"No, my friend, but it comes to the same thing. Think about it. You have on your side, in the crowd, the poor old people who took candor as far as getting up at dawn to come to the fountain; they'll be mocked, abused, knocked down, trampled underfoot; they'll make a carpet of them. Against you, you have the unemployed, who won't be able to sell their places because no one can get to them any longer: discontent, followed by fury. They'll want to console themselves with a drop of elixir, and if you don't open the gates, they'll climb over. Dilemma: gate, or pillage."

"Good..."

"There remain those who are coming from behind, three-quarters of whom are your enemies. Their principled hostility won't prevent every one of them, individually, from carrying away a liter of existence under his arm, two if he can. Thus, they'll come in through the open breach like the rest and pillage what remains, if anything does remain—which seems improbable."

"Improbable." Auguérand took out his watch. "Seven minutes to," he said.

"Your distribution of elixir is advertised for nine o'clock. "In ten minutes, the grounds will be invaded."

"Just so," said the inventor. "In ten minutes."

---

[78] The system of Pneumatic Tube Transport invented by William Murdoch, which propelled small packages contained in capsules, was more extensively developed in Paris, from 1866 onwards, than anywhere else. In actuality, it survived for some years after 1941, not being finally abandoned until 1984, but its importance had been declining throughout the 20th century.

VI. The Tragic Morning

There was amazement all over the world when people learned about France's attitude. Since midnight, the telegraph had launched the disconcerting news all the way to the antipodes: *Paris opposes the adoption of longevity*. At first, people hesitated to believe it, and when certainty imposed itself, they could hardly comprehend it. Then the successive dispatches brought the arguments against the Macrobians.

The arguments obtained, in the main, scant success; people were glad to find an opportunity to observe once again the stubbornly paradoxical character of the French mind, and almost everywhere they mocked our incoherence. The United States of North America, which still practiced tyranny and where people counted for very little, were almost alone in thinking like us. The English on the contrary, with their marked respect for the individual, came out strongly in favor of the liberty that everyone ought to have to live or not to live, at their own risk. Spain and voluptuous South America could ask for no more than to enjoy blissful existence for as long as possible, and rejected the worrying problems with the flick of a fan. Italy, where so many races are hybridized, hesitated and was divided. But black Africans persisted in dancing with joy in honor of Auguérand. The people of the Far East, imbued with respect for their ancestors, were religiously indignant that anyone might refuse the prolongation of old age. The Panslavists, strong in numbers and rich in space, even more than the Pangermanists, had sound reasons for adopting a system that would increase their importance. In brief, with the exception of the United States and a few northern Italian provinces, the concert of world opinion condemned us, in order to align themselves with the German theory: "Let us first welcome the benefit, and we shall deal with the difficulties it will provoke."

That was very easy to say, but not to do.

"France is her own mistress; Auguérand is in France, and his formula also. Who will insure humankind against the perils of Parisian bluntness? There is everything to fear from the impulsive mob, for which the head of a scientist is of no more account than that of a king, and which will raze a clinic even more readily than a Bastille."

This hypothesis—which, moreover, was not lacking in plausibility—inevitably gave rise to an immediate question: "Is it tolerable that the caprice of Paris should deprive humankind of a conquest that belongs to everyone?"

Thus posed, the question admitted but one answer: "No!"

Everyone was unanimous on this point. Even in the United States opinion was against us; in spite of their administrative despotism, they professed too fervent a worship with regard to inventions to consent to a crime against such a precious godsend.

"But how can we obviate the evil that is in preparation? Declare war on France? Send aircraft armed with bombs over Paris? They'll arrive too late. Paris has the means to respond; their victory would be uncertain; their advent would exasperate the capital and the worst excesses would be even more to be feared. Demand that the government protect the inventor and save his discovery? If the government cedes to the injunction of the powers, popular fury will turn against it and overturn it before it can act."

The morning telegrams aggravated the anxiety; with the day, the apprehensions of the night became a reality. When the magnitude of the agitation in the Schools and the Faubourgs became known, when news spread of the defection of the administrative services and that—more serious—of the police, and when accounts were read of the ever-increasing rush of the people toward Neuilly, a bleak discouragement of disturbed minds everywhere. It was, however, of short duration almost everywhere; Negroes, Muslims and the Chinese were able to resign themselves by virtue of religious habit or innate philosophy. The others rose up in revolt.

"Paris is in possession of the life of the world, and will not hand it over!"

Consciences waxed indignant against the abuse of power; the bankruptcy of a delightful hope irritated two billion disappointed egotisms; the Auguérand discovery appeared more precious as the risk of being deprived of it increased. The philanthropy of a scientist who would deliver his formula to the human family gratuitously rendered more odious the exaction of a people who were taking possession of something that belonged to everyone in order to destroy it. From the depths of steppes and the slopes of mountains, from every country that the sun scorches or neglects, a long murmur rose up, and, as in the times of barbarian migrations, the eyes of races, charged with wrathful envy, turned toward the garden of France, where people lived in comfort and were never content.

In the majority of financial centers, Stock Exchanges registered considerable falls. In various places, our residents and colonists were insulted, their businesses boycotted, and some were pillaged. In Ohio, the populace lynched and revolverized three negroes, in the capacity of French citizens, and thus responsible.

These local measures were far from sufficient. It became urgently imperative to give a more solid satisfaction to world opinion. Governments provided it without delay, on the initiative of the Pangermanlich Republik; at eight o'clock in the morning, Berlin convened a telephonic Diplomatic Congress for eight thirty. The session did not open until eight thirty-three, however; the delay was due to France, which was expected, but did not appear—not because the French Republic was refusing to talk to the other powers, but simply because the general strike, by shutting down the power stations, isolated our ministries, even though the ambassadors maintained Hertzian communication with their respective governments and particular individuals, more favored than those in power, still benefited from automatic correspondence.

In spite of the precautions normally surrounding these kinds of conferences and protecting them against the curiosity of reportage—precautions that had been increased for such a grave circumstance—the secret got out. As the measures of prudence had been exceptional, the hypotheses they provoked were no less exaggerated; the fact that the diplomats were trying to hide served to prove what the whistle-blowers were able to suppose.

By eight forty a still-vague rumor of unknown origin was circulating in Paris, and at eight forty-seven the *Balai* posted a categorical pantogram: *Comminatory injunction of the powers; they are taking Auguérand under their protection.*

Immediately, the *Drapeau Rouge* replied with another pantogram: *Ministry refuses to take part in Berlin Congress.*

Paris became indignant at the first, and cheered the second, erroneous though it was. The two parties created a national solidarity in the face of the foreigner, legitimated it and necessitated it; the people and the government were marching in convoy for once. If the intrusion of the foreigner lent the demonstration a patriotic character, the adhesion of the government conferred a legitimacy upon it; henceforth, all action would be licit, as an expression of national pride, and the disorder itself, implicitly approved by the authorities, became equivalent to order, or even better, being summary and more rapid.

People did not reason in respect of these things; they felt them; a psychic electric current united the crowd. A shameful anxiety ran through the sparse Auguérandists, who began to doubt that they were right, and were dissolved even more than before in the great wave. At the same time, an enormous clamor rose up on the long hill that extends from the Étoile to the Seine: "Vive la France! Down with the Alboches!"

At the same moment, too, by a sort of telegraphic repercussion, the world learned this news: *The Parisian rioters are invading the villa at Neuilly.*

There was nothing to it, however. The most determined, the most impatient and, above all, the nearest, were now hesitating to risk the adventure. Some were even giving up, and trying to get away.

In fact, at eight fifty, the *Balai* had displayed a new pantogram in Neuilly, formulated in scarcely reassuring terms: *The Direct Action Committee informs citizens that they will be risking the most serious dangers if they penetrate the Macrobians' residence.*

No one was unaware that the Committee made it a point of honor never to issue vain threats; thus, they were going to take action.

"They're going to blow it up!" The Clinic's butler, on duty at the door, ran to advise his master. He found him in the drawing-room, in company with Thismonad.

The doctor replied calmly: "That's all right. Warn the sanatorium; it has to be evacuated. Then come back."

"Shall we open the gates at nine o'clock?"

"No."

"What if they climb over?"

"Let them—and take care of yourself."

A more furious howl thundered outside: "Down with the Alboche! Death to the Alboches!"

"Monsieur hears that?"

Without further response, Auguérand went to the window and placed a hand on the handle. The butler withdrew.

The pitiless Thismonard was only able to respect his friend's meditation for twenty seconds. "You're looking at the trees for the last time? Bid them farewell, my friend—and the lawn where the young octogenarian deer are dancing, and the grass that your cows have been grazing for a third of a century, in order to inform you of the means of being like a God, you who wanted to give human beings as much as God had given them. Go and see the flasks and alembics, before they're smashed! Go and inspect the sanatorium and make a tour of the menagerie for one last time, while their stones are still standing. Let's go pat an adieu on the withers of the beautiful beasts and the hands of the brave people that you've rejuvenated out there in the depths of the park. If you want, we can release the tiger, as its brethren will be coming in..."

Auguérand cracked the knuckle of his middle finger against his palm. "You're annoying me with your infantile lyricism. Shut up."

Thismonard was only susceptible in favor of his great man. He shut up. But his mutism was not to last long; to occupy himself, he immediately consulted his watch—and shook his head, for the hand had rotated; then he went to the barometer, which he started tapping with his fingernail, and shook his head again.

"That's the only thing that can save us! The artillery of a downpour is the most effective against a mob...but the imbecile's rising!"

Auguérand did not hear him. Rigid at the window, pale in the green-tinted light that was falling toward him from the treetops, his features set, his hand still resting on the handle, he was staring at the curtain of foliage veiling the gate to the grounds, and his lips were moving feverishly in silent speech.

"You resemble a pilot who can hear a storm coming, but can't see anything..."

With these words, as if his remark had revealed the evidence of a verity that he had formulated without comprehending it, Thismonard saw himself in exactly the same situation as a shipwreck-victim on a reef in mid-ocean. In that house, besieged by a human tempest, there was against him—against the two of them—the monstrous force, rumbling there behind the foliage, ready to mount its assault, of a still-invisible rising tidal wave, which was about to appear, with its surf of red faces, in the gaps in the verdure: the anonymous wave of a hundred thousand angers. Death, without a doubt.

Clearly, with prescience that beasts possess, his flesh perceived the approach of death, and in the depths of his being a magnetic certainty notified him of the supreme moment. Of his artificial cheerfulness and his energy, nothing now remained; an animal fear numbed his muscles. In order to be less alone, he wanted to draw nearer to the other, and he observed that his legs were trembling.

"Oh, no!" he said. "Not that way!"

With a vigorous effort, he shook his soul and went to the window.

"Well? Have you decided?"

The inventor did not move; his tall figure seemed petrified.

"Wake up!"

Already, Thismonard was raising a hand to bring it down on Auguérand's shoulder, but his gesture remained suspended, for he had just perceived on the master's impassive profile a tear, which ran through the grooves of his wrinkles, and thought he was seeing a statue weep. Before that august dolor of the imagination, before those tears of the mind, he became aware of his pettiness, and the indignity of bestial fears. What was the death of the flesh compared with such a calvary, in which the work was about to perish in the person of the man who had brought it into the world, and knew what he had brought?

Thismonard took a step back, seized by respectful pity; the marble that he saw weeping was no longer his friend, but took on a symbolic majesty, like an outraged Christ: genius divining itself through insults and ingratitude.

VII. *The End of a Dream*

At that moment, above the human rumor, a metallic bell rang, clear and firm, like an alarm bell in the midst of a tempest.

"Nine o'clock!" said Thimonard.

They only heard the first stroke, greeted with an acclamation that drowned out all the rest.

"It's now..."

Only then did the inventor turn his head toward the confidant of his work, and say: "Do you believe that it's necessary?"

"What?"

"To punish them."

Horrified, Thismonard understood. The demigod was holding the life of the world in his hand and weighing it. That immobility, which a superficial examination had taken for dejection, was the sternness of the judge before which the world had been summoned, and was hesitating over his own verdict! Had he shed the two tears still shining on his face for humankind, before the condemnation, or over the work, before its abolition?

"Oh, Master, you're thinking...of..."

"I'm thinking about it."

Since the clock had chimed, the unemployed, with an imperious rhythm, were intoning the appeal: "El-ix-ir! El-ix-ir!"

"You want to?" Thismonard continued. "You could?"

"I no longer know where duty lies. I no longer know what my rights are."

Suddenly, an immense clamor of triumph drowned out all articulate voices.

"Are they climbing over?" Thismonard asked.

But Auguérand pointed at the sky. The other raised his eyes sand uttered an exclamation. The Direct Action Committee's airplane was arriving over the villa, the yellow letters DA on its violet wings: an enormous butterfly of death floating on the wind of menace.

"Quickly! The caltrops!"

Thismonard raced to the handle controlling the blades lying in the grass, which were stood upright at night in order to prevent nocturnal landings; the meadow was covered with lances.

Auguérand slowly raised both hands, in a despairing gesture that might have been a blessing or a curse.

"They wanted it..." He let his arms fall back, then, forcefully: "Come on!"

"The DA have seen the blades. They're turning."

"Their presence is protecting us. No one dares come in while they're here, for fear of bombs. They're giving us time. Come quickly."

"Where?"

"The laboratory."

"You're decided?"

They cross the room. As they reached the door, a telephone bell brought them to a halt."

"Should we answer it?"

"What good would it do?"

"Let me listen. One never knows. I'll catch up with you..."

"As you wish. I'll give you thirty seconds."

"Hello...? Hello...? Yes, the Clinic... No, it's Thismonard, his friend... Him? Impossible—busy... As if to him...who's speaking?"

Framed in the doorway, Auguérand waited. Thismonard's face, leaning over the apparatus, expanded and reddened. His eyes, illuminated with joy, were raised to extend toward the door with a gaze like that of a dog wanting to impart some good news to its master.

"I'll pass to your message, Monsieur l'Ambassadeur. Please wait. Patrice!"

"Speak quickly."

"The German Ambassador, by order of the Congress, offers you shelter with the benefit of diplomatic immunity. I addition, the Pangermanliche informs you confidentially that it is disposed to adopt your system for itself: honors, an annual pension or immediate capital, name your figure. The ambassador's aircraft is on its way to pick you up. Your response?"

"That which another Frenchman made at Waterloo. Get lost."[79]

"Patrice..."

"Get lost, I tell you."

"Think about it! Cambronne survived the battle, but our fate is sealed, I can feel it—it's the end! Patrice, think of your work, which would be saved..."

"To serve what end? Hatred! He's just admitted it—they'll use me against people, and I've worked for people. They're perverting it. So much the worse for them."

"You're speaking in anger..."

"In complete discouragement. What you're going to tell them translates my whole thought; I can't put it any more exactly. Go on."

"Patrice, we'll die badly...."

"I've lived well."

"Irrevocable, Patrice?"

"Yes."

"Let the future judge, them and you!"

"Let them judge us, since I'm judging. Hurry up and join me."

Auguérand went out. Slowly, Thismonard returned to the apparatus, initially with a plaintive expression.

"Well, perhaps he's right." He shrugged one shoulder. "Bah!" Then, with a devil-may-care gesture, he gripped the receiver "Hello...? Monsieur l'Ambassador...?

Perfectly: I've transmitted your proposals to the doctor. His response...yes, well, his response: that of Cambronne, Monsieur l'Ambassador. My respects."

He hung up, and then burst out laughing in the corridor, as he galloped in pursuit of his friend. On the front steps of the building, however, he recoiled under the pressure of the almighty din coming from the street.

"The laughing's over, now."

To reach the laboratory it was necessary to cross half the park; having slid momentarily through the bushes, the pathway went around the lawn in the open.

---

[79] I have translated "Vas-y," accurately enough, as "Get lost," but the dialogue makes it clear that this is a euphemism, and that we are actually dealing with what 19th century French literary parlance called "the word of Cambronne"— i.e. something unprintable. When General Cambronne's command was surrounded at Waterloo and invited to surrender, he refused, and the rumor was swiftly put about that he had replied: "The guards do not surrender; they die!" It was closely followed by a counter-rumor alleging that what he had actually said was "Merde!"—which can be translated, in the appropriate context, as "Fuck off!" rather than the literal "Shit!" French writers frustrated by not being allowed to represent speech as Frenchmen actually spoke, led by Victor Hugo, began referring to "the word of Cambronne" whenever they wanted to signal to the reader that an obscenity of that kind had been uttered.

Thismonard, still running full tilt, went into the shade of the trees; his pace caused him to collide with flies that were trying to buzz amid the human racket.

"My word! They don't seem to suspect that they're hearing the vibration of a unique moment in the history of the world. They're circling around, as they did yesterday, as they will tomorrow...uh! Tomorrow? Their arbor won't be so comfortable tomorrow."

At the edge of the wood he perceived the doctor, fifty paces ahead, hastening along the uncovered pathway. Almost immediately, he heard the roar of an engine, and a shadow passed close by. Twenty meters from the ground, the Direct Action airplane, coming back after describing a horizontal circle, was now heading for the laboratory. Two human silhouettes were profiles between its wings; one as holding a rigid object, a staff or a rifle, which dipped. A detonation, as sharp as the crack of a whip, clicked imperceptibly in the din, and then a second.

Thismonard saw Auguérand throw his arms wide, in an attitude of crucifixion, and fall to his knees on the threshold of the laboratory. He raced forward, paying no heed to the airplane, which was already passing over the roof.

"Patrice! Patrice? You're hurt?"

Auguérand, raising himself up on his elbow, held out a bunch of keys, and murmured, feebly: "Everything...quickly."

"Everything? Destroy it?"

"Yes."

Thismonard tried to search for the wound.

"No...go!"

"My poor old..."

"Quickly, go."

The dying man collapsed, and his forehead struck the step of the building in with the work had been born with a dull thud. The stone was already stained red.

Thismonard said: "The end of a dream!"

He had to step over the corpse to enter the laboratory. The sanctuary as still entirely impregnated with the master and his night's toil. There, four hours earlier, he had been laboring to complete the work of half a century, full of joy at being able to extend his benefit of the races of humankind...

Thismonard knelt down momentarily—but it was not the time for meditation; he chased away his own.

"Quickly, and everything! We have but to obey. I'm the executor of his will."

Then, methodically—for he had a very methodical mind—he started destroying. First, he emptied the carboys of elixir into the sink, in order that no one could use them, and while the years of human existence glugged viscously toward the sewer, he smashed the flasks, bottles and alembics, in order that no analysis could reveal the chemical composition of the liquids therein.

"His formulae! His treatise!"

He opened the writing-desk and took out armfuls of paper, catalogues, labeled files, stacks of notes; he stuffed the stove, in which the flames sizzled. The task did not take long; five minutes sufficed to annihilate a life.

"Have I forgotten anything? Oh! An idea! Of course, yes—that's the safest way."

With a liter of gasoline, he made a pool on the floor and set fire to it; he scarcely had time to throw himself backwards; his clothes and hands caught fire.

"A pyre for you, my great man! I'll offer you the funeral rites of Hercules."

He ran outside in order to lift up the cadaver and drag it into the conflagration, but, to his great amazement, Auguérand had disappeared. Only the bloody stone step attested to the scene of the drama.

"Someone's picked him up, carried him away, perhaps saved him. Who?"

A hired aircar was flying straight ahead, over the trees. The caltrops on the lawn had been retracted into the grass. How? In the distance, in front of the sanitarium, silhouettes were running away; others, closer, emerging from the trees, ran forward howling. The unemployed had climbed over the gate.

"There he is!"

"It's not him!"

"Yes!"

"No!"

"Elixir! Elixir!"

"Death to the Alboche!"

"Death to the traitors!"

"Elixir! Elixir!"

In an instant, Thismonard was surrounded by faces, fists and cries, and driven back against the wall. Behind him, the fire was crackling; further away, to the left, the animals in the menagerie was roaring and bellowing in terror.

"Fire!"

"It's been set on fire!"

"It's the Action!"

"It's the Alboche!"

"Elixir! Elixir!"

In the deafening racket it was scarcely possible to make out the voices, and he rubbed his burned hands with a mechanical gesture.

"Where's the elixir, you?"

"Thrown away."

"Auguérand?"

"Gone"

"His formula?"

"Burned."

"The elixir, you were asked!"

"Down the drain, I told you."

"Take that, you bastard!"

Thismonard fell, his left eye and brain traversed by a bullet.

They searched the house and the outbuildings for the inventor, without finding him anywhere. The already dense crowd in the garden mounted an assault on the balconies, came in through the windows, crowded into the rooms and smashed everything, only looting with difficulty for want of sufficient freedom of movement. Those who had succeeded in stealing some work of art were soon forced to let go of it, because it was digging into their sides, but they did so in such a way as to leave nothing but shards. Almost everything was destroyed within a hundred minutes.

The massacre of the animals offered the amusement of a sport; the tiger, rendered furious by blows of canes and human baying, lashed out with its claws and was riddled with bullets.

At eleven ten, fire broke out on the first floor of the house, lit by a prankster. The youth of the Schools arrived; it generously set out to put out the fire that it had demanded the previous day. That disaster might yet be circumscribed.

At one o'clock, nothing more was rising above the clinic but swirls of inoffensive smoke. In the absence of any kind of brigade, the students had spontaneously taken on the role of the police, and carried it out with the conviction that young people bring to the exercise of any temporary authority. They evacuated the area, only permitting their own people to go into the buildings. They could be seen prowling around inside, in quest of things they would not specify to anyone; it may be supposed that they were searching for a forgotten flask, some vestige of the great secret, the fortune.

These efforts had no compensation at all; the Auguérand formula remained as undiscoverable as his person.

The fact spread into the streets and throughout the world. Already, Paris was experiencing a vague sadness; no one admitted it out loud, very few people having dared, and the newspapers made no mention of it, but it was not necessary to express it to feel it. All thinking people estimated that they had undoubtedly been too hasty; they blamed it on the panic.

They went to bed with that thought that evening, and the on the morning of the twenty-seventh, Paris had a very clear notion of having experienced a fit of madness the previous day.

The public services resumed their normal functioning as if nothing had happened. In spite of that affected reserve, however, the sentiments that the world had professed against us the day before spread among us against the perpetrators of the vandalism.

The curiosity-seekers who had headed on foot toward Neuilly that day were almost as numerous as the protesters of the day before. Their ranks filed slowly along the avenue, with long gazes at the twisted gates, the devastated gardens, the brown-tinted fragments of walls, which they pointed out to one another in low voices. Until nightfall, the march-past continued, reverently, at the pace of a funeral.

During the week that followed, the ruins of the villa were the goal of an incessant pilgrimage; people came from far and wide; a few cities sent wreaths; the mourning as affirmed, opinion settled. Auguérand's discovery became inestimable from the moment that it was lost.

For a long time, the doctor's disappearance invited speculation; no one had seen him except for Thismonard, who was no longer there to say anything, and his testimony would not have cleared up the mystery anyway. The Direct Action claimed the honor of having "set fire to the glory-hole" but not of having shot the inventor. He was generally believed to be dead, but some claimed that he was still alive; some even claimed that an ambassador had taken him away in a hired aircar.

Might he not be in hiding, in Germany or elsewhere? Might he not reappear one day? Some conserved the hope, but they grew old waiting.

One certainty, at least, remained granted: human life could be prolonged.

What had been found once could be found again.

Everywhere, people started searching.

Gaston de Wailly: *The Murderer of the World*

Le Meurtrier du globe *by "Commandant G. de Wailly," here translated as* The Murderer of the World, *was originally published as a 26-part feuilleton serial in the* Journal des Voyages *between 15 May and 23 October 1910, the fifth of the six serials that the author contributed to that publication between 1886 and 1915. It was subsequently reprinted as a paperback book by J. Tallandier in 1925 and reprinted by the same publisher in 1933.*

Gaston de Wailly (1857-1943) came from a notable literary family, of whom he was by no means the most distinguished member. He published a few further books in addition to reprints of the five full-length feuilletons from the Journal de Voyages, *but they were all in ultra-cheap paperback formats at the bottom end of the literary marketplace. All of his novels are melodramatic adventure stories, mostly set largely at sea, in the Vernian mode in which the* Journal des Voyages *specialized, but he also wrote in a very different vein for the theater.*

What makes Le Meurtrier du globe *interesting, in spite of its crudity, is the fundamental speculative notion that provides the novel with its title and its climax. In terms of its plot, the story is a standard chase thriller in which a small band of heroes is harassed by an uncannily powerful villain, through whose claws they slip continually in a series of hairsbreadth escapes. In that regard too, it is unusual, by virtue of the pressure of melodramatic inflation on the evil character of the villain and his various unlikely accomplices, but the eventual effect of that exaggeration is merely ludicrous. The nature of the theory that motivates the action of the mysterious scientific genius who is the object of the chase, and the project he has completed in consequence of that theory, might be deemed ludicrous too, but certainly not in any mere sense, being possessed of an admirable flamboyance that gives the novel a certain eccentric panache.*

B.S.

Prologue

I

That evening, the Hôtel Continental was exceptionally animated. A crowd of mostly young and intelligent people, vibrant with warm and generous gaiety, filled the large hall beneath the sparkling chandeliers.

"Centrales"[80] of today, yesterday and the day before yesterday, with their families and occasional chosen guests, were sharing the delicate joy of a fine expected pleasure, anticipated in total security, promised by the theater curtain masking a stage erected at the back of the hall. Laughter was prepared in advance on all lips, and hands were getting ready to applaud. That was because a comrade, the son of a great Parisian director, and a clever and zestful author, had written one of those special revues that year, Aristophanean in its liberty, in which, among the incidents of the school, reflected in the Gallic fashion, the tics of the various teachers would be wittily parodied. They would be the first to salute their young charges with their bravos, joyfully and without resentment.

A good audience! The raising of the curtain had been announced for nine o'clock, and it was half past nine, but no one was bothered by that delay. Chatting, laughing, exchanging handshakes, evoking memories, confiding successes or hopes and talking cordially about absentees, occupied the young and old comrades sufficiently to wipe out any hint of impatience.

One replete individual installed in the front row, however, did not seem to be participating in the general forbearance. Senator Dupeyroux, to whom the committee had offered the presidency of the celebration that year, was squirming incessantly in his seat, making it clearly manifest that even senatorial patience has its limits. Unable to stand it any longer, he stood up abruptly, traversed the hall, in spite of the deferential objurgations of two young Centrales bearing the badges of stewards, and went into a small reception room serving as a vestibule and controlled entrance to the hall, transformed for the occasion into a theater.

He addressed himself to the chief steward, who was busy checking the invitations of a few latecomers

"Well, he hasn't arrived, then, your famous Mining King?"

"Monsieur Williamson is certainly a little late, Monsieur le Sénateur."

"I'm certainly a supporter of courtesy, even exaggerated, with regard to foreigners," affirmed the "conscript father," in a slightly acidic tone, "but since we're all subject here to the pleasure of that republican monarch, I'm wondering why your committee didn't offer the presidency to him rather than me!"

Embarrassed, the steward busied himself with the classification of variously-colored pieces of cardboard.

"That's all right," the elect of the restricted suffrage went on. "I incline before the modern majesty of the dollar and I'll go back inside to set an example of patience. Oh, by the way, I asked for a place to be reserved next to my seat for my new secretary. I'd be obliged to you, as soon as he arrives...he's a tall, dark-haired young man, with the bronzed complexion of an African explorer..."

---

[80] The École Centrale in Paris, founded in 1829, is the oldest and most prestigious school of engineering in France, long renowned for its production of technological innovators and entrepreneurs.

"Is Monsieur le Sénateur now involved in colonial politics?"

"It's the best thing..."

"For the future of the country?"

"For bringing down recalcitrant ministries. My secretary, a precious fellow, very knowledgeable, is named Rolland."

The young commissioner raised his head. "Rolland? An explorer? Claude Rolland, perhaps?" he enquired.

"Do you know him?"

"He was a comrade of my older brother at the École Centrale."

"Bah! He's an engineer and didn't say anything to me about it! It's a pearl of knowledge and modesty that I've found there. Look—here he is!"

Claude Rolland had, indeed, come in, very late but with his excuse on his arm: Mademoiselle Edmée Rolland, as tall and slim as her brother; as blonde as he was dark; better than pretty, beautiful—but with a slightly grave beauty that seemed poorly adapted to the tender shade of her abundant, slightly curly and hectic hair. In particular, she had two superb large blue eyes, gentle and profound, and, at the same time bright, with a determined and energetic gleam.

Claude introduced her to his new "boss."

"I understand," said the latter, bowing a trifle ponderously to the young woman, "why you've renounced the glory of your distant expeditions for Mademoiselle your sister; she's charming!"

"Our mother, who was our only remaining parent, having passed on, duty recalled me to Edmée..."

"Only your duty?" questioned the young woman, mildly.

"And my tender affection, Sister, as you know very well!" Claude replied, in his masculine but musical voice.

In a gallantly pretentious fashion, Dupeyroux added. "You'll doubtless hold it against me, Mademoiselle, if I take possession of your brother in order to talk about our great report?"

"Not at all, Monsieur—the interests of the State before all!"

"Always at your orders, Monsieur le Sénateur," said Claude. And he called: "Furet!"[81]

"Present, Commandant," said a blond and thickset fellow who had come in behind the fraternal couple, and had remained respectfully to one side until summoned.

"Take charge of our coats," the young man said to him, throwing him his overcoat, "and I confide Mademoiselle Edmée to you."

"Have no fear, Commandant," said the other, hastily rejoining the young woman.

Dupeyroux took his secretary by the arm.

---

[81] *Furet* is the French equivalent of the English "ferret."

"My dear chap, that's the second time that fellow has called you Commandant, but..."

"I'm not. This is the explanation: Jean Guitard, nicknamed Furet, is a brave and skillful sailor, who has navigated numerous rapids on the great African rivers under my orders. That's when he acquired the habit of calling me his Commandant, and he's never wanted to get out of it, any more than he consented to leave me when his official service to the State ended."

"I understand. Let's talk briefly and to the point. Where are you up to in our work?"

"The first part, the list of accusations, is already in your in-tray."

"Terrible, isn't it, the charge sheet? It's necessary that every paragraph be a stick of dynamite, in order that the whole ensemble is blown to smithereens, minister and ministry together."

"Alas, the task is only too easy; it's sufficient to content oneself with telling the truth."

"So much the better!"

So much the worse, thought Claude, who, not being a politician, had the naivety of thinking of the country first and foremost.

"And the second part—the reforms? For it's all very well to demolish, on condition that one takes responsibility for rebuilding. Everything is there, you understand!"

Claude Rolland understood only too well. It was not without a certain coldness, the mask of an honest scorn, that he replied: "My notes are organized; I've just begun writing them up."

"Do a good job! When will you be finished."

"In a week at the latest."

"Good—the interpellation is in a fortnight; I'll have time to work on my speech. Now..."

He was interrupted by the sudden arrival of one of the celebration's stewards, at a run, exclaiming: "Monsieur le Sénateur, we're only waiting for you to give the signal."

"Your rich Yankee has arrived, then?"

"A moment ago."

"Impossible—we'd have seen him!" said the chief steward.

Laughing, the comrade who had just arrived explained: "Weren't we told that he's the greatest eccentric in North America? He came in through the rooms reserved for the performers. He's flatly refused the seat that was reserved for him next to Monsieur le Sénateur and demanded two chairs for himself and his groom, a puny chap with an insolent and stuck-up manner, and has sat down in the passage leading from the wings to the reception room. That way, he can leave easily if the performance bores him. He's an eccentric!"

"In that case," said the chief steward, "we can't give him an entrance?"

Dupeyroux, who was already heading back into the hall, stopped, and in a tone shot through with irritated jealousy, said: "You'd arranged an ovation for that fantasist?"

"Out of professional admiration for the foremost geologist in the world!"

"Oh!"

"It's not saying too much, Monsieur le Sénateur. Every time that astonishing man, a prospector without equal, points his finger at the ground and says: 'Dig a shaft there,' they find the coal, the oil or the minerals predicted. Never a hesitation, never an error—hence his colossal fortune."

"Legend... or bluff!" protested Dupeyroux, shrugging his senatorial shoulders. Then he went into the hall of the celebrations, followed by Claude Rolland.

Their appearance was saluted with the rhythmic salvos of an ovation, which the vanity of the parliamentarian attributed to himself, although it was actually addressed to his comrade, whose intrepid youthful glory as an explorer reflected on everyone and made the École proud.

The performance had scarcely been running for ten minutes when a person of rather rude appearance, with a long bushy beard and no moustache, wearing a long frock-coat and a vast hat, arrived on the threshold of the little control room, debating in a low voice with one of the hotel footmen. He seemed the complete type-specimen of the Yankee, as popularized by caricaturists in the Old World.

"Very close to the stage, on the right, with his groom," the footman indicated, before making off, with an anxious expression.

The bearded man head toward the door of the hall with meter-long strides, where a steward stopped him.

"Green card? Or pink?"

"No ticket. Just off the train, no time to get one. No need, anyway. Jonathan Loeb, chief of the Knights of Labor,[82] member of the general staff of the Salvation Army..." As the steward pursed his lips with courteous irony, the red-bearded man said, in a surly tone: "You still have the right to smile at Salvationists in France; you'd bow if we were in America, or even in India."

"Unfortunately, Monsieur, we're in Paris, where those titles don't have the power to impose orders."

---

[82] The Noble and Holy Order of the Knights of Labor, founded in 1869, was one of the largest and most powerful American labor organizations of the late 19th century, but it dwindled rapidly in the 1890s, eventually disappearing in 1939. Modeled on the Freemasons, of whose august society the newcomer is obviously also a high-ranking member, it maintained a secrecy of membership in order to prevent employers taking reprisals. It had considerable support within the Catholic Church, but was regarded with suspicion by left-wing labor unions because of its staunch Republicanism.

"And this one?" said the tall, robust individual, standing up straight. He rapidly placed his open right hand, with the fingers extended and together, on his stomach, and then raised it to his forehead, made what is known in military terms as a half-turn, and immediately returned to his original position.

The commissioner looked at him, amazed and amused. "Are you in pain?" he asked.

The newcomer sketched a scornful gesture.

At that moment, a pale young man irrupted into the same vestibule. He had a curly moustache, a fur coat over his arm, and was clad in an evening suit of the very latest fashion: an accomplished specimen of the "dandy" or "snob," one of those elegant high spirits of Parisian high society who, without any entitlement whatsoever, are at all the premières, welcome in almost all salons, and make up the most specialized or reputedly most exclusive social cliques.

He came in casually. Proclaiming in a serenely shrill voice: "I'm late, I'll wager? Damn it, I was in such exhilarating society..."

He stopped dead. As he turned in the direction of the great hall, after having thrown his invitation negligently on to the green baize table of the chief steward, his gaze had just alighted on the tall and singular transatlantic individual, who, looking at him fixedly, put his hand to his stomach and then to his forehead for a second time.

"Damn it!" muttered the elegant latecomer, between his teeth. "That's the first time that I've encountered..."

And, awkwardly, because he was somewhat intimidated in spite of his aplomb, he took a step toward the man with the red beard and the small, steely eyes, placing his right hand, with the fingers extended, in front of his throat, and then touching his right shoulder, before letting it fall slowly again to dangle alongside his thigh.

The hollow and rigid features of the man who had named himself Jonathan Loeb to the Centrale steward relaxed in satisfaction. "Good, an apprentice," he murmured.

With a stiff gesture he extended his hand to the pale young man, and their handshake, devoid of any warmth, was nevertheless long enough for an observer to have the sensation that they were carrying out some kind of secret ritual.

"Delighted to meet you," said the American, coldly.

"What can I do for you, Monsieur?" asked the dandy, in the same tone.

"Get me in, although I haven't had the leisure to get myself a ticket."

"Difficult..." Suddenly, he slapped his forehead. "But no, in fact," he said. "The Senator who's presiding is..." He finished the sentence whispering in the American's ear.

With an abrupt gesture, Jonathan Loeb took from his pocket an enormous worn leather wallet, and took a card out of it, on which he wrote, below his name:

Chief of the Supreme Council of New York.

And then: *Necessity to attend celebration.*

He slipped the card into a gummed envelope, sealed it and handed it to one of the young stewards, saying: "To the senator president immediately. Interest of a superior order."

The steward, with a rather poor grace, rang for a messenger, whom he charged with carrying the missive to its destination.

Loeb turned to his pale and perfumed companion and said, in a brusque and trenchant tone: "Thank you. If I can ever be useful to you in my turn..."

"Of course. I'm glad to have run into you. I'm expecting to visit the United States soon..."

"Pleasure trip?"

"No, it's a matter of establishing the death of a relative who disappeared."

"A long time ago?"

"We last had news of him, by chance, twenty-five years ago."

"Difficult. Tell me anyway."

"Permit me first to introduce myself. Grégoire de Montalpé, well known in leisured Parisian society, great hunter of stars...the terrestrial kind: an astronomy full of charm but costly. And, well, it's a good time for me to get a feel...."

"A feel?"

"That is to say, to get my hands on a certain inheritance."

"I understand. This disappearance, only dating back twenty-five years..."

"Will tie up the funds for another five years. I can't, however, wait that long."

"French, presumably, this disappeared individual?"

"No, Russian. Muscovite genealogical branch, extinct with him, I believe. Oh, if you could help me to get the death of this Lobanief certified..."

The Yankee shivered from head to toe. "What did you say?" he articulated, hoarsely.

"I said Baron Lobanief, aristocrat of Valchow."

"Him!"

"You know him?" said de Montalpé, stupefied.

"I've been looking for him for twenty years! That's the man that it's important for you to discover?"

"Not alive, you understand."

"Trust me—vengeance is a sure guide."

"Vengeance?"

"Listen! The Russia of today is almost mild, but that of old...! My father was a Jewish serf. His overlord, young Lobanief, had him exiled to Siberia, where I was born to hate. When my father died I quit the icy inferno to search for our torturer. The latter, disgraced, had left the country. I followed his trail—too old, alas!—across Europe and then the Ocean. In Chicago, one day, I found evidence that he had passed though, but then I lost the trail, and I spent my last dollar without being able to pick it up again. Then..."

"You abandoned the game?"

"Never!"

"Without money, though..."

"What need do I have of money when I have an army at my service?"

"Don't understand."

"I have the soul of a leader. I became a Knight of Labor, in order to become one. Of the Salvationists, countless all over the surface of the globe, I'm really in command, as chief of the general staff, although the Marshal and his wife reign...and collect.[83] As a Freemason, I'm at the head of all the rites recognized in America. Strengthened by that triple occult sovereignty, the master of a million men of all nations and social classes, to convert into loyal agents, I've extended my nets."

"But you haven't found him?"

"Not yet."

"That's because Lobanief is dead."

"It's because he isn't. Tombs are loquacious; living lips know how to keep quiet. Not all, however."

"You have a clue?"

"Yes—a report from a Salvationist has identified a man who, thinking himself alone, has twice pronounced the name of the man I hate."

"And that man...?"

"Is in this hall. Nothing is as propitious as the neutral terrain of a celebration to make contact with a power who is almost unapproachable elsewhere."

"He's a prince, then?"

"He's a king—one of our American kings, sovereign by grace of the power of gold."

"The famous Williamson, perhaps?"

"The very same."

II

That conversation was interrupted by the appearance of the bellboy coming back to invite Loeb, on the senator's behalf, to take his place in the armchair next to his presidential seat.

---

[83] The Salvation Army launched in the U.S.A. in 1880 was established by Salvationist emigrants from Britain, under the command of Commissioner George Scott Railton, but it functioned thereafter independently of the British military hierarchy organized by William Booth, with its own command structure. General Booth was still alive in 1910, when this novel was written, but would not have had any effective authority in the U.S.A. The "Marshal" to whom Loeb refers is fictitious, and the organization as he imagines it bears no resemblance to the actual one.

Loeb hastened forward, followed by de Montalpé, and the spectators, disturbed in the midst of their amusement, were surprised to see that caricaturish individual cutting through the joyful crowd unceremoniously, welcomed with marks of the greatest consideration by the most auspicious of the conscript fathers. The latter were quite scandalized to see that their advances were welcomed no better than a downpour at a picnic.

That was because the unpolished Jonathan had experienced a great disappointment: the chairs that had been indicated to him as being occupied by Williamson and his groom were empty.

Did Loeb's arrival have anything to do with the sudden disappearance of the Mining King?

Not at all. Williamson was completely unaware of Jonathan. Since the curtain had gone up on the Aristophanean and truly quite witty Centrale Revue, his broad face, carefully shaven, whose colors remained almost juvenile in spite of the approach of his fortieth year and his blue eyes, devoid of any gleam, had not expressed the slightest interest and had remained phlegmatically disinterested, although the audience was crackling with increasingly enthusiastic bursts of laughter.

Suddenly, his closest neighbors had seen him stand up tranquilly and go away without the slightest gesture, accompanied by his inseparable Toby.

Loeb and de Montalpé had scarcely left the vestibule when the chief steward was surprised to see the celebrated mining industrialist come in by another door. "Our revue doesn't have the good fortune of pleasing you?" he asked, contritely.

"It bores me."

"To judge by the welcome our audience is giving it, however..."

"Too much laughing," declared the billionaire, in a plaintive voice. "It makes me feel ill. I'm as nervous as a woman."

He spotted an armchair, pushed it into the middle of the room, and made a sign to his groom, who brought forward a chair, on which Williamson put his feet, saying: "Cocktail!"

"Yes sir!" replied the stiff and starched flunkey, pivoting on his heel and disappearing through the service door.

Nonplussed, the steward thought he ought to intervene.

"Pardon me, but the hotel bar is only a few steps away, if you..."

"I'm all right here."

"It's just that...it's not really...the place, and..."

Very calmly, in a soft voice, as if wearied by the effort of making it audible, he said: "I don't mind. I have a horror of convention...like that revue at which they're laughing...leaving business behind, I have a poetic temperament...too many men in that theater hall. I like women's voices, for their charm...I'll wait here until it's finished."

"Your desires are law..."

"I know," said the billionaire, conclusively.

His eyes half-closed, Williamson remained still, and it was in silence that he absorbed, with indifferent slowness, the drink that his groom brought him.

Although the untimely arrival of Jonathan Loeb had not caused the exodus of the nonchalant billionaire, it had had the effect of forcing Claude Rolland to give up his seat next to the senator. As there was not a single free seat left, he retired to the back of the hall. Several stewards hastened to try to find him a place. He did not want the entire assembly to be disturbed on his account, however, so, offering the pretext of needing some air, he headed back to the little reception-room-cum-vestibule, where he certainly did not expect to find the other American. The chief steward informed him, as best he could, about the singular person who had forced the explorer's retreat, adding that he thought he had understood that Loeb had come with the intention of seeing Williamson.

"Pfft!" said the latter, emerging from his mutism without interrupting his absorbing occupation. "Doubtless some mendicant. Everyone in New York knows perfectly well that I never give anything."

"Rich as you are, Monsieur, I can hardly believe that," protested Claude.

Williamson looked at him sideways. "Charity," he declared, flatly, "creates paupers and ingrates, so it's acting badly. Life is a battle; so much the worse for those killed in action."

"That's a cruel theory."

"It's true. Anyway, I'm too warm-hearted to give alms."

Rolland and his comrade the steward looked at one another, legitimately surprised.

"That's...quite a paradox," the explorer could not help exclaiming.

"Not at all," affirmed the billionaire, in an icy tone. "I've very sensitive; hearing plaints makes me feel ill."

That was too much for Claude's natural generosity. "You prefer," he said, sarcastically, "to plug your ears."

"Yes...I'm so good!" And Williamson's voice softened with intimate emotion to add: "No one since Adam has been as good as me!"

"Theoretically!"

"Practically. I pay those I employ well and punctually. At Christmas, I even give them imperial gratifications."

"And in case of catastrophe, unexpected misfortune, you..."

"Wait. I like regularity. Anything that troubles it makes me feel ill. This year, one of my engineers—a Frenchman—in order to save the honor of his family, he said, asked me for an advance on his salary..."

"You refused, evidently," said Claude Rolland, with increased sarcasm.

"No. I can't refuse—I'm too good. I just invited him to seek employment elsewhere."

"Mining King, perhaps," Claude whispered to the steward, indicating Williamson. "King of Egotists, for sure."

From her place in the celebration hall, Edmée had seen her brother make his rapid exit, and as she did not know the reason for it, the incomprehensible departure had astonished her greatly. Claude was everything to her; she loved him as much as she was proud of him. Not seeing him come back in, her astonishment was transformed into anxiety, which increased with all the customary rapidity of the feminine imagination. No longer able to contain herself, she left in her turn, followed by the faithful matelot, in search of news.

"Oh, there you are! I was afraid you were ill," she said to the explorer, emotional but reassured.

Williamson had turned his head negligently. "Is this your wife?" he asked.

"Who is this gentleman?" Edmée asked.

"Williamson, the rich Yankee," he replied, in a low voice. To the American, he said: "Mademoiselle is my sister."

"Good! Charming! How much?"

Claude started, and his face went red with anger. "Monsieur!" he said, menacingly.

"Oh, don't get upset...it's just habit...I was joking."

"In a singular fashion!" The young man took his younger sister's arm, and headed back toward the hall.

"Hey!" said Williamson. "You interest me. Come here!"

"Me?"

"With your sister."

"Not in this life, damn it!"

A sullen veil covered the clean-shaven features of the Mining King. "You're annoying me," he said. "In that case, I'm leaving."

The chief steward ran to Claude, his expression pleading. The latter stopped.

"All right," he said. "Out of regard for my young comrades." With a rather ill grace, he sat Edmée down, and asked the Yankee: "What do you want with us?"

"To know who you are."

"Claude Rolland, civil engineer," the young man announced, dryly.

"And the explorer that all Paris is talking about at the moment," the young woman added. Like her brother, she had a warm, musical and captivating voice.

"You have a delightful tone of voice, Mademoiselle," Williamson remarked. Addressing Claude, he said: "Explorer? Yes, I've heard mention of you. To get yourself massacred for the profit of others is very brave, but very stupid. Would you like to be the director of one of my mines? How much?"

"Nothing."

"You're refusing?"

"I came back to France to devote myself to my sister."

"Mademoiselle will accompany you."

"Your behavior just now would forbid me to take her."

"You're not very flattering?"

"I'm not trying to be."

An expression of blissful satisfaction illuminated Williamson's face. In a brisk tone that contrasted with his previous phlegmatic morosity, he said: "Well, so much the better; that makes a change. Your European princes see spines curbing before them; with me, it's consciences. It flattered me for a time; now I'm blasé. I've run around the old continent after America, and it seems to me that I always have the same shop-window in front of me, by dint of always being pursued by the same offers of sale. I have four hundred million dollars; I'm tired of buying things…and people… too easily. Life obsesses me…your attitude is new to me, and I haven't been bored for the last five minutes."

Edmée looked at him with a pensive ingenuousness. "You're suffering from being too rich," she said.

"One is never rich enough. Gold gives one everything one can desire."

"Except for what it can't buy."

"And what is it that it can't buy, down here?"

"Disinterested sentiments, of course."

"They don't exist. No one does anything for nothing."

"Unless," Claude put in, "the motive is honor, or duty, or glory?"

"There's no other motive in human actions but money," the billionaire declared, almost brutally, becoming cold again. "Honor, duty and glory are masks that disguise the true goal."

"Monsieur," said Claude, "just now your words made me indignant. I was wrong, Now, I feel sorry for you."

Williamson opened his eyes wide, looked the young explorer up and down, and then emitted a formidable burst of laughter. "Feel sorry for me—me, whom everyone envies! Ha ha ha—that's funny. Is that your opinion too, Mademoiselle?"

"Sincerely, Monsieur, yes."

"Perfect! Oh, what fun I'm having! I'm indebted to you both for that pleasure. Williamson never leaves debts unpaid. Since you don't want to run one of my mines, I'll find some other way to acquit myself." He tipped back his armchair, shaken by inextinguishable laughter. "Someone feels sorry for me! Oh, I'll laugh about that for a long time!"

The racket of a storm of applause and cheers next door cut his hilarity short.

"That's the end of the final sketch in the revue," said the steward.

"Oh, already!" said Williamson, regretfully, his features resuming their expression of froideur and ennui.

Edmée stood up and drew her brother aside. "That man is very famous and very rich, Claude," she said, "but I don't think he's happy. Really, I pity him."

128

A flood of spectators irrupted into the reception room; among the first were Dupeyroux, who, followed by Loeb, headed straight for the Mining King, his heart in his mouth.

The latter stopped the first spectator who came to hand and, pointing at the conscript father, demanded laconically: "Who's he?"

"Monsieur le Sénateur, the president of the celebration," was the reply.

"A politician," murmured the billionaire, with a scornful grimace.

Dupeyroux bowed to him ostentatiously, but did not have time to open his mouth.

"Oh, no speeches," said Williamson. "They bore me. You want to thank me for having come? Well, shake my hand and let that be the end of it."

Nonplussed and vexed, the senator replied: "You'll permit me, at least, to introduce you to one of your compatriots, who asked me to do so? Monsieur Loeb, chief..."

A rude tap on the arm cut off the speech again. "Thanks—I'll take it from here," Jonathan declared.

"What boors these Yankees are!" muttered Dupeyroux.

Loeb and Williamson were staring at one another coldly and stiffly, at close range.

"You are...?" the latter demanded, through pursed lips.

"Your equal," said the other. "You've elevated yourself above men by gold, I by domination. You buy, I command."

"Loeb? Good. I remember...I know. What do you want?"

"To talk."

"Between eight and nine, at my hotel."

"Same time at mine."

There was a glacial silence between those two gigantic prides, without any movement, without the slightest play of the physiognomy. From the first moment of contact they had been measuring one another with a superb calmness.

Dupeyroux, in whom long parliamentarian habits had killed all sterile self-respect, pulled himself together urgently. "I have a hunt, an hour from Paris, in which fur and feather abound. If, tomorrow, for example, Monsieur Williamson would like to do a little shooting, I hope that Monsieur Loeb wouldn't refuse to join him?"

"Neutral ground," said Jonathan, without ceasing to stare at his compatriot, who maintained his silence.

"You'd have complete independence, Messieurs," Dupeyroux added. "I'll be there on my own to receive you, with my secretary, Monsieur Rolland."

"Monsieur Rolland is your secretary?" articulated Williamson, who appeared to unfreeze. "He interests me, that young man. I'll come to kill a few of your beasts tomorrow."

"Bravo!"

"Unless...." He shouted: "Toby! The New York *Herald*, quickly!"

Like a flash of lightning, the groom opened a path through the increasingly dense crowd of engineers and Centrales that were almost filling the reception room, where the Mining King was a powerful magnet for curiosity.

"What!" exclaimed the senator. "You need to consult the New York *Herald* to know…?"

"Whether it's permissible for me to be your guest? Yes. You're astonished that I, who disposes at my whim of the work and time of others, don't have complete liberty in my own actions? That's the case, however; every day, for fifteen years, I've been waiting for an item of information to which death alone will prevent me from responding."

The reception room had suddenly immobilized. People scented a mystery, and all ears had become curiously attentive, none more so than those of Loeb and his interested satellite, Grégoire de Montalpé.

The Mining King had the distinct impression that the general movement was sympathetic to him, and, submissive to a kind of subconscious impulse, since he had thus attracted an interest that his fortune of which his fortune could not, in all sincerity, furnish him a complete aliment, he raised his voice slightly, and addressed the whole room.

"Messieurs," he said, "the prestige of an exceptional wealth is sufficient for me, and I don't want, before men of science, to usurp that of scientific genius. Fifteen years ago, when I was a poor reporter, I pulled an old man out of the Hudson whom I cared for in my home. Having recovered consciousness, he began by cursing me for having thwarted his suicide. Suddenly, however, after having looked at me as if he were searching the utmost depths of my soul, he asked me to tell him my story.

"It didn't take long. A foundling, picked up half-dead by English soldiers at Fort William—hence my name—I'd been brought up by them on that Canadian territory, until the day I ran away to the United States to attempt to make my living freely. Of my early childhood I had but one memory: a heart-rending cry and the ground opening up ahead of me.

"When I'd finished talking, the old man closed his eyes for a long time, and then he said to me: 'Williamson, you were well-inspired to save me. I'll make you the richest man in the world. You only have to dig the ground where I tell you to do so in order to extract mineral treasures. Now, Old Sinker doesn't lie'"

At that name, gravely pronounced, Jonathan Loeb shivered. "Old Sinker," he murmured. "The old well-digger. What a flash of light, perhaps!"

"Who's Old Sinker?" de Montalpé asked Loeb, in a whisper.

The other replied, in a troubled voice: "A singular monomaniac who, it's said, spends his life fathoming the depths of the earth, without any apparent objective."

Meanwhile, Williamson continued: "I never saw him again. I've never known where in the world he was drawing breath. But for fifteen years, without asking anything from me in return, he's indicated to me the precious deposits that have made my fame and fortune. I've often repeated that story, before this evening, in all humility, but no one wants to oppose the legend; they prefer not to believe me."

"Then...he writes to you?" asked Loeb.

"Old Sinker has never written to me."

"You see him in revelatory dreams, then?" Dupeyroux joked, ponderously.

"I receive, without any indication of provenance, a fragment of a map of the designated country, with the initial of the nature of the deposit and a red dot. That's it! I give the map to an engineer, whom I make responsible for the exploitation, and once the land is bought, I'm the master of one more superb mine. It's perfectly simple."

"So simple," observed the senator, "that any practical joker could send you to the ends of the earth to waste your efforts."

Williamson smiled. "Impossible! There's a 'sign.' For, in telling you that the man has not demanded anything of me, I was only talking about money. He imposed a tattoo on me—oh, something trivial, hardly visible—and an oath to come without delay in response to his summons when...he judged the moment had come, he said, to give me the means to be the master of the world."

"How?" demanded Loeb.

"That's his secret."

"It's the height of fantasy...or mild madness," declared the future minister, laughing. Then, on seeing Jonathan's somber face he added: "You're not laughing, Monsieur Loeb? Such pretension doesn't merit anything else, though."

"How do you know?" retorted the occult dominator, violently. "Nothing is impossible...in America."

The orator of the Luxembourg shrugged his shoulders.

The groom reappeared, carrying the great transatlantic paper, of which his master took possession unhurriedly, and unfolded it, saying: "It's purely to acquit my conscience. It would be very extraordinary if, after fifteen years of waiting, this very evening..."

Suddenly, he shuddered, in spite of all his phlegm. His finger on the newspaper, his voice rendered uncertain by an emotion stronger than his will, he articulated: "He's summoning me!"

Loeb, who had rapidly slipped behind Williamson, uttered a hoarse cry and exclaimed: "The sign! And the two letters: L. F. That's all I wanted to know: Old Sinker is Lobanief!"

That name was repeated in a triple echo, by de Montalpé—for reasons we know—but also, simultaneously, by Claude Rolland and Edmée, whose brother squeezed her wrist and whispered in her ear: "Shut up!"

De Montalpé ran to Loeb, heart-broken. "He's alive then?" he said.

"What does it matter, if I'm now sure of finding him? How much money do you have left?"

"A hundred thousand."

"Dollars?"

"Francs."

"It's enough. You'll have your inheritance and I'll have my revenge."

Transported by such a firm assurance, the elegant Grégoire seized Jonathan's powerful and bony hand: "Oh, it's my lucky star that caused me to run into you. Thanks to you, the cousins are sunk! To the lucky de Montalpé, the hoard!"

Someone touched him on the shoulder. It was Claude, with Edmée on his arm, who looked him in the eye and said, ironically: "Evil designs rarely succeed, Monsieur de Montalpé."

"Pardon me, but...?"

"Why am I interfering, no? What do you expect—I'm interested in those poor cousins."

"Bah! Petty paupers that I've never seen, and who'll never know anything."

"It would have been necessary, for that, not to inform them."

"What?"

"Our maternal grandmother—my sister and I—was named...Lobanief."

"Like mine! Damn it! They're the cousins! What a gaffe, my emperor!"

"Chatterbox!" whispered Jonathan, in his ear. "Don't worry—I'll take care of them ...as well as *him*." He indicated Williamson with a glance.

At Loeb's exclamation, the Mining King had bitten his lip, but he had immediately expelled any expression of annoyance, and traced a few figures in his notebook. He tore it out and handed it to his groom. "That dispatch to Camper and Nicholson at Gosport, to send me the steamer *Astrea*." Then he went straight to Loeb. "You've discovered my secret. You can't have any interest in it?"

"Yes—that of catching up with your Lobanief."

"You won't reach him."

"We'll reach him!" proclaimed de Montalpé, incorrigibly loquacious, adopting the attitude and tone of a braggart.

Williamson looked at the reckless snob disdainfully and called out: "Monsieur Rolland!"

The latter came forward, with Edmée.

"I heard just now, while writing in my notebook," the billionaire said to them, "that you have an interest in your relative Lobanief."

"It's of little consequence to me," said Claude, "but for the benefit of my sister, certainly. Unfortunately, our means..."

"I've told you that I'm indebted to the two of you. I'll offer you a voyage."

"Us?" said the two young people, looking at one another.

"Unless your prejudices against me..."

"The frankness of your story has dispelled them," said Claude.

"So?"

After a brief hesitation, Edmée nodded her head, gravely. Without the slightest reticence, the young explorer said: "We accept, Monsieur."

Bowled over, Senator Dupeyroux hastened toward his secretary. "What? You're leaving? What about my interpellation? And your unfinished work, which is the lynch-pin? Such a defection is impossible! It would mean disaster for me...and ridicule...and...." He dared not add: *and my portfolio up in flames!*

"That's true," Claude sighed. "I've promised..."

Williamson intervened. "Can you not, Monsieur Rolland, do the work during the journey?"

"But what about the time it will take to reach me!" protested Dupeyroux. "The interpellation is fixed for a fortnight hence."

"Good. You'll have plenty of time. I'll have it cabled from New York."

"But that will cost..."

"A bagatelle. Come on, it's agreed. You two, rendezvous tomorrow at the Le Havre express, eight twenty-five. Toby, hat and overcoat..."

While the groom ran to fetch his master's hat and coat, the latter felt Jonathan Loeb take hold of his arm and draw him to one side.

"Do you know how that infernal Lobanief intends to make you master of the world?"

"What does it matter to you whether I know or not?"

"I've had strange reports regarding Old Sinker. That accursed demon is capable of anything, perhaps even stealing some frightful secret from God. Whatever infernal power he's conquered, he won't transmit it to you."

"Because?"

"I don't want that."

"I'm not afraid of you."

"While I'm alive, you won't go to meet that man!"

"I shall."

"Be careful—I'm powerful!"

"It's war, then."

"You'll have brought it on, and you'll see what I can do!"

Phlegmatically, Williamson put on his overcoat, which the groom was holding out to him, took his hat and replied: "As you please."

As he left, he darted a cold glance at Jonathan Loeb, who was standing with his arms folded and his lips pursed in a satanic rictus, gazing at him with hatred and defiance.

III

The next day, at a quarter past eight, their baggage having been registered, Claude appeared, with Edmée on his arm and escorted by Jean Guitard, on the platform of the Gare Saint-Lazare.

133

The young explorer's energetic face respired an intense satisfaction. He was about to quit the office job for which he was so ill-made to lead the life of the open air and vast horizons that he loved, and not only without ceasing to take care of his sister, but for her and in company with her.

Edmée was a little anxious in confrontation with the double unknown of the adventure and the eccentric and scarcely sympathetic traveling companion that hazard had abruptly imposed on them.

As for Jean Guitard, the prospect of reacquainting himself with the pitching of a vessel and the briny air put quicksilver into his veins.

On the station platform, the voyagers found Toby on watch. He led them silently to the corridor carriage in which His Majesty the Mining King was already installed, very democratically for such a rich individual. Claude and Edmée, who had expected that he would have mobilized some special carriage, were a trifle disillusioned.

"Monsieur," said the explorer, greeting Williamson, "having not had the possibility of settling anything in agreement with you yesterday, I've taken the liberty of bringing my faithful manservant and former companion of my African excursions. As intelligent as he is devoted and brave, a clear-headed sailor second to none, I'm convinced that you'll have every reason to praise his services in the course of an expedition like the one we're undertaking under your benevolent and generous tutelage."

The celebrated Yankee raised his indifferent gaze as far as the meager height of Furet, who, utterly uninhibited, saluted militarily, putting his hand to his cap. "Good," he said, in a soft voice. "He can keep Toby company. Go away."

The two servants disappeared in response to a signal, to go to a nearby compartment. Williamson invited Edmée to come into his own and said, with an awkward smile: "Mademoiselle, on the railway, I'm accustomed to choosing the place with the most passengers, because the noise of conversations lulls my somnolent wait until the arrival. Because of you, I reserved a compartment. You'll have to chat a good deal between the two of you."

That kind of "consideration" left the young woman somewhat nonplussed, and her brother bit his lip in order to hold back a hostile reply.

Without paying any more heed to them than if they did not exist, Williamson nestled into his cushion, prepared by Toby, and closed his eyes.

Edmée arranged her meager feminine hand luggage, and whispered softly in her brother's ear: "Well, that's promising!"

The blast of a whistle cut through the mist. The train pulled away.

Until the express went through Mantes-la-Jolie station—which is to say, for about forty minutes—Williamson did not make a single movement.

At that moment, Edmée, who had only exchanged a few commonplace comments with her brother, embarrassed as she was by the obsessive gaze that she sensed gliding over her beneath the billionaire's eyelids, and very nervous, exclaimed: "All in all, Claude, you'll admit that it's a wrench to be on our way to the New World like this, without even knowing where we're going, nor what route we'll be taking and what stations we'll be passing through with that unknown objective."

"Why torment yourself like that, dear?"

"Things might be indifferent to you, as a man, but they're of the utmost importance to me, a woman. A man can. If necessary, go around the world with a simple valise for his underwear and toilet necessities, but it's not the same for a woman. On your advice, I've only bought two two-piece costumes, one of which I'm wearing. I'll have to complete my wardrobe at Le Havre, according to the circumstances—so it's necessary to know what they are. A woman can't dress the same for a crossing on a liner or a yacht. And when we're on the other side of the Atlantic, if Monsieur Williamson takes us to some sumptuous palace, as his residence must be, I can't present myself among elegant American ladies dressed like an errand girl delivering a hat. A Parisienne has the honor of the flag to defend! I need to know..."

That speech was intended for the Mining King—who, as Claude observed from the corner of is eyes, did not flinch.

"Little Sister," the young man decided to say, "I understand, and within the limits of my ignorance, reasoning by deduction, I'll try to enlighten you, at least partially.

"First of all, it seems evident to me that we'll be making the Ocean crossing aboard a yacht, undoubtedly superb, that Monsieur Williamson must possess."

"What makes you think so?"

"The suddenness of our departure on a Wednesday, when the Company liners only leave on Saturday. If we were taking one of them, we'd have set off three days early."

"But there isn't only the French line that goes from Le Havre—if it's really to New York that we're going!"

"Certainly, but the Holland-America Line stops over at Boulogne and the Hamburg Lines at Boulogne and Cherbourg."

"And the English liners?"

"Leave from England, and we're not going to England."

"How do you know?"

"Because then we'd have headed for the Pas-de-Calais. Our generous guide wouldn't have wasted precious time taking the slow route from Le Havre to Southampton."

Without changing his posture, Williamson finally deigned for the first time since the departure, to unseal his teeth. It was to affirm laconically: "Both in error: I have no yacht, and no residence."

Edmée uttered a brief burst of laughter, whose nervousness attenuated its pretty sonority somewhat. "Do you, by chance, intend to have us cross the Ocean swimming, and make us sleep under the stars on the other side?"

The eccentric billionaire threw back his fur, sat up, suddenly put an amiable expression over the customary nonchalant morosity of his visage, and explained: "A yacht is a chain. It's necessary to go to its home port to board it, or wait for it a long way away when one sends for it, which is incompatible with my humor.

"I've arranged with the world's principal naval constructors that they should always have a comfortable ship ready for my use at various points of the globe: Gosport in the English Channel, Hamburg in the North Sea, Rothsay on the Clyde for the Irish Sea, Libau in the Baltic, Marseilles and Brindisi in the Mediterranean, Bordeaux, New York and Rio de Janeiro in the Atlantic, Colombo in the Indian Ocean, Hong Kong in the Far East, Sydney, San Francisco and Guayaquil in the Pacific, and the Cape in South Africa. Thus, whether I'm in France, England, Scotland, Germany, Russia, Scandinavia, Spain, Italy, Greece, Turkey, India, China, Australia, South Africa, or anywhere on the American continent, I always have at my disposal, with the minimum delay, a means of traversing the seas, at home, to go wherever my fancy takes me.

"As for the residence, I'm not stupid enough to burden myself with a fixed dwelling, with a staff more master than the master, and the obligation of coming to anchor myself there to satisfy the demands of Society, when my desire is to breathe freely under another sky. As a true Yankee, my home is the hotel—that way I'm at home anywhere in the world.

"I have three hundred palaces combining all perfect comforts, thousands of valets whose hope of a princely tip exalts their zeal. All the museums of the continent are my gallery, so that I can enrich myself with some exceptional work whenever the whim takes me, and I don't have to take the risk of paying fifty or a hundred thousand dollars for a fake signature to a dealer who'll laugh at me while banking my dollars and showing off the daub to a heap of snobs who'll ecstasize over it and a few connoisseurs who'll consider me an imbecile.

"You seem surprised, the pair of you, to hear me talk so much in spite of my principles. That's because I understood that you'll keep quiet if I don't put in my share, and your voices, especially that of Mademoiselle Rolland, are a music that has an extreme charm for me. Your turn now."

"So, Monsieur," said Edmée, pulling a face that, unknown to her, made her even lovelier, "it's because the timbre of our voices pleases you that you decided to take us with you?"

"Why do you want me to do it?"

"One isn't so frank."

"I'm not the billionaire Williamson in order to embarrass myself with hypocritical formulas."

"So it's not only to do a favor for worthy young people like us, too poor to be able, without assistance, to take care of their interests?"

"I never do favors, on principle."

"And to attract their sincere gratitude?"

"That word represents something non-existent."

"Admit, at least, that my womanly pride might be wounded on seeing myself reduced to the role of a music-box."

"I'm very fond of music-boxes. I have several of them in each of 'my' hotels, and they're all marvels. I give myself concerts, all alone, in my room, to put me to sleep…as your legendary Montaigne used to put himself to sleep in childhood. As regards feminine pride, I have the right to ignore it, never having encountered any example of it."

"I shall therefore impose on myself, from this moment on, the most absolute silence. And if my voice is agreeable to you, I shall have the regret, for the sake of my demonstration, of deriving you of it."

"Oh, you're always annoying me!"

"The music box having become voluntarily silent, you may abandon us, if you wish, at Le Havre station."

"What about your fortune?"

"I wouldn't even pay for your fortune with a single humiliation."

"What if I take you at your word?"

"We'll take the first train back to Paris, won't we, Claude?"

"Certainly, my dear," the explorer agreed.

The Mining King fell silent for a long moment, making a grimace of irritation. Then, suddenly, he said: "In that case, you'll accompany me to the end, because I retract what I said and apologize. You're both so strangely new to me, who has thus far only encountered servile complaisance. I'll take you all the way to Lobanief, and tell him what independent individuals you are. And I'll hear your charming voice, Miss, even if I have to talk myself from here until New York to get you to reply to me. Is it like that that it's necessary to speak?"

"Yes, Monsieur," said Edmée, intimately flattered by the small victory that she had just won. "To demonstrate your kind dispositions, tell us about our strange relative, whom we're going with you to meet."

"No, not that—not here at least. When we're between the sea and the sky, yes; here, there are too many ears, in spite of the noise of the machinery—free ears, I mean."

"At least you'll tell us where we're going to meet him?"

"No."

"May we know why not?"

"The best reason in the world—because I don't know, and will only learn myself when we make landfall."

"Which is where?"

137

"I can reveal that even less than everything else," Williamson declared, his expression preoccupied, darting an anxious glance through the closed interior door at two passengers who were going along the corridor of the carriage.

"I have no luck!" exclaimed Edmée tapping the floor of the carriage with a petulant foot.

"Listen, Miss Rolland—I may call you that, may I not, since we're going to a country where English is spoken, and it's easier for me to pronounce than your incommensurable Mademoiselle—I shall have a great deal that is very curious to tell you concerning...the man who is summoning me. I told the exact truth yesterday at the Continental Hotel in relating publicly the rescue that was the origin of my great situation, but I didn't reveal the profoundly strange circumstances that had led the unique individual to whom you are distantly related to the waters of the Hudson. That story, I promise the two of you, but only when I judge that prudence will permit me to tell it to you. Between now and then, grant me the credit of a little patience and...let's talk about anything except the objective of our voyage."

And all the way to Le Havre, Williamson, who had been traveling the world in fantastic zigzags for fifteen years and had seen everything, with an eye that had only gradually become blasé and indifferent, revealed himself to his companions as an agreeable conversationalist full of memories and verve.

It was a sudden metamorphosis, with which Edmée's keen feminine intuition made her understand that she was not unconnected.

Animated by that unexpected success, she made her own contribution of wit. As that wit was one of the most lively—she surpassed her brother in that respect—Williamson, enchanted, declared that she alone had more humor than all the daughters of Eve that he had encountered during his existence as a rich nomad.

On arrival at Le Havre, the Mining King, having engaged in such a copious and light-hearted dialogue, had a glint in his eye and color in his complexion. Toby was open-mouthed; he no longer recognized his master. How could he have recognized him, when the true Williamson—the one behind the mask—was unknown to everyone, including himself?

Terrible events were about to furnish that repellently enclosed soul and that triply-immured heart with the opportunity to release themselves from their prison.

1. Battle is Joined

By a miracle of feminine magic, it was an almost amiably loquacious Williamson who set foot on the platform of Le Havre station in the company of Claude and Edmée Rolland. There is nothing like the taciturn for not knowing how to stop, once they have broken their customary morose mutism.

That abnormal state explains why the Mining King, who had promised himself to maintain a particular vigilance, did not perceive that when he left the station, two men, one of whom was very tall, with the peak of a traveling cap pulled down over his eyes and a muffler covering the lower part of his face, followed the three new arrivals at a distance, climbing into a vehicle that followed their own, and, having seen them get out at the Hôtel de Normandie in what is now the Place Gambetta, had themselves taken swiftly to the extremity of the harbor, to the point where the jetty begins, level with the Hôtel Frascati.

There, the taller one said to the other: "Go back to our sleazy hotel—you'll get in my way otherwise—and don't come out before I come to fetch you. Above all, on your life, not a word to anyone of what I've allowed myself to tell you on the way about Old Sinker!"

"Unnecessary recommendation," the other replied. "I'm not naïve enough to go telling tall tales of that sort!"

"Go!" commanded the first, in a rude voice.

While the hired vehicle conveyed his companion to the Rue de Paris he muttered: "It's as well that that fellow's a Frenchman. He's not worthy to be a Yankee."

Turing stiffly on his heel, he went at a long stride to the Chamber of Commerce, where he addressed himself to the watchman.

"Has the steam-yacht *Astrea*, announced on your list, been sighted?"

"Not yet," was the response.

Retracing his steps, the interminable individual went to pace back and forth along the embarkation quay for the boats from Le Havre to Honfleur, Trouville and Caen. From there it was easy for him to keep watch on the exit from the Rue de Paris to the harbor.

In these two individuals you will have recognized Grégoire de Montalpé and Jonathan Loeb. The previous evening they had left the Hôtel Continental on the heels of Claude and Edmée Rolland, accompanied by the faithful Jean Guitard, alias Furet, who were following as they retreated by the Mining King, escorted by the inflexible groom.

Then, while the "Williamson camp" had put off their departure until the following morning, Loeb had demanded that de Montalpé, exceedingly but futilely recalcitrant, impose on himself the fatigue of a seven-hour train journey on the slow train leaving the Gare Saint-Lazare at forty-five minutes past midnight, the eleven-thirty express not leaving them enough time to make the most summary preparations.

What was Loeb going to do in Le Havre, where no liner was leaving for America or England, and why had he wanted to get there ahead of Williamson? That can be partially explained by the following dialogue, between him and his companion and travel-cashier, the previous night, on the train.

"Why have ourselves jolted around all night—a real party what!—when there's an express in the morning!"

"Williamson will take it."

"Exactly. It's the best means of not losing track of him."

"We haven't only to follow the Mining King. If we get ahead of him at Le Havre, we might have a stroke of luck—not probable, but possible."

"What?"

"That of finding out what ship he's using to cross the Atlantic."

"That's easy, since the transatlantic liner that will leave on Saturday is in dock at..."

"He won't take the liner."

"How do you know?"

"I know; that's sufficient."

"Then we're going to lose track of him when he leaves Le Havre."

"Yes."

"In that case, it's not worth the trouble of hurrying."

"Yes, one of two things must happen: either I'll be able to take action in Le Havre, in which case we can wait tranquilly until the French ship leaves on Saturday, or I won't, and it'll be necessary for us to go to Boulogne, Cherbourg or Liverpool in order not to miss the first Dutch, German or English ship...for it's vital, at all costs to reach the American shore twenty-four hours before him."

"A race! And a long distance! Oh la la! I'll be worn out! Try, then, to take 'action' in Le Havre."

"I will, if chance favors me—as it probably will."

"And from New York, where are we going?"

"Straight for that demon Old Sinker."

"Otherwise known as Lob..."

"Shut up! On your soul, never pronounce that name."

"On the train, who do you think...?"

"What do you know? Anyway, if it ever emerges from your mouth without my permission, I'll cut out your tongue."

"What? No stupidity!"

"Take that as read."

"Sure! And where will we find him, this...Old Sinker?"

"That's the sole point that I need to elucidate. It doesn't worry me, I've discovered, in two minutes, all the rest of Williamson's secret."

"When?"

"Before your very eyes a few hours ago, at the Continental."

"What secret?"

"Capital: the sign and...something else."

"What sign?"

Loeb took a copy of the New York *Herald* from his pocket, bought immediately after he had left the Centrale celebration with de Montalpé. The American newspaper was folded to display the personal ads. With his finger pointing at the right place, he showed the newspaper to his companion.

140

"This one!"

"Oh! That's odd, that...but...it's a globe run through by a dagger."

Loeb furrowed his bushy eyebrows gravely.

"I've had strange reports about that damned Old Sinker! Many years ago, he said something terrible, something corroborated in a redoubtable fashion by that sign, devised by him for his secret correspondence with the Mining King."

"Get away! The hieroglyph is naively clear! A man who, you told me, spends his life digging holes in the ground..."

"O futile Frenchman, who stops at appearances and explains everything in a word, without ever delving deeper!"

"What do you want me to delve into? The holes that your Old Sinker digs? No thanks—I'll leave subterranean enterprises to the moles."

"Know that the man in question has said: 'The earth is malevolent to humans; it deserves to die.'"

"For the good of humanity? That's a lunatic's reasoning! To summon the end of the world to embellish existence, when it would simply destroy it? If he really used that incoherent language, my excessively-alive relative has a spider in his skull."

"Make no mistake—Old Sinker is a genius. That he's inspired by Hell, I don't doubt, but he's nonetheless capable of anything."

"Not of icing the planet, I imagine!"

"Who knows?"

That was too much for de Montalpé, who nearly choked with laughter, and exclaimed: "Oh yes! The sign! The dagger-thrust...in the fashion of our apache cut-throats! Ha ha ha! That's a good one, my dear!"

Loeb was not laughing. He looked at his traveling companion with a gaze in which irritation attenuated the scornful pity.

When de Montalpé had recovered a little of his seriousness, he concluded: "Anyway whether the fellow is as made as they say, and whether all Yankees are the same way, or not, is an irrelevant question. The only thing that interests me is whether, alive or dead, genius or madman, he'll let me get my hands on the inheritance in suspension...before the final deadline. That's the only serious thing; I'm risking everything I have left on you, and I expect that still holds, eh?"

"More than ever. My hatred will answer to you for that."

"Good! That's talking in human terms. Let's leave it there, if you please, and try to get some sleep. If we don't have time to get some tomorrow night, it's only prudent to get a little in advance. Good night! Oh, no—cutting the throat of the world...that's a good one."

Shaken by a slight residue of hilarity, the elegant Grégoire went to sleep, while Jonathan Loeb, his eyes fixed, pursued some somber dream, wide awake.

When, after an ample lunch, such as one obtains in good provincial hotels, Williamson, Claude and Edmée emerged in a carriage from the Rue de Paris on to the waterfront, with Toby, as stiff as a stick, beside the coachman, Loeb took cover swiftly, and then, seeing the adverse trio get down on the edge of the north jetty, followed them at a considerable distance, but in such a fashion as not to lose sight of them.

As he went past the post office, which forms the corner of the street and the quay, Jean Guitard, alias Furet, came out, having gone in to expedite a few postcards that Edmée wanted to send to her friends before departure.

At the sight of the tall silhouette of the Yankee, the mariner shivered. Without being exactly well-informed with regard to Loeb, he had discovered or divined enough to esteem the presence of that individual in Le Havre abnormal at the moment when Williamson and his young masters were passing through.

Moving adroitly, he observed him, and soon saw him go to the edge of the dock, take a pair of binoculars from his pocket and study the sea, and then turn around abruptly and draw away at a rapid stride, heading directly away from the sea.

Furet then hastened to rejoin his masters on the jetty, where, following the billionaire's example, they were busy observing a ship that was heading toward the harbor from the open sea under full steam.

"The *Astrea*, Commandant?" he asked Claude.

"Yes. What a mover, eh? She'll be in the harbor within three-quarters of an hour."

The mariner tugged gently at the young mariner's sleeve, drawing him to one side.

"You have something to tell me?"

"Yes, Commandant. You know the individual who took your seat beside the senator last night...?"

"Jonathan Loeb. Well?"

"He's here and he's spying on us. He saw the *Astrea* and veered away from our wake."

Rolland immediately informed Williamson of the fact. The latter shrugged his shoulders. "The effort will be futile," he said, pursing his lips disdainfully. And he resumed observing the ship.

Forty minutes had not gone by when the superb yacht, rigged as a three-masted schooner, approached the jetties at half-speed, stopped in the outer harbor and then moved slowly to the level the Quai Notre-Dame. There she moored on a cathead anchor and, there being no danger of any encumbrance because the tide was going out, immediately made her dispositions to turn around and head westwards, in case she had to sail at a moment's notice.

Several small boats presented themselves to bring mooring ropes, and their assistance was not refused by the mate who was responsible for the maneuver, while the commandant, the launch having been lowered, had himself taken to the shore.

Williamson and his companions, who had quit the north jetty and were following a course along the quay parallel to that of the *Astrea*, but at a lesser speed, had scarcely arrived at the corner of the Quai Notre-Dame than the commandant of the yacht set foot there.

The Mining King advanced toward the officer and introduced himself. "Williamson!"

"Captain Burner," replied the impeccably-dressed and extensively-braided mariner, saluting.

"Good. Are you ready to put to sea?"

"Immediately, if you give the order."

"What! What about my clothes, my indispensable purchases, my preparations?" said Edmée, in alarm, to her brother, on whose arm she was leaning elegantly. The latter gestured to her to be quiet.

Captain Burner explained to Williamson: "I'll make the observation to you that we'd only gain an insignificant amount of time in the crossing by making ready to sail now. The embarkation of baggage and the formalities will take at least an hour. Only two hours would remain before low water, which means that as we headed out to see we'd encounter the incoming tide, with a head-wind, which wouldn't permit us to make much progress. By sailing this evening, an hour after high water, we'd have the current to take us out of the Channel, and there's a chance that the fresh breeze blowing in mid-Channel will have calmed by sunset."

"So be it. Ready to sail at..."

"Eight o'clock."

"Did you hear?" asked Williamson, addressing Claude and his sister, who nodded. "Free time until then. Oh, wait a moment, Miss Edmée!" He turned to the captain. "When I cabled for the ship, I asked that a chambermaid be embarked...?"

"She's on board."

"Well chosen?"

"The best available, given that we only had three hours to search, at night. Not young or pretty, but she's sailed before, which is an important point, and has references. Does the Miss want me to disembark her?"

"No thank you, Captain—I don't have time to make her acquaintance while running round the shops. I'm very grateful to Mr. Williamson for his attention, and most of all for having thought of it. What is her name?"

"Grace."

"Ah! A promising forename."

"More than it delivers, I warn you, Miss," said the Captain, who was a handsome man, still young, sketching a smile. "Grace Strangestorm. Look—there she is."

The mariner pointed at a tall individual with a jaundiced complexion, clad in black, who appeared to be very busy listening to what a man in an oilskin and coifed in a mariner's sou-wester was saying to her.

Edmée pulled a light face. "She has a rather tempestuous name and doesn't look very lively," she said, laughing, "but for the little use I'll make of her, she'll still be sufficient."

"I'll go aboard with you, Captain," said Williamson. Addressing the fraternal couple, he added: "Until this evening. We'll have supper as soon as we're out of the harbor. Be on time for casting off."

The Mining King got down into the launch with the Captain, and Edmée, on Claude's arm and escorted by Jean Guimard, headed back to the Rue de Paris cheerfully, in quest of her numerous and various purchases.

At eight o'clock precisely, the steam-yacht *Astrea* churned up the waters of the harbor with her double propeller, *en route* for a night at sea and the waves of the Atlantic.

At the extremity of the north jetty, two men watched the nocturnal departure. When the yacht began to salute the slight swell that welcomed it at the port entrance with its prow, one of them articulated in a hoarse voice, with a satanic rictus on his lips, a "Bon voyage!" replete with hateful irony.

His companion, warmly wrapped up in a fur coat with the collar raised, said to him, in a tone of mediocre satisfaction: "They've gone, though, all the same."

"Let them go."

"What about us?"

"We'll wait tranquilly for Saturday's steamer."

"You've taken action, then."

"Yes, since the imbeciles left me the time to do so, when they could so easily have slipped through my fingers by taking to the sea when their boat arrived, Oh, Monsieur de Montalpé, if the old crackpots of the mysticism of Albion didn't exist, it would be necessary to invent them. When they put their minds to it, they're worth ten men. By Jove, I need to laugh this evening. There's a music hall here—let's go, as men satisfied with a good day's work, to finish the evening joyfully there."

2. The Catastrophe

Whoever has not spent at least a few days traveling on a great yacht is ignorant of the most perfect delight that fortune reserves for its exceptional elect, as well as their parasites...on condition, of course, that none of them are subject to the disagreeable symptoms *sui generis* that can be produced by the sway of the swell.

144

Williamson and Claude were vaccinated against all the choreographic fantasies of the waves. Edmée, who was entering for the first into enduring coquetry with Neptune, would perhaps not have been insensible to the serious rudeness of the sea, but the latter, by the eighth day of the voyage had not yet wearied of giving evidence of a gallant clemency with which few voyagers can flatter themselves that they have been favored to such an extent.

There was only a little fatigue on departure, for the breeze, as Captain Burner had hoped, had softened while the *Astrea* waited in port for the tide, and when, on the afternoon of the next day, the yacht doubled the isles of Scilly—which the French call the Sorlingues—situated south of Land's End and making a pendant with our Île d'Ouessant to mark, in the north, the extreme limit of the Channel, she found a calm in the Atlantic that was not belied by the following days.

The voyage was a genuine enchantment, and, the human mind having a tendency to consider a fortunate beginning as a favorable augury with regard to ensuing events, everyone aboard should have been manifesting a confidence full of security.

"Everyone," however, would be saying too much. It is necessary to make an exception for the chambermaid of the young and lovely passenger Edmée Rolland, the tall, thin, jaundiced, mature and sectarian Miss Grace Strangestorm. Was it the predestination of a tempestuous name that influenced the character of the nautical maidservant? At any rate, correctly stiff and opposed to any physical movement, she was mentally the most unquiet, the most exalted and the most troubled and troubling of creatures.

"It's the most extravagant type of old Anglo-Saxon spinster that, in complicity with hazard, you've given me for a chambermaid, Monsieur Williamson!" Edmée said to the Mining King that evening, when, between him and her brother, she had stretched herself out comfortably in a padded wicker armchair after supper, in the vast saloon of the yacht, offering her finely-shod Parisienne feet to the sunset.

"What has she said or done now, your Grace?"

"It amuses you when I relate my little arguments with her, and the continual surprises she causes me?"

"You recount them with so much humor, Miss Edmée, and your voice takes on even more charming intonations. I can assure you that if your chambermaid provokes astonishments in you, they bear no comparison to those you provide for me. You're both changing and fixed, prettily cheerful and, at times, as serious as a man...and with that, so intellectually correct and independent! I've never seen that before."

"That's because you haven't taken the trouble to look."

"All the women I've encountered before you have always put on a performance in my intention, either of laughter or of sentiment. You, you're just yourself, as if I weren't here."

"That's doubtless because your millions of dollars don't dazzle me."

"That's extraordinary. You're an enigma."

"Not very difficult to decipher…isn't that so Claude?"

"Little Sister, your portrait can be painted in three strokes: good and brave heart, honest and frank character, served by a keen wit and an open intelligence. There is, besides, the spontaneity of a true young Frenchwoman, which you are in the fullest sense of the term."

"I protest," declared Williamson, *ex professo*. "Miss Edmée is an exceptional individual."

"For you, perhaps, who have only seen human societies under the mirage of your…how shall I put it?…your royalty, but not for the young men of my homeland. Ask Claude! Come on, Monsieur Williamson, I don't have any pretention to being a phenomenon, and it annoys me considerable to be considered as such, for I have a horror of phenomena, of whatever nature they might be. So, if you'd like my…ancillary story…?"

"Please."

"Well, here it is: you know that the respectable Grace doesn't give me a minute's…grace on the question of my salvation. I've already told you that she wakes me up by intoning a psalm, helps me to get dressed while talking to me about our final destiny, and in the evening, never lets me go to bed without warning me about the eternal torments of Hell. I wonder why I don't dream, every night, about horned devils, and damned souls that have our faces writhing in the flames. Fortunately, I have a tranquil conscience as well as a sound stomach, and, in consequence, no tendency to nightmares. But now preaching no longer suffices her zeal for my eternity; she's passed from somberly lugubrious exhortation to action."

"How so?"

"Listen, Brother. This morning, woken up by the first rays of the sun sliding through my porthole, delightfully rocked by a gentle swell, I experienced a desire to linger in bed a little later than usual. So, when Grace entered discreetly, I watched the woman through barely-parted eyelashes, who contemplated me in silence with an expression simultaneously ecstatic, dolorous and…ardent. When she was quite certain of the profundity of my sleep, she unhooked, with a rapid gesture, the lifejacket that a forethought with which I have no argument had placed aboard within reach of passengers.

"What an odd idea!" exclaimed Claude.

"The action did, indeed, demand an explanation. As she beat a retreat with the fruit of her larceny, I called out: 'Why, Grace, what are you doing?' She turned round without making any attempt hide the…*corpus delicti*.

"'Miss,' she said to me, gravely, 'our existences are in the hands of the Lord. His divine wisdom has fixed their term, and it in His hands alone that we should put ourselves with regard to our final hour down here. An object such as this one is impious, in that it marks a pretention on our part to oppose the verdict of Heaven. If Our Lord sends us to shipwreck, it's because he has decided to re-call us to Him, and out obedience to his decisions forbids us to do anything to exempt ourselves from His will.'

"And she went out deliberately, taking the lifejacket with her."

"The woman is mad!" protested the Mining King. "I'll give the order to have the flotation apparatus in your cabin replaced immediately."

"What's the point, Monsieur Williamson? We'll soon be arriving in Amer-ica, the weather is superb—and then, why disturb the poor soul in her crazy mysticism? I can assure you that I surprise, at times, the expression of a mar-tyr...although it's true that at others..."

"At others?"

"Perhaps I shouldn't say this, and you might accuse my changing humor of being in haste to demolish the saint as soon as I've put her in her niche. After all, *honni soit qui mal y pense*...but ten times in the last three days, I've sur-prised my austere quakeress[84] deep in conversation with a crewman—a tall fel-low with a somber air, whom I've often seen at the helm."

"A helmsman! Wait a moment, Sister. Dark-haired, isn't he, will a full beard, sort and bushy...and a scar on the right side of his forehead."

"That's the one."

"I've noticed him too, and I asked the Captain his name, which is Smith. He's apparently very serious in service, but has one foible, which is that of not wanting to go to his bunk when his watch finishes. He claims that he finds it sti-fling in the crew quarters, and as he's found it uncomfortable there twice he's been authorized to sleep on deck."

"I understand, then, why Miss Strangestorm is always sure of finding him there," said Edmée, smiling maliciously.

"An idyll in tarpaulin," said the billionaire, with a mocking expression.

"It's more likely, I presume," the young woman retorted, "that he's a neo-phyte that my chambermaid is catechizing, doubtless with more success than me, given that I'm as far from fanatical excess as from incredulity."

Williamson shrugged his shoulders slightly.

"The foundation of the feminine character being hypocrisy..."

"Thanks!"

---

[84] The author inserts a footnote at this point translating "Quakeress" as *Trem-bleuse* and adding the remark: "a Protestant sect further exaggerating our Jan-senism," which is by no means an accurate characterization of the Society of Friends, the most sober and determinedly pacifist of all Christian sects. Edmée, as a devout Catholic, might not know the difference (extreme as it is) between a Quaker and a member of the Salvation Army, but it is not an error that reflects well on her or her author.

"I've told you, Miss Edmée, that you're an exception! Thus, for this Grace, I believe her to be quite capable of allying the most exalted religious mysticism with…with…"

Edmée came to his aid, laughing. "With preoccupations as terrestrial as they are profane?"

"That's right."

"Well, I don't share your opinion. I have the conviction that Grace lives as little as possible on earth, and hat her ardent eyes, which seem to be getting more hollow by the hour, are solely hypnotized by visions of a sacred beyond. Since we've been aboard, she hasn't belied her role as a living Bible, except on one point, on the subject of which you know that I share her curiosity."

"The agreed point to which I need to go in case of a summons from Old Sinker?"

"Yes, Monsieur Williamson. I understand that, once we were embarked, you wanted to keep the secret for the first few days after we had quit Europe, but now that we're so close to disembarking and heading toward the unknown rendezvous…for it's true, isn't it, that we're approaching New York?"

"Miss, when Captain Burner took a point at midday, we were at 70° 55' 45" west longitude…."

"From the English Greenwich meridian?" specified the young engineer/explorer.

"Naturally."

"Well, as Greenwich, 5' 45" east of London, is 2° 20' 40" west of the zero French median, that's 73° 16' of west longitude…"

"Exactly, but as the United States, like almost everyone in the world, has adopted the Greenwich meridian…"

"Oh, I don't have any self-respect invested in it, Monsieur Williamson—except that, as I've brought a French chart of New York and its maritime approaches, I'm underlining the differences aloud in order to engrave them on my memory and rectify my own calculations with regard to the English baseline. Forgive me for having interrupted you."

"I was saying that at midday we were at 70° 55' 45" of longitude west…of Greenwich. As, since then, we've been heading due west and making an average of sixteen knots, and as the distance between two consecutive degrees of meridian, which is, at the equator—employing your metric measures for convenience—one thousand eleven hundred meters, is no more, at our latitude, than about forty-four miles, or eighty-one and a half kilometers…that means that presently, at nine ç 'clock in the evening, we ought to be…well, calculate it, Monsieur Engineer."

"I've already done it, while you were talking," said Claude, completing a rapid operation in his notebook. At this moment we're 75° 30' of longitude west of Paris, or 73° 9' 45" of longitude west of Greenwich."

"Good. Now, as New York is, in round numbers, at 74° west longitude, in English terms, the distance that separates us is ten minutes less than a degree, which is..."

"Fifty-one and a third miles, or ninety-five kilometers, just less than a hectometer."

"Still as far as that?"

"Oh, it's child's play, Miss Edmée. At our speed of sixteen knots we'll be there in...in...Oh, I'm too lazy to calculate. What is it, Mr. Rolland?"

"Three and a quarter hours."

"With the result that we'll be entering the Hudson in the middle of the night. And I was so looking forward to the spectacle of that arrival! I shan't see a thing."

"Unfortunately, that's true, Miss, but on the other hand, we have every chance of passing unnoticed and leaving New York before anyone catches wind of our presence on American soil—and I have serious reasons for considering that as good fortune."

"Then it's almost as if, from now on, we're on our way to the unknown rendezvous point to which you're taking us?"

"That's exactly right."

"In that case, I don't understand what interest your excessive prudence has in keeping it from us any longer."

"In truth, Miss, you're logic personified."

"So you're finally going to tell us?"

"Shortly. But as it would be rather difficult to explain, insofar as you don't have all the geographical details of North America presently in mind..."

"Not precisely, in fact..."

"I'll need..."

"A map?"

"Yes. And I don't know if I'll find one easily on board, where the collection of marine charts is certainly complete, but as regards terrestrial map...."

"I have what you need."

"You?"

"Not me, but that illuminate Grace Strangestorm. Outside of her minimal service, when she isn't preaching, praying or absorbing herself in some poignant meditation, she contemplates a large map of North America suspended in her cabin. Do you want me to ring for her?"

"Do...and give her the order yourself; it's so agreeable to listen to you."

Edmée pressed the call button and Toby appeared immediately, in his immaculate high collar.

"Fetch the chambermaid, right away."

Grace Strangestorm, more jaundiced and stiffer than ever, in her narrow black dress, soon appeared on the threshold of the sumptuous saloon.

"Do you still have that map of North America that I've seen in your cabin, pinned to the wall?"

"Yes, Miss," the Englishwoman replied, with difficulty, so much were her bloodless lips trembling, and in a hoarse voice, her throat having suddenly contracted, while her sunken eyes lit up with a sudden gleam.

"Will you bring it to us, please. We have to look at it for...something."

The chambermaid turned on her heel and departed like an arrow.

"Did you see her eyes light up with joy?" said Edmée to the two men.

"I didn't suspect that compassed creature of having such an intensity of gaze," observed Claude.

Without having made a movement, Williamson muttered between his teeth from the depths of his armchair: "I don't like such a violent and inexplicable curiosity—for you haven't promised, I suppose, Miss, to take her with us when we disembark?"

"I haven't even given it a thought, but in her holy ardor for the salvation of my soul, perhaps she's hopeful."

"Well, she'll be wrong, for I beg you, if you please, not to accede to her pleas if she addresses any to you. As I'm convinced that you'll keep to yourselves what I'm going to...indicate to you, her shocking curiosity won't be satisfied, for she won't know, even if she's listening—of which I think her perfectly capable—whether it's to the north, west or south that we'll be heading before daybreak."

Grace reappeared, holding her unfolded map. This time it was without haste, very calm in her stiff dignity, that she went to set it out on the large table with castors, in old mahogany, edged with marquetry. Without Williamson, who was about to do so, having any need to order her peremptorily to go away, she withdrew discreetly, and closed the door behind her.

That attitude brought a frown-line to the billionaire's forehead, which was immediately effaced. He went to the table.

"Open your eyes, both of you, because I won't pronounce a name," he said. "I shan't articulate a single word, and you'll do me the favor of following my example."

He took a pencil from his pocket, of which he broke off the lead, and, after having taken a moment to get his bearings, he placed the point of the stick on a spot close to which the sinuous line of a river could be seen to run.

The two young people looked at him interrogatively. Only his eyelids responded positively. Then leaving the brother and sister time to take account of the designated geographical point, he put his index finger across his lips and, quitting the table—from which Claude and Edmée also drew away—he went to press the call button.

As before, Toby presented himself and received the order to summon the chambermaid. The latter returned in response to a sign, picked up the map and drew away at a measured pace, after having bowed ceremoniously, attentively followed by the gaze of the Mining King.

When the door closed again, the latter shrugged his shoulders slightly and dubiously. He would not have done so if he had seen her, once in her cabin, throw herself to her knees, her arms forming a cross, her gaze ecstatic, exhaling in a single breath: "Lord, you have finally wished it! Be glorified by your humble servant, who places herself in your divine hands!"

Then she took the map, which she had deposited on her bunk, folded it up carefully, inserted it into a flat metal case which she slid into her corsage, and leaving her cabin silently, went up on to the deck.

In the saloon, Edmée said to the billionaire: "I'm very grateful to you, Monsieur Williamson, for granting my wish. Now that I know what fatigues await us I ask your permission to take advantage of the brief hours of travel that remain to us to prepare myself for them with a little sleep."

"That's reasoning and acting sagely, Miss Edmée. Unless something unexpected occurs, I don't think you'll have to leave the ship until three or four o'clock in the morning."

Edmée Roland retired to her cabin and, glad to have avoided her lugubrious preacher for once, went to bed and, very happy with a life that was both opulent and mildly adventurous, did not take long to fall asleep with a smile on her lips.

"The night is splendid. If it would interest you as much as it would me to see the lights of the American coast appear on the horizon, come and smoke a few Havanas on the bridge."

"Delighted to follow you, Monsieur Williamson, and believe that, for my part, I wouldn't have missed it."

On the bridge they found Captain Burner, who, by reason of the imminent landfall, had come to take up his command post. The mate and the first lieutenant, the officer of the watch, were with him.

"Well, Captain?"

"I proclaim, sir that you can never have made such a fine crossing. Since emerging from the Channel we've scarcely seen a cloud, and one couldn't ask for a more splendid night to conclude the voyage."

"You haven't seen anything yet?"

"Not so far, but it can't be long. And look, there's a light fore and starboard, emerging from the water. Perfectly...blinking at fifteen second intervals. That's the floating light at Sandy Hook!"

"My compliments, Captain. It's impossible to make landfall with more magisterial precision."

"Commanding a ship in these conditions in very easy; everything has gone as one would wish in the marvelous voyage."

151

"Including my famous work," said the senator's former secretary, smiling. "Thanks to the constantly calm sea, I haven't suffered any interruption or inconvenience, and I can guarantee that Monsieur Dupeyroux will be content. If, with that redoubtable document, he doesn't acquire the morocco that is the object of his ardent desire, he'll have been very maladroit—and if, by following the indications once in power, he doesn't achieve fortunate results for the country, it will be because he really doesn't want to!"

"On that subject, Monsieur Rolland," declared the billionaire, "as we're only going to be passing through New York by night, I've given your manuscript, and a check, to Captain Burner, who will take charge of cabling your copy tomorrow morning, as agreed. Tomorrow evening, the future minister will be in possession of the political weapon that you've forged for him."

Claude thanked him, and as, when the cigars were lit, the conversation on the bridge became general and animated, he took advantage of it to stretch his legs by taking a turn around the deck. Almost at the foot of the iron ladder he found Jean Guitard, who, with his hands deep in the pockets of his blue bell-bottoms—since Le Havre he had been exchanged his suit, too terrestrial for his taste, for a matelot's uniform—was pacing back and forth, head down, like a wild beast in a cage.

"What's the matter with you?" asked the young man, amused.

"I'm eaten up with boredom, Commandant, and bogged down in a dull anger. It's high time the crossing ended, or I won't be able to contain myself any longer, in spite of my desire not to cause you any annoyance...and watch out, if Furet brings his fists and his kick-boxing into play!"

"Good God! Who's upset you?"

"All of them...and one in particular."

Come on, calm down. Tell me about it—that will help."

"Commandant, you know as well as I do how it is between French *mathurins* and English *bluecoats*. The *entente cordiale* only ever existed in regulation manifestations and on the surface, in mutual receptions during political visits of squadrons. Apart from that, their mariners and our mariners are as friendly as cats and dogs. All those here, since I've been assigned a bunk in their quarters, have had less regard for me than if I were cockroach; none of them talk to me, and in their midst I'm more in quarantine than an infectious case stuck in an isolation ward. At least, when I'm obliged to ask them for something, in the good English that I've learned on your instructions, most of the *rosbifs* content themselves with looking at me and replying *yes, no, over there* or *I don't know*—but there's one of them who affects to turn his head and switch his tobacco plug from side to side without unclenching his teeth. Oh, the dirty caulker!

"I've had to hold myself back several times from ramming his fat belly all the way to his throat with a good kick in the...figure! Three days ago I look at him in such a fashion that he understood and since then he's been avoiding me—and it's me, since then, who's been sticking to his wake."

"Why seek him out? If it's to provoke a quarrel, you know, I'd be extremely annoyed."

"No danger; I only follow him at a distance. It's because, Commandant,
I'll tell you, he's got a shady manner that I don't like, the dirty dog.
Look...under the bridge..."

"But that's...if I'm not mistaken...the one called Smith."

"Exactly, Commandant."

"And who seems to be paying court to the maid put in my sister's service,
unless it's the other way round?"

"She came here not ten minutes ago, bringing him something that he hid in
his jersey double quick."

"Some sentimental token."

"They don't have an amorous look about them, those two. I've had my eye
on him since Le Havre; we were already on board when he came back, hoisting
himself up on a bit of hawser that a comrade threw down to him. I understand
that a man might have shore leave, but since the ship's boats were going back
and forth all the time, why would the mysterious seaman do that? On top of that,
he has somber and searching eyes. In sum, he's a fellow I don't like. I believe
him to be capable of more dirty tricks, and I can do other than keep track of
him."

"Leave it, Jean. We'll be arriving soon, and as we'll be leaving the coast as
soon as we've disembarked, you won't see him again."

"That will be with please, Commandant."

"You know that we're within sight of the Sandy Hook lightship, anchored
only a few miles from the entrance to New York Bay, formed by the Hudson
estuary?"

"I've seen it, Commandant. Look, there it is...and, look!"

"What!"

"There's a ship in sight, just beyond the Sandy Hook lightship."

"What eyes you have! I have excellent eyesight, and I can't see anything.
I'll go back up the bridge and borrow the watch officer's binoculars."

Claude did exactly that. Through the instrument, he observed that the ship
in question was carrying three lights in a triangle, of which the positional
lights—of which the green was visible to his right and the red to his left—
formed the base and a white light the apex. He concluded that it was a steamer
heading toward the *Astrea*, and following exactly the same course in an opposite
direction.

He signaled his discovery to the officers, who did not even take the trouble
to confirm it, the appearance of a distant ship being of absolutely no importance
in current navigation.

It was not the same when, a quarter of an hour later, when the two boats
were a good deal closer, a rocket went up from that same ship, streaking the
night with a thin luminous track, and, almost immediately, a rocket responded

almost immediately from the Astrea, bursting above the bridge into white, red and green stars.

Captain Burner leaned over the rail of the bridge immediately and shouted, angrily: "What are you doing, Smith?"

The man addressed, who had returned to the helm, replied: "The rocket at sea aft is obviously a distress signal. I fired immediately to signal *seen*."

"Who gave you the order?"

"I thought it a duty..."

"You thought wrong! It's a serious failure of discipline, unforgivable on the part of a serious and punctilious helmsman like you. And why have you fired, instead of an ordinary rocket, a particular rocket used as a recognition signal between ships of our line?"

"In my haste I mistook the compartment in the locker."

"You'll be punished! To begin with, when we arrive in port, you'll be confined to quarters until further notice."

The punishment must have been indifferent to helmsman Smith, because his lips creased in an ironic smile.

"Steer for that ship," the Commandant commanded him. Addressing Williamson, he added: "We'll go and see what they want, inasmuch as it won't take us off course. If it really is in distress, as its speed and the fact that's its steering away from land doesn't seem to indicate, it'll renew its signal rocket at brief intervals—which doesn't seem to be its intention."

For ten minutes, the two steamers continued to head toward one another. Now, scarcely half a mile separated them. To judge by the height of the position lights above the water, the ship maintaining the course opposite to that of the *Astrea* had to be a large cargo-vessel, unladen—which rendered the eastward course that it was following rather abnormal, for a ship would not use up the amount of coal necessary to cross the Atlantic without at least being compensated by the price of the cargo it was transporting.

Captain Burner thought about that, and expected to see the cargo-vessel change course at any moment toward the north or the south, heading toward some American port.

Nothing of the sort: the distance was still decreasing. Captain Burner ordered the helmsman: "Two quarters to starboard!"

The "quarter" of the compass being 11° 15' of the circle of the "rose," steering two quarters to starboard would reset a course west-north-west instead of west. According to the international shipping regulations, the cargo-vessel ought to do the same, and both of them, both steering to the right like road-vehicles on a boulevard, would mutually move out of one another's path.

But Smith, doubtless distracted, delayed turning the helm until he had received a second order from the captain. It was high time, because the ships were only a few lengths apart...

Damn! What did that mean! The cargo-vessel was steering to port instead of starboard, and, in consequence, continuing to head for the yacht instead on turning away from her!

With a brief blast of the siren, Burner emphasized his regulation maneuver to starboard, announcing it to the other vessel. The latter did not respond, and did not rectify its false maneuver.

On the bridge, everyone held their breath. Even the imperturbable Williamson went pale, and recoiled instinctively.

"My God! Are they dead or mad in there?" cried the captain.

Bounding to the apparatus communicating his orders to the engine-room—which the mechanics call the "telegraph"—he manipulated the levers feverishly, almost howling, as if he could be heard in the bowels of the ship: "Stop! Reverse engines, full steam!"

The yacht shivered in its entirety under the gigantic effort of the propellers churning the water in reverse—but what could the *Astrea*'s maneuver, still too slow, achieve against the massive cargo-vessel traveling at twelve or fourteen knots?

Captain Burner, who, until then, had been acting in conformity with the regulations, understood that, since obedience in the presence of a ship that was doing the opposite would only render the imminent catastrophe inevitable, the moment had come to infringe them audaciously.

Stiffening himself, and calling all his mariner's composure to his aid, he measured with his eye the short distance that separated his vessel from the adverse and menacing prow, told himself, in less time that a lightning-bolt takes to cleave the darkness, that, the collision no longer being avoidable, he had just enough seconds left at least to attenuate the terrible consequences of the formidable impact.

The means to do that was that as the two ships came together, to provoke a glancing collision, scraping one hull against the other—which would very nearly demolish one side of each vessel, but might perhaps only inflict rips above the flotation line, which would avoid fatal inrushes of water.

Bounding to his telegraph that captain shouted, at the top of his voice: "Full speed ahead!" and "Hard to port!"

At the risk of breaking everything, the propellers changed the direction of their rotation almost instantly, producing such a pressure that the yacht almost capsized—but the rudder, in the hands of helmsman Smith, instead of turning left, as ordered, steered to the right...

Instead of her bow, it was her flank that the unfortunate *Astrea* offered fully to the high prow of the cargo ship, which advanced with frightful speed through the darkness.

There was a sinister clamor aboard the yacht. Everyone, understanding that they were doomed, remained motionless, breathless and horrified.

Only Claude Rolland had leapt backwards, slid down the stairway to the deck, and run like a madman to the lead of the stairwell descending to the cabins. With a few catlike bounds he had reached his sister's cabin, the door of which gave way under the impact of his shoulder.

He had grabbed his sister, who was sitting up in bed anxiously, and carried her away at a run, scaled the stairway as if he had not been bearing his precious burden and emerged on to the deck at the exact movement when, with a bang, and formidable and frightful ripping sound, the prow of the cargo-vessel opened a gaping wound in the side of the ship, through which the sea flooded.

On board, in the midst of indescribable chaos, people were rushing in all directions, some running for the boats, others toward the high iron wall of the ramming ship, in order to try to scale it and find a refuge from death.

The latter were immediately disappointed in their supreme hope, for as soon as the impact had occurred, the rammer disengaged, reversing its engine. It did not, however, depart into the night entirely alone. Smith, as soon as he had delivered the fatal twist of the wheel, doubtless terrified, had run to the exposed hull and, at the moment of impact, had grabbed a rope that, surely by some miracle, was hanging down from the murderous prow, and had started climbing....

But he felt his legs seized. A supple body, with an apelike agility, passed over his back, climbed on to his shoulders, and hoisting itself up by the strength of its wrists, arrived on the deck of the cargo-ship ahead of him.

Smith reached it in his turn, and coolly hauled aboard the rope to which he owed his salvation, and might perhaps have saved some of his comrades.

It was then that the rammer disengaged, abandoning the yacht, which, no longer being sustained and already having three meters of water inside her hull, rapidly heeled over to port.

Claude Rolland, his sister having fainted from shock in his arms, sensing the *Astrea* going down with an anguishing rapidity, judged that within two or three minutes the yacht would have sunk completely. Although he had never been shipwrecked—at least at sea—he thought about the whirlpool in which it was vital not to allow himself to be caught. He did not hesitate, but climbed over the side and, holding his sister solidly in his left arm, squeezed her nostrils and blocked her mouth with his right hand, and leapt into the sea.

Returning to the surface, he sustained the beautiful colorless face above the water, and started swimming vigorously with his right arm.

His objective was, having got far enough away not to fear being dragged down in the turbulence the ship would produce as it was engulfed by the waves, to get closer to the cargo-ship—the only place from which help might come.

He swam courageously, but, hampered by his clothing and having an inert body to support, he rapidly became fatigued. Soon, following the din of a violent explosion, a wave that seemed enormous lifted him up...

That was all. He understood that the yacht had just sunk, and that, if he had delayed in diving into the water, he would have been dragged down with it.

At hazard, conserving his strength, he began calling for help, in case a boat put into the water by the cargo-vessel was within range of his voice.

To his second appeal, it was a familiar voice that replied, from close by, saying with the greatest calmness: "I believe, Monsieur Rolland, that we have very little chance of getting out of this. However, if I can be useful, I'm at your disposal."

"Monsieur Williamson! You jumped too?"

"From the footbridge, as soon as I understood that the yacht was about to sink. I preferred to avoid the explosion that would not have left me the time to collect myself before passing into eternity. I wanted to delay the annoying moment slightly."

"It's necessary to fight until the end, and in order to fight better, don't give up hope."

"I'm envisaging the situation coldly, that's all. Oh! But you've saved Miss Edmée! Toby followed me—we can help you to sustain her."

"Thanks—I'm beginning to have difficulty."

"Don't talk any more—it saps the strength. Toby! Come here!'"

"Yes sir!"

Williamson and his groom took charge of the poor unconscious Edmée, which permitted Claude, relieved, to get a little of his strength back. Futile, alas, for the shipwreck victims had distinctly seen the dark mass of the cargo-boat vanishing into the darkness. They were abandoned!

Devoid of hope, silent now and increasingly breathless, the two men and the adolescent swam for nearly twenty minutes, taking turns to sustain the inert body of the young woman. They were at the limit of their strength, especially Claude, who had expended an excess of energy since the very beginning.

Feeling himself becoming numb, the young man did not want to let himself sink without uttering one last appeal. He collected his last forces, and, vain as the attempt seemed, cried "Help!" one last time.

A sudden start electrified him, rendering him an energy of which he had thought himself incapable. Distantly, and as if involuntarily muffled, a human voice replied to him: "Shh! Don't shout! Hold on! I'm coming!"

3. Maritime Disasters

It was a Wednesday evening when the steam-yacht *Astrea*, in consequence of the collision within sight of the American coast, went down with all hands.

Two days later, the Yankee newspapers published the following dispatch:

Norfolk, Virginia, 20 November. Entered port last night, the cargo-boat Awful, *registered at two thousand four hundred tons, Captain Lodgehead, coming from New York to pick up cargo for Montevideo. The* Awful*'s hull was broken four feet above the flotation line and the sheet metal had been staved in be-*

tween the prow and the sides of the bow. The captain declared that he had been in collision in the open sea off Cape May the previous night with an unknown steamship which, in spite of his warnings and by virtue of a maneuver contrary to the rules of navigation, had thrown itself into his path.

The unknown ship sank in less than four minutes, and although the Awful *remained on the site of the disaster and put her boats to sea with all possible haste, one of which was lost, no crewman from the sunken vessel could be recovered, nor any wreckage permitting a conjecture as to the nationality and provenance of the ship, which must have gauged approximately fifteen hundred tons and appeared to be heavily laden.*

The Awful *will be put in dry dock today in order to repair the serious damage, and will not be able to moor at the Jamestown docks to embark her cargo for at least a fortnight.*

Captain Lodgehead is a well-known and highly reputed mariner, and there can be no doubt that his conduct must have been eminently correct in this unfortunate circumstance.

Although that dispatch informs us of the names of the ramming cargo-vessel and its captain, it contains, on the other hand, several serious counterfactual statements, deliberate or otherwise.

The disaster had not taken place in the open sea of Cape May, situated to the south of New York State, at the eastern extremity of the bay formed by the mouth of the Delaware, but near the entrance to New York Bay—which is to say, a hundred and sixty-five miles further north. It had not been caused by a false maneuver by the vessel that was rammed, but by the rammer. Finally, it was not true to say that the *Awful* had attempted to save the crew, since it had sailed away thereafter, fleeing that strict duty of humanity, or to affirm that no one from the *Astrea* had survived the wreck, since Smith, and...someone else...had scaled the high wall of the cargo-boat. As for the indications so opposed to reality given regarding the appearances of the sunken ship, it leaps to the eyes that they were tendentious. There is no reason, moreover, to be astonished that Captain Lodgehead, being unable, in his own conscience, to consider himself as other than wholly responsible for the disaster, desired, by means of interested precaution, to mislead the subsequent research of the Naval Department.

It is well-known that from one shore of the ocean to the other, pilots embarking in proximity to one of the terminal ports of the transatlantic liners, bring aboard fresh news in the form of the latest newspapers to appear at the moment when they take to the sea. It was naturally thus for the Compagnie Générale Transatlantique's *Touraine*, when, the following night, it arrived in its turn within sight of the Sandy Hook lightship.

The article concerning the collision that had claimed so many victims in the very area that the liner was traversing, leapt to the eyes of all the passengers, and particularly to those of Jonathan Loeb, departed from Le Havre with Gré-goire de Montalpé three days after the yacht chartered by the billionaire.

He read the dispatch from Norfolk carefully and, without a word or a single feature of his thin face having twitched, held out the newspaper to his companion, marking the passage to which he was calling his attention with his thumb.

The latter read the article conscientiously and, raising his eyes to look at the Yankee with an uncomprehendingly interrogative gaze, said: "It's doubtless a misfortune, but why are you drawing my particular attention to it?"

"You don't understand?"

"I understand that a cargo-ship has sunk another, probably quite a long way away from here. It's an accident that happens all too often, alas."

Loeb shrugged his shoulders. Standing up unhurriedly, he took Montalpé by the arm, drew him out of the lounge full of passengers and then on to the promenade deck. There, he made sure that no one was close enough to overhear him, and in his hoarse and caustic voice he said: "You haven't understood, then, that you're alone in the ranks, once Old Sinker is out of the way, relative to the inheritance on sufferance of which you have need?"

"You're not going to tell me that the ship lost with all hands was..."

"His."

"It says a cargo ship, not a yacht, and places the accident off Cape May, which isn't near here, so far as I know, and, in consequence not on Williamson's route."

"Would you have wanted Captain Lodgehead to sign his ramming? I couldn't demand such a stupidity of him."

"You? It's frightful, what you're suggesting to me! Obviously, you're making fun of me. How could you have...too bad, I'll say the word...commanded a disaster to occur while we were in mid-Atlantic?"

"Didn't I tell you, on the evening after our arrival in Le Havre, that I'd taken action?"

De Montalpé recoiled instinctively.

"It...was sufficient for you..."

"Poor brain, which hasn't yet understood the power I have!"

"Brrr...I've got cold chills down my back. But I don't understand..."

"Not one word more here. Everything will be explained to you in a few hours. Let's go back to the lounge. Come on!"

De Montalpé followed his terrible companion, but almost at a distance, as a fearful dog follows its master, in whose hand it can see the cruel whip.

Not another word was exchanged between them until the *Touraine* was moored at its arrival dock. As soon as the gangplank had been set up, they were among the first to descend to the shore. On the quay, in the first rank of the waiting porters, there was a man in a check suit with a scarf around his neck and a bowler hat pulled down over his eyes, to whom Loeb made an imperceptible sign.

That man, rendered almost unrecognizable by his change of costume was the helmsman Smith. He followed the two travelers at a distance, taking the ferries and trams at the same time as them, and rejoined them when they stopped, in an Avenue near Central Park, outside a door above which two luminous words were legible: *Salvation Army*.

Loeb rang the bell.

A thin, ageless woman, clad entirely in black opened the door, and, at the sight of Jonathan, stood aside respectfully.

"Come with us, Colonel," said Lobanief's enemy to her, in a low voice.

"At your orders, General," she replied, closing the door and triple-locking it.

An elevator carried Loeb and his three companions up to the third floor. There, with a key extracted from the depths of one of his pockets, he opened a door, turned an electric commutator, traversed a severely-furnished antechamber and went into a drawing-room that Williamson himself would not have denied, so much expense did the furniture and wall-hangings solemnly proclaim.

Jonathan threw his damp overcoat and hat on to a silken pouffe, sat down and put is his dirty boots on a sofa, and, without wasting time inviting his companions to sit down, addressed himself to Smith:

"Well?"

"It's done, Master."

"Lodgehead?"

"Received your encrypted order cabled from France and didn't hesitate, grave as the requested action was. He hastened the unloading of his ship, put to sea on Wednesday evening, just in time to meet the *Astrea* at sea, which I identified to him by means of a rocket, and which I offered sideways on to his prow by means of a false maneuver."

"You were able to get aboard the *Awful* immediately?"

"Thanks to a rope lowered from the bow."

"Alone?"

"One man, whom I wasn't able to recognize, took advantage of it, passing over my back, but the most scrupulous search mounted on board proved that he hadn't taken refuge there. He was climbing like a madman, and must have fallen back into the sea when he reached the smooth part of the side, by virtue of the shock produced when the *Awful* disengaged."

"What's this lost boat the newspapers are talking about?"

"An unconscious and quite natural impulse on the part of two crewmen who, without waiting for orders, wanted to put it into the sea to help the shipwreck victims. In his haste, one of them, according to the other, cut the supporting ropes, and the boat, falling nose-first, must have sunk immediately, for there was no trace of it when we turned south."

"It definitely sank?"

"There's not the shadow of a doubt about it?"

"So the loss of the *Astrea* is definitely total?"

"Absolutely. Complete surprise, explosion of the boilers, and lightning disappearance, having not had time to embark a single boat. I'm the sole survivor."

"Do you hear that, Monsieur de Montalpé?"

The Parisian dandy was unable to reply; he was literally frozen with horror. Loeb, as cool and calm as if it were a matter of a child's toy boat sunk in the pond in the Tuileries, went on: "Pass on to Grace Strangestorm."

The woman in black started abruptly.

"Yes, Colonel Camden," said Jonathan, lifting his booted feet on to the arm of sofa, "it is indeed a matter of the adjutant-major that you accommodated last year. A fortunate hazard dictated that I found her embarked aboard the *Astrea* as a chambermaid. Reply now, Smith."

"Oh, the worthy girl," said the helmsman, with a hint of emotion. "From the departure onwards she knew that she had to die before reaching the American coast, and didn't betray herself by an instant's weakness!"

"A martyr to our faith! Our Lord will give her a throne of light in Paradise," murmured Miss Camden, in a tremulous voice.

"She obeyed, as was her duty," Loeb articulated, dryly. "But she had a particular and capital mission. Did she complete it?"

"She told me to give you this." Smith held out to the chief of the Great Council the flat metallic box that that the chambermaid, a Salvationist officer, had given him less than an hour before the catastrophe.

Loeb, to the disconcerted amazement of his subordinates in the sect and the secret society, who had always been seen draped in a mantle of rude calm and brutally authoritarian coldness, so economical with his gestures, the living negation thus far of any impulse sentiment, bounded to his powerful feet and fell upon the proffered object like a wild beast on its prey, took possession of it, and held it momentarily in his vast, bony hands, which were trembling, his features contracted and his staring eyes flashing.

With a prompt gesture, he tore off the lid of the box and, running to a sidetable, he pulled from its protective sheath the very map that Grace Strangestorm had "lent" to Williamson and his friends.

He did not even look at the map. Taking a knife from his pocket, he nervously sliced through a corner and, that section showing that the map was doubleply, he carefully slid his blade between the two leaves, which he separated from one another, with the aid of a slit rapidly made along the four sides. Leaving the map, he took the sheet of the lining, held it up before his anxious eyes and, observing a single minuscule black dot thereon, uttered a kind of roar of triumph.

"Finally!"

Heedless of the silent attention of which he was the object, he first extended the map on the table, placed the lining sheet exactly on top of it, set the tip of his knife on the black dot and leaned on it heavily, saying, in a tone of grim joy: "There!"

Then, with a single gesture, he tore the sheet away from around the blade, threw it on the ground, and avidly leaned over the point on the map pierced by the tip of the knife. Having done that, he straightened up, replaced the knife in his pocket, folded up the map methodically, put that in his pocket too, and, resuming his customary mask of harsh coldness, turned round.

"Grace Strangestorm fulfilled her mission superbly and executed the orders of the commandment. If it had been possible for her to survive, another double stripe would have been her legitimate recompense. Where she is, I can do no more for her, Let's not mention her again.

"You, Smith, make arrangements to be in New York on the twelfth of January, the day of the great convent. I'll speak to you and the Great Council, and you'll see how grateful I am for services as exceptional and secret as yours.

"For the moment, go to the house of Barthleit, the surgeon, and tell him that I'm going to send him a client who mustn't be seen by anyone. It's you who'll introduce him in the manner that will be indicated to you. Go.

"You, Colonel, return to your apartment and remain at my disposal."

As soon as Jonathan and de Montalpé were alone, the later exclaimed; "Damn! You have means and ways of action, you! You did well not to let me glimpse them in Paris or Le Havre, for I'd never have gone along with it."

"Monsieur de Montalpé," said the Yankee, slowly, string at his companion, "know that when one enters into the direct zone of attraction of Jonathan Loeb, one always 'goes along' and one 'goes along' as far as he desires."

"Hang on!"

"Have you forgotten your oath of apprenticeship?"

"Oh, those oaths only engage one for form's sake. It's a simple means, a precaution, a guarantee—insurance, if you wish—against the contingencies of life, in our epoch of political and philosophical evolution."

"You can see that Smith, who thus far hadn't put a foot wrong in his duties as a mariner, didn't understand it that way."

"You Americans, perhaps, but in France..."

"You're no longer in France, and to employ your language, you're under the blade of my guillotine."

"You think so?"

"I demand passive obedience."

"Permit me..."

"Without restriction."

"I'm not a Grace Strangestorm. I have no vocation for martyrdom, myself."

"I don't know what I shall have to demand of you, but whatever it is, you'll obey whether you like it or not."

"Threats! You know, after your trick regarding the collision with the *Astrea*, it's necessary not to take such a haughty tone. There are judges in the United States."

Loeb uttered a dry burst of laughter, as trenchant as a blade. "Jonathan Loeb makes his own law—otherwise, he wouldn't be the 'Powerful.'"

"Ta ta ta. What if I took it into my head to spill the beans?"

"You'd lose your head, Monsieur de Montalpé, before having had time to open your mouth dangerously."

That was said in a tone that made the dandy shiver. Adopting a tone of coldly ironic bonhomie even more frightening for his interlocutor than the harshly authoritarian one in which he had begun, he went on: "That said for our guidance. I'm certain that you won't ever force me to resort to such extreme means. So, a truce on idle words, with which we don't have time to waste. We're awaited at the surgeon's."

"You have an operation to be carried out?"

"On you."

"What? But I'm not ill. I don't want..."

"Don't worry. It might be a little long, but not too painful and not at all dangerous."

"Oh! No joking..."

"I never joke."

"What do you want to do make of me?"

"A satisfied heir, as I promised you."

"Are you going to explain?"

"No. Get your coat and hat, and let's go."

"But..."

"Enough! I think I've made you understand that I expect to be obeyed without question!"

Grégoire de Montalpé was prodigiously anxious, but also checkmated. He dispensed with any further protest, and, pale and with an ill-assured step, followed the master out of the drawing-room.

Before going out, Loeb had rung. He found Miss Camden on the landing and said to her: "I won't be coming back here before midday, before leaving New York for an indeterminate time. In case anything important comes up, telegraph me at..." He stopped, reflected, and then, while tracing a few brief lines on a page of his notebook, he went on: "No, not you. With an adversary such as Williamson was, it's necessary to guard even against the improbable. Miss Camden, you're coming with us."

The Salvation Army Colonel could not dissimulate a sudden pallor. In the end of Grace Strangestorm she had had a further proof of the risks involved in being charged with "missions" by the redoubtable Major-General. High-ranking, however, she had the example of discipline before her. She contented herself with objecting: "What about the Temple? And the service of the Army Corps?"

Loeb tore out the sheet of paper and handed it to her, replying: "Here are the orders. Pass command over to Major Klebbs. He's second to you on the general staff in New York?"

"Yes, General."

"Wait for us at daybreak at the Western Railroad Station on the right bank of the Hudson. No luggage: we'll make arrangements on the way."

In a tone that had become firm again, the Colonel replied: "Yes, General."

4. A Miraculous Rescue

Shortly before nine o'clock in the morning, having crossed the Hudson River by ferry, Loeb, followed by Grégoire de Montalpé—who was very pale, his back arched, his eyes feverish and his features revealing acute suffering—arrived at the Western Railroad Station, where he signaled to Miss Camden, who had been standing sentinel for some time, to come and join him.

As all three of them went into the hall, heading for the ticket window, a young and thickset individual with leather gaiters, coifed with a large "cowboy hat" and enveloped in one of those vast ulsters that are the glory of Anglo-Saxon travelers, suppressed an exclamation on seeing them and, pulling his hat swiftly down over his eyes, murmured between his teeth: "Thunder! It appears that I'm fated to run into that bird, here, as in Le Havre. It's a pity that I daren't give chase, since, when one hasn't been seen, it's necessary not to try to get too close. But have no fear—if it only depends on me, your account will be settled, and you'll lose nothing by waiting, word of a matelot!"

You will have recognized Jean Guitard, alias Furet, the faithful mariner so attached to his former expedition-leader, Claude Rolland.

How did he come to be there, very much alive, and not at the bottom of the Atlantic with the yacht *Astrea*, Williamson and his dear masters, Claude and Edmée?

That is what will be explained without delay.

Let us go back to the moment when Williamson, Claude and Toby, sustaining Edmée's inanimate body, exhausting their last strength struggling against the cold and fatigue, in order not to let themselves sink, heard a voice call out to them in the darkness, telling them to keep quiet and hold on for a few minutes more.

We have seen the poor shipwreck victims, at the end of their tether, recover their courage and hope at the same time. Galvanizing their exhaustion, if one might put it like that, they turned in the direction of the voice, which continued its encouragements, saying: "Come on, one last effort! I'm coming! I'm pushing a float in front of me made of three oars tied together. That will give you a rest while waiting for something better."

Alas, how distant that voice sounded! Would the unfortunates have the time and the strength to meet up with that providential aid?

164

They thought it was still far away when a few brasses away, in the slight splashing of the black water, one of the ends of the blessed bundle of oars suddenly appeared. Breathless, kicking with their heels, they reached it and clung to it, the unconscious Edmée in her brother's arms and her head slumped on his shoulder.

"Good! Just in time!" was all that Williamson said, uttering a sigh of relief.

"There," said their savior, in a low voice. "Everybody stop moving; it's a matter of not letting the cold get us now!"

"You, Jean?" said Claude, finally finding the power of speech, and already having recognized the mariner's voice.

"Yes, me, Commandant. My God, the poor demoiselle! Not dead, at least?"

"I…I don't think so."

"Give her to me, so that I can hold her up. I've been able to hear you for some time, Commandant, but one doesn't move very quickly when one's swimming with a boat in tow."

"What? You've brought us a boat? Oh, you're a brave fellow, Master Furet! I can't see it. Where is it?"

"Not a quarter of a cable away. Except that it's only sticking out of the water by three fingers. It's full of water. You understand why it took me such a long time to tow it this far."

"Full of water? That's very inconvenient."

"It's very fortunate, in fact, Monsieur Mining King. Otherwise, we wouldn't have it, for I wouldn't still be alive and wouldn't have been able to bring it to you."

"What do you mean?"

"I'll explain in a little while. Let's get to it first. The three of you push the float toward it. I'll stay at the front to guide it."

The shipwreck-victims took ten minutes to reach the launch floating at surface level, which even the intelligent pilot had difficulty locating.

Jean Guitard recommended that his companions remain silent; they maintained themselves on the side of the boat while he hoisted himself aboard cautiously at the stern. Immediately, using his beret for want of anything else, he started emptying the water from the boat with thrusts of his arms. As soon as he judged that it could support the weight of a second person without danger of capsizing the launch, he helped Toby aboard, who followed his example, scooping with his hat, which the impeccable groom had retained in spite of everything he had gone through.

After several long minutes of effort, the water inside had descended beneath the level of the benches. Then the mariner, assisted by the groom, hauled the icy and inert body of poor Edmée aboard, and laid her down to dry out on a bench. Then they both resumed their labor.

165

Finally, Williamson first, and then Claude Rolland, were able to come to join them, but, without lending any assistance to their endeavor, the rich Yankee having sat tranquilly down at the rear and the engineer devoting all his efforts to the attempt to bring his sister back to life, by means of vigorous massage.

The launch was empty before he was able to bring the slightest warmth back to the young woman's lovely and supple body. She remained as unconscious and cold as a beautiful antique marble.

Claude was in despair, hot tears mingling with the sweat that was running down his face in spite of the low temperature of the November night, born as much of anguish as fatigue. Jean, his task terminated, dared not propose that he assist him in his tortuous endeavor, out of respect for decency. It was Claude who invited him to do so.

The young mariner took off his short woolen blouse with a high collar, and then his jersey, and gave them to Toby in order that he could wring them out, until not a drop of water remained within them. Opening his shirt, he applied the poor little bare feet to his chest, the contact of which was as painful as if he had placed two blocks of ice on his skin.

Claude understood the naively-set example, and did for the arms and hands what Jean was doing for the feet; leaning over the poor child, he also strove to warm up her neck with his breath.

At the rear, Williamson, numb, was shivering on his bench. Abruptly, he stood up. "By Jove!" he said. "It would be too stupid to catch pleurisy now; let's make a useful reaction."

He came forward, arrived at the middle bench where Edmée was lying and asked: "Well? Is she coming round?"

"Alas, no!" groaned the unfortunate brother, sobbing and raising his head. "She must be completely dead."

At that moment, the first ray of light from the waning moon, outlined the eastern horizon and came to strike Edmée's closed eyes and mortally pale features.

"Oh! Oh!! Oh!!!" said Williamson, repetitively. And he added, in a penetrating tone that no one had heard in his voice before: "It will be a great pity if she's dead; she's regally beautiful, that young woman!"

Momentarily, he contemplated the soft and grave marmoreal face, framed by the golden algae of her wet hair...but the cold made his teeth chatter again, and self-consciousness reclaimed its exclusively empire over him. He took note of the fact that his admiringly contemplative pity was not increasing the beautiful victim's chances of a return to existence in any way, and that no one had any desire to go and keep her company in the icy shades of death. In consequence, he took possession of two heavy oars and stared rowing with a hysterical fury.

At the appearance of the first ray of moonlight caressing Edmée's face, Jean Guitard had experienced an exceedingly sharp sensation, with which the resplendent, solemn and sad beauty of the rigid and icy features of the young woman had nothing to do. It was a sensation of violent disquiet, which was translated into a glance of extreme anxiety directed at the sea in a southerly direction—but it disappeared immediately. Under the white radiance of the nocturnal star, the ship that had caused the catastrophe only appeared as a minuscule distant silhouette cut out in black against the silvery and scarcely undulating surface of the sea. At such a distance it was utterly improbable that the little launch was perceptible, and the mariner breathed out, relieved of a dread that had not quit him for an instant during the time—nearly an hour—since the yacht had been swallowed up.

Claude was at the limit of his strength and his mental suffering. No sign of warmth was manifest in his beloved sister, and his eyes, drowned, ardently fixed upon her, could only see her through a mist.

"It's finished!" he murmured, dolorously. "It's finished! She won't wake up again."

Desperately, he struck his ear against the icy young breast, and suddenly raised his head, abruptly, transfigured, his eyes wild with crazy joy.

"The heart! The heart's beating! How faintly...but it's beating! She's alive!"

Jean held out his jersey to his commandant, which Toby had finished wringing out, so conscientiously that it seemed almost dry. Quickly, aided by the groom and not without difficulty, Claude passed it over his sister's inert torso, and, taking off his wet jacket and waistcoat. Seized her in his arms and pressed her against him, addressing touching maternal words to her, which implored her not to remain any longer in the limbo of unconsciousness and apparent death.

Finally, the long velvety lashes twitched and the eyelids lifted effortfully, allowing a vague fearful gaze to slip through. The pretty lips parted slightly, having become less pale, to allow the passage, in a fragile breath, of a few scarcely-perceptible words.

"I'm cold...where am I?"

Bewildered by joy, the young man lifted the resuscitated loved one from the bench, and sat down in the bottom of the boat, holding her on his lap, while Jean enveloped the numb gracious body as best he could in his matelot's blouse and Claude's jacket, duly wrung out.

Williamson, his reaction now complete, had stopped rowing, and was watching the unexpected resurrection with a very keen interest. Then he too took off his jacket and gave it to the groom to be wrung out, so that it could be added to the means of bringing back a little warmth to Edmée. It was the first time in his life that the billionaire had made an altruistic gesture.

Under that multiple improvised covering, she gradually warming up and he exhausted by fatigue and emotion, the fraternal couple fell asleep.

167

Jean and Toby, henceforth free, took up oars, following the example of the Mining King, who, to compensate for the loss of warmth caused by the reduction in his clothing, had resumed rowing energetically.

The matelot had taken up his position between the last bench and the stern of the boat, manipulating the most powerful oar—a scull—and steering the boat as skillfully as if it were a rudder. With a few vigorous thrusts he had brought the skiff round in a semicircle, and the latter, which Williamson had moved a few cables toward the America shore, became to glide instead away from the Sandy Hook lightship.

The King of Mines perceived that.

"What are you doing, Master Jean?"

"Our duty is to make sure that none of our unfortunate companions survived the shipwreck in addition to us."

"A pointless waste of time. I listened while you were occupied in recalling Miss Rolland to life. No cry for help reached me. The entire crew of the *Astrea* has gone to the bottom. Evidently, that's extremely regrettable, but we can't do anything about it. Let's take care of ourselves. Set a course for Sandy Hook, my lad, and..."

He interrupted himself. His port-side oar had encountered an unexpected resistance.

"What's that?" he said.

The mariner had leaned over the side. Swiftly, he resized the boat's landing-gaffe, saying: "Your blade has encountered a body floating just beneath the surface. Hold on, while I hook it...come and help me haul it aboard, Toby."

"Not necessary. Just see who it is."

"It's a woman...the chambermaid...the eyes are vitreous; she's definitely dead, poor creature. Shall I let her go?"

"No!" said the billionaire, urgently. To his groom, he said: "Toby, help him haul her in."

"Are we going to take her to New York?" asked the mariner.

"Not your business...I only want..."

Without completing his thought, Williamson pulled in his oars. Moved cautiously toward the rear and, with a preoccupied expression, searched for the dead woman's pocket and rummaged therein. He pulled out a coin-purse, which he replaced, and a little wallet, which he kept.

"Let her go," he commanded, "And let's get moving."

Grace Strangestorm's corpse was reintegrated with its damp tomb, and the boat resumed its slow progress, briefly interrupted.

"Tell me now, lad," said the Mining King, addressing Jean, "how you were so fortunately able to bring us this boat."

In sentences punctuated by the rhythmic effort of plying the oar, Jean Guitard, alias Furet, explained.

"It came of keeping watch on the helmsman Smith...and I wasn't wrong, as you'll see...something pushed me...and there were the sideways glances he gave me...to keep my eye on him. I was under the footbridge...not far from the helmsman's post...when the cargo-boat came toward us...and I wondered if it wasn't doing it on purpose..."

Williamson fixed the mariner with his gray eyes, with extreme attention.

The other continued: "When Captain Burner...ordered 'Hard to port!' I distinctly saw Smith...push his assistant away...and spin the wheel...as hard as he could to starboard...offering the side of the ship to the rammer."

"That Smith...good! Go on," said Williamson, phlegmatically.

"My blood ran cold...I leapt to the helm...too late for a thrust in accordance with the order to do anything to avoid the crash. I saw Smith quit the post at a run...I bounded after the bandit like a tiger...I saw him, at the moment when the *Astrea* was gutted...grab a rope dangling from the bow of the cargo-ship...and not by chance, no one will ever convince me of that...and quit the deck of the *Astrea*, hoisting himself up...

"With one bound, I grab the rope myself...and then that scoundrel Smith by the legs...I hoist myself up after him, sure that he wouldn't let go...I pass over his hips, his back, his shoulders...I grab the rope above him...I get to the rail of the cargo-ship first...and jump on to the deck...I run like a madman to the nearest boat...I can see its silhouette hanging from the davits...I cut the seals with my knife, tear away the tarp. A crewman's there...I shout at him, in English: 'Launch in the water, now! Captain's order!'

"The man helps me shove the boat out over the side, above the water...I jump into it immediately...and while the other unwinds the rope from a pulley-block, I cut through one of the safety-ropes with my knife...one turn of the suspension-rope...on to the second safety-rope...which runs free...the boat tips up, nose down to the sea, and I find myself taking a header into the big drink...the shock has made the comrade up top let go, and the support rope unravels...the boat falls, nose first...while I'm coming back to the surface...

"It was a very lucky that it had fallen...given that, by a chance I can't yet explain...it floated, full of water...I say very lucky because the men on the cargo-ship...which, after having backed up to disengage, put on full steam to run away...thought that it had sunk, while it and I passed under the canopy in the wake of the propeller...and they didn't worry about it any more...otherwise...

"Finally, I heard...and the rest you know...I steered for the Commandant's appeals...not making fast progress...in spite of my efforts...because it's not easy to tow something like two tons of water...understanding from the voice...that the poor Commandant...was near to letting himself sink...I tied the oars together to make the float...and while replying very quietly...in case anyone on the cargo-ship might hear...I shoved the float toward you...that's it."

Williamson had not interrupted the faithful mariner for a second time. After a moment's silence, he contented himself with saying, his voice having become calm, indifferent and bank again: "Good. You're a clever fellow." A moment later, he added: "I owe you my life. I'll pay."

"Oh, that, no, damn it!" exclaimed the mariner, his tone brusque and angry.

"Why not?" demanded the billionaire, in a tone once again surprised. "I value it highly."

"First of all, for me, adrift on the big drink, one man's worth as much as another. And then, to offer a French mariner money for having done his duty in working to save shipwreck victims, is to humiliate and offend him. Where we come from, those services, when there's a great deal at stake, are rewarded by a bit of ribbon, by which the minister distinguishes those who've proved that they're not afraid to drink a cup. And then, to tell the truth, you know, I can't say that I wasn't also thinking about you, but only in third place. My Commandant and the pretty mam'zelle Edmée, so good and not proud, came first. If, of the three of you, I'd only been able to save two, it would be you who'd be in the soup."

The plump face of the Mining King blossomed in satisfaction. "All right!" he said. "You belong to the same free-minded nation as those Rollands." He added, as an aside: "Well, I accept the debt to be settled *sine die*." Then, in a louder voice: "Understood. Enough about the past. Let's look forward. Have you been to New York before?"

"A little. I know the harbor and the rivers like my pocket. Before going into the service I was a novice, and then an able seaman, aboard a four-master that spent six weeks there for repairs."

"All right! Can we land by our own means, with this boat?"

"This thing? A little heavy, but a first-rate model. If I were sure of a crossing as calm as the one that just finished so badly, and could scrounge a little canvas, I could take you all the way to Havana in her."

"Perfect, lad. I have reasons for landing, not in New York or Brooklyn, but, for example, at Newark on the Passaic River."

"Known! Through the Kill van Kull, between Staten Island and the tongue of land at Bayonne, then the bay at the mouth of the Passaic. I can see it from here.

"Oh, very good—from now on, you're our captain."

"Fine."

"At five dollars a day. I don't want you to say no. That's what I paid Captain Burner."

"Since it's a wage, I've nothing to say. Although, for the command of a transatlantic of...two tons... Anyway, so be it!"

"Only, I don't want us to stop, or to be seen too closely, until Newark, where I want to land tonight."

"That's what I would have done without you telling me," declared the young mariner, winking. "Necessary that no one has a little act of war in store for us like last night's...have no fear. Count on me."

"You're a perspicacious fellow."

"Oh, it would be necessary to have a tarp over one's eyes not to see…the sun at midday!"

"Good. You can dispose of our arms."

"Oh! Damn it, yes—I can't do everything, can I? In our situation, it's necessary that everyone puts his best foot forward. The Commandant will play his part too."

"Let him sleep a little longer. He's had a great deal of trouble and…he's keeping Miss Edmée warm."

Toby looked at his master with astonishment. He had never heard him show such concern for anyone else.

Aided by a weak current, the boat doubled the Sandy Hook lightship, a distant witness to the loss of the *Astrea*, prudently keeping a mile to the south, at about half past midnight—an approximate time that the new captain, a very modest commandant, estimated from the height of the moon, the castaways' watches having failed to resist such a long immersion.

Seeing the mariner studying the numerous lights in view with some preoccupation, Williamson asked him: "Are you hesitating over which route to take?"

"It's more a matter of studying the routes to avoid, because they're frequented by ships. In front of us, a little to starboard, is the Gedney Chanel, marked by eight luminous buoys, which we can see a trifle confusedly, as one can see a constellation like the Pleiades in the sky with the naked eye. That would be a wasps' nest for anyone wanting to pass unperceived.

"I'll set a course for the double red light of the Scotland lightship. I know that it marks the southern channel, leading via the Swash Channel to the main channel that all the big ships entering or coming out New York take. So, from there we'll head westwards, leaving the terrestrial light at Sandy Hook further and further to starboard."

"But that will take us straight on to the coast of Sandy Hook."

"That's what I want to do. I recall that on that tongue of low-lying land closing the bay of New York to the south there are isolated houses where we can, I hope, without raising the alarm, in spite of the late hour, find indispensable fresh water and food, clothes that we need badly—especially the poor demoiselle, who was surprised by the collision in her night-dress—clothes that, along with the advantage of being dry, will have that of modifying your appearance, too obviously that of shipwreck victims. Not to mention that the jersey I've given to Mademoiselle bears on the front, in red letters, the letters S.Y.A.R.S., for "Steam Yacht *Astrea*, Royal Squadron." Might as well shout out loudly who we are."

"Well reasoned. But rescue stations are numerous in the approaches to New York. I seem to remember that there are at least two on the coast of Sandy Hook. Won't we run into one?"

"Well, only if we're unlucky—but before landing, we'll take precautions. We can't appear in daylight as we are."

"You're right again. Go on."

It was at that moment that Claude Rolland woke up. In a low voice, he called on the faithful Jean to help him. With infinite precaution, they laid Edmée, finally warmed up and sleeping peacefully, in the bottom of the boat, in order that he could add his recovered strength to that of his companions in misfortune. They succeeded in doing it without waking her, covered her up as best they could, and the rowing resumed, activated by that vigorous reinforcement.

At about half past two in the morning, after having maintained an average speed of four knots since the accident, covering thirty-three kilometers in total since ten o'clock in the evening, the launch ran aground gently on the beach, not far from a modest fisherman's hut. Jean Guitard leapt on to the shore, his pockets duly ballasted with dollars by Williamson, and set out on reconnaissance.

After half an hour he came back, escorted by a family of "toilers of the sea," bringing almost everything they possessed of spare clothing, warm and dry. The mariner was carrying a heavy acquisition of which he was prouder than anything else: a mast and a dinghy-sail, with a coil of strong new rope. In addition, the fisherman's wife deposited on the sand a heavy basket full of provisions, solid and liquid.

All of it had been acquired at a high price, which ensured the silence of the couple, delighted with that stroke of luck.

While Edmée, who had woken up when they landed, exhausted but fully lucid, got dressed on the strand, assisted by the fisherman's wife and veiled by the shadows of night, the moon having been temporarily eclipsed by cloud—her brother had brought up to date with the shipwreck, which she only remembered confusedly, the rescue effected by Jean while she was unconscious, her laborious recall to life and their present situation—the men transformed themselves into Yankee fishermen and the real fisherman and Furet set up the mast and sail.

Afterwards, Jean donned the costume destined for him, and the maritime couple, after having helped the young castaway aboard, shoved the launch out to sea.

The mariner, full of joy, adjusted the rigging, set the "rudder," and, leaning slightly under the effort of a light south-easterly breeze, the launch disappeared into the calm night extended over the plaid sea.

The first light of dawn found the vessel, carried by its sail, waiting in Gravesend Bay, Long Island for the nearby light on Norton Point to go out. "Captain Furet," as Williamson had baptized Jean Guitard, having not wanted to engage by night and without a searchlight in the bottleneck some fifteen hundred meters wide—less than a thousand of which are usable for those unfamiliar with the coast—that separates the upper and lower New York bays, guarded by four forts, one of which, Fort Lafayette, is on an islet emerging from the bosom of the waves.

As soon as it was bright enough for him to steer, the boat set off and went through the bottleneck, three nautical miles long. When it entered the upper bay, its crew, who had not attracted any attention in the estuary of the Hudson, where the navigation is so intense—contented themselves with saluting the famous Statue of Liberty on Bedloe Island from a distance, skirted Staten Island to the north, went past Factoryville and Port Richmond, and traveled the entire length of the lower bay of Newark, just in time to have a frugal midday meal in a modest inn, where they represented themselves as a small party undertaking a nautical excursion. As they had taken care to rebaptize themselves in whimsical fashion for the occasion, there was no danger that the incognito of the overly famous Mining King would he unveiled.

More than ever, Williamson did not want to be recognized. As soon as daylight had permitted him to do so, he had set about attentively examining the little wallet that he had taken from the pocket of Grace Strangestorm's dress during the night, after his oar had chanced to trouble her final slumber in her vast liquid tomb. Among a few letters of no interest and pious images, he found the identity card of an officer in the Salvation Army and a piece of paper on which a few lines had been scrawled in pencil by the dead woman—Williamson had no doubt of that, although there was no signature. They read:

General, I have been faithful to the end to the discipline of our sacred cohort. Your orders have been carried out. Now, strengthened by duty passively accomplished, I await calmly the death that will not be long in coming, for I have just heard it said that the America coast is in sight. Pray that the great general in Heaven will give me a modest place among the martyrs of the faith.

The paper was folded in four, and bore the subscription: *Mr. Smith, Helmsman, Yacht* Astrea.

On reading that notes, born of the imperious desire to write that few women can resist when an idea or a sentiment occupies them wholly, and which it had not been possible to confide to the man charge with conveying it to its true addressee, a flash of enlightenment had illuminated in Williamson's eyes the full extent of the web of intrigue to which he had so nearly fallen victim—aimed at him alone, he thought, although so many others, who has nothing to do with the matter, had found death therein.

He did not hesitate for a moment to add the name of Jonathan Loeb to the title of General traced by the Salvationist. He understood that such an adversary was not to be disdained, and that when Loeb had said to him in Paris that it was war and that he would show him how he could wage it, he had not been formulating a vain threat.

The Mining King, who was fundamentally very brave, in spite of all his sybaritism and his monumental egotism, did not entertain for an instant the possibility of renouncing his expedition, or even delaying it by an hour, but he recognized the necessity of tightening his game and taking serious precautions.

The first of those, the one most immediately indicated, was to take advantage of the belief that Loeb must have that his criminal plan had succeeded—a belief that would incite him to act openly, and, in consequence, to become more vulnerable to his alerted adversary. Williamson was under no illusion; a person of his notoriety could not hope to preserve his incognito for long on American soil unless he went to ground, which he did not want to do at any price, being honor bound to respond to the appeal of Old Sinker/Lobanief. It was, however, at least necessary for him to go unnoticed for as long as possible, and that would not be easy to do, from the very start.

The castaways landed in the New World in a state of complete deprivation. Williamson had seen the liquid money that he had carried with him in the form of banknotes go down with the yacht. Ordinarily, the wealthy nomad would only have had in his possession the small sum—relatively speaking, of course—of a few tens of thousands of francs. Like all princes of fortune, he proceeded by means of checks, having deposits in all the great banks in the world.

It followed that the peerless billionaire became, so to speak, all proportions maintained, as poor as Job as soon as he could no longer show his face in the sunlight. That was a difficulty whose resolution was extremely delicate.

As they left the inn after the meal, the groom went away, and, taking every precaution to maintain the secrecy of the conversation, the billionaire made his companions party to his predicament, as well as the vanity of his efforts, since daybreak, to figure out a way of vanquishing the difficulties.

Very frankly, he did not hide anything of the discoveries he had made concerning the plot made by Loeb and the perils to which that war to the death would expose in future those who attached themselves to his paces. He proposed to Rolland and his sister that he should leave them behind, promising that if, in spite of ambushes, he succeeded in reaching their relative, he would speak to him about them.

He was profoundly surprised by the headstrong simplicity with which Edmée rejected the idea, which she qualified as desertion in the face of the enemy, and affirmed her determination of not depriving Williamson, by pusillanimously accepting his proposition, of the devoted assistance of two supporters as valiant as Claude and his matelot.

Once again, the pretty Edmée, a simple young woman discovered by chance in the French bourgeoisie, overturned all his most stubborn theories, which he judged to have been severely put to the proof by the musicality of her voice, and then, successively, by her proud susceptibility, her disinterest, her intelligence, her impressive beauty revealed under the appearances of death—and now the young feminine soul was offering the unexpected grandeur of generously virile decisions and a reckless bravery of which his trenchant philosophy and misanthropic lassitude had disdainfully deprived the weaker sex.

Decidedly, in a matter of days, the brother, and even more so the sister, had caused that American to discover…America!

And that little matelot Jean Guitard! How that child of Gaul, to whom the prideful prince of the dollar had not deigned to pay any attention previously, had imposed his alert and clear-sighted personality on him, since the day before!

In the embarrassment of the present problem, it was the mariner, once again, who found the elegant solution, in a trice. What did he need to take care of the most urgent needs?

Three or four thousand dollars, Williamson affirmed.

The latter wishing to pass temporarily for having been swallowed up with the *Astrea*, and none of his companions possessing the slightest fraction of the necessary subsidies, was it not impossible to avoid introducing a third party into the secret of the miraculous rescue? Evidently—but it was necessary that the third party in question could advance the funds discreetly, and with the security of absolute discretion.

It was with regard to that point that "Captain Furet," had an idea that seemed to him quite natural, but which was a stroke of genius.

During his sojourn in New York a few years earlier, the young mariner, who was not a man to repudiate the pious traditions in honor among worthy maritime populations, had found himself in communication with an old priest of French origin, in whom he immediately inspired a paternal sympathy.

That priest, the founder of a mission in New York State, seeing the number of his flock increasing, had dreamed of building a beautiful church, to which he would devote all his personal wealth—modest, alas, and very insufficient—but had despaired of ever accumulating donations proportional to the goal he was pursuing, his congregation being almost exclusively proletarian or belonging to the world of small tradesmen.

"That's the banker you need, Monsieur Mining King," the matelot proclaimed. "Promise him his church, and everything he has will be yours. As for guarantees; the disinterest of a man devoid of needs, the discretion of a confessor doubly sealed by his apostolic interests. Oh, if only the good God could allow us to find him again!"

"Try," concluded Williamson, giving his new captain *carte blanche.*

Finding the priest in another district of the city, not without difficulty, bringing him to Williamson—who made the deal with royal generosity—realizating and handing over the funds, took forty-eight hours.

During his first sortie in Newark, Jean Guitard had procured a globe-trotter's outfit that disguised him sufficiently in case Loeb had retained some memory of him, after having seen him at the Centrale celebration. He had come from Newark to collect a small residue of funds when he found himself almost face to face with the said Loeb at the Western Railroad Station, departing for the interior in company with Grégoire de Montalpé and Colonel Camden.

When, having rapidly returned to Newark, the mariner gave an account of his encounter, and the time and place at which it had taken place, Williamson went pale.

Does Loeb know where I need to go to pick up my guide? he wondered. But he reassured himself. *The direction he's taking can only be a coincidence. And then again, even if he's going...there...he won't obtain anything. He doesn't have the sign.*

More anxious than he wanted to appear, however, he said to Edmée: "Miss, I would have liked to give you two days to recover completely, but it's important that we arrive...you know where...as soon as possible."

"Whenever you wish, Monsieur Williamson; I'm strong, I assure you."

"Good. Captain Furet, do you have the revolvers I asked you to buy?"

"Four large ones for the men and a real jewel for Mam'zelle Edmée, plus fifty cartridges apiece."

"All right! Let's eat quickly, and be on our way!"

5. The Sign

Wisconsin, as everyone knows, is a western state bordered in the north by the western reached of Lake Superior, in the west by the St. Croix River and then the Mississippi, and to the south by the state of Illinois, whose famous capital is Chicago, on Lake Michigan. Finally, it is limited to the east by the shores of that same lake, from slightly below Racine to the south as far as Marinette, on the Menominee River, and Green Bay in the north. It is a vast, flat territory, heavily wooded, except for the north, where there are high hills in the approaches to Lake Superior.

From the center of the state, situated close to the great Rapids in the Wisconsin River, if one travels east-north-east for almost two-thirds of the radius that would end at the common frontier of the states of Wisconsin and Michigan, at the point where it plunges into the waters of Green Bay, one finds a small rectangular territory some sixteen miles long and twenty-four wide, traversed in the middle from north to south by the Wolf River.

That territory, minuscule in proportion to the immensities of America, a little more than sixty square leagues, is the Menominee Indian Reservation, left to the Indians of that tribe.[85]

What a gigantic human drama—or rather inhuman; let us say "ethnic," to employ the correct term—is contained in that word "reservation," apparently so calm and innocent. "Reservations," of which the number and extent is diminishing as rapidly as the last resides of their populations are thinning out, are the cemeteries of races.

---

[85] The Menominee Reservation now has its own website; the representations imply very strongly—and there is no reason to doubt them—that the present plot calumniates that people in its depiction of them, albeit not to the same extent as it calumniates the Salvation Army and other organizations that the author seems to consider fairer game.

The autochthonous Indians, driven back by the formidable white invasion, decimated by gunfire, and destroyed, most of all, *en masse*, by the treacherous and mortal "firewater," being for the most part unassimilable, have gradually been confined within increasingly narrow limits, pressed from all sides by the brutality of the inexorable conquering civilization. There, incapable of finding the elements of their existence in the native fauna, destroyed like them, the last vestiges of one-powerful tribes, sovereign rulers of an immense continent, can only count, in order to sustain their precarious and condemned life, on the parsimonious and insidiously calculated liberalities of the white man, whose invading masses are submerging them like an implacable, continuous, untiring tidal wave.

You will have an idea of the miserable existence of these rare temporary fugitives for the ethnic inundation if you care to penetrate with us into the Menominee Reservation whose situation in east Wisconsin we have just identified.

Near the center of the minuscule hunting-ground—where hunting is virtually proscribed, for lack of big game—on the right bank of the Wolf River, in a small clearing open in a vast woodland in which oak and maple abound—too much for the long security of the present and last occupants—around a fire whose ruddy glow merges with the last red gleams of the sunset, is an assembly of strange, or, more accurately, dolorously grotesque, appearance.

In the center of a great circle formed by a few hundred men and women, warriors and squaws, clad in ragged costumes half-Indian and half-civilized, a dozen old men—old more by virtue of appearance than real age—are seated around their chief.

That chief, who is only forty-six years old, although the numerous silvery threads mingled in his long black hair, falling in thick hanks over his shoulders, and the lassitude of his features seem to indicate a much more advanced age, is the only one who is almost entirely dressed in traditional costume: moccasins on his feet, bottomless leather trousers whose longitudinal seam is fringed externally with long goat-hairs for want of human scalps—the heroic era of the warpath being long gone—and a hide blouse decorated with a few emblematic hieroglyphs. But a threadbare manufactured macfarlane is thrown over his back, while instead of a feather bonnet, it is a heavy rigid bowler hat that coifs him, grotesquely.

The sachems, or tribal elders, who are assisting him do not all have moccasins on their feet. Two of them are sporting, without any pride, strong hunting boots, another "cowboy boots," a fourth a mariner's jersey under an ample cotton blouse frayed by usage, etc., etc., and the series of headgear offers a lamentable disparity. As for the "warriors" and the "squaws," one might think that a blind fairy had gathered together a lot of old costumes worn for a century, as many in New York or Chicago as on the Prairie, and made a magical distribution of them at random. One woman might wear, beneath her Indian shirt of tanned leather, a fluttering skirt, another might secure her torso within an obsolete military uniform-jacket, and more than one warrior, dressed in an incomplete three-piece suit, envelops his shoulders in a shawl as feminine as it is civilized.

Only one young woman, slender and gracious, sitting a few paces behind the chief, dressed in a perfectly correct cycling costumes in gray cloth, with a short skirt, her hair gathered into a heavy plait, might be mistaken for a "Miss" from Washington or Cincinnati, not having very much Indian color in her face.

There is nothing about all the individuals thus clad, however, so great is their gravity, so evident their suffering and so visible the dull and terrible anger that inflames them, that could lead anyone to smile.

Leaning on their rifles, the men wait, gazing fixedly at the torches and the ardent coals of the hearth of the "council." An uninformed traveler would hesitate to recognize them as the "redskins" that they really are, so pale to they seem by comparison, for instance, with the Sioux of the neighboring state.

The chief gets to his feet. In a sonorous but singular language, incomprehensible even for those who know most of the Indian dialects of the New World, and in a strong but unemphatic voice, as somber and sad as the features of those who are listening to him, he says:

"Menominee warriors, it is with grief that I see you in the miserable state to which we have been reduced by the false promises of the Palefaces, who have stolen all our lands and are completing the destruction of our race by famine.

"When I think that my voice can be heard simultaneously by all those who remain of the people that the first Palefaces who came from beyond the great lake without limits called the white Indians, by reason of the scant difference between our faces and theirs, all those who remain of a proud, wise, and intelligent nation, the most beautiful of all those which freely hunted the bison on the boundless Prairie, I ask the Great Spirit what crime we could have committed to be thus afflicted by slow and yet frightfully rapid annihilation!

"The Menominees have, however, always maintained the respectful worship of the Ancestors whose bones, piously collected, repose in this forest, our final refuge. In our nation, fathers never cruelly abuse their sacred authority, sons never show themselves disrespectful or disobedient, and squaws have always been good mothers and valiant wives.

"But it is unworthy of us to lament. The force and numbers of the Palefaces has reduced us to their mercy. Let us at least not give them the joy of hearing us complain, like women. Let us not give them either, by allowing ourselves to be dominated by our anger, legitimate though it is, a pretext for shedding the last blood of our race and coming to plant their great wooden tents on this land, our last refuge, our last homeland.

"Yes, certainly, while not leaving is enough territory in which to hunt and with which to supply our needs by ensuring the primary necessities of life, they promised to furnish us with indispensable support, and still, today, they are not keeping their word. The season of frosts is beginning, and we are hungry, and for half a moon we have been waiting in vain for food supplies.

"My beloved daughter, Snow Rose, who has lived for a long time in the stone huts of the Palefaces, has been to make claims of the white chiefs in their great city of Milwaukee. She has been assured that the convoy would be rapidly formed and sent, but in spite of that promise, the sun has set nine times since she has returned, and we are still waiting."

A man detached himself from the circle and brandished his rifle. "We can't wait, and don't want to wait, any longer!"

"Silence! The venerated sachems of the tribe have deliberated with your chief. They recognize that your anger is just, and your suffering great, and the anxieties we have for our existence legitimate, since we even lack powder in order to attempt to hunt, but they know to what misfortunes any act of violence on our part would give rise. They say: 'The promised convoy will come; we are suffering, but let us be patient still.'"

"The sachems are old men; their needs are less imperious than ours," grumbled the warrior.

"Silence, Black Bison!"

"In that case, Chief Manitoba, give me firewater so that I might forget that my squaw's teat has dried up at the lips of my new-born."

"Even if I had any, I would not give you that deadly water!"

"You have none! Gillette, where the smoking carriages roll, is overflowing with it, as with clothing and provisions. We still have enough powder and bullets—let's go take them!"

"Shut up, serpent's tongue! At the next sunrise, Snow Rose will depart again. At least wait for her return!"

"And my child will be dead, as his elder brother did, of the same cause, last winter!"

"No, your child will not die. I have a single goat with replete udders. My daughter will give it to you."

"So be it! In that case, I can wait."

"We shall wait," approved the unhappy Menominees, "but let the convoy make haste, or we shall follow the counsel of Black Bison."

Snow Rose stood up, and interjected in her clear voice: "You will follow the counsel of the White Avenger, who forbids any talk of using powder against men, because men, all being victims of the Great Monster, ought not to kill one another. And he has promised that he is the one who will avenge all men!"

"I did not yet have the strength to carry a rifle when he shared the tent of the chief and said that. Since then, he has disappeared, and his vengeance is still is the state of a promise, like the Paleface convoy!"

"Know, Black Bison, that Old Sinker has not disappeared for me, who, throughout last year, lived on his bread and his teaching! Know that the hour is near when he will keep his promise to make you all the fortunate people, for he

179

has told me to wait here and guide to him the one who is to be witness to his mysterious work. And look! All of you, look!"

Opposite the clearing, on the other bank of the Wolf River, five people, emerging from the edge of a nearby wood, had paused: three men, one of whom wore the woolen jersey, beret and reefer jacket of a mariner, a boy of fourteen or fifteen, whose tight costume, high stiff collar and cap gave the impression of livery, and a woman.

The tallest of the men shouted in English, in an imperious voice that easily carried over the watercourse, which as narrow by America standards: "Chief!"

The latter advanced to the river's edge.

"Manitoba is the chief of the Menominees!" he replied.

In the same tone, the stranger shouted: "Williamson! Come in response to Old Sinker's summons."

"What did I tell you!" cried Snow Rose, triumphantly.

"Welcome!" said Manitoba, making a sign to a group of Indians to go and meet the travelers.

The Redskins gathered on the river bank, each picking up two long poles from a large number disposed in rows close to the water's edge.

Winter had come early. Already the Wolf River was carrying large ice-floes. The Indians, plunging one of the extremities into the bed, while holding the other end in their muscular hands, launched themselves forward. In three "giant steps" separated by brief pauses on an ice-floe chosen because it offered solid supper, they crossed the Wolf River, carrying extra poles for the use of the newcomers, who passed from the far bank to the nearer one by the same procedure.

When they arrived at the council fire, the one who had already spoken asked: "Is Old Sinker here?"

"No," replied Snow Rose, "but he warned me of your arrival, and I am waiting in order to take you to him."

"Perfect, lovely squaw. When do we start?"

"Shortly after the second sunrise."

"Why not right away?"

"First, I have to go and demand the provision convoy that the administration owes us, and for which we've been waiting in vain for two weeks."

The stranger winked imperceptibly at one of his companions, who was wearing an elegant traveling costume, and who immediately came to join him, while the others remained behind.

"No need to delay for that; I'll do what's necessary to make sure that your tribe has what it needs tomorrow."

A few approving "Ahs" departed from the popular circle. No promise could assure the Palefaces of a more enthusiastic welcome from the exasperated and famished Indians.

"I'll set forth," said the chief's daughter, "as soon as I've seen the convoy arrive."

"You don't trust me?"

"Old Sinker has always told me to believe in facts rather than words."

"Oho! Since when has a squaw cackled so loudly among the Redskins?"

"If Old Sinker, the White Avenger, has chosen the daughter of the great chief Manitoba for his confidential missions, after having had her educated by the Yankees and initiated to formidable secrets, it is because he knows that her soul is prudent, her will firm and her judgment circumspect. In raising me to his level, he has given the Americanized squaw the right to speak loudly."

"I can see that," said the other, ironically. "My apologies, Miss…Miss?"

"Snow Rose."

"Good. Miss Snow Rose will not have, henceforth, any follower more devoted than me…provided that she does not delay in showing us the way."

"I shall only indicate it to Williamson. It is under is responsibility that he takes others with him. He has not given me instructions on that subject."

"The others? They are, in addition to this mariner, who is my servant, and that boy, who is Williamson's, my sister Edmée Rolland and me, Claude Rolland, cousins of the man that Snow Rose calls the White Avenger."

"You are not Williamson, you who have spoken thus far?"

"No, this is Williamson," he said, indicating his immediate companion.

"I'm the King of Mines," confirmed the other, in a soft voice.

The daughter of the great chief Manitoba looked at him fixedly. "In that case," she interrogated him, "you have the sign?"

"That I can assure you," he replied, in a singular intense tone of certainty. Swiftly taking off his overcoat and jacket, he rolled up the left sleeve of his shirt, and laid his arm bare.

The young Indian woman had gone to fetch a flaming brand from the fire, for the daylight was fading rapidly, and she approached it to Williamson's pale and thin arm.

"On the left arm," she said, "and it is indeed the sign, but…"

"But what?" demanded Claude Rolland, in a hoarse voice, furrowing his bushy eyebrows.

"Nothing. Since it's the sign, I have nothing more to see."

She said a few words to her father in the indigenous language, and then said to the newcomers: "The chief will have tents set up for you next to the fire."

"And sleep on the ground? Brrr!" said Williamson.

"When it would have been so easy to avoid that accursed chore by leaving right away!" said his companion. "You aren't taking us, I think, into regions where nocturnal travelers are in peril?"

"First, we're going to Chicago," said Snow Rose.

"By Jove! That's retracing, all the way to the Railroad, the easy road that we've just traveled. Come on, yield to our haste, since I give you my word…as a

Frenchman...that the convoy you're waiting for will be here tomorrow, and let's leave immediately."

"The Menominees have learned from their ancestors to speak with cordial respect to the people of that nation, for they were, in the times when we were strong and considered, with our great allies the Sioux, the first of the men of the distant East who settled in our lands. The relationship that our nation had with them was all justice and amity, and we have retained the traditional memory."

"Then since I, a Frenchman, promise you, and affirm the certain arrival of the convoy, you'll consent...?"

Snow Rose remained silent and indecisive for a moment, moving her dark gaze from one stranger to the other, and then, in a clear and resolute tone, she said: "No. We shall leave as soon as the convoy is in sight. I have spoken."

A dark flash passed through the eyes of the taller of her two interlocutors, who suppressed a gesture of anger.

The tents were erected and, in spite of the penury to which the tribe had been reduced, Indian hospitality succeeded in assembling the elements of a meal, which was served to the travelers: a picturesque meal that was finished by the light of resinous torches, night having fallen, very dark.

The Menominee families, still seething with their contained anger, and resolved to wait for the promised convoy at the assembly-point, had dispersed in groups to the neighboring clearing and along the river bank, where they made arrangements to spend the night around rapidly-lit fires.

Having finished their meal, the white travelers had slipped inside their conical shelters, after having received wishes for happy dreams from Chief Manitoba, who went back to his own tepee in the wood.

Snow Rose had not followed her father.

Sitting on the ground, her folded arms enclosing her knees, she remained pensive next to the dying council fire, and her gaze frequently went to the tents occupied by the white men.

In the narrow tepee that they shared, crouching side by side, the pale and jaundiced Williamson and the tall, rude Rolland were not sleeping either.

"Why that preoccupied expression?" said the former, in a low voice. "The dispatch you received on getting off the train in Gillette, announcing our adversaries? What does it matter, since everything is going well, in sum? Haven't all the precautions been taken?"

"Yes—but all the same, I'd have preferred to be *en route* this evening to meet Old Sinker. To be immobilized is to leave a flank open to surprises."

"Our half-breeds, back there?"

"Will fulfill their mission well, that's certain. Each of those fellows, who are the terror of the region, is worth four men on his own. But that defensive organization caused us to lose precious time, and we're inconvenienced here by the fact that the little Indian girl is the ransom of our delay. I'm thinking of completing our safety precautions with the aid of the two companions we've brought, and in order to ward off and further difficulty coming from this night of forced rest."

"What a terrible man you are! What need is there always to be imagining dangers, instead of letting events take their course while everything is going well?"

"It's only by anticipating too much that one is sufficiently prepared. Stay here and sleep, I'll go and give instructions to our people, if the circumstances arise."

Slipping out of their common tepee, Williamson's companion went to the one to which their traveling companions had retired, and shut himself in with the mariner and the groom.

He was still there when a shout rang out and caused Snow Rose to leap abruptly to her feet.

"Chief!"

"Who wants him?" demanded the young Indian woman sharply, trying to penetrate the nocturnal darkness with her gaze.

From the other side of the Wolf River, a voice that was evidently forced, doubtless unaccustomed to long-distance dialogues, replied: "Williamson! Come in response to Old Sinker's summons."

The same sentence that had already resounded on the arrival of the other Palefaces!

Manitoba's daughter shivered violently. She was certainly not alone, for the white men who had already arrived were all standing up in their tepees.

"Wait!" commanded Snow Rose, in a troubled voice. Immediately, she modulated a bizarre sound, simultaneously reminiscent of the call of a blackbird and the mewling of a cat.

It could only be an alarm signal, for, almost instantaneously, the entire underwood surrounding the big clearing lit up, as did the river bank, with flickering torches. In less than two minutes, all the warriors of the tribe, rifle in hand, Manitoba and the sachems at the head, came to gather beside the ruddy embers of the council fire.

By the light of the torches, the same passage of the river, back and forth, as effects. In the same way as before, too, the new band of white travelers was composed of three men, a woman and a boy of about fifteen. But if the latter wore a livery similar to his predecessor, none of the three men indicated by their clothing that one of them was a seaman. And furthermore, they had a guide, who, in response to the welcome given to his clients, had not thought it appropriate to cross the watercourse with them.

The young Indian woman, her brows furrowed and her eyes flashing, advanced toward them. "Which of you claims to be Williamson?" she demanded, abruptly.

"Me."

"You're lying. Williamson is here!"

"Well, I expected that. Who is designated by Old Sinker to take William-son to him?"

"Me."

"Very good," said the newcomer. "Will you observe the sign?" He un-dressed partially in order to lay his arm bare.

Nervously, Snow Rose took hold of a torch that a warrior passed to her and gazed at the minuscule tattoo representing a terrestrial globe pierced by a dag-ger, which illustrated the very pale flesh of the arm, almost feminine by virtue of its roundness. She looked at it with extreme attention, slowly moving her finger around the design.

Finally, with a completely changed expression, she said: "You really are Williamson? Then...the other...."

"May I see him, if he hasn't fled when we arrived?"

A rude voice replied to him, rising up a few paces behind the group formed by the chief and the sachems.

"The true Williamson doesn't flee before an impostor. Here he is!"

And, pushed forward by his tall Barnum companion, the pale and frail Wil-liamson number one emerged into the yellow torchlight. A loud burst of laugher greeted his rather pitiful appearance.

"What! Cousin de Montalpé, you've suddenly become a billionaire and the Mining King? Truly, you don't look the part! No matter, all my compliments!"

For his part, Williamson number two, addressing the spokesman of his counterpart, said ironically: "Did you think, Monsieur Loeb, that those whose ship you sank within sight of Sandy Hook would really be obliging enough to disappear from the world of the living? As a good believer, as the great General of the Salvation Army ought to be, don't you see, in this resurrection, a miracle from On High and a sign of supernatural protection, against which such a great chief of the Servants of God ought to forbid himself to struggle any longer?"

"I only see one thing, and that's a false Williamson, who wants to deceive the friends of Old Sinker, in order to be taken to him, the devil only knows with what unacknowledged design, and that false Williamson is..."

"Him!" interrupted Snow Rose, forcefully, pointing at the young traveler with the appearance of a dandy, whom the pretty companion of the new arrivals had just called cousin, and who appeared, as the common saying has it, not to be very sure of himself.

"That's false!" thundered Loeb. (You will have recognized him long ago, and there is no point henceforth in designating him by circumlocutions.)

"That's false!" repeated de Montalpé, like an echo, in response to a fierce glare from his brusque companion.

"It's true!" proclaimed the Indian woman. "The proof was given to me by examination of the signs. The second one I've seen is very old, and had faded to the point of being half-effaced. The one I saw first was, as you know, only accepted by me with certain reservations. That's because it's so recent that the in-flammation of the needles is intact, and the swelling clearly visible."

"Cousin de Montalpé," said Claude, ironically, "will have the regret of having suffered the pain for nothing!"

Loeb bit his lips until they bled.

Suppressing his internal rage with difficulty, he shouted: "Are you going to put your trust in the absurd words of a squaw who is surely slightly mad?"

"It's obvious," said the brave young rescuer Jean Guitard, "that Mr. Loeb hasn't looked very closely; it's not with two beautiful big velvet eyes like those, which radiate a limpid gleam of clear intelligence, that one can accuse someone of poor sight. I'm only a matelot, Mademoiselle Indian, but as such, I've already traveled to the far ends of the earth, and, well, faith of a mariner, I've never en-countered a gaze as… beautifully impressive as yours."

"Come on, enough nonsense!" thundered Loeb. "If the squaw declares her-self for the imposture, it doesn't matter to me. Before daylight comes, she'll know, as will you all, which of the two Williamsons she's going to take to Old Sinker—I'll guarantee that!"

So saying, he brutally took hold of the exceedingly nonplussed Grégoire by the sleeve of his jacket, turned him around without the slightest regard for a pre-tended American king, pushed him into his tepee.

He then strode away and plunged into the trees bordering the clearing.

In groups, the warriors dismissed by the chief—who did not know enough English to have understood very much of the scene that had just unfolded before their eyes—went back to their respective encampments.

Around the council fire reanimated by the young Indian woman, William-son, Claude, Edmée, Jean Guitard and Toby sat down in company with Manito-ba and his daughter.

It was decided with the latter that the departure to meet Old Sinker would take place as soon as the band of impostors had left the area—which the chief promised to obtain, whether they liked it or not, in the course of the following day.

They were counting without their guest; Jonathan Loeb was not one of those who leave the battlefield before being victorious or dead.

6. *The* Coup de Jarnac[86]

---

[86] A "*coup de Jarnac*" is a violent, unexpected and expert thrust, with an impli-cation of underhand practice. It is named after a thrust delivered by Guy Jabot de Jarnac in a duel fought in 1547 against the champion of the dauphin, which sliced through his opponent's hamstring. The move was, in fact, not illicit, but Jarnac was a Protestant, and it was described as treacherous in the Jesuit ency-clopedia that was responsible for the phrase entering common parlance, before the 19th century lexicographer Émile Littré called attention to the real cheats.

Williamson had refused, on his behalf and that of his companions, Manitoba's offer to set up tents for them.

So close to his implacable enemy and hateful competitor of "Power," he judged it prudent to stay together and on watch, armed and in the open air, les propitious to surprises.

Not wanting to be reckoned pusillanimous, in the opinion of the Indians in communication with Old Sinker, he gave Manitoba and his daughter a brief account of the criminal collision engineered by Loeb of which he had been the victim, and how he and his companions had survived the shipwreck, thanks to the initiative, decisiveness, boldness and agility of the young French mariner.

That story occasioned two very different reflections of the scantly loquacious lips of the two Redskins.

"So this Loeb," said the Menominee chief, "is also a very great chief among the Palefaces, to have been able to provoke such a catastrophe at such a distance!"

Snow Rose, looking directly at Jean Guitard, who had not enough eyes to gaze at her, declared gravely, in her half-Yankee half-Indian fashion: "Captain Furet is a great warrior, worthy of his ancestors, whose honesty out ancestors held in high esteem. If he were Menominee, all the squaws of the Reservation would be proud to feed the fire of his tepee."

The mariner did not understand that very well, but he felt distinguished by the beautiful and slightly strange Indian, and in truth, felt a sharp emotion in which his self-esteem was not the only thing in play.

Manitoba and Snow Rose having decided to stay with the strangers in order to cover them with the protection that their mere presence constituted, Snow Rose went to fetch a bison skin from the paternal tepee in which Claude could wrap his exceedingly weary sister. The men, smoking slowly, chatted for another full hour by the council fire.

It was, naturally, about Old Sinker that Williamson, Claude and Edmée—whom curiosity kept awake—wanted to hear from the father and daughter with the slightly ardent complexion. To get the Indians of the American prairie to talk, however—particularly about a desired subject—is a task before which Hercules himself would have recoiled.

All that they were able to learn was that the White Avenger had been the guest of the Menominees for the last time two years before, and had taken Snow Rose away with him, having previously had her educated at the girls' school in Milwaukee; that he had only stayed for an hour in Manitoba's tent, and that the young woman had been initiated by him for twelve moons in the redoubtable

---

The phrase was repopularized by Honoré de Balzac in his essay-sequence *Petites misères de la vie conjugale* (1830-46), who, like the present author, retained the Jesuitical implication.

secrets that she was to impart to Williamson alone when the moment came; and that the prudence of the venerated and strange individual had instructed Snow Rose to guide Williamson without having revealed to him in advance the itinerary that she was to make him follow.

That was all, although it was as insufficient to satisfy the curiosity of the travelers as it was to permit them to keep the dialogue going for a long time. Thus, the first hour of the watch having passed awkwardly, the periods of mutism became so long that Edmée went to sleep and her companions had to struggle desperately to vanquish the drowsiness that was increasingly overtaking them, thanks to the warmth of the fire. All being tranquil around them, a peaceful and reassuring silence as reigning in the enemy tents as well as the entire Indian camp, Williamson proposed that they yield to natural solicitations, without departing from a prudent surveillance, thanks to sentinels ensuring everyone's security.

It was decided that "Captain Furet"—the mariner seeming immune to the drowsiness of his companions—would take the first watch. After two hours—or sooner if he feared that he was about to succumb to sleep in his turn—he was to be relieved by Claude, who would be relieved in his turn by Toby, Williamson naturally reserving the most prolonged quietude for himself.

Rapidly, the Mining King, Claude Roland and the groom lay down, rolled up in their mantles, while even the Indian chief, inclining his head on to his arms, folded over his knees, allowed himself to be carried off to the land of dreams.

Snow Rose seemed no more inclined than the matelot to imitate her father and her white guests. After making sure that his revolver was quite loose in its holster, and having paced around he sleepers for a quarter of an hour, moved gradually closer to the motionless young Menominee, who was watching him covertly.

Under various pretexts, he exchanged a few remarks with her, banal at first, and then came frankly to sit down beside her—and a whispered conversation was established between them, which became increasingly animated.

It does not require an expert in such matters to understand that a naïve and spontaneous flirtation had been established between the two young people. What they were saying must have been very interesting, at least to them, because they did not perceive that a rumor—almost imperceptible, it is true—had risen in the underwood, son to give way, abruptly, to a silence so complete that it would have given Fenimore Cooper's Leatherstocking pause for thought.

Suddenly, Redskin instinct awoke in Snow Rose.

She seized the mariner's arm, stood up, and darted her dark gaze around her in an anxious glance—only one, for it was already too late!

From all directions around the almost-extinct council fire, beings bounded like wild cats, and before the sleepers, who had stood up in response to the a cry of alarm, could even put their hands on their weapons, they were knocked down—including Snow Rose—and all resistance was rendered impossible.

No hand had committed the near-sacrilege of touching Manitoba, but the chief found himself surrounded by a dozen men as respectful as they were determined not to let him intervene in favor of the travelers who were victims of the aggression, sand when he raised an angry voice to demand an account from his warriors of such an inexplicable attack, it was Black Bison who replied: "The chief has been deceived by odious impostors!"

"The impostors are those who presented themselves first. My daughter, Snow Rose, established that before the warriors."

"Snow Rose left the tepees of her brothers the Menominees too young and too long ago. Among the Palefaces she has lost the keen senses of the children of the Great Spirit, living free in the prairies and the forests. The fact that you were all surprised a moment ago proves that Snow Rose is unable to see."

The young Indian woman had freed herself from those who had knocked her down, and who evidently permitted that liberation, which could no longer hinder the execution of the forcible strike now accomplished. She protested: "The inflammation of the swelling around the sign proves that..."

Black Bison interrupted her forcefully: "Proves only that Snow Rose was not able to discern the cause, being a stranger to tattooing. The man who protects Williamson—the first and true one—has convinced the warriors of that."

"The Menominee warriors are naïve children!"

"Let Snow Rose not insult her brothers! The Menominees do not want to be duped like her! Williamson and his friend, who is a great chief among the white men, are the friends of the Menominees, and the newcomers are their enemies, who want their death."

"That is false!" protested Manitoba, is a loud voice.

"It is so true," howled Black Bison, "that it is them, the accursed sons of pigs, who have prevented the expected convoy from reaching the hungry, and which the powerful friend of the man who calls himself the White Avenger will bring tomorrow, on condition that we make it impossible for our starvers to hinder his efforts in favor of the children of the Great Spirit! Let those filthy reptiles be tied to trees and put under guard, until the assembly of warriors decides their fate."

Manitoba and his daughter, now freed, looked at one another. Their eyes said, mutually, that to try to struggle overtly against the furious anger of the tribe would be to expose their friends to worse and immediate danger. It was necessary to appear to give in to the unexpected torment, with the hope of subsequently bringing back the unfortunates, exasperated by suffering, to saner ideas, and a comprehension of the role that an infernal cleverness had caused them to play.

"The light of the Great Spirit has been withdrawn from the hearts of my sons the Menominees," Manitoba said, "but they are right, if they believe the newcomers to be guilty of such a great crime against us, to take precautions that a near future will make them regret. But let the warriors be wise! Once those they believe to be their enemies are immobilized, let them not hasten to judge them without proof!"

"The chief has spoken well, and not otherwise than the powerful protector of the friend of Old Sinker and the Menominee nation," proclaimed Black Bison. "The great white chief asks nothing more. 'Let them be rendered incapable of doing harm,' he has said, 'and when I have proved their crime and repaired the effect of their machinations, let the Indians do justice to their enemies.'"

Without waiting for the mute acquiescence of Manitoba, the Mining King, Claude and Edmée Rolland, Jean Guitard and Toby were taken away and tied solidly to nearby trees with the aid of lassos, and a picket of a ten armed Indian guards was posted nearby, around the council fire, reawakened by the addition of a few dry branches.

The warriors went back to their respective encampments. The chief and his daughter went back to their tepee, under the suspicious surveillance of the indigenous leader of the rebellion, who, without wanting to injure the person, or even the authority, of the leader of the "nation," had substituted his will, in a specific instance, for the *vox populi*.

Not one of the victims of that aggression, of whose Machiavellian origin they were all too well aware, weakened under the blow of that new catastrophe—not even Edmée. The young woman had only uttered one cry, quite natural, when, awakened in anguish by the alarm call given by the chief's daughter, she had seen two of the red demons hurl themselves upon her, their customary grotesqueness dramatized by the darkness. Valiantly, she had stiffened al her will, and had not allowed any plaint to escape when she was brutally tied to a tree between her brother and Williamson.

The latter had suffered the surprise, just as he imagined the consequences, with a phlegm that, in the circumstances, equaled the firmest courage. Whereas Claude had only uttered one word—a name, Edmée!—absolutely forgetting himself in his fraternal alarm, the mariner, in his impotent anger, had allowed an oath to escape, and that Toby's correctness had not been able to retain a fearful: "Help, sir!" the billionaire had been content to hiss between his teeth a "Good!" synonymous with: "Well, it's gone wrong...and this time, it's serious!"

When the clearing had emptied, the mariner, who had been biting his tongue for some time to combat the urge to... say something, remembered that he had always been "the Parisian"[87] aboard the ships on which he had served, said to the billionaire: "Well, Monsieur Mining King, I believe that Loeb, this time, is well on the way to freeing you from the concern of Captain Furet's wages!"

---

[87] The author inserts a footnote here to explain that "Parisian," in this sense, means a joker, no matter what the provincial origin of the sailor in question might be.

Williamson did not reply to the mariner, firstly because a joking tone never found a reply on his part, secondly because "Captain Furet" was occupying the position furthest from the river in the line of prisoners, and it would have been necessary to raise his voice, which he never did except in cases of urgent necessity, and finally because a preoccupation—and a saddened preoccupation, to boot—was absorbing all his thought.

It was toward Edmée that he turned his head—the only thing he could move—to say, in his customary tranquil tone: "You would not believe, Miss Rolland, how desolate I am on your account for what is happening, and what reproaches I am addressing to myself for having dragged you with me into such disagreeable adventures."

"You're not doing yourself justice, Monsieur Williamson," the young woman replied, in a weary but firm tone. "Whatever happens to us—and it's to be feared that the imminent consequence of this treacherous attack will not be pleasant—you ought not to accuse yourself of anything in my regard. You insisted sufficiently in Newark that my brother and I, and our brave Jean, should allow you to depart for the interior alone, in company with our young Toby. We wanted to come with you. If our destiny is to finish as soon as the journey has begun, be sure that, like Claude and our faithful Jean, I shall hold my head up and look ill-fortune in the face."

"Miss, your words only drive the dagger more deeply into my heartsickness. You have revealed to me the existence of a kind of woman that I thought non-existent, as I've told you—and now you add to the surprise I have already had the astonishment of discovering in you a firmness of soul that even yesterday I would have sworn to be incompatible with your sex in general, especially in the Old World."

"Because you've only seen the uninteresting flighty individuals who were attracted by the shine of your millions and your celebrity. It's among those, infinitely more numerous, who hide themselves, wounded by the overly brutal glare of an arrogant human sun, among the silent and retiring army of the proud and the modest, that it's necessary to search, there that it's necessary to take the trouble to look, in order that your judgment will not be misled, by virtue of being superficial."

"Good! I greatly regret that I might not live to follow your advice. Since hazard had involved you in it, my life, which was so indifferent to me, had begun to interest me in a fashion that amazes me."

"In that case," said Edmée, making a valiant effort to be cheerful, "I think that in philosophizing, flattering as it might be for me, you're wasting precious time. Our exceedingly precarious fate might depend on a fortunately opportune idea coming to illuminate your thought, as only you know our adversary and these demi-savages that he's employing against us. Whatever the obsession might be of the horrors that wait us, we must search until the last minute for the means of getting out of it…if there is one."

"Never despair! By Jove, from what a human race you're the issue! I'm not talking about North America, which is a composite of all the races in the world, nor of myself, who have no idea where I emerged from, but I understand the people of the Old World who say, with one of the great poets, who is only misunderstood by us: Every man has two fatherlands: his own and France!"[88]

After that unexpected fit of lyricism, perhaps fatigued by an effort so extraordinary for him, Williamson fell silent and began reflecting ardently.

Claude, a man of action in any circumstances, twisted repeatedly in his bonds, exhausting himself in attempts—vain, alas!—to break them.

Jean Guitard, knowing as well as any mariner how to judge knots, did not renew a first attempt of the same kind, having understood its futility. He avenged himself with mocking and vituperative sallies addressed to the savage guards who were crouching around the council fire, mute and attentive, with their rifles on their knees.

Toby, white with fear but correct, remained stiff, his dilated eyes fixed in his master, unable to believe in a prolongation of his captivity, and expecting to see him cast of hi shackles at any moment and come to set him free, and say to him tranquilly: "Toby…*cocktail!*"

Soon, a great silence reigned in the clearing—a poignant, anguished silence for the prisoners, a feline silence of predators sure of their prey for the Redskins.

That silence had lasted for more than a quarter of an hour, without anything having troubled it, when Jean Guitard felt something touch his shoulder, and a scarcely perceptible voice that had recently become as familiar to him as if he had known it for years, whispered in his ear: "Don't move, and don't say a word! Just turn your head slowly and negligently to the left. I'm behind the tree. Good, like that. Now listen. Reply to me without moving your lips, so quietly that your breath couldn't lift a down feather.

"My father and I don't expect anything good for you all, although we'll try to save you, when the stars pale in the first light appearing in the Orient.—but I don't want you to fall victim to the impostor. At great risk for both of us, I'll cut your bonds, and while I distract the guards' attention, take advantage of it to flee."

"No," Jean replied, simply.

"Captain Furet refuses his life?"

"Without being assured at the same time of those of my companions, yes, Mam'zelle Snow Rose. Among us, it's like this: all or none. I'm deeply touched

---

[88] The author includes a reference to "Vicomte Henri de Bornier, *La Fille de Roland*." The quotation is usually attributed to Thomas Jefferson, when he was the American ambassador to France, but it might be apocryphal; undoubtedly, however, Henri de Bornier had Jefferson's alleged remark in mind when he put the same words into Charlemagne's mouth in his 1875 play.

191

by your good intention in my regard, but I'd be a wretched dog if I took advantage of it."

"The white warrior has a great heart. I had no need of that new proof to save him. But let him reflect—I can only attempt to save one."

"Then let it be Miss Edmée, the weakest, too good and too pretty to die like this."

The Indian woman's dark gaze launched a double flash into the darkness, immediately extinguished. "It would be in vain if I freed her; she'll be recaptured before taking twenty paces. It's only Captain Furet that I can save, firstly because he's at the tree closest to the heart of the woods and most distant from the fire where the guards are on watch, and secondly because, having the suppleness of a serpent, the cunning of a fox and the speed of a deer, he alone has a chance of escaping the Menominees' pursuit, and finally because...because I want him...to owe me his life."

"That's very nice, what you're saying, Mam'zelle Snow Rose, and be sure that if we can't avoid the bad quarter of an hour, not being able to prolong our acquaintance will be what I regret most in quitting life...but a French mariner fleeing alone and leaving his comrades face to face with their executioners has never been seen and never will be, you understand? You could cut my ropes and I wouldn't budge."

"If you don't lose a moment you could reach a Paleface village, warn the police and come back to get your companions..."

"And find nothing but their dismembered bodies. No, not that. Thanks, Mam'zelle, but don't go on."

"Oh!" murmured the young Indian, clenching her fists. "It's necessary that I save you, even so."

And, as light as a bird, hardly disturbing a blade of grass, she disappeared into the depths of the wood.

Another quarter of an hour went by in the lugubrious silence.

Suddenly, the five prisoners looked in surprise at the opposite side of the clearing. A man appeared there, moving with precaution. That man was the false Williamson, Claude and Edmée's cousin, Grégoire de Montalpé.

He advanced toward the group of armed Indians, and with a tempting mimicry, showed them two bottles whose necks were sticking out of the inside pockets of his overcoat.

For the Menominees, deprived by the long delay to the convoy, the temptation was too alluring. After a semblance of resistance, they yielded to it. Five minutes later, the two bottles of firewater were empty, passed round and their contents silently swallowed. De Montalpé took two more from the same hiding place, and ten minutes had not gone by when the ten guards had fallen to the ground, struck down by the effects of the alcohol.

Then, deliberately, the dandy headed for the prisoners.

"This time," he said to them, "you have no chance of escaping Loeb's hatred. Oh, he's taken his measures jolly well, that fellow. A good idea, stopping the convoy—or, rather having it stopped a band of half-breeds recruited and mobilized in a trice. If you'd come via Gillette, like us, things would have gone without so much fuss; you'd have been caught without suspecting it by an ambush set by three of the Prairie bandits, who were charged with preventing the drivers of the convoy and their escort from untying themselves—for they've been temporarily transformed into black puddings, just like you, my friends. Then, a few bullets that wouldn't miss their mark, and it would all have been over.

"The trouble is that you got off that the preceding station, Shawane, south of the Reserve instead of East, and came here along Lake Shawane, then up the left bank of the Wolf River. That meant that you didn't see the convoy, avoided the trap, and that satanic Loeb, who's a hell of a lot smarter than you, has been obliged to create a revolution among the Indians to get rid of your inconvenient persons definitively.

"You're wondering why I'm telling you all this and taking the trouble to get your guards drunk? Well, me, I'm not bloodthirsty. I want the inheritance, that's all. That Loeb has a score to settle with the Mining King—a royalty that he must be regretting rudely at present—but I couldn't care less. They can settle it between themselves—in private, of course. But it's not the same for you, cousins. I'm not a bad fellow, I don't insist on your demise.

"You can see that I've put your guards to sleep. Sign a renunciation of the Lobanief inheritance for me, which I have here in my pocket, all ready, with pen and ink, and I'll untie you, advising you to clear off...you'll be done for otherwise.

"That's generous on my part, isn't it? Life is well worth, as is sung in the *Noces de Jeannette*, 'a name at the bottom of this page?'[89] Agreed, isn't it? I can take out the piece of paper?"

"On one condition," said Claude, "and that's that we're all free."

"Ta ra, ta ta! I can see you coming with your big clogs. Once all four of you are free, good old Grégoire is knocked down, and you make off, after having taken the piece of paper back. No fear, my jewels! This is how we're going to proceed: I detach one of the cousin's arms, just enough so that he can sign, with my help. I tie him up again and do the same with his sister. Then, as I keep my word, I detach the brother definitively, and hold a revolver to his sister's head while inviting the excellent Claude to keep twenty paces away, under pain of causing damage to that dear head. When the girl is freed in her turn, they'll

---

[89] *Les Noces de Jeannette* [Jeannette's Wedding] (1853) is a one-act comic opera with music by Victor Massé and a libretto by Jules Barbier and Michel Carré. The highly improbable plot revolves around a marriage contract, which a reluctant groom is tricked into signing.

both do me the pleasure, still under threat, of going somewhere other than where I am. Is that understood?"

A violent conflict then took place in Claude's heart and mind. He honestly did not care about the fortune, but it would be extremely repugnant to him to abandon Williamson. Alone, he would not have hesitated for an instant, but what about his dear sister? Out of chivalric sentiment with regard to an egotist he had only known for a fortnight, was he about to let his beloved sister die?"

"Sign it," advised Williamson, smiling internally at a hidden thought, in which he could not prevent himself hoping that, thanks to Manitoba, he might succeed in thwarting Loeb's hatred once again.

"I need five minutes to think," said Claude.

"As you please, cousin. The fellows I've laid out here aren't going to wake up any time soon. We have the time. You can even discuss it with your companions. I'll go to the river bank, discreetly. I'm very obliging. Only, decide before I get back, or I'll go back to my apartment, and then…you can guess the rest. Without adieux, my dear."

When his back was turned, Snow Rose suddenly stood up beside the mariner.

"The opportunity is exceptionally propitious," she said. "Does Captain Furet still refuse to escape?"

"Now? Oh, no!" said the brave mariner, swiftly. "On condition that you come with me to carry out a little operation I've thought of."

"Not saving the others? If the Menominees here are drunk, the others are watching in the woods. A mass escape is bound to be perceived."

"Don't worry—I'll leave alone…with you."

"Come on, then!" said the Indian, urgently, cutting Jean's bonds.

Gliding like shadows, they both disappeared under the somber branches. Toby, who was next to the mariner, was the only one who perceived the desertion, but the unfortunate boy was too fearful to pay attention if lightning had struck at his feet.

Grégoire de Montalpé returned to Claude.

"Well?"

"Oh," said the other, "it's miserable and cowardly, what I'm doing! Forgive me, Monsieur Williamson."

"Don't sign it, Claude!" protested the young woman, bravely.

"Sign it…for her!" the billionaire pronounced, forcefully and emotionally.

"I'll sign," declared Claude, nervously.

"Well I won't!" said Edmée, closing her eyes as if to drive away the tempting vision of life and liberty reconquered.

"You'll sign too, Miss, or I'll never forgive you!"

Edmée did not reply.

De Montalpé set about freeing one of his cousin's arms. While acting attentively and prudently, in order not to give the prisoner too great a liberty of movement, which he judged dangerous to his security, he said: "You see, my dear, how well precautions have been taken for the operation to proceed smoothly. I certainly wouldn't have thought of it myself."

"Loeb knows?" asked Williamson, abruptly, his expression darkening.

"He organized the whole ceremony."

"He authorized you to get our guards drunk! Oh, be careful, Monsieur Rolland! What trap is still hidden here?"

It was, indeed, a trap, but aimed at the one who suspected it the least. Just as Claude's right arm was finally freed, a volley of guttural cries rang out on the far side of the clearing, where a band of Menominees surged forth.

They pointed at the tree left vacant by the flight of the mariner, and then de Montalpé, still occupied with Claude's bonds. They rushed upon the fake Williamson, caught—in their view—*in flagrante delicto* freeing the prisoners. In spite of his cries and protests, he was dragged away brutally and tied up in the fugitive's place.

In response to the tumult the entire tribe was not long delayed in arriving, and with the strangely picturesque horde, Loeb, the terrible architect of the mortal scheme.

With a cruelly ironic curl in his lips, he did not even deign to glance at his adversaries, so magisterially vanquished, and went straight to his accomplice, who, suddenly riveted to his tree, was writhing like a devil in a holy water stoup and howling like a polecat.

"Be quiet!" he commanded him, rudely. "You only have what your humanitarian fantasies merit. When one wages a war like the one with which you've associated yourself, one doesn't stop at the violence that the circumstances warrant, more or less. Too bad if, in fighting to the death the man who proudly titles himself the Mining King, it happens that these Rollands, about whom I don't give a damn, are swallowed up in his defeat.

"You wanted to take care of your petty affairs alongside mine and spare the accomplices at the moment of the final settlement, but you didn't think that one doesn't play games with a host one has launched into revolt and whose savage passions one has excited to paroxysm. You've been caught red-handed in complicity with the escape of the prisoners, whose death these furious fellow desire. I can't prevent your sharing their fate and, in truth, I confess that your stupidity will rid me of an inconvenient and, by the same token, compromising companion.

"Get yourself out of it, my dear, if you can. But I want, at least, to give you this information: the Indians never sacrifice their victims except in broad daylight, because they want to enjoy their suffering. You therefore have a few hours before you to prepare to be brave, or to think of a means, if any can be found, of dissociating yourself from the condemned before the fatal moment.

"With that, Monsieur de Montalpé, good night—I'm going to bed. Oh, I'll also warn you that they'll surely start with you: all the advantages, my dear! That will spare you a spectacle as painful as it would be demoralizing."

And without paying the slightest attention to the fearful supplications and desperate sobs of his accomplice—whose funds he was keeping—he drew away from the clearing, shrugging his shoulders scornfully.

For half an hour the crowd abused the prisoners, in particular the breathless Grégoire, the most culpable of all, in their eyes, for having wanted to deprive them of their imminent vengeance.

Then the Menominees returned to the wood, and took away the dead drunk guards, who were replaced by a new and wide-awake squad.

And the lugubrious watch recommenced.

Great as their courage was—Grégoire and poor Toby excepted—the prisoners' strength, energy and resistance to anguish was exhausted when, without, Chief Manitoba having wanted or been able to do anything to save them, a pale pink light rose above the Wolf River.

It was daylight…it was death.

There was a rumor in the underwood. The executioners were making their preparations.

Soon, with the chief and the sachems in the lead, they advanced processionally into the clearing.

It really was the end! The prisoners exchanged in a glance—and what a glance!—a mute and supreme adieu.

Suddenly, there was a stir within the crowd that had invaded the lugubrious theater of the quintuple execution. After a moment of indecision, it moved *en masse* toward the bank of the Wolf River.

What was that distant noise, those cries, that the savages' ears perceived in spite of the distance?

The sinister preparations were suspended. A few warriors broke away, crossed the river, and went to see what was happening.

The wait lasted a quarter of an hour at the most.

Suddenly, between two thickets, moving at a rapid trot, three heavy wagons appeared, in the midst of whipcracks.

"The convoy! It's the convoy!" howled the Menominee crowd, in a delirium, no longer of vengeance, but of joy.

The first wagon approached the river, escorted by the warriors who had departed as scouts, who were capering around it frantically. And standing at the front of the wagon were…Snow Rose and Captain Furet, making grand gestures of victory!

The first wagon, now launched down the slope leading to the watercourse, comes to a halt a few yards from the bank. The mariner and the Indian woman try to get down, but they are seized by enthusiastic arms, which bring them across the river holding them high above their heads, and they make their entrance to the clearing carried in triumph.

Imposing silence with a gesture, Snow Rose shouts: "A band of half-breed scoundrels, on the orders of the infamous companion of the false Williamson, had stopped our convoy, tied up the drivers and the escort, whom three of them were guarding under the menace of their rifles. The great Paleface warrior and Snow Rose took them by surprise, killed the Prairie bandits and freed the escort. Here is the convoy for which the Menominees were waiting, and of which the infamous impostors deprived them!"

A tempest of "Ouahs!"—Indian cheers—accompanied by a hectic dance, welcomed these words. Then, while the crowd crossed the river and fell upon the wagons, under the guidance of Manitoba and the sachems, desirous of preventing pillage and organizing the distribution. Snow Rose ran to the prisoners and started setting them free.

On arriving in front of Grégoire de Montalpé, his replacement, the mariner stopped, in amazement.

It was Claude Rolland who cut his cousin's bonds, saying: "You wanted to sell us our salvation; personally, I'm setting you free without condition. I'm not forgetting, anyway, that it was your loose tongue that must have informed my intrepid and wily comrade Jean of the existence and location of the intercepted convoy, which he was able to bring here…just in time. Take advantage of that great service involuntarily rendered to those you considered as enemies. Try to get away, because I think that very soon, this won't be a good place for you to be."

More dead than alive, and as crestfallen as a fox caught in a trap, the dispirited Grégoire disappeared hurriedly into the woods.

Williamson's first action, once freed, was to come to Jean Guitard and shake his hand vigorously, saying to him, with a frank and amicable emotion: "You're a brave lad, Captain Furet!"

Jean replied, bluntly: "No trouble, Monsieur Mining King. At your service!"

If Toby, collapsed unconscious at the foot of his tree, had been able to hear and see his master, he would have been less able to recognize the old Williamson than ever.

On the other side of the river, the first wagon had been unloaded, as if by enchantment. The driver had unhitched the horses, which hastened to drink, and then drew away to browse a few hundred paces away. The poor animals were naturally desirous of a well-earned rest.

While the Menominees were uniquely occupied with unloading the precious cargo, three people who had crossed the Wolf River half a mile upstream and had then slipped back under the trees, creeping through the grass, leapt on to the three most distant horses, and, striking them repeatedly with sticks, launched them at a triple gallop eastwards.

A cry of anger rose up among the Indians, twenty of whom set off in pursuit of the fugitives. It was in vain. Loeb, de Montalpé and Colonel Camden were out of reach. It was in vain, too, that they searched for the false mariner and groom. As soon as the convoy appeared, the disguised half-breeds had fled on foot and reached safety.

On the afternoon of the same day, Williamson and his companions, having been fêted as gods by the same Indians who had wanted to torture them, departed for Chicago with Snow Rose.

7. The Immense Beast

Some forty hours later, in three separate and successive groups, clad in overcoats purchased in various stores—Williamson having also, as an additional measure of prudence, by reason of having passed through Chicago on several occasions, donned a superb false beard—the Mining King and his companions, augmented by their Indian guide, had installed themselves in a hotel in one of the giant buildings known as skyscrapers.

Since then, they had not gone out, even to stretch their legs on the sidewalk of the broad street, for two reasons, each as important as the other.

On the one hand, Snow Rose was waiting for an indication of the route to follow, which was to be given to her, as to Williamson in Paris, by way of the New York *Herald*, but in a different fashion, which could only be recognized by her, in an advertisement that would be repeated once a week until further notice emanating directly from Old Sinker.

On the other hand, it was important for the travelers to avoid their dogged enemy, who was not unaware that they had to come to Chicago, Snow Rose having unfortunately not concealed the first stage of the journey to the man she had then believed to be the real Williamson.

In the hotel, they occupied, under false names, four separate rooms, Claude and Edmée on the eighth floor, Williamson on the ninth, the young Menominee on the seventh and Captain Furet and Toby on the thirteenth. Except when they slept or took their meals in the dining-room on their own floor, however, they all gathered by day in the Mining King's apartment.

You can see that their precautions had been carefully taken.

That day, after the midday meal, at about half past two in the afternoon, Williamson, swaying in a rocking chair, and Edmée sitting on a sofa on the back of which Claude was leaning, saw Snow Rose come in at a more rapid pace than usual.

"Well? Do you have news?"

"Yes."

"The indication."

"I've read it."

"Good. Are we going to leave, then?"

198

"By this evening's train, if you wish."

"May we know on which line?"

"The Great Western line."

"All right! And will it take us long to reach Old Sinker?"

"Only he knows."

"What precautions!"

"He can never take enough."

"Like us," Claude observed.

"You have only one enemy to avoid, who is also one of his; he has a legion," said Snow Rose, gravely. "There are still a great many who haven't forgotten the scenes that unfolded fifteen years ago."

"What scenes?" asked Edmée, curiously.

"I believe," said Williamson, consulting the young Indian woman with his gaze, "that I may speak now?"

"Yes," she approved, "And me too, since we're well on the way to joining him."

"Well," Williamson began, "you'll remember, my dear Miss, that I confided to you aboard the *Astrea* that I'd only told part of the truth in our presence, in Paris, about the event to which I owe the acquaintance of Old Sinker. It's quite true that I pulled him out of the Hudson, where he wanted to put an end to his days, but he hadn't thrown himself in there entirely voluntarily, and the desire for suicide had only come to him after he had sought instinctively, on the contrary, to avoid death."

"That's an opposition difficult to comprehend," observed Claude Rolland, smiling.

"It's quite simple, however. He had sought refuge in the river from a crowd that wanted to lynch him, and it was in the middle of the river that uncomprehending disgust for the material instincts of the crowd, combine with the sudden conviction that it would be impossible for him to realize his scientific dream, that inspired him with the sudden idea of ending his existence."

"They wanted to lynch him because he was a great geologist?"

"For another reason, my dear engineer. Old Sinker had an opinion on the subject of our planet that will perhaps seem strange to you, if not insane, as a man nourished on official science, but on his part, it's more than a conviction; it has risen to the level of an ardent faith, a sacred scientific religion.

"You're pricking our curiosity," said Edmée, her elegant body leaning forward.

As Old Sinker so often pricks the earth to your profit," Claude joked.

"Never sufficiently!" said Snow Rose, gravely. "The evil one can never endure too much suffering!"

Claude and Edmée looked at the young Indian in amazement, wondering whether they ought to laugh at her strange exclamation. Williamson's face, nowadays generally smiling, had also taken on an almost mystical seriousness.

The young French couple fell silent, somewhat bewildered, awaiting an explanation for which the Mining King did not keep them waiting long.

He said, in fact: "You'll soon understand the imprecation of that child nourished on the faith of your relative of genius. If he was fleeing, as I've just told you, the lynching with which a furious crowd was threatening him, it's because Old Sinker had just revealed, in a meeting, that he had discovered—and he gave reasons that his audience approved at first, and found persuasive—that the terrestrial globe is not the inert mass that present-day science believes it to be, but a living being: an organism."

"What!" exclaimed Claude's sister. "Something like an immense beast, then?"

"Yes."

"That's an extravagant theory, damn it!" exclaimed the young engineer-cum-explorer.

"Wait before judging, and let me finish my story first," said the billionaire, phlegmatically. "In America, you, see, people aren't astonished by the extraordinary; they even have a tendency to admit it as soon as it's announced, with all the more reason if it's supported by strong evidence and profound knowledge. If Old Stinker had restricted himself to his demonstration he would have been, so to speak, deified by the delirium of spontaneous disciples. Unfortunately for him—and fortunately for me—he let himself get carried away by a singularly dangerous speech.

"'Yes,' he cried, 'the earth that bears us is a living being, but it is also a gigantic monster of cowardly malevolence. And will the Man who shall punish the evil mother of all his misfortunes not be the quintessential Man, the Man pushing well beyond all human power, the Man-God, in a word, because he is almost equal to a god: *the man who will be the murderer of the world?*'

"At first, there was amazement...and then a general egotistical madness. To kill the Earth was to annihilate humankind! Would not the prodigious man who had discovered the living nature of the globe be capable of becoming the murderer that he was praising so highly? The instinct of conservation exasperated the crowd. Speakers surged forth who proclaimed with loud cries the necessity of forming a Club, or a League, of World Defenders.

"Another, more practical, declared that the best thing would be to nip in the bud the possibility of such a...global assassination, by suppressing the man whom an evil genius might make the author of that capital crime.

"Frantic hurrahs welcomed that proposition. Old Sinker fled...and you know the rest."

"I know now," said the young engineer, "that American credulity in fantastic folly must be raised to the nth power. I knew it was extreme, but not to that immeasurable degree." And he gave free rein to the desire to laugh that, out of respect for Williamson, he had so far contained, with great difficulty."

The Earth a beast, with its mines, its productions, its spherical rigidity, its icy poles...its atmosphere! It was simply too baroque!

His fit of hilarity, which Edmée had begun to share, was abruptly cut off.

Snow Rose had bounded, as if moved by a spring, from the far side of the drawing room, where she had been standing, attentive and reserved. Arms forward, her eyes launching an angry glare, an expression of almost ecstatic faith animating her features, she came to a stop three paces from the sofa, shouting in an exalted voice: "Don't laugh! It's impious to laugh at Old Sinker's sacred dogma! It's impious to laugh at the truth!"

"Eh? That's exactly what I'm contesting. Let our amiable guide deign not to anathematize me if my common sense puts in doubt—very great doubt—the first article of the dogma to which she accords her genteel faith!"

"I believe it, because it's true!"

"Oh!"

"And you ought to believe as I do, a paltry creature whom Old Sinker has deigned to educate."

"As I'm not in your situation, you'll surely admit that..."

"No, it's necessary to believe, I tell you!"

"You'll permit..."

"It's necessary to believe, because you have no good reason to support your incredulity."

"That's not so!"

"The Earth is a living being; everything proves it."

Claude Rolland, surprised at first by the sudden fit of fanaticism on the part of Manitoba's daughter, was now very amused by it. He resolved to push her to see how far she would go in the development of what he considered to be an imaginary scientific fantasy in the manner of Verne, who had long been a master of the genre.

"My beautiful Indian," he retorted, "it seems to me that everything demonstrates the contrary."

"Because you don't know or don't want to see."

"I swear to you that I'd be delighted to see through your eyes, which must only see beautiful things."

"They see the truth, which isn't always beautiful."

"No matter—I'll risk it. Enlighten me."

"What objection do you have?" demanded the young Redskin, with a certain hauteur that suited her svelte and elegant person very well.

"First of all, my dear Master, it appears to me that our planet does not exhibit anything in its constitution that could make you assimilate it to a living organism."

"How do you know?"

"But..."

"What do you know on the Earth other than its epidermis?"

"Pardon me. I've descended..."

"Into mines? Then let's say that you've penetrated to the outermost level of the dermis—you're a long way forward! Is it the case that one of the microscopic beings that pullulate on us could claim, because it had plunged into the opening of a pore of our skin by a few hundredths of a millimeter, to know the human organism?"

"So, according to you, the terrestrial crust is the skin..."

"Of the monster, yes. It isn't me who's speaking—I'm only a poor ignorant girl, in spite of the studies I've carried out at the white girls' school. The person who is expressing himself through my voice is the Master, Old Sinker."

"Let's see, you've just made, with regard to humankind, a comparison with parasites living on our surface—a perfectly just comparison. I'll appropriate it in order to observe that the different organic parasites of humans—I won't go into detail; everyone is familiar with them from having suffered them—have, at least a constitution that resembles ours more or less distantly: a head, a body, locomotive apparatus, respiratory, digestive and circulatory systems, organs to touch, vision, hearing, etc., etc., whereas the Earth..."

"One moment, if you please Is it the case that, in order to be alive, nature requires all its creations to have a form and organs similar to ours? Is it not the case that in running the gamut—already vastly extensive—of the organisms we know, and which belong to the Earth, we find many that are totally different from us in their external and internal structure, as of their ways of life, but which are nonetheless alive? It's not an educated man such as Old Stinker's friend tells me you are who needs me to tell him that one finds living beings that are spherical, like the Earth, and not offering anything more in the way of external and clearly visible organs."

"Undoubtedly, by searching in the ultimate series of the animal kingdom..."

"Well, it's not among those sketched beings that it's necessary to classify the Earth, but among those possessing a more perfect organism."

Claude marveled at finding so much knowledge in the young Indian and hearing hr speak with such surety in scientific terms. Edmée was looking at her in amazement, and Williamson was listening gravely, his eyes half-closed.

The engineer exclaimed, not without irony: "You're not classifying the planet among the vertebrates?"

"It's not, however, the projections of the vertebrates that it lacks. What about the great mountain chains? But I don't insist, that similarity not yet, so far as I know, having been proved by the Master. In any case, there's no lack of other similarities. You mentioned a circulatory system?"

"So?"

"What else are its subterranean rivers, seething in the depths of the terrestrial dermis? And take note that they're only tiny cutaneous veins carrying the excreta of the skin in the form of dissolved salts, like the blue blood of our tiny microscopic veins.

"So, for you, the blood of the Earth is water?"

"Pure in the arteries buried in depths that humans have not thus far attained, impure in the veins that we know, and which are the most superficial."

"And respiration? Does your monster breathe?"

"Yes, but more grossly than we go."

"Aha! You admit a difference there?"

"Capital, but normal. Need creates the organ. The Earth has no need of a respiratory apparatus similar to ours, not having to introduce into itself a dense gas like air."

"What does it breathe, then?"

"It absorbs the element in which it moves—the element that we call, vaguely, the ether. Ether is much subtler than air, and the Earth respires it in the fashion of our trees, which assimilate air through the intermediary of their leaves. The penetration takes place by endomosis, and the ether, like air in us, is used to aliment the eternal combustion.

The engineer smiled. "*Si non e vero, e bene trovato!*"[90] he murmured. And he added: "That suppresses the difficulty of…the lungs."

"The Earth possesses two kinds: one internal, which is everywhere, and one for the external or superficial circulation, which is the sea, where the cold veins, or rivers, discharge in order to purify them of their saline water."

"And nutrition?"

"Our rotating and floating beast nourishes itself on solar emanations, that nutrition taking place by a process analogous to the phenomenon of respiration."

"I expected as much. I confess that the theory is insidious and adroit. It has only one great fault—that of colliding head-on with the theory of the central fire, which is demonstrated by a hundred various effects.

"In what way? It's merely a matter of reaching an understanding regarding the expression 'fire.' For us, it's organic matter possessed of a great deal of heat. Now, is it the case that, proportionately speaking, one of the microscopic organisms living on our surface, like those I mentioned to you a little while ago, wouldn't suppose that we had a central fire? Isn't it the case, for example that, progressing into our skin by infinitesimal degrees, it would find heat increasing with depth, given our vital heat and the relative coldness of our normal external habitat?"

"But what about volcanoes, which are the outlets of that chaotic central molten matter?"

---

[90] "If it isn't true, it's well conceived." An Italian saying, usually credited to Giordano Bruno's *De gli heroici furori* [On Heroic Furies] (1584), although it might have existed beforehand.

Snow Rose shrugged her shoulders. "An unhealthy accident provides nothing, except for accidental purulence. Volcanoes are the bursting of boils—of which they have, in fact, the general structure, and lava is merely pus, which is no more a constituent of the body of the Earth than ours.

"Damn! They're long-lasting bursts!"

"Relative to the longevity of the Earth, a volcano that remains active for a hundred centuries doesn't last any longer than one of our sores, which disappears in a few weeks."

"You have an answer for everything."

"You've hardly raised any objection yet, and I have many other arguments to develop. Is it the atmosphere that preoccupies you? Doesn't a mare, after a long gallop, radiate vapors, especially in cold weather? Aren't all animal mouths misty in winter? Now, what is the heat of minuscule beasts by comparison with that of the terrestrial beast, and what is our great winter cold but a parallel with that of the ether, tough which the monster's frantic trajectory moves.

"Are reeking fogs—which, by the way, your theories explain so poorly—a subject on which you would care for some enlightenment? What, pray, is the meaning of your expression: 'It smells feverish?' when you go into a sick-room, if not that the invalid's whole body is giving off an odor, and is therefore carrying a mist invisible to our poor eyes? Often, the terrestrial beast also has a fever on some point of its gigantic body, and emits the relative rarity of those special and more or less deleterious exhalations.

"Would you like to talk..."

"Enough, thanks!" exclaimed Claude, in a tone deprived of gravity, but whose ironic tone had evaporated somewhat. Come on, beautiful and knowledgeable Snow Rose, it's necessary to spare my self-respect a little, as a white European instructed in the errors of the old science.

"You're playing in the unlimited field of hypotheses like an airplane doing stunts over its experimental field, with vertiginous rapidity, precision and a disconcerting assurance. The objection hasn't got time to arise in the mind before it's bowled over by an unexpected outline before which I remain with closed mouth. That's all to the honor of the arguments that Old Sinker has given you, and we admire the fact that you've profited so marvelously from their education—but for us it's very humiliating."

"You're joking about such a grave subject. You're very French."

"I swear to you that I'm not joking. I sense, in your bizarre arguments, certain naiveties of form that, as soon as I try to get past them, present themselves to my judgment like screens partly masking disquieting depths. If they aren't persuasive, I confess that they cause a certain trouble in the mind, and I'm asking you...to let me breathe."

"So be it," said the Indian. "The cup of truth requires to be drained in small sips by those guided by a strong reason, for it ought not to intoxicate them as it does less cultivated minds. It ought to penetrate their cerebral substance gradually, in order to melt into it and transform it. I'll await the opportunity to pursue my demonstration, but I won't let you off today without having deposited in your reason one argument of scientific philosophy that I defy you to refute."

"Go on," said the engineer, reluctantly but curiously.

"From the infinitely small to the infinitely large, nature is unified. The sublime law of universal gravitation applies not only to terrestrial, planetary and sidereal bodies, as the genius of Newton indicated, but also to the most infinitesimal elements of all bodies

"It was anticipated for a long time, and an as-yet-incomplete proof has been provided by the discovery of X-rays, that every solid body is formed by particles cemented together. Exactly the same thing happens in microscopic beings as in the worlds voyaging in the infinity of Time and Space, passing through a drop of water, a blade of grass, humans and mountains to planetary systems. It is the universal vortex, of atoms as for suns. Is that true?"

"Undoubtedly."

"Well, if the universe is unified with respect to movement, by what right do you claim that it is not so with regard to life? You admit that a drop of water contains thousands of organisms animated by an intense life, because the microscope has shown them to you. You think, rightly, that those tiny creatures contain creatures infinitely tiny in respect to them, and so on. You therefore consent to the existence of organic beings in the sense of the descending progression, but you deny it in entities of superior dimension to the animality wandering over the surface of what you call the terrestrial crust? So that animal life rises from the infusorium to the elephant and the whale, but stops there? Why?

"Reflect on that, and you will say, with Old Sinker, that the living organism extends from the 'minus infinity' to the 'plus infinity,' passing through the infusoria, via humans and the Earth, the sun and all the suns we perceive, which are perhaps no more than formidable atoms composing some great being decillions of decillions of miles in extent, microscopic itself with regard to others...and so on, indefinitely!"

"Enough!" begged Edmée, in her turn. "I'm getting vertigo."

"Let's leave it then, Miss, with our petty Earth, which is a very malevolent beast—which explains why there are so many malevolent ones among those which crawl upon its surface. Another time, I'll tell you about its misdeeds. I'll tell you how that monster..."

Snow Rose as unable to finish. After having rapped summarily on the door and entered without waiting for authorization, Jean Guitard came into the drawing room like a gust of wind and ran to Claude Rolland.

"Commandant, I've just come face to face with your cousin."

"De Montalpé?"

"The same."

"Hmm!" aid Williamson, getting up from his rocking chair. "Then Loeb isn't far away!"

205

"Probably."

"And Grégoire saw you?"

"Since I've told you, Commandant, that we nearly bumped into one another."

"What bad luck, only a few hours before our departure!" Edmée declared.

"Oh, Mam'zelle, if the Great American Shark hasn't discovered our niche, it isn't the cousin who'll let the cat out of the bag."

"You're dreaming, Jean. Isn't he allied with the man you've so aptly baptized?"

"Allied like the mouse and the cat, Commandant."

"How do you know?"

"He told me so, of course."

"You talked to him then?"

"For sure. Or rather, it's him who talked to me, because I received him like a smoker in a Sainte-Barbe!"[91]

"He's fallen out with our enemy, then?"

"He's had enough of being treated like a lame dog by him, especially after the trick that he played in Mam'zelle Snow Rose's father's place, with regard to which his flapping tongue worked out so well for us. Then again, he thinks that the dirty dog of a pirate is using...methods compromising for anyone who sails in convoy with him. He thinks that one can't go around sinking ships and provoking worthy people to rebellion without the police getting involved, especially when it's a matter of a person like Monsieur Mining King. So, he thinks it would be prudent to get away from Loeb, to obtain your pardon, to offer you his amity and to pursue the recovery of the inheritance in concert, which he'd rather share than risk being electrocuted someday—which is the way they guillotine people hereabouts."

"And what did you reply?"

"I put on my amiable expression of a steel mask to tell him that I'd deliver his message. I came up double quick to tell you about it, via the elevator to the fourteenth floor, in order that he couldn't follow my route."

"Might this offer of reconciliation conceal a trap?"

"On your cousin's part, Commandant? Word of a matelot, I don't think so. He's not clever enough for that."

"I agree with Captain Furet," Williamson opined. "Nevertheless, it's necessary to look twice before making him welcome. His incompetence makes him a precious auxiliary...but in the hands of the adversary. The adventure among the Menominees proves that.

---

[91] Sainte Barbe [Saint Barbara] is the patron saint of artillerymen, military engineers, miners and anyone else who works with explosives, so "Saint-Barbe" became slang in Catholic France for ammunition-dumps, dynamite-stores and so on—and also for booby-trap bombs.

"In that case, Monsieur Williamson, it would be more advantageous to us to constrain him to stay with Loeb?"

"I think so, Monsieur Rolland. But in that regard, there's an accessory question. It's not the accomplice that worries me. If he's staying in this hotel, as it's his first time in Chicago, it's because Loeb brought him or sent him here. Now, is that choice a mere coincidence, or has our exceedingly skillful and powerful adversary has discovered our retreat?"

As if in response to that question, the electric bell situated beside the fire place in a metallic box sealed into the wall, connected to a pneumatic tube, signaled the arrival of a visiting card, which the Mining King went to collect, without his phlegm deigning to hasten a single one of his strides.

"He's the answer," he said, in his most tranquil voice. Without the slightest trace of emotion, he read aloud: "*Jonathan Loeb informs Mr. Williamson that he can take off his false beard and cease to cloister himself. J. Loeb, president of the reconstituted Club of World Defenders, is waiting for you to come alone to the landing of this floor, neutral and public ground, setting aside any possibility of an ambush, for an urgent conversation and an interesting proposition.*"

Claude, Edmée and the mariner looked at one another, anxious and troubled. Snow Rose furrowed her black eyebrows. Only Williamson seemed no more emotional than is the incident were happening in Tokyo or Valparaiso, and concerned someone else entirely. In his nonchalant tone, he said: "Good. I'll go."

"Let me go with you!" exclaimed Claude and the matelot, running toward him.

Williamson stopped them with a gesture. "It says *alone*. So stay here, and whatever happens, don't budge."

He put his hand to his belt to make sure that his revolver was in its holster, and, that gesture alone betraying his secret opinion of the gravity of the situation, he went out.

8. A Drama in an Elevator

When he arrived on the landing, Williamson scanned it in its entirety with a rapid glance. In the center, the twin elevators were in action, dispersing residents or visitors to all the floors. On the monumental stairway with a double revolution, its steps covered with a thick carpet, members of the service staff were going up and down, crossing paths with residents who were only coming or going between the neighboring floors, disdaining the mechanical elevators. On the landing itself, two of the numerous doors were not closed.

Satisfied with that entirely reassuring examination, observing that his enemy had not lied about the "neutral territory," the Mining King marched toward Loeb, who, quitting his station in front of the elevator-shafts, came striding to meet him, with his hat on his head.

"You wanted to see me. What do you want?"

"To finish."

"With?"

"An absurd situation."

"Your pursuit?"

"You've escaped me twice."

"Only because the attack was, on each occasion, badly planned."

"It's too many machinations for a simple suppression. I've had enough."

"Good. I'll be glad to have peace."

"Complete. I've come to propose an arrangement that will give it to you."

"Go on."

"First, I want you to know that I don't have any direct hatred against you."

"Your actions, however..."

"Are aimed over your head."

"Old Sinker?"

"Lobanief, yes. You understood my card?"

"President of the Club of World Defenders. I thought that was an old story."

"I've rejuvenated it."

"To make yourself a weapon?"

"Against Lobanief, whom I hate, and to whom I don't want you to bring the help of your millions and the incredible luck that favors you."

"The fact is that you're not fortunate against me."

"It doesn't matter to me that you're alive, as long as you don't get in my way."

"It's you who are getting in my way."

"Solely because it indicates mine. I want Lobanief choking under my foot, and I need your guide to reach him. You're rich enough. Let me do my work and I'll let you live."

"You can see that I'm conserving it quite well without your permission."

"Renounce joining the man who has summoned you."

"No."

"Tell me where I can find him."

"He hasn't made me that confidence."

"Then let me take the girl that's guiding you; I'll be able to force her to guide me."

"A thousand regrets."

"That's...no?"

"No—today, tomorrow and forever."

"It's you who are forcing me to kill you in order to render myself master!"

"She has other guardians."

"With you out of the way, they scarcely count Do they have the domination of men, as I do? The power of gold, like you?"

"They have intelligence."

"That's good to serve."

"Courage."

"Useful to die. Let's leave those negligibilities. It's between the two of us that the struggle is circumscribed, since you don't want to give up."

"Never."

"Do you know something?"

"I will when you've told me."

"It's that my life has been entirely guided by my hatred, and now that I'm within reach of my vengeance, my hatred is my entire life."

"Which means?"

"That I'm only living to satisfy my hatred, to the accomplishment of which you're raising the supreme obstacle."

"Conclusion?"

"Be good players. Instead of wasting time and effort in plans of attack and defense let's settle the future like good Yankees, revolvers in hand. The survivor will be free of all cares."

"That's neat. I like it. When?"

"Ah! Right away. Rightly or wrongly, I thought you'd refuse… tomorrow, perhaps?"

"Because?"

"Of…those who are accompanying you."

"Then you're mistaken. I don't want to expose them to your ambushes any longer."

"It's a point of view."

"But we can't do it here. At the first shot, people would come running. And I think it would be in bad taste to give the spectacle to…my companions."

"Yes, besides, we'd be hindered…wait! I have the means."

"Where?"

"Without leaving here."

"Which is?"

"The elevators."

"Practical?"

"You'll see."

Taking a voluminous chronometer from his fob pocket, Loeb said, in his hoarse and imperious voice: "Let's synchronize our watches."

"Three-fourteen and twelve seconds," Williamson said, having taken out his own.

"I'll set mine to your time."

"You can—it's that of the Observatory in Washington. Now?"

"At three-thirty exactly I'll take one of the elevators, alone, from the roof of the skyscraper. At the same time, also alone, you take the other from the ground floor…"

209

"Good. When they meet, fire at will..."

"And, arriving at the bottom before any word of the affair has spread. I'll make myself scarce, to avoid any annoying complications."

"What about me?"

"Oh, no one will cause any disturbance to the famous Mining King. Anyway, it doesn't matter—you'll be dead."

"Or you. I'll have on me a declaration certifying that there was regulation duel."

"Me too."

"Agreed for three-thirty."

"Agreed."

The two adversaries turned their backs, and Williamson, very calm, almost smiling, went back to his apartment.

He found his friends there, their expressions distraught with anxiety. Claude and Edmée ran to him.

"What happened? Condemned to remain here by your order, we were in mortal dread."

"Nothing happened," said Williamson, with a forced cheerfulness, "that isn't, fundamentally, very advantageous."

"For us?"

"Certainly. Loeb declares that he's tired of tracking us."

"Him?"

"And regrets the needless trouble it has caused you."

"He'll reach a settlement?"

"I think I can bring him to one. We'll be having a second... private conversation about the subject shortly."

Edmée, fixing the billionaire with her large profound eyes, velvety and limpid, said to him, choosing the most harmoniously soft notes of her beautiful voice: "Why, Monsieur Williamson, aren't you telling us the truth?"

"Me?"

"Don't be astonished; I sense that there's something else, or something more, than what you're expressing. I swear to you that you can confide in us, who have open hearts with regard to you."

"You have, then, some amity toward me, Miss Edmée?"

"A great deal, Monsieur Williamson, and a little more every day, because every day I discover a little more of the secret man that you hide within you, under the disabused mask of the billionaire that villainous humankind has spoiled."

The Mining King did not reply immediately. Then, adopting a detached tone, he said: "I assure you, Miss, that there's nothing but what I've told you."

"As you wish!" said the young woman, a trifle sadly, still visibly incredulous In the midst of the somewhat constrained general silence that followed, she added: "I also sense that our presence embarrasses you at the moment, and that you'd rather be alone."

"For a moment, yes, perhaps. I need to reflect on the fashion in which it will be necessary, momentarily, to engage the combat…of words…with my adversary." Seeing his companions sketch a movement toward the threshold, however, he swiftly added: "But don't go away. There's no need to return to your rooms. Go in there, into my bedroom. I'll only be a few minutes."

He doesn't want us to appear on the landing, thought Claude Rolland's sister. But she did not breathe a word, and, contenting herself with nodding her head graciously as a sign of acquiescence, she indicated the discreet retreat route to her brother and the mariner—and to the young Indian, who never ceased to devour the latter with his eyes.

Williamson's gaze followed Edmée until she disappeared.

When, with urgent politeness, "Captain Furet" had closed the door behind Snow Rose, the expression of the American King changed abruptly, and a crease of anxiety was hollowed out in is smooth forehead.

He sat down rapidly at a writing-desk. On the first sheet of paper that came to hand he traced a few lines:

I declare that, having been killed in a duel, my last will is that my adversary not be either sought or troubled on account of my decease.

He folded up the paper and put it in his pocket.

On another, he wrote:

I bequeath all that I possess to Miss Edmée Rolland, who, with her brother, is accompanying me on the present voyage. I designate Monsieur Claude Rolland, her brother, to continue on her behalf, with the title of managing director, the exploitation of my mines and associated factories. She will not forget that Toby has served me well, the Jean Guitard has twice saved our lives, and that Snow Rose is a friend of Old Sinker.

He put the address of a solicitor on an envelope, unhooked a telephone and said: "Hello? The hotel manager… It's you? Good. Would you care to come up tight away to the ninth floor, number 174, with three or four people that you have ready to hand. Understood? All right!"

Three minutes later, the manager of the skyscraper and the requested assistants appeared in front of Williamson. The latter said to the master of the immense caravanserai: "I'm present here, as are my companions, under a false name. I'm Williamson, the Mining King."

"I know."

"Ah! Since when?"

"An hour ago."

"Naturally..." And the billionaire thought: *That simplifies things*. Aloud, he went on: "You and these gentlemen are going to establish in writing that it really is me who signed these documents in your presence."

When the signature had been countersigned and the witnesses dismissed, Williamson put his testament into the envelope he had prepared and, handing the later to the Hotel manager, whom he had retained, he said: "You will only hand this letter back to me, in person. If I...judge it appropriate not to do so today, before nightfall, you will immediately send it or put it into the hands of its addressee. Here's twenty dollars for the errand-boy.

The hotel manager acquiesced, and left. Williamson looked at his watch. He only had four and a half minutes left. He took his revolver from its holster and examined the barrel, replaced the weapon methodically to his belt and quit his apartment, at a tranquil pace.

While all this was happening in the Mining King's room, another brief scene was unfolding on the landing of the floor.

As Loeb, having quit Williamson, strode toward the ascending elevator, he had made an authoritative sign to an individual resembling a Quaker who emerged therefrom and immediately disappeared into the stairwell. At that moment, Grégoire de Montalpé, coming down from Jean Guitard's room, where he had gone to wait the response he expected from the latter, appeared on the ninth floor landing.

At the sight of him, Loeb frowned. "I ordered you to keep watch in the ground floor grill room," he said, brutally.

The accomplice baulked. "I revoked the order myself. I've had enough of being treated like a whipped dog in order to go after my money."

"What are you saying?"

"That I'm finally rebelling! That I'm changing uniform! That I'm leaving, if you want it in a word."

"You think so!" exclaimed Jonathan Loeb, with a dry, sinister snigger of sinister irony.

"I'm so convinced of it," said the other, raising his head like a bloody and de-plumed cock at the end of a losing fight, "that it's now a settled matter. My re-entry has been negotiated into the grace of my cousins and Williamson, whom you have failed to stop for a second time."

"Because of your stupidity."

"Not with regard to the collision at sea, though! And then, you know, please keep your insults for others. Whether you like it or not, I'm handing in my resignation. That's it!"

"Cretin!"

"Ah! There you go!"

"Peace, then! What about my permission?"

"I'll do without it."

"Listen. I'd like nothing better than for you to go over to the enemy."

"What?"

"You had twenty thousand dollars; we've spent four. Are you going to give me the remaining sixteen?"

"Give them to you? That's not going to happen."

"If you don't give them to me willingly, you'll be found tomorrow lying on the bank of Lake Michigan, unburdened to my advantage."

"What about the police?" de Montalpé countered, unable to help shivering.

"Half those in Chicago are under my control—so, no idle threats. I'll take the cash and you'll go to Williamson to betray me...if, in a quarter of an hour, that's still necessary. But remember this: you're going into the enemy camp with my permission, to serve me there."

"Never!"

"I've put down better men than you, my lad. Not having the leisure, at the moment, to take care of such a small matter, I'm content to scorn this vain attempt at rebellion, which you'll redeem by showing zeal and trying not to be stupid. You're going to run to the square at the end of the street. On the sidewalk outside the entrance door, you'll find a gentleman Ask him whether or not his dispositions are presently made, wholly or partly, in accordance with my orders. Whatever his reply is, I need it here before three twenty-five. You have exactly five minutes. Go!"

"But..."

"Would you prefer the lake or two inches of steel between the shoulder-blades?"

"Me? I'm...going. But when I get back I warn you..."

"You'll receive my instructions on the nature of your role in the Williamson camp, if they make the mistake of letting you in. Go!"

De Montalpé made a grand gesture of heroic decision...and took to his heels, in order to obey more rapidly.

Loeb shrugged his shoulders and murmured: "Oh, if he didn't represent the sinews of war...never mind. If I'm rid of Williamson shortly, all will be well. If, impossibly, the encounter turns to my disadvantage, I've woven a net around him that he won't escape."

And, striding back and forth on the landing, he waited, frequently consulting his watch.

The five minutes were up. De Montalpé had not reappeared. Leaning over the cage of the elevators, Loeb waited two more minutes, tapping his foot angrily.

He saw Williamson come out of his apartment. He only had the time strictly necessary to get to the top of the skyscraper. With a gesture of annoyance, he activated the handle of the elevator, which immediately stopped in front of him, jumped into it and started it moving toward the summit of the immense building, while Williamson went down to the ground floor in the same fashion.

213

Almost immediately, the anxious faces of Claude, Edmée and Jean appeared on the threshold of the apartment, ahead of that, equally anxious, of the young Indian woman. From the depths of their retreat, their ears, on the alert, had caught the sound of the billionaire's unusual exit. Infringing the prohibition, Edmée had gone into the deserted drawing room. They had all headed for the landing then, having understood that Williamson's intention was to keep them out of the way—which caused them to suppose that something serious was about to happen.

They were not mistaken. They had only been there for five minutes, consulting one another anxiously with their gazes, when, before their anxious eyes, the paths of the two elevators crossed. A series of detonations departed from the one that was descending, followed by a cry, and then a raucous oath.

The descent continued on the one hand. The other vertical transporter, which had stopped at the floor, opened, and in the midst of a general exclamation emerging from numerous doors suddenly disengaging a surprised population, a bare-headed man bounded on to the platform, his face bloodied, beating the air madly with his arms, and fell almost at the feet of Edmée and Claude, who cried out at the same time: "Montalpé!"

Aided by the mariner and the young Redskin, both of them bent down to help the unfortunate man. Meanwhile, guests and members of the hotel staff hurried down the double stairway in pursuit of the murderer.

The hero of the adventure, however, must have been more frightened than hurt, for, getting to his feet, he started howling in French: "Help! Murder! He's killed me!"

Suddenly recognizing his cousins, he implored them, in a fearful voice: "Protect me! Hide me! The killer will come back!"

"What killer?"

"*Him!*"

"Who's *him?*"

"Don't pronounce his name! Shut up, for pity's sake! He'll kill me again!"

"Damn it! For a dead man, you're making a lot of noise!" Claude could not help remarking.

"Come on, be quiet and let us look at your wound," added the engineer's sister, using her delicate handkerchief to mop up the blood, already quite abundant, that was reddening the dandy's forehead.

"Be careful!" the latter moaned. "The bullet went through my skull."

"Damn it!" exclaimed the former explorer, holding the terror-stricken man still be force. "If your cranium had been pierced you wouldn't be moaning so much. Your wound is a long graze, that's all. There's no reason to scream as if you were being flayed alive."

"You think so?"

"Yes, there, at the top of the head."

"I don't have a fractured skull?"

"I'll admit that you've had a narrow escape. A centimeter of difference in the trajectory and you'd be the late Montalpé."

"De Montalpé, my dear!" rectified the Parisian fop, vaingloriously.

Claude burst out laughing. "The pride is uninjured," he said. "You can see quite clearly that the brain hasn't been damaged. A little iron perchloride lotion and it'll be fine. Jean!"

"Commandant?"

"Fetch a bellboy."

"Done, Commandant; there's one coming now with a first aid kit."

While Claude bandaged the wounded man, Edmée murmured: "How did this happen? What's become of Williamson? My God, where is he?" Her features were distressed. In an emotional voice, she said to her brother: "Claude, leave our bad relative, who scarcely needs treatment except for fear, and run to help our great friend. I'm sure that his life is in danger! Go quickly, with Jean. Find him, protect him…ward off a frightful misfortune that I can sense hanging over him."

"Here's the man Old Sinker summoned," Snow Rose announced, pointing at Williamson, who was coming up the stars, tranquilly.

"Oh!" said Edmée, taking a step toward him. "I was afraid that you'd been killed."

"Don't worry, Miss. Things have passed in a satisfactory manner, if not without an unexpected hitch, and I've made sure of my adversary's retreat."

"Ah! My presentiment wasn't mistaken. It was a duel, and an odious duel! Oh, it was wicked of you to hide it from…"

She did not finish. Suddenly weakening, she almost fainted in her brother's arms.

"That's extraordinary," murmured the Mining King, with an anxious astonishment. "Miss Edmée waited so intrepidly for execution by the Menominees."

"Her soul is strong in common peril," Claude explained, "but her heart is generous and feeble before a danger run by a friend without her sharing it."

Williamson said nothing more. He was visibly troubled by that nervous weakness, so inexplicable for his psychology, and a hard labor began in his brain, to which the young woman's prompt return to self-possession put an end.

"Excuse that sudden weakness," she said, smiling a little awkwardly. "I don't understand it myself, but it's over. Now, tell me quickly how it came about that those bullets, of which I felt the impact deep within me, and were surely addressed to you, were fired—one of them, at least—at Monsieur de Montalpé."

"You see, Miss, they say that a man doesn't walk toward his misfortune, but that he runs to it. Now, it wasn't only at a run, it was by violence that my adversary's companion took my place in the elevator, in which I was waiting until the exact second agreed before going up to encounter Loeb."

215

"Hold on, damn it!" cried the man wounded in error. "My murderer had enjoined me, on pain of death, to bring him an answer urgently, and I was nearly five minutes late."

""What answer?" demanded Williamson, staring at him imperiously.

"You're asking too much. I was to find out from a gentleman whether something—I don't know what—was ready."

"Well," said the Mining King, in a harsh voice that was not habitual to him, "since you're so slightly wounded that you can screech and lie like this, why don't you run off and make your report to your master."

"Know, Monsieur Williamson, that Grégoire de Montalpé doesn't recognize any master! Then again, I've had enough of running his errands and spinning like a top in the hands of such a man. The miracle is that he didn't kill me just now, and I don't want to find myself in his presence, and that of his revolver, again. Besides which, you ought to know that I want to break with that bloodthirsty man and attach myself henceforth to your fortune. The mariner in the service of my cousin Rolland ought to have told you..."

"Faithfully," declared the billionaire, in the same tone. "I had postponed my response until now. Here it is: I won't accept into our company a traitor, a spy...or an imbecile."

"Monsieur! I do not accept such epithets!"

"Oh, I won't impose them cumulatively—you can choose. But what I want most of all is for you to liberate us from your presence."

"You're throwing me back into the power of that pitiless man?"

"Of your ally."

"See how he treats me!"

"Error doesn't count."

"I'm doomed, then!"

"That's not my concern. Let's leave it there, please."

"No. I won't leave!"

"We'll leave you, then. Let's go back to my room, my friends."

"I'm not budging from here, and you'll have to come out again. Then, I shall follow you..."

Grégoire de Montalpé did not have time to say any more. At a sign from Williamson, now known to all of the hotel staff, two of the employees had put their hands on his shoulders and were leading him away without his consent, forcibly dragging him to the elevator, into which they pushed him before getting in with him. The dandy protested in vain, his exclamation rapidly fading away into the distance of the lower floors.

"But if I understand the conditions of this fortunately abortive duel correctly," said the young engineer to the Mining King during that forced descent, "your adversary had all the advantages. Descending like that, he could see you for some time, while the metallic floor of his elevator protected him until the two machines crossed paths. How were you able to accept such dangerously un-equal conditions?"

Resuming his habitual indolent voice, Williamson replied, smiling: "Bah! What did it matter to me? I have faith in my lucky star, and you can see that it didn't betray me. That's the third time in a matter of days that I've escaped Loeb's attempts on my life, and he's a strong player. 'It's written,' as the fol-lowers of Mohammed that you've frequented in the course of your African ex-plorations would say.

"Oh, Monsieur Williamson, don't talk to me about Africa—don't awaken my remorse!"

"Your remorse?"

"For having broken my promise to Senator Dupeyroux. It's today that he was to make his famous interpellation. And when I think that my report was swallowed up with the unfortunate yacht, and that, without it, the senator was unarmed...how he must be cursing me!"

"Perhaps not. Who knows?" And, smiling amiably, the billionaire added: "Perhaps, like me, your Monsieur Dupeyroux has a lucky star. Anyway, it's not your fault, is it?"

"Certainly not."

"Having nothing for which to reproach yourself, expel all vexation from your mind on that subject, and let's think about us." Raising his voice and ad-dressing the small circle of his companions of both sexes, he added: "As it would be ridiculous to try to maintain an incognito that can no longer deceive anyone, we'll be able to get a little air. I'll go to the bank to get a hundred thou-sand dollars, the dollar being a weapon of attack and defense superior to bullets that miss their target, and of which we've deprived ourselves for too long since we've been on American soil."

"We'll go with you," declared Claude and Edmée, swiftly.

"That's what I want, for it would be wise never to split up. It will procure me the pleasure of employing the few hours that remain to us by showing Miss Edmée around Chicago, which she's doubtless curious to see. Rendezvous in ten minutes in my room, where I'll telephone for an automobile. Until then!"

And, as tranquilly as if no drama had taken place there, he left the land-ing—where numerous groups, already including a few reporters, were comment-ing on the "terrible duel" between the Mining King and an unknown enemy.

9. The Rain of Gold

For a simple excursion in the city, to which a certain slowness would add charm and interest, Williamson could have contented himself with one of the large elegantly harnessed carriages or automobiles that the hotel kept conscious-ly at the disposal of tourist clients. If he had preferred an automobile of a pres-tigious make with a powerful engine, it was not without reason.

As soon as Claude Rolland and Edmée had rejoined him in his drawing room, he asked the latter to do him a small favor in order to keep her occupied momentarily, and he took the engineer to one side.

"Can you drive an automobile?"

"Certainly."

"Good."

"But...we'll have a driver?"

"It might be the case that I'll decide to dispense with him."

"Ah!"

"In any case, you'll need keep a very close eye on the man at the wheel."

"You can't suppose that an unknown driver who might be absolutely any-one, could be...?"

"I don't suppose anything, but I'm wary of everything. Don't be distracted because of your sister; I'll look after her very carefully. Tell your brave Captain Furet to keep his eyes on the young Indian, along with Toby."

I believe that instruction's unnecessary, the former explorer thought, smil-ing involuntarily. To the legitimately suspicious billionaire, he said: "You think that Loeb, having failed to catch you in the trap of that infernal duel, will set up some new ambush for us?"

"The ambush—I don't know what—is certainly planned and perhaps al-ready set. I need no more proof of that than the urgent mission with which he charged your cousin a little while ago. Be assured, though, that as soon as I feel the banknotes in my pocket, I'll no longer be content with a passive defense that will end up by doing us a bad turn, for there's no chance that he'll let up. Not another word. Don't worry anyone, but be ready to understand me at the slight-est sign."

"You can count on me."

"I know."

Five minutes later, the little troop, fully equipped, were heading at top speed in the direction of the bank indicated to the driver by Williamson. From there, they went to an agency of the New York *Herald*, into which Snow Rose went on her own—under incessant surveillance, without being aware of it—in order to insert a small ad, the secret of which she wanted to keep.

The Mining King had never seemed to be in such good humor, even aboard the steam yacht *Astrea*, where the presence of Claude, and especially of Edmée, had alleviated his long-standing ennui. It was because, as a man accustomed to the power of money, having had his chest solidly padded with banknotes and his pockets ballasted with dollars at the bank, he felt his strength renewed, and had become proudly confident again.

It was in an almost jovial tone that he said to the young Frenchwoman: "Miss Edmée, it's up to you now to give orders, and dictate the itinerary that your Parisienne whim requires. What would you like to see in Chicago? The pig factories? No, I understand. The monuments? I fear that by comparison with your prestigious Paris, they'll be disappointing. The shores of Lake Michigan, perhaps?"

"Oh yes, said the young woman. "I only glimpsed them from the railway—Erie first, then Michigan—and from a distance. I'd like to see one of those inland seas at closer range."

"The ladies and gentlemen could take a little trip to the former site of the World's Fair, from which there's a superb view over the lake, and where numerous attractions are gathered: music halls, circuses, velodromes and all kinds of sports clubs, including the Aero Club, for which a special factory producing lighting gas has been built, and another producing hydrogen."

"Is that all right, Monsieur Williamson?"

"I repeat, Miss, that we're entirely at your orders."

The auto pulled away at a moderate speed, and then, when it reached a broad straight avenue, launched forward at forty an hour, which soon brought it to the edge of a vast liquid plain, some five hundred and seventy kilometers long and as much as a hundred and forty broad, in comparison with which the largest lakes of Europe are mere ponds.

In the immense gathering of various amusements, it was so quiet, the numerous visitors being thinly spread as they strolled or watched the sports with placid and joyful conviction, that Williamson after a long moment contemplating the lake, saw no inconvenience in the excursion continuing on foot, with pauses in a music hall and on the edge of a golf course, a cricket pitch, etc.

When the little troop emerge from a giant cinema, where they had been diverted to the extent of forgetting momentarily the terrors of the past and their anxieties for the future, they did not find the automobile at the place where they had left it. They only had to wait for a few minutes, for the rapid vehicle did not take long to come to pick up its passengers, but that displeased Williamson, who was not fully satisfied by the excuse furnished by the driver. He decided, in consequence, to resume the effective and direct command that he had relinquished temporarily—in appearance, at least—to gracious feminine whimsy.

With a rapid wink, she showed the engineer a pocket map of the State of Wisconsin, on which he rapidly traced several large zigzags with his finger, whose significance Claude understood immediately.

For Williamson, in fact, the present excursion was merely an adroit feint to put Loeb off the track.

Ostensibly, the little troop was to leave that evening by the Western Railroad. Orders had been left at the hotel to transport the travelers' meager baggage there. In the meantime they were killing time visiting Chicago.

In reality, Williamson was using the excursion to make a real clandestine departure. The auto being a hundred HP,[92] he was about to launch it at top speed

---

[92] The author inserts an entirely gratuitous footnote at this point: "The author cannot protest too much here against the incurable malady of our sportsmen that

across country, changing direction so as to avoid and pursuit, and connect with the railway at a distance, in good time to satisfy the peremptory instruction formulated by the young Indian guide.

It was improbable that, until that moment, Loeb and his sleuths had not been taken in. If he had prepared some immediate *coup de Jarnac*, it was evident that the blow, whatever it was, could not fall until they returned from the excursion, between that return and the advertised departure, quite probably at the railway station.

Now, Loeb would wait in vain for the return to the city and the departure, and if he launched himself in pursuit of the auto, it would be at the very moment that the travelers were boarding their Pullman car.

If, by chance—which possibility, at the moment, Williamson was not far from admitting—the chauffeur was under orders and tried to prevent the execution of the plan, excellent by virtue of its very simplicity, we know that the Mining King was resolved to throw him overboard.

Thus, as he climbed into the auto, Williamson said pleasantly to the engineer and his sister: "If you don't mind, we're going to put on a little speed."

"Oh," said Edmée, with a disappointed expression. "Aren't we continuing this amusing and interesting excursion?"

"Yes, but by going on to Hyde Park, a few miles away."

---

consists of always Britannizing necessary technical terms. "HP" is an abbreviation of the expression 'Horse-Power,' which is exactly similar to our '*cheval-vapeur*,' or, word for word, '*cheval-puissance*.' It is observable that only the expressions are synonymous, not existing between the English HP and our *cheval-vapeur*. That one employs the English expression in a country where English is spoken, as is the case here, is normal, but in France it is simply ridiculous Anglomania. If one objects that the expression "*cheval-vapeur*" is no longer adequate to internal combustion engines which are, in fact, a French invention, let it be replaced by, for example, "*cheval-force*" (CF), but let us not, by borrowing a foreign locution, Britannize, so to speak, our own invention, so fecund and so beautiful, and to which it is necessary from every viewpoint to leave the glory of our fatherland, so fertile in the work of progress." The first commercially viable two-stroke internal combustion engine was, in a way, French, having been developed in Paris by the Belgian emigré Étienne Lenoir in 1859, and describing its capability in terms of "*cheval-vapeur*" [literally, horse-steam] was, indeed, always silly—although "*cheval-force*" is no better (and positively ridiculous if translated literally into English). The problem vanished of its own accord, however, when the comparison with horses was largely abandoned, being conventionally replaced in the context of automobile engines by measurements of their cylinder capacity, and in other contexts by the unit named after the displaced term's inventor, James Watt (thus reflecting the glory of Scotland, alas for the French).

220

"We're not stopping beforehand at the Aero Club, whose landing-ground I can see over there, surrounded by a fence plastered with posters?"

"On the way back, if you wish."

"What if it's dark? Since we've arrived at the edge of the lake I've been gazing enviously at the colossal sphere of the captive balloon rising up—so high!"

"It goes up half a mile—eight hundred and eighty yards," the driver made haste to inform her.

"What a view one must have from up there, in such clear weather! One must be able to see the whole of the lake, and beyond it, the state to which it gives its name. Who knows whether one might be able to see Erie, the Saint-Clair River and the tip of the great peninsula the Canadian Ontario extends into the lacustrian cranium of the United States?"

"Miss Edmée," Williamson replied, putting on a jovially sulky expression, "I appeal to your sense of justice. If demoiselles have these whimsical desires, which are laws so far as they're concerned, gentlemen are not spared fashionable neurasthenia, and I have to take into account its nervous demands on the temperament. Personally, in an auto, I experience an irrational need for speed. If I don't satisfy it, I sense that I shall become peevish for forty-eight hours. Just grant me thirty minutes to calm that unhealthy irritation. I promise you that we'll make the ascension that appears to be tempting your heart immediately thereafter."

Edmée pursed her lips, not without chagrin. "Are you quite sure," she said, with an enigmatic smile, "that this little crisis is really neurasthenic, and not simply egot..."

She stopped dead. Her gaze had just met her brother's, and she had read therein...that something was at stake. "In fact," she exclaimed, laughing, "as you wish. After all, deep down, I don't care about the famous ascension anymore."

"I expected no less of you, Miss," said Williamson, seriously. And he turned to the driver, who was staring at Edmée, doubtless astonished by such a sudden change of mind. He showed him the road that led due south and ordered, in a dry tone: "Forward! At forty-five and hour!"

The man seemed hesitant. "That's the maximum my engine can manage," he observed.

"I know."

"I've never yet demanded that speed of it. I won't take the responsibility, and I can't guarantee anything."

"I'll pay for any damage to the auto...and there's five hundred dollars for you if I'm satisfied."

"I'll try."

In a matter of seconds the automobile reached the long fence alongside the aerodrome where Edmée had wanted to make her first excursion toward the zenith; in a few more seconds, it had been surpassed...when all of a sudden, the driver cut the ignition and applied the brake.

"What's wrong?" interrogated the billionaire, a trifle rudely.

"What I feared. I can hear a rattle that worries me. It must have overheated. I need to take a look."

"How much time do you need?"

"Five or six minutes, I think."

"I won't give you any more."

The vehicle stopped, the driver jumped out, and Claude Rolland got out with him.

The man exposed the engine, looked. Scrutinizing it with minute attention, and hence with a slowness that appeared to irritate Williamson, watching from his seat.

"You can't find anything?" Claude asked him.

"No, nothing. Everything's working normally. It's doubtless a loose bolt that needs tightening. I'll go underneath."

Armed with a monkey wrench, he slid under the automobile.

The engineer had scarcely raised his eyes than he met the imperative gaze of Williamson, obviously reproaching him: *What are you doing? You're interrupting your surveillance!*

Claude threw himself flat on the ground. He saw the chauffeur busy tightening a bolt, who said to him: "The gentleman can see. It's what I thought—a little looseness in the thread. It's fixed."

The man crawled out from under the vehicle while Claude stood up. The latter saw that the Mining King was standing up in his seat, pointing in the direction in which the vehicle was heading.

"What's that?" he demanded, curtly.

That was a black mass of people marching along the road, heading for the Exhibition site that the travelers had just quit.

"The ones in the lead are carrying a banner," announced Jean Guitard, making use of his keen eyesight.

Unhurriedly resuming his seat after the engineer, the driver said, disdainfully. "It's a troop of the Salvation Army, who march singing hymns, supposedly for the purification of these places of amusement, which they qualify as dens of iniquity. Don't take any notice of them. They'll move out of the way."

He put his hand on the gear-stick, but Williamson stopped him abruptly.

"Turn round!" the commanded. "Go the other way. Take us to Evanston instead of Hyde Park."

"Because of those people?"

"Do as you're told," said the billionaire.

"Oh, as you wish. The road north is as good as the road south."

Starting it in motion, the man turned the vehicle around. When it was heading in the right direction, he put it brutally into fourth gear, and without anyone having been able to anticipate the insensate action, leapt out on to the road, where the acquired velocity laid him out on the ground.

The leap might have been fatal. The voyagers did not even have time to make that reflection when a violent detonation resounded, and the auto lifted up as if it were about to take off.

But for the composure and promptitude with which the engineer bounded into the driving seat, cut the ignition and maintained the direction, there would have been a catastrophe. Under the firm and skillful handling of Claude, the auto, mastered, came to a halt.

"It's a burst tire," he explained.

"By the driver, when you took your eyes off him," said Williamson, in a dull voice.

Turning around swiftly, he saw the man, fifty paces away, get to his feet and draw away, limping, still suffering the effects of his voluntary fall.

"Scoundrel!" growled the billionaire. "I promised to pay you well for your services. Here!"

His arm extended, holding a revolver. He fired.

The chauffeur beat the air with his arms and fell backwards.

A clamor in the ranks of the Salvationists responded to that execution, and the troop started running.

"Quickly, everyone out!" Williamson commanded. "Run to the aerodrome!"

As the little company, out of breath, reached the southern end of the fence, they perceived another mass of people, running flat out, coming from the north.

"Those," announced the mariner, "have a big triangle at the end of a pole by way of a flag."

"It's decidedly serious," murmured Williamson. "Loeb doesn't waste any time! The Knights of Labor now! We must at all costs reach the entrance to the Aero Club before those people do."

They started running again, Claude and Jean supporting—almost carrying—Edmée, who was incapable of maintaining the pace.

They arrived level with the captive balloon, the dome of which, gilded by the rays of the sun going down in the west, emerged gigantically above the palisade. At that moment, the leader of the fugitives realized that it would be impossible to reach the entrance, still more than three hundred yards away, in time.

"Halt!" he commanded. "Backs to the palisade and get enough breath back to make our shots count. I think we can hold them at bay long enough for those inside to come to our aid."

"Counting on others is borrowing on the inheritance of the living, always a bad move," philosophized the mariner. "Only counting on oneself is more reliable. This accursed fence is more than two brasses high—no matter; let's try. Without commanding you, Commandant, brace yourself. I'll put Toby on your shoulders. Climbing over the two of you, I can reach the top. Then you'll see!"

Acting while talking, the nimble matelot hoisted himself up to the top of the fence.

Inside, there was a narrow roof, under which equipment was stored, including suspended coils of rope. To grab one of them was a matter of seconds. He threw one end over the palisade, shouting: "Hold on!" As agile as a squirrel, he used that point of support to resume his place at the top of the planks.

"Send up Mam'zelle Edmée!"

In a trice, the young woman, lifted up with delicate energy, was deposited on the interior roof, where Snow Rose joined her, in the same fashion, in a matter of seconds.

For the men, Jean contented himself with mooring his rope solidly to one of the joists of the little roof and letting them climb up, while he occupied himself with getting the young women down to the ground, where everyone was gathered when the first vociferating crowd arrived and stopped, momentarily disconcerted, beside the fence.

Several employees of the aerodrome had run toward the travelers, who had introduced themselves into it by somewhat unorthodox means. At their head was an individual clad in a jacket with dull metal buttons and a helmet with a flat peak, decorated with a badge that depicted an aerostat in gold filigree. It was that individual who shouted to them: "What are you doing? Who are you?"

"I'm Williamson, the Mining King."

"Ach!"

"Pursued...no time to explain...give us shelter...out of range of the miscreants."

"The only shelter I have is the nacelle of the captive balloon, whose captain I am."

"I'll buy it, Captain."

"It's not for sale."

"Yes it is! Ten thousand dollars? Twenty thousand? Here they come!"

"But an aerostat nacelle isn't a fortress. There's no more precarious shelter."

"Excellent, on the contrary—and we'll climb out of range."

"Today's ascensions have finished."

"There'll be an extra one."

"I don't have my staff."

"We'll make do. Go on, take the banknotes. Quickly, let's go!

"So be it," said the Captain, taking the wad of bills that was twice the value of the aerostat. He addressed the club's employees: "You loosen the ropes of the nacelle. I'll operate the winch myself."

Alas, rapid as the negotiations and the embarkation were, they had not been as rapid at the two cohorts, now reunited, who had traversed all the obstacles and invaded the field. As Williamson had anticipated, the Knights of Labor had reinforced the first troop, fusing into a single legion; the individual banners had vanished, to give way to long streamers, on which was displayed the communal, frightfully significant motto: *World Defenders*.

That was the old idea and the old formula so actively and adroitly reawakened by Jonathan Loeb: the idea and formula of the implacable hatred of popular self-preservation against Old Sinker and all those who might serve his criminal genius.

And that crowd headed straight for the captive balloon serving as a retreat for the fugitives.

"Release all!" shouted Williamson.

The balloon oscillated, and…that was all! A hundred hands had seized the attachments, representing a human weight of seven tons, which retained the balloon, ready to launch into the atmosphere, on the ground.

A few dolorously critical seconds went by, but it is extreme peril that provokes ideas of genius, and Williamson had one. Standing up before the howling horde he raised his two fists full of dollars, which he hurled with all his strength into the crowd, shouting: "Yours!"

The effect was devastating. Under the rain of gold, which he renewed three times in different directions around the vast nacelle, their hands instinctively let go of the ropes to seize the sovereign manna that was falling from heaven…

Abruptly liberated, with such force that the steel cable, tightened too soon, snapped, the liberated captive launched forth into the sky like a cannonball, carrying Williamson and his fortune, along with his five companions, far away from Loeb and his acolytes.

Five? No; it is necessary to say "six companions." There was one person who had grabbed hold of the ropes to retain the nacelle and who had not let go during the rain of gold launched by the billionaire. That one had been carried away into the air like a wisp of straw.

In spite of the fury of his fourth disappointment, Loeb uttered a kind of hiccup of laughter on seeing the unfortunate Grégoire de Montalpé flying toward the zenith, hanging beneath the nacelle like a ridiculous marionette, also relieved of the weight of his wallet, which his implacable master had made him hand over.

10. The Latter Day Saint

Let us take a leap—a truly American leap—of some twelve hundred and sixty miles, as the crow flies, and enter the famous metropolis, at least so far as its inhabitants are concerned, of Salt Lake City, situated in the north of the state of Utah, about ten miles south east of the Great Salt Lake on the Jordan River linking that Lake to Lake Utah.

At the back of a vast courtyard, on the stone steps, tinted green by damp, of a vast house offering the ugly aspect of a single-story barracks, an obese man with a fleshy and thick-lipped face, clad in a dark ulster with a long black jacket hanging over trousers of the same negative shade, coiffed in a slightly furry and prodigiously tall top hat, shod in robust clogs, was scolding five women who were escorting him in submissive attitudes.

This five women, the youngest of whom was not twenty and the eldest certainly about forty, clad in black costumes whose style dated back at least a third of a century, where the dejected spouses of the Latter Day Saint, the great pontiff of the Mormon sect, the patriarch of that essay in religious Orientalism in the midst of the desert of the Far West, the absolute and tyrannical master of the New Jerusalem, as the inhabitants of the city of the Great Salt Lake considered it to be.[93] That Saint, that pontiff, that patriarch, that master, the husband of the five wives, the grotesque fat man dressed as we have just seen—because it was raining heavily—closed his huge umbrella, and left his muddy clogs on the threshold.

"Mabel," said the Saint to the oldest member of his harem, a tall ugly woman as stiff as a plank, shivering in her mantle under the icy downpour, "I ought to make you serious reproaches for your coquetry. You want a new dress...at your age! You're not thinking enough about the poverty that the Lord, in his mercy, imposes upon us for the expiation of our sins, and that after having once known the seven fat cows, we're now under the reign of the lean cows! Don't get angry, I'm not saying that for you.

"As for you, Betsy, your accounts are very neatly written, but full of errors. You've recorded as fifty dollars the fine to which I condemned Andrew Sweetish for having permitted his only wife, under the fallacious pretext that she was too rudely beaten, to flee to the land of the Infidels. It was a hundred dollars that I demanded of him, and it's a poor price, in view of his difficulty in living. Betsy, no more favors or...errors of that sort. Such a great sin, when women are so desolately scarce in the New Jerusalem, merits no pity, especial when, as Andrew has, one dares to rejoice in having become solitary again, which is only permitted to children and old men fallen into decrepitude. And then, times are hard...and I need cash.

"Meg and Bella, both receive my anathema for having managed so poorly, one of you the kitchen for the satisfaction of my palate, and the other the keeping of my house, which is not in accord with my dignity as a Latter Day Saint.

---

[93] This depiction of the Church of the Latter Day Saints is of course, as bizarrely inaccurate and ludicrously insulting as the depiction of the Salvation Army. The Church had, in fact, abandoned polygamy in 1890, and although it was deeply in debt at that point, the adoption of a tithing system had ensured that it was thriving financially by 1910. By that time, its members were increasingly taking prominent roles in such national political movements as the Women's Suffrage movement and the Temperance movement. Far from it being an authoritarian institution, many Mormons were members of the Utah Social Democratic Party, carrying forward a long-standing cooperative tradition within the Church.

"As for you, Maud, your youth is no excuse for taking so little trouble to please me. A little more zeal, if you please, in your privileged functions as secretary! Go put on your beautiful white negligee made of silk and lace, for which I sent away to San Francisco, and wait for me in my study. We have all day to occupy ourselves with matters of Religion, and know that a wife can never be too beautiful when it's a matter of the Lord and his wife."

The four older women had meekly bowed their heads under the mercuriality of the Master. Young Maud, very irreverently, made a grimace significant of the lack of attraction that the favor of spending a long day in private with her illustrious, vast and mature husband had for her.

The sonorous vibrations of the bell at the main entrance, agitated violently, put an abrupt end to that scene of multiple domesticity. The Saint's Olympian eyebrows furrowed.

"By Abraham! Only an impious man would dare to ring like that on my venerated threshold. Maud, go and see to it. Put the infidel in the parlor and come and tell me what he wants." Addressing a magisterial gesture to his other wives, he ordered: "Go inside!"

Five minutes later, Maud came into the study and handed the Mormon pope a visiting card on which he read: *Jonathan Loeb, chief of the general staff of the Salvation Army.*

He started so violently that his abdomen quivered five or six times before resuming its normal equilibrium.

"One of the great chiefs of that invading and damned sect dares…!"

His indignant expression disappeared, however on reading the two handwritten lines, which were evidently much more agreeable to him.

"Bring the stranger in," the Saint commanded the bewildered Maud.

"Here?" she queried. "Where not even the most notorious of the faithful are allowed to enter?"

"Refrain from judging, brazen hussy…and do as you're told."

It was sitting in an armchair that was too high for his short fat legs, further elevated by the semblance of a stage, enveloped in the tails of his long black coat and with his "stove-pipe" hat on his head that the pontiff of the Mormons greeted with an ample suprasacerdotal gesture the Salvationist general—whose generalship was only the slightest string of his redoubtable bow.

The Saint's welcome was doubtless not to the taste of the newcomer, for the relied to the exaggerated gesture full of junction in a curt and hoarse voice: "No mannerisms, if you please. They waste time and words—time and words as valuable as gold…when they're mine."

"Speak—I'm listening."

"Not like this. Leave your sham throne; you're mistaken if you think it will impress me. We're working in the same cause, my friend: the profitable exploitation of credulity and human fanaticism. The founder of your church had a desire to give Oriental liberties to Occidental Christians; in order to be able to defy

Christian laws with impunity he made himself an apostle. In the same way, our late Marshal, in order to conquer and omnipotent and fortunate situation, created a sect that, thanks to his appropriated means of military organization of its propaganda and its faithful, is in the process of making an oil-stain on the surface of the world."

"Alas!"

"Good—there's a frank sigh! Salvationism is a seed-bed of old women, while Mormonism demands a plethora of young ones. So much the worse for you if we're harming your interests. It's the struggle for existence—every man for himself. But that's too many superfluous words. Come down from your splendor. Let's sit down together, like good colleagues, for I need to talk to you, and for both our sakes, no ear should catch what we say."

The Saint hesitated momentarily; then, ceding to his visitor's reasoning, he gave him satisfaction.

Then Loeb said: "You lack women, and the gold in your coffers is diminishing..."

"What makes you think that?"

"I don't think, I know."

"It's a calumny!"

"Peace, damn it, or we'll never finish. I also know that Mormonism is breaking up. From numerous deserters..."

"Oh, it's from those accursed wretches! In spite of the terrible punishments with which I threaten perjurers, I realize that defections..."

"Are increasing from day to day, eh?"

"Since you're so well-informed. I won't feign a confidence that escapes me. The New Jerusalem is in trouble."

"You're under no illusions about the cause, are you?"

"Of course not! I only have five wives, when my predecessor had twenty. I'm also obliged only to have one official one, in order not to be at war with the whole of Utah, and to call the others maidservants. If we were prospering, I wouldn't hesitate to maintain our fundamental dogma by the force of independent practice, but..."

"Instead of increasing, you're thinning out."

"How do you expect it to be otherwise, without reestablishing slavery with regard to the sex that's depriving you of its indispensable support? Four-fifths of the men of the Faith are reluctantly monogamous, and the rest are languishing in an involuntary celibacy that takes away their only reason for staying with us."

"You need..."

"Well, yes, we need women, and gold to attract them."

"Indeed. On that subject, I can propose a bargain to you."

"Which is?"

"To furnish you with a woman, a pearl such as Salt Lake City has never seen."

"I'll finally be able to attain the half-dozen?"

"You haven't lost the taste…and gold…"

"Much?"

"Enough to recruit a regiment of…amazons!"

"Isaac and Jacob be praised! How much?"

"Seventy-six thousand dollars."

"By Job's dung-heap—my mouth's watering. And from where does this celestial manna come?"

"From Chicago, in a straight line, for that's the key. A man withdrew from a bank there, four days ago, exactly ninety-six thousand dollars, of which he's spent twenty thousand to make the journey."

"He must have been throwing handfuls of gold to the crowd along his route, then."

"You don't know how right you are, except that it wasn't on the way but on departure that he threw the handfuls. But let's stop talking in enigmas. These are the facts: a genius vomited up by Hell, intends to provoke the end of the world…"

"By the holy prophet Daniel, that would be the abomination of desolation…if it were possible."

"Can one assign limits to the forces of evil? Anyway, impossible or not, all of the American north-east—Maine, Vermont, New Hampshire, Massachusetts, Connecticut, Rhode Island, New York, New Jersey, Maryland, Pennsylvania, Ohio, Michigan, Indiana, Illinois and Wisconsin—is astir. Secret meetings have taken place, and I've been charged with finding the monster and annihilating him before he can attempt the demonic work."

"That's practical. While laughing at the pretention, it's still good to suppress the audacious person in advance, just in case."

"Listen to the rest. The accursed one has summoned to an unknown meeting-place where he's hiding, for some experiment that might, if nothing else, provoke a disaster, a man who is carrying with him the power of gold. That's the man I mentioned to you."

"It's necessary to prevent him reaching him, that's all."

"I've tried three times, in vain, to block his route, and I've come to ask you to help me."

"In an endeavor that is certain as agreeable to the Lord as it is profitable to Mormonism…personally, I'm all yours."

"Good. This man, who is accompanied by four men, one an adolescent, and a Redskin girl…

"Oh—there's another woman?"

"That one I'll keep, for she's the guide, the only one who knows the retreat of the man I have a mission to exterminate."

"Hmmm! She might be colored, but if she comes here, it will be difficult for her to get out again!"

"Don't worry about that. I'll take charge of it."

"In sum, you want me to keep all these people?"

"I want you to get rid of them for me…for good."

"That's more serious, but possible…except in one case…"

"What?"

"If they become Mormons—for then their lives would be sacred."

"The Mormons are in your absolute dependence, aren't they?"

"I'm the master and judge of all the faithful."

"Then I have no anxieties: you won't Mormonize, at the very least, the one that I have in view."

"We have terrible means to force conversions."

"Incapable, in spite of everything, of bending certain obstinacies."

"We'll see about that…when you've put these individuals in my hands."

"They'll be yours when you want to take them. Before then, in return for a gift that I've brought you, gratuitously—which is to say, without keeping anything for myself—I want you to make a formal engagement, which is a condition *sine qua non*…"

"Which is?"

"Not to demand anything of the man in question except for what he has on him, and to be inexorable in his regard, even if he promises you a hundred millions."

"By the poverty of Agar, is he that rich?"

"You can see that it's already given you pause for thought, and that I was right to take my precautions. You'll content yourself with the seventy-five or seventy-six thousand dollars, or you'll get nothing. Choose!"

"I'll take the guaranteed sum."

"Good. But I need a guarantee. You'll have to authenticate and sign this."

Loeb held out a piece of paper to the Saint, on which the latter read, not without an intimate frisson:

I forbid all those faithful to the Religion to trouble on the matter of my death the bearer of the present document, Jonathan Loeb, chief of the general staff of the Salvation Army. I have killed myself voluntarily in his presence to expiate my violation of a formal agreement into which we entered.

"What does this mean?"

"That you recognize my right to blow our brains out with impunity if you fail, in any respect, to fulfill the terms of the agreement we've just made.

"And if I refuse?"

"I'll take the celestial manna elsewhere."

The Saint reflected, a conflict taking place within his brain between lesser and immediate cupidity and vast but eventual cupidity."

He very quickly fell into line with the old proverb that a bird in the hand is worth two in the bush.

He certified the document as read and approved, and added the sacred seal to his signature.

"Are you satisfied?"

"Yes."

"And you'll deliver me these impious individuals for conversion?"

"When you've put at my disposal the means of finding them."

"You don't have them, then?"

"As good as. Listen: they slipped through my fingers, so to speak, in Chicago, by virtue of the rupture of the cable of a captive balloon, in the nacelle of which they'd taken refuge. The balloon leapt up eight or nine thousand yards, but one of the people is a skillful engineer, who was able to render himself master of the aerostat, which came back down to a moderate height and, pushed by an easterly breeze, set off toward the setting sun. I've had its position signaled to me by telegraph continually, for everywhere."

"Your correspondents can't have mistaken one balloon for another? There's so much aerial navigation nowadays."

"No. One of the travelers, who fears me and wants to keep on the right side of me as long as I have custody of his paltry funds, has taken care to identify the aerostat by throwing notes addressed to me over the side by night. I've been able to track the balloon until it passed over the Wabash Mountains at Ogden. It flew very low over that paltry city, following the line of the railway track that traverses the Great Salt Lake for a distance of thirty-five miles."

"In which they've doubtless drowned!" exclaimed the Saint, alarmed.

"They must have done everything possible to avoid it and come down on land, being unable to get over the Lake Side Mountains, in the Great American Desert, with what denouement I leave you to imagine. In any case, I have proof that they haven't crossed the desert. After landing, having no food, the fugitive troop must certainly have set out to reach the Great Salt Lake, where their only chance of encountering a few people and help lay in following the shore."

"What if, on the contrary, they headed west, into the desert?"

"No, Williamson, a great traveler, knows only too well..."

"Williamson!" exclaimed the Saint, with a start. "It's a matter of Williamson, the Mining King?"

"Yes, since my tongue has let the cat out of the bag."

"Oh, if I'd known...!"

"Too late. You've signed and I'll hold you to it!"

The obese patriarch nearly collapsed in despair. He was about to protest, quite uselessly, against the surprise, which he considered as shady dealing, when Loeb imposed silence on hm. Someone knocked softly on the door.

The Mormon pope, with a heart-broken expression, answered that appeal, in which he recognized the light hand of his youngest wife.

Through a narrow gap in the doorway, Maud informed him that a band of seven faithful, two of whom were women, dying of hunger and cold, had been picked up by Hugh Neumann, a salt-farmer at Lake Point. Neumann was a Mormon of Silesian origin, rich enough to possess three wives, fifteen sons and a dozen daughters, which made him the most important person in the Church after the corpulent Saint—who, moreover, in spite of his quintuple marriage, had no descendants.

Loeb and his worthy partner looked at one another; Williamson and his companions had thrown themselves into the net; they had not put their enemy to the trouble of finding them.

Hugh Neumann had come to ask where he should take the people he had picked up.

"To my Cabin of Proofs on the bank of the Jordan," the polygamous patriarch replied. And as Maud went away, he explained to Jonathan: "There's no better prison. No one has ever come out without being duly Mormonized."

"What about the others?"

"The river," replied the gentle apostle laconically, with an odious smile.

11. The Cabin of Proofs

For forty-eight hours—or, to be strictly accurate forty-seven hours—the fugitives escaped from Chicago, Williamson, Claude and Edmée Roland, Captain Furet, Snow Rose, the ever-correct and tremulous Toby, and their involuntary, if not entirely unintentionally, companion on the aerial voyage, Grégoire de Montalpé, whose dandysism had fled under the rude tyranny of the implacable master to whom the unfortunate had given in himself, have been prisoners in the Cabin of Proofs.

About what happened during the four days and four nights of their journey from the famous city on the shore of Lake Michigan to the similarly famous—albeit from another viewpoint—capital of the sad land of the Mormons, it is sufficient to say a few brief words, interesting as they have might been with regard to adventures. The situation into which hazard, rather that the implacable hostility of Loeb, had delivered them this time, requires our story to be distracted as little as possible.

The departure from the aerodrome in Chicago had, as we know, by virtue of the ascensional force of the aerostat, very insufficiently ballasted, had the brutality of a fall in reverse.

Although they were all stunned and suffocated, like their companions and Toby, Williamson, Jean and Claude had conserved their composure. Although the first two did not know what to do in order to ward off the danger of rising like an arrow to altitudes where low atmospheric pressure leads to death, the first concern of the third, less of a novice in aeronautical matters, was to find the cord of the valve. When he located it at last, he clung to it desperately—and only just in time, for they were all on the point of losing consciousness.

The aerostat descended again rapidly toward the breathable layers.

As he strove to discern the terrain through the sparse clouds that were traveling between the aerostat and the ground, in order to discover the moment when he ought to arrest the descent, Claude discovered Grégoire de Montalpé swinging in the void, suspended by one arm from one of the lateral mooring ropes of the nacelle, which had, fortunately for him, formed a virtual knot around his shoulder at the moment when it had been whipped away by the sick of the vertiginous ascent.

Abandoning the cord of the valve, the engineer began, with the aid of the mariner, to haul the unfortunate and uninteresting incompetent into the nacelle where he remained inert for several hours before coming to, with a rather intense alarm.

The sympathetic practitioner of wild sprees, quickly showed evidence of great devotion by introducing surreptitiously into the sacks of ballast notes addressed to the person whose domination was so burdensome to him but from whom, as we know, he had been unable to free himself. That was because Loeb had, by means of threats, forced Grégoire to confide his funds to him, and Grégoire, very anxious on the subject of his treasury, was doing everything he could to draw the custodian of his fortune into the wake of the balloon. By introducing his notes, rolled up into balls, inside the ballast sacks, among the prospectuses that the ingenuity of American advertising had inserted therein, he was able to convey messages to the balloon's tracker via the fugitives' own hands

As soon as the aerostat had been equilibrated at an altitude of a thousand yards, in a current heading due west, Williamson and his companions had a discussion. Should they descend as soon as possible? That was not the billionaire's opinion. He wanted to take advantage of the unexpected means of locomotion furnished by circumstance to distance himself from his redoubtable adversary, and, thanks to the velocity of the wind and the rarity of roads practicable for an automobile, the further west they went, at least to try to shake him off once and for all.

The sovereign mistress of the situation, in that regard was the Indian guide. When consulted, Snow Rose declared that the route was good, and that she would tell them when it needed to be interrupted, provided that she was kept up to date with the names of the regions they traversed.

It was decided, in consequence, to continue the aerial navigation for as long as possible, while drawing nearer to the ground from time to time in order to inform themselves about the inhabitants they might encounter in proximity to aggregations of population.

They traveled in that manner all through the night following their evening departure, and then all though the following day.

Nothing is comparable to, and nothing is as delightfully restful as, the silent peace that the adherents of aerial navigation experiences in the bosom of the atmosphere. It seems to the aeronauts that they have forgotten all the quotidian miseries, great and small, of terrestrial life, including the earth itself.

That special influence made itself felt with regard to Williamson more than any of his companions, doubtless because he was naturally less adept than them at escaping his overly important personality in order to let his thoughts vegetate and his heart beat freely. For him, therefore, the entire journey was merely one long conversation with Edmée Rolland, in which he ingenuously gave vent to the increasingly strong emotion that he experienced in the presence of the young woman—who, as we know, had long ceased to consider him as an overgrown brat spoiled by a great fortune for which the difficulties of his early life had not prepared him. If he experienced an increasing enthusiasm for her, she, for her part, saw blossoming in him, one by one, strong and simple qualities that he was almost naively grateful to her for bringing to light.

It was not a flirtation between that young woman and that man, still frankly young, but something better: an awakening within the man of a new man, as superior to the old as a flamboyant sun is to the pale night star, by virtue of the action of a beautiful feminine soul that took an interest in its work much more intense than it realized.

Similarly, there was no longer a flirtation between the good and brave matelot Jean Guitard and the lovely and brave Redskin, but infinitely more: an honest, loyal, naïve and spontaneous tenderness. Both of them had received the mutual "thunderbolt" during their first dramatic interview in the Menominee Reservation. All the time that the operations commanded by Claude Rolland left to "Captain Furet" was dedicated by the latter to his sentimental romance, and all the time that Snow Rose thought she could consent to distract from her role and guide and the apostolate of the scientific faith she had acquired from the lips of Old Sinker was given to giving her reply, in all confident sincerity, to the inflammable mariner.

Toby did his best to be of service to the engineer transformed by necessity into the captain of an aerostat. When Claude judged that he could grant himself a few rare and brief moments of repose he did his best to assist the mariner who had become the first mate, maintaining a vigilant watch and being ready, at the slightest disquiet, to wake up the Commandant—who had never merited that title more.

As for Grégoire de Montalpé, needless to say, he was kept in such rigorous quarantine by everyone that he made few efforts to break the legitimate ice that he sensed around him. Besides which, if the dandy had a firm footing in society, he was no more an aeronaut than a mariner, and he suffered prosaically during the voyage in the sky from airsickness, just as he had suffered on the Atlantic from seasickness—which did not prevent him from committing the infamous perfidy of letting Loeb know the course the balloon as following by means of short notes slipped into the sacks of ballast, but did not encourage him to take any interest in the strange and troubling theories of which the ardent faith of the young Indian was the echo.

It would have been necessary to follow the existence of the little troop hour by hour to note the continual similarities between life on earth and the intimate life of the Earth-Monster that Snow Rose continually identified, with regard to everything and nothing, as evidence of the similar vitality of the planet.

The violent incidents of the struggle between the two human powers named Williamson and Loeb do not permit us to relate those disquieting theories in as much detail as they merit. We cannot go more deeply into the strange parallel that she established in the course of that aerial journey between the sensitive atmosphere of the globe and what the occultists call the "astral body" of human beings, that sort of nervous emanation of being, invisible and yet so existent that it is perceptible at a distance. And with what acuity the atmosphere—and, certainly, through its rigid skin, the body of the Earth—perceives those sensations! It is troubled, stirs and writhes under the slightest influence of neighboring beings, and it is not only the light spasmodic breath of the sun that it senses, and instantaneously translates the effects, but the magnetism, the nervous manifestation common to all the living colossi—relative to us, of course—that populate the universe.

But let us pass on—very regretfully, because, like Claude, Edmée and even Williamson, although long prepared for those vertiginous concepts, we would be profoundly stirred and impressed by them!

On the evening of the second day of aerial navigation, the balloon had lost so much gas—not so much by virtue of exomosis through its envelope as frequent descents to obtain information about the route it was following—that it was visibly deformed and was only maintaining a relative stability with the aid of reiterated maneuvers and continual sacrifices of ballast. It was evident that it could not sustain them above ground for very much longer when the glistening surface of the Great Salt Lake appeared in the evening twilight.

Fortunately, the easterly breeze remained strong enough, and steady enough, for them to hope that by sacrificing, for lack of mobile ballast, the equipment and even parts of the nacelle, they could avoid a fatal descent into the bosom of the bitter waves. Claude Rolland acted with so much skill, propriety and prudence that a fortunate result was obtained; the liberated captive was even able, by a supreme effort, to go through a low-lying pass in the Lakeside Mountains and came to rest definitively, after a long and perilous drag, on the sands of the Great American Desert.

Then a terrible ordeal commenced for the castaways of the air, in which only the energy of some and the instinct of self-preservation of the others permitted them to triumph. After having resisted as best they could forty-eight hours of privation of food and water, isolated in arid and uninhabited terrain, the unfortunates found themselves in darkness, with the prospect of perhaps having another twenty or thirty miles to cover before encountering any help.

Without losing a moment, they set forth, retracing their route in the direction of the lake, just as Loeb had reasoned and anticipated. Fortunately, an abundant rainstorm permitted them to slake their devouring thirst and recover sufficient strength to reach the eastern slopes of the Lakeside Mountains, and, by going southwards through the foothills, the few houses of Dunstein, where they were able to restore themselves as best they could.

From there, after a few hours of indispensable rest, they reached the shore of the lake and followed it, walking painfully until the fall of night, which they spent shivering in the open.

The next day, they finally found the road from the desert to Salt Lake City, and the point where it turns around the north of the little chain of the Stansbury Mountains, made their only meal in Grantsville and, in the darkness again, ran aground in Lake Point, where the Mormon farmer Neumann picked them up, in order to take them in a cart—preventing them from taking the railway in spite of their protests—to Salt Lake City...and the Latter Day Saint.

That individual—who has certainly seemed grotesque but at whom one would be wrong to smile, even in the Old World, for it is only in his form—had resolved to receive those he referred to, by antiphrasis, as his "guests" in a manner to impress them, with a view to their future conquest.

He summoned a few notable households—which is to say, as polygamous as the present emaciation of the sect permitted. The ladies put on clothes with tempting pretentions; the gentlemen submitted temporarily to the humble role of servants. And when Williamson, sufficiently recovered from the frightful fatigues of the four previous days to attempt to clarify the new and once-more-disquieting situation of the little troop, imperiously demanded to be put in the presence of the person who was arbitrarily detaining a free citizen of free America and his friends, it was in an indescribable parody of a harem that they were introduced—a harem in which, in a gold-spangled robe, the Saint was the supreme Pacha.

It was thus, to a world-weary individual like Williamson, Parisians like the Rollands and de Montalpé, a widely-traveled young man like Jean Guitard and a civilized Indian who, by virtue of atavism, was astonished by nothing, that the Saint hoped to make the charms of Mormon life appreciated!

All the suavity of that setting did not prevent the high priest of occidental polygamy from signifying to his "guests" that his duties as the supreme apostle of the Mormon faith obliged him to attempt their conversion by all means possible, and that, to his great regret, he could only part from them when it had been proved to him that he had no chance of saving their souls.

Williamson having protested that he did not have time to waste with such nonsense the obese patriarch added that, in order to be agreeable to him, he would arrange from the work of persuasion to proceed by giant strides, and not prolong the proofs beyond forty-eight hours.

In order to demonstrate the consideration that he intended to show to visitors who, he had no doubt, would have the wisdom to become his dear sons and daughters in Mormonism, he wanted to cede to them the very room in which he had just welcomed them as persons of distinction..

It was a rather vast room with only one visible entrance, with, by ways of annexes, two small rooms devoid of exits. One large window illuminated it, overlooking the River Jordan from a sheer height, which was deep and rapid at that point, full of turbulent eddies that would extinguish any idea of an exodus by the liquid route.

It was there—without neglecting a frugal but sufficient sustenance, mysteriously delivered—that the little company, imprisoned in great secrecy, completed the forty-seventh hour of detention under the pretext of proselytism out of the forty-eight that the Saint had fixed as the extreme duration of the "proof."

Now they understood the value and the only too rigorous exactitude of that word. In the beginning, Williamson and his companions had suffered without overmuch alarm that attempt made, in their respect, on right of people to individual liberty. Harassed and exhausted, they experienced above all else an immense need for repose, which, on bunks that were almost sufficiently comfortable, they spent the first twelve hours in such physical annihilation that none of them found the leisure to think about what they all considered, at first glance, to be a perfectly ridiculous contretemps.

When they awoke, the found a basket full of victuals, to which they did great honor, while wondering how it could have been delivered to them. Before going to sleep, in fact, the prisoners had built a barricade of furniture against the only entrance, which was still intact.

As they finished their meal, rendered relatively cheerful by the wellbeing they felt, they heard a noise, and at one point in the partitions serving as walls they saw a large envelope swinging without any apparent form of support.

Are we in the home of Robert Houdin? wondered the Parisians.

It's sorcery! Toby and the pretty Redskin thought.

"That," murmured the matelot to himself, "is as odd as navigating at twenty knots, keel in the air. Hmmm…have to see!"

Williamson did not even take the futile trouble of any conjecture. Practical above all, he went to take the envelope, which yielded to the first solicitation of his hand, and opened it in order to discover its contents.

They were as many copies of the dogmas and rigorous regulations of the Mormon sect as there were prisoners, with, at the bottom, a formal certificate of conversion awaiting a signature.

To the set of printed sheets was appended a manuscript bearing advice that was singularly reminiscent of an ultimatum:

You only have another thirty-four hours to decide. Know that no one but a Mormon has ever got out of the place where you are.

Silently, the prisoners took cognizance of the printed sheets, on which each of their names was accurately inscribed in the margin, although only Williamson had declared his loudly—without anyone appearing to suspect what that name was worth.

The mystery was further complicated, unless Loeb...? But it was considered implausible by all of them, except de Montalpé, that the enemy, so fortunately thwarted in Chicago, could have picked up their trail again so soon.

Leaving his companions to discuss those matters in low voices, not without some anxiety, Jean Guitard, primarily inclined to action, first wanted to assure himself that there was no means of escape. After having interrogated the walls with his first—almost all resonant but offering no indication of a hidden door—he noticed the grooves of a small trapdoor in the ceiling, between two joists. With the skill of an acrobat and the composure of an able seaman, he formed a pyramid out of tables and chairs, and succeeded in reaching the ceiling, but the trapdoor resisted all his efforts.

Nevertheless, it must logically be up above that it was necessary to explore. Leaning out of the window, he observed a rope hanging from the roof—well out of reach, of course. With a few handkerchiefs torn into strips he manufactured a cord, to the end of which he tied two of the pieces of iron cutlery that had been supplied with the meal. With the aid of that improvised grapnel, he succeeded after several fruitless attempts, in drawing the rope toward the window, to the interior of which he attached it. Then, raising himself up over the void by the strength of his wrists, he reached the roof, broke the glass of a skylight and found himself in a loft that contained a large quantity of straw and discarded or broken utensils.

There was no exit from the loft but a trapdoor, whose heavy bolt he withdrew. It was by that route, disappointingly, that he set foot once again on his fragile scaffolding and rejoined his companions.

"No means of taking advantage of darkness to escape via the roof, as I'd hoped," he told them, dejectedly. "On the three sides that don't overlook the river the building is surrounded by smooth walls fifteen or eighteen feet high. No illusions are possible; this really is a prison, and a serious one. No point thinking about the river, with its only-too-visible turbulence; the best swimmer would down in it.

"Oh, if we only had several nights in front of us to weave cables with the straw that's up there, I'd construct a raft and we could get away by the liquid route, thumbing our nose at the turbulence, but with only one poor night before us, we can't undertake such a long-term endeavor."

In order to acquit his conscience, however, the young mariner unscrewed the bolt of the trapdoor to the loft and wove a solid rope with the straw, long enough to establish a facile and sure means of communication—for a good climber—between the room and the attic.

Nothing is as depressing as isolation under the latent, imprecise threat of a blow whose nature one cannot foresee, any more than the manner in which it will be struck. So, for the prisoners of the collective, the hours went by with both hectic rapidity and desperate slowness. They would have liked to be able to hold them back, and yet they seemed to last for centuries. Williamson, especially, was agitated.

"Why don't they tell us in good faith what they're going to do with us?" he repeated, incessantly. "Better a grim threat, even mortal, than this waiting!"

None of them, except for the tearful Grégoire, had considered for a second the idea of giving in to their jailer's ultimatum. Setting aside any question of religious commitment, was the Mining King about to place under the domination of a Latter Day Saint and settle, in the fullness of youth, his independent life as a nabob in that odious region of the Great Salt Lake? Such a hypothesis did not even warrant being formulated. Were French citizens like Claude, Edmée and Jean Guitard going to become Mormons, and by intimidation? Could Edmée, most of all, a sincere Catholic, swell the grotesque harem of some farmer as fat as the one who had captured them, rather than rescuing them, at Lake Point? The question could not even arise, any more than that of the young Indian, so ardent and fanatical a disciple of Old Sinker, suffering the same fate.

Such modest valors, such strong and superior humanities, were not accessible prey for the base and brutal proselytism of a Mormon pope.

That evening, the question continually formulated, aloud or mutely, by Williamson, received its response—and what a response!

After a summary and frugal supper, hastily absorbed by pale starlight—for no lamp or candle had been left at the disposal of the internees—the prisoners had lain down silently on their bunks, although not to sleep, for they were too acutely anxious for the arrival of slumber to calm their nervous exasperation. Suddenly, a dry click resonated in one of the partitions, making them all sit up.

Williamson struck a match, by the light of which—without anyone having come in, so far as they knew—they all saw a piece of parchment pinned to the wall by a dagger, and bearing the significant words: *No more than eighteen hours! Our Lord will enlighten you! Sign or die!*

This time the threat was undisguised.

"Ah!" exclaimed Claude Rolland, dully. "If that wretch Neumann, at Lake Point, hadn't taken advantage of our weakness to disarm us, we could attempt to break down that door and open up a passage, revolvers in hand, to flee this accursed city!"

"That would be futile folly, even armed," said Williamson coldly, "for now I'm convinced. Taking our weapons without touching the banknotes I have on my person might have been the work of a fanatic, but this imprisonment without my being robbed, without any allusion being made to the question of money, and no one wanting to seem to suspect the importance of my person, which is not unknown in any corner of the United States any more than in any major center in the world, proves that the head directing this assault knows exactly what I'm worth and intended to avoid the purchase of visible guards, which is always easy when price is not an issue. This is abnormally clever."

"From which you conclude?"

"That the new blow has indisputably been struck by Loeb, whose dispositions have undoubtedly been made, outside as well as within."

"Come on," Claude objected. "It's impossible for that Argus to have eyes everywhere. There are multiple currents in the atmosphere, and we could have found one that carried the balloon southwards or northwards as easily as due east. Even if he affiliates are innumerable, he could only proceed by elimination, which would not have permitted him to be informed so rapidly of our actual direction."

"Unless we took care to guide his search from on board."

"You don't believe, at least, that I've betrayed you?" de Montalpé protested, forcefully. He bit his tongue immediately, but it was too late.

Williamson replied with cold irony. "I didn't ask you for that confession, Monsieur. The advertisements that the sacks of ballast contained would have sufficed, without you, to mark our trail."

That's true! What an error! thought the two cousins at the same time, but giving very different meanings to their regret. Claude was deploring his carelessness, Grégoire the futility and danger of a treason that had already caused him so much anxiety and had delivered him into the peril of immediate reprisals.

Cry of anger that rang out in the scornful silence struck terror into de Montalpé's entrails. The Indian woman had just understood the role played aboard the nacelle by Rolland's malevolent relative. Atavism reacted spontaneously on the civilized individual. She ran to the dagger fixed in the wall in order to make it a weapon of just vengeance, while Grégoire, breathless with terror, hid behind Edmée.

But the dagger was firmly embedded. The vindictive Menominee miscalculated the force of her gesture, and, disconcertedly, extracted nothing from the wall but a broken blade.

"Oh, Mam'zelle Snow Rose," the mariner reproached her, softly and tenderly, "Why were you so hasty? A weapon that our enemies had given us, and which, with a little patience, we might have had in good condition!"

"Snow Rose," said Williamson, tranquilly, in his turn, "We are above the office of executioners in the cause of justice, with which Loeb had charged himself. Isn't it evident that if the master Monsieur de Montalpé has chosen had not wanted to get rid of a follower he now judges to be useless, he would have taken steps to ensure that he did not share our imprisonment?"

Williamson was preaching indirectly to a convert. Grégoire was informed as to the amenity of Loeb's sentiments in his regard, and was very well aware that, now that Loeb had custody of his money, he was at least indifferent to the life of the man to whom it belonged. So, he resolved, in order to escape both the dangerous domination of Loeb and the fate that awaited him, to sign, as soon as the first light of dawn permitted him to do so, the certificate of conversion imposed by the Saint.

Three times during the night the same macabre advice was given, in the same symbolic fashion. Each time, with silent and patient effort, it was the mariner who detached the pitiless parchments, and at daybreak, Williamson, Claude Rolland and Toby each hid beneath their clothing a blade whose temper had been assured by experiment.

As soon as the sun rose, dead on time, the unfortunates saw the conditional condemnation renewed by the same mysterious means—except that, to the great chagrin of the brave Jean, no symbolic weapon fixed the ultimatum to the wall on this occasion.

You can imagine what such a day must have been like, after such a night. After exhausting themselves in vain searching for a means of escaping their destiny, they had recognized the inanity of any attempt. So the forty-seventh hour of their detention found them dejected and desperate, and when the last warning—*Beware! In one hour you will be Mormons or dead!*—appeared on the ensorcelled partition, no one looked up, knowing only too well what it contained. No heart among them had weakened; all of them were determined, when the moment came, to sell their lives as dearly as possible. Their nerves were jangling, their brains, overworked by anguish, seemed to be voids within their burning skulls.

They were no longer talking. What was the point? They were no longer even thinking. They could do no more...

And mechanically, they counted the seconds, adding up the minutes.

Then, the material imminence of the crisis provoked an almost violent reaction.

Edmée was the first to rise abruptly to her feet from the chair in which she had been slumped, next to the table, squeezing her temples with her fragile clenched fists. She went to her brother, placed her hand on his shoulder and said, in a slow, grave voice: "Brother, you love me truly, don't you? Well, as I have no weapon, when the fatal moment comes, before striking yourself, kill me."

"Edmée!"

"Would you want your sister, when your blood has been shed, to become the living prey of these monsters?"

Williamson jumped up. "Oh, Miss Edmée, don't talk like that! You, so beautiful...you,, whose soul is so noble, whose heart is so good...you, who are grace, charm, purity, intelligence and valor personified...you, who have no equal, fall into the gross hands of the repugnant and grotesque chief of this sect—that shall not be! You, die! You, who are made for life, for happiness, to reign as a sovereign over humankind...you, wanting to die...wanting no longer to be, very soon, anything but an inanimate statue in order to escape the claws of these predators! Oh, I will not have it! I will not have it! I will not have it!"

"Alas," said Edmée, moved to the bottom of her heart by the exaltation that transfigured the man she had known so cold, so disillusioned, so scornful of his fellow humans, and of women in particular, "what can you do to oppose our fatal destiny?"

"I shall do…I don't know what I shall do! But I want you to live, and to live happily! And I want to live in order to see you live, and live happily! I want you to live, Miss Edmée, because…because you have made me experience what I did not know that my heart could ever experience…because I admire you above all others…because I venerate you…because, in sum, I love you!"

"What a moment for such a confession!"

"Well, exactly—it's when a man sees himself on the threshold of the eternal unknown, when he knows that he might perhaps have only a few more moments in possession of his terrestrial thought, that his soul bursts forth in the brightness of truth, inundated by the supernatural light that shows his sentiments in their true grandeur, and reveals them in their powerful intensity. And it's under the empire of the serene truth that dazzles and guides, imposing itself imperiously upon him, that his voice, obedient to the command of a superior will, translates that truth of that sincerely great and totally liberated soul.

"For a long time—yes, a long time, for in the existence we've been leading for several days, the hours have been days and the days months—I've understood that a complete transformation has taken place within me, of which you are the cause and the goal. But my consciousness, still fogged by all the tenacious errors of my pride and my false past experience, resisted all the intimate forces that extended toward you, refused to admit something so beautiful and so natural, and prevented me from seeing clearly within myself.

"Today, confronted by death—perhaps imminent, unless we receive some miraculous aid from God—at this poignant moment when neither the soul, nor the heart, not the mouth can lie, I repeat to you, Miss Edmée, that I love you."

Edmée gazed at him with a heart-rending smile, and said, emotionally: "Believe, Monsieur Williamson, that your words descend into my utmost depths, and that they are engraved there forever…which is to say, for the few moments that it is still granted to us to be able to see and hear one another…but I'm a Christian; these supreme moments ought no longer to belong to the earth. Let me pray."

She knelt down.

A scene of a similar nature, if not similar expression, was taking place a few paces away between Snow Rose and the brave young mariner Jean.

They did not have to make the confession that their eyes, and then their mouths, had confided even before leaving Chicago. Their mutual tenderness was determined to protest against the evidence, still wanting to believe, in spite of everything, that their lives might still be saved....

Jean Guitard, devoted as he was, forgot about Claude and Edmée, whom he cherished both profoundly and respectfully; for him, at that moment, nothing any longer existed but the almost furious determination to get the adored Indian woman out of that fatal cabin and that deadly city.

He had to do something...

But the minutes went by, flying on the dial of the large antique clock whose tick-tock caused the partition wall to vibrate.

He uttered a muted growl of exasperated despair, seized Snow Rose in his arms and carried her to the thick straw rope that he had fabricated, which was hanging through the gap of the trap-door in the ceiling, obliged Manitoba's daughter to cling to is back, and, charged with that precious burden, climbed up to the loft. From the loft he intended to go out on to the roof, and from there, by the grace of God...it would be necessary for him finally to invent some means of escape, since he loved Snow Rose and it was necessary for him to save her.

As the two of them disappeared into the loft, the clock chimed.

It was time.

Williamson, Edmée, Claude, Toby and even de Montalpé, although his hand was on the point of the cowardly submission that he considered as an aegis, raised their heads at the same time, their faces contracted by an inexpressible anxiety, and instinctively retreated to the wall opposite the only door, through which they were expecting...the unknown!

The door opened.

The Saint appeared—alone!

What! He had the incredible aberration of presenting himself alone? He was not Daniel, however, to renew the Biblical miracle of the lions' den.

After two seconds accorded to surprise, Williamson and Claude exchanged a glance, gripping the hilts of the daggers concealed within their clothing.

They had waited too long. Just as they launched themselves forward, the panels of the wall behind them pivoted, giving passage to six Mormons who, after treacherously seizing the male prisoners by the neck, knocked them brutally down on their backs and, pressing their knees into their breasts, rendered it impossible for them to attempt the slightest defense.

The Saint smiled; the operation had been executed perfectly.

He made a sign to the two unoccupied "faithful," to whom he indicated the trapdoor in the ceiling, and, aping courtly mannerisms ridiculously, headed toward the astounded Edmée.

"Miss Rolland," he said, in a honeyed tone, "welcome to the New Jerusalem. You are the first Frenchwoman to enter the seraphic choir of my beautiful Faithful, all of whom you surpass in personal ornamentation. An envied honor is reserved for you, whom the Lord has blessed; it is the roof of the Latter Day Saint himself that will shelter your felicity. Mabel, Betsy, Meg, Bella and Maud, who already know that they will be your servants even more than your companions, are waiting for you on the threshold of the cabin to take you to your new dwelling in great ceremony. On the way, they will explain your duties and my tastes. Don't worry, I'm not very demanding! Your hand, divine Edmée!"

And he extended his toward the young woman, who shuddered in disgust and, before anyone could stop her and prevent her action, leapt to the window, opened it wide and cried, with her foot on the sill: "One more step by you or your men and I'll throw myself in the river!"

Anxious as well as nonplussed, so much did Edmée's tone testify to the unshakability of her decision, the obese pontiff dared not advance any further, and signaled to the two men who were in the middle of ascending into the loft, on their mission of pursuit, to stop. Gently, he sought to soften the resolute Parisienne.

"Enough!" the latter commanded him. "I swear before God, who will forgive me, that you won't take me alive!"

Without taking her eyes off the Saint, she climbed on to the window-sill. Between her and the abyss there was no longer room for the slightest movement.

"Don't jump!" begged Loeb's accomplice, taking a step back.

"Don't jump!" repeated, like an echo, a young and warm voice that seemed to fall from the sky. "Don't jump, Mam'zelle Edmée—here I am!"

From the trapdoor of the loft, sliding down the straw rope, "Captain Furet" brought his heels down on the skull of the higher of the two Mormons who were in the process of climbing up it—who, stunned, fell on to his comrade, who let go and fell backwards on to the floor.

"And two!" proclaimed the mariner.

He reached the floor almost at the same time as them, threw his arm around the throat of the Saint with a single bound and put the barrel of a revolver to his temple, threatening: "If any one of you budges, I'll shoot!"

The advice had come to late…for the Mormons. With a single impulse, at the sight of the danger run by the patriarch, they had turned their heads and half risen to their feet, rendering, for a split second a partial liberty to the felled prisoners—who took advantage of it.

In the blink of an eye, Williamson, Claude and Toby—the last-named opportunely aided in his weakness by the valiant Edmée, had disengaged themselves from the relaxed grip, seized the throats of their aggressors, knocked them down in their turn and were holding them immobile with the threat of daggers held above their hearts.

"A change of view, eh, Papa?" mocked the matelot, under the nose of the Saint, who was white with terror. "You didn't expect that? Nor that my little Snow Rose would have had the presence of mind to hide her shooter from the search of the rogue who disarmed us in such a cowardly fashion at Lake Point. It's necessary to go gently, fat Papa! Orders, Monsieur Williamson!"

In the tone that was always calm in the midst of the most violent crises, Williamson remarked: "What's become of Snow Rose? We're going to need her."

244

Stifled cries and the sound of a brief struggle on the floor above replied to him.

Jean Guitard uttered a cry of rage and despair. Someone was attacking, up above, the woman he loved, whom he had disarmed in order to save everyone, and for whom, under the pain of losing all those for whom he had once again shown his devotion, he might have liberated the Saint from the mortal threat in order to fly to the Indian's aid.

At Snow Rose's first exclamation he had almost launched himself forth…but, heroically, with an anguished sweat pearling on his brow, he had remained at his post.

"Have no fear for her," Williamson said to him, who now understood what the mariner must be suffering. "She's too necessary to Loeb for him to allow any harm to come to her."

"Is it him who's grabbed her, then? Oh, woe betide him! I don't know if I can refrain from blowing out the brains of the ape who's trembling in my arms! I could give chase to the abductor!"

"Don't kill that man, Jean!" Edmée begged.

"Don't kill a man who might be useful to us, Captain Furet! But I have a strong desire to get rid of the one who's under my knee. I need to be free in my movements without delay."

"I'll take your place, Monsieur Williamson," Edmée declared, resolutely. "I understand that there are times when a woman's hand mustn't hesitate before the horror of bloodshed, if it's necessary for the common salvation I'll guarantee that the man won't budge until Jean can come to relieve me."

"With a simple energy, she matched her words with action, leaving Toby alone, face to face with his enemy—who did not attempt to take advantage of the groom's weakness, because he knew that any assault would pass a death-sentence on his chief and his companions.

Rapidly, Williamson took over Jean's revolver and his role. The latter, with a terrible gleam in his eyes, relieved Edmée of the dread of being constrained to plunge steel into living flesh.

From then on, things moved swiftly, for Williamson commanded as a harsh and inflexible master. Under his dictation, the Saint was obliged to write:

I deplore the violence carried out in Salt Lake City against Mr. Williamson and his friends at the perfidious instigation of Jonathan Loeb, and humbly leave it to the generosity of the Mining King to spare myself and the Mormons legitimate reprisals. I order all those of the Faith to give aid and assistance, in full obedience, to the said Williamson, and will punish with the chastisement of perjury any Mormon who attempts, in any fashion whatsoever, any action that might be prejudicial to him.

The Latter Day Saint

Then he demanded that the latter order his six men into one of the rooms with no exit, including the two injured men who had not yet recovered consciousness, and placed Toby on the threshold, revolver in hand, a dagger being sufficient henceforth for the Yankee king to suppress any whim of independence on the part of the Mormon pope. The latter obeyed without hesitation.

Finally free to think of himself, poor Captain Furet sank into a chair and began silently to weep his worthy amorous tears. The loft had fallen silent again. What had become of his beloved Snow Rose?

"I can see her!" Edmée suddenly announced, from the window. "That's surely her, thrown into the bottom of a boat that Loeb is rowing himself, alone, with great strokes of the oars. And wait! She's got free of the gag—which Loeb has immediately reattached—but she had time to utter a cry...no, not a cry! A word!"

"What word?" demanded Williamson, urgently, without letting go of his hostage. "A name, perhaps?"

"I don't know," said the young woman...it ended in an *o*."

"Think!"

"It was something like *fricot*."

"Frisco!" cried the Mining King, exultantly. "Oh, the worthy girl! Captain Furet, don't measure with your eyes the distance that separates us from that river mortal to swimmers. I now know where we'll be able to find your Snow Rose. And Loeb will become my guide! Let's not lost a single minute—they're precious."

The, addressing the Latter Day Saint, who was very depressed by the turn that the adventure had taken, Williamson said: "You're nothing but a base scoundrel, a mere accomplice in this ugly affair, and the scorn I have for you goes as far as pity. Your excuse, if there is one, is to have wanted to bring, at my expense, a momentary prosperity to your sect, which, as all America knows, is crumbling like an old rotten wall.

"First of all, you're going to return our weapons, or furnish us with others, if your Germanic Mormon has appropriated our little arsenal for himself. Then, as befits important visitors who have given Salt Lake City the too great and entirely involuntary honor of the presence, you're going to conduct us respectfully to the railway station and you're going to wait until the first train we can catch has carried us away for us to relinquish the guarantee of your presence.

"That done, you'll refrain from any annoyances still possible, and, that way, you'll render us a service. Now, as Williamson has never received a service for which he hasn't paid handsomely, you'll receive in your hand, at the moment we hear the signal to depart, a check for twenty thousand dollars."

That program was followed in every detail. Soon—with what a sigh of relief!—the little troop quit the New Jerusalem for good, including Grégoire de Montalpé, who had nearly ended his days as a Mormon.

That scarcely creditworthy socialite had truly had more luck than he deserved. It was fear alone that had stopped in his throat the proclamation of his apostasy, at the moment of the surprise attack in the tricked-out cabin—which he judged it appropriate to keep secret when he saw things turn so promptly and so unexpectedly to the advantage of Williamson and his relatives.

He was, of course, the only one not to have mastered his aggressor, but he had understood that all danger had disappeared for him, the Mormon who had flattened him having been condemned to inertia under pain of provoking the death of his Saint and his coreligionists.

Loeb still had his wallet, to be sure, but now that he had obtained the desired guide, he would be able to find and hatefully put to death this Lobanief, the cause of all the trouble. So casually abandoned by Loeb, de Montalpé would have the misfortune of having to share the suspended inheritance with his cousins, but he knew that half would be more than sufficient to compensate him for his losses. That was all that could be pulled out of the fire, and he would have to settle for it.

12. The Broken Thread

Eight days have gone by since Williamson and his friends left—triumphantly but after having endured inexpressible suffering—the city of the Mormon popes. They have been in San Francisco for seven, for it was definitely "Frisco"—the popular diminutive of the name of the State Capital of California[94]—that Snow Rose's last cry had given as a rendezvous to those to whom she had faithfully attached herself, because they were the ones summoned by her piously venerated master, the demigod, the prophet and the genius that she placed so high above other men...in other words, Old Sinker.

For a week, the Mining King had been strewing gold around generously, mobilizing police officers and private detectives, scouring personally or through the intermediary of his companions the whole city, from dives to palaces, and all the surrounding agglomerations on the shore of the vast closed by of the Pacific, especially Oakland, its sister city—and had not found a trace, not a single clue to the whereabouts of Loeb and his prisoner.

It was certainly not for lack of trying. If Williamson, temporarily occupied with some other concern, had sometimes shown a slight slackness in his research, poor Captain Furet, now pale and exhausted, mad with chagrin, always on his feet, no longer sleeping, only eating what was strictly necessary not to collapse for lack of nourishment, incessantly imagining some tiny new trail, had spared absolutely nothing in the attempt to find his beloved.

The engineer had also gone on campaign very energetically, albeit with no more success. His ardor had been subjected to a pause, however; the steps taken

---

[94] The State Capital of California is actually Sacramento.

in the first few days only having yielded negative results, he had understood that the discovery of Loeb and the Indian, assuming that they really had come to Frisco, would require long days, if not weeks. He had told himself that his personal attempts, as a foreigner, could scarcely add to the chances of success, when the local police, official and unofficial, were working on it. In addition, a case of conscience had imposed itself on his intransigent honesty.

He had not been able due to *force majeure*, to fulfill his promise to Senator Dupeyroux, and the non-reception of his report must have been a disaster for the latter. But might not his sojourn in San Francisco, which would, in all probability, be prolonged, permit him to repair that disaster to some extent?

Dupeyroux might have been able, not having received the promised oratorical "bomb" in time, to have the famous interpellation postponed, a postponement perhaps announced by the desperate cablegrams that had been unable to catch up with the little troop during its journey across the North American continent. If, from San Francisco, Claude was able to cable, if not a complete report like the one swallowed up with the unfortunate *Astrea*, at least sufficient elements to form a basis for the virulent attack projected by the parliamentarian, the disaster would be partly averted, and the former secretary would at least be conscious of having done everything humanly possible to keep his promise.

What if it had the good fortune to arrive in time! And why not? From the collision within sight of the Sandy Hook lightship to the present moment— which is to say, forty-eight hours after his arrival in San Francisco—that frightful series of dramatic events, in which the travelers had seen death at terrible close range four times, and which was sufficient to fill the entire life of a modern adventurer—had only lasted, in total, twelve days, and the term fixed for the interpellation was only five times twenty-four hours in the past.

Claude no longer had his notes, of course, but the facts, dates and figures registered in his excellent and faithful memory were sufficient to edify a very appropriate and hurtful series of accusations.

The young explorer therefore decided to leave to others the ingrate and disappointing labor of man-hunting and to shut himself away, pen in hand, in order to acquit his debt. As he could do nothing without Williamson, for whom the expense would be aggravated by the telegraphic traverse of the vast United States, he explained his project to him.

To his great surprise, the latter turned him down, not without some vehemence. He suggested to him that a parliamentarian in want of a portfolio would not miss an opportunity to scale the heights of a ministry because his documentation was wanting; and that in a week he had had plenty of time to fill the gap with serious information—or not, if he had not even bothered to solicit it, because all the disappointed ambition and rancor, or even some dilettante ironist, might have shown him that the comedy of the political kitchen amuses everyone, and excites indulgent disdain. In any case, what did it matter whether one brought to the tribune solid arguments or baseless enormities, given that the orator is addressing himself to others even more ignorant than himself, and, in consequence, incapable of discerning the true from the false, the political result being the same?

And the Mining King, in a vein of sarcastic humor, concluded with the sally: "In any case, my dear friend, it's probably better for your senator that things turned out as they did. Armed with your work, drawn from sources of truth and experience, he'd probably have failed, because, to the ignorant, the truth appears implausible, whereas, if he stuck to adroit deceptions seasoned with a few facetious quips, it's a good bet that your Monsieur Dupeyroux, if he isn't completely stupid, is vaingloriously enthroned in the ministry he covered."

Claude dared not persist, and, as a distraction from the remorse of his conscience, threw himself wholeheartedly into the search for the undiscoverable.

It goes without saying that His Opulence the Mining King was staying at one of the most luxurious and expensive hotels reconstructed on the still smoking ruins of the tellurian disaster in which—no one has forgotten the frightful seismic catastrophe—the superb city engendered in a few years by the demon of gold had collapsed.[95] He had a vast apartment for his exclusive use on the first floor overlooking the mouth of the Golden Gate. The similar apartment on the next floor up was occupied by Claude, Edmée and their faithful Jean. Grégoire de Montalpé had been disdainfully relegated almost to the eaves, where he was literally cloistered, deeming it imprudent to collaborate in a search whose success, in addition to risking putting him back under the hand of a pitiless master, ran exactly counter to his own interest, which was not to impede Loeb's vengeance. Only the death of Old Sinker/Lobanief, in fact, would permit him to get his hands on his inheritance—henceforth, alas, to be shared.

If the hotel was an appropriate official residence for the dignity of the Yankee majesty, however, it was too public for the conferences inherent to the nature of police work, to which Williamson, Claude Rolland and Captain Furet were devoting themselves with various energies, and young Toby too, who had gradually recovered from the traumas of the previous days and was visibly resuming the formal correctness that had been singularly compromised by the hectic terrors that he had endured since the shipwreck. For business meetings they had chosen the bar of a modest "posada" situated near the south-western exit from the city, on the road that, after the last few houses of the great maritime city, extends along the extreme foothills of the Santa Cruz Mountains, heading toward the suburban township of San Bruno.

Rendezvous there were frequent, but, more often than not, Williamson sent Toby in his stead. A very powerful magnet retained him in his lodgings: Edmée.

It was not that he dared the incorrectness of aspiring to keep the young woman—obliged to rest after fatigues and emotions too powerful for her nervous system is not her courage—company in the absence of her brother. That

---

[95] The great earthquake that devastated San Francisco occurred in April 1906.

would have been good for the Williamson of before the journey across the United States, to whom the transformed Williamson of San Francisco bore as little resemblance as the beautiful summers of France to the Arctic, or the Clitandre of *Les Femmes savantes* to the ex-King of Dahomey,[96] but a few days had sufficed to mutate the omnipotent and cold egotist, the being of immeasurable and splenetic pride, for whom a scornful impoliteness constituted the acme of originality, into a fearful, respectful, almost modest man, to whom a new and spontaneous intuition to given a grasp of tact, and the most subtle delicacies of the heart.

The beautiful eyes of a woman, mirrors of the noble, valiant and pure soul of an intelligent and refined Parisienne, had worked that miracle. Edmée, like a breath, had melted the heart that had believed itself to be unassailable behind a triple armor plating of gold, ice and scorn for humankind, and which, for its debut in the sweet martyrdom of love, had contracted in the cruel hothouse of a first great suffering.

In fact, Williamson had not waited until the arrival in San Francisco to confirm to the young woman the cry of respectful adoration that, at the poignant moment in the Cabin of Proofs when they had all believed that they no longer had anything to expect but death, has escaped from his entire being, so long concealed. In the saloon carriage speeding toward the Sierra Nevada, the high summits of which were profiled in the west, the Mining King had taken the brother and sister into a corner, and there, with a simple and timid eloquence, had asked Edmée to consent to share her entire life with him, as she had just shared such terrible dangers.

Very emotional, the young woman had closed her long-lashed yes momentarily, and then, with a grave smile and with a slight gesture of the head, she had replied: "No."

"Why not?" the astounded billionaire had implored, his breast transfixed by a stabbing pain.

"You're too rich, and I'm..."

"What for pity's sake?"

"Listen. Without comparing you to our relative Old Sinker, whose fantastic and immense scientific ambition attacks the worlds that populate infinity and aspires to enslave them—ours, at least—to his will, you, my dear Monsieur Williamson are a power ambitious for supremacy by way of gold, as your great indirect enemy Loeb, is by way of his tyrannical domination of the human herd. Well, my friend, I too am very ambitious..."

---

[96] Clitandre is the young hero of Molière's *Les Femmes savantes* (1672), whose desire to marry the beautiful Henriette is opposed by the eponymous "learned" relatives, who want to marry her to a "scholar." The French abolished the political authority of the Kingdom of Dahomey in 1900, but were obliged to bring the exiled king Agoli-Agbo back for ceremonial purposes in 1910, maintaining him in a certain celebrity, which did not extend to his looks.

"You have the right, adored Miss, to all ambitions; there are no heights of which you are not worthy, and the worthiest!"

"I have only one of them—the highest, in my opinion, to whose conquest a human being of the feminine condition can and ought to aspire: that of happiness in a legitimate love, as perfect as the present state of the thinking race, ruler of Creation, presently permits."

"But my love is at your feet, Miss Edmée, complete limitless and absolute, having no law but to make you a happiness envied by all!"

"I believe that, because I know it. I knew that you loved me before you were aware of it yourself, well before the expectation of the fatal blow excited your soul as far as the confession."

"So why, then, that cruel 'no'—the 'no' that breaks my heart?"

"Wait! The happiness of two people, the only one that I understand and want, is only possible in a shared love in which each of the two gives himself or herself to the other entirely. That is true, especially when there exists between two individuals a disproportion of social condition that, in our case, is pushed beyond the most extreme limits."

"That's not important!"

"It's very important. Suppose that I consent, that we're married, and that one day a dissension erupts between us..."

"Never!"

"On your part, perhaps, but it might be me who renders myself culpable. Then, you would be able to think, if not to say to me, that another ambition is allied to my ambition for happiness...and the happiness would be destroyed. In order that that cannot be, it's necessary that I should be conscious, in a complete and absolute fashion, that the elect of my heart is uniquely that of my heart, and that not the slightest shadow, not the most infinitesimal suspicion of a reflection, can diminish in me the pure frankness of the invincible attraction that draws me toward him."

"And that consciousness?"

"I do not have in its plenitude."

"Ah! You don't love me!"

"Yes, too dear illustrious companion in peril, I experience for you, such as I have learned to divine you and know you in spite of yourself, a profoundly tender amity, but..."

"But?"

"I'm not absolutely sure; nothing furnishes me with the dazzling proof that, in the sentiment that I experience, the Mining King has completely disappeared behind the features of Williamson."

"Is that such a great evil? Oh, how I permit you to unite those two, who are but ne, in your thought!"

"But I cannot permit it. The happiness of which I dream can only be attained if, in the tribunal of my own judgment, I can swear before God that I know I am giving as much as I receive, that I love as much as I am loved. Then, I will not care whether there is a billionaire behind the mask, since I shall only see the elect. Then, he will know that he is truly loved, and can savor ideal happiness in peace, forever exempt from suspicion. But so long as I cannot be sure that my tenderness is what I want and need it to be, I shall maintain the 'no' that my conscience and my sentimental ambition have just ordered me to formulate."

"And...when will that certainty come to you?"

"Perhaps tomorrow, perhaps never. It is my heart that will tell me. If it speaks in the direction you desire, I will tell you immediately. You know that I am frank and honest, and you have my word—my oath, if you wish. Wait!"

"Alas! And that's...your final word?"

"I never have two of them."

"I'll wait. But if your heart rejects me for wanting too much, or if it is too slow in becoming clement, I shall die of it."

Since that conversation, every time Williamson's eyes met Edmée's, they imported: "Is it today that you will tell me that you love me?"

And every time, the young woman's gaze responded: "Wait!"

And it was that waiting that riveted the languishing lover to his sumptuous apartment, which seemed to him to be so ugly and so sad. But up above, on the chaise-longue on which the unique object of his thoughts was resting her dear and adorable feminine fragility, the heart of the beloved might suddenly speak, and he wanted to be there to receive immediately the confession on which his life was suspended—if it came!

That evening, however, Williamson came to the meeting at the posada. That was because Edmée felt better, and had resolved to go there in order to embrace her brother.

At the agreed time, in the corner opposite to one in which three belated clients were finishing their consumption, Edmée and her companion saw Snow Rose's poor inamorata arrived, exhausted, dejected and hardly able to stand up, escorted by Toby.

"Well?"

"Nothing—still nothing! I have however, repeated the tour of the two bays of San Francisco today, asking questions everywhere. It's impossible that it's to Frisco or its surrounding area that the filthy dog of a woman-stealer has brought her! Damn! I have nothing left to do than to go bury myself alive in some convent in Mexico, for I'll never see her again."

"Come on, courage, Captain Furet! You must never despair. I still have hope! Have a glass of brandy, and tell us about our day."

Slightly reanimated by a few drops of alcohol, the mariner began: "You know I told you that I thought I'd picked up a trail?"

"Yes that kind of ancient cowboy—or 'peon,' as they say in this Mexican state of the Union—whom we found so often on our heels, following us, but who fled as soon as we approached him, and whom you intended to try to follow in our turn."

"I said to myself: he must be one of Loeb's spies..."

"That quite probable, in fact."

"Well, no, Commandant. I ended up clarifying the matter. I found out where he lives and informed myself in his regard. He's a fisherman from the hamlet of Purissima, not far from here on the Pacific, a mile south of Half Moon Bay. His name is Santos Miguel and he's considered a harmless lunatic. For about a month, his monomania has consisted of running around Frisco in all directions, without ever speaking to anyone, looking at all the passers-by, listening to what they say, and especially never missing the arrival of trains on the Great Western Railroad, at Oakland as well as San Francisco. He watches the passengers go by, then goes back to wandering or to bed. It seems probable to me that, less crazy than he's believed to be in Purissima, he's a police informer. At any rate, he can't have anything to do with us, in spite of his persistence in our regard, since, having been following that bizarre trade for a month, he can't be spying for Loeb, who wasn't in America then."

"That's true."

"With all that, we're no further forward than the day we disembarked here. I have to don my mourning-dress, I tell you, because I'll never find my beloved Snow Rose, just as you'll never find Old Sinker, since you have no guide."

Poor Captain Furet was in despair.

"It's a crime," he moaned, "to have put a treasure of grace like Snow Rose in the situation of becoming the victim of a ferocious beast like this Loeb! What has he done to that dear creature by now? He might have tortured her, to force her to guide him to the place to which she was only supposed to guide Monsieur Mining King! Courageous as she is, she won't have wanted to betray him in favor of his implacable enemy, whom she venerates and calls Master and genius. And perhaps he'll have killed her, without me, unfortunate and powerless, having done anything to defend her!"

"Come on, my worthy Jean, calm down and reflect! To harm Snow Rose is entirely contrary to Loeb's interests. Be sure, on the contrary, that he'll treat her as a precious hostage, and try to get round her, but will avoid attacking her head on for fear of not obtaining what he desires from her."

"Who knows, Commandant?"

Williamson intervened. "Monsieur Rolland is right, Captain Furet. There's more reason to be anxious, at present, for the fate of Old Sinker than the gracious guide that he gave us, whom we've unfortunately allowed to be abducted, and who has so profoundly touched your heart."

"Oh, Monsieur Williamson, what makes me want to blow my brains out in furious despair, is that I've been the cause of that misfortune, by taking it into my head to leave her hidden in that fatal loft in order to try to keep her out of the hands of that filthy dog of a diabolical Saint!"

"No, Captain Furet, I alone am the guilty party, because, lacking composure at that terrible moment, I wasn't able to foresee what happened and obviate it, within the limits of the possible. In the interest of the strange man who made me what I am, I should not have allowed myself to lose sight for a single moment of the person who was to guide me to him, and whom, by virtue of that fact, he entrusted to me.

"Be careful," said Edmée. "That remorse is almost a reproach addressed to me."

"Oh, Miss Edmée, how can you say that? To reproach you for something when, on the contrary, I'm accusing myself so bitterly for the sufferings that you're endured because of me!"

"Come on," said Claude "let's cease these futile recriminations. I can see that it's up to me, who is untroubled by any intimate emotion, to be calm and practical for everyone. Let's leave the past and, in order to make resolutions for the future, let's envisage the present situation clearly. In that regard, one thing is of primary importance: Ariadne's thread is broken."

"Alas," said Williamson, "to the extent that I'm permitted any other concern by the suspension of my life on a word that hasn't yet been pronounced, that's what upsets me the most. I made an oath to respond without delay to Old Sinker's summon, but it's materially impossible for me to keep it."

"Let's reason it out," the young engineer continued. "That conductive threat, we must try to reconnect at any price. There are two means to do that: the first and most urgently imposing was to try to pick up the trail of our guide. It seems increasingly evident to me that every passing hour diminishes the chances of succeeding in that. The remains the second, which I submit to Mr. Williamson: to inform Old Sinker about the difficulty that had stopped us by the anonymous and secret means that he has given us to communicate with him—the worldwide publicity of the New York *Herald*—and request instructions from him. That might take a long time or a short one, depending on whether Lobanief is far away or close at hand, but it seems to me that it's nevertheless the best thing to do. What do you think?"

Williamson put his head in his hands and reflected carefully, He was about to open his mouth to reply when the door of the bar, now empty of other clients, as shoved brutally and opened with a bang.

Williamson, Edmée Claude and Jean leapt to their feet and stood there for a few seconds, eyes staring and mouths agape, literally paralyzed by surprise.

In front of them, rigid and rugged, the tall, thin silhouette of Loeb was outlined, clutching Snow Rose.

What did it mean?

Laconically, his voice hoarse, Loeb explained:

"I'm returning your guide to you, Williamson, because she's useless. Old Sinker is making a fool of you. I regret having tormented you—for as I've said, I have no hatred against you—and of having given myself so much trouble to end up in a cul-de-sac. I've forced the Indian to confess the whole truth to me. Her mission was only to bring you to San Francisco, and she has no idea where the man I hate is hiding. I refused to believe in that ignorance for a long time; I've set all the traps imaginable for the Indian; I've used all means, and it's necessary for me to yield to the evidence. She doesn't know anything. She can't guide either you or me to the man whose retreat, as I have twenty proofs, she doesn't know. She's useless to me; I don't want to encumber myself with her any longer, and I'm returning her to you.

"Williamson, I'm also ending my war against you. Our struggle, like your journey, is over. The advice on which you set out on campaign, with me in your wake, was a joke in poor taste on the part of the man whose entire life, in fact, is one vast bluff, as is his pretended science. In his regard, I've reawakened passions in the United States that I'll make haste to extinguish. I'm not in the habit of persisting in a still-born affair. I'm cutting my losses and quitting the game, regretting the time wasted."

Throwing a wallet on to the table in front of the friends, amazed by that unexpected denouement, he added: "Give back, I beg you, to that imbecile named Grégoire de Montalpé, what remains of the campaign subsidies with which he furnished me. Follow your path, which I don't envy, having proved to you that I'm stronger by means of domination than you are by means of millions.

"Adieu...and no hard feelings!"

And Loeb, with a shrug of the shoulders that expressed his scorn for having put so much effort into a vain project, turned on his heel and left, leaving his enemies of the day before still immobilized by amazement.

It was Captain Furet, obedient to the supreme law of living beings, who broke the charm. He advanced toward Snow Rose, his arms open wide and tears in his eyes, pronouncing her dear name—and the Indian allowed herself to fall into them, murmuring: "Captain Furet! Oh, my dear!"

Extracting herself very quickly from the candid effusion, with a modest gesture, Snow Rose came to Williamson and said: "What that evil man has just said is true. Old Sinker limited my mission to San Francisco, without any other indication..

"Then...what are we going to do now?"

"I don't know."

"Who might know, then?"

"Old Sinker."

"When and how will he let us know his wishes?"

"I don't know."

"Monsieur Rolland advised me to solicit him via the New York *Herald*."

"It's not necessary. Old Sinker hadn't said so."

"If we do nothing, the situation could last forever."

"Old Sinker will make provision."

"After all," Williamson concluded, "it's up to him, in fact. If, as it seems, he hasn't taken precautions, there's nothing we can do. We'll have made a voyage that, for my part, and even though, time after time, it has brought us frightful anguish, has been the best of my life, for I've discovered something better than America therein.

"My friends, let's go back to the hotel, and live, since we're rid of Loeb, as if we had no other goal than to visit the city, the Queen of the Pacific, come what may…or what might. Will you deign to grant me your arm, Miss Edmée"

They had been walking for ten minutes through the city, still partially reconstructed, when Claude, who was walking beside Williamson, said, in a low voice: "There's the man."

"What man?"

"The monomaniac my matelot says is named Santos Miguel."

"Where?"

"Behind us. He went past the couple formed by Jean and Snow Rose and immediately attached himself to their paces. They're both too preoccupied to have noticed him. I'll inform the mariner."

"Don't do anything, my friend. Total passivity is now our law."

At the moment when Snow Rose and her great friend Jean, following Williamson and Rolland, went into the hotel, the Indian started. Behind her, almost in her ear, a voice had said: "Manitoba."

"My father?" said the gracious Redskin—who was hardly red at all—turning round and finding herself face to face with the Californian fisherman that Jean recognized immediately.

"Menominee," added Santos Miguel.

"My nation?"

"Your name?"

"Snow Rose."

"Finally. I've been waiting for you for a month."

That interrogation was not to the taste of the young mariner. He was about to criticize the manner in which the individual permitted himself to interrogate Snow Rose while she was on his arm when the latter uttered a significant "Shh!" and addressed herself to the supposed monomaniac.

"Is it the great chief of the Menominees who sends you to me?"

"No. It's an old man with long white hair who passed through Purissima a month ago and asked me to carry out a commission, paying me in advance.

"He didn't tell you his name?"

"He said that it wasn't worth the trouble, and that you'd recognize the origin…"

"Of what?"

"The letter I have for you."

"A letter? Why didn't you say so right away? Give it to me, quickly.

"Here it is."

"And that's all?"

"That's all."

"Dear Captain Furet," said the young woman, urgently to the young mariner, "give this man all the dollars you have on you. Mr. Williamson will return them to you."

Jean obeyed. The man drew away, calling down all the blessings of heaven on the generous young people, and Snow Rose ran after the Mining King and his friends. She signaled to them at a distance that she had to talk to him.

Intrigued, the billionaire took everyone into the drawing room of his apartment.

Then the young Indian took the letter from beneath her mantle, where she had hidden it, opened the envelope and took out a fragment of a map, which she handed to Williamson.

The latter had scarcely glanced at it when he stifled a cry of surprise. In the corner was the sign.

"My friends," he said, very emotionally, "Admire the wisdom and the prudence of the man who is summoning me. It was deliberately that he broke the connective thread—a rupture to which we owe Loeb's renunciation and Snow Rose's liberation. At the same time, though, he's taken care to re-knot it, for he's undoubtedly given me this time, via the intermediary and emissary so well-chosen, the indication of the definitive place where we'll find him."

"Which is?"

"I shall imitate the prudence of which he has given me such a marvelous example. I'll tell you as soon as we've left San Francisco."

"We're retracing out steps?"

"Oh no! On the contrary."

"But we're leaving?"

"In two or three days' time. Loeb is still so close! We're going to organize ourselves as if we were going to stay here for some time, and then disappear abruptly. It's the end of our voyage, Miss Edmée. May I flatter myself with the hope that it will make me happy?"

"To one of the questions you asked at the posada a little while ago, Snow Rose replied that Old Sinker would make provision. To the one you're asking I can only reply, at this moment, that God will make provision."

Williamson bowed his head, not without discouragement, but, in spite of himself, with a vague…very vague…hope.

13. The Fantastic Murder

The surprise at the posada—a surprise of deliverance and partial happiness—followed by that of the letter, had taken place on a Monday evening.

Exactly two weeks later, and, in consequence, on the second Monday thereafter on the incommensurable and implacable Clock of Time, a supplementary liner of the America-Japan Line, after having left the large military port of Yokosouka to port, moored a little before nightfall in the harbor of Yokohama. To general surprise, from that liner of nearly ten thousand tons, whose vast flanks could accommodate more that thirteen hundred passengers, only six passengers emerged.

Having not found, at first glance, a steamer departing from the great California port at his convenience, and wanting to be able to traverse the north Pacific as rapidly as possible, in order to render a repeat of the shipwreck off Sandy Hook impossible, the Mining King had chartered one of the modern giants of the sea for his personal use.

Loeb surely ought to have been a long way from San Francisco two days after his abrupt renunciation of pursuing his campaign of hate, but Williamson was determined not to neglect any precaution, no matter how exaggerated it might seem. To that effect he had ostentatiously rendered a villa in Berkeley, near Oakland, directly opposite the broad entrance to the bays, had transported his friends and hearth there, as if he intended settling in for a long sojourn in California, and, via the intermediary of Captain Furet, had arranged a seemingly-fortuitous encounter with the director of the Transpacific Company.

The latter invited the celebrated Yankee king to participate in the trials of a new ship, which had its coal-bunkers full and set forth, at an average speed of seventeen knots...all the way to Japan.

Claude and Edmée could not be dupes of the stratagem, although Jean Guitard had maintained an obedient silence regarding the step he had been secretly instructed to take, but what about Snow Rose, who was hesitating so dolorously between the duty of returning to the paternal Reservation now that her mission was accomplished and her great desire to see Old Sinker again, in the company of her brave and joyous sweetheart? In any case, she was, intimately, infinitely grateful to the Mining King for having thus disposed of her without consulting her and for having imposed a long voyage upon her "in convoy," as Jean put it, with her dear Captain Furet.

As for Grégoire de Montalpé, Williamson had simply left him in Berkeley, alone with his recovered wallet, which was not too badly breached, the procedures of the dominator of men having been—for that very reason—fairly economical.

In the little group, now so amicable, that was following the fortunes of the Caesar of the dollar, de Montalpé was the only one who, in Williamson's scale-free eyes recalled the moral vileness of the human rabble that his old misanthropy had once generalized. Thus, the presence of the gentleman, who had not even redeemed his sins by a little virile courage, was intolerable to him, and he had deprived himself of it—not sorry, fundamentally, to do him the bad turn of making him miss out on the goal for which he had associated himself with Loeb in Paris.

The surprise of the workers at the port of Yokohama on observing the small number of passengers disembarking from such a large ship come from so far away was completed by the breathless arrival of the United States consul, escorted by the principal authorities of Yokohama, one of the largest of the nine Japanese ports open to commerce.

That was because, on arriving within sight of the coast of the Isles of the Rising Sun, the Mining King had thought he ought to announce the fact by means of a skillfully courteous cablegram. He would have need of Japanese complaisance to reach the rendezvous signed to him, traveling across country in the minimum possible time. Knowing the mistrust of the conquerors of Korea, having experienced it previously, he took his precautions.

It was, therefore, as an important person that Edmée's "suitor"—whom the voyage had left sighing, as before, in spite of the long intimacy of the crossing and a few hopeful glimmers that he had seemed to observe in the young woman's eyes—was welcomed at Yokohama, and it was with quasi-royal honors that he was received in Tokyo.

Given the delicate negotiations between the victorious isles of the Far East and Washington, sage governmental diplomacy considered it an honor to give an extraordinary reception to an individual of primary influence in the great American Republic. Whether he liked it or not in spite of his haste, it was necessary for Williamson to submit, for forty-eight hours, to diurnal and nocturnal festivities, with gala performances, mousmé ballets and sumptuous meals, which were only tolerable because the Parisian grace, beauty and wit of Edmée was magnificently triumphant thereat.

Finally, on Thursday, he was able, with his companions, furnished with all the necessary licenses to travel through the fantastic insular empire, to depart via the Tokyo-Mito-Sendai-Hachinohe-Aomori railway for the north of great Nippon.

It was between the last two stations that he left the railroad and the little troop, mounting horses brought from the capital in a wagon added to the train, set off in the company of reliable guides toward the volcanic chain that gives Japan the appearance of a gigantic antediluvian reptile with a dorsal crest, asleep in the waves, its slumber sometimes troubled by profound shivers.

A grave emotion rendered the voyagers silent as they approached a mountain higher than its neighbors, whose conical summit, partly veiled by light vapors, dispersing liked ripped gauze in the breeze, rose up arid and bare above the cultivated fields, which, in that winter season, dressed its base with a gray and brown checkerboard reminiscent of the fabrics favored by Anglo-Saxons.

When they arrived sat the extreme limit of cultivation, Williamson, after having consulted for the hundredth time the map received in San Francisco, halted the little troop, made them dismount, dismissed the guides and horses, and, following the detailed indications of a large-scale plan drawn on the back of the sheet of paper, beckoned to his companions to follow him.

For two long hours, marching in his wake, they went around the vast cone, scaling blocks of lava solidified in bizarre forms, sometimes disappearing into narrow corridors, going up and coming down again, in order finally to arrive at the threshold of a somber portal, from which a warm breath emerged, which seemed to be the entrance to a disquieting tunnel plunging into the heart of the mountain.

In a voice rendered tremulous by emotion, the Mining King formulated the brief words: "This is it."

Torches were lit and, with a stride as firm as the uneven nature of the ground permitted, they advanced, their staring eyes searching the darkness.

Avoiding the projections of rock that sometimes threatened their heads, they descended a slope that was often steep for more than an hour.

Suddenly, the vault of the tunnel rose up abruptly above their heads. They went into a vast cavern...

A hundred meters in front of them, a luminous dot was shining, which was raised and lowered three times in a sign of greeting.

Their hearts squeezed by an oppressive anguish, they headed toward the beacon.

By the light of their torches, a tall old man appeared, clad in animal skins, his head crowned by abundant white hair falling in snowy waves over his shoulders. He was holding up a heavy lantern at the end of a robust arm.

"Old Sinker!" murmured Snow Rose, in a tone of devotion that was both ardent and almost fearful.

The old man stopped some fifteen paces away. The steel of a large caliber weapon suddenly gleamed in his right hand.

"Williamson?" he interrogated.

"I'm Williamson, and I've come in response to your summons."

"Advance alone!"

The Mining King obeyed, his lantern raised to the level of his face.

"I recognize you," said Old Sinker—and, accompanied by Williamson, he approached the immobilized group and inspected them with a rapid glance.

"Snow Rose!" he recognized. "Why did you come all this way, child? Anyway, it's Destiny." Then, indicating the rest of the group, he said to Williamson: "Who are they?"

"This is Mr. Claude Rolland, an engineer, and his sister Edmée, two noble hearts, French, and your relatives, their grandmother having been a Lobanief. Next to them is a valiant mariner of the same Gallic race, their servant, or rather their devoted companion, an intelligent and intrepid seaman who has saved us all from death three times in the course of the voyage. Finally, my groom Toby, a faithful and taciturn lad."

The strange old man seemed to collect himself. Then he said: "All right. Come."

260

Following him, the little troop traversed the vast cavern without saying a word. Claude noticed, in passing, that the uncertain light of their torches, penetrating the darkness vaguely, revealed in its depths a series of giant windlasses capable of unrolling tens of kilometers of steel cable.

Having arrived at the wall, Old Sinker lifted up a heavy opaque door made of several bearskins sown together, and the visitors went into a large natural chamber copiously illuminated by several incandescent bulbs.

That redoubt, in which a company of infantry could easily have assumed various drill-formations, simultaneously resembled a laboratory, by virtue of the immense furnace laden with retorts, crucibles alembics, and electric and other heaters; the generating plant of a factory, by virtue of its powerful steam engine and its dynamos; and the study of a geologist who was also an advanced mathematician, by virtue of its collection of minerals of unknown forms and gleams, its blackboards covered with figures and equations, and its colossal table heaped with books and pieces of paper blackened with calculations. Only a heap of furs serving as a bed, a few kitchen utensils and a few stacks of food-tins announced that it was also a place of residence.

Claude's curious gaze noticed immediately, first of all a fissure in the wall into which the fumes of the furnace and the steam engine disappeared, which doubtless communicated, doubtless a long distance away, with the crater, and thus served the endeavors of a single man as a chimney, and then the continuous noise of a trickle of water into a full basin.

Then his surprise, as an engineer, at finding in that profound cavern, in a site distant from any human aid, a laboratory, a factory and a habitation, disappeared. That was because they all saw, fixed to a low part of the vault, an iron chain from which hung a terrestrial globe pierced through by a dagger: the sign.

The engineer—the others not having minds free enough to deliver themselves to observation—did not have the leisure to take his investigations any further. With a grave gesture, Old Sinker had invited his visitors to sit down on rocky outcrops forming natural seats, and, standing up, having slowly caressed his long snow-white beard, began to speak:

"In the fifteen years since we met, Williamson, in very dramatic circumstances. My work, then merely sketched, has passed from the domain of theory into the domain of precise, palpable facts.

"I told you then, roughly and without insisting, that the terrestrial planet is, like us, like everything, a living being, whole pellicular surface we inhabit as parasites

"I charged my intelligent, docile and unique neophyte, Snow Rose, to prepare you with some knowledge possessed by her, for the striking truth that awaited you here. I assume that she has done that."

"Yes, Master, albeit in the insufficient fashion corresponding with my feeble strength."

261

"I have no doubt, Snow Rose, that the little that it was in your power to say has been well said.

"I told you, Williamson, at the time of our abrupt and definitive separation fifteen years ago that I would summon you after you had enriched yourself more than other men, when I was in a position—in collaboration with you—to be the master of the destiny of the world. That day has come.

"It is you alone that I wanted to instruct and enable to assist at the supreme moment the proof crowning an entire life of effort to discover the Truth. You will know shortly why I am tolerating other presences, including that of these two French people, to whom I am sympathetic as much because they are French as because a little of my blood runs in their veins, and above all because you like them and answer for them.

"So, listen, Williamson, about whom I have not ceased to think since our former encounter, and whom I have made the richest of men, I hope…and listen, all of you!

"Geologists, who, if they had the slightest sincerity, if not modesty, would call themselves simply 'dermologists,' since it is not the Earth that they can discover but only the epidermis of the monster, because it is only the epidermis that they have been able to penetrate to a feeble depth and determine its contents…those, I say, who have baptized themselves, as falsely as pridefully, 'geologists,' have, from the heights of their professorial chairs, informed humanity of a host of errors to which a few rare intellects have refused to subscribe—such as Lord Kelvin, who recently disappeared from the number of insects living on the substance of the Immense Beast.

"They have represented it as a mass of molten minerals surrounded by a crust solidified by contact with the cold of space, without pausing at the impossibility of the resistance of that crust—the thinness of which even they observe—to pressures due to solar and lunar, not to mention planetary, attractions, without taking into account the fact that the rapidity of translation of seismic shocks is far superior to what is achievable traversing a liquid medium.

"It would be cruel for human science to persist.

"That the Earth is solid in all its parts, and that, in consequence, the story of the central broth, transforming the globe into an immense chaotic cauldron, is a myth and a dream, I have known for a long time, because I assured myself of it directly a long time ago."

At that formidable assertion, Old Sinker's listeners raised their heads.

"Yes," he said, tranquilly, it is already ten years ago that I traversed the famous terrestrial crust and I, a pygmy, commenced to delve into the flesh of the monster, boldly compiling an anatomy of the basis of that vivisection. That is why you find me in this region, which I chose for two reasons, one technical— which would have been sufficient on its own—and the other political.

"Technically, it was necessary for me to find a place where the 'hide' was very thin and where the vital organs came, in a sense, to touch it—a place comparable to the human temple, where, almost beneath the thin skin, the artery beats that creates a vulnerability.

"Politically, it was necessary for me to work in a region where the people, mentally very different and very preoccupied with their social development, would let me work without paying any heed to me, a people having, in the mass, very little science and too much superstition to come prying into my solitary labor.

"I found here what I needed: in the ten years since I transported into this cavern the necessary tools and provisions, the simple agriculturalists, even those on the slopes of the mountain, have, I believe, quite forgotten me. As for the limited thickness of the terrestrial dermis, I had rightly anticipated that this tormented ground, punctured by volcanoes, guaranteed a sensitive area and present inflammation of the immense body. I discovered the 'flesh' eighteen and a half kilometers down, a flesh less hard than the skin—and by 'skin' I mean the rocky dermis, not the epidermis, and even less the superficial dirt of twenty or thirty million years, a dermis that we incorrectly label the subsoil, the region of quarries and mines utilized by our existence on the ultimate surface. That flesh is, as I say, less hard than the skin, but of a variable hardness and nature, as the cellular composition of our bodies differs between muscles, fat, nerves, bones, etc."

Old Sinker saw Claude Rolland agitating his fingers with some impatience. "Do you have an objection to make?" he asked, with a certain arrogance.

"No—a question to ask."

"Go on."

"The increasing heat...?"

"It only increases in traversing the envelope, at the inner surface of which it reaches it maximum—which is to say, that of the body, which no longer varies, at least in the limited thickness of that which I've been permitted to reach, and which I firmly believed to be very similar throughout the Monster's mass."

"And that temperature?"

"Is a hundred and forty-eight degrees centigrade."

"How were you able...?"

"To survive there? Certainly not without a refrigerant suit and a provision of air at a respirable temperature. It is not an environment into which a man can introduce his body, which is adapted to environments proximal to the cold of infinite space, without the protection of his industry, nor one where it is prudent to torment the Beast in person. When my tools were operating, I was able to keep myself out of reach, far away in the inert matter that overlies the epidermis.

"Once, however, in spite of that precaution, I nearly failed to return to the extreme surface. My scalpels had attacked and sliced special very distinctive fibers—as I observed later—of a substance and contexture that I shall call 'ambient tissue.' The consequence of that was a general tremor that was translated, in the sunlight, into seismic shocks, which, I subsequently learned, had repercussions, unfortunately mortal for too many human beings, in several regions some distance away from here. I believe I can affirm that I encountered that day a significant 'nervous filament.'

"In addition to that exceptional case, however, I observed, by the evidence of inexplicable pressures to which my implements were subjected in spite of the resistance of their massive metallic alloy, superior to that of modern chrome steel, that the mass is, in general, like our flesh prone to reflexive reactions against anything that troubles its normal harmony. Thus, it was only after my tools had finished their work that I went down to study the results."

"But how," Williamson asked in his turn, "while your strange experiments were taking place here, were you so often able to indicate to me, in America, the existence of mines that..."

"The labor that I carried out here necessitated frequent interruptions, superficial healing, without which my carnal fragment, robust as it is, would not have resisted that superhuman labor. It was then, Williamson, that I undertook expeditions to America, where my expert eyes read the so-called subsoil and threw into your coffers a few more millions of dollars."

"Your fabulous work, then...?"

"Save for an improbable error, is complete. Two months ago, I set my tools at rest, because I had certainly encountered one of the entity's organs."

"An organ?" queried the troubled auditors of the fantastic lecture, in chorus.

"An essential organ, if I can believe the rhythmic beats, at intervals of twelve hours, to which its rather tender and very elastic envelope is subject, which I hesitated to perforate. Is it the Monster's heart? I cannot believe so, given its proximity to the surface. Is it an analogue of the carotid in the human neck, rendered by its outlying position easy to reach? Everything gives me that conviction.

"Then a formidable problem arose before my conscience, whose eventual solution has been simultaneously the torment, the goal, the terror and the desire of my entire life.

"I believe that I am sure of having put my finger on a vital organ of the planetary Monster that carries us. Ought I to surrender my secret in order that others, after me, can push on even further with the study of the living sidereal body that carries us through space in its rolling course, as a swallow carries a spider with hooked feet through the sky from north to south? Or should I mortally wound the rolling giant, taking revenge for the countless voluntary cataclysms that, since the beginning of time, have doomed so many millions of human brethren, as well as billions of inferior animal brethren?

"Its death, doubtless slow, would bring about the slow disappearance of all the parasitic lives that struggle and suffer in order that fewer of them might die. But could there be any more transcendent benefit than that general annihilation, and, as I once said, would not the man who was able to become the 'murderer of the world' be sublimely wise and good?"

Williamson and his companions had risen go their feet, breathless. Lobanief extended his arms in a gesture of supreme authority.

"Wait, before replying!

"I hate the Earth! It is because it has revealed itself to me as the infamous devourer of human creatures that it has enabled me, in one horrible minute, always present in my mind, to divine its living and malevolent nature.

"More than thirty years ago, exiled from my fatherland, I came with my family in search of forgetfulness and repose, to an isolated and almost deserted location far from human grandeurs, which are often very heavy to those who assume them.

"I had bought a small plot of land on the border of Canada and the Union. From the house where I lived, my view extended to the horizon over the calm majesty of the immense and beautiful Lake Superior. I hunted, and I fished in the abundantly-populated Pigeon River, which ran at the foot of my wild property. I meditated for hours or cultivated the sciences, for which I had always had a pronounced penchant, and I relaxed in the bosom of a numerous and tenderly cherished family...

"I was happy!

"One evening, a terrible storm burst over our house, which oscillated but resisted. Then, without there being any volcano, or even mountains, in the most distant vicinity, the ground opened up beneath my dwelling, which I had quit momentarily in order to go to the stables to make sure that my horses had not been carried away.

"It was into an unfathomable abyss, which closed as soon as it had opened, like a demonic rictus, that my house was swallowed up, with my adored wife, two sons already grown up, who were my pride, and an adorable daughter, who was an angel, and my last-born son, scarcely emerged from infancy, who was a cherub!

"Mad with terror, I leapt on to a stallion, whose halter I broke, and I fled, galloping aimlessly, until my mount fell dead, leaving me inanimate on the ground.

"I was picked up by Menominee Indians, who took me to their Reservation, then as vast as a kingdom, and cared for me. It was among them that I recovered my reason, and thus my dolor, among them that I acquired the conviction of the living spasm of the Earth, and the burning desire for cold vengeance was implanted in my soul.

"After thirty years, the hour of that vengeance has chimed. I have seen so many human beings suffer, one after another, due to the Earth, that in avenging myself, even at the price of the annihilation of everything it bears, it is humanity entire that I can and want to avenge!

"It is futile now, you will have understood, to talk to me about the other solution, of preserving the gigantic Beast, which is perhaps nothing but an immense invalid rendered evil by its own suffering, of learning to know its organism in order to care for it, to regulate its functioning, so that the humanity of future ages might succeed in playing the role of benevolent microbes in human and animal organisms

"If I said these things to humans still to new on the surface of the turbulent being, still poorly detached from the animality of their material nature, they would not believe me, would persecute my disciples, and continue for many centuries to come to languish in error and suffering.

"No! The moment has come for my vengeance and for the worldwide benefit of extinguishing all life in the world, by means of the sacrificial murder of the world! A Being as formidable as that, the vital duration of which is measured in millions of centuries, does not die immediately of a small wound, even if it is mortal. The present generation, at least, will have time to complete its career before the monstrous death-throes commence, and your life, Williamson, will be beautiful; the only one informed, having the supreme and sovereign power of gold, you will extract from the end of the world all that it can offer of joys; you will be the last fortunate man—which is what I want, because I love you!

"The moment has come! Lift up your hearts! Watch the judiciary strike of the Avenger of Humankind, the Master of Death, the Murderer of the World!"

The fantastic old man had stopped speaking, but his listeners were still stunned, astounded and terrified...

Only Williamson darted at Lobanief a singular glance, whose fixity seemed to want to read in Old Sinker's soul something that he had not said, something that extended his entire being in an intense and mute interrogation.

The tall old man, who, his expression inspired, appeared to have become even taller, summoned the billionaire to come toward him with a broad authoritarian gesture, into which a nuance of emotion nevertheless intruded.

He said to him: "In spite of the long-meditated precautions that I've taken, the immense action that I'm about to take is subject to contingencies, because our embryonic science can't anticipate everything.

"I'm going to go down in order to judge the force of the thrust that I must deliver to the Monster. Every two thousand feet I've set up a refuge, but in case I don't come up again—and only then—you must swear, once you have acquired the certainty that the avenger of humankind cannot reappear alive in the sunlight in order to delight in the progress of his murderous work, that you will open this letter, in which is recorded my final revelation and my last will."

So saying, he took from his bosom a sealed envelope, which the billionaire received in a tremulous and distracted hand.

The tall old man fixed Williamson with a long stare in which there was a strange, intense expression...and advanced majestically toward the exit from the chamber into the large grotto, heading toward its dark depths, followed by his stunned guests, oppressed by a kind of tremulous, admiring and quasi-religious horror.

Suddenly, ten arc-lamps inundated that opaque obscurity with light, and, at the extremity of the series of enormous windlasses that Claude Rolland had glimpsed in passing, illuminated the gaping opening of a large fissure, a black and mysterious gulf, to the rim of which Lobanief advanced.

He called to Snow Rose, and, showing her the lever of a commutator fixed into a block of lava, ordered: "At the precise moment that I disappear!"

Eyes dilated, with a double gesture, abrupt and catastrophic, the young Indian seized the lever and nodded her head, saying: "Yes."

Then, Old Sinker/Lobanief shoved, as he jumped into it, a kind of metallic skip or nacelle, which oscillated momentarily directly above the abyss.

In a voice that showed a hint of emotion for the first time, the old man shouted: "*Au revoir*, Williamson...or adieu!"

The windlasses having been immediately set in motion, he plunged into the warm darkness of the gulf.

At that moment, the engineer pulled himself together. "Come on!" he said. "It's frightful and it's insane, all this! We need to stop..."

Detaching himself from Edmée, who was clinging to him, he leapt toward the Indian.

Too late.

Snow Rose had lowered the lever.

He stopped, dazed by anguish.

A sepulchral silence reigned, only troubled by the unctuous friction of the axle-trees of the windlasses in their groves.

Of the six human creatures who were there, none was breathing...

Suddenly, muffled, mysterious and formidable, the sound of a multiple detonation, compounded out of explosions, gigantic cracking sounds and sinister rumblings, as if a thousand cannons had started firing simultaneously in the distant entrails of the earth, rose from the terrible abyss.

At the same time a dense column of vapor surged forth, rendering the intense light of the lamps vague, and the ground shook, oscillating.

Uttering cries of fright, Toby, the Indian, who had been grabbed and was being dragged by the mariner, and Edmée, gripped in her brother's arms, raced toward the corridor through which they had come when they arrived, the only exit from the cavern.

They did not reach it.

A terrible shock shook the grotto, the vault of which collapsed, opening a huge gap in the mountain-side to the sky.

As they fell, the blocks had crushed the windlasses.

Terrified, the fugitives hastened toward the new exit, rendered accessible by the piles of fallen rock.

Only one remained. Standing on the edge of the gulf, extending his arms desperately, Williamson shouted in the silence that had almost been restored:

"Him!... Him!!... Him!!!"

Edmée tore herself away from the fraternal grip, violently. Climbing over the collapsed rocks she ran to Williamson.

"Come!"

"Him!... Him!!"

"A few seconds more and it's death!"

"Run away! Leave me!"

"Those hot and poisonous vapors...that are coming out of it. In spite of the hole, they're filing the cavern...irrespirable!"

"Run!"

"A few more seconds and we'll suffocate!"

"Oh, run, run away, Miss Edmée! I can't...I can't! Him! Down there! Him!!!"

Struggling against the efforts of Claude to drag her away, the young woman begged: "Come, if you love me!"

"I...I can't!"

"Then...then I'm staying—we'll die together!"

Williamson uttered a mad scream and turned to Edmée. "You want...?"

"If you want to die, I don't want to live!"

"You love me, then?"

"Until death!"

"Ah! To live! To live! I want to live!"

With a clamor of wild joy, Williamson seized the young woman in his arms, his strength multiplied tenfold, and carried her away toward the light, toward the sky, toward life. Claude helped him in the climb, difficult with a human burden.

Behind them, in the midst of incessant trepidations, an increasing din rose up, similar to that of a tumultuous tide forcing itself through a narrow bottleneck.

The two men hastened recklessly, but they were out of breath, blinded and strangled by the hot and fetid vapors, whose column now hid the exit.

Fortunately, help was at hand. Jean Guitard, after having set his beloved Snow Rose down on a safe path, came back to aid his dear masters.

After a great deal of effort, and after having thought twenty times over that they would not reach the portal, the little troop was finally reunited in the open air, on the flank of the crater, beyond the emanations of the subterranean exhalation.

Just in time!

A shock, a hundred times more violent than the first, completed the dislocation of the vault of the cavern...

Before the frightened eyes of the fugitives, with a sound that no comparison can approach, the entire vault collapsed, opening a gaping, fuming hole several hundred meters in diameter.

Although, very fortunately, they had only stopped on the part of the mountainside beyond the scope of the vast subterranean cavity, Williamson and his companions nevertheless remained in a situation that was, if not immediately critical, at least very worrying.

Backed up against an outcrop of volcanic rock, unscalable without ropes, ladders and outside assistance, they saw the vast cavity that had opened up in front of them cut off the other direction of escape. They had no alternative but to wait where they were for assistance that seemed unlikely to arrive, exposed to the risk of falling victim to some further convulsion of the mountain.

Their eyes, widened by anguish, could not tear themselves away from the gaping circle, from which smoke was rising, alternately gray and yellow, and from which Williamson was still vaguely hoping that, by some miracle, the tall and disturbing old man who had caused the cataclysm might emerge.

When, after half an hour of anxious waiting, the vapors had finally thinned out sufficiently to allow them to penetrate it with their gaze, it was not Old Sinker that appeared but a lake of thick mud, punctured here and there by bubbles from which jets of smoke emerged, and the overflow of which was pouring into a broad groove that ran down the side of the mountain, destroying in its passage a number of symmetrical rectangular crop-fields.

"It wasn't an artery or an organ," murmured Snow Rose, sadly. "It was only a tumor or an abscess. The master, in losing his life, wanted to wound the monster mortally…perhaps he's only given it relief."

For his part, Williamson, renouncing his impossible hope, let out a long sigh.

"It's really your opinion," he asked Edmée and her brother, "that your unparalleled relative, to whom I owe everything, is definitely dead under that burning scum emerged from the depths?"

"He's dead," replied Edmée and Claude, gravely, in chorus.

Then, the Mining King, with a trembling hand, took the sealed envelope from his pocket, opened it and started reading. At the very first lines he straightened up and uttered a stifled cry. Holding out the unfolded letter to the young people, he cried, with sobs in his voice:

"I suspected it, and wasn't mistaken. Old Sinker was my father!"

The child found and brought up by the Canadian garrison at Fort William was the last-born of the noble Russian exile Lobanief, who had miraculously survived the catastrophe in which the rest of his family, save for his father, had been swallowed up. And when, as a young reporter, Williamson had saved from the Hudson and despair the author and apostle of a discovery or a new scientific faith, the latter had recognized his son. Not wanting any human affection to deflect him from his bitter, fantastic and murderous determination, however, he had resolved, while heaping the greatest terrestrial benefits upon him, to remain a stranger to him, and only to summon him on the day of the frightful experiment, which would be that of his death, when the two would be reunited!

269

Williamson, his eyes moist, turned to Edmée. "My father," he said, "wanted to give me the mastery of the world, by means of the knowledge of its imminent end. The surety of the progressive and constant diminution of the vital intensity of the world's surface was an element of fortune even greater than the reliable discovery of mineral wealth.

"By an error of his genius...or madness...the Earth, the object of his hatred, swallowed him up without him being able to keep his promise. But he did something better for me. The fact of his supreme appeal put in my cold and egotistical path, and intimately involved with my life, to teach me to know its value, an angel descended to earth with the features of a woman!

"My father hasn't given me the mastery of the world, but may his great shade, which floats here above his Titanic tomb, be blessed! Thanks to him, via your love, Edmée, my soul has finally awakened to communion with the Great Secret of the World!"

14. Conclusion

For a long moment, Williamson and Edmée, standing side by side and hand in hand, dreamed silently, delightfully and gravely, their gazes wandering over the horizon, no longer veiled by the smoke of the subterranean mud, already cooling.

Claude contemplated them fraternally, while "Captain Furet," with the eloquence of his gaze, gradually dispelled the grave and tragic shadows in the dark eyes of Snow Rose.

Suddenly, above them, an abrupt and hoarse voice shouted: "There they are! They've been surprised and delayed by that sudden eruption of mud. We've arrived in time!"

The six fugitives raised their heads and, at the top of the outcrop of volcanic rock, recognized Jonathan Loeb, flanked by a Grégoire de Montalpé who, having recovered his sufficiency, was more a dandy than ever, accompanied by several Japanese authorities and the highest representative of the United States in the Empire of the Rising Sun.

"You have, on the contrary, arrived too late to encounter the noble genius Old Sinker, who is no more, but very much in time for me, since you've been gracious enough to bring the most important representatives of this Empire and our Republic. If you please, gentlemen, will you give us the means of getting out of the situation we're in and coming to join you?"

Men equipped with climbing equipment rapidly organized the liberation of the six prisoners of the mountain, who were welcomed with the greatest respect by the Japanese and the Yankee diplomat, with a suspicious hostility by Jonathan Loeb, and with a Southern loquacity by de Montalpé, to whom the "official" news of the death of the inconvenient Old Sinker gave a crazy desire to dance with joy.

"It was naughty of you to leave poor Grégoire kicking his heels all alone in San Francisco, when you were heading for the beautiful land of Japan! Fortunately, the worthy Monsieur Loeb hadn't left the place; he'd caught wind of the flight and, having no doubt of its objective, freed me in order that we could come here at the gallop, with the aid of these powerful Messieurs, warned about the catastrophes of which their country, by virtue of facts of which you're aware, might eventually become the theater. Then..."

"Enough!" said Loeb, immediately obeying.

Williamson went to the American diplomat and, handing him the envelope whose seal he had broken a short while before, said: "I'm depositing these papers in the hands of the senior representative of the United States, which, in the circumstances in which they were given to me, establish the decease of the noble Russian Baron Lobanief, my father."

"What!" cried de Montalpé, who had reasons for not being content with the general surprise. "You're the son of..."

"These papers establish it officially.

"But then...the inheritance?"

"A thousand regrets, my dear...relative. But perhaps you were also ingenuous, in so often thwarting the plans of an...adversary who thought of nothing but getting rid of me?"

"Oh, what a gaffe!"

Williamson addressed Loeb.

"Our paths were different; I dare to hope that we shall no longer be adversaries?"

"Well, we might, in the circumstances, now that we've made one another's acquaintance, even become allies, for I've never been directly your enemy."

"As regards an alliance, it's not that, for the moment, that I desire," the Mining King replied, diplomatically. He took Edmée's hand. "Gentlemen," he proclaimed, bowing slightly, "the new Baron Lobanief, American Citizen, has the honor of introducing you to his fiancée, Miss Edmée Rolland, of Paris."

This time, the unfortunate Grégoire thought he would faint from stupor and jealousy. As pale as his immaculate shirt-front, he stood there open-mouthed, unable to articulate a single word.

Addressing the diplomat again, Lobanief/Williamson went on: "As soon as we return to Tokyo, I shall have the honor of asking you to be kind enough to marry us, in conformity with the law. My mourning forbids any ceremony; we shall proceed with a simple civil ceremony; the others will take place, in accordance with Mrs. Lobanief's desire, in New York or Paris. I beg the Japanese authorities, whose welcome was so pompously gracious on my arrival, to be kind enough, for the same reason, to allow me to pass through Tokyo and Yokohama incognito in order to return to my ship.

"Oh! Let's not forget, in personal happiness, the happiness of others. I desire that, at the same time as the marriage of Miss Rolland and myself, the union should also be sealed of this brave mariner here, whom I shall continue to employ in the position and with the salary of a captain, with Miss Snow Rose, to whom I shall give a dowry of two hundred thousand dollars."

Finally, Grégoire de Montalpé was able, through a throat taut and obstructed by tears, to articulate a cry of despair: "And...and...and me? What...what...what will become of me?"

With an exaggerated and cold politeness, Lobanief/Williamson said: "Your presence here, my cousin de Montalpé, proves that you have a pronounced taste for long voyages. Let's see, my dear future brother-in-law and Director General of my mines, can we not find an exploration or a residency...somewhere?"

"A residency, certainly...I'll take care of it."

"Where?" moaned the discomfited dandy.

"Madagascar."

That was Claude Rolland's only vengeance with regard to Grégoire de Montalpé.

One final amazement was reserved, not for the unfortunate Grégoire, but for Claude.

On arriving at San Francisco, he found a dispatch from France addressed to New York, which had been forwarded by post to the Californian port by reason of the notoriety of the second name contained in the address: "M. Rolland, care of M. Williamson, Mining King."

Claude opened it and read:

Many thanks. Report perfect. Effects tribune devastating. Ministry slain. Am minister. If politics tempting, return quickly. Reserving situation cabinet chief.

Dupeyroux.

Claude's features expressed such a prodigious bewilderment that his billionaire brother-in-law, who was watching him from the corner of his eye, could not help smiling.

"But...I wasn't able to send my work, since I didn't reconstitute it after the shipwreck!"

"My dear Claude, it was received anyway."

"*My* work?"

"Not entirely. Thanks to the intermediary of the Catholic priest who rendered me a service in New York—and who will get a true cathedral for his pains—I had a critique of French colonial administrative methods compiled by an adroit American humoristic journalist and cabled..."

"And it was a fantasy concocted by trickery that...?"

"Brought down one ministry in order to consecrate another. Don't be surprised. In France, people believe so easily that which isn't serious, especially when one senses a foreign brand on it. I don't advise you to quit me to follow the senator; a man of real value, knowledge and honesty like you would make a deplorable politician, out of favor as soon as you opened your mouth. You'll stay with me eh?"

And, with good hearts, the two brothers-in-law shook hands firmly.

Eugène Thibault: *Radio-Terror*

Eugène Thébault's Radio-Terreur, Grand roman du Mystère, *translated here as* Radio-Terror, *was initially published in a serialized version in the magazine* L'Aventure *Nos. 1-30 in 1927-29, then collected by publisher Arthème Fayard in 1930. It was that version that had the honor of being one of the very few French works selected by Hugo Gernsback to be translated by none other than Fletcher Pratt, the well-known author of* The Well of the Unicorn, *and it was published in the June, August and October, 1933 issues of* Wonder Stories.[97]

Eugène Thébault was born in 1864 in Arthenay, a small village in the Charente region in Western France. He died in Viroflay, near Paris, in abject poverty, on January 5, 1942. Thébault was a journalist and a prolific popular novelist, who made his debut in 1894. He collaborated with a wide range of newspapers and magazine including L'Écho de Paris, L'Aurore, Le Matin, La Petite République *and* La Revue de Paris. *He was a renowned art critic from 1896 to 1906. As a novelist, he penned many thrillers and romance novels, such as* Mademoiselle Midinette, Sauvé par l'Amour *[Saved by Love] and* Les Chevaliers de la Croix Noire *[The Knights of the Black Cross]. In 1909, under the pseudonym of "Paul Zahori," he wrote a Holmesian pastiche,* Mademoiselle Sherlock, *which was first serialized in* Le Figaro, *and later collected in book form by publisher Tallandier (Le Livre National No. 840, 1932). In it, an 18 year-old Parisian woman, obsessed by Sherlock Holmes, becomes a detective.*

Thébault also used the nom-de-plume of "Amaury Kainval" to pen a series of popular detective novels for Ferenczi. His science fiction novels include Le Magicien de l'Air *[Wizard of the Air] (19??),* L'Aile Invisible *[The Invisible Wing] (1918),* Le Surhomme *[The Superman] (1928),* Le Soleil Ensorcelé *[The Spellbound Sun] (1930),* Nina, Australe Mystérieuse *[Nina, The Mysterious Austral Creature] (1930) retitled* Les Deux Reines du Pôle Sud *[The Two Queens of the South Pole] by Publisher Tallandier when he reprinted the book in 1932. This novel is about the descendants of an ancient Babylonian civilization living secretly in the Antarctic and gifted with powers between science and sorcery.*

J.-M.L.

---

[97] For *Wonder Stories*, Pratt also translated S. S. Held's *La Mort du Fer* (1931) (as *The Death of Iron*), *Wonder Stories*, Sept., Oct., Nov. & Dec. 1932) and Charles de Richter's *La Menace Invisible* (1934) (as *The Fall of the Eiffel Tower*), *Wonder Stories*, Sept., Oct. & Nov. 1934.

1. The First Broadcast

On October 18, 193*, the weather in Paris was marvelous, and numerous groups lingered along the boulevards in the early afternoon to yield themselves lazily to the caresses of autumn.

At the Place de l'Opéra a great crowd had gathered before the perfected loudspeaker which had just been installed there for the benefit of the public. Its powerful voice dominated the clamors of the traffic which rolled unceasingly past like a triumphal parade.

The loudspeaker, with a clarity and tone that delighted the assembled public, was reproducing the sounds of a cleverly assembled concert in which eight educated dogs, three elephants and a dozen parrots were performing a rendition of Beethoven's *Ninth Symphony*. The eight dogs were in London; the three elephants were in Calcutta, where one of them was tooting a trombone, the second a bassoon, and the third an oboe especially constructed far this gigantic and rather unusual performer. The dozen parrots sang (if one could call it that) from Buenos Aires; and everything had been arranged by the world radio commission so that all the different members of this extraordinary choir could be heard by wireless enthusiasts in any part of the universe.

As a matter of fact, the reception was all one could hope for. The elephant oboe player had just finished a solo, executed with deafening virtuosity, when all at once the thread of the animal concert was broken, to be replaced by an absolutely insupportable sound of frying.

"Well!" remarked someone, "what's going on? I don't seem to be able to understand the words anymore."

People laughed, imagining that the disagreeable sounds were part of the program.

A blonde *midinette*,[98] declared gaily:

"I know what it is; they've tuned in on some pigs asking for their soup."

"It's extraordinarily well imitated," affirmed a young radio enthusiast in a tone of conviction.

Suddenly, the sound of frying ceased, and after a few seconds of incomprehensible silence, a voice came from the loudspeaker, a sharp, dry, tearing voice, but so clear that every syllable enunciated was heard.

"*Listen!*" said the voice. "*Listen! The world is coming to an end!*"

A burst of laughter greeted this announcement. The first speaker cried:

"Is that all?"

A serious-looking gentleman shrugged his shoulders. "Wait. A new publicity trick," he explained.

But the voice in the loudspeaker began anew, trembling with vibrations of hate and anger:

---

[98] A Parisian salesgirl.

275

"Listen! I, whom you do not know and who hate and despise all of you, announce that I have found a method of annihilating mankind and destroying the world! Listen! In an hour the world will be destroyed! In an hour, do you hear? Nothing will exist anymore, neither you nor the Earth that supports you! I am the master of unknown forces and of waves possessing an infinite power of destruction. I am the master, the only master of the universe! And I desire that the universe shall perish."

The only result of this emphatic speech was to raise an even greater hilarity.

"Too bad," shouted the joker, "that I didn't know about it three days ago. It would have saved me paying my rent."

A tall young man who was tranquilly lighting a cigarette chipped in:

"—And with me getting married next week!"

And the *midinette* added:

"The radio's a bore today—just when the animal concert was going so well, too! Somebody ought to call up about it."

The general opinion seemed to be that some practical joker was amusing himself at the expense of the crowd. But the crowd did not go away; everyone waited for the words that would show what the clever speaker was advertising. The cloudless sky held an autumn sun so warm that everyone felt amused and indulgent; at certain times of year it takes very little to please Parisians. The loudspeaker began again:

"I hate humanity and I have condemned it. All human beings are criminals; they injure themselves, they kill each other, they deserve to be punished. I, who speak to you, I, against whom you can do nothing, I, who can do everything, am going to precipitate all of you back into the nothingness from which you should never have emerged! I am going to give you a proof of my power. You see what time it is? Look at your watches; in ten minutes the Sun will disappear; the shadows will cover the whole Earth and become thicker and thicker; no light at all will be able to shine in the night that I create...

"Listen! Listen! In 20 minutes a glacial cold will replace the present warmth. Your limbs will be paralyzed and then you will begin to believe what I tell you. I hate you, all of you, you living people, who, in an instant, will be nothing but so many corpses. Your bodies will not fall to dust—they will be annihilated! Have you never thought what it would be like—not to exist? Well, you have 50 minutes to prepare yourselves for it."

A frightful laugh, amplified by the loudspeaker, sent a tremor through the crowd. The voice continued:

"I hate you. I wish your agony could last for centuries. But in 50 minutes no living thing will exist anymore."

The voice fell silent; a silence filled almost with agony. But the clear laughter of the *midinette* dissipated the general sensation of terror.

"I have it!" she said. "It's an ad for a fur company! If it weren't so warm, I'd take my 30,000 francs and buy me a moleskin."

The serious gentleman added:

"The joke is in bad taste. Why don't the police do something about it?"

Nevertheless he pulled out his watch and glanced at it, an action imitated by the major portion of the hearers of this unlikely discourse. Then, as though in spite of himself, he looked at the sky.

Not a cloud! The benevolent Sun shone down on them, reassuring and magnificent. Decidedly, the *midinette*'s idea was the most likely explanation of this unexpected and ultra-modern method of getting people's attention.

All the same, in this crowd which remained so skeptical and so little moved, there was one person who seemed to take this incredible announcement hurled on the ether, apparently by some melancholy joker, at its face value. It was a young man of some 22 years, who wore the smock and cap of a Parisian laborer. His thin, serious face bore an expression of the keenest attention, as making play with his elbows, he worked as close as possible to the loudspeaker and waited to hear it again. But no one paid any attention to the growing surprise and fright that spread over his visage.

The Place de l'Opéra was black with people, and hurrying crowds of the curious overflowed down the boulevards, filling the Rue de la Paix as far as the Place Vendôme, flowing down the Rue Auber and into the Rue du Quatre-Septembre, growing larger every second through all the streets where one could hear the voice of the loudspeaker. The clever merchandiser who had thought of this scheme to advertise his wares, had certainly attained his object. He must have been a clever psychologist to thus play on idle dolts with a display of superior doltery.

Meanwhile, a good many of the strollers, thinking the show was over and that the interrupted concert would hardly be resumed, began to go their separate ways when the loudspeaker began again.

"*Watch!*" clamored the gigantic voice, "*watch the Sun! It is going to darken, and in two minutes the cold will begin.*"

At these words, the young workman made desperate efforts to get away. He succeeded in escaping from the crowd, got around the Opera House, and raced as fast as his legs would carry him down the Rue Auber. It was time; there was a terrible surge among the mass of people and cries of fright rose from all sides. A sinister shadow, like that of an eclipse, spread rapidly from west to east, hiding the Sun and then spreading rapidly across the heavens to plunge the whole city into a nightmare dream. And in every direction, propagated by terror with the speed of an electric current, the news that a frightful and inevitable catastrophe was upon the world spread through the city, invading every district, racing down every darkened street.

In the sudden obscurity there was the wildest disorder. As the voice had predicted, it was impossible to light either electricity or gas; and in the crisis produced by this abnormal night, no one thought of taking steps to insure order and quiet movement—not that any such steps would have been of the slightest use.

In that wild crowd of men and women who had suddenly become the prey of an inexpressible horror, nobody had the cool-headedness even to think of the supernatural individual who had boasted of being able to destroy the world and who seemed in a fair way to do it. Everyone thought of the horror; no one of its author.

Was the unknown really going to realize his terrible prediction? And in destroying the Earth and all its living beings, would he not destroy himself as well? Was the same thing happening all over the world as in Paris? So many problems, so many questions—and no one able to answer them, all were incapable of intelligent thought. The movement in the streets and boulevards was completely halted, an agonized silence weighed down the crowd, as everyone heard only the oppressed breathing of his neighbor.

Suddenly cries of despair broke forth, heart-rending appeals, wails, shouts of rage and the dumb sound of blows, revealing the combats for life the dark concealed. It was for anyone who could to make his way through the crowd by main strength, to find his way through the opaque black toward his home, there to exchange a last farewell with his family before plunging into nothingness. The prediction was being realized; a brief and final agony was beginning for the human species, brief, but so terrible that seconds seemed to last for centuries.

Once more the voice of the loudspeaker rose above the crowd, sarcastic and insulting:

"Everything I promised you is really going to happen... Now prepare for the cold! The polar cold, which you would not be able to resist even if I should renounce the joy of destroying the Earth and all its inhabitants. In a few minutes, in 30 minutes at most, there will be no more people alive."

And in fact it was as though an icy blanket fell suddenly upon Paris. Then, after a few seconds the cold was accentuated, it became so bitter that no one among the victims of the diabolic unknown had even the strength to shiver. In an absolute silence, like that of the tomb, in a night as profound as that of the sepulcher, the loudspeaker counted the last moments of the world, before it should be re-absorbed in the infinite,

"Still ten minutes more!...Five minutes more!"

Near the loudspeaker a single soft voice rose in a sobbing plea:

"My God!"

As though the prayer had been heard, the enemy of the world cried from the loudspeaker:

"Two minutes more—and the world will be destroyed."

2. The Helium Lamp

At the exact moment when the crowd in the Place de l'Opéra was finding itself much amused by the concert of the dogs, the elephants and the parrots organized by the three amusement trusts of London, Calcutta and Buenos Aires, the engineer Gribal was preparing to leave his little apartment on the Rue Boissy-d'Anglas. His wife, daughter and son were meanwhile listening in on the performance.

When little Roger, a boy of 14, saw his father take his hat and start toward the door, he called out, in a tone of regret:

"Oh, papa it's a shame you have to go. The elephants are simply wonderful; the one with the oboe just made a trill in *sol!* Didn't he, Paulette?"

Roger's sister, whose 18 years conferred a musical sense a little less uncertain than that of her brother, corrected him with a smile:

"I think the *sol* was a *re*. But it's true that the elephants are good."

Roger protested:

"A *re*! Never! Women have no ear for music!"

Having delivered himself of this sage maxim, Roger took up his headset again, for the radio in Gribal's apartment, an improvement on the usual models, rendered to perfection the sound of the instruments and voices which are always a little distorted by a loudspeaker.

Madame Gribal, a little less interested than her children in the virtuosos of Calcutta, laid down her listening helmet to say to her husband:

"No overcoat? You'd better take one; the evenings are getting quite chilly now."

Gribal laughed:

"Bah," he said, "it's as warm as a summer's day. Don't worry—this is not a good day for catching colds. Run along back to your concert; I'll be back in a couple of hours, anyway. Have a good time."

"Don't get run over."

Gribal smiled. Every time he went out his wife gave him the same good advice. She knew that her husband was always mulling over some scientific problem in his head, and was quite as likely to stop in the middle of the street to calculate a formula as not. But Gribal had two qualities sufficient to protect even a pedestrian in a city—he had a quick eye, and in spite of his 42 years was as supple and active as a young man of 25; moreover, he was not as absent-minded as he seemed. For he had a sort of double mind; his intelligence went ticking along without in the least interrupting his physical reactions.

And, moreover, what was there to fear? He worked hardly two doors from where he lived, in the Avenue Champs-Elysées, at the Office of Scientific Research, a bureau of the new Ministry of Science. And he had a good position; he was at once the disciple, the friend, and the main reliance of the director of the office, the celebrated Mazelier, the great scientist whose discoveries for the last two years had been upsetting the usual concepts of physics and chemistry.

Gribal had to go up the Champs-Elysées as far as the Rond-Point. He walked gaily along, filled with the joy of life, totting the sweetness of the exquisite autumnal day which seemed meant for a holiday. The engineer, naturally, knew nothing, and could suspect nothing of the drama which was proceeding only a few hundred yards from him, for the dismal announcements of the loudspeaker reached him only as an indistinct murmur. Therefore his surprise was extreme when, as he arrived at the door of the office, he saw the Sun suddenly darkened, and the shadows descend rapidly upon the city.

At first he thought:

"What's this? Night already? My watch must be decidedly slow."

But as rapidly as lightning, another reflection crossed his mind. It was hardly half a minute since he had glanced at the Arc de Triomphe, bathed in sunlight. The Sun was still high above the horizon. No doubt possible; his watch was not slow. But then, what did this sudden darkness mean?

Naturally Gribal was in the habit of searching for a scientific explanation for every phenomenon he observed. This time, to his astonishment, he could not find any.

His stupefaction was such that he expressed it aloud:

"This is too much; I don't believe it," he remarked.

And like any other scientist with a theory upset, he added:

"It's incomprehensible!"

The event that produced such a statement was surprising indeed, for Gribal held it as a fundamental principle that the human mind was capable of understanding everything, and as a consequence accomplishing anything. But, for the moment, there was nothing for it to accomplish. Alone in the Avenue des Champs-Elysées, whose habitual and joyous noises had given place to the silence of the tomb, he was ready to admit that he was dreaming wide awake, and that some kind of an absurd delusion was in possession of his brain.

Suddenly there was a voice at his side, a voice vibrant with inquietude, and which he recognized without difficulty:

"It's you, Gribal? Quick, quick, come here!"

"Ah, you're there, Professor Mazelier?...What the Devil is going on, anyway?"

Gribal felt much reassured. Mazelier was there! The explanation of the phenomenon would not be far behind him. But without replying to Gribal's question, the director of the office repeated, in a voice dominated by a kind of terror:

"Quick! Quick! For Heaven's sake, hurry, Gribal!"

"Wait. I can't see a damned thing. I'm going to light a match."

"No use. Your matches won't light. Here! Take this."

A feeble light, then another, burned suddenly in the shadows. Gribal could make out the face of his superior as he handed him a little torch of singular shape.

"It's a helium lamp," said Mazelier, "the light is resistant to the influence of most kinds of waves. Fortunately, I had a couple with me. But quick, open the laboratory door. You have the key, haven't you? Quick, quick! We haven't a second to lose."

When such a man as Mazelier made a display of uneasiness, there must be some danger both grave and immediate. Gribal ceased asking questions and began acting. He hurried along after his superior, bearing like him, the providential lamp. The two ran through the complex corridors of the laboratory. The sound of a voice was audible, issuing from a loudspeaker placed at one side—the same voice that was carrying terror to all Paris, and doubtless to all the world beside. Gribal paused a moment to hear and grasped a part of the truth. A madman—it could only be a madman—in possession of a frightful power over matter, had conceived the project of annihilating every existing thing.

"In fifty minutes," clamored the voice, "it will be all over with humanity."

Fifty minutes! The threat had the curious effect of providing Gribal with a clear head and a confidence in his own and his superior's powers. With Mazelier, they would need 50 centuries!

"Ah," he said to Mazelier, "what can I do to help you?"

For he was certain that Mazelier would save the world.

The scientist, leading the way without halting, crossed the laboratory proper where he labored daily surrounded by the juniors of the office. He pushed the door of an inner room where no one was permitted to enter, not even Gribal, who was to a certain extent the depository to whom Mazelier confided his theories, his experiments and his secrets—to draw them forth again, refreshed and altered by the clear intelligence of the engineer.

In this inner room, Mazelier put into practical application his most audacious theories and constructed many pieces of apparatus that had never reached the outer world. But he was a somewhat secretive character; some of his experiments he never mentioned, even to his faithful collaborator, before being certain that the experiment had reached a dead end or would be one more of those successes for which he claimed so little personal credit.

In the latter case, he was in the habit of taking the successful piece of apparatus into the general laboratory, where he revealed its mysteries, and complacently answered the questions of his subordinates. Gribal had never quite dared to question him on what he kept in this mysterious inner room.

He hesitated therefore, at the door of the forbidden chamber, when Mazelier called him:

"Come on, my friend, come along."

Gribal went into the sanctuary, which was sufficiently illuminated by the two helium lamps to make objects visible. To his extreme surprise, he saw no extraordinary pieces of apparatus; there was no arsenal of the sorcerer of modern science he had expected to find. There was only, alone in the whole room, a little table on which was mounted a brilliantly polished sphere of metal—a sphere of copper apparently. Two round legs bore a double ring which encircled the sphere; and in each corner of the table were dials and a maze of little levers; before the sphere itself another dial with a needle on its face indicating the zero point on a scale whose purpose was obscure. That was all. Gribal dared not say, though he thought, that this seemed a very slight apparatus with which to combat the terror of the unknown. But he had not followed his superior to make an argument; he was there to help and to obey.

Feverishly, Mazelier gave the example. He bent busily over the apparatus, his forehead furrowed with frowns, breathing hard. Gribal had never seen him like this before.

Without a word, Mazelier worked one of the levers. As he closed some connection a musical note, low and sustained, came from the sphere, as though it were turning within its supports like an enormous top. But Gribal could perceive that the sphere remained perfectly unmoved. The scientist touched another lever; the sound became sharper and sharper, soared beyond the limit in which the human ear could follow its vibrations. He moved the running members. Suddenly to the sharp, almost intolerable shriek, there succeeded a hammering like the rapid fire of a whole battery of machine-guns! The needle on the dial oscillated, and Mazelier, bending over it, followed its course. It must have satisfied him, for the expression of strain left his face and a sudden flash of pleasure streaked across it.

All the feverishness had disappeared from his motions. He seated himself tranquilly before the little table, and said, in the quiet voice which was his usual manner of speaking:

"Do you know where the enemy of the human species is, Gribal? Not two kilometers west of where we are! Between Passy and the Etoile."

Gribal started and said:

"Can't we do something? Call up the police? Warn the people?"

Mazelier smiled:

"My friend," he said, "begin your research by saying nothing to anybody. To anybody, do you hear? For I do not wish to have to regret confiding in you. And then reflect—this fiend could realize his threat, or at least cause a terrible catastrophe, long before you could find him. I can deal with him more easily from here—perhaps."

An icy hand gripped Gribal's heart. "Perhaps!" His superior had said "Perhaps." Then he was not sure of winning out. The engineer dared to ask:

"I hope you don't believe in the threats of that lunatic?"

Mazelier's reply fell into the little silence:

"Humanity has never been in greater danger. Never! But leave me alone now—I can work better. I still have 30 minutes to do what can be done. It's more than I need... but at a certain moment the defense must move as rapidly as the attack, and you are holding me up. Run along, Gribal; I will try to do it alone."

Gribal could not conceal his emotion:

"My duty is to watch over you," he declared.

"No, no, Gribal. I am running no more risks here than anyone else is running anywhere in Paris. Your duty is to go back home and reassure your family. They must be worried. Run along, Gribal, run along. You can find your way with the lamp. But when you get home, turn on your radio and don't lose a word of what you hear."

What would Gribal not have given to assist, even by his mute presence, in that strange duel in the dark between his superior and the invisible enemy of the human race? But Mazelier's orders were not the kind one discusses.

The engineer, alone and a little frightened, was about to leave when he heard the voice of the unknown—so loud, so close and so clear that Gribal jumped. "Here comes the cold," it said, "the polar cold. In 30 minutes, at most, there will be no more world!"

It was necessary to admit that the unknown was no liar. Both the engineer and the scientist could remark the astonishing and rapid decline in the temperature. But Gribal turned back to find Mazelier's calm unruffled.

"Do you notice," his superior remarked coolly, "that it is becoming easier to breathe?"

Even in the hour of peril his spirit of scientific observation did not desert him. Shivering as he was, Gribal dared to pause for a last question:

"How is it you can hear him so clearly in this inner laboratory? Is there a loudspeaker here?"

"Certainly, my friend. That sphere, which you see before you. It's not metal, it is—but, run along, Gribal! I'll tell you all about it later. Leave me, leave me. Don't hold me up any longer."

Gribal left, his heart constricted, realizing that what he had always thought impossible had occurred; a man, or rather, two men, in possession of the innermost secrets of matter, the one striving to use his knowledge to annihilate it, the other to maintain it in its eternal form. Human intelligence, then, did it dominate all things to such a point?

Gribal found it difficult to admit. Nevertheless, he was a scientist, and the marvels he was witnessing, did they not confirm the most extreme claims science had made? Why not admit, in that case, that matter was vanquished, the secret of atomic and electronic forces discovered at last?

Such ideas filled the mind of the engineer as he hurried homeward at the utmost speed at which his legs would carry him. He was so busy with them that he hardly felt the cold, which was, nevertheless, enough to freeze the hair on a monkey. He hurried along toward the Place de la Concorde, past the Marigny Square and the Avenue Gabriel, all enveloped in night and silence. Not a voice, not a sigh, not the slightest sound in the immense avenue of the Champs-Elysées. 20 minutes had hardly gone by since Gribal, from that same spot, had admired the brilliant light of the Sun and the incomparable spectacle of the Parisian crowd, gay and moving. What had become of all the strollers, of all the autos that crowded the streets? Paris was deserted.

In the Champs-Elysées the first threats of the unknown, heard at first from the Place de l'Etoile, and in the flicker of an eyelash carried the length of the avenue to the Place de la Concorde, had produced an immediate terror. While Gribal, busy with his thoughts, had been strolling toward the office, walkers, bus-drivers, automobilists, obeying one of those singular mass movements which seize on crowds, had been hastening toward any refuge they could find. What Gribal in his distraction had taken for the ordinary vigorous movement of the avenue's life had been, in reality, a rout, a flight. And the shadows had descended upon the last fliers hastily seeking refuge in the little cross streets.

Meanwhile, as he felt his way along the Avenue Gabriel toward the Rue Boissy d'Anglas, Gribal looked about him to see whether he could not help some person in distress. But he was alone. The feeble light of his lamp was reflected from no human form. Along here everyone had fled, while at the Place de l'Opéra, the curious crowd, victims of their own inquisitiveness, dared no longer make the least effort to disperse.

3. The Great Illusion

And it was thus that at a dozen steps from his door, Gribal was seized with a sudden sensation of fear. Would he find his wife and children alive? His wife, Paulette, and Roger? As a scientist, he had faith in the ultimate victory of Mazelier, but as a father, as a man, he feared the worst.

Trembling more with agony than with cold, the engineer hurried into the silent house; the door stood ajar. He mounted the stairs, listening for any noise that would be a sign of life. But one would have said that all the inhabitants of the building were sunk in some supernatural sleep. And Gribal, so anxious to arrive a moment before, now hesitated to unlock the door, nerved himself to the effort and flung it open. At the sound there was a triple exclamation:

"Pierre? Is it you?"

Madame Gribal, as rapidly as she could in the obscurity, ran to her husband, and Roger, suddenly became joyous and confident once more on the arrival of his father, cried out:

"We're in the front room, papa. Wait till I get this chair out of the way, so you won't stumble over it."

Gribal replied from the hallway:

"Stay where you are. I have a light."

Paulette, in her turn, gave a little cry:

"A light! Then we are saved."

284

His children were worried no longer; their father was there and he was a scientist.

It was just at that moment that the wave of cold became doubly severe though nobody paid any attention as there was a babble of rapid conversation and embraces that ended only when Roger asked:

"Papa, why is it so cold?"

Madame Gribal remarked:

"You see, we've got all the overcoats and furs in the house on. Wait a minute, I'll get you some blankets from the bedroom to wrap yourself in."

"Oh," said Roger, looking at the helium lamp, "what's that?"

"Don't touch it," warned Gribal.

He perceived with satisfaction that it was unnecessary to reassure them. For Roger, the threatened cataclysm was nothing but an exciting adventure. The words transmitted by the loudspeaker had not frightened him at all, for the simple reason that he had not believed them. As for Paulette, who had been for some time her father's most brilliant scientific pupil, she was too curious to be scared. She asked:

"But father, explain to me why we can't light any matches. There is not a light in the streets, and we can't seem to light any of the fires; everything went out in the kitchen. But we are breathing all the same, just like before. So there isn't any lack of oxygen—but why isn't there any combustion?"

The fact had already struck Gribal; for that matter Mazelier had warned him of it; all matches would fail in the midnight atmosphere. But everyone was breathing, full and deep, as though the air of Paris had become suddenly richer in oxygen.

Meanwhile, if Gribal's family had ceased worrying, he himself felt more and more uneasy as the minutes passed. He replied, almost half-heartedly:

"I don't know how to explain it. We will ask Mazelier."

"Did you see Professor Mazelier?"

"Yes."

"Oh, then he must have told you all about it."

Gribal did not think it quite prudent to gratify Paulette's curiosity; and as his children became more and more reassured, his own inquietude, if not his fear, grew greater. The decisive moment was at hand. The prodigious duel would soon be over. But he dared not reveal to his family the existence of that combat, unknown to all but Mazelier, himself, and the mysterious organizer of the catastrophe.

He closed his eyes in spite of himself; then remembered something, and reached for the listening helmet, signing to his wife and children to imitate him.

"Is there something to hear?" asked Roger. "But it's all over, papa."

Gribal insisted:

"Put on your helmets."

"I don't hear anything," murmured Paulette.

"Naturally!" said Roger. "They always cut the most interesting parts. Probably the silly man has gone to get himself warm."

"Do you know?" said Paulette, after a minute, "I think it's less cold than it was."

"Of course," put in Roger, "such a temperature in October is hardly natural. It couldn't last."

At any other time Gribal would have been amused by the superb confidence of his son. How happy the quietude of ignorance was.

Suddenly, the receivers brought the characteristic noise of static that preceded a world-broadcast. Roger remarked:

"Ah, the chap has unfrozen himself! Now he's going to tell us some jokes. You'll see that—"

He did not finish. A cry came to the ears of the listeners, a cry of fury, rage and fright, ending in a sort of desperate rattle. And then, a voice which Gribal had no difficulty in recognizing, pronounced calmly,

"The world is saved. Everything's all right. The danger—"

The sentence was interrupted by a sound which no human being could analyze correctly; resembling, more than anything else, a million electric discharges letting go at once. Then came a complete silence. Gribal imagined that his radio was out of order, some essential part smashed, no doubt, by the combat of radiations between the two adversaries.

Had Mazelier won? Suddenly, all the electric lights of the apartment, which had been switched on, flashed into activity, then died again, as though a sudden burst of current had caused a short-circuit. But the room filled swiftly with light and the helium lamp now looked no more than a candle in the bright glare.

And filled with the joy of victory Gribal cried:

"We are saved! See how the day is coming back!"

He went to open the window, but recoiled, overwhelmed to see in the distance the red light of an enormous conflagration.

The engineer closed the window quicker than he had opened it to shut out the vision. Overwhelmed, he murmured:

"Paris is burning."

Even Roger no longer cared to joke. Paulette, pale, looked into her father's face for some reason for condolence which she did not find there. Madame Gribal was frightened. To the north and east of them the whole city seemed ablaze, with enormous flames roaring up into the skies.

And thus this extraordinary business of night in the middle of day, of winter cold at the beginning of autumn, this boast of the unknown who swore he was going to destroy the Earth, everything that had at first seemed a gigantic conjurer's trick was ending in a genuine drama of fire and ruin.

And what a drama! The world might indeed be saved, but Paris would be destroyed. Radiation of a force and character thus far unknown would not dis-

solve the planet, but Paris, at the heart of the disturbance, would be itself dissolved by the fire and nothing would remain of the most beautiful city in the
world but a pile of ashes.

What had Mazelier and the unknown been doing? The scientist must be in
danger, for his announcement of deliverance had been interrupted. He must certainly have tried to break the silence which the other had imposed upon him; he
had not succeeded, and the city was afire. Gribal thought but a moment.

"I'm going back to the office," he announced.

"With the city all afire?" said his wife. "I beg you, don't leave us like this."

Worried and stirred by her plea, Gribal hesitated, then became firm. With a
resolute reasonableness, he declared:

"Mazelier is in danger. My duty is with him at this moment."

The sacrifice was hard, but there could be no question of the necessity.
Madame Gribal, with damp eyes, showed that a Paris wife could show the qualities of a Joan of Arc.

"Go, then," she said. And she added, simply: "Come back as soon as possible, but not before you are sure you can leave."

As she spoke the doorbell rang. Roger ran to open as though the unexpected visitor brought safety itself with him, and Gribal could not repress the
feeling that it was no less that, that he brought when Roger returned to announce
joyously:

"It's Professor Mazelier!"

Gribal hurried to greet the scientist:

"I was just leaving to come to the office," he cried. "Why do you risk coming all the way here?"

"Risk? I haven't risked anything."

"What? With Paris all afire?"

"Paris afire? Where did you get that idea?"

Gribal opened the window again, pointing toward the Concorde, the Tuileries and the Seine:

"Look, look. It's frightful!"

Mazelier contemplated the flames that had alarmed the engineer and began
to laugh:

"There's nothing burning. It's an illusion."

"An illusion?" repeated Gribal, stupefied, but delighted.

"Yes, and the proof is that I am going to take you into the middle of that
furnace, I will guarantee that you will be no more exposed to the fire than you
are at this moment.

And turning toward Madame Gribal, he added: "I believe I came into your
parlor without wishing you good afternoon? Permit me to make my apologies,
Madame. And Paulette, how is everything with you? Hello, Roger, I see that you
have borne up well under the dark wave and the cold wave we have just been
having."

And the boy, at once respectful and familiar, replied like a true child of his age:

"Oh, me, Professor Mazelier, you know how little things like that bother me."

And he added, expressing the feeling that they all felt:

"We knew there was nothing to worry about when we found out you were on the job."

"Ah, you think that—"

"That if something was going to happen, and it didn't happen, it was because you were there to keep it from happening. And that's all there is. It isn't difficult to understand."

Mazelier and Gribal exchanged glances, while Roger went on:

"After all, only a nut would think that the world would come to an end, just like that, while people hadn't had time to finish their lunch—"

"Do you know, Gribal?" said Mazelier, visibly amused by Roger's remarks, "do you know that everybody in Paris will be thinking like that tomorrow, and even more than that? Just as Roger has told us."

"Of course, it couldn't have been anything but some kind of a joke," insisted the boy, "the world didn't come to an end, did it, and there isn't any fire?"

This simple explanation was a long way from being satisfactory to Paulette. The strangeness of the phenomenon had upset her elementary scientific knowledge; if there was really no more danger there still remained a good deal of inexplicable mystery.

Impatient to learn the explanation, she questioned:

"But really, Professor Mazelier, what has been happening? What's going on?"

The scientist was vague: "We'll talk more about it some other day, Paulette. For the moment the scientific problems involved are less interesting than some others. I need Gribal with me, and I must ask your permission to take him away. And if you wish to go out yourself, Madame, don't let anything keep you. There is not the least danger. I repeat it, not the least. You will only have the impression of seeing fireworks all around you, but without any smoke."

"What, everything we see, it isn't—"

"Nothing at all. A coloration of the atmosphere, that's all. An enormous rainbow above us, in such a fashion that we don't see all the colors at once. They will penetrate the air one after another, beginning with the red. It will end with an indigo apparition, so that Paris will be successively enveloped in purple, topaz, emerald, sapphire and amethyst. And then the Sun will come back and it will be all over."

"All over," said Gribal, with a little retrospective shudder.

"Yes, all over—for this time," added Mazelier in a voice which only his companion heard.

Neither Roger, Paulette, nor Madame Gribal heard these last words. Only Gribal grasped their significance, and they brought him back with a start to reality, reminding him that Professor Mazelier's tranquil air was assumed to impress the others. But why did he thus seem to encourage such incredulity and joking references as Roger's? And why, Gribal asked himself, this grave reserve behind, those mysterious words "for this time?"

In any case, there was one gain. The catastrophe announced by the radio had thinned out into a series of queer atmospheric effects. The affair had not ended badly—thanks to Mazelier, the silent victor in the unknown and terrible struggle. What a singular situation! An hour ago, seeing Mazelier go by, a little round-shouldered man with graying hair and a little beard cut to a point in the old-fashioned manner, no one in the world would have selected him as the savior of humanity. He would have been passed by with a glance and a remark—"That old chap? Looks like one of those goofy professors, with those thick glasses."

But behind those glasses, few would have observed that the eyes were young and modest, too modest to seek public applause for anything the brain behind them conceived.

But Gribal knew. He wished to cry out, to tell the world:

"Ah," he said, "what would have happened to all of us if—"

Mazelier interrupted him brusquely.

"Come along. We'll be late. You must hurry if you want to get back in time for dinner; we have a lot to do. And then Madame Gribal would not pardon me, and what a fix you would have me in."

The scientist accompanied these words with a wink so unmistakable that Gribal understood at once that he was to say nothing. He shrugged his shoulder: "All right, I'm ready any time."

"Let's go, then. We have a rather delicate calculation to make at the office."

A calculation! Nothing would have pleased Gribal better under the circumstances. He knew without a word being said that the calculation had something to do with the mysterious promoter of the end of the world.

At the corner of the Rue Boissy d'Anglas and the Avenue Gabriel, with the immense panorama of the empty Place de la Concorde and the Seine spread before them, Mazelier suddenly gripped his assistant by the arm:

"Look," he said, "what do you see there?"

4. The First Clue

Gribal made no effort to restrain his cry of astonishment. To the flamboyant red along the skyline, which had so frightened him before, there had succeeded an orange fog, light and transparent, here and there thinning off into clear yellow as though the rays of the Sun were trying to pierce it.

289

"It is exactly as you predicted," declared the engineer. "But I confess that I don't understand why."

Mazelier smiled a little quiet smile.

"And I am willing to bet that you imagine I understand everything that is beyond your depth? Alas! my ignorance is almost as complete as your own. For what's the use predicting something when the reason why it is taking place is unknown to you?"

And with the same expression of a half-smile which accentuated the expression of a good-natured old professor he habitually wore, he added: "Listen, Gribal, try to put yourself inside the head of the individual about whom we won't know anything till we've read tomorrow's newspapers."

"Tomorrow's papers. You're joking."

"Not a joke. We're reasoning in a vacuum—at least until we have news from all over the world. What has been happening in Paris is only a detail. We need the complete picture."

"But," objected Gribal, "the newspapers know as little as we do. In fact, they know less; nobody has any idea of what you've been doing. Instead of getting exact information by tomorrow we will be drowned in thousands of bughouse lies."

"Bah! We will try to read between the lines. But do you notice, my dear Gribal, that we are alone, absolutely alone, on the Champs-Elysées. Our countrymen have not dared to stick their noses out yet. They're going to laugh at each other soon. Here we are, at last. But who is that pulling up at the office?"

A powerful car, emerging from the cape of fog which was already taking on a greenish hue, had halted, not indeed, before the main entrance to the office, but a few yards further along at the corner of the Rue de la Boëtie. A tall man, with a soft felt hat pulled down over his nose and a scarf that concealed his chin, leaped swiftly from the vehicle, took several steps toward the office, and then, his eye falling on Mazelier and Gribal, turned, and leaped back into the auto.

"Wrong address," said Gribal, with a laugh, "you'll find the bar a little further down the street, old man."

The explanation apparently did not satisfy Mazelier. The engineer heard him grumbling:

"And why should that car drive up and then go off again as soon as we get here?"

"Pure coincidence. Anyhow, we have seen the first auto that has been moving in Paris since the end of the world. That's one rarity at least."

This mild pleasantry had no effect on Mazelier. Before entering he turned again to look after the car, which was moving rapidly away in the direction of the Rond-Point.

"And not a cop in sight to pinch him for speeding," said Gribal. "Whether this fog is green or not it is certainly a fog; that chauffeur ought to switch his lights on."

"The chauffeur?" asked Mazelier. "By the way, did you get a good look at that chauffeur?"

"No, why should I look at him?"

"I'll bet anything he is a Chinese. A pure Manchu."

"The Devil!" exclaimed Gribal. "We're in the fashionable world. A Chinese chauffeur, that's something clever."

"Anyway," replied Mazelier energetically, "his employer was not afraid of the fire, like you."

Gribal was impressed by the accent of the scientist. What did he have up his sleeve? He risked a sharp answer to draw his superior's ideas:

"If he wasn't afraid of the fire, what's more natural than that he should take a little ride around the town? We're doing the same thing, only on foot."

Mazelier shook his head:

"Listen, Gribal. Would we have gone out if we were not sure that we would find nothing wrong in the streets of Paris? But who informed that chap there that everything was all right? How did he know what we are the only ones to know?"

The engineer was silent, struck by the force of the observation. Mazelier went on, jerking along at a nervous stride in a manner that showed his preoccupation as he spoke:

"Therefore the man in the big car must be an accomplice of the bandit whom we are trying to discover. And what if it were he, himself? He, whom we have seen…"

The engineer had followed his superior into the inner laboratory as they talked, eager to assist at the calculation the latter had promised him; that remarkable calculation, which had so much and so extraordinary an importance. For he did not doubt that Mazelier would reveal to him the double secret of the attempt to destroy the world and the means by which he had overcome the destroyer.

"My friend," said the scientist, "we are about to work on a document of the first importance. Come over here; turn on that commutator. Good… Can you see clearly?"

"That map? But it is a map of Paris."

"Certainly. It's a map of Paris. Did you expect something else?"

"I admit it."

"And I understand why. Only, my dear Gribal, what worries me at this particular moment is not the nature of the phenomena we have been seeing. There are no theories to be deduced from them, nor any warnings for the future that we can draw from them. We can do all that sort of thing later—if we have time. Today, we must work at top speed."

"That is to say—"

"That is to say that we must first discover who it was who tried to destroy the Earth, and at any cost, at any cost whatever—do you understand?—keep him from trying it again. For if we leave him alone he is sure to have another whirl at it, Gribal."

And lowering his voice instinctively, Mazelier added: "And he might be stronger than us the second time."

Gribal protested by shaking his head.

"No! A thousand times no, Professor! Don't exaggerate the powers of that man. Don't underestimate your own abilities—you have just beaten him at every point."

"No doubt. I have beaten him, as you say. But how badly? We can only tell later. And while we are waiting—to work, my dear Gribal."

"But," protested the engineer, "the unknown must necessarily work alone. It is impossible to imagine that anyone would help him in such an enterprise. No matter how mad he is, he certainly would not have confided in anyone. While we—"

"While we? Well, well, Gribal; go on, finish your sentence."

"We have all the police forces of the world, all the civilized governments, everyone to whom we choose to appeal. With so much help we could surmount any difficulty."

"You fool, don't you understand? Don't you know what your contemporaries are like? Tell the world about the existence of the unknown, make it known that instead of a joke he really meant business, and all the imaginations in the world will go to work. An army of madmen, of criminals, of unknowns, will spring up, will be arrested on every hand. We should never find the real criminal. And depend upon it, our unknown has taken good precautions to prevent just such a public search."

"But, Professor, what then?"

"Then we must get busy ourselves, my dear Gribal, with our own resources; we must search him out ourselves. A long and difficult task no doubt. Of course, the police could set up the same inquiries we could—less secretly, naturally. But they have two faults; this is a scientific problem and they know nothing of science, and they lack the necessary persistence. By tomorrow the police themselves will be issuing statements that there has been nothing serious going on. If I contradicted them, they would laugh—and all the other police forces in the world would laugh in chorus with them."

And rapping out his words, Mazelier went on with his tirade:

"It's up to us to undertake the job. And it is a dangerous job, don't kid yourself on that point. We will risk everything we have, our lives and the lives of everyone we touch. We can ask help from no one, we must beware of everyone in the world. If we go down, no one will even know, and if we succeed, I fear there will be no applause for us. Under such conditions, Gribal," are you prepared to go on with me? There is still time to say no."

For his only reply Gribal bent over the map of Paris that Mazelier had showed him.

"I am ready," he said. "What shall I do?"

"Simply this. Get yourself a compass, a ruler and a pencil. Good. Of course you know that just now my first care was to find out from precisely what point the cold and dark radiation was coming; or rather, the interruption in the radiation of light and heat. Well, we will follow out on this map the course I have traced by means of my implements."

Mazelier drew from his pocket a sheaf of notes.

"Here Find the place where we are now; Rue de la Boëtie, at the corner of the Avenue. Now, trace along the line of the Rue Pierre Charron a line 900 meters long, on the scale of the map."

"Done."

"Where are we?"

"Place d'Iéna."

"Place d'Iéna. Remarkable! I imagined a little while ago that I had made a mistake in saying at first that the source of the trouble was between Passy and the Etoile. But now I imagine that we will not have to look elsewhere. Now Gribal, at the end of your line draw a perpendicular 300 meters long on the same scale. We are...?"

"At the corner of Rue de Lubeck."

"Good. Rue de Lubeck. Ah, there's something wrong about here; I almost lost the trail. Something happened of which I'm not quite certain. But I tuned in on another circuit. At the extremity of the perpendicular of 300 meters, make another of about 1000 meters long. Wait, that's it! Hold it there, Gribal. Where's the spot?"

"Rue Cortambert, near the Place de la Muette."

The two men looked at each other, a little pale.

Mazelier was the first to speak. "We must go there, Gribal."

And almost thoughtfully, he added, "The Rue Cortambert! One of the quietest and most aristocratic streets in the quiet and aristocratic quarter of Passy."

"Yes," said Gribal, following his thought, "it seems impossible that the person we are looking for has not been noticed in a district of that kind. If only by the size and importance of his laboratory."

"True. True. At least, if... *Parbleu!* At least if he has not succeeded, like me, in simplifying his machine to an extraordinary degree. But why should he not have discovered the same things I have?"

Gribal had a thousand questions on the tip of his tongue, but he kept silent, knowing that his superior was not yet ready to answer them. For that matter, there would hardly have been time. As Mazelier rose, preparing to go, there was a knock at the door of the laboratory.

Mazelier frowned. Who was daring to interrupt in spite of the strict orders he had given that he should not be disturbed? Gribal went to the door and found Père Bibent, the old concierge of the office.

"What is it, Père Bibent? You know very well that Professor Mazelier will not see anyone when he is busy in his laboratory."

"I beg your pardon, Monsieur Gribal. But it is a young electrician who says he'll tear the place apart if he doesn't see Professor Mazelier. He insists he has something of the utmost urgency and importance to tell you. Here he comes, now. He looks honest, so I ventured—"

Gribal, in spite of his annoyance, could not repress a smile. Poor old Bibent! He imagined himself a psychologist.

But the indiscreet visitor pushed Bibent aside, and with the desperate hurry of the very timid, addressed Gribal, speaking rapidly:

"Monsieur, I have a revelation to make concerning the events which have just been happening. Pardon me for interrupting you, but I must tell you about it. It's important."

Gribal regarded the unknown. The young workman really did look honest, and his air, at once modest and decided, spoke in his favor.

Bibent was eclipsed and vanished across the laboratory in the direction of the door whose watch-dog he was.

Gribal set himself to put a few preliminary questions:

"What is your name?"

"Monsieur, my name is Roland Duplay. I'm an electrician, and I have just finished my course at the Breguet school."

"And why did you come here instead of going to the police?"

"Monsieur, because what happened this afternoon is so extraordinary that only a scientist like Professor Mazelier can find the explanation for it."

"And you have something to tell him?"

"Yes, Monsieur. I know who it was who declared he would destroy the world."

"Well, who was it?"

"It was the Marquis de Saint-Imier, who lives in the Rue Cortambert."

"Rue Cortambert!"

Instead of barring the door before the young workman Gribal seized him by the shoulders and literally pushed him into the laboratory.

"Quick, speak, my boy. Tell us everything you know. Did you hear, Mazelier? Rue Cortambert!"

Mazelier gazed calmly at the newcomer without the slightest surprise. He asked coolly: "How do you know?"

Duplay replied: "I was at the Place de l'Opéra when the voice came through the loudspeaker. I got as close as I could to it to hear better. And I swear to you that I recognized the voice. It was not two weeks ago that I was doing some work at the Marquis' house. I was astonished at the things he had me install there. And his voice, Monsieur! It's impossible to forget it when one has heard it a single time. That man frightened me, Monsieur. It could only be him."

"But you should go tell that to the police, my boy."

"They wouldn't believe me, Monsieur. The Marquis is rich, he has a lot of pull, everybody knows him. They wouldn't even listen to me at the police. They'd tell me I was crazy. While you, you are a scientist, you can tell whether I'm right or not."

"And why should I know any better than the police?"

"Because you're a scientist. I have read your books, Monsieur,—oh, if I could only understand them better. I have followed everything you have done."

Gribal and Mazelier exchanged a glance.

"Thank you, my boy," said the scientist. "And what can I do for you?"

"I don't dare ask for any reward," babbled Duplay. "I'm so ignorant."

Mazelier divined the thoughts that were agitating the young electrician.

"Well, Monsieur Duplay," he said, accenting the word *Monsieur*, "I advise you to stick to your profession, but if you have any leisure time you may employ it at this office if you wish. Gribal will show you the research we are carrying on, if you think you would like to see them."

Overwhelmed with emotion and gratitude, the workman stood before them, incapable of pronouncing a single word. But his attitude and his glance showed that the two scientists had gained the undying devotion of the young man.

"Now," said the scientist, "one last question. Here's a map of Paris. Would you mind showing us the exact point where the Marquis' house, where you made the installation, stands?"

Duplay bent over the map. Then with a visible astonishment:

"It's exactly at the point that is marked with a blue cross."

And he looked up with wondering eyes.

"Did you know, then?"

"Faith!" said Mazelier, "we know what hole he was in, but we didn't know the name of the rat. Good, Monsieur Duplay, you may come back here whenever you like. I have the conviction that you will be a scientist someday."

The electrician bade them farewell, his face alight.

"Do you think he's all right?" asked Gribal.

"Entirely! And now, let's go have a look at the Rue Cortambert. It will be a nice little walk, and I am curious."

Gribal glanced out into the Avenue.

"The Sun has come back," he announced. "Look, look! What a crowd. What animation!"

"Yes, of course. Everyone knows it was only some kind of a joke or nightmare now. They're all telling each other how brave they were."

5. New Development

He was not far wrong; it was the end of the nightmare. One would have said that every inhabitant of the great city had come out to salute the return of the light of day in a public and universal joy like that of some grand holiday. For

295

a few moments the people of Paris seemed strangely purified; their delight, their happiness bade farewell to all hatred, envy and despair as a breeze drives away a pestilential mist.

From the Etoile to the Concorde a human tide flowed without ebb. Mazelier and Gribal even had some difficulty in making their way through the crowded streets.

"Ah," said the engineer, "this makes the Sun-worship of the barbarous ages comprehensible."

"Yes," said Mazelier, "but just at the present moment I would be more appreciative of the benefits of civilization in the form of a bus."

"But look how everybody is moving around," cried Gribal. "Decidedly the Parisians are easy to reassure. Here, let's get up to the Boulevard Haussmann and take the electric."

The electric monorail car, quick, light and silent, which ran from the Carrefour Drouot to the Muette, was right on their route. 15 minutes later the two amateur detectives descended at the Avenue Henri-Martin, near the Rue Cortambert.

Mazelier explained:

"There are enough people in the streets so that we won't be noticed. We'll go along slowly as though we were out for a stroll. Unless I'm much mistaken, we will know very quickly when we come to an interesting place."

"And how will we know?"

"Oh, a little trick of my own, Gribal. Look, this will give us the signal."

Mazelier drew from his pocket a little round object.

"What's that? A watch? And how will that signal us?" asked the engineer, surprised.

"It's rather like a watch, true. But it isn't one all the same. There's a little buzzer inside—oh, a very little one—that will sound when we get close to the emission source of any unusual wave radiations. If, as I expect, our adversary is still at work, it will reveal his presence, and we will know both where he lives and where he carries on his labors. Look, I'm going to wind it up; that will set it to catch any radiation."

Mazelier had put on a different pair of spectacles and held in his hand a sporting journal in which he seemed to be deeply interested as he strolled along. For the passers-by he was the perfect model of a little shop-keeper intensely interested in the outcome of the bicycle races, but whose personal devotion to athletics does not extend beyond a two-block walk after dinner.

As for Gribal, he lighted a cigar and assumed the air of a boulevardier whose ambition is limited to eating two well-chosen meals a day and making the circuit of the most famous cafés of Paris for a drink in each afterward. Both of them paid no attention to each other. These precautions were hardly exaggerated, considering the fact that they knew nothing either of the ability of their adversary or his means of defense. His means of defense?—rather, his means of attack.

Thus they arrived at what Gribal called the "hot spot." Mazelier slackened his pace, and then halted, holding his watch to his ear like a man who doubts whether it is in running order. And his face showed a lively surprise, followed by some irritation.

He went on to the end of the street, followed at a little distance by Gribal, who understood that the apparatus invented by his superior was not giving the hoped-for result. Had Mazelier made a mistake in the house? No, for he had turned back and resumed his patrol before the same building.

All at once the bugle of a large auto sounded a blare of notes, and people crossing the street leaped out of the way of a huge car which arrived at high speed, pulled up suddenly and swung through a double gate that opened to receive it. The auto was swallowed up in the inner court of the mansion; a building decorated in the most sumptuous style, but too modern in character to catch the eye of an artist.

On the sidewalk, near Mazelier and Gribal, two passers-by halted to watch the entrance of the big car.

"Who's that?" asked one of them.

"Don't you know?" asked the other in the superior tone a butler in a grand household would employ in informing a new porter of his duties. "That's the Marquis de Saint-Imier. There's a chap who doesn't worry about a thing—even the end of the world don't keep him from running around the town."

Gribal felt someone nudge his elbow. Mazelier motioned him to follow at a little distance.

"Did you see?"

"*Parbleu!*" said the engineer, "the chauffeur was a Chinese."

"Did you recognize the car?"

"I recognized the chauffeur even more vividly."

"Wait a minute."

Suddenly Gribal jumped. The sound of a little buzzer came sharply to his ear, causing him more fright than the voice of terror on the loudspeaker.

"All right, daughter?"

"I should say so, father. And you, mother? We ought to amuse ourselves a little from time to time; we have had so much to worry about. Are you coming with us?"

Madame Gribal was slightly scandalized:

"Me? To go to a reception at the ministry? You're crazy, child. I'd be bored to death. And who would get your lunch for you?"

"Ah, that wouldn't matter. For once in our lives we could do with some chocolate and cakes."

"Yes, yes. It's easy to say that beforehand, but when the moment came I think you'd want something a little more substantial. No, no, run along with your father to the reception. I'll stay home and take care of Roger."

"Thanks very much, but I don't need it," said the young man of whom she spoke.

But Gribal came to the rescue of the maternal authority:

"You stay home, young man. You'll see too much of receptions and ministries when you grow up. But you can go to the movies tomorrow, and let Paulette get lunch for you."

Paulette was genuinely enchanted with the invitation to the reception, which had arrived no later than that morning. Even a girl whose heart is set on becoming a scientist sometimes enjoys putting on her best dress and going to parties. She found the Minister of Science a delightful person and was quite prepared to vote him into office for life. She was even so happy over the prospect that she forgot the mysteries of the day before and the scientific questions they aroused and which she was so anxious to resolve with her father. Paulette was not ignorant of the fact that the Minister of Science was at once a politician of some prominence and well known in the fashionable world. His invitations were as much in demand among the smart set as among the universities.

But Paulette could not but wonder why the Minister of Science should organize one of his most elaborate receptions on the very day after the extraordinary event which had alarmed all Europe for the space of several hours.

Gribal thought he understood, but said nothing. He had talked the matter over with Mazelier, also one of those on the invitation list. But the scientist had told him:

"I don't think I'll go. I will hear so many stupid remarks that I would end up by laughing in their faces, and being in an official position I haven't the right to laugh. You go, Gribal. Look around you, listen to everything they say. If you find out anything interesting, you can give me the news at the office tomorrow."

"Don't you think it a little—premature, this idea of the Minister's, of having a kind of *fête* so soon after the attack of the unknown?"

"My dear Gribal, I think the Minister is perfectly right. I'm going to tell you the truth—in official quarters they are absolutely terrified. They don't understand in the least what has happened. They only want to reassure the public, and what better means than a big society reception as though it were all nothing to worry about? It will be a fete in honor of Science—do you get the idea? In the honor of Science, which defends, protects, and sometimes ultimately explains the inexplicable. The Minister is pretending a tranquility which he is really very far from feeling."

"Did you see him?"

Mazelier smiled slightly.

"Now do you really doubt it? The Minister summoned a whole army of meteorologists in the greatest urgency yesterday evening. There was a great deal of discussion about currents in the upper atmosphere, the Heaviside Layer, the effect of charges of electricity on abnormal atmospheric depressions. And as nobody understood what anybody else was saying, they wound up by cooking up a story to issue to the public. When you get to the heart of it, it is quite meaningless. Oh, a good story, you understand…Something about a wireless amateur who got the atmospheric electrical currents all tangled up, and who has now been arrested."

"But," cried Gribal, "such a yarn can't be believed for a moment. And the cold? And the sudden darkness? And the impossibility to make any light? And—"

"Yes, yes," said Mazelier, "all of that. But you forget that the crowd forgets quickly and thinks not at all."

"Good. Suppose we admit that. But even the crowd reads the newspapers. And the newspapers this morning had the news that the cold wave spread over all the eastern district of France and most of the rest of Europe, beginning with the meridian of Paris. We know that the wave of darkness did the same and only ended at the line that passes through Riga and the tip of Greece. We know that west of Paris nobody noticed any effect except that all the wireless sets went out of order. But how in the world can anybody take the combination of all these phenomena for a mere joke? Who would believe it?"

"Who? Everybody. The public has become used to the marvelous. When there is some new miracle every day, you get bored with the next one very quickly, and end up by not paying attention to any of them"

"Don't you wish to see the Minister and tell him what you know?"

"Once more, no! And after all, what do I know? Reflect, Gribal. What do we really know? Just what the papers have printed, no more. Three quarters of Paris felt the effects of the cold and dark waves. Auteuil and the Bois de Boulogne were only relatively dark. Further west the Sun went right on shining. And then?"

"Then," said Gribal, "I deduce that someone in the Rue Cortambert succeeded in—"

"Oh, yes. The Marquis de Saint-Imier. The moment has certainly not come to reveal what we have discovered or even to be sure of the guilt of a man we have never seen. Go to the reception, Gribal, amuse yourself. I doubt whether you will find the key to the mystery at the Ministry of Science however."

"And you, Professor, what will you be doing?"

"Me? I'll work. At least up to midnight. See you tomorrow, but be careful who you talk to about it."

The engineer, although obedient to Mazelier's advice, could not resist the impression that he was overcautious. Why should he, Gribal, in an assembly which would include the most eminent and respected scientists of the country, be careful about whom he talked to? There would be women there, naturally, but none of the women one would find at a ministerial reception would be at all likely to even understand a scientific theory. He determined to establish himself in some quiet corner and watch what went on, obeying Mazelier's command to the extent of not talking about anything with anybody.

Paulette, naturally, was in an entirely different state of mind. Her pleasure had no alloy. Arriving at the ministry, she was at first a little frightened by all the splendors, to which she was a such a stranger, but a Parisian of Paris itself, her embarrassment was only momentary.

Besides, chance brought her under the eye of one of her school professors in the very first moment, and before she had time to think about it had been presented to ten different people and drawn into the midst of a particularly interesting conversation.

"I assure you," Madame Reynier-Vitral was saying, "that my husband doesn't see anything at all extraordinary in what happened yesterday."

"Really!" exclaimed a woman who had a doctor's degree and lost no opportunity of letting people know it. "What sort of thing must happen to astonish a chemist?"

"But the affair yesterday was nothing but a kind of chemical experiment that could be reproduced any time one wished."

There was a unanimous chorus of protest. A woman lawyer's voice rose above the rest:

"Oh, do tell your husband not to repeat the experiment right away, please! What jolly jokes these chemists make—to turn our temperature into 40 degrees below zero on a moment's notice."

"Without mentioning that it was so dark you could cut it with a knife," added Madame Brasseur. "To be cold, that's all right, we can understand it, but not to be able to see people's teeth chatter—it's absolutely ill-bred."

Senator Moutonneau intervened:

"But, dear lady," he said to the lawyer, "who told you that it was 40 below? I'm certain that it was a lot nearer 80."

"Impossible!" said the learned dame, impolitely.

"But, asking your pardon a thousand times, it is not only possible, it happened."

"Oh, Monsieur, I will pardon you ten-thousand times, but not for your 80 degrees below zero. But look—we wouldn't be here talking if it had been that cold, we would all be dead."

"It's a singular fact," remarked Monsieur Perignon, "that there has been no epidemic as the result of the cold wave—not even a single case of bronchitis."

"Which proves that the human body can support extremely reduced temperatures."

"Impossible!" declared the doctor again. "I know from my personal experience how easy it is to catch a cold."

Paulette ventured timidly to toss a question onto this sea of conversation:

"But what was the cause of the dark and the cold?"

"Well," said Madame Reynier-Vitral, "according to my husband it was this way—it was a question simply of the absorption of light by the agitated electrons of matter. The American physicist Millikan,[99] in 1927, predicted the possibility of such phenomena."

But nothing in this ordinary banal drawing-room conversation predicted what was to follow a few minutes later.

Nevertheless, Paulette had a vague presentiment of something about to happen, for which she could not account.

She insisted: "Good. That answers for the dark. But the cold?"

"Couldn't that be explained by an almost total absorption of the light in the upper atmosphere, thus producing a drop in the temperature?"

But Paulette, now less bashful, plunged on with the question she had already put to her father: "But, Madame, how do you explain how we managed to breathe while all combustion had become impossible?"

Everybody looked toward the wife of the chemist. As a matter of fact all had noticed it; nobody had been able to relight the lights that had gone out. Therefore, there was no oxygen for combustion. Then how was it that every being plunged into that sinister and sudden night had had the impression of breathing more deeply and freely instead of succumbing at once to a lack of oxygen?

Madame Reynier-Vitral, fortified with the science of her husband, did not hesitate a second: "My husband," she said with becoming modesty, "thinks that radioactive gases were somehow set free in the atmosphere yesterday. Everywhere in the laboratories they were following the experiments of Messieurs Bayeux and Vaugeois. Therefore the composition of the air was modified, but without being changed in a fashion dangerous to living beings. The proof is that we could live in the modified atmosphere."

5. The Secret Exposed

This explanation, which really explained nothing at all, enthused Paulette. She believed she saw the first rays of the light of truth. And why should it not be possible, in the secrecy of the laboratory, to create and then to spread abroad, unknown gases, rays up to now unfamiliar since their number and power of expansion was theoretically infinite?

Nevertheless, Monsieur Perignon was not at all satisfied. He spoke slowly:

"I would like to know what Monsieur Gribal thinks about all this."

And, addressing himself to Paulette, he added, "Your father must have made some observations on the affair?"

---

[99] Robert A. Millikan (1868-1953), American experimental physicist and Nobel laureate for his measurement of the charge on the electron and for his work on the photoelectric effect.

The young girl was about to reply when she was interrupted by an occurrence. Monsieur Perignon's question had been heard by a personage whose elegance, at once athletic and aristocratic, was remarkable even in that assemblage. His face was expressive and his eyes almost incredibly active. There was a sort of concentrated irony in his smile as he approached Senator Moutonneau, and asked:

"Gribal? Who is that Gribal? I don't remember having heard that name before."

The senator replied, loudly enough to be heard by the whole group: "That name, my dear Marquis, belongs to a man of the first rank. Gribal is the principal collaborator of the famous Professor Mazelier."

"Mazelier! Faith, I didn't know that he was so famous. In any case, that young lady is certainly a beauty—hardly what one would expect of the daughter of a scientist."

And the man who had been addressed as a Marquis, went on, with a little laugh: "Tell me, Senator, if someone succeeded in disassociating matter, wouldn't it be a shame to dissolve such a beautiful assembly of atoms as Mademoiselle Gribal?"

Had this rather impertinent speech been made deliberately in a tone of voice a little loud? In any case, the reflection was distinctly audible to Paulette's ears. The young girl blushed, then turned her back to hide her chagrin at the remark, by which she was not at all flattered.

But the Marquis, as though he had not noticed her annoyance, advanced toward the group with the ease of a man of the world whom nothing upsets. He saluted Madame Muserolle and extended his hand to Professor Perignon. Then, excusing himself for having interrupted the conversation, he bowed before Paulette with a courtesy that was more than a trifle exaggerated.

"I believe I overheard them addressing some very interesting questions to you?" he said in a tone of inquiry.

"Yes," said the senator, "they were asking her what Monsieur Gribal had thought of the events of yesterday."

All eyes turned toward Paulette, and she felt as though she had never in her life so much desired to give a sharp answer to anyone: *How can you find the observations of a man you never heard of interesting?*

But instead of saying the words that leaped to her lips, she lifted her eyes to those before her and saw them so attentive, so respectful, so little like what the remark had led her to expect that she felt ashamed for her thoughts. After all, he was also one of the Minister's guests. She replied, a little confused: "I don't think my father made any special observations. In fact, I am sure he didn't."

And she went on, rather naively: "If he did make any, he hasn't communicated them to me." Was it possible that what she had just said seemed to afford a certain pleasure to the Marquis? But Monsieur Moutonneau lifted his head:

"It is impossible that a man of Gribal's intelligence should not have made some extremely interesting notes in a case like this."

"Really?" inquired the Marquis in a tone that contained a good deal of sarcasm.

But Paulette did not perceive the undertone.

"Certainly!" declared the senator positively. "Gribal would not know whether it was 40 degrees below zero or 80, but he has, I am willing to wager, some extremely interesting opinions on the dissociation of the atom and the destruction of matter."

"Brrr!" said the lady doctor. "Let's talk about something else."

"Let's not," said the Marquis. "Tell me some more about it, I beg you. I am as ignorant as a herring, and would like to obtain a little information while I'm in such scientific company. You think it's possible to destroy matter completely?"

"Oh," cried Paulette, carried along into the discussion in spite of herself, and excited by having her father's name dragged into the conversation, "Oh, it's just impossible."

The Marquis cast her a furious glance, but it was in a suave voice and with the most charming smile that he replied:

"Ah, really, mademoiselle! I am glad to hear that Monsieur Gribal thinks so."

"My father has always told me that to dissociate matter is not to annihilate it."

Monsieur Perignon approved:

"*Parbleu!*" he said, "evidently an atom dissociated into its electrons is not destroyed any more than a piece of sugar that has been dissolved in coffee. Only a madman could dream of the destruction of the world."

Paulette, delighted at this approval, went on:

"Certainly. Matter once dissociated, resolved into its simplest form, which is energy, would simply reform in another shape, and that's all."

The Marquis seemed pensive:

"But," he objected, "if I understand what you are saying, Mademoiselle, if one dissociated matter, it would simply result in the creation of a new world. Faith, the one we are living in is so poorly made, that it's almost worth the trouble of doing it to get a new one."

And he added, laughing:

"Don't you think so?"

There was no echo of his gaiety. Paulette had a sensation that his laugh had something grating and unpleasant in it. And that voice, with its curious vibrating inflections, where had she heard it before? She felt a disagreeable impression, as one does in the presence of people one detests instinctively.

She watched the Marquis slyly from the corner of her eye—an art which all girls possess from the cradle upwards. The result rather astonished her. He radiated an atmosphere of superior intelligence; his eyes yielded to no one's. But there was something vaguely antipathetic about him.

All at once Paulette found the key of it; the emotion he aroused in anyone who looked at him was fear.

But the doctor was speaking:

"Well, you can make your new worlds in the laboratory if you wish. I admit that I did not find the remaking of this one a pleasant affair. The darkness that came on the city last night found me at the door of a client with no way of getting in."

"And you, my dear senator?" asked Madame Reynier-Vitral.

"The Senate was in session at the Luxembourg, Madame. We simply waited calmly, for it is the duty of the French Senate to give an example of calmness to the world."

The Marquis suggested: "You didn't even try to telephone home?"

Monsieur Moutonneau admitted; "We did think of it. But the telephones weren't working."

"And at the Chamber of Deputies?"

"*Peuh!* They say that some of the deputies were really terrified."

"Oh, the deputies," said the doctor, "they're young. The senators for my choice." And she smiled archly.

Then, she turned toward the Marquis: "And you?" she said, "what did you do about those uncomfortable phenomena and the threats on the radio?"

Paulette glanced at the man thus addressed:

"Me, Madame?" said the Marquis, "I am sorry to admit it, but I saw nothing. I was in the Bois de Boulogne. At a certain moment it seemed to me that it became a trifle chilly, and I came back to Paris too late—like the police. The show was over."

"You didn't even see the discoloration of the atmosphere? It was really superb."

The Marquis replied dryly:

"No, Madame. I missed the whole thing."

He put into that simple phrase a certain intonation of profound distaste, almost of anger. But he recovered with wonderful quickness, and added in a tone too lively not to be sincere:

"It's queer. I, who saw nothing at all, I am more astonished than you who were in the middle of Paris. I see the whole thing less clearly than you, Madame Brasseur, in front of your client's door in the dark. The events of yesterday seem so incomprehensible. And what is queerer still is the way everyone talks about it. Look—I'm not dreaming am I? I'm really in a circle of the greatest scientists of France? Well, when they told me about yesterday, I thought they were having a joke at my expense. I said it was impossible. Now you others, ladies and gentlemen, you are scientists, you say that it was possible, and you add, if I understand this, that it was simply a sort of laboratory joke. Is that correct?"

"Faith," said Perignon, "hardly. I think as you do—it was impossible."

The Marquis smiled. But it seemed to Paulette that his color changed. The senator remarked in a serious tone: "It's a good thing you came to this reception. Now, if the world does come to an end, you will understand why."

"You are right, my dear senator. As you say, I'll understand why next time. I'm glad I was a boyhood friend of the Minister of Science, for he certainly did not invite me here because of my knowledge."

And in a new burst of his mad humor, the Marquis went on:

"Then the only thing certain about it is that yesterday some millions of human beings were convinced that they were about to perish. Unfortunately, most of them were unable to see the senators giving an example of calmness to the world. Well, since we have arrived at the moment for confidences, perhaps Mademoiselle Gribal will tell us her impressions?"

It was said in a perfectly natural manner. Paulette carelessly—for why should she be on her guard—replied with her ordinary frankness:

"*Mon Dieu!* I was more interested than disturbed, I assure you."

"Brave child!"

"My brother jokes all the time. And he was particularly amusing when he put on mother's old coat to protect himself against the cold. And we were all very much reassured when father arrived with his little lighted lamp.

The Marquis gave a start of surprise so marked that the others gazed at him.

"Ah!" he said, "your father—"

"Father had a helium lamp that Professor Mazelier gave him. And then, it was Professor Mazelier who explained to us that the red light was not caused by a big fire as we thought."

"Ah!" babbled the Marquis, "that Professor Maz—"

He did not finish his sentence. His smile gave place to a kind of convulsive and horrible grin, and he became so pale that the doctor said:

"Do you feel ill?"

But the Marquis was not one of those to be so easily overthrown. He bowed to Madame Brasseur:

"It is a trifle warm here," he remarked. "Thank you, Madame, but I shall not need your help this time."

At this moment an eddy of the crowd formed around the entry of a woman whose extraordinary beauty caused a murmur of admiration to arise as she came in. It was Madame Ghislaine Roberval, the widow of the celebrated inventor who had produced the electric automobile that was driving gasoline cars from the market.

She entered the salon at the precise moment when someone was saying to Gribal:

"Mademoiselle Paulette is making conquests."

"Yes?" he answered, non-committal but flattered.

"Her conversation seems to have drawn to her the most intelligent and fashionable man in Paris. Don't you know him? It's the Marquis de Saint-Imier."

The name struck Gribal like a flash of lightning. He excused himself to seek his daughter, all unsuspicious of the danger she was in. Or was it already too late? Had Paulette already said more than she should?

But the crowd separated him from her. He could only wait, his heart beating rapidly with fright. Saint-Imier was there! The audacity of the man was beyond anything he had imagined. And in spite of himself, Gribal became the witness of a singular scene.

Near him, Ghislaine Roberval was passing by, majestically beautiful followed by Saint-Imier, whose hot eyes burned with an extraordinary fire as he looked after her. The Marquis approached the beautiful widow and said something to her that Gribal could not avoid hearing very clearly: "Will you come tomorrow? I will wait for you." Madame Roberval looked on the Marquis with a contempt she made no effort to conceal: "You're crazy," she said. "You give me the horrors."

She turned her back on the Marquis, leaving him pale with rage. Tenaciously, he maneuvered through the crowded room to regain her attention. But no less obstinately, she fled him, without disguising her dislike and her impatience. It was so pointed that people began to watch them, the more so since the Marquis, for once in his life, seemed to have lost all control of himself.

Finally, at a moment when Saint-Imier was about to rejoin her again, Madame Roberval, without affectation, took the arm of a young man in the adjoining salon. Someone said:

"It's Monsieur Gabriel de Neuville, the young diplomat."

For a moment it looked as though the Marquis would leap on his rival, but he contented himself with giving him a glance of pure hatred, and moving slowly away as though the public snub had not affected him. He even smiled—but with what a smile!

Gribal was able to get to Paulette finally, and to her great astonishment, led her toward the cloakroom.

"Are we going already, father?"

Then she noticed her father's agitation and did not insist. But in the taxi which was taking them back toward the Rue Boissy d'Anglas she did not hide her annoyance:

"What's the trouble? Did I do something wrong? Why did we have to leave so early?"

"No, daughter, what happened is hardly your fault. You don't understand?"

"Understand what?"

"That Marquis, who was talking to you—"

"Well?"

"You had better avoid him, daughter."

"He is not a nice person?"

"No. What did he say to you?"

"He asked me what you thought of the end of the world."

"And you mentioned Mazelier?... And the helium lamp?"

"Yes... Shouldn't I have?"

"No."

"Why?"

"I'll tell you in a moment. But be reassured. You couldn't know. I should have told you not to say anything about it, about anything that happened yesterday. For that matter, I couldn't know that you would meet that man."

"But that man, can he do you any harm?"

Gribal made an evasive gesture.

Paulette was not stupid; her brain was working furiously.

"Then," she said, "I must have touched on a dangerous secret without knowing it?"

"Perhaps."

"This secret—do you know it, father?"

"No."

"Does Professor Mazelier?"

"I don't know. He may know no more than I do."

Paulette did not dare to ask confidences her father was unwilling to give. She said in a meditative voice:

"That man, father, he really frightens me. And his voice... It seems to me that I have heard it somewhere. Ah, if I could only remember."

All at once, she gave a little cry:

"I know, father. I know where I heard it. It was yesterday, on the radio. Therefore, it was he who—"

Gribal took his daughter's hand:

"Hush, Paulette. And above all, don't talk like that to your mother or to Roger."

Was any further doubt possible? Paulette also had identified the man who had threatened the world so madly and shouted his hate for the whole human species over the radio.

The cause of this hate? A matter of no importance—the important thing was to defend oneself against the man as against some wild beast, and to bring him down like a mad dog.

7 The Maid and the Chinese Man

At the office, where Mazelier and Gribal were discussing the matter in the silence of after-hours, they arrived at a single determination to use any possible means to suppress the adversary who, pretending ignorance of things scientific, nevertheless possessed powers of the first order.

307

Mazelier repeated for the 16th time: "It's going to be a hard fight."

"Are you discouraged, Professor?" asked Gribal, worried. Mazelier lifted his head: "I will carry on the fight to my last breath," he cried. "I only wanted you to understand that from now on we two are directly threatened."

"What can we do?"

"Nothing. Wait."

After a moment of silence Mazelier added: "Listen, Gribal: if he gets me, you will have to take my place immediately. If you are the first to fall, I will do anything on earth to make him pay for it. Now, I must put you in touch with what means of defense we possess. For we have some—and not so feeble, either. Do you see that sphere? What do you think it is made of?"

Gribal looked at the gleaming ball with its electrical connection and dials which the scientist had used in calculating the center of the emission of the cold and dark waves.

"I don't know that metal," he admitted.

"It is not metal, my friend. It is made of solidified air. I had to experiment a long time before finding a means of producing it. And this globe of solidified air is also, as you have reason to know, an excellent loudspeaker. But it contains a special apparatus which is at one and the same time a radiometer and an emission-generator. It is from the interior of that sphere that the emissions went forth that counteracted those of Saint-Imier. You must learn how to use it, Gribal. But I warn you that it is impossible to use it without producing always some very strange and unpredictable effects."

"Dangerous effects?"

"Sometimes, if one is not careful. In any case, of such force that they would not pass unnoticed. What would you say if at a given moment all the motors in Europe suddenly stopped? All the autos, all the electric railroads, all the subways, everything but steam engines?"

"You could do that?"

"Easily, Gribal. By the use of the same apparatus I could blow up at the same moment all the explosives, all the projectiles and all the other munitions within a given field of radiation. Unfortunately for war use, those nearest would go first! I imagine that I could also act upon the nerves and muscles of living beings. You see why I cannot confide the use of this apparatus to everybody?"

"Professor," said Gribal, stirred, "I will be worthy of your confidence."

"I know it, my friend. But be careful of the consequences of the slightest indiscretion, of the slightest overheard remark. Ask yourself only what would happen if the Marquis de Saint-Imier were aware of the method I have followed. I would have to bend all my efforts to undoing everything I have done. Singular situation!

"With my sphere, I opposed the radiation emitted by Saint-Imier with more powerful emissions. No doubt you noticed that I was worried yesterday. It was because I was not at all sure of the effects of the radiation I discovered. I might very well have intensified the catastrophe instead of preventing it. But I had to risk everything to gain everything. And fortunately it turned out well. In that single hour of combat I learned more than any time in my life."

These reflections had a peculiar effect on Gribal; he had a certain sensation of retrospective fear.

"Ah," he murmured, "what would have happened, if you had not been here?"

Simply and calmly, as though he were delivering a lecture, Mazelier went on: "This is what would have happened. In all the countries under the influence of the radiation emitted by the Marquis de Saint-Imier there would not be a single living being at this moment."

Mazelier went on: "Reynier-Vitral was right. Living beings can exist in an atmosphere composed differently than ours. He is right to remember the precision oxygenators invented by Bayeux. But he was wrong in imagining the phenomenon could have lasted. A frightful poisoning would have finished us all off, not to mention the cold. We would not have been far from the 80 below zero Paulette mentioned."

"But how was it that the phenomena of destruction were localized, if I can put it that way, in the region east of Passy? The Marquis threatened the whole world, and more than half the world escaped. *Parbleu!* I see, though... The Marquis arranged it so that he was outside the effects!"

Mazelier shook his head.

"No, Gribal, don't think that. The dark, the poisoned air, the cold, the destruction of cellular matter would have manifested themselves to the west as well as to the east. It was only a question of minutes."

"But in that case the madman would have shared the fate of his victims!"

"Who knows? Perhaps that madman, as you so justly call him, was anxious to die. He is not the first who has wished that everything should go down when he went."

In his turn, Gribal made a negative gesture:

"Oh, come, Professor! Be reasonable. The man is still young; he is not more than 45, Paulette says. He is rich. He is the center of the Paris fashionable world. He has everything he needs to make him happy. And he wished to die—to die amidst the destruction of the world. It is inadmissible; it is hardly possible that he is as crazy as that."

"That is his secret," replied Mazelier gravely, "and I admit to you that I don't know the reason. It's enough that I know the fact. The man is a danger to humanity; he must be reduced to powerlessness."

"And if he repents some day?"

"Well, Gribal, the Church tells us that we must pardon those who repent. But we must also be pitiless to those who persist in evil."

"Doubtless. But how can I believe that this man wishes to do the same thing as some people I knew at Marseilles?"

"Good," said Mazelier with a laugh, "you're going to tell me some tall story, but go on."

"I swear it is nothing but the truth. You remember that in 1910 there was a good deal of talk about whether Halley's comet would hit the Earth and reduce it to fragments? Well, my Marseilles friends climbed up to the belfry of the cathedral, there to have a better view of the end of the world."

"You're right, at that, my friend, not to take the matter too tragically. Too bad we can't have young Roger with us—he knows how to look at these things."

The name of his son recalled to Gribal that he was keeping his lunch waiting.

"We're going to be late getting to the table," he said, pulling out his watch.

Mazelier, who never knew what time it was, approved.

"Well, let's get something to eat then. Come back right away, Gribal, and we'll get busy on it immediately...Ah, by the way, do you remember that work you did on yttrium, zirconium and tungsten? You remember that you established certain analogies and called them the 'masked bodies?' "

"I remember perfectly, although it was some time ago."

"At the time I gave you my own notes on the subject. You have them still?"

"I should say so. They are locked in my desk along with the most precious of my other papers."

"In that case, I suggest that you bring them back to the laboratory when you come. We are going to need them."

"Nothing easier."

"All right. Goodbye, Gribal."

"Till after lunch, Professor."

Gribal arrived at his home in a state of enthusiasm difficult to describe accurately. The previous worry had fled; he felt only the high spirits of the fighter who has become certain of victory. What he now knew of the labors and discoveries made by Mazelier reassured him completely. Who in the world could equal him? Nobody, he answered himself; Saint-Imier was already beaten, for Mazelier saw into scientific depths to which the other was a stranger.

He leaped up the stairs four at a time. But a surprise was waiting for him; there was no lunch ready. Madame Gribal met him in the entryway:

"Did Suzie come back with you?"

"The maid? Of course not. I haven't seen her."

And perceiving that his wife looked a little worried, he inquired:

"Has she gone out, then?"

"Yes, father," answered Paulette, "and it's so queer! She went out to do the marketing at about 9 a.m."

"And she hasn't come back?"

"You can see. And it's now 12:40 a.m."

Gribal grumbled:

"That's carrying things a little far."

"Something must have happened to her," declared Paulette.

"Oh, I hope she hasn't been run over," said Madame Gribal. "There are so many street accidents nowadays."

Roger, philosophical as ever, offered a more comforting hypothesis:

"Probably gone to a talkie and forgotten what time it was."

His mother replied severely:

"You know very well there aren't any morning talkies anymore."

This delay was really worrisome. Suzie, who was from Brittany, a native of Saint-Guénolé, was a pearl among housemaids. Clever, a hard worker, careful and honest, quick to obey and speaking little, she had been in the employ of the Gribal household for over a year. She never asked for extra evenings out, never had to be reprimanded. She appeared for work with such regularity that the concierge of the apartment was in the habit of saying:

"Ah, that Suzie must have a clock in her middle. You could run a railroad by her."

"What shall we do?" asked Madame Gribal, a prey to somber imaginings.

Gribal was perplexed.

"Faith," he said, "let's wait a little longer. What should I do? If she doesn't show up, I'll report the matter to the police."

And then, to reassure his wife, he added:

"I don't think there has really been any accident. They would have let us know, and she's been gone long enough for them to send word."

But he himself was not really convinced. Meanwhile, he decided to look up the notes of the experiments of which Mazelier had spoken. He knew exactly where they were—a little secret drawer at the back of his desk.

He took out the key for the drawer and—stupefaction! —found it wide open. Hardly believing his eyes, Gribal called:

"Paulette! Have you been in my desk?"

The young girl ran to him:

"Of course not, father. You know very well that no one would touch your—"

She did not finish. Gribal gave a cry of astonishment and annoyance; the secret drawer had been forced; the notebooks and the package that had contained them were gone.

Roger and his mother, hurrying to the scene of the disturbance, looked in astonishment at the too-evident traces of the robbery. After a moment of silence, Madame Gribal spoke:

"But it's impossible! Impossible!"

"Yes," said Gribal, controlling himself with an effort, "it's impossible, but it happened! Look, has anyone at all been here during my absence?"

"Nobody, absolutely nobody."

"And you didn't go out yourself?"

"Not for a moment."

"Who has been in this room?"

"Suzie. And Suzie alone. She did up the room before going for the food."

"In which room does she usually begin?"

"She usually begins in the dining room instead of this one."

"And which room does she do last?"

Paulette and her mother replied together:

"Your office."

"And she went out immediately afterward?"

"Yes, but—" demanded Madame Gribal, "all the same I hope you don't suspect her."

No, Gribal did not suspect her. All the same there was the evidence. Drawers do not force themselves; papers don't take wing and fly away. Who else could have entered the room?

Most important of all, who would have gained from the crime? Certainly the missing documents were of the greatest importance, since Mazelier had been so urgent about having them at the office. Now, what possible advantage would they be to Suzie, an illiterate servant from Brittany? And who could have told her of the existence of the secret drawer or what it contained?

In any case, no further hesitation seemed necessary; the police must be called in. Gribal clapped on his hat and hurried off to the nearest station, but on the very doorstep remembering Mazelier's counsels of prudence, said nothing of the loss of his papers.

"A servant four hours late?" The affair seemed to the policeman on duty one of the smallest importance. Nevertheless he asked the usual questions, taking notes:

"What was the name of your maid?"

"Suzie Kerdel."

"Ah! A Bretonne?"

"Yes, from Saint-Guénolé."

"Oh, in that case, she will be easy to find. There's a peculiarity about the women of that neighborhood, I know it. They look very Chinese. A skin almost yellow, slanting eyes, long black hair. Doesn't that describe your maid?"

"Perfectly," said Gribal, surprised and strangely moved by the observation, which had never struck him before. *Chinese type*—the idea roused in him curious associations and memories.

"Any special details? How was she dressed when she left your house?"

"As usual; that is, she wore a regular Breton costume."

"That will make the search very much easier. There are not too many of those queer Saint-Guénolé bonnets running around the Paris streets."

"Where did she live?"

"She went home every evening; 43 Rue Faber."

"At Grenelle? Good. I thank you, Monsieur. Go home to your lunch; I promise you that before your next meal you will have news of her."

And the policeman added, with a smile:

"Even if she was 48 that makes no difference. Women can do their running around at any age."

Gribal did not answer, and for a good reason. His suppositions cut considerably deeper than those of the policeman, but they seemed so absurd that he rejected them as untenable.

The most reasonable thing to do at present was to wait for the results of the police inquiry and to warn Mazelier as soon as possible. There was still time to put the police on the track of the stolen notes if the scientist thought the effort would be worthwhile.

Gribal was so much affected by the loss of the notes that he was a little apprehensive about seeing his superior again. The engineer moved toward the office, but emotion seemed to halt his footsteps. The scientist would never believe such a fantastic story—a theft on the very morning when he had asked for the notes! And at the best, he could not but draw the conclusion that Madame Gribal paid very little attention to what went on in her house. It was both ridiculous and painful; in fact, nothing can be worse than the situation of a victim to whom one can say, "It was your fault." As he passed the concierge's lodge, he stuck his head in to ask Père Bibent:

"Has Professor Mazelier come back yet?"

"He went up just before you, Monsieur Gribal."

The engineer sighed. He hated to face it. But he consoled himself with the thought that after all, he had not much with which to reproach himself.

8. The Mysterious Saint-Imier

He encountered the scientist at the door of the inner laboratory.

"Ah, there you are, Gribal! I was afraid I was late and was keeping you waiting. Come along in."

"Professor," babbled the engineer nervously, "I'm sorry to have to tell you that—"

Mazelier, as he was taking off his hat and coat, had looked around with the experienced eye of the methodical worker to see that everything was in its place before beginning. And now suddenly, like Gribal before the forced desk, and while the other was in mid-sentence, the scientist gave a cry of pain, surprise and anger. Then, clutching at his heart, he would have fallen, had not Gribal sustained him and assisted him to a chair.

"Are you ill? I'll open the window"

Clumsy and hurried, like anyone else in such a case, Gribal fumbled with the catch, but was called back by Mazelier:

"Gribal! Look! The sphere... the dials... disappeared!"

The engineer turned, rubbing his eyes, refusing, in his turn to admit the reality. The dials, the connections, the sphere, had all vanished.

Underneath his frail-looking exterior Mazelier concealed more energy and decision than his assistant. He made no complaint, expressed no regret. Recovered from his momentary weakness, as calm as though he were giving directions for some minor experiment, he said:

"Someone has stolen the whole apparatus. Not an hour ago. Let us discover how it was done—if possible."

"Didn't you lock the laboratory door when you went out to lunch?" asked Gribal, restored by his superior's magnificent cool-headedness.

"Yes. I remember it perfectly. Besides I have just opened it again with my key, and in opening, found nothing unusual about the lock. Let's have a look at the window."

It looked out on the Avenue des Champs-Elysées. The laboratory was on the fourth floor, and it was impossible that a thief, in broad daylight, had managed to climb to such a height to get in. Moreover the glass was intact, the catch still closed. Nobody could possibly have touched the window.

"Therefore," said Mazelier in his calm voice, as they ended the examination, "someone got in with a false key. Let's go see Père Bibent. But don't say anything that might frighten him, nor anything that would rouse his suspicions about what happened. I don't want him talking."

Père Bibent himself had one of those honest, rock-hewn faces; Mazelier had known him for too long to suspect the old man himself of such a piece of thievery.

"Tell me, Bibent, did anyone call to see me while I was out?"

"Oh, no, Monsieur."

"I expected someone, and when I went out I clean forgot to tell you. Look, try to remember—you didn't see anyone at all?"

"No, no one asked for you Professor Mazelier, I'd swear. The only person here this noon was a kind of huckster selling little statuettes. A yellow man."

"Ah, a huckster? That's funny; those chaps are black for the most part."

"Ah, if you had been five minutes later going out to lunch you would have seen him as clearly as I did. You had hardly gone out, both of you before he arrived."

"What sort of little statuettes did he have?"

"Oh, ivory ones. I chased him along. He looked like a bad egg with his big mouth and yellow skin and his nose all flattened out. A kind of a Chinese, I tell you, Professor Mazelier."

"A Chinese!" cried Mazelier and Gribal together.

"Yes. I shut the door in his face and didn't see him again. That's all. But aside from that, nobody has been here during the lunch-hour. Sure and certain."

"Thank you, Bibent."

314

The two men returned to the office. In the laboratory they looked at each other.

"Well, Gribal?"

"Well, Professor, It was probably the Marquis' chauffeur."

"Do you think so?"

"I don't think so, I'm sure of it. But if I can explain what happened here, I am at a loss to explain what happened at my own house."

"At your house?"

"Yes. My desk was forced this morning, and someone took—"

"Someone took?"

"The notes on the experiments, Professor."

The expected words of blame did not come. Instead, Mazelier said simply:

"That does not surprise me, my friend."

And he added, after a minute:

"Never mind those notes. We can write it all up again. I remember them fairly well."

"After ten years?"

"There are certain things one does not forget, Gribal. You will see when we get to it. But I understand how the theft was committed here. Do you know the means at your place?"

"I can only suspect my maid, and I can't believe it was she."

"Have you talked to her?"

"No. She went out this morning to do the marketing. She had not yet come back when I left."

"Well then, Gribal, it was she. She stole the notes and then ran away."

"But that would be so stupid. By this time they have certainly found her. The man at the police station was right. A Bretonne in a Saint-Guénolé bonnet would be easy to find in Paris. Especially since I have her home address."

"Did you say she was from Saint-Guénolé? She must have been a descendant of that colony of Orientals there, in that case"

"She looked quite Chinese, as a matter of fact."

"It was she, Gribal. Decidedly, we have very little luck with the Chinese today."

Was Mazelier quite undisturbed by the double theft, since he found the heart to joke about it? Gribal himself was the prey of a considerable feeling of uneasiness, which he did not seek to conceal from his superior. The marvelous sphere, the machine that had saved humanity from disaster, Mazelier's greatest discovery, was in the hands of the redoubtable enemy of the race, who thus sent his agents everywhere. Would he not make it the instrument of new crimes, perhaps an ultimate disaster?

"Ah, my friend, there never was a more useless burglary! The Chinese man had hardly got out of here before the sphere vanished from his hands. The solidified air of which it was composed became gaseous again. And as to the radia-

315

tion-generators within it, they are completely gone by this time. The whole apparatus was kept in a state of abnormal equilibrium by radiation emitted by another apparatus within this laboratory—look. Our friend, the Marquis de Saint-Imier has stolen nothing but a mirage, Gribal. And every time he does something like that he leaves another trail pointing to himself of which we can make use. He thinks he has us now, whereas it is we who have him."

"Well, what do we do next then?"

He interrupted himself, prey to a sudden nervousness, and began to pace back and forth in the laboratory.

"You will see, my friend. We will make another solidified air sphere, better and more easily handled than the first. We will get to work on a whole group of new forms of radiation. The atom is going to yield up to us its last secrets. For everything is possible, Gribal. You hear—everything, absolutely. This Saint-Imier is an imbecile, in trying to limit something that has no limits. Doesn't he see that matter cannot be destroyed?"

He halted, thoughtful for a moment. Then he continued his train of thought, speaking, one would say, more for his own benefit than for Gribal's.

"Yes, *parbleu!* The Chinese man slid into the stairway and went up the minute Bibent's head was turned. Yes, the maid at your house had precise instructions. But all that has no real interest. What I would like to know is—yes, yes, the only important detail is how Saint-Imier discovered the existence of the sphere and the notes. He found it all out in the course of a few hours this morning. How in the world did he do it?"

And replying to a question which Gribal had not pronounced, Mazelier went on:

"How did he see what went on here and in Gribal's house?"

That same evening Gribal found at his house a communication from the police. They announced that their inquiry had received a complete setback. Suzie Kerdel remained unfound.

A single significant detail. In the Rue Faber, at the address she had given, no one knew of her. The pearl among maids was, according to all appearances, nothing but a crook. Madame Gribal, ignorant of the whole truth, could not understand. Suzie disappeared? She must have been the victim of gangsters who had first robbed and then killed her, probably thrown the body into the Seine or cut it in pieces and hid it somewhere. The poor woman was really in despair.

As to Paulette, she did not partake of these kindly illusions, but she kept her opinions to herself, and this silence pleased Gribal considerably. He was still more pleased with his daughter when she offered to help her mother with the household duties instead of hiring another servant. "Economy," she said to her mother, and then in her father's ear whispered, "economy—and take no chances."

Gribal understood that although Paulette knew nothing, she had guessed nearly everything, and realized that if things became complicated he had an assistant he could rely upon.

For the moment there were no complications. At the office the work went on as usual, and as though nothing had happened. Mazelier, however, was more careful than usual to let the press and public know about all the work he was carrying on and the results hoped for from it. Nothing to hide, was the key, nothing to hide, and nothing sensational being done. But would these precautions really hide from the Marquis de Saint-Imier the fact that Mazelier and Gribal, in the silence of the inner laboratory, were continuing their secret research?

The Marquis himself was equally open. Apparently he was enormously busy about everything but scientific research. For one thing he was out of the city. The newspapers were full of a big *fête* he was giving at Nice, where he had assembled performers to give a series of all the known dances from all the different parts of the world, ending up with the massed performance of a troupe of 500 dancers in the open air, including the best artists of the Paris stage.

At Pau, he was organizing a series of boxing matches; next he was at Chamonix in the midst of a mountain-climbing expedition. He went over to Algiers and held a camel race, he arrived at Touggourt and played practical jokes on the grave Arab sheiks there. His success at Naples was less striking, his efforts to reproduce the destruction of Pompeii on the scene, having aroused the anger of influential Italian circles.

He was next heard of in London, organizing a race among the "superhorses" of the British Empire, ridden by an assemblage of the best jockeys in the world. In fact, he was living the life of a superman of fashion, throwing money out of all his windows, and as he was as polite as he was generous, as distinguished as he was extravagant, he enjoyed a considerable esteem in his world.

Could one possibly suspect such a person of having conceived a gigantic and savage attempt on the lives of millions, and even more, of having tried to carry it out?

Mazelier and Gribal had almost arrived at the conclusion that they were wrong. The Marquis was surrounded by people, by servants; perhaps one of them, keeping carefully in the background, was the real criminal. It was not at all impossible.

But always they ran up against Paulette's observations: the voice that had come over the radio, and which had been heard by everyone, she remained certain that it was the same voice she had heard in the minister's drawing room. One can be deceived in voices, but she insisted.

One morning, on opening his paper, Gribal noticed a small item in the society column. The Marquis de Saint-Imier was returning to Paris. He was going to give a series of costume balls at his house in the Rue Cortambert. It would attract the whole smart world of Paris; one could not consider oneself in style if one did not receive an invitation.

317

Meanwhile the days were going by in absolute calm for Gribal and Mazelier. Paris had already forgotten the strange autumn night in the middle of the day; the judicial inquest that had been opened to discover the identity of the "practical joker" had been quickly closed without result. Would Mazelier have time to complete his experiments without any further interference?

One afternoon in March, Mazelier was working in the laboratory at the office. He had sent Gribal to the library to consult Reynier-Vitral's latest work on isotopes; he was in the main laboratory. About him the other research workers were watching an electric furnace in which the scientist was carrying on, with improved apparatus, the experiments of Wöhler and David in the production of synthetic diamonds by means of boron. Mazelier was seated at his desk, busily working out chemical formulas.

All at once he felt his chair move and sway, as though from a powerful earthquake shock. The movement was so violent that Mazelier was thrown from his seat, his head striking the sharp point of a magnetic instrument that he had placed on the desk that very morning. As he fell, the scientist cried out; the others gathered round him and lifted him up half-conscious. Fortunately the wound was insignificant, but a quarter of an inch in either direction and it might easily have been fatal.

The assistants could not understand the accident. They had felt no shock, perceived no movement. In the whole laboratory nothing had moved but Mazelier's big armchair.

"Decidedly, I'm getting clumsy in my old age," the scientist explained when the wound had been treated. "I must have moved too quickly."

He had no more to say on the subject. But he moved the magnetic instrument away and had workmen take from his office every object that possessed dangerous corners. And when Gribal arrived, he took him into the inner laboratory and locked the door. The assistants noticed that Gribal looked worried when he emerged some time later.

Nevertheless, during the following days, everything went along in order. Mazelier carried on his work as usual, without making any further allusions to his accident.

But one morning Gribal, who felt in the most excellent health when he went to bed, woke up with a frightful headache. He took an aspirin, but without the slightest effect. What was worse he felt extremely weak, and even for him to go to the office demanded an effort that took the last bit of his energy. As he got out of the taxi at the door, he crumpled to the sidewalk, and Bibent had to help him upstairs, and as he arrived at the laboratory he fainted.

The scientist was alone in the office at that moment; it was early and the assistants had not yet arrived.

"Shall I call a doctor?" inquired the concierge.

"Yes, yes, hurry up. But before you do that, help me get him into the inner laboratory."

Alone with Gribal, inanimate in the big armchair where he sprawled, Mazelier acted quickly and with certainty. Near the big sphere of brilliant metal on the table, he found a button, touched it, and then pulled a lever. There was the sound of a low humming, a vibration made itself felt, and the hum deepened to the sound of the lowest tone of some great organ. After a minute or two Gribal opened his eyes, then moved in his chair, sat up and said:

"I think I must have fainted."

"You certainly did, my friend. Do you feel better now?"

"I feel quite all right. *Parbleu!* My headache is gone. It was really stupid of me to pass out like that. Something must be wrong with my digestion."

9. Attempted Murder

Mazelier maneuvered another lever and the vibration ceased.

"Ah," said Gribal. "You have been using the sphere."

"Yes, to cure your headache."

"Ah. Indeed. But—"

"But, my dear fellow, you never had headaches like this before."

"I should say not. What happened to me, anyway?"

"You were poisoned, that's all."

"Poisoned!"

"Literally. Poisoned by radiation let loose in your bedroom, where you were quite alone; poisoned by the Marquis, our little friend, who seems to be taking active measures. Your wife didn't have a headache?"

"No; she got up an hour before I did."

"Well, that's what saved her. And if you had not come down to the office—"

Gribal grew pale.

"Will it happen again do you think?"

"We shall see. The other day, I just missed killing myself. This morning you just missed dying. I just managed to save you. But it's all right now. The danger is over."

"For the time being."

"Yes, for the time being. But it was really my fault that you were in danger at all."

"Oh, come."

"Certainly. I've been working in the main laboratory as you know, and so didn't want to have on me the little apparatus with the buzzer that warns of the presence of unknown forms of radiation. That's how it happened the other day that I wasn't warned of the attack on me—or rather, on my chair. And for the same reason, not having one of these revelators at your house, Gribal, you were not warned this morning that you were in danger."

"Doubtless. But how is that your fault?"

"You should have one of these revelators with you all the time. And take Paulette into the secret, too. Your wife and Roger can think that it's some queer kind of watch which strikes the hour. I only hope they don't try to wind it up. And you, whenever you hear it, no matter where you are or for what, go away from there fast. You will be in real danger. And now Gribal, let's get busy. We must make one of these revelators for you; better make another for Paulette."

"But if he invades this laboratory with his radiations?"

"He can't. I have set up a barrage-curtain of counter radiation."

And Mazelier pointed to the sphere:

"There's our defense-machine. Always on the job. Unfortunately, I can't extend the curtain to cover us when we get out of these four walls."

"And won't the Chinese man come back?"

"Certainly not. Oh, for that, he will hardly try; he will know that we will be on guard. But if he does get in, he won't get out again alive. That's why only you and I are permitted to come in here. But wait, Gribal, I must show you; it's possible you will have to get in some day without me. I'll show you how to do it. Look here—"

Mazelier rose and opened the door of the inner laboratory.

"You see the key-hole? And the glass plates above and below? Well, when I go out, I press on this place here, which is attached to the upper plate. Before going in again, I press on the lower place. That's all, but you mustn't forget. Do you understand?"

"I think I see," said the engineer, "pressing on the upper button actuates a curtain of deadly radiation; the second stops the generator and permits one to go in."

"Right, Gribal. And note that the buttons are hidden under the form of the screws that hold the glass plates. I defy Saint-Imier or any of his assistants to find them. But you see—in the whole wide world, we have only this one place that is absolutely safe. But admit that you thought me crazy in doing so much work on the doors of my inner laboratory."

"Professor," said the engineer with a smile, "you know very well that a good soldier obeys without asking questions. We are now engaged in a war; I am a soldier."

"Admirable, my friend. The more so, since like a good soldier you carry out all orders to the letter, even when you don't understand them."

As he spoke, Mazelier had been working over a watch-case, in which he was installing a tiny apparatus.

"Your revelator will be ready tomorrow. I will still have to put something into it which I don't have at the moment. I hope only that I won't be interrupted tonight in my work."

"Do you think he's going to invade your house too?"

"Anywhere, I repeat, he will follow us anywhere."

320

"But," demanded Gribal suddenly, "can't we send him the same kind of a visiting card?"

Mazelier shook his head.

"Do you think I haven't thought of that? Unfortunately, before I can do that—you see, I might make any number of innocent victims. The apparatus for attack waves, which I have been developing as well as he, is not yet refined enough to enable me to concentrate on a point like that. I must be able to direct the wave action where I wish and they must act nowhere but on that spot."

And Mazelier went on, with a cold fury that astonished his companion:

"On the day I find out how to do that, we can be at rest, for I swear I will not hesitate."

"But he has attack waves, and is not hesitating to use them, whether he can control them or not!"

"Doubtless. But he is a criminal. I wonder how many innocent people he struck down this morning, trying to reach you? Or how many other accidents he caused the other day, trying to cause one for me? Ah, the monster!"

And coming back to the idea that obsessed him, Mazelier went on:

"But how was he able to see? For he did see, Gribal! How did he know the exact placing of my chair and your bed. I must know or lose the game!"

Paulette was not an athletic young woman. Nevertheless she had been an enthusiastic bicyclist since her 15th year, fearless even of the Paris traffic, amid which she maneuvered with an agility and cleverness worthy of a professional. She managed her wheeled steed with a gay carelessness that nearly gave Madame Gribal tremors, but which Roger found the most natural thing in the world.

On this particular day, returning from the university, Paulette realized that she was distracted. People often ask what young girls think about; this one on a bicycle thought about dodging buses, automobiles and pedestrians, not counting the new high-speed "motos" that whizzed through the streets like meteors.

A traffic jam brought Paulette to a halt at the Pont de la Concorde. The Boulevard Saint-Germain, as far back as the Ministry of Foreign Affairs, was packed with vehicles, and the tumult of their horns was infernal. But there was nothing to do but wait till the police untangled the mess. Mechanically Paulette looked around.

All at once, she gave a little "Ah!" of surprise. Quite close to her, separated only by a taxi, a huge auto had halted. Paulette's gaze fell on the chauffeur, who was quite exceptionally unhandsome. Buck teeth, slanting eyes, mouth that reached from ear to ear. Paulette expressed it to herself, "Where in all China did they find him?"

Naturally the young girl's curiosity extended from the chauffeur to the proprietor of the car, and as she looked at him Paulette could not restrain an exclamation of astonishment. She recognized him; it was the Marquis de Saint-Imier. She had seen him only once before and then for hardly five minutes, but she would have recognized him a thousand years after, so forcibly had his features been imprinted on her memory by the circumstances. She looked at him almost fascinated as he lounged among the cushions of his car, disdainful and haughty, not considering the sights of the street worthy of a glance.

Had he seen and recognized Paulette Gribal? It was not at all probable. In any case, there was not a movement, not a change in his face to indicate that he had. The girl only saw him pick up the end of the speaking tube and give some order to the chauffeur. And then it seemed to Paulette that the chauffeur was looking at her attentively, but out of the corner of his eye. She shivered; then the policeman blew his whistles and the line of vehicles began to trail across the Pont de la Concorde.

As she emerged from the bridge an open space was before her; she had to turn to the left to reach the route to Marly, and prudently looked around. On her right a street-car was coming down the Quai; straight ahead, the autos coming from the other direction were still at some distance; on her left the Cours-la-Reine was quite empty. Paulette turned into the open without the least apprehension.

She had not covered 20 yards when she felt herself suddenly lifted from the ground, turned round and then—It lasted only a split second, but it was like a century, and it was enough for Paulette to recognize that she had been hit from behind by an auto, and that in another fraction of a second she would be rolling with her wrecked bicycle beneath the wheels of the car. She saw herself dying; and then in the third fraction of a second was astonished to find herself on her feet and in the arms of a young man who was asking respectfully:

"Are you hurt, mademoiselle?"

She replied: "Of course not," as though the question had been "Have you a cold?"

Then, suddenly recognizing that she had been miraculously saved from certain death, she cried:

"Oh! Why it's you, Monsieur Duplay."

She was hardly astonished to see him there, for she had met him frequently of late, at her father's office or just near it. Roland Duplay, who had proved a research student of the first order, had been admitted to a considerable degree of intimacy by Gribal. Madame Gribal found him altogether sympathetic, and he had been a caller at the house, where he had told the story of his life's struggle.

His parents had been in business and had sent him to the best technical schools. Then came a change in the family's fortunes, and Roland found himself obliged to abandon his education. He worked; he became an electrician. By means of his labors he procured the funds to buy books and continue that pursuit of pure science which alone could lead him to the fulfillment of his ambitions. And finally his dreams were realized: he had received the powerful protection of Mazelier and Gribal.

His dreams? Perhaps he had other dreams when Paulette shared the lessons which Gribal was giving him. And it was with delight that he had accepted the commission of watching over the girl; from a discreet distance naturally, in a way that she should not suspect. Gribal was anxious; Mazelier had told him to expect anything at all from the Marquis. They had been right. But Saint-Imier did not even know of Duplay's existence.

Paulette, on her part, found it neither surprising nor disagreeable that he should be on hand. "Your poor bicycle," said Roland. "It's in fragments."

The news had a singular effect on Paulette. For the first time she became fully conscious of the fact that it was by a miracle that she had escaped being crushed under the auto, and in the same moment remembered that before the shock, she had recognized the Chinese at the wheel. And if Duplay had not been on hand to catch her, she would have gone under the wheels. She experienced a shiver of retrospective terror.

Nevertheless, she gathered herself together, not wishing her mother to know how narrow an escape she had. To get home now, that was her only desire.

Roland Duplay guessed at her desire. As the crowd of curious persons began to collect and the policeman on duty advanced, thumbing his notebook, the pair were already on their way up the street leading to the Champs-Elysées, and beyond the reach of official inquiry.

They went rapidly as far as the Crystal Palace. There, seated on a park bench where no one would pay any attention to them, they consulted.

Roland was overwhelmed.

"You're more scared than I am!" accused Paulette.

"I admit it."

"Nevertheless, that didn't keep you from saving my life. You pulled me to the left just as I was toppling under the wheels of that car."

"I was lucky enough to be there in time," said the young workman, blushing.

"Tell me, did you have the impression that the accident was...on purpose?"

Roland murmured:

"It isn't an impression; it's a certainty."

"Then that man is a criminal."

Roland did not answer. But he made an affirmative movement with his head.

"What have I done that he should hate me and wish to kill me? Do you know?"

"It isn't because of you yourself. He's aiming at your father and Professor Mazelier."

"But why?"

Roland spoke out clearly:

"Because that man is afraid of them. And he's afraid of them because they are stronger than he is."

All at once Paulette perceived something. Her father had bound her to secrecy on the subject of the incidents at the ministerial reception. Now, Roland Duplay evidently knew both the name of the Marquis and the part he was playing in the drama in which all of them were engaged. But how had he acquired this information?

In answer to her question, the young man did not hesitate to tell her the story of the day of darkness.

"Good," said Paulette, when he had finished, "then we are accomplices."

She was no longer frightened. A combat was begun, and she was now as much engaged in it as anyone; it amused her to think of herself as a soldier. And moreover, she realized that she had a friend and helper in Roland. She held out her hand to him.

"Thank you a thousand times. Till tomorrow, then?"

"I will try to come. Monsieur Gribal is so good to me."

"And you also, you have been good to me. Come tomorrow, and you will see what beautiful lies I can tell. Naturally I don't want mother to know anything about this, she would worry too much. But father, that's something else again. I'll tell him first thing!"

Paulette, entering the house, had her explanation ready:

"Mother!" she cried with all the gaiety with which one would announce a piece of very good news, "do you know, I've lost my bike,"

"Oh yes, I knew you'd forget it someday," said Madame Gribal.

"But I think someone must have stolen it."

Madame Gribal could not avoid noticing the exuberance of her daughter, her rapid and joyous gestures, as though she were possessed of some happy secret.

"My word," she said, "anyone would think it was a pleasure for you to lose it."

This simple observation left Paulette a little confused; she did not know what to answer. But Roger, without realizing it, saved her face for her:

"She ought to be happy about it, mother. If someone swiped that old bike of hers, she'll have to have a new one."

But Paulette was blushing, for she had discovered the cause of her joyous feeling. It was because the loss of the bicycle had been compensated by the gain of an admirer.

10. They Try a Disguise

The next morning, Gribal, who had been informed of the details of the adventure through which his daughter had passed, recounted them to Mazelier. The scientist, when he himself was the object of attack, was accustomed to oppose an unruffled calm to the frown of Fate. But this time he gave full rein to his anger. Their opponent had descended to attacks on young girls—nothing equaled the atrocity of such an attempt except perhaps its cowardice.

"I wonder what one would find in the past of this man if we could pry into it. Well, we must get busy, Gribal. I have been delaying too long. Let us attack from our side."

Mazelier was really furious. Let the Marquis attack him if he wished, him an old man, and without family—that was a matter of no importance. When Gribal became an object of attack, it was already a little too much. But Paulette, so intelligent and so cheerful, who seemed destined one day to be a genuine collaborator in the research of the laboratory; Paulette, in the springtime of her life, who deserved so clearly to be happy; Paulette, whom Mazelier loved like one of his own daughters—that was intolerable! The punishment ought to be made to follow the crime with the rapidity of lightning.

"I can strike," said Mazelier, "and I will strike."

But one had to be sure of one's blow. And another difficulty—Mazelier stoutly refused to take any step that might make innocent victims. The forms of radiation he was about to liberate must be made to go straight to their target with the precision of a bullet aimed by an expert marksman. For all those who were even touched by these terrible rays would never recover, even from the simple contact.

"First we must try to find out where we can most easily strike at the animal. Then, Gribal, we will go for him, taking precautions which I trust will be sufficient. I will punish him without remorse, but I would never forgive myself if I made other victims."

"Not even the chauffeur?"

Mazelier hesitated:

"He's only an instrument," he offered.

"Oh, come. He's an accomplice. Saint-Imier gave him the order to run down Paulette, but the chauffeur did not hesitate to do it."

"You are right," said Mazelier reflectively. He went on: "What would you say if we could strike them together?"

"That it would be justice. But how are you going to do it?"

"Look. We don't know anything about the interior arrangements at the Marquis' house. In what room does he live? Where is his secret laboratory, the place where he has perhaps discovered new laws in physics of which I am ignorant? Where does he sleep? We can't do anything against him, under the conditions, without striking at some poor folks around him who are in ignorance of what their master is doing."

"Evidently."

"But suppose—yes, suppose that Saint-Imier gets into his car, driven by that horrible chauffeur. If we could be certain that at a given moment he would pass a certain point, I believe, Gribal, that we could do justice to him. Look, that idea is much more practical than the one of getting at him where he lives; much better than my previous project."

"What was your previous project, Professor?" inquired Gribal, curiously.

"I was going to direct against him radiation that has a terrible effect. They cause the flesh itself to rot, by disintegrating the cellular structure, but the individual subjected to them would doubtless live on for several weeks, the prey of the most acute agonies. They do not kill, you understand; on the contrary, they cause the processes of life to be speeded up. But while the individual who is subjected to them seems to be in the most excellent health, his body is rotting until the day when he becomes nothing more than a skeleton covered with skin. Then—"

"But this radiation," murmured Gribal, "doesn't the Marquis know about its effects?"

"No, my friend. He certainly does not know about this form. For if he did, we would now be rotting, both of us. No, this form of radiation is known to me alone. And you wish to know how I know their effects. Well, do you remember Sully Tavernier?"

"That young pupil of Henri Poincaré, with so much talent, who committed suicide after disappearing from Paris so mysteriously?"

"Poor Tavernier! It was he who discovered this form of radiation, Gribal, by chance, in the course of an experiment—and they bit him. He suffered frightfully—even beyond the limits which imagination can give to pain. He told me about the discovery that was killing him, making me promise never to make the secret public. And then he made his young wife shoot him through the head. She did it, for pity's sake—and then she went insane, Gribal."

"Horrible. My God!"

"What would you have?" said Mazelier, melancholically. "That's the risk we all take in this kind of research. Well, anyway, you see what I was going to do. For this Tavernier radiation, with my apparatus I can project it to a distance, and I hope, concentrate it on a point. But I doubt whether I could do it without striking innocent people, and that is a thing I will never do."

"And I approved," declared Gribal, "but what do you intend to do now?"

"To apply the *lex talionis*," answered the scientist. "He tried to kill Paulette through an auto accident; well, we will give him an auto accident. And we will see whether he escapes as easily as your daughter."

There was a moment's silence between the two, interrupted by a remark from Gribal: "May I make a request?"

"What is it?"

"If I understand you correctly, you intend to wreck the Marquis' car while it is going at full speed."

"Something like that, Gribal."

"And you can produce the accident from here, seated in your chair?"

"Certainly."

"Without the slightest risk?"

"Without the slightest."

"Well then, let me do it instead of you."

Mazelier gave him a sudden glance of illumination.

"I understand, Gribal," he said. "Yes, the idea which you did not formulate in words has come to me too. I am fighting a scoundrel by rather *scoundrely* means. And you think that I, Mazelier, who has nothing on his old conscience, ought not to descend to the level of a criminal, even to chastise a crime; you fear the effect on my tender sensibilities. Have I guessed it?"

"Professor, I think it is our duty to bring down this bandit. But since we cannot do it in public and under the forms of law and honesty, I beg you to let me take your place. It would be unworthy of you but my position is different; I can take the responsibility. I am the father of the child he tried to kill; that gives me rights you do not possess. And besides, if it comes out, I am only Gribal. While you, you are Mazelier! Your name must remain irreproachable."

The scientist shrugged his shoulders.

"You talk like a boy, my friend. Your scruples are very fine and even re-fined, but I avow that I see nothing in them whatever. You yourself have made the point that my name is irreproachable. And do you think that an irreproacha-ble man would be so easily dishonored by employing against a man capable of any crime the only means that would really bring him to book? Run along, Gribal, go to the police station and make a formal complaint against Saint-Imier for having tried to assassinate your daughter, and see whether the complaint will not be turned against you. You were speaking of justice a few minutes ago; well, go try the official means of justice. The Marquis will be delighted, I assure you!"

Gribal felt the force of his remarks. But in spite of them, he hesitated, and Mazelier perceived it. The scientist went on, interested by this exaggerated case of tender conscience.

"My friend, remember that it is a case of life and death, not only for us two, but for your family. Remember that I would prefer, like you, to take the matter up with the authorities, and that I would not hesitate for a moment to de-nounce the Marquis, if it were not evident in a hundred ways that in doing it, I would be playing right into his hands."

"Yes," said Gribal. "I suppose I should not make so much talk about the means chosen to shoot a mad dog. The Marquis, if he is not outside the law, is at least outside humanity."

"Why certainly! The only thing we can do is level all our artillery against him. And that brings up some problems."

"Yes. We must know, first, when the Marquis will make a long trip in his car; second, what road he will take, and third, what time he will leave, his prob-able speed and the probable moment he will reach the chosen point. Right?"

"You have stated the problem admirably. But one of the pieces of information we already have, to wit, the speed of the car. The Marquis always travels at 50 miles an hour on the open road. His chauffeur is really very skillful. Monsieur Perignon, who has traveled with him not a few times, has informed me on that point."

"Good. But how are we to find out the rest?"

Mazelier was embarrassed. All at once Gribal saw him run to the window of the laboratory which looked out on the Rue de la Boëtie and fling it wide open. A sonorous voice floated up from the street:

"Ol' clo's! I cash ol' clo's."

Mazelier leaned out.

"Hey, there!"

The old clothes merchant lifted his head. Mazelier motioned to him to come up.

"What!" Gribal exclaimed, stupefied, "are you going to sell some clothes?"

Mazelier laughed:

"Just the opposite! I'm going to buy."

The engineer, curious though he was, did not dare to ask questions before the old clothes man who had now entered the laboratory, a pile of hats on his head, and the picturesque cloak of old garments flung over his shoulder.

"Wanna sell something?" he asked, a trifle suspiciously, gazing around the laboratory open-mouthed.

Mazelier was so self-effacing, his natural air was so modest, that the merchant selected Gribal, tall, strong and with the visage of a leader, as the man to whom he should address himself. But Gribal said not a word. He looked toward Mazelier, who began:

"We haven't anything to sell you. But we might like to buy."

"But," objected the merchant, "I haven't anything new."

"Exactly. What we want are some second-hand clothes. Let's see what you've got."

The man spread out his packet, his face lighting at the prospect of doing business, There were workmen's smocks, ragged and stained with rain; old trousers which no doubt knew by heart the names of all the streets of Paris; a few dirty old collars, ties without energy or prestige, and a few other articles that he had the nerve to offer, in his regular patter, as "the very latest models from the fashionable houses on the Boulevard."

Mazelier picked here and there among them, regarding each garment attentively, and calmly offered half the price the man demanded. The offer, after a moment's haggling, was accepted. The seller left, convinced that he was dealing with two men who were quite utterly insane, and promising himself to come back at the earliest occasion to take fuller advantage of their lunacy.

At last, Gribal was free to ask:

"What the Devil do you mean to do with that truck?"

"Try them on, of course! I hope they will fit us."

"What! You want—"

"Yes. I want you to go with me for a little walk near the Rue Cortambert. And for such a walk, it would hardly be a good thing to dress in new morning coats. Look, this ought to be about your size."

"It's frightfully dirty," said Gribal with a shudder. "Well, since we have to..."

"Ah, you understand?"

"I think so. We'll have to dirty ourselves up a bit."

"I assure you that it is indispensable."

When their curious toilet was done, Gribal gave a cry of astonishment to which Mazelier replied with a satisfied grunt. They were completely unrecognizable.

"What in the world do we look like, anyway?" inquired the engineer, more amused than disturbed by the adventure.

"We ought to look like what we are," said the scientist, "that is, a pair of bookkeepers out of work. We're dirty, but respectable. It's a terrible thing not to have a job! Well, let's go eat all the same."

"In the Rue Cortambert?"

"Where else? I noticed a little restaurant there. All the chauffeurs of the quarter take their meals at it. The roast beef must be something wonderful."

"Is it near the Marquis' house?"

Mazelier dropped the joking tone in which he had been speaking:

"It's right across the street."

"We'll be in the lion's jaws."

"Yes, but they won't close on us. He'll never imagine we are so close."

"All right," said Gribal, with another glance at his companion. "We certainly look like a fine pair of birds. We mustn't let Père Bibent see us like this, though. Our reputation would be ruined."

Mazelier shrugged his shoulders:

"Decidedly, Gribal, you would never do for a conspirator! Come along and take your first lesson in camouflage."

"Ah!" said Gribal, in enthusiasm, "you are the limit, my dear Professor. I never imagined that you were such a Sherlock Holmes!"

Mazelier made no reply to this compliment, but opened a little cabinet in the corner of the laboratory where various chemicals were kept, for the most part alkaloids newly developed and still under investigation. From this group of choice poisons, the scientist chose a little bottle:

"Listen, Gribal, we ought to perfume ourselves a little. That will make up for the lack of clean linens. What do you say to this attar of roses?"

Uncorking the bottle, Mazelier held it under Gribal's nose, then sniffed at it himself.

"*Parbleu!*" said the engineer, "I would say that your attar of roses smelled rather more like a fish that had been around for some time. Eh! But my voice has changed. What a curious impression. I don't recognize myself anymore."

Mazelier replied, in a voice equally unrecognizable:

"Isn't that a swell perfume—capable of changing a bass into a soprano with a turn of the hand? Our larynxes will keep the impression for a couple of hours at least. All ready, Gribal?"

"Let's go, Professor Mazelier."

As they passed Bibent's lodge, the old man's head popped out:

"Where are you going?" he asked.

"We're translators. Official diplomas. And we're looking for some work," offered Mazelier.

"But there isn't any in this madhouse of yours," added Gribal.

"Yeah? Well run along and do your translating before I give you something you won't be able to translate," answered the concierge angrily. "Translators, indeed, with pants like that!"

"Well?" inquired Mazelier, when they had attained the avenue.

"Wonderful! The experiment is a success. Too bad we haven't more time; I'd take a run home to see whether they recognized me there. What a voice you have given me, Professor! The voice of a siren—but the siren of a tugboat!"

"And me? Would you recognize this rattle?"

Gribal was filled with confidence. At last, the long nightmare of terror was about to have an end. Nobody would have to worry any longer about the threats of the strange bandit whose social position rendered him so immune to the ordinary methods of attack. Mazelier was right; he would have to be struck as with the hammer of God, unforeseen, almost treacherously, and without pity.

11. Exposed!

The engineer and the scientist were seated before a table in the little restaurant in the Rue Cortambert, looking at the dinner usually given to clients who had large appetites and small purses. They honored the repast without repugnance. They were silent, maintaining the air of men intimidated and humbled by fate. Gribal had his back to the window, and could see, in a mirror facing him, a little of what was going on in the street outside; Mazelier was so placed as to miss nothing of what went on in front of the Saint-Imier mansion.

Such a vigil was capable of lasting a long time without producing any particular result. But Mazelier was patient. He felt sure he would sooner or later make the acquaintance of some member of Saint-Imier's staff and draw interesting information. Neither he nor Gribal had the slightest fear of recognition. Only Saint-Imier himself might possibly be capable of penetrating their disguise, but certainly he would never set foot in such a restaurant.

"This is a good place," said Mazelier aloud for the benefit of the others around them. "We ought to come here again. Ah, if we could only find a job in this section of the town!"

"We can try," said Gribal, entering into the spirit of the occasion.

And in the high, sharp voice which he now used without effort, he added:

"You, you're a stenographer; you ought to be able to find a job in some big house around here."

A chubby-looking chauffeur at an adjoining table, overhearing the remark, as he was intended to, glanced them over rapidly with the penetrating eye of the Parisian workman who can so quickly take the measure of a man. His examination apparently had a favorable result; Mazelier particularly made upon him the impression of a good old chap who was bearing up with dignity under undeserved misfortune.

Poor old man! His shoulders were rounded, his chest pinched, his thin face, cracked and rattling voice, bore the marks of incipient tuberculosis. He was evidently incapable of such feats as piloting a taxi from Montmartre to Vaugirard without missing a single turn or drawing a rebuke from a policeman.

The chubby chauffeur turned a protective glance on Mazelier: "Well, what's the matter, things not so good?" he asked in a sympathetic tone.

"They could be better," Mazelier avowed.

"No use kicking, though," said Gribal, adding after a moment: "Just the same, it isn't because we don't want to work."

"Nor because you don't want to eat either," observed the chauffeur, with a burst of laughter.

"True for you," answered Gribal.

"Certainly," said the chauffeur, "what do they take us for anyway—cows that can eat straw? That's always the way. But what do you do when you have anything to do?"

"We are bookkeepers," replied Mazelier.

"Yes," agreed Gribal, "but we were even better than that at one time, weren't we Martin?"

Mazelier understood that the name of Martin fitted him like the paper on the wall.

"Ah!" he sighed, "much better. When I remember that I was once the stenographer for the Chamber of Deputies—"

The chauffeur opened his eyes to their full extent:

"Not really? And the deputies, they let you go unemployed like this? That's not decent. I know a little about them on my own hook, me. That astonishes you, no? But I know how to speak in public. When the elections come around, the deputy from our district is right on my trail asking me to help him every time. And when I go to see him and ask him for some little favor, you know what he does? Lets me gather moss waiting in his outer office!"

331

He emptied his glass with a noble gesture and went on: "You look all right, Monsieur Martin. If you'd like me to, I'll look around for something for you."

"Get back my job at the Chamber, for example? I've grown older since those days."

"Of course. Of course. I understand, the old hand isn't as supple—I suppose one has to go like lightning to keep up with the remarks of those johnnies. But, as your friend was mentioning a minute back, you could still hold a job in one of these houses around here."

"Oh yes, I think he could do that all right," replied Gribal.

The chauffeur regarded Mazelier with a sagacious air:

"You must have an education, now? Yes, I know, you know how to do almost anything except find a job. I know. I have a cousin who is taking a course in pharmacy, and he hasn't found a job yet. He'd have died of hunger long ago, if he hadn't got him a job on the railroad. And he's really educated, too; he knows the names of more than 50 laxatives. And he can reel them off in Latin!"

Mazelier gravely lifted his head: "That's wonderful," he approved.

"Yes, but what use is it to him? Well, it's not quite the same thing with you is it? Well, I'll see—you're looking for a secretary's job, in some fashionable house, huh? I know quite a few people in the fashionable world, me. Secretary to a dancer from the Opera, that would hardly do. You're not well enough turned out—oh, nothing personal you understand. I'll find it though. You see."

Mazelier was only giving a minimum of attention to the rambling assurances of his new-found protector. All at once the chauffeur began to gesticulate, lifting his arms in the air.

"Hey! Over here. Come on over, you, I want to say something to you."

A woman had just entered the restaurant and was threading her way among the tables toward the bar. Gribal turned his head mechanically to see the newcomer, and then became as petrified as though he had seen Medusa and both her sisters. It was not the Medusa who was ordering a vermouth-cassis at the bar; the woman in the Breton bonnet had nothing terrifying in her aspect. But Gribal recognized the former maid, Suzie Kerdel!

"Hey, you from Brittany," called the chauffeur, "bring your drink over here, and we'll buy you another one if you're nice."

And when the Bretonne, enchanted with the offer, brought her glass over and seated herself by the chauffeur, the latter continued: "We'll even buy you a couple, if you'll help us out."

Gribal kicked Mazelier significantly under the table. But he might have spared himself the trouble; the scientist had recognized at once the woman for whom the police had searched in vain.

The situation was becoming more complicated than the engineer had foreseen. He busied himself with his plate, and Mazelier imitated him. Would their rashness be turned on them after all? What would happen if the Bretonne recognized them and announced their real station in life in that rough crowd?

Suzie began by swallowing her vermouth-cassis in a single gulp. Then she said: "Ah, but I'm in a hurry today, I must pack the trunks for this evening."

"Your boss going away?"

"I'll say so! Leaving this evening for Biarritz."

"With the Chinese?"

"Who else would he go with?"

"Of course, of course. Well, one has to admit it; there are damn few chauffeurs like that one. He knows how to handle a wheel. Biarritz, you say? He'll make it in eight hours."

"That," said Suzie, "is their business. Is that all you got me over here for?"

And she glanced at her empty glass. The chauffeur understood.

"What will you have with us, little one?"

"Oh, a snifter of curaçao to start with," said Suzie.

Gribal, dumbfounded, did not move. Mazelier tried to keep his self-possession by cutting up a piece of meat into tiny morsels with great care. Suzie paid no attention to them. She went on:

"What was it you were going to ask me? Hurry up; I tell you I've got to get away."

The chauffeur pointed to Mazelier, who, keeping up his role, replied: "It's about me, Madame, if you would be so good—"

"If I would be so good—?"

He played to perfection the part of one of those timid old people always asking for help, but always hesitating and bashful about asking.

"This good man has a regular education," declared the chauffeur, with authority. "Would you consider speaking to your boss about him? You have been there long enough, he ought to have some confidence in you. And he is rich enough to hire a good secretary."

"A secretary?"

"Yes, someone who will do his letters for him. Your Marquis writes plenty of letters, doesn't he?"

"That is, he has someone write them for him," observed Suzie.

"Exactly. Rich people like that don't do anything for themselves. Well, you'll do it then? You'll speak for Monsieur Martin?"

Suzie repeated slowly:

"Monsieur Martin?"

"I live in the Rue d'Arcole," declared Mazelier.

"Good. Write it for me on a piece of paper, will you? When Monsieur comes back from Biarritz I'll bring it to his attention."

The chauffeur threw a triumphant wink in Mazelier's direction:

"Well, old man," he said familiarly, "you see how it works?"

Martin was so much touched that he brushed away a tear.

"Ah, Madame," he cried effusively, "what will you have to drink?"

It was the best means of thanking her.

333

"This time it will be a little cognac," replied Suzie.

Gribal stifled an exclamation of horror and surprise. This was his model servant, so faithful, so punctual, so temperate, who only rarely, and upon being urged, accepted a little beer or cold tea at his house. What an actress she had been while preparing the way for her theft.

And what was still more incredible, but undoubtedly true, she had not the air of having recognized her former employer.

All at once Suzie looked at Mazelier and began to laugh. The scientist and the engineer were shaken with a single shiver of terror.

"Fortunately," said the Bretonne, "you want a job as a steno and not a singer. Because you have a voice that would kill mice. When I get you the job at our house, don't come into the kitchen. The sound of that voice would curdle the milk."

And she rose to go. The chauffeur still plied her with questions:

"You won't have time to say anything to the Marquis right away, now that Martin is here?"

"Oh, I couldn't do a thing for two weeks yet," said Suzie. "Monsieur is leaving at 9 p.m. And it's already 6:45. I must go. So long!"

"So long, my dear," replied the chauffeur, gallantly. Mazelier, in a tone of emotion, tried to express the depth of his gratitude.

"Madame, I am your servant for life."

"What a lovely remark, and what a musical voice," laughed Suzie.

And she added: "I know. When someone gets married they can have you sing serenades."

And she left on this note of mild pleasantry, to the great relief of her former employer, who had never believed himself well disguised.

Three quarters of an hour later, Mazelier and Gribal were back at the office. As their normal voices had returned, they had only to sing out as they entered:

"Good evening, Père Bibent!"

And the good fellow replied:

"Good evening, Professor Mazelier. Good evening, Monsieur Gribal."

He did not come out of his lodge to watch them go up, unsuspecting the singular spectacle he had missed. But ten minutes later the engineer and the scientist, dressed in their normal fashion, were ready to meet any eye."

"Do you know?" said Gribal, "I was uncomfortable."

"True," said Mazelier pensively, "I had hardly foreseen such an encounter."

"And the chauffeur who mixed in our affairs to get us the protection of that female, that drunkard. And me, I confided the keys of my cellar to her!"

"Did she ever take anything?"

"*Parbleu*, no! She stole nothing but my documents. But there is no longer any doubt possible, she is one of the Marquis' creatures. The important thing is that she did not recognize us."

"Are you certain?"

"What!" cried Gribal, to whom that simple question was like a draft of ice-water on his enthusiasm, "you think that—"

"My friend, I think that woman was quite capable of acting a part for 15 minutes, after having acted one for a year."

"True," said Gribal, discouraged. "But what shall we do?"

"Do the impossible," replied Mazelier.

At the same moment the bell of the door rang.

"Who's calling on us at this hour?" said Gribal. "Don't get up Professor. I'll see."

"Be careful."

"No fear."

A moment later Gribal was back.

"It was only Père Bibent," he announced. "He brought up a note that someone left to be delivered to you."

And Gribal held out an envelope with Mazelier's address upon it. The other tore it open:

"Doubtless a card—ha! Gribal, it was he! Read, read what he wrote."

And he held out to his companion a correspondence card upon which beneath the Saint-Imier coat of arms, appeared in a handwriting, at once elegant and vigorous the following words:

Monsieur Martin may rest assured that I will find a situation for him in which he will be treated as he deserves.

For the first time the Marquis had threatened Mazelier directly and in person. The masks were down; the two adversaries now in open combat.

This bothered Gribal, who was, moreover, affected by so rapid a check to their little plan. But the scientist remained calm.

"*Parbleu!*" he said, "really I like that better. You can no longer reproach me with wishing to stab him in the back. Our clumsiness, or rather our rashness, has brought a good result after all."

"You will not abandon the attempt?"

"Less than ever. The Marquis tried a collective crime against the world; it did not succeed, but the fact remains that he tried, and this gives anyone in the human species the right to suppress him. Moreover, he has committed against you, two crimes under the common law: he stole something from you, and he tried to kill your daughter. This gives us the right—no, this confers upon us the duty, to defend ourselves. And the best defense is an attack."

"But he'll be on his guard now, won't he?"

"I don't think he'll believe we are going to make an attack on him during his journey, and that's just what we are going to do."

335

"And if he goes by another route?"

"We will know it."

"But we can't follow him."

"I beg your pardon. Without leaving this office, we will take up his trail. For the first time, I am going to apply my newest apparatus; that for which he stole the notes, to a particular case. It's about 8 p.m. now, isn't it? At 9:45, Gribal, turn this little lever here to the left, two centimeters on the scale. That will do the job."

As he spoke, Mazelier indicated one of the maze of attachments leading off from the enormous sphere which replaced the one the Chinese had gotten away with.

"Now, let's get things in order," the scientist went on. "I must direct the concentration of radiation exactly on the point selected, insulate them during their journey, and halt them exactly at the point."

"Can you do it?"

"I hope so."

12. To Biarritz

Before the sphere on the table Mazelier set up a tripod upon which he mounted a box like a small self-contained radio receiving apparatus. But instead of the usual installation, with its bulbs, rheostat, condensers, the box contained nothing but a complex of prisms set at varying angles and a multiplex of lead-sheathed wires. Prisms and wires were detached and re-attached in different combinations, finally appearing at the base of the box in order of size, while on the table before them other prisms were connected up in the opposite order.

"You know, Gribal, that invisible and unsuspected forms of radiation can, when concentrated, upset and confound everything that has been known, up to the present, as a law of nature. Since I have been experimenting in this field, I have become convinced that the so-called natural laws have no real existence. Does that scandalize you?"

"Yes, it does, I admit it. But you have already convinced me laws of nature are nothing but convenient conventions which give us some ground to work from while we are roaming in the prodigious field of phenomena nature presents."

"Right! One must admit that radiation has an existence of its own; the rays have caprices, angers, individual tastes and sympathies. They behave as they like; they do whatever they wish, and to use them one has only to find their preferences. They are comparable to certain people sitting down to dinner, who only eat the dishes they like. Now let's see whether I have succeeded in pleasing this lot. At least I have neglected nothing that ought to please them."

Mazelier closed the box, and attached to its cover another tripod with long sharp points. Then, he carefully turned the whole apparatus this way and that, pointing it in the direction of the Rue Cortambert with the aid of a map of Paris. Finally, he regulated one of the dials placed before the sphere.

"What time is it, Gribal?"

"Exactly 8:30 p.m."

"Good. We have plenty of time. Nothing will happen before 9."

"You think that the Marquis will stick to his program of going out this evening?"

"I am altogether persuaded that the Marquis will think me incapable not only of preventing, but even of defending myself against his attacks at present."

"Just the same he ought to remember that you have escaped him up to now."

"Yes, but his dispositions were not well taken, his apparatus far from complete. Even without my intervention something happened to upset his calculations. But remember what he accomplished that day last October. It was really prodigious."

"What! You still believe that that man is a genuine scientist?"

"Yes, and a scientist of genius."

"You astonish me. I take him for one of those clever amateurs like those courtly gentlemen who studied the structure of the atom under the Cardinal de Rohan in the time of Louis XVI while they were hunting for the philosopher's stone. But a genius—I rather doubt it. But tell me, about that note he sent you—?"

"Oh, I deserved that crack, my dear Gribal."

"All right, I don't want to argue with you about it. Anyhow, it's a declaration of war."

"It would seem like that."

"Then why is he running away to Biarritz after having threatened you?"

"And who told you he was running away? What time is it now?"

"8:55."

"It's time."

Mazelier pressed a button at the base of the box he had set up and bent over it, listening.

"Nothing yet. Wait a minute. Let me take your watch, Gribal. I am the limit; I completely forgot to wind up my own. Thanks. 8:56, 7... Ah, listen. The Marquis' chauffeur is starting up his motor."

A sort of soft purring, like the sound of water boiling in a teakettle, came from the great sphere.

"Do you hear?" inquired Mazelier, who could not conceal his nervousness. "Now watch my direction indicator. There, Gribal, the tripod on the box. It is suspended so that it can make a complete turn. Automatic, Gribal, it's automatic. Look, it's swinging to the left. Good—now a little to the right. Look, look, what a sharp swing to the right. The Marquis must be about passing the Palais-Royal. What did I tell you? We can follow him wherever he goes. Ah, see, the tripod is

337

pointing to the south. The Marquis' car is headed for the Porte d'Orléans. He must be going to take the Estampes road. Good, good. Now he's slowing up. Ah, he's opened her up again, always in the same direction. Look, the dial indicates 30 kilometers and it's only been 15 minutes. We'll have to act sooner than we thought."

The purring from the sphere continued, synchronously, one would have sworn, with the sound of a big motor, powerful and regular. The direction indicator no longer wavered. It seemed to Gribal that he could hear the beating of his heart answered from the center of the shining sphere. What he was seeing, here in the midst of Paris, in the laboratory of a government establishment, did it not resemble some scene out of a book of medieval magic?

Mazelier no longer busied himself over anything but the slow flight of the hands on the face of Gribal's watch. All at once, he cried out:

"Ready with the lever, there. I'm going to count to ten. At the tenth count, swing it to the left. One...Two...Three..."

The seconds went past with a desperate slowness; an effort of will-power was necessary for him to restrain himself from throwing the lever before the signal. After a century, it arrived.

"Ten!" said Mazelier.

Gribal swung the lever. And suddenly the sphere was silent; the tripod oscillated violently from left to right, then swung completely around and came to rest, pointing northward.

Pale with emotion, Gribal, not daring to say a word, held his breath. Mazelier, also, was paler than usual. But he consulted dial and sphere, and then in his grave, quiet scientist's voice, indifferent to the emotions that were stirring the engineer, he said:

"Monsieur de Saint-Imier's auto has turned over on the Estampes road, 50 kilometers from Paris." And he added tranquilly: "Let's go along to bed, Gribal. Tomorrow morning the newspapers will tell us the rest."

On the next morning, as a matter of fact, nearly all the papers had on the first page an account of the mysterious accident that had occurred on the Estampes road, near Chamarande. But after he had read the story, Gribal rubbed his eyes and then read it again, and leaped from his breakfast table to run to the office where he would find Mazelier. The account ended in this fashion:

One of the most striking personalities in the fashionable world of Paris, especially well known in artistic circles, the Marquis de Saint-Imier, was the victim of an inexplicable accident last evening. The Marquis de Saint-Imier had left Paris at 9 p.m. to go to Biarritz in his car, which was driven by his chauffeur, the Indo-Chinese Pou-Hi, an experienced driver who has been in his service for some time. While traveling at high speed near Chamarande on the Estampes road, about 50 kilometers from Paris the accident occurred.

Police investigation has established that the Marquis' car was alone on the road at the time, and that it was without obstacles. All at once the car stopped short although the motor was still functioning perfectly and the tires were undamaged. There was a considerable shock and the car turned completely over, hurling the Marquis de Saint-Imier and the chauffeur out. The latter has a broken arm and possible internal injuries. The Marquis escaped with cuts and bruises.

From declarations made to the police the accident remains completely inexplicable. An examination of the car, which was badly damaged, showed that the motor, tires and other running parts were without defects.

Another auto passing the scene of the accident five minutes later, carried the chauffeur Pou-Hi to Estampes where he was placed in the hospital. The Marquis de Saint-Imier, after having received medical treatment, was able to take the Bordeaux express and continue his journey to Biarritz, where he is to be the guest of Señor Cuchillo, one of the most prominent members of the Argentine colony in France.

Gribal dashed into the laboratory, brandishing his newspaper.

"Did you see it, Professor? Decidedly, these scoundrels have all the luck."

Mazelier smiled.

"Never mind, Gribal, be calm. You forget that we also have had our bits of luck. Remember that Pou-Hi didn't succeed in running down Paulette either."

"Yes. But you saw that the Marquis alluded to some unknown force during the investigation. Don't you think that remark was addressed to us?"

"There is not the slightest doubt of it."

"And don't you think he will try an answer?"

"It is highly probable."

"And that doesn't stir you?"

"No use being emotional about it, my friend."

"Right. But that leaves us in the position of a condemned man waiting for the executioner. How are we going to defend ourselves?"

"Always in the same way that has been successful in the past."

And without giving Gribal time to answer, Mazelier went on:

"It mentions a Señor Cuchillo, Gribal. Do you know that *caballero* by any chance?"

"Cuchillo? *Parbleu!* He's a big race-track man and has a chateau in Corrèze. And I believe he is the author of what they call the Cuchillo syllogism."

"Ah, a syllogism. What is it?"

"Well, it was at a banquet last year that Señor Cuchillo said something like this—There are plenty of sheep in the Argentine. Now with sheep, one can make wool. With wool, one can make tapestries. Therefore we have a tapestry industry in the Argentine."

"Not a bad piece of reasoning if one admits that wool is all there is needed for tapestries."

339

His superior's calm and humor succeeded in reassuring Gribal.

"Well, Professor, what do we do next?"

The scientist replied: "Well, if you are willing, we will take a little trip. It will give us a change. Would you like to go with me?"

"Professor, you know very well, I would go with you to the end of the world."

"Take it easy, my friend, take it easy. The end of the world, that's quite a distance. And I can't leave for three days yet. So, in three days—"

"Yes," said Gribal, "a good deal can happen in three days."

"Things will happen, never doubt that. Then you will come?"

"And where will we be going?"

"To Biarritz," said Mazelier simply.

It is evident that if the Marquis de Saint-Imier had not lived in the center of society, the newspapers would have been silent about his auto accident. The celebrated "unknown force" which alone could have stopped Pou-Hi's car did not arouse much curiosity, for the very good reason that no one believed in its existence. Everyone who knew the Chinese—and these were a considerable number in the Passy section—had very clear opinions on the subject; Pou-Hi was a two-fisted drinker, and though he was also a splendid chauffeur, there was some talk. But Pou-Hi was one of those silent drinkers whose potations seem to make them more careful and more skillful.

When one intends driving from Paris to Biarritz in a single night, one has need of an extraordinary degree of strength.

Pou-Hi had strengthened himself by means of glasses of whiskey, taken in company with Suzie. Nobody doubted that the "unknown force" was a force from inside the bottle. Pou-Hi, sobered by the force of the accident, had simply told his master a likely story, and the latter had pretended to believe him.

Therefore, nobody in Paris thought of the Marquis any more, and Gribal was astonished to find the world very calm and very much inclined to mind its own business. The journey to Biarritz had to be held up; the scientist was having a series of interviews with the Minister of Science on the subject of the personnel of the office and its budget for the coming year.

But if Mazelier did not make his voyage, Madame Ghislaine Roberval took precisely the opposite decision at about the same time. Since the night when the fashionable world had seen her snub the Marquis at the ministry, she had decided to marry Monsieur Gabriel de Neuville, and she was distinctly worried. She knew the Marquis for a man capable of terrible revenges, and was certain that he would avenge the slight somehow. But when? And how? This rich and beautiful woman, who had everything needed to make her happy, could not avoid melancholy presentiments. It seemed to her that once she was married again, she would be in considerably less danger.

Her fiancé certainly made no objections. But Madame Roberval did not wish to be married in Paris. She feared some *contretemps* arranged by the Marquis, some noisy scandal that he might bring up.

"But what do you expect him to do?" inquired de Neuville. "I will notify the prefect of police, my dear Ghislaine, and I assure you that we will be thoroughly protected against anything of the kind."

Madame Roberval shook her head:

"No, Gabriel, no! We must not be married in Paris."

"But I must stay here for the present. I have been appointed secretary of this new international conference; the minister would never let me absent myself now."

"Try to accomplish the impossible, then. We must get away—to Italy or England."

"I would like nothing better. But I repeat, it is impossible. Besides, you know very well that the Marquis is at Biarritz now."

"Are you certain that it is not only done to deceive us?"

"Oh, certainly. He is there all right, and very busy. The fashionable world is talking of nothing but his eccentricities there."

Madame Roberval did not seem convinced. She did not know quite what she feared, and hardly wished to annoy her fiancé with nameless terrors.

What was she concealing? This: that in the voice of the loudspeaker in the Place de l'Opéra she also had recognized that of Saint-Imier! How could she confide to anyone, even her future husband, the terrors so vague that they seemed ill-founded which were stirring her? Neuville would certainly have laughed at her fright and remarked that the best loudspeakers deform the human voice to a greater or less extent. And after all, had the Marquis succeeded in his effort? No. Had he tried again? No. The fact was that he seemed to have even abandoned his effort to pursue Madame Roberval.

These arguments, which her spouse-to-be would certainly have advanced, were a long way from convincing Ghislaine. She was quite certain that the Marquis had not in the least given up. And a strange thing had happened; she had seen him, in flesh and blood, following along the street, approaching as she went in the other direction, moving away when she approached, at the very moment when the society columns were publishing the news of her persecutor's being in another city and far away. The unhappy woman had arrived at the state of asking herself whether she were not the victim of hallucinations, but she confided her fears to no one.

Nevertheless, the day arrived when Gabriel de Neuville arrived with good news; the trip to Italy had become possible and with it a prolonged honeymoon. Madame Roberval found her lost tranquility in the announcement. She felt sure that as soon as she had become Madame de Neuville, she could arrange things so they would stay in Italy or somewhere else, anywhere else, provided it was not Paris.

Ghislaine was going to take the express to Vintimille. Her fiancé would follow by auto and meet her at Nice. Naturally Gabriel de Neuville accompanied her to the station and saw her safely installed in her compartment. They stayed, chatting for a few minutes while the train prepared for its departure. After about 20 minutes de Neuville glanced at his watch.

"The express is late already, my dear. If this keeps up I'll be in Nice before you are."

He laughed, not really annoyed at a delay which permitted him several moments more of conversation with her. But suddenly, glancing out of the window, he noticed a singular stir in the station. It looked as though all the travelers were getting out of the train. He got out with them. A hasty announcement was made:

"Breakdown somewhere. They're going to change locomotives. It will take at least 45 minutes. Take the express on the other track."

Neuville would have liked to ask more precise information, but the functionary who made the announcement had already disappeared, surrounded by a crowd of impatient passengers. The diplomat returned to Ghislaine and told her the news.

"Do you really believe that?" asked the young woman, incredulously.

"But... Anyhow, that's the official explanation."

"It won't hold water, my friend. You ought to know more than that about official reasons for things."

Madame Roberval spoke in a joking tone, but a strange feeling of disquietude rose in her.

"A breakdown before the engine has even started," she went on. "It's incredible. And that long to change locomotives. It's impossible. Well, let's change trains anyhow."

"I'll carry your bags. What a mob! It's odious."

The confusion was general, and everybody was talking at once. A voice arose, dominating the individual voices:

"The trains aren't running!"

Neuville, annoyed, grumbled:

"Ah, no, what are you telling us now? A joke, a little heavy, that joke. Why aren't the trains running? They arrived here, didn't they?"

As a matter of fact there were several trains stalled in the station.

But one had to admit it; none of them were moving.

13. The Voice Again

Soon the news was coming in from every station of Paris, the inexplicable, phenomenal news. The fact, quickly verified, was that for some reason, not a train was running. The incoming trains rumbled in as usual; but they stayed.

342

The travelers, after having delivered the usual noisy protests which such a situation might be expected to call forth, went home. A good many of them, like Madame Roberval, did not give up their intention of traveling. If the trains were not moving, autos were. She, defying the conventions in this case of necessity, got into Neuville's car.

Neuville was delighted.

Unfortunately, when his comfortable car arrived near the city limits, he noted with annoyance that he was preceded by an interminable jam of vehicles of all kinds and descriptions, vibrating solemnly with the running of their motors, but utterly immobile. It was the world's record traffic jam.

Their horns made an infernal concert of noise. In the midst of it, Ghislaine and de Neuville noticed an employee of the *octroi* [100] running down the line, waving his arms and crying out something that nobody heard.

As he approached they heard him. "You can't get past!" he was shouting. "Autos and airplanes have been halted like the trains. Nobody has got out of the city for an hour."

This time Ghislaine was very frightened, and Gabriel was powerless to comfort her. What was happening was not the effect of chance; all the autos, all the vehicles of Paris, brought to a stop, but only when they tried to get out of the city.

Somebody was stopping them at his own good pleasure.

And who was this somebody if not the individual mad with hate who had already sown abroad so much terror?

"I tell you it must be him!" insisted Ghislaine.

"My dear," replied Gabriel, tenderly, "don't be frightened. One lone man would certainly not be able to do so much. This is probably due to some curious cosmic perturbation which we will read all about in tomorrow's newspapers."

Ghislaine shook her head but did not insist. All the same, the evident optimism of her fiancé reassured her a little, and she did not wish to destroy it. She kept her secrets to herself. But Gabriel secured her promise to see him in the morning, when they would go for a walk in the Bois and discuss the date of their marriage, which would take place in Paris since it could not be performed elsewhere.

But, that same evening in the capital where every inhabitant had found himself literally made a prisoner, and where the dumbfounded scientists were trying to explain the affair by means of scientific theories which they did not understand, the abhorred voice again took possession of the radio.

It was during a lecture given by Monsieur Reynier-Vitral on "the food of the future." The eminent chemist was developing the theme so often taken up and abandoned by successive generations of biologists that there is no such thing

---

[100] A tax collecting body. *Octroi* was a duty on various goods brought into certain towns and cities in France. It was abolished in 1948.

as life; the human animal being nothing but a machine, and that the best means of repairing the worn parts of this machine is not necessarily food as it is generally understood; that the stomach is not necessarily made to digest food, the teeth to bite it, or the palate to taste it; that everything can be expressed in the form of energy, and the energy the individual needs to recuperate himself can be furnished in the form of electrical currents of a certain character by special electrical machinery.

As the lecture was being delivered at the hour when most people had just finished well-rounded dinners, it amused them very much. Monsieur Reynier-Vitral spread his theories before a sympathetic audience, and if he had been able to hear the comments of his auditors, he would no doubt have been surprised to discover they were laughing at him.

Suddenly, at the moment when the speaker, lifting his voice, was about to introduce a touch of pathos, he was interrupted by a dry and somewhat insolent comment. The loudspeakers said:

"Enough! Monsieur Reynier-Vitral, shut up. You have said enough stupid things to last a year."

Immediately there was a reply. Monsieur Reynier-Vitral had evidently heard the remark, for he said:

"Oh, come, that's, not decent. Are you drunk, my friend?"

The lecturer must have thought that the voice came from the announcer just behind him.

"Monsieur Reynier-Vitral, don't insist! Your lecture is over. Nothing that you say will be heard. I am the only one who will be able to hear what you say. What? You say you will complain to the authorities? Complain ahead, I wish you luck."

The public was amused, thinking it was something arranged in advance, like one of those scenes in the theater in which confederates in the audience answer the actors on the stage. That a person of the eminent respectability of Monsieur Reynier-Vitral should take such a part was a bit odd, but Paris contented itself with thinking that he must have been paid extremely well to take so ridiculous a part, a part which made all the other scientists of the world ridiculous at the same time.

A farce improvised by means of the radio, that was something really new! It was doubtless the first announcement of a great new discovery for once Reynier-Vitral had heard the other speaker, it was evident that it had become possible in some way for the hearers of a program to make the speaker hear them. What a vista! To be able to make the artist hear one's applause, hisses, or caustic comments, while one remained comfortably seated in one's armchair before the fire.

Or was it a joke on Reynier-Vitral? He would be the object of all the jesters of Paris the next day, and would probably sue the radio company for having asked him to lecture, and that would be the funniest of all.

Suddenly, amid the universal gaiety, the familiar voice fell like a douche of cold water.

"*Listen! It was I who threatened you all on the 18th of last October. You have already forgotten; you did not wish to understand. Remember the sudden dark, the terrible cold that you passed through. I wished to destroy the world, and you thought, I was crazy, didn't you? Because I did not complete the experiment, you said, 'It is impossible.'*"

In the different parts of Paris where loudspeakers were installed in public squares the crowd listened, curious but not scared. The unknown no longer frightened them; his bluff would end in a check, as before.

The voice went on: "*Haven't I given you sufficient proofs of my power?*"

In the Place de l'Opéra, a single voice rose:

"Razzberry!"

At the same moment, near the Etoile, another voice cried out:

"You'd think he was claiming he didn't do it."

The voice replied, with an indefinable accent of disdain:

"*I didn't do it? You poor idiots; do you think I'm excusing myself, like a practical joker whose joke didn't come off? Listen! I am going to tell you my conditions; the conditions, Parisians, on which I will permit you to continue living.*"

The voice was silent for a moment, then went on with increasing violence: "*Listen! Listen! If you don't all want to be killed at the moment I have chosen, you must give up three victims to me. Two men and a woman. I wish the two men to perish like two animals, surrounded by the execration of their kind. Whoever tries to help them will perish with them.*"

The actions of the crowd on hearing this singular explosion of anger resembled defiance more than fear.

Nevertheless, there were no voices raised in protest. The unknown, who struck from a distance, as though he were endowed with the gift of hearing and seeing everything on the spot, paralyzed the indignation of those who heard him because he remained hidden. Where could one find him, how could he be struck at?

A sort of savage laugh vibrated from the loudspeakers. Then the voice went on. "*I will give eight days to those I have mentioned to put an end to their existence. Let them be grateful to me for permitting them to choose their own forms of death, to commit suicide easily. If they have not died within the eight days there will not remain a single living being in the whole of Paris! All you who hear me now will die in the midst of the most frightful sufferings. But not all at the same time; for I have thought the matter over. Instead of killing humanity off at a single blow, I will slaughter it in detail.*"

And the voice added, with another of its abominable laughs:

"*It will be much more amusing that way. Now listen; this is my last public communication. I will not again warn you of my intentions. But you can expect some unpleasant surprises. Since last October I have perfected my apparatus. This time, nothing can halt me."*

And suddenly, the voice became louder, more sonorous, to pronounce these terrible words: "*Have no pity on the men whose death I demand. They are nothing but highway robbers, assassins. I am going to give you their names, for they are cowards, they hide so that the people of Paris cannot find them to tear them in pieces. They are named—*"

The two names which should have been uttered were never pronounced! The loudspeakers carried to the crowd the noise of a brief clatter which was succeeded by silence, all the ordinary radio programs were off the air. Was it some new mystery? Then the voice came back, reinforced with new fury.

"*Those who are trying to interrupt me would do better to be demanding my mercy. No one can leave Paris without my permission. I have today given you all proof of that. What more do you need? Victims? You will not have long to wait. Beginning tomorrow I shall punish all those who are in my way. Listen! Listen! I am going to give you the names of the two men who shall die. They are—*"

As on the first occasion, there was nothing but a confusion of burbling sounds. And then laughter—the laughter of the listeners was clearly audible. But the strange communication to the public was not ended.

"*Listen, you who are laughing! You won't find it so funny tomorrow. For I now revoke the delay of eight days which you do not deserve. Tomorrow morning the first victims shall fall. I shall not stay my hand until you deliver the woman I hate over to me. The day after tomorrow she will be alone, in the middle of the Place de la Concorde. I shall go, I alone, to take her away from there, before all of you, who care to watch. For I do not fear you. You will see me tomorrow; I who challenge all of you will be there. And beware of trying to interrupt me; the man who attempts it will be struck by lightning. Do not try to deceive me; you will not succeed. The woman I demand, who is to be my slave is named—*"

An agonizing silence. Then a voice, breaking on a note of rage and powerlessness:

"*She is named—*"

Another silence. A power as strong as that of the unknown was opposed to the appeal he was making to the fear and the egoism of the multitude. And rightly; if the three names were pronounced how many cowards in the crowds that heard the voice might not have hurried to carry out its bidding in the hope of saving their own lives?

But the names were never pronounced. The vast majority of those who heard were convinced they were listening to a supreme and unique exhibition of bluff. If the names were not given, it was because the man of hate at the other end of the broadcasting line had decided, at the last moment, not to give them.

People thought so. But the general curiosity was held at fever heat by the number of curious communications that came in during the night. In London, a voice, speaking the most perfect English, had declared through the loudspeakers there:

"From this time on, no French vessel will be able to reach any port in the British Isles. No airplane coming from France will be able to land on British soil."

The London public is less easy to stir than that of Paris. But the communication caused a lively emotion of surprise, for it was thought to be an official announcement. What did it mean? Was war against France to be declared?

A denial from the First Lord of the Admiralty and from the authorities in charge of aeronautics came a few minutes later to calm the aroused public. The denial was followed by the statement that the author of the false information was being searched for and would be punished.

But, on the following morning the news came in that the same announcement had been made over the radios of Brussels, Rome, Berlin, Moscow, Madrid, Lisbon, Athens and New York. When the differences in latitude and longitude were calculated it was discovered that all these broadcasts had followed each other within 15 minutes.

Eight more official denials followed each other in rapid succession.

What was it—a joker's syndicate abroad on the air? The same person, even granting the utmost speed of transmission, could certainly not have made himself heard in so many places at the same time. Evidently, the chief of this mysterious band must have assistants in all these cities.

But the international astonishment grew still greater when it was discovered that the different countries forbidden to French ships and planes, by the voice on the radio, received no more visitors from France. Some magical influence immobilized the great liners at a distance from the coasts. The airplanes were forced down before they had crossed the frontiers of France. And what was worse, it soon became evident that the international trains that left Paris were not arriving either. It touched various interests in their most sensitive spot; it upset the European equilibrium like a war. The situation was impossible.

But it had to be made possible all the same. Shipping companies, airplane companies, railroad companies, took the necessary steps to limit the disaster as much as possible. The halting of the international trains had brought with it the stoppage of the trains within the borders; long lines of immobilized railroad cars crowded the tracks. The ports along the Mediterranean and the Atlantic were less overcrowded, but they were rapidly becoming encumbered as the captains of ships hesitated to put to sea. At the airdromes, all was silence and stagnation.

A final surprise was yet to come for France; for all Europe. An attempt to organize traffic in trucks was begun; and every truck halted, out of order at the edge of the country.

This time doubt was no longer possible. The mysterious voices which had made their announcements in the cities of the world were not those of jokers. But they remained mysterious. And the opinion of Europe turned back to the threats made in the previous October and the phenomena that had followed them. What object had the man who was thus girdling France into immobility? And if he was, indeed, serious, who were the victims he had demanded?

It was noticed that the states of Central Europe had not received the mysterious communications, nor had any county outside Europe with the sole exception of America. All the scientists of the world turned their resources on the problem, to solve the questions it aroused, but above all to put an end to the blockade of France, for her isolation menaced all with some unknown disaster. And the scientists of the world remained in complete darkness.

But how had the communications been made? For it had to be admitted that France and all the other countries that had received the messages were covered with an enormous network of radiation.

14. The First Victim

At the National Office of Scientific Research there was feverish activity under Mazelier's direction. The Minister of Science had never hidden his view that this office should be a sort of discovery-factory. Consequently, it was Mazelier's duty to make discoveries.

Mazelier had smiled when this viewpoint was presented to him, and then said:

"Your Excellency may count upon me."

The "Excellency" discovered in this statement a sort of promise to get immediate results, and communicated the good news to the cabinet.

"You see! I called in Mazelier. I admit that I don't think a great deal of him. He is a little too sharp with that tongue of his. But I know men, and I touched this one on his weak point. I said to him, 'Mazelier, you must discover the means of restoring peace and security to the world.' And he answered, 'Excellency, I will do it at once.' Isn't that a bit of all right?"

Mazelier was even more on the right trail than the minister imagined. In the laboratory, for the tenth time, he was discussing a matter of tactics with Gribal.

"But I don't understand," said Gribal. "You only have to make a single motion to return things to normal. Why don't you do it?"

"Can't you imagine, my friend?"

"No. Time is passing. The delay which the Marquis has been so gracious as to grant us for our double suicide is already half over."

"Are you afraid, Gribal?"

348

"You know very well I'm not, Professor. Just the same, I admit that I would like to know how we're going to get out of this. The scoundrel has got himself a whole new set of teeth and claws."

"Let's look things over, Gribal. The Marquis wishes to get rid of us. Has he succeeded? He tried a vague allusion to us when he spoke of highway robbers. But he couldn't do more without revealing his own name. Before leaving for Biarritz, he tried to turn the minister against me, but he didn't push the point hard enough and the poor minister didn't understand. Finally, he wanted to give our names to the crowd, and I cut him off after having let him make his little speech. And since then, what has he done? He has made use of the same forms of radiation we used on him on the Estampes road. I admit that he has made progress. But he must be allowed to believe that we are still behind him. That illusion will help us a lot."

"And the woman he threatened at the same time as us?"

"Wait and see who she is, Gribal. As to seeing her alone in the Place de la Concorde, I would like it very much. Things wouldn't turn out the way the Marquis expects."

"But he will make victims."

"He says so. We shall see tomorrow. He can't do as much as he thinks."

"If we only knew where he is!"

"I would like to know that myself."

"Haven't you calculated?"

"Result, nothing. The only thing I can be sure of is that he has left Biarritz for Paris to try to stir up a mob against us. Since then I have lost track of him. And I admit that I cannot make out how he was able to speak in eight or nine places at once in so short a space of time. It's really quite wonderful."

"What he's doing now doesn't help you in locating him?"

"No. Perhaps he has an automatic apparatus. But anyway, there is no hurry, Gribal."

"What, no hurry? But we'll really have a catastrophe on our hands if this keeps up."

"Yes, but it won't keep up. We can end it whenever we wish. Only, the lesson must be rubbed in on the public. Do you remember the day after the catastrophe of last October? Nobody took the destroyer of the world seriously. Now he is stalling our economic life, and there is unanimous indignation. If I had intervened too soon, what would have happened? Do you see? Well, I will tell you if you don't—you and I, Gribal, would be finished. For nobody would have believed us when we came to reveal what we know."

"And now?"

"Ah, now it's a little different. Fear is decidedly the mother of wisdom. The minister sent for me a few minutes ago."

"And what did you say to him?"

"Naturally, that I was still in the dark."

"But…"

"But, Gribal, you forget that the Marquis de Saint-Imier is a personal friend of the Minister."

"Ah," cried the engineer, "really, you have a good deal of courage to continue the combat under such conditions."

"True," said Mazelier placidly, "the conditions are not too good. But I have a date tonight; in fact, I'm going there right away. Will you go with me?"

"Where is it?"

"To the Elysée."

"To the President of the Republic?"

"The same. It will not be the first time that the President has shared a state secret. Come along, Gribal, this time, they will believe us; there is a national danger."

The two men rose.

"The Devil!" said Gribal, "we're stepping out. To the Elysée Palace! But it's a little embarrassing; I am not used to places like that and I warn you that if it's going to be necessary to go through my paces before him, it might not turn out right. I think it would be a good job if I stayed here instead of going along to try out life among the flunkies."

Mazelier was ordinarily grave, silent and even a little reserved. But Gribal's fears sent him off in a burst of laughter.

"What an idea of etiquette in a republic you have! Haven't you had enough practice in the art of bowing? *Mon Dieu*, what will happen to us? I don't know any more about it than you do—they'll probably have us guillotined for kissing the floor at the wrong moment."

And the scientist added, with genuine sincerity:

"As a matter of fact, I probably know less about etiquette than you do."

And then, went on, with another laugh.

"We can practice a little before we start, if you like."

It was Gribal's turn to laugh.

"Bah," he said, "they will excuse us in view of what we have to say."

"Ah, this time you have touched the mark. And now, Gribal, listen—I have never met the President, but they tell me he's a good sort; just the kind of man we need, in fact. I don't think the etiquette question will worry him much."

Calmed by this soothing thought, Gribal started toward the door of the laboratory. He was about to open it when Mazelier cried:

"Stop! Don't open."

In the scientist's pocket his radiation-indicator was giving forth its characteristic buzz.

"You see, Gribal! The Marquis is not going to wait for the expiration of the 24 hours he gave us before we popped ourselves off. He's taking matters into his own hands. The good fellow actually thinks he can get us before we get to him."

"I ought to have thought of that," said the engineer. "Would you believe it?—I actually thought the Marquis would keep his word, and that we still had some time before us."

"Do you know what this rushing the program proves, though? That things are not going quite as well as our gentleman would wish. If he anticipates himself, it's because he's afraid of something. And that's queer, too, because except for shutting him up when he was about to give names, I have let him go ahead as he liked."

The revelator continued its buzzing.

"Hunt, go ahead and hunt for us," said Mazelier. We're safe here, old scout. My turn will come, too."

But Gribal could not repress a little shiver at the thought that a tiger's cage would have been a slightly safer place than the outer laboratory beyond the protection that Mazelier had thrown around their inner walls.

The indicator continued its annoying and hateful buzz.

"Decidedly, he must have determined to make an end of us today," remarked the engineer.

"Yes, but I have taken the necessary precautions."

And Mazelier continued with a statement that surprised his companion:

"If he can see and hear at a distance, he at least can't see and hear into this room."

To see and hear at a distance? Had the Marquis solved this problem also? And was Mazelier still undisturbed?

These questions hurried through Gribal's mind and he was the victim of a sort of discouragement. It was impossible to blink at the facts; Mazelier and he had before them an adversary as strong as themselves, provided with fully as much inventive genius and having the advantage of a lack of scruples that permitted him to do things they would not do.

Mazelier had understood from the start that they would have to use the same weapons as their antagonist. But that might injure innocent people at a distance— and all at once the engineer was terrified by the thought that the Marquis might be pursuing a parallel line of research. The man who had made his voice heard in all the great cities of Europe and America would certainly be able to distribute his malignant radiations abroad in several different places at the same time. And if one of these projections touched Gribal's house? He himself was safe—but his wife? and the children?

He could not remain still.

"Professor! I must try to get out!"

"You're crazy. Why?"

"Who knows what's happening at my home?"

Mazelier replied in a tone of authority:

"Nothing is happening there. Be calm. While he's busy here, he can't be thinking of other attacks."

"Are you certain?"

"Absolutely."

But Gribal's disturbance gave rise to several useful ideas for Mazelier. As a matter of fact the Marquis might very well be looking elsewhere than at the office for his enemies. Already, he had attacked the engineer at home, and had struck the exact spot. As a consequence, Gribal must not go home at all. And as a second consequence, his family must leave the Rue Boissy d'Anglas as soon as possible.

"You must move, my friend, to some distance from Paris, and without saying a word to anyone. Madame Gribal had better pack a few indispensables in a valise and clear out at once—but listen, tell her not to pack any trunks or make any ostensible preparations. Send all of them away this very evening."

"And how are we going to let them know? We are imprisoned here."

The rattle of the revelator continued.

"True," admitted Mazelier. "He's keeping us in here. I could get us out, but to do so would be to reveal to him that I know the forms of radiation that he is using, and that I have an answer to them, and he must be kept in ignorance of this. Patience, Gribal! He'll get tired of the game before we do, I repeat it."

Suddenly, the ringing of the revelator came to a stop.

"Quick! Let's go," cried Gribal.

"Wait a minute. No hurry."

Mazelier waited silently, his head on one side.

"Listen, Gribal. What did I tell you? It's starting again."

The buzzing started again; then halted, and went on in a series of fits and starts at irregular intervals.

"Good thing I'm on the job," said the scientist. "But something isn't going right with the Marquis."

There was a sort of pulsating of the buzzer and then as though the emission apparatus had reached the limit of its power, there was complete silence.

"This time I think we can risk it," said Mazelier. "Now, let's move fast when we do move."

Gribal, mad with impatience, threw open the door, and dashed down the corridor, followed by his superior. The two men arrived at the vestibule of the office. A tenth of a second and they were in the street; a half a minute and they were in the avenue. All at once, Gribal sank like an inert sack of corn to the pavement, and at the same moment the revelator vibrated for a second and then became mute once more. But Mazelier had the time to hear a sarcastic voice, which seemed to come from someone standing directly at his side, murmur:

"Got one!"

He looked around; he was altogether alone, with the inanimate Gribal at his feet.

Not altogether alone; for Roland Duplay was hurrying to help him.

15. The House of Silence

Paulette, like everyone else, had heard the new series of threats addressed to the people of Paris who had been guilty of incredulity in the face of the approaching destruction of the world. But this time, Roger's little jokes brought no smile to her lips. She understood the full significance of these threats, which left her mother so indifferent. After all, why should the good woman pay any attention to words which had no special significance for her?

And Paulette had been careful not to say: "But it is father and Professor Mazelier whose deaths are demanded." It would have uselessly frightened her mother and her brother. But the young girl's agony was all the greater because she had to conceal it.

And who could the woman be that the Marquis threatened at the same time? Paulette imagined that it might be herself. The Marquis must hate her because he had tried to assassinate her.

And thus, the girl had two good reasons for silence.

But, though waiting for her father's return, she refused to go to bed, overwhelmed with anxiety. It was even with some annoyance that she listened to the chatter of her brother, who rattled along:

"Isn't that amusing? There's a story for you. He's going to stop the trains, the airplanes and the ships. Pretty smart, that fellow. I'd like to know how he does it? I'll get it, though, and soon. I'm working on it like anything. I've been studying radiology, magnetism, chemistry, and electricity. I'll get beyond you one of these days. And then, you watch what I do!"

Roger was not really indulging in useless boasts. As he said, he was working hard and making genuine progress; and Paulette was watching him with not a little envy, for she was making no progress at all.

Since the afternoon, when Duplay had drawn her from the jaws of death, Paulette had not once seen him. The young man seemed bent on avoiding her. What a bashful youth! He was actually afraid to hear gratitude expressed in a harmonious voice accompanied with a charming smile and a glance from a pair of eyes filled with good wishes and sympathy.

To see him again would have been a real pleasure to Paulette. She searched for reasons to explain his over-discretion and finally found only one that satisfied her:

"He's afraid that I'll keep him from working," she told herself.

And then she scolded herself.

"But why should I worry about it. He's not accountable to me for his actions. I hope he's not sick, but if he isn't, then it's none of my affair."

She forced herself not to think about him, and thought she was succeeding. But Madame Gribal, worried at her uneasiness, kept asking her:

"Don't you think it's queer that your father hasn't come home yet?"

"No, mother. You know very well that father and Professor Mazelier were to work late tonight."

"Yes, that idiot on the loudspeaker again. But when your father has to work late, he always sends some message. And he hasn't sent any. *Mon Dieu*! I hope—"

"No, no, mother," Paulette hastened to say, though she herself was still more worried.

At midnight, Madame Gribal could no longer restrain herself.

"I'm going to the office," she declared. "You wait for me here."

Paulette replied:

"Mother, let Roger and me go with you."

"But if your father comes while we are out? He will be worried about all of us."

"I'll leave a note for him, on the table here. He can see it right away."

Paulette got a piece of paper and wrote on it: "Father, we have gone to the office to look for you. Well be right back."

"There. He'll understand when he sees that. Are you coming, mother?"

The girl hurried into her wraps.

Roger asked: "Are you going to take a taxi?"

"Yes, yes," said the worried mother. "Come on, let's go. Hurry up, please!"

Three minutes later she was knocking at the door of Père Bibent's lodge.

"What are you doing here, Madame Gribal?" Her face showed so much worry and strain that he added: "What's the matter? Has something happened?"

"My husband has not come home. Is he still here?"

"I believe so... But certainly, Madame. I haven't seen either one of the gentlemen go out."

"Will you tell him I'm waiting for him here?"

"Right away, Madame Gribal. But you know, Professor Mazelier and he have stayed shut up in their laboratory all day long. I had some letters to take up, and when I knocked at the door no one answered. I think they didn't want to be disturbed."

Paulette was about to say: "You see, mother. They are busy."

But Madame Gribal, at the limit of her patience, would no longer listen to anything. She ordered: "Go on up. Knock until they open up. And if necessary, break in the door!"

Père Bibent was scandalized, but did not let it be seen. He went up the stairs as fast as his old legs would carry him. Five minutes went by—five centuries!

Père Bibent came back down. He was alone.

"I knocked and shouted," he explained, "but no one answered. I don't think there's anyone there."

Madame Gribal felt her knees giving way beneath her. Paulette had more courage; her father had repeated to her many times that she was never, under any circumstances, to lose her coolness of head. Neither fear, nor despair, nor pain, could prevent her brain from registering impressions, from reasoning, unless deprived of her senses.

"But you say that you haven't seen them go out!" cried the girl. "Then they must be in."

Afraid there would be a scandal, Père Bibent lost his head completely.

"But look," he babbled, "I haven't left my lodge."

"Think. You are certain? You haven't left your lodge for a moment, and you haven't seen anybody asking for Professor Mazelier or my father?"

"Oh, on that point, I'm certain, Mademoiselle. Nobody has asked for them."

"Then they must still be up there," repeated Paulette. "I'm going up to see for myself."

Père Bibent thought it over. All at once he struck his forehead with his hand, and said:

"But how stupid I have been! I was out three times during the day. Oh, not for a long time—a minute or two. Listen, Madame, the last time was not 20 minutes ago, possibly 15. Am I crazy or losing my memory? I went down to the corner of the Rue de Marignan for some tobacco. Just long enough to go there and back. Mademoiselle, it must have been then that they went out. Look, Madame, it could not be otherwise. For, as to being up there, they aren't. I made enough noise to wake the dead. They must be out."

Like a faithful echo Roger repeated: "Evidently. They must have gone out."

Paulette, somewhat more at ease, added: "See. Everything is explained now."

Père Bibent went on: "Madame, you must have missed your husband on the way. At the same moment you were coming to look for him, he went to find you."

"Let's go quickly, mother."

Thus brought back to hope, Madame Gribal permitted her children to lead her along. Moreover, the *concierge's* explanation was not impossible. And for that matter, in a few moments it would be decided.

As the taxi drew up at the door Paulette leaped out, leaving Roger the duty of accompanying their mother. She climbed rapidly up the stairs. Then she rang, hoping her father would open the door. But the door did not open. Paulette had to get out her key to get in.

In the entry she called: "Father! Here we are!"

No answer.

"Are you there, father?"

Paulette hurried through the dining room, her father's office, the bedroom, her own room and that of Roger.

Nobody! All the rooms were empty.

Madame Gribal and her son came in. When she looked at Paulette, it was unnecessary to ask a single question; she understood without words. Incapable of keeping up any longer, she gave one feeble cry and fainted.

Paulette perceived that it is sometimes difficult to keep one's head cool. A single sentence danced through her brain, "Father has not come home!" For a moment, she stood overwhelmed, inert, filled only with an immense distress. But the sight of her mother, flat on the floor before her, brought her back to her senses, and she bent to help her.

From her bedroom she brought the smelling salts, a carafe of water. What did one do? Paulette hesitated for a second, and then held the salts under her mother's nose.

After a moment she opened her eyes and began to move uneasily.

"Get some pillows!" called Paulette.

Roger hurried off to do it.

"Help me lift mother up. Good. Mother, mother! Are you comfortable now, mother? Do you hear me?"

Paulette, by a kind of instinct, knew that she must distract her mother's attention by an excess of words. But her mother had not quite come out of her faint; she was in a state of semi-consciousness in which she certainly did not understand the words her daughter was pronouncing so rapidly.

But Paulette, while continuing her chatter, found time to whisper over her shoulder to Roger: "Quick! Bring a doctor."

The boy did not even wait to put on a cap. He leaped for the door with the intention of racing down the four flights even more rapidly than he had descended them that morning, when he had slid down the banister.

But, having made a single bound, he came to a full stop before the door.

Paulette, surprised and angry, called to him: "Hurry up, you little fool! What are you waiting for?"

"Listen. Someone's coming up. They're right here."

"*Mon Dieu!*" cried Paulette. "Ringing our bell!"

Through her head flashed the thought:

If it were father he would come in without ringing?

She had not the strength to go to the door, but she braced herself for a shock. Only a bearer of ill news would call at so late an hour.

Roger had opened for the visitor. Paulette looked at her mother; Madame Gribal had heard the bell. She too, her hands joined and tense, awaited the blow of fate.

With a step that had an appearance of firmness she got to her feet and advanced toward the entry. Why didn't the visitor come in quicker? What was he saying to Roger? She wished to know, and at once.

At this moment, the visitor, accompanied by Roger, came into the dining room. Paulette gave an exclamation of surprise that was almost joyous. It was Roland Duplay!

"You!" she cried.

Then, suddenly, she was in confusion, hardly daring to lift her eyes. Roland placed a finger on his lips and held out a slip of paper, indicating that she was to read it before speaking.

Paulette read: *I have come on a mission for Monsieur Gribal. But, on your life, don't say a single word about it, aloud.*

Paulette passed the paper to her mother. The unhappy woman, at the end of her strength, lacked neither courage nor hope.

She glanced at the young man in a way that said more plainly than in words: "You have come from my husband. Is he dead or alive?"

Roland looked back at Madame Gribal and his severe face relaxed in a smile; the first Paulette had even seen on his face.

He took back the slip of paper and wrote upon it: "*Monsieur Gribal is now out of danger. He is waiting for you. I have a letter from him to give.*"

And Paulette wrote at the bottom of the paper:

"*Mother, Monsieur Duplay is all right. You can rely on him.*"

The young man pulled from his pocket an envelope, which he tendered to Madame Gribal at the same moment that Paulette passed her the paper, with the news concerning her husband.

Roger understood nothing of this singular scene. Why did everyone write notes instead of speaking? But as his mother and sister observed the same silence as their visitor, he imitated them.

Madame Gribal, meanwhile, was reading the letter from her husband:

My dear wife and beloved children:

I have just escaped from a terrible danger, but don't be worried, I am safe now. The danger threatens you, however, as long as you remain in the apartment. Fly, fly immediately. Don't wait to take a single thing with you. Follow the bearer of this letter; he will bring you to me. Don't speak to a living soul. I beg you, fly. In two hours we will be together again.

Gribal.

No doubt possible; it was the handwriting, the signature of the engineer. Nevertheless, Madame Gribal, happy though she was over the assurance of her husband's safety, was a trifle suspicious. Fly—but why? Immediately—but what about money? And where? And how would they go?

Ah, what a lot of questions remained undecided. But with Paulette it was otherwise. All worry disappeared, she felt almost joyous, as though she were already beyond all alarms and peril. What had already happened had been only the expected. As to what would happen in the future, she felt only that once the family was reunited they would be invincible. And moreover, Roland Duplay, once before her savior, was at hand.

357

She had become so habituated to the idea of miracles, among the extraordinary events through which they had been passing, that the appearance of the young man, at this time and place, seemed altogether natural. And as her father's wishes accorded exactly with her own, she had only to obey without discussion.

As soon as the fugitives had left the apartment, Paulette closed the door noiselessly. The concierge let them out without being spoken to, and there remained only the people who lived on the floor below, who must have thought they were going to the theater rather late in the evening.

In the Rue Boissy d'Anglas, Duplay silently motioned for them to follow him. He led the way up the street, almost to the Madeleine, turned into a covered passage at the left, and came out on the Rue Faubourg Saint-Honoré. There, a powerful car was drawn up at the curb. The young man opened the door.

"Get in, mother," whispered Paulette.

Madame Gribal thought she must be dreaming. To bolster up her courage she repeated to herself the words her husband had written: "In two hours we will be together again." Two hours in an auto—at least 75 miles. She got in. Roger and Paulette took their places beside her. The girl left the door open, thinking that Duplay would join them.

"But where is the chauffeur?" asked Roger, forgetting the injunction to silence.

Madame Gribal understood no better than her son what danger there could be in speaking aloud a few feet from the Rue Royale. Roger's question seemed to have something in it; she glanced at Paulette.

She, who looked at the door with something like regret, silently indicated Duplay, who had installed himself at the wheel.

The sight left her a little thoughtful, for Roland could hardly have a very clear notion of the right way of piloting a 100 HP car.

Nevertheless, everything went well. Duplay apparently knew the geography of Paris to perfection, for with singular accuracy, he followed all the least frequented streets, and those where there were the fewest encumbrances. He conducted them thus to the Place des Ternes, turned to the right, ran along the length of the exterior boulevards and arrived at the Porte de la Chapelle.

By this time Paulette was certain that the wheel was in experienced hands.

But he stopped 100 yards from the *octroi*. What was there to stop them? Roger, with his cap pulled down over his eyes, stuck his head out for a peek.

"Traffic jam," he whispered.

Fifty or more vehicles, with more coming up every moment, waited, silently. Paulette understood. Roland had run into that unknown force which was blockading all the Parisians in Paris.

But, what now? For Paulette recognized that this second blockade could very well have been established to keep the car, for which Gribal was waiting somewhere, in Paris. She understood that the injunction to silence had not been imposed upon them without some reason. And Roger had twice broken it, and her mother, who sighed out her impatience and renewed fear in a series of gasps.

She glanced at Duplay. He turned at the same moment, met her eyes, and gave her a nod which signified: "Don't worry."

Then, while the rest of the lineup made a terrific hubbub with their horns and voices, he descended from the driver's seat to draw down all the curtains that seemed to be made of leather, and were placed outside the car.

In the interior the darkness was complete. Madame Gribal was the prey of terrors. She would not have hesitated to leap from the car and return to the Rue Boissy d'Anglas had she not held her husband's letter firmly clutched in her hand. As to Roger, he would certainly have made a racket if his sister had not suddenly placed her hand over his mouth.

But neither the fright of the mother nor the annoyance of the son were of long duration. The interior of the auto was lit with a strange and feeble luminescence, sufficient for the occupants, but not enough to pierce the outside curtains. At the same moment there came a terrific racket outside, the sound of many voices.

"At last! Not too soon, I'll say."

"Let's go."

"It was a joke."

"Farewell, dear heart. I'm off to the country."

"Hey, everybody! Good-bye and thanks."

Shouts of all kinds came from the chauffeurs of the vehicles in the line ahead of that which held the Gribal family. They felt the car slowly getting into motion, following the others which were crossing the barrier.

But to their profound surprise, it seemed to Roger and Paulette that cries of rage and imprecations were coming from the drivers of the cars behind them, and then from the drivers of those which were all about.

Had they not moved after all? It sounded as though a hole in the invisible curtain had opened before Roland to shut down again immediately behind him.

But the auto began to travel with a velocity that gave Madame Gribal the sensation that they had left the earth and were flying. Then they gradually slowed down; the pale light went out suddenly, the auto stopped; the leather curtains went up again, and a voice pronounced the following delightful words in the midst of the peaceful night:

"Madame, we are safe, and we will arrive in ten minutes. You can speak as loud as you wish now."

Roger profited by the permission to say: "Don't let anything keep you from going as fast as you like. Speed is very agreeable to me."

16. An Audience With the President

Ghislaine Roberval had guessed better than Paulette at the name of the woman the Marquis had wished to announce to the mob. Why had Saint-Imier not given it after the preliminaries? The idea that a power as strong as his own had prevented him did not occur to her.

She had promised her fiancé to meet him in the Bois de Boulogne. Dare she keep the appointment? Not to go would be to worry Gabriel de Neuville, who, like everyone else, had heard the Marquis' threats, and already knew enough to be able to guess the rest. But to go—would that not be to place herself in the lion's jaws?

But after all, what would she be risking? She would go—and immediately. Nevertheless—fear paralyzed her. If the Marquis should have accomplices? If one of them had been told to kidnap Ghislaine Roberval? A kidnapping in broad daylight—Saint-Imier was quite capable of so audacious an action.

Ah, how she regretted the past, when still a young girl she had been flattered to see the Marquis paying attentions to her. She had imprudently accepted his advances until the day when chance had allowed her to see his basic character, vile and cruel. She was certain, now, that the Marquis would stop at nothing... Well, in that case, the thing to do was to be with her fiancé, who would be able to defend her.

She went to the Bois. Gabriel was already waiting near the Pré Catalan. As usual, he was calm and smiling, and seemed unconscious of any possible danger.

"My dear Ghislaine, I hope that the ridiculous announcements that everybody has been hearing, have not disturbed your sleep?"

"Alas, yes! I'm really frightfully worried."

Neuville began to laugh: "Why? Because a practical joker wants to gather a big crowd around the Place de la Concorde this afternoon?"

"You're laughing? But why has the crowd been invited? Can't you imagine what woman he was talking about?"

"My dear, keep cool, and don't worry. Of two possibilities, one must be a fact, either it's the Marquis de Saint-Imier with one of his excesses again—and if it is, I promise you that I, for one, won't hesitate to denounce him. He's beginning to be annoying, that animal. Now, if it isn't he—"

"But it is, Gabriel, I don't doubt it for a minute."

"In that case, he can come to the Place de la Concorde as he has announced. He will find me there to pull his nose for him."

"Gabriel, don't go."

"I beg your pardon. I shall be the first one on the spot."

"But this man has extraordinary methods of..."

"*Parbleu!* Do you think so?"

"But this blockade of Paris and then of all France?"

"My dear Ghislaine, according to what I heard at the Ministry of Foreign Affairs, the Marquis had nothing to do with that. Do you know what caused it? A Japanese scientist living in Russia has made an enormous electromagnet with extraordinary powers, and he is performing some experiments at our expense, that's all."

"But the Marquis is using the results of those experiments. He has said as much."

"Bah! He's a boaster. It's another of his lies."

Ghislaine and Gabriel were alone, all alone, in a little glade. All at once they heard a voice near them murmur:

"Diplomats who talk too much never get anywhere."

Gabriel cried: "Who is following us?"

He looked around, but saw nobody.

Madame Roberval, trembling, had let go his arm. She was about to say: "It's the Marquis' voice."

But she did not have time. Gabriel de Neuville, as though struck by lightning, rolled at her feet.

"Got two!" cried a strident voice.

Ghislaine would have cried out, screamed for help, but she remained mute with terror; the Marquis, grinning terribly, stood suddenly before her. It was like an apparition; for he vanished as he had come…

A suddenly-organized search failed to find any trace of anyone. The examination of Gabriel de Neuville's body failed to show the slightest trace of a wound. It was thus established that what Ghislaine declared to be a crime was nothing but a sudden heart-failure on the part of her fiancé.

Mazelier did not care much for official society, and the President of the Republic was reported to be not particularly fond of that of scientists. But Mazelier had to lay before the head of the country, who understood nothing of such subjects, the reasons why France was cut off from the rest of the world and Paris from the rest of France. How would he manage to do it?

On his side, the President expected to see before him a man filled with the pride of recondite information who would tell him a great many incomprehensible things and make a lot of demands he did not wish to meet. It was impossible to believe that the man who, they told him, was the only one in France capable of saving the situation, would not ask for very considerable rewards.

Mazelier and the first magistrate of the Republic were, therefore, equally on their guard when they found themselves in each other's presence in the presidential office. They looked at each other…and suddenly their strained faces relaxed a little. They had, by a species of telepathy, seen themselves in each other, equally simple, equally enemies of bunk and useless words. The ice was broken immediately.

"Professor Mazelier," said the President, "I beg you to be seated."

"Thank you, Monsieur le President. I have not yet slept tonight and—"

"You have been working continuously, and I have doubtless interrupted you in sending for you. But you understand the situation. This blockade, to which we are submitted, is both ridiculous and terrible. Can you get us out of it?"

"Very easily."

"And when?"

"Right away, if you insist. I may add that if I have not already ended it, it is for excellent reasons, which I ask your permission to lay before you."

"Speak! Speak!" cried the stupefied President.

"I have voluntarily allowed this state of affairs to continue, although it is truly embarrassing, in the hope that the man who brought it about will be obliged to come out in the open."

"But we know who it is!"

"Really, Monsieur le President?"

"The information is certain. It is a Japanese scientist, with a new electro-magnet, who has caused it."

A burst of laughter, in defiance of etiquette, shook the presidential assurance a trifle.

"You don't agree with that, Professor Mazelier?"

"Not for a minute, Monsieur le President. The author of the blockade of Paris is in possession of formidable weapons. He is threatening the most abominable crimes and he has already committed some this night."

"What?"

"Yes; it is the same man who dared to invite the public to a new type of spectacle at the Place de la Concorde."

The President remained incredulous:

"I believe," he said, "that you are confounding two things; a joke and a scientific experiment. Both of them are guilty of upsetting the—"

"Both are criminal, Monsieur le President."

"In any event, it is hardly permissible to play a public joke of that character. Well, Professor Mazelier, since you can open the frontiers of Paris and of the country, I ask in the name of the country that you do it without delay."

It was an order. Mazelier bowed: "I cannot obey you as yet," he declared clearly.

"Because you are unable?"

"I left Paris tonight, Monsieur le President. I had to take to a place of safety, outside the city, because my collaborator, Gribal, was struck down under my very eyes, by the murderous radiation with which the criminal is menacing the entire population."

"And you said nothing to the police?"

Mazelier risked a slight shrug of his shoulders:

"The Prefect of Police can do nothing against a man whose very name is unknown to him, and which he will be unable to discover unless I tell it."

"You know, then—this individual?"

"Yes, Monsieur le President."

"And you will not give the name to the officers of justice?"

"No; for it would be to make certain of failure."

"But will you tell it to me?"

"I came here to tell you everything. The man, whose science and audacity make him so dangerous and so capable of escaping justice and who has not been touched because of his position, is the Marquis de Saint-Imier."

The name made the President start. "Saint-Imier! Impossible! But you are—"

The President stopped himself, just in time, from saying "You are crazy." He went on: "You are certainly mistaken. Saint-Imier! Everyone in the cabinet knows him. He has a colossal fortune."

"Yes, Monsieur le President. That is all true, and more. But in running down the person responsible by means of my scientific apparatus, I found the Marquis de Saint-Imier. That is the plain, brutal fact."

"But, if your apparatus made a mistake?"

"Impossible. Besides, I have checked it in a dozen ways. I am certain of what I am saying."

"Your name and your attainments inspire the utmost confidence, but I must tell you that I don't believe you."

"Time will tell, Monsieur le President."

"Time! Time! But time has been running on without bringing any information but the unlikely hypothesis you have just advanced. This is hardly very good. You can liberate the stalled traffic of Paris and of all France and you refuse to do it because you have a theory about who is causing the trouble."

"If you were persuaded that I were telling the truth, would you blame me, Monsieur le President?"

The question touched the heart of the matter. The President, who was becoming angry, became calm again.

"Perhaps," he conceded. "Unfortunately, I am not persuaded. Saint-Imier! But it's absurd. And you—"

The ringing of the telephone interrupted the conversation and the President must have found the information it gave him interesting, for with a gesture, he invited Mazelier to take an extension. The scientist heard:

"...there are more than 50,000 persons gathered around the Place de la Concorde to see the arrival of the man of the radio. It is now 2:45 p.m., and nobody has come, naturally. People are already beginning to leave. Order is perfect and the crowd is calm."

"Come," said the President, "admit that you were wrong to take a bad joke so seriously. Believe me; relieve the blockade if you can, and think no more of the poor Marquis who doubtless does not even know you are talking about him."

The audience was over, and Mazelier was left in confusion. The scientist was about to rise and take his leave, when a sharp voice resounded through the room from the loudspeaker which the President, like the meanest citizen of France, kept in a corner. And the voice in mocking accents, was making a new series of threats:

"*Parisians, you are laughing because I didn't keep the appointment I made for this afternoon. Wait for a few minutes and you will laugh no longer. I have already accomplished a portion of my vengeance; the woman who should have been given to me is mourning her dead fiancé now. Let her take her lesson from this. And I have already demanded once, that you sacrifice the two men I hate. Professor Mazelier and Gribal! Mark those names. Gribal was already struck down last night; now let Mazelier tremble. He will not escape me, even behind the barred doors of his office. And his death will be frightful!*"

Silence. The President of the Republic gazed dumbfounded at Mazelier. The scientist, in spite of the injunction, was not trembling.

Sharply the voice went on: "*Parisians, you will now feel the weight of my anger. I could kill you by the hundreds; but I prefer to kill you one by one. I will exterminate you in detail; it will be more amusing.*"

A laugh at this lugubrious joke came from the mouth of the loudspeaker. And the voice continued:

"*In an hour you will have 20 victims to prove that I can do what I say, and that I meant what I said when I demanded the sacrifice of the three persons as the price of your lives. And that is not all; ten children will fall dead. Every day, do you hear, every day, there will be ten more deaths, chosen by chance in the city. Nothing can prevent them; useless to try.*"

Mazelier was by now as overwhelmed as he had been calm before.

"There is not a minute to lose!" he cried. "Monsieur le President, give me permission to act."

A suspicion crossed the mind of the head of the state. He wondered whether Mazelier himself had not organized this affair with the aid of some accomplice. But the absurdity of such a suspicion was all too evident. And then?

Mazelier was on his way to the door when a servant appeared.

"Monsieur le President, a lady in mourning insists on your receiving her at once. It is Madame Ghislaine de Roberval."

This name, though unknown to Mazelier, was not unfamiliar to the President. What could the most beautiful and fashionable woman in Paris be wanting?

"In mourning?" inquired the President. "I thought she was about to be married."

He gave the order that she should be admitted. It was a day of surprises, and the normal order of etiquette must give way before the necessities of the situation.

Ghislaine entered, pale as a ghost.

"What can I do for you, Madame?"

"Monsieur le President," she said in a voice broken with tears, "I ask for justice. Justice against the cowardly assassin of Gabriel de Neuville."

"What? Monsieur de Neuville…"

"…Was struck down this morning at my side while we were walking in the Bois de Boulogne. It was a crime. And I swear that the author of the crime was the Marquis de Saint-Imier!"

The President turned: "Go, Monsieur," he said to the scientist. "I believe you and I place the resources of the state at your disposal."

"Alas!" said Mazelier, "this time I am arriving too late."

17. Unmasked

Mazelier was fully aware that he would not have received the presidential carte-blanche without Ghislaine's sudden and dramatic interruption. He had stirred, but not convinced his auditor. Doubtless the President had been ready to admit that the director of the Office of Scientific Research was beyond suspicion, but so was Saint-Imier. How could he suspect the personal friend of half the cabinet, the man whose money, liberally disposed, had done so much for science and education? Mazelier had seen for himself that the head of the state did not take the radio threat seriously. Alas, these threats were only too serious. The Marquis had announced that the first deaths would occur within an hour. In ten minutes Mazelier would be in his laboratory ready for the struggle. He would begin by lifting the blockade as he had promised the President. And then he would undertake the counter-offensive against Saint-Imier. But where was he? In the Rue Cortambert? It was unlikely. And Mazelier asked himself:

"For that matter, will I reach my laboratory alive? The brigand can see and hear at a distance, and he must be watching me. By going to the office, won't I fall directly into the trap? He thinks Gribal is dead, but he knows I'm still in the ring. Should I expose myself? Well, so much the worse, my duty is clear. Roland is waiting for me at the office."

And as he hastened along, Mazelier-continued to himself:

"He's right, that Marquis. I should not leave my laboratory. He has made use of the time while I was away at the Elysée, and he has been able to give my name and Gribal's to the mob. Well, we will see. At any event, he has not divulged the name of the woman he pursues so furiously. That name—I know it now, it is Ghislaine Roberval. Well, well, Marquis, we'll see."

Mazelier, having just arrived in the Champs-Elysée, was about to go up to the Rue de la Boëtie, when he encountered a veritable tide of humanity. A shouting crowd was pushing in the direction of the Etoile, crying: "Assassin! Death to the assassin. Down with the baby-killer!"

It was the sound of a revolution in birth. But what revolution, and against whom?

This is what had happened: the crowd of the curious assembled around the Place de la Concorde, at the moment when Mazelier was having his conference with the President, amused themselves with their own remarks at first. Everybody was perfectly sure that nothing at all would happen. The public mind had been made up; the experiments of the person they had come to consider as a kind of scientific acrobat, juggling with radiation as an athlete with dumb-bells, were doubtless very curious, but were always a little behind the program he laid out for himself.

Briefly, he was bluffing. The end of the world had been promised; the transport of France had been disorganized, and for what? Nothing at all, when you came down to it. The Earth continued its march through space; the Sun rose every morning, and people went about their business. The unknown made continual threats and then did little or nothing. But what he had said this time had a personal interest for the whole population.

"It's him again? Bah, I'm too much in a hurry to listen. Tell me about it next week," said a man who was taking a bus in the Rue Chateaudun.

"Yes, yes, but listen. It's really amusing this time. Listen," called someone from a table on the corner, where he was seated before a glass of vermouth-cassis.

A circle of auditors gathered around the loudspeaker whose voice dominated the noise of the vehicles in the busy street.

When the voice pronounced the names of Mazelier and Gribal, they produced a veritable torrent of jokes. The two scientists became famous in a second; and they attained the notoriety to which their genuine discoveries entitled them without having to work for it.

"The guy's a nut," cried one gentleman comfortably seated at his café table. "Bright idea, to use the radio to announce that he's having a quarrel with Mazelier and Gribal!"

This was the common opinion. But a wave of uneasiness went over the crowd when the voice raged on to announce the deaths of ten persons taken by chance. It was a little beyond the license permitted to jokers. Nevertheless, the threat would not be carried out. At this moment Mazelier and Gribal would have received a public ovation if they had appeared. As the oration from the radio ended, there were murmurs of disapproval:

"It's time somebody squelched that idiot!"

And there was a general shrugging of shoulders. There are certain crimes impossible to commit, especially when one announces to the public that they are about to be committed. Nobody doubted that the prefecture of police had been warned and detectives were already on the job. And the individual who had already been looked for could expect a rough handling when they found him. It would not be too hard—broadcasting stations are not difficult to locate.

As a matter of fact the prefecture and the police were working. The news that they were searching for the origin of the voice, followed the voice itself without a moment's delay and had the effect of calming the mind of the public still more.

All at once there came a piece of news that was like a clap of thunder. While people were listening in the center of Paris a terrible drama had been taking place in the outskirts. Ten children in Passy had been stricken, covered with terrible burns. The crime had been committed, and the assassin had not even had that kind of cynicism which permits a criminal to keep his word exactly; after having sought the aid of the Parisians, he had deceived them. As cowardly as he was cruel, he threatened at one place and struck at another.

But could one believe what was said; the horrible details that were passing from one quarter of the city to another by word of mouth? Alas, to those who would have liked to have doubted the crime and its terror there came confirmation from the criminal himself as the loudspeakers once more resounded with the well-recognized voice:

"Parisians, do you believe me now?"

The assassin was triumphant and his laughter an insult. He went on: *"I have kept my promise. Justice is done on the wicked city!"*

There was in the crowd a ground-murmur that contained at once the seeds of fury and revolt.

The scoundrel dared to speak of justice! He went on: *"For today, that is all. You are at liberty. All of you can go about your business. But I warn you that if Mazelier is still alive by tomorrow, 20 children will pay the forfeit for him; on the following day 40, and the day after that 80, and so on. Until the day when you have obeyed me and given him up to justice! I want that man! Good night, Parisians; I have no more to say to you but that nothing will stop me now."*

Fists were clenched toward the loudspeakers as though the inanimate machines could have transmitted to the unknown these evidences of the general anger.

And it was almost as though they had, for the voice took up again: *"You didn't take me seriously, did you? Don't complain now, I gave you plenty of warning. But be warned; if you do not obey me, I will kill every child in Paris, and then the rest of you, one by one. I hate you, citizens of Paris; everything you suffer only increases my pleasure. Your anger, your fears are delicious. I hate you, all of you!"*

The entire city was literally in the street, moving aimlessly about, and resembling one of those prodigious tidal waves which carries everything before it. The formidable murmur of revolution mounted; a breath, a sound, would turn it in one direction or another. There was not one person in a 100,000 of those who heard who had ever seen or heard of Mazelier and Gribal, but the two names, let loose in a dozen streets by voices raised in genuine anger, became the symbols of the resistance and defiance the crowd offered to the unknown menace.

"Vive Mazelier! Vive Gribal!" shouted thousands of voices in different parts of the city.

A final mockery came through the loudspeakers:

"Yes, Vive Mazelier! But add Death to Paris! afterward."

The voice said something more but nobody heard or wished to hear; the mob was up; the church bells that had sounded for the deaths of kings, tolled in Paris, and the sections were choosing delegates to call on the President. There, they were received with courtesy and given the latest details in possession of the authorities.

Ten children had been attacked by the mysterious forms of radiation at regular intervals of three minutes. A half an hour had been enough for the multiple assassination. But, among these ten children, one had miraculously escaped the agony of the others. The escaped child lived in the Rue Duphot; attacked at exactly 3:45 p.m., he had suffered agonies for a few minutes, and then his tortures had ceased and his burns had quickly disappeared.

The other nine had succumbed under conditions which left the witnesses altogether incapable of describing the event. What kind of radiation had been used? How was it that the first child attacked had escaped the danger? These questions would be studied later; for the moment, the entire population had a double duty; first to prevent more crimes and second to discover the criminal.

Now, at the Elysée, chance or providence had ruled it so that the servant who had introduced Madame Roberval had waited in the outer office. He had good ears, and the name of Saint-Imier, pronounced with such energy by Ghislaine, repeated with stupefaction by the President and with an accent of triumph by Mazelier, had reached his ears. And when the delegations from the sections arrived he could not restrain himself from affirming:

"It's the Marquis de Saint-Imier!"

Nobody thought of doubting, such is the unreasoning passion of a French mob, once aroused. From the courts of the Elysée to the Faubourg Saint-Honoré, from the Faubourg to the Champs-Elysée and the Place de la Concorde, the news ran like a fire through a train of powder, and a few minutes later, as the cabinet was in session, it was hurled even there into the midst of the discussion. The Minister of Science, vibrating with indignation, cried:

"I protest against the calumnies which are being spread abroad! An occasion for public mourning should not serve as the pretext for absurd accusations."

But it was noticeable that the President of the Republic did not support the protests of his minister. Nevertheless, the latter went on:

"Come, come. It's foolish to raise such accusations against a man of the importance of Saint-Imier without cause and without proof. I dined with him only yesterday evening."

The Minister of the Interior answered:

"Ah, my dear fellow, if every other murderer only knew that a sure means of avoiding suspicion was to invite you to dinner!"

Everyone recognized that because a man was rich was no reason for exempting him from justice. But what could be done without proof? And there was no proof.

It was the President of the Republic who cut the knot of the difficulty:

"There is no reason," he declared, "why we should not make an investigation. In a moment as grave as this, I need not add, I suppose, that we should take precautions that the inquiry should not be influenced from any quarter whatsoever. Justice must be done without weakness. But on the other hand, such an inquiry will keep the people of Paris from being carried away by momentary impulses."

It was impossible to object to these words of wisdom. The Minister of Science no longer opposed, and his colleague of the department of Justice went into immediate conference with the heads of the prefecture of police.

Meanwhile, the President had another subject of worry. What had become of Mazelier? The scientist, when he asked for complete liberty of action, had doubtless intended to signify that he would pass into a prolonged eclipse from the public gaze. But only one of two things was possible; either the scientist knew nothing of the Marquis' latest crime, and therefore, since he was ignorant, was inferior to him, or, Mazelier knew about it and his efforts to prevent the crime had been futile. For if Mazelier were aware of what was going on, it was impossible to suppose he would not have done everything to prevent the crime.

Also, the head of the state wondered whether the child who had been saved had not owed his life to Mazelier. But why had only one escaped? In any case, bound by the promise he had given to Mazelier, the President could not confide his impressions to anyone.

Meanwhile, events were driving on in a manner altogether unforeseen.

While the official powers were discussing the method of an inquiry, which was considered a matter of extreme delicacy, difficult and extremely confidential, the people, stirred by the obscure atavism of self-defense, were on their way to perform the same task without official permission.

From all directions, without an order being given, the people were gathering. Let the assassin defend himself by the emission of his murderous radiation. The people would see whether he was capable of striking down an entire population. The radiations tamed by the Marquis made him redoubtable, no doubt, but could his powers really extend to infinity?

Every street of Paris became filled with a human river, all flowing in the direction of the Rue Cortambert and the home of the Marquis. The crowd was all the more formidable because it remained silent. Not a cry, not an imprecation, not a gesture. But silently, it moved along, every member animated by the same thoughts like different drops of water in a tidal wave.

In a few minutes the Rue Cortambert was filled by that flood, which halted before the great mansion of Saint-Imier, with its double doors, the back-eddies piling up in all the adjoining streets.

With the irresistible force of a tide the mob went through the doors, and then, despite the protests of the doorman, into the grand hall of the building itself.

Then, and only then, was the invasion provided with some sort of organization.

Two companies were formed to explore the different parts of the building. One remained in the entry hall to question the domestics and centralize whatever information was obtained. A footman, with a suspicious eye and proud lips, tried to halt the invaders at the foot of the grand stairway. He was seized by iron hands. Frightened, he babbled:

"What do you want here?"

"We wish to see your master!" said a rude voice.

"But Monsieur the Marquis has gone out."

"We will wait. Get your comrades, the other servants, together, and bring them here."

Between two bodyguards the footman led the way toward the office, while the searchers began to explore the four floors, the cellars and the vast garages of the Marquis.

What would they find?

18. The Secret of the Stairway

It must be remembered that the different incidents of this inquest all took place together, although they are narrated here in sequence; and the intervals between them are intervals of a few seconds only. It was swiftly established:

1. That the servants of the household were all there, with the exception of a housekeeper called Suzie la Bretonne and the chauffeur of the Marquis, the Chinese, Pou-Hi. Where were they? The others could give no information on this point.

2. All the servants were agreed in stating that the Marquis de Saint-Imier had gone out, alone, about 20 minutes before, in the little town car he kept for running errands around Paris. The fact that he had taken this car indicated to the others that he intended to return early.

Nothing abnormal about any of this. But suddenly they were in the midst of impossibilities.

The servants, after having said there were but three loudspeakers in the mansion, one in the little salon on the ground floor, the second in the Marquis' room and the third in the rooms reserved for the use of the help, added that they had as usual turned it on during their lunch. That a little later, their loudspeaker, as well as that in the little salon, had suddenly ceased functioning in the midst of

370

the concert, and that afterward, having heard nothing else, they imagined something had gone wrong with the apparatus. Questioned as to the threats which had come over the air subsequently, and had been heard from every radio in Paris, they affirmed, with the utmost apparent sincerity, that they had heard nothing at all.

Thus there were two possibilities:

Either the servants were all in agreement to tell the same lie, and in that case, it would be necessary to assume that the Marquis had extended his circle of accomplices to a dangerous size,—for when there are so many, the result is that one of them always tells.

Or, they were telling the truth, and the disconcerting fact must be admitted that, alone in all Paris, the loudspeakers in the Marquis' mansion had remained silent at the precise moment when the assassin was boasting of his crimes.

If this fact was not directly incriminatory it was at least indicative. It could mean that the Marquis de Saint-Imier had found a means of speaking to the rest of the world without being heard in his own household.

A second report, from the group which was searching the rooms on the second floor, added to the uneasiness which everyone felt in this luxurious house. The Marquis' bedroom was on this second floor, reached through an ante-chamber next to a bathroom. There was a striking contrast; all the furniture of the ground floor, including the dining rooms, was of an extraordinary richness, almost too rich and elegant; all the furniture of the second floor was made up of pieces of surprising elegance, veritable museum pieces.

But the ground floor furniture was garish and absurd, that on the second floor, refined and in the best of taste. Second contrast; the windows on the ground floor contained jewels, set in the worst possible style; but, on the second floor, the windows were stained glass in indisputable taste. The same thing was true of the pictures which covered the walls, but in a different way.

The ground floor was filled with the latest works of the moderns, hideous and popular. But the enormous bedroom contained only a single canvas, a wholly admirable portrait of a woman. In a corner of this portrait a card had been placed. It bore the name of Saint-Imier and these curious words:

I loved her. Now I hate her.

No one in the mob could recognize the portrait as one of Ghislaine Roberval.

But the visitors were not in the Marquis' private residence to look over his art treasures and furniture; they were there to find proof that an atrocious crime had been committed in the house. There ought to be a wireless station in the building. But no such place had been found, though it would be in the upper floors near the bedroom, in the most reserved part of the house.

The search party was about to go back over its tracks, when one of its members, an interior decorator, whose models of new designs for furniture bore witness to a remarkable originality, signaled them to wait for a moment. The big four-poster bed interested him. At a glance it was evident that it was a perfect example of the art of—but no! it had no particular style, it was unclassifiable.

This mass of carvings of unequal excellence, these motifs, so curious and unusual. An intuition flashed through the head of the decorator; he remembered the legends that clung around certain princely beds of the Renaissance, veritable secret chambers in themselves, in which stores of weapons or poisons were concealed, or which contained huge strong-boxes for the reception of money.

The decorator, to the astonishment of his colleagues, began to feel every carving, every sculptured motif. As he had the air of examining it solely from the standpoint of artistic taste, there were murmurs:

"We're losing time. Can't be anything here. Let's look somewhere else."

And in fact, if there were secret drawers, like those in the famous chamber of Catherine de Medicis at the Chateau de Blois, they were a long time in coming to light. The curious inquirer was about to abandon his task, when, suddenly, he felt something give under his fingers. At the same moment, behind the head of the bed, a large panel swung open in the wall, presenting to view a stairway large enough for three men to have mounted abreast. The movement had certainly lit an electric light somewhere, for the stairway was bathed in its glow.

The decorator was triumphant. But where did the stairway lead?

The group divided into three parts; the first was given the duty of climbing the stair; the second that of going down it, for it led down as well as up; the third remained in position.

Meanwhile, the visits to the rest of the house went on without incident. One group arrived at the garage and found it locked. The key was asked for in vain from the porter and the other servants; all declared that the Marquis usually carried it on his person. They added that there was a second key, but that the Chinese chauffeur always kept it.

The inquisitioners were not long in coming to a decision. They would break in the door.

Here, a remark is necessary. Crowds, like individuals, are capable of the most contradictory actions. Among those who burst into the Marquis' mansion were people of all classes and all types of morality. If some of them had arms on them, they never thought of using them. And others, whose morality had not always been of the highest character, thus participating in an act of public policy, never thought of committing the slightest theft.

They were incapable of stealing anything; but at the least sign of resistance, or the first suspicion, they were capable of destroying everything.

The garage door gave way at the first push. And the pushers halted suddenly, with the same exclamation of surprise as their companions on the second floor, at the sight of another secret stairway.

And, at the precise moment when the garage door gave way, a powerful touring car, all its lights ablaze, clashed suddenly into gear and charged away from them, directly at the rear wall of the garage!

Who was within? Who, rather than let himself be taken alive, was willing to dash himself and his car against the wall of the garage?

To the general stupefaction of all, the wall opened and then closed behind the auto as though it were made of gauze. The disappearance took place so swiftly that it seemed altogether unreal. A cry of rage swelled up behind the first cry of surprise.

"The brigand! He was in it! He's getting away!"

"Not for long. You can't lose an auto."

"Not when you have the number. But we haven't."

"Gentlemen," said the chief of the searching party, "we must continue our hunt."

Everyone was afire to discover the secret of the wall through which an automobile could pass. But this new incident, added to that of the bedroom when communicated to the group in the entry hall, and thence to the crowd in the streets, and so on its way through all Paris, aroused the liveliest emotions. A little amplified, perhaps, even a little deformed in the telling, it arrived at the room where the ministers were still busily discussing the proper forms for an official inquiry into the Saint-Imier house.

It was decided to begin the inquiry without delay. But the machinery of justice is slow about getting in motion. And the responsible magistrates hesitated to issue the proper warrants, for they found no evidence of any reason for beginning official processes against anyone but the crowd who had invaded a private residence.

The crowd, meanwhile, was unembarrassed by these scruples. In the eyes of everyone present, the discoveries made so far justified pushing the search still further. That was why, instead of patiently looking for the opening in the rear wall of the garage, it was judged simpler to take it apart brick by brick, with chisel and pickaxe. In the twinkling of an eye, amateur house-wreckers were at work. They discovered immediately—and this did not surprise them—that the wall was nothing but a concealed partition, which contained neither bricks nor steel. A very ingenious system was quickly laid bare by the inexorable picks, by means of which the door was rolled back. Its ingenuity did not impress the observers; the only question they asked was:

"What are we going to find behind the wall?"

The reply was not long in coming. The wall once down, the searchers found themselves in another garage. And its doors were wide open on the Place de la Muette. The auto which had disappeared, with its lights ablaze, must be a long distance away by this time, on the Bois de Boulogne. The second garage contained two machines; another touring car and a low-bodied racer. Did they belong to the Marquis? Evidently not, for a guardian in livery appeared on the scene, at once angry and frightened, to protest against an intrusion, which in truth, could not be justified. But from questioner he was quickly turned into questioned. He must have known what had aroused the grumbling mob around him for he ceased his complaints, immediately, when he heard cries of: "We want to punish the baby killer!"

He was an individual with the olive skin of the typical South American, and he spoke with an accent:

"Gentlemen, I beg of you, don't hurt me."

"Good. But answer! Did you see an auto go out just now?"

"No, I swear to you. I was in the kitchen when I heard the noise of your pickaxes. It is for that I came out. But I saw nothing. I swear it!"

"Who owns this garage?"

"Señor Cuchillo."

"Ah, and where is Señor Cuchillo? We want to talk to him."

"Señor Cuchillo is in Biarritz."

A sly light appeared in the eyes of the guardian, but the crowd did not perceive the difference. Neighbors came to confirm the fact that house and garage did indeed belong to the rich Argentine.

The fact that the two garages were backed up to each other was not really abnormal. But another fact was at once curious and troubling; the two garages communicated with each other by means of a secret door, and the Marquis' auto had left the door of the rich Señor open.

"Bah!" said someone. "The police will clear that matter up. Let's go back to the Marquis' garage and see what other surprises we can find."

As a matter of fact, what was needed was a complete search, carried on, as rapidly as possible, to surprise the enemy in action if possible. A second sooner and they would have had the auto. Therefore speed was essential.

And as the search-party returned to the first garage, they seemed to hear behind the wall forming an angle with the demolished partition, footsteps and the sound of voices. Was this wall too, a fake? In any case, there came the sound of blows.

"Pickaxes up!"

The demolishers had already seized their tools and were preparing to tear down this second partition, when it opened suddenly—like that in the bedroom, and like that which had let the auto pass.

"It's us!" cried a voice. "Don't strike."

The picks fell to earth again. The new arrivals were part of the party which had been searching the upper floor, and who had gone down the secret stair to find out where it led to.

So, the secret stair led to the garage.

Therefore the Marquis could come in and go out without anyone in his house knowing about it, by using his private stairway and the Cuchillo garage.

The inquest was advancing—but without any direct proof of culpability. But had the garage delivered up all its secrets?

Before going back to the vestibule to report to the party in charge, the searchers resolved to make an inventory of everything in the garage. But as they began a terrific clamor came from the upper floor, spread abroad to the vestibule and the Court, and they left their task to run after the new discovery. There was a tempest, a hurricane of imprecations, a collective fury carried to the last limits, a release of one of those popular passions which nothing is capable of resisting. Fists were clenched, voices went high and hoarse, broken sentences were shouted.

"Death to the assassin! Lynch him! Death! Lynch him!"

What had happened?

The party that had gone to the secret stair had stepped on a landing corresponding to the third floor. The Marquis had been so certain that he would never be discovered that he had not even taken the precaution of turning the key in the door on this landing. The searchers penetrated into a huge bedroom, furnished with that elegant sense of luxury which is found only in the highest circles. The room had no lights but interior ones, no issue but a small skylight heavily barred. And it contained nothing but furniture.

But the searchers went on, certain that they would find something. There was another flight of stairs; they climbed to the fourth story, and penetrated into another room which opened on the hidden stairway; and here they gave an exclamation of triumph. For this was, without the slightest doubt, Saint-Imier's secret laboratory.

The first things to draw their attention were two huge mirrors, one concave, the other convex, mounted on universal joints which permitted them to be turned in any direction. Then the trituration tubes, the retorts, the glassware of the ordinary chemist; an electric furnace of extraordinary design and great power; a series of radioactive compounds in tubes; a radio receiving apparatus which at a first glance seemed like commercial apparatus, but in which certain details were peculiar, as for instance, the presence of two brilliant discs on the lateral faces; other machines, invented and made, certainly, by no other hands than those of the Marquis, whose use could only be told with certainty by experts, but which did not at first draw the attention of the searchers, and beyond, a doorway, leading to a private office.

On the table, papers were spread out. They were examined, at first cursorily; what interest or importance could scraps, of paper covered with figures, mathematical signs and hieroglyphical formulas have? But one of them was easier to read.

"Look, names and addresses. And figures. The Marquis' list of creditors with what he owes them."

There would have been a laugh at this pleasantry, had not one of the searchers cried:

"But that's the list of the dead children!"

19. The Duplicate Assassin

Every eye was directed at the tragic paper. The truth was as clear as day. On the scrap of paper, the Marquis had written the names of the children who had been struck down. And the list was too old to have been made after the crime.

Ten names, with the corresponding addresses were written in ink. Nine were struck out in pencil. The only name not crossed out was that of the child who had escaped, living in the Rue Duphot. And between the lines were written in pencil, the names of nine more children.

Opposite every name there were figures. What did they mean? Never mind, that could be discovered later—the important thing was that the proof was found at last. But the angry crowd need not worry now; they were certain of their game.

More pieces of paper were discovered. They were carefully classified. The first bore the heading: *Tomorrow evening, at 5*, and contained a list of 20 names. The second was headed: *Day after tomorrow, at 4*, and it contained 40 names. They corresponded exactly to the frightful program announced by the loud-speakers. The third scrap of paper was a sketch map of the streets at the east of the Halles Centrales. A semicircle, traced in blue crayon was around a section of it, and there were 20 points indicated in red crayon accompanied by mysterious numberings. A fourth slip of paper bore a similar sketch of the Montmartre district with 40 similar numbers and indicated points.

Thus, in the silence of his room, believing himself hidden from all eyes, disposing of forces against which there was no defense, this man had studied, in cold blood, and prepared the way for, the assassination of the population of a capital.

In the explosion of anger provoked by the discovery of these documents, one detail was not perceived; the secret stair led to the fifth floor and the room of the Chinese chauffeur, Pou-Hi. When it was finally discovered, the odor of the cigarettes the Chinese smoked habitually was still in the room; Pou-Hi had evidently left only a short time before. Further on a door communicated with the room of Suzie la Bretonne, and on the bed was a headdress in the style of Saint-Guénolé, newly pressed. It was therefore natural to conclude that the two servants were accomplices of their master. They, alone, could know of the existence of the stairway.

Moreover, everyone noticed that the lists of the persons the Marquis meant to slay bore their names, their first names and their ages. How had he been able to get such precise information and why? Would it not have been simpler to strike by chance?

Such questions the crowd relegated to the rear. What everyone wished was the immediate punishment of the criminal. And while waiting for that why not destroy his instruments? Yes, break everything in the laboratory. What did it matter what might still be discovered? The terrible pieces of paper were enough. The importance of a decisive proof is not helped by secondary proofs, no matter how good. As to giving the criminal to the ordinary processes of justice, what use would it be? No—violence was the only remedy.

Who gave the signal for the beginning of the destruction? Nobody. One would have said that everyone gave it at once. The sack of the laboratory began at the moment when the police, impotent against the gigantic crowd, appeared on the scene.

At the Elysée, the council of ministers was over. The President of the Republic, alone in his room, was reflecting on the grave events of the day. He had been kept advised, in some measure, of what was happening in the Rue Cortambert. The President's decision was made; the Marquis de Saint-Imier had escaped and it might not be easy to capture him. A call to arms of the whole country might be necessary. It was necessary to proclaim the Marquis a public outlaw.

All at once the telephone sounded. The features of the President expressed delight and surprise as he heard the voice of the Prefect of Police. The Paris police are ideally the best in the world! The Prefect announced that one of his inspectors had discovered the Marquis at the cabaret of the Cercle des Arts. He was taken immediately before an Investigating Magistrate. The Prefect added that all necessary precautions had been taken to prevent an escape. Delighted with this news, whose effect would be immense, the President hung up the receiver. But he was immediately recalled to the instrument. This time it was the Director of the secret police who wished to speak to the President in person. And the President in person gave signs of stifling when he heard the news:

"What? You say, my dear Director, that three of your inspectors have just arrested the Marquis de Saint-Imier? At the Cercle des Arts? What, what? They arrested him as he left the Princesse de Lezigny's house? Rue de Varenne? Are you certain? No resistance, hmm? They have taken him before an Investigating Magistrate. Well, tell me the news. I am curious to know the results of the questioning. Yes, thanks. Goodbye, my dear Director."

The President forgot to congratulate the zealous official who had thus transmitted a piece of news of the first importance, and who thought himself entitled to at least the ribbon of the Legion of Honor.

But the President, perplexed and troubled, suspected an unforeseen complication, also of the first importance.

How in the world could the same individual have been arrested in two spots widely separated from one another? How had the inspectors of the police department been able to meet the Marquis de Saint-Imier at the Cercle des Arts, two steps from the Etoile while the inspectors of the secret police were arresting him in the Rue de Varenne? Someone had lied or been deceived.

The President sighed. He knew the vagaries of public opinion. He knew that the Parisians have always been delighted by those good stories which permit them to laugh at government officials. That the frightful drama of the Rue Cortambert should become a means of laughing the government out of office, even before it reached its conclusion, was a little shocking. Something must be done to evade it.

But which one, the prefect or the director, had been deceived? And suddenly, the President thought:

What if neither of them had been deceived? With a man of Saint-Imier's type, anything can happen. I'm going to call the Ministry of the Interior.

He did not have time. The Minister of the Interior called him first, on a question of importance. The Saint-Imier mansion was in flames.

The arrest of the Marquis de Saint-Imier at the Cercle des Arts had not been attended by the slightest difficulty. The captain of police for the Muette quarter knew the Marquis very well and was on familiar terms with him. Saint-Imier affected to live in what he was pleased to call a "glass house." He took no kind of precautions, apparently, in his private life. Everybody seemed to know him. The papers took notice of his appearance at all the official solemnities, at all the notable receptions, the leading sporting events and society weddings.

Thus it was, that everyone knew that the Marquis had the habit of stopping in daily at the Cercle des Arts. A couple of good man-hunters, had been posted there without any great hope of finding their game, for nobody imagined that the game, so clearly unmasked, would have the impudence, or the imprudence, to come to his usual haunts.

Nevertheless, he came. He came late, but he came, and his lateness was only another reason for supposing, that at the time of his usual visit, he had been committing a crime. The Marquis had not even thought to provide himself with an alibi.

At the Cercle a half-dozen regular habitués were on hand, no more. These few were chatting about the wonderful progress being made in radio, which permitted a single individual to mystify all Paris.

The Marquis agreed with them, and added with indignation, somewhat surprising in a skeptic, that the police ought not to permit that sort of thing. Then, with a volubility not quite usual in a personage ordinarily reserved, he had expanded on the way in which crowds will believe anything at all. His six auditors remarked that he spoke rapidly, and without replying to remarks made by the others, as though he did not hear their questions, or rather, stared off into the distance as he spoke, as though unaware of their presence.

After which, he rose, passed into the reading room, ran briefly over the evening papers, which bore scare heads:

TEN CHILDREN KILLED BY UNKNOWN RADIATION
Police Search for Criminal

A copy of a later paper was handed to the Marquis by an employee of the establishment. He read aloud in a monotonous voice, and as though bored to death:

MOB ATTACKS ST.-IMIER HOUSE
Mysterious Auto Escapes Through Garage Wall

One would have expected him to be a little more stirred by this news. But he showed no sign of it if he were. He refolded the paper, put it in its rack, and with his monocle in his eye, stepped out into the hall of the Cercle, where he was pounced upon by four policemen, their revolvers in their hands, for they expected a furious resistance. But there was no resistance at all. The Marquis only asked, with a smile on his lips:

"*Sapristi!* What haste! What would you like, gentlemen?"

"You are Monsieur le Marquis de Saint-Imier?"

"Yes, but I regret to say I do not know you."

"We are police inspectors and we have a warrant for your arrest."

"That's odd," said the Marquis calmly, and then added:

"I am arrested then. Would you mind telling me what I ought to do? It's not usual for me, you understand. I have never been arrested before, but once, and then it was by a fog while I was flying over the North Pole."

The scoundrel dared to joke. An automobile drew up in answer to the policeman's signal.

"Get in quick," advised the inspector, "if you don't want to be lynched in the street."

The Marquis got in docilely beside his guardians. The position he was in seemed to leave him altogether unaffected. The auto went to the Palais de Justice, where Monsieur Blondel, the Magistrate in charge of the investigation, was to question him.

The other arrest of the Marquis took place almost simultaneously in the Rue de Varenne, and was due to a happy accident. Opposite the residence of the Princesse de Lezigny was a little wine merchant's shop. From time to time inspectors of the secret police came there to take a glass or two of *mousseux*. Now one of these, remembering having seen the Marquis' auto frequently halted before the Lezigny's, and knowing that Monsieur de Saint-Imier was usually to be seen at society receptions, placed himself on guard at the bar. He had the delight of hearing the wine merchant say:

"Ah, there comes the Marquis. He hasn't Pou-Hi with him today."

"Who is Pou-Hi?" asked the inspector.

"His chauffeur, of course. The Chinese."

"Ah, yes. True. The Marquis is driving himself."

It was the little car which the porter at the Saint-Imier mansion had mentioned to the invaders.

The inspector saw the Marquis go in, and telephoned for reinforcements.

About the same time, the Marquis, entering, perceived that he was alone in the salon.

"Ah," murmured Madame de Lezigny, "it's so good of you to have come. Do you know, I am dying of fear? Did you hear the radio?"

"Oh, yes, and I agree that it made a very disagreeable noise. Just the same, I see nothing to be frightened about."

"What, don't you know then—?"

"Oh, I never know anything. What happened?"

"The threats have been realized," said the princess, in a low voice, which seemed to be trembling with genuine fear.

The Marquis started:

"What do you mean?" he said.

"I just heard that ten children have died, as the loudspeakers predicted."

"But it's frightful."

"Isn't it? I don't dare to move any more. I hardly dare to breathe. It's frightful, Marquis, frightful."

"And incredible," said the Marquis. "Are you certain?"

"My brother just telephoned me about it. He said they were holding a ministerial council about it."

Monsieur de Saint-Imier could no longer doubt that the news was true. Madame de Lezigny's brother was an ambassadorial secretary attached to the foreign ministry, and would know at first hand.

The Princess went on:

"My brother told me I ought to join him. But I didn't dare to go out alone."

"Would you like me to accompany you as far as the Quai d'Orsay?"

"I would like it very much. With you, there would be nothing to fear."

The Marquis bowed.

On the sidewalk, as he bent to open the door of his car to show the princess in, he was rapidly surrounded by the vigorous agents of the secret police, while the head of the detachment made his excuses to the Princesse de Lezigny, explaining to her that he had a warrant to bring the Marquis de Saint-Imier in for questioning.

Fixing his monocle in his eye the latter turned to the princess:

"I am overwhelmed with regret at not being able to accompany you," he said with a smile. "But you see, what these gentlemen ask is impossible to refuse. I must go with them. Farewell, Madame."

He saluted with the grace of a gentleman and mounted into his own car between two of the detectives while a third took his place in the rumble-seat.

Ten minutes later, the Princesse de Lezigny was recounting this incredible story to her brother—to wit, that the most elegant man in Paris and perhaps in the world, had just been arrested. The Director of the secret police must certainly be crazy.

When she learned the truth, she had not even the strength to be surprised; she fainted with terror. She had been alone with the assassin for some minutes. She had placed herself under the care of the monster to drive about Paris. The story spread rapidly, and as soon as the unfortunate princess recovered from her faint, she was surrounded by an army of reporters, all of them wanting interviews with the woman who had seen the bandit arrested.

But the journalists, who had been prevented by the fire in the Saint-Imier mansion from visiting the secret stairway, the laboratory and the bedroom with its curious decorations, did not get all they hoped for.

In the first place, to avoid the popular tumult, the arrest of the Marquis was not officially announced until late at night. And the reporters could not know of the strange scene, the absolutely incredible scene that took place before the examining magistrate.

Monsieur Blondel was preparing to interrogate the Marquis de Saint-Imier arrested at the Cercle des Arts, when the Marquis de Saint-Imier arrested in the Rue de Varenne was brought in.

Very much astonished, the honorable Magistrate said to himself that one of the two was obviously not the man wanted. Which? It ought not to be too difficult to find out. Some of the policemen had made a mistake; that sort of thing happens every day. When they were confronted with each other, the unfortunate individual who had the bad luck to resemble the Marquis would be sent on his way, and the blunder of the police would be made good as soon as discovered.

But when Monsieur Blondel summoned the two, and saw before him two identical Marquis de Saint-Imiers, his stupefaction passed all bounds. He looked at his bailiff, who as astonished as he, stood by with his mouth open. Never, within the memory o the Msagistrate, had two accused persons resembled each other so much as this pair. Physically, the resemblance was absolutely perfect. And what finally upset the Magistrate was the fact that the two were dressed in exactly the same manner. Everything, even in the smallest details, was repeated.

"My word!" said Monsieur Blondel, rendered severe by his doubts, "has this been arranged in advance? But—but—they are absolutely interchangeable."

And the Magistrate, leaning over to the bailiff, whispered an order. Immediately, two athletic policemen placed themselves one behind each of the duplicate Marquis.

But the Magistrate reassured himself with the thought that the false one would certainly not wish to be confounded with the genuine.

20. Escape!

It was a delightful illusion. The two Marquis, identical in face and in costume, were also identical in their attitudes. The first Saint-Imier seated himself calmly in the chair that was placed for him; the second Saint-Imier, in the same 100th of a second, did the same. With the same gesture, they adjusted their monocles in their eyes; together they crossed their right legs over their left, and waited, the same ironic smile on both visages.

Monsieur Blondel had recovered his equilibrium. He threw a glance at the bailiff which signified:

"Patience! They'll come to their oats."

And he proceeded to the questions of identity.

It was dumbfounding. The two Marquis replied at the same time, articulating exactly the same words in the same voice, with the same intonations so exactly timed that one would have said it was a single voice that answered.

Monsieur Blondel wiggled his heavy eyebrows, and turning to the one on his right, he said dryly:

"You ought to understand, both of you, that it is not to your interest to perform such tricks before the bar of justice. The charges against one of you are exceptionally grave. I must recall to you that these questions of identity are for the purpose of distinguishing the innocent from the guilty person."

The facts were self-evident. Since it was impossible that there were two copies of the Marquis de Saint-Imier, it must be that one of the two before the Magistrate was a joke of a too original character abusing his incredible resemblance to the true Marquis. Saint-Imier's double was amusing himself? Well, he would not amuse himself for long. He risked having to pay a high price for his fun.

Monsieur Blondel went on:

"I address myself to you at my right. Are you the Marquis Guy-Gontran de Saint-Imier?"

The two Marquis inclined their heads with the same movement, and replied in unison:

"I am the Marquis Guy-Gontran de Saint-Imier, living at the Rue Cortambert, Paris."

"But I said nothing to you!" cried the Magistrate to the Marquis on his left. "Your turn will come, be quiet. It's not worth the trouble to tell me, both at once, that you are the Marquis de Saint-Imier. The Marquis de Saint-Imier is in danger of losing his head."

These words should have shot fear into the hearts of the two mummers. They replied only by the same smile of ironic appreciation. Monsieur Blondel, who had expected to interrogate the two together, before bringing in the evidence against one of them, was disconcerted for the moment.

Was he dealing with a pair of accomplices? But in that case, what was their game?

He repeated his question to the prisoner at the left:

"Do you declare that you are the Marquis de Saint-Imier?"

The two voices replied as one:

"I declare that I am the Marquis de Saint-Imier."

Monsieur Blondel was tempted to have the guards take away one of the two. But he gave over the idea, persuaded that the extravaganza could not be of long duration. Two individuals claimed the same personality they would therefore be subject to the same punishment, and let them beware!

And the Magistrate put a question that should end the difficulty:

"Where were you arrested?"

The two Marquises made together this stupefying response:

"I was arrested first in the Cercle des Arts in the Rue Presbourg, and then in the Rue de Varenne, in front of the Lezigny home."

This was really too much. What—the two individuals before the Magistrate pretended to be a single person? Evidently, the pretence could not be sustained. Nevertheless, they acted, they spoke as though the pretence were a reality. Moreover, they had the air of being ignorant of each other's existence; the Magistrate noticed that they never looked at each other. But the synchronization of their replies, made in the same words, with the same intonations of the voice, remained absolutely perfect. One would have said they were two automata, fabricated in series, and wound up so as to utter the same words.

Monsieur Blondel again addressed himself to the Marquis on his right:

"You were really arrested at the Cercle des Arts and again in the Rue de Varenne?"

"Yes," declared the two prisoners together.

The Magistrate lifted his head and said to the stenographer:

"Write down the double response."

"You are indeed the Marquis de Saint-Imier? And you, too, you are the Marquis de Saint-Imier?"

"I am the Marquis de Saint-Imier," repeated the two.

"In that case," pronounced the Magistrate, "for the first time in my life, I am going to give one order for two persons. Do you know of what you stand accused, gentlemen?"

The two Marquis lifted their heads, adjusted their monocles and replied in unison:

"Monsieur, do not give yourself the trouble to insist. I recognize the facts."

Monsieur Blondel could not restrain a movement of irritation:

"Be careful. The facts are of exceptional gravity. You cannot both be responsible. Look—you still have time to think it over between yourselves."

The two Marquis had the air of understanding no better than if Monsieur Blondel had spoken in Hebrew. Collective warnings decidedly were not going to have any effect. The Magistrate came back to the direct method, and this time, turned to the one on his left.

"You know, then, what it's about. Endangering the safety of the state; collective homicides…"

The two prisoners interrupted together:

"I know all that. Haven't I told you, Monsieur, that I recognize the facts?"

And in a tone of mockery, the two voices continued:

"You speak, Monsieur Blondel, of acts against the safety of the state. It is hardly sufficient. I wished to destroy, not the state, but the entire world. Not merely the world, but the universe. That is what I tried to do. The rest is only a detail. I suppressed two or three scoundrels who insulted me in the streets. I have also killed a few children—it's a detail, I repeat. Your laws are so stupid that this last act has become the principal accusation against me. It's enough to make one laugh. Monsieur Blondel, if you please, consider me as the assassin of the whole human species. You will tell me that in fact, I have assassinated only a small part of it, and the intention does not make the fact.

"But, yes, I tell you. That which I have not yet realized, I will soon accomplish. You can thus consider that I am guilty, not of killing a score of humans but of millions, since I am going to make everything living disappear; then everything which contains the seeds of life. In a word, I admit all the charges that can be brought against me. I admit anything you wish. I declare that I regret nothing, and that I will complete my program. Will that do, Monsieur? Do I make myself clear? I am prepared to repeat these declarations to you if you have not understood them. But hurry up, for otherwise I will tell you nothing."

And the two prisoners made a slight bow in the direction of the judicial seat.

Monsieur Blondel was one of the most distinguished Investigating Magistrates of the Paris bench. He had handled numbers of celebrated cases. But never had he heard of a double personage charge himself with such audacity and such cynicism. As he heard the accusations the accused made against himself, he felt the hair on the back of his neck rise with terror. The two men before him were mocking justice. But they were no more than men. Their double comedy could not last much longer; the rude hand of justice had been placed on their shoulders, and justice would have the last word in this singular dialogue.

"They are held," he thought, and this thought helped his head cool; for a Magistrate must never lose his head. The Marquis and his companion were outraging justice—very well, justice would make them pay. Monsieur Blondel replied:

"I take cognizance of what you have told me, both of you. But I doubt, if you persist in that attitude, whether you will find a lawyer willing to defend you."

This unpleasant prospect did not seem to disquiet the two prisoners. Seated before the Magistrate, they kept their easy and impertinent calm, which they had kept since the beginning of the questioning. They never looked round at the guards placed behind them. The bailiff did not seem to exist for them. Nevertheless, when the judge announced that the record of their declarations was about to be read, they answered, always in perfect unison:

"Don't trouble yourself, Monsieur. But you may add that I declare this also—the people of Paris have sacked my mansion and set fire to it—"

Monsieur Blondel interrupted, stupefied:

"What? What are you saying?"

"The simple truth. The mob has set fire to my house."

"But how did you know that, since you left before the crowd arrived, and have not returned to see the spectacle of its just indignation?"

The Magistrate's question brought no reply. The two Marquis went on:

"I could complain of a crime committed against me also. Well, I do not complain. The imbeciles who believe they have disarmed me will soon discover that they have not limited my activities in the least, and I will now be pitiless: Paris will be destroyed! Every Parisian will be destroyed; not one will remain alive. But, you may be certain, Monsieur le Juge, that I will act correctly. Before striking, I will warn my victims. These victims will believe they will have time to escape. They will be very much surprised to find themselves unable to move. Yes, everyone will have time to fly, but no one will be able to. Don't you find the situation a bit comic, Monsieur Blondel?"

And the two sinister personages, in the presence of the Magistrate, the bailiff, the stenographer and the guards, began to laugh:

"Enough of this cynicism!" declared Monsieur Blondel, with a voice of thunder. "Stenographer, give the declarations to the prisoners to sign. Committed for trial!"

The stenographer had the impression that they would refuse to sign, on the usual pretext of prisoners who are interrogated without their lawyers being present. But the legal formalities must be observed, even with monsters, and he half rose to hand the pen to the nearest of the pair.

He fell back into his seat with a cry of astonishment and terror which was echoed by the Magistrate and the guards.

The two Marquis had disappeared! But their laughter was still vibrating through the room, and neither window nor door had been opened.

It was necessary to admit the fact; the two Marquis had escaped and the escape had been effected in a split second.

21. Mazelier Sacrifices His Beard

The escape—or if one wishes, the double escape—of the Marquis de Saint-Imier, was not printed in the papers. The public supposed that the fantastic and redoubtable individual was under lock and key awaiting the inevitable hour of punishment. Nobody was surprised at the slow course of justice; everyone knew that she goes with one foot lame, especially when the Magistrates have so many mysteries to solve. But everyone was certain now; he, who had so audaciously announced his intentions over the loudspeakers, the noble who was now known under the name of *Radio-Terror*, was awaiting his punishment.

The greatest tranquility reigned in Paris. Thanks to Mazelier, normal life went on once more; the barrier of invisible radiation had been lifted from the capital and from the frontiers; there remained of the whole fantastic affair only the memory of an immense upheaval. And no one suspected the really decisive role that Mazelier had played in the solution of the problem. Already the story of the blockade was half forgotten. But, what no one did forget, what aroused the indignation of everyone when he thought about it, was the silent and cowardly assassination of the nine children. But now, thanks to the outburst of an angry people, all danger seemed over.

Three or four days after the burning of the Saint-Imier mansion, the newspapers contained the following note:

A terrible accident, which has provoked a considerable stir in scientific circles, occurred three or four days ago at the Office for Scientific Research, Avenue des Champs-Elysées. Monsieur Gribal, the distinguished collaborator of the director of the office, Professor Mazelier, was electrocuted in the course of an experiment. There have already been several accidents of this character, particularly in the field of radio-therapy, and this makes only one more martyr to that science.

Professor Mazelier, himself, was gravely injured in an explosion following the accident. His laboratory was wrecked. With Monsieur Gribal's assistance, he was engaged in studying the forms of radiation which brought about the blockade of Paris and of the borders. The distinguished scientist has been replaced as director by the well-known chemist, Monsieur Reynier-Vitral.

In a little house hidden away in the bois of Ville d'Avray, two men were reading this note, and one of them was laughing.

"Well, I'm dead now, my dear Professor. You have already resuscitated me twice, but I wasn't officially killed then. How are you going to bring me back this time?"

"Patience, Gribal! The moment has not yet come to show ourselves in Paris. It is absolutely necessary that he think we are out of the way."

"*Parbleu!* Do you think he will dare to continue the combat?"

"I don't think it; I am certain of it. The man who was able to escape in that strange manner from the Investigating Magistrate will never be wholly disarmed."

"All right. But he must be a little worried. And he knows very well they are looking for him without officially announcing the fact. His photograph is everywhere."

"Yes. And he is nowhere. It bothers me that he doesn't come out."

"He's hiding."

"No, preparing for a new attack."

"But his laboratory is destroyed. What can he do without his apparatus. Nothing!"

386

"I hope so. Meanwhile, let's be on our guard."

"All right, my dear Professor. We'll watch. But I assure you that I do not partake of your fears. And the proof that I am right is that Roland never brings us the slightest bit of news. I assure you, I think we have gotten rid of that titled scoundrel for good. He has all Paris against him."

"We can wait, Gribal. But be careful."

"I will be. Just the same I would like to walk about Paris."

"I forbid you."

"And I will obey. What can I do anyway—I'm dead. It annoys me a little that no one has noticed I have had no funeral."

"You can be sure that *he* has noticed it."

"Oh, come. He can't do everything. He doesn't know everything. He's only a man, after all."

Mazelier lowered his voice:

"Listen, Gribal. There are certain moments when I doubt even that. Look— remember the circumstances of that double arrest. Those two doubles before the Magistrate. If the fact were not certified to me by the President of the Republic, I wouldn't believe it."

"And I," said Gribal, "I don't believe it yet! Well, since you wish it, we will wait."

The wait was prolonged for a month more. Roland Duplay, who could not be known to Saint-Imier, was the news-agent between Mazelier and the Elysée. Every evening, he came to Ville d'Avray, and every evening, he came without any news of importance. He was also given the duty of watching discreetly over the residence of Madame Roberval in the Rue Godot de Mauroy. This watch also yielded nothing. The Marquis had apparently ceased to hate the woman he had never ceased loving.

But one day Roland came earlier than usual, bearing strange news, but news not at all well verified.

A servitor of the Ministry of the Interior swore that he had seen the Marquis in the very office of the minister. Two members of the Cercle des Arts declared that they had seen him on the same day, at the same time, appear in the foyer of the opera house to disappear again immediately.

Gribal heard the news with a laugh:

"*Parbleu!*" he said. "It's not ordinary at least; a collective hallucination. You will hear tomorrow that the Marquis has been seen in Rome, in Chicago, at Timbuktu, and at the South Pole. And always at the same time."

"But," interrupted Roland timidly, "I think I saw him myself. Not at the same time but about two hours later."

"What, you too, Duplay? I should have thought you immune to such delusions."

Mazelier asked the young man:

"Where did you see him?"

"Rue Godot-de-Mauroy, 20 yards away from Madame Roberval's house. I assure you I was wide awake."

It was evident that Mazelier did not partake of Gribal's skepticism. On the contrary, he gave decided attention to the words of the young workman.

"And this...this vision, did it last long?"

"Not more than a couple of minutes."

"The Marquis went away. In what direction?"

"Monsieur, he didn't go away. He simply disappeared."

Mazelier did not laugh. Gribal became impatient.

"Oh, we can't discuss manifest impossibilities," he said. "Come, Professor, we—"

Mazelier interrupted:

"I think, Gribal, that I have never been able to see the limit which separates the possible from the impossible."

"Then you believe that several copies of the same individual can appear simultaneously in Paris?"

"I believe nothing, my friend. I deny nothing either. I think only of well-attested facts, whatever they may be."

Gribal was a man of good sense. It was difficult for him to admit anything but the most obvious explanations of a phenomenon.

"This fact," he said, "can be explained simply, in two ways. For example, if the Marquis has some accomplices who imitate his appearance and bearing, and if they show themselves in different places where he certainly is not present—"

"This hypothesis won't go, Gribal. The Marquis has no accomplices."

"What do you mean, no accomplices? He has at least two—the Chinese chauffeur, that's one—and that miserable Suzie. But there is another supposition equally reasonable."

"What is it?"

"That the Marquis' *Radio-Terror* has become a popular type like Cartouche and Fantômas. Jokers are amusing themselves by making up to resemble the Marquis de Saint-Imier, and startle people around them. There are always idiots who would think that sort of a masquerade funny."

Roland approved:

"It's possible," he admitted. "I thought of that, too."

Encouraged, and thinking he had now convinced Mazelier, Gribal continued:

"You speak of facts. Well, I'll give you another. Your revelator for radiation has been silent ever since they sacked the Marquis' mansion."

"Yes," admitted Mazelier, "nothing from that quarter since then. And my revelator is more powerful than it used to be. Saint-Imier cannot emit any forms of radiation without my hearing them now."

388

"Well, then? If the Marquis has not made a counter attack, it is because he has been reduced to powerlessness. Otherwise, as angry as he certainly must be, we would certainly hear from him. In consequence—"

"In consequence—?"

"*Parbleu!* I repeat it—we can go out and take the air and not stay shut up here. And that poor Madame Roberval, who remains shut up; won't you lighten her captivity? We are prisoners; it's simply ridiculous."

"You don't fear that the man who almost killed you will take the offensive again?"

"Not for a minute. He got his knock, that's enough to put some sense into his head."

"It should be, anyway. But it doesn't matter. Listen, Gribal, we must wait. And you, Roland, tell Madame Roberval from me, to be more careful than ever."

Gribal knew very well that Mazelier, once he had made his decision, would not alter it. Moreover, the scientist no longer heard his protests; he was sunk in a reverie so profound that he did not even notice when Paulette came in to ask the latest news from the Rue Boissy d'Anglas.

Three days went by like this, bringing no change in the situation of the voluntary prisoners. One afternoon, about 3 p.m., Mazelier and Gribal were at work in the laboratory where the scientist had installed his latest pieces of apparatus.

All at once the revelator began to vibrate.

"Oh, oh, it's waking up," cried Gribal, paling a trifle.

Mazelier was inspecting the movement of a needle across a dial and noting down figures.

Ten minutes later, another ringing from the revelator. No further doubt possible; the Marquis was neither disarmed nor inactive. He alone could have emitted the radiation which had stirred the revelator from its sleep. Mazelier and Gribal looked silently at each other, without the necessity of speech. What would Roland Duplay have to tell them?

He came in earlier than usual.

"Well, well?" questioned Gribal impatiently at his appearance.

"Nothing serious," replied the young man, surprised that his interlocutors already knew that something had happened. There was a little fire at Madame Roberval's, but they got it out quickly."

"At what time?" asked Mazelier.

"3:10 p.m. or thereabouts."

The engineer and the scientist exchanged glances.

"What caused the fire?"

"Nobody knows. It was queer. The fire started in her bedroom. A short circuit, they think."

"And at exactly 3 p.m.," Mazelier persisted, "didn't anything happen?"

"At 3 p.m.? No…Wait a minute, I forget. Something quite sensational did happen. But something that doesn't touch us at all. At 3 p.m., as the Minister of the Interior rose in the Chamber to make a speech, he fell dead."

Gribal was disconcerted:

"At 3 p.m.," he cried, "that must be it! But why should the Marquis wish to strike down the Minister of the Interior rather than anyone else?"

"What, Monsieur Gribal, was that death the work of the Marquis?"

But it was Mazelier who replied to Roland:

"Yes, my boy. And if you wish to know why, remember that the Minister of the Interior is the man who is said to have led the cabinet to pursue the judicial inquiry against Saint-Imier. Do you remember, Gribal? It was the Minister of the Interior who said to his colleagues: 'If every other murderer only knew that a sure means to avoiding suspicion was to invite you to dinner!' He has just died for having made that smart remark."

"And we, Mazelier, what are we going to do about it?"

"We? I think we have waited long enough. We must get busy without losing a minute."

"What? Now that there is really danger, we are going to go out?"

"Exactly. The moment has come. Roland and I, we will go into Paris together in a few minutes. We will separate at the Gare Saint-Lazare. Roland will tell Madame Roberval that by tomorrow she will be at liberty to come and go as she pleases. Understood? Whatever happens to her, she is never to forget that she is really safe and that unseen protectors are watching over her. Right?"

"Right, Professor Mazelier."

"Then, Roland, you will meet me again about 8 p.m. in front of No. 20, Rue Fabert. Ah, wait a minute…as you probably will not recognize me, I had better show myself to you as I will appear when I meet you there. I have already camouflaged myself once—not so, Gribal? And they picked me out right away. But this time! You will see. A moment, if you please."

Mazelier went into his room. 15 minutes later he came back, quite unrecognizable. He had cut his beard and curled his hair. No more and no less, but the change was extraordinary.

"Who disguises himself too much, does not disguise himself at all," he remarked with a laugh. "That's axiomatic. Don't I look like a retired mailman, Gribal? Well, Roland, come along. After meeting in the Rue Fabert, we will take a little walk toward Grenelle. And be sure to have a gun with you."

"And me?" asked Gribal. "Are you going to leave me shamefully inactive?"

"You, my dear friend, you are dead. Don't forget it. There's nothing more compromising than to go for a walk in Grenelle with a dead man! And besides, you can't change your face as easily as I can. Tel me, am I ugly enough?"

The fact was that Mazelier, without his little beard and corona of white hair, was far removed from manly beauty.

Gribal resigned himself to inaction with a bad grace. He had to give in, however, without understanding the hazardous project on which his superior was engaged.

22. Triplex

Ghislaine Roberval had attached no particular importance to the minor fire in her bedroom. She received with an inexpressible sense of relief the message from Mazelier. Yes, beginning the following morning she would go out to fulfill her duty of placing new flowers by the tomb that held the remains of Gabriel de Neuville.

The next morning, about 8 a.m., she called a taxi which was passing her door. To her great surprise, the chauffeur—he had doubtless misunderstood her directions—took the Rue Royale and went toward the Place de la Concorde. That was the wrong direction. She knocked on the window; the chauffeur half-turned. He had a singular face, yellow of tint, with a cruel mouth.

Where had Ghislaine seen that mask of a face before? All at once she remembered—the Chinese chauffeur! The familiar of Saint-Imier. She gave a cry of terror, and half rose to leap from the car, in spite of the speed with which it was going down the Rue de Bourgogne, when a voice seemed to murmur in her very ear:

"Don't be afraid! There is not the slightest danger."

She almost fainted with terror. The Marquis was seated by her side! Ghislaine tried to open the door at her side; she did not succeed; the door seemed to be locked solidly into the side of the machine. She reached for the door on the other side, and then fell back with an exclamation of terror. For her arm had passed through the body of the Marquis as though it were not there, as though it were nothing but a ghost. And the Marquis, his hands on his knees, remarked calmly:

"No danger, I assure you. You will understand that I have taken every precaution."

The precautions signified that any attempt at escape would be futile. Trembling, Ghislaine sank back in the corner of the car, and then recalled, suddenly, the message from Mazelier: "No matter what happens, unseen watchers will guard you."

But how had she been so easily trapped?

Tearing along, as though it were running a race, the auto did not stop till it reached the Rue Javel, where it pulled up before a sordid-looking building. The Marquis got out first, and with his characteristic politeness, removing his hat, said:

"Will you follow me, my dear? I would like to have you attend my house warming in my new home."

What audacity! Ghislaine leaped from the vehicle, resolved to fly down the street, to cry for aid, for there were some passers-by in view.

But she neither cried nor fled; she followed her captor, trembling, as though enchanted, dominated by some inexplicable force that rendered her as inert as the hands of a watch.

Saint-Imier, preceding Ghislaine, and by this sign, certain that she was following him, went up a dark and narrow stairway. Decidedly, his new house had not the elegance of the old. Nobody had apparently paid any attention to the strange couple. The Marquis marched gaily ahead with long steps; Ghislaine following as rapidly as she could not knowing by what miracle she was able to move limbs paralyzed with fright.

At the fifth floor, she felt a sudden return of her forces, and would have turned and fled; and then she turned back again with an exclamation of horror. The Marquis was behind her! She went up another step or two—the Marquis was before her. The two Saint-Imiers, who had already been seen by the Investigating Magistrate, had surrounded Ghislaine, and she, overcome with terror, was sure that nothing could save her. And the ironic voice of her double kidnaper announced:

"Don't hurry, my dear. We have all the time in the world. Besides, it's only two more flights to *our* apartment."

The terrible ascent went on. On the landing of the seventh floor, the trio halted. Ghislaine no longer dared to look at her captors. Finally, a narrow door opened and an African in livery, with a silkily polite voice, bowed before her:

"Enter, Madame. We are pleased to have the honor of your presence."

Ghislaine went in. She took several steps and found herself in a room only feebly lighted. Windows and blinds were closed tight. Suddenly, she perceived that she was alone. What had become of her two guardians? She did not have time to look for them; at the other end of the room a door opened, and the Marquis—a single Marquis—came in.

"Good afternoon, Ghislaine," he said, as though he had not seen her before. "Sit down, I beg you. Are you not a little astonished at what has been happening to you?"

She did not answer. First, because she did not wish to answer; and secondly, because she was trying to assemble her whirling thoughts. It seemed to her that the man who stood before her had a more sonorous voice, a more lively eye, than he—or those who had accompanied her. Yes, she might almost have said that the others were his reflections.

By no means disconcerted by the silence of his victim, and at ease as much as in the salons of which he was an ornament, Saint-Imier seated himself in an armchair beside a table surmounted by gleaming instruments.

"You permit?" he murmured and lit a cigarette. Then: "Listen, Ghislaine, I owe you an explanation. I will give it to you completely. You must have been astonished, in your taxi as well as on the stairway, to see me appear, and to redouble myself the better to escort you up the stairs. Here, look at this machine."

Ghislaine noticed on the table a sort of rectangular box, and emerging from the box an object which resembled a metal ball with a wire which ran round the outside of the container.

"Look," said the Marquis, "I close a contact here. I turn this button. Observe the lights that appear around the ball and the velocity with which it turns You don't understand what it is for? Well, it produces two more Marquis de Saint-Imiers, that's all. Oh, *Mon Dieu*, yes, it's perfectly true, as I have the honor of telling you. I am seated comfortably in my armchair. I put this apparatus in motion and two emanations, two projections of myself, are materialized. Isn't it practical for making calls you don't care to make in person?"

He laughed; and then a note of pride crept into his voice:

"Very convenient," he went on. "My projections go immediately to any spot where I want them to go; whatever anyone says to them, I hear it here; whatever is going on around them, I see; whatever I wish them to say, they say. In brief, they are two other selves which I can cause to appear and disappear as I wish. They have only this disadvantage, that both of them must act alike. Do you understand, Madame? In a few minutes, we will have a little experiment with them, with the object of amusing you, Madame."

The last words were pronounced with such an indefinable accent of cruelty that the blood seemed to freeze in the veins of the prisoner.

He laughed gently, exaggerated a trifle by his super polite air of a man of the world:

"If you permit, we will begin now. And you will see."

He approached his box, made a contact, turned a button and then another. The ball began to turn; colored balls of light appeared, surrounding it, gyrating in the opposite direction. A soft purring sound filled the room. And slowly, out of the whirling clouds of light, the two personifications of Saint-Imier appeared, immobile before him like two well-trained servants.

"Do you know where I am going to send them?" asked Saint-Imier, addressing himself to Ghislaine. "They are going into various well chosen localities in the world of society to tell a few little stories about you and your private life. We will start with that, my dear. They will add that you are in a sanitarium, recovering from the effects of your last excesses. And it was you, of course, who furnished me with the list of children destined to be killed."

"You scoundrel," cried Ghislaine.

"Oh, there will be lots of other touches, my dear. And in any case, with my two agents here who can penetrate any doors, and who can speak to anyone and be questioned by no one without my permission, I will be surprised if I do not finish by laying on your shoulders the responsibility for what has happened."

He turned the little lever.

The two phantoms did not move.

An exclamation of surprise escaped the Marquis. But he did not glance at the two reflections of himself which had risen before the astonished eyes of Ghislaine.

"What's wrong now?" he said aloud, bending over the opened box.

"I ought not to keep you in ignorance, Ghislaine. It was I who lit a little fire for you yesterday afternoon. If you hadn't gone out this morning, there would have been another. I was intending to smoke you out, do you see? Ah, yes, and another thing. I believe that about the same time, I damaged the Minister of the Interior who was so injudicious as to defend your interests a little too strongly against me. I gave him the same dose that Gabriel de Neuville got. You remember? Would you like me to show you how it's done? I can try it on some other subjects."

Ghislaine rose. The Marquis turned toward her.

"Ah, dear lady," he said, "we're really going to have a good time. You can't go out, you know, but you can do anything you like in here."

He threw the little lever again. The two phantoms moved no more than they had the first time. The Marquis cried, impatiently:

"This is annoying. There is certainly something wrong with this machine. Well, we'll hold over the little trip through the Paris salons for another day. I must return the emanations of my corporeal body to nothing."

He broke the contacts, an act which should have produced the immediate disappearance of the two. But instead of vanishing into thin air, they advanced a step toward the Marquis, and cried in a single voice:

"I am the Marquis de Saint-Imier!"

The genuine Marquis did not lose countenance. He remarked:

"Well, well, and now we have talking machines that express opinions, and in voices unlike their master's. It's queer to say the least."

The two reflections turned toward Ghislaine together.

"That woman is mine," they declared.

And they continued to advance toward Saint-Imier, who moved back a step.

"What a good idea!" he said. "That's it, Ghislaine, how would you like to belong to two Saint-Imiers?"

But the two apparitions, now become rebels to their creator, continued to advance without another glance at the young woman. The moment arrived when the Marquis found himself so pinched between his two doubles that it was only by physical effort that he could escape them.

In an instant the fantastic adventure became a drama. As though in a frightening dream Ghislaine found herself the spectator of a combat between the two copies of the man and the man himself. Three Saint-Imiers were fighting among themselves with an extraordinary violence. The Marquis was like a man fighting with his image in a mirror; every blow he struck was returned to him with double force; and nothing could be stranger than this triple combat in which two members acted exactly alike. Saint-Imier, his face showing his sudden fright at the discovery that the beings he had created, had, like himself, flesh and bones, essayed to seize one of them by the throat; but as he did so, his own throat was seized in a double grip and he fell at the feet of Ghislaine overwhelmed with horror.

Whether the death of the Marquis brought about the disappearance of his reflections or not, or what strange medley of projections and images had brought the thing to pass, Ghislaine did not know. She knew, only, that in an instant she was alone, and at her feet was the dead body of the *Radio-Terror*.

Alone? No, for the door through which the Marquis had come, opened again and through it appeared—Mazelier and Roland Duplay!

For the scientist had gained his greatest and final victory. Substituting, with more powerful radiation, his own control for that of the Marquis, he had directed the phantom figures against their creator, and, at bottom, the combat among the three Saint-Imiers had been not a combat but a suicide.

Before the corpse of the aristocratic and heartless scientist, Roland paused a moment to say:

"At last his victims are avenged!"

But Ghislaine added in a tone of sadness:

"Alas! Your vengeance does not give me back those I weep for."

Mazelier did not try to console her. Without a word he took her arm, and the three of them left without even another glance at the remains of the man, who, made mad by pride, thought of accomplishing everything by intelligence without the admixture of a generous heart and clean hands.

Jean-Marc Lofficier: *Dad*

This is a story I wrote for Tales of the Shadowmen *No. 9 in 2012, and as I was short of a couple of pages to wrap up this book, it seemed like a good idea to reuse it here, especially since it fits the theme.*

J.-M.L.

Bobo says, I must kill Dad. Dad, he brings another hoe today. That's how he says, but I don't know what a hoe is. Dad, it makes him laugh. He put her in the pit, like the others. I'm the one who dug the pit in the cellar. The walls are smooth. Once inside, you cannot get out. I am five, but Dad, he says I look fifteen. I am very strong.

I went to see the hoe in the pit. She is not like the others. She has pretty red hair. She looks like Mom. Mom, I did not know her because she died when I was born. But I've seen her pictures. Dad, he keeps a big book with pictures of the hoes and the results of his speriments. It is in a locked drawer, but I found the key. I am also very smart.

Bobo, he is my monkey. He is my best friend. Dad began his speriments on Bobo before the hores. It was full of tubes with blue, green and red liquids that he sinks into their belly with a needle, and after, he put his sausage in their bellies, and the hoes, they scream a lot. Dad, he goes, han-han-han, but he loves it. Sometimes I wonder if his speriments are not an escuse to dip his sausage. Once, after, Dad looked at me funny, he laughed and asked me if I wanted to dip my sausage too, but I started squealing. Because I can't talk.

The hoes, they all die after Dad's speriments. Except one who got all big. Dad was very excited. And then, little brother broke her belly with his claws and teeth, and she died too, and Dad eutanazed little brother. He was not pretty with all his scales. Except his eyes. He had blue eyes like the hoe. Later, Dad asked me to take the body to the Rock. Because I have a Gift.

It came when I was two. I went to the Rock. It's like a little island of black rock, lost in a sea of red liquid fire red. Dad, he says he don't know where the rock is, elsewhere or in my head, but it's useful to get rid of the bodies. He says that, with the Rock, the fuckincops won't find anything. And he laughs. I told Bobo of the Rock. He says it can't be the only place I can go. There must be other rocks but prettier. Where we could go and live, me and him. Because I suffer.

The new hoe who looks like Mom, she is nice. She begs me to get her out. All the hoes, they do the same, but I dare not disobey Dad, because he beats me with the electric thing that hurts. I squeal loudly when he beats me, it's like he go crazy. He calls me names I don't know, like mongolide, mutant... So I hide or I go to the Rock but I can't stay long because the air there, it feels like what Dad use to clean everything, and it's very hot. And I really hurt and I cry.

Glinda is the name of the new hoe. Yesterday, Dad pushed a new bright green liquid in her head and belly. Then he dipped his sausage. I cried a lot. I don't know why.

Glinda, she saw the Rock. Since yesterday, she sees like noodles of colors that twist around me. The one that goes to the Rock is a red. I can't see them too, but Glinda, she can. Bobo, he says that with her, we can find other places to go, Glinda, me and him. Bobo, he says that we don't need Dad. Bobo, he says to kill Dad. Glinda puts her hand on mine and looked at me. Now, her eyes are very blue and they shine. She's very pretty. I'm happy.

Tonight, I grabbed Dad and took him to the Rock and threw him into the sea of fire, like all the other hoes. Then Glinda, Bobo and I, we follow another noodle, all blue, all pretty. I take Glinda's hand, and Bobo take mine, and I push really really hard. And we got there. The soil is full of rose petals and the sky is very blue. And in the distance, there is a yellow brick road and a city made of green glass. It's very pretty and I'm sure people will be very nice. Now I am happy.

IN THE SAME SERIES

www.ingramcontent.com/pod-product-compliance
Lightning Source LLC
Chambersburg PA
CBHW020255030726
47499CB00001B/206